# JULIA
# DEFIANT

ALSO BY CATHERINE EGAN

*Julia Vanishes*

# JULIA DEFIANT

## THE WITCH'S CHILD, BOOK 2

## CATHERINE EGAN

DOUBLEDAY CANADA

Doubleday Canada and colophon are registered trademarks of
Random House of Canada Limited.

This book is a work of fiction. Names, characters, places, events and incidents
are either the product of the author's imagination or are used fictitiously. Any
resemblance to actual persons, living or dead, is entirely coincidental.

Library and Archives Canada Cataloguing in Publication

Egan, Catherine, 1976-, author
Julia defiant / Catherine Egan.

Issued in print and electronic formats.

ISBN 978-0-385-68468-2 (hardback).—ISBN 978-0-385-68469-9 (epub)

I. Title.

PS8609.G34J83 2017          jC813'.6          C2016-905218-4
C2016-905219-2

Published in Canada by Doubleday Canada,
A division of Random House of Canada Limited,
A Penguin Random House Company

www.penguinrandomhouse.ca

10 9 8 7 6 5 4 3 2 1

Penguin
Random House
DOUBLEDAY CANADA

For David—

it can't have been easy being the littlest,

or captive to my relentless story making,

but every story of mine is still for you

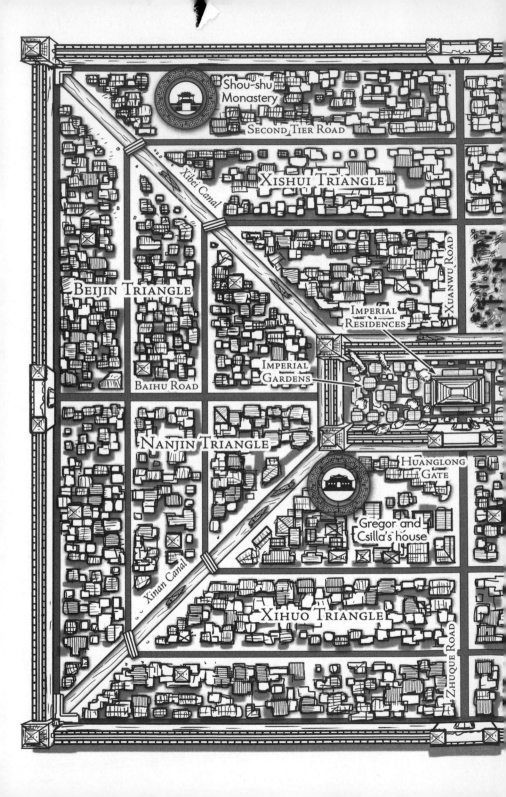

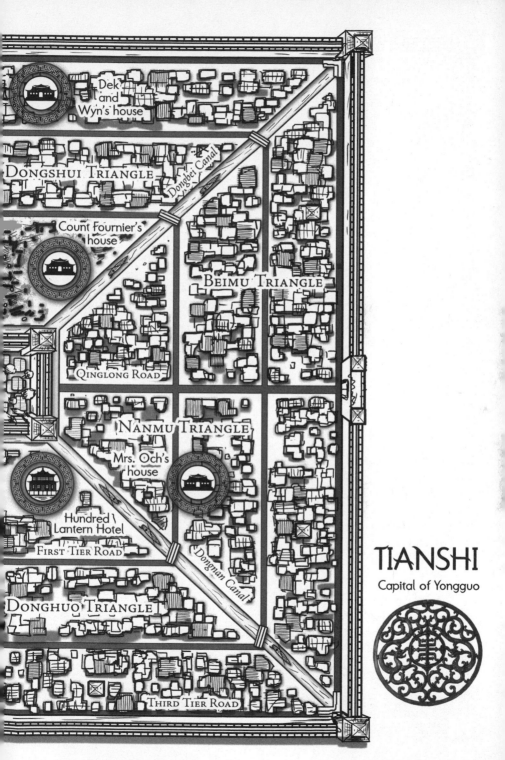

Dek
and
Wyn's house

DONGSHUI TRIANGLE

Dongbei Canal

Count Fournier's
house

BEIMU TRIANGLE

QINGLONG ROAD

NANMU TRIANGLE

Mrs. Och's
house

Hundred
Lantern Hotel

FIRST TIER ROAD

Dongnan Canal

DONGHUO TRIANGLE

THIRD TIER ROAD

TIANSHI

Capital of Yongguo

# PEOPLE, PLACES, AND THINGS

**Ammi:** A witch; Julia and Benedek's mother

**Professor Baranyi:** A scholar, once jailed for heretical writings, now employed by (and devoted to) Mrs. Och

**Benedek:** Julia's brother

**Bianka:** A witch; Theo's mother

**Casimir (Lan Camshe):** One of the Xianren, seeking to reassemble all three parts of *The Book of Disruption*

**Csilla:** An actress turned con artist; Gregor's lover; a member of Esme's gang

**Esme:** A Spira City crime boss, now employed by Mrs. Och

**Count Fournier:** A Fraynish aristocrat living in Tianshi; Lady Laroche's nephew

**Frederick:** A brilliant young student; Professor Baranyi's assistant

**Gangzi:** The elected leader of the Shou-shu Council

**Gennady (Zor Gen):** The youngest of the Xianren, imprisoned by Casimir; Theo's father

**Gregor:** An ex-aristocrat con man working for Esme; Csilla's lover; a drunk

**Agoston Horthy:** The prime minister of Frayne

**Jun:** An able spy; Count Fournier's associate

**Ko Dan:** One of the Shou-shu monks; a famous witch

**Lady Laroche:** A witch; the head of the Sidhar Coven in Frayne

**Lidari:** A general of the Gethin; Marike's associate

**Ling:** A smart young woman from Tianshi; Benedek's girlfriend; Mei's sister

**Marike:** A witch; the first Phar and founder of the Eshriki Empire

**Mei:** Ling's sister; Wyn's lover

**Mrs. Och (Och Farya):** The eldest of the Xianren, trying to keep Theo (and the third fragment of *The Book of Disruption*) out of the hands of her brother Casimir

**Pia:** Casimir's terrifying assassin, sent to Yongguo to find Theo . . . and Julia

**Si Tan:** The grand librarian of Yongguo, a position second only to the emperor's

**Lord Skaal:** A dignitary from Frayne; an associate of Agoston Horthy

**Theo:** The toddler son of Bianka and Gennady, with a fragment of *The Book of Disruption* bound to his essence

**Wyn:** An orphan and a crook; Esme's adopted son; Julia's ex-lover

**Zara:** A Fraynish girl hiding in the Shou-shu Monastery

**The Ankh-nu:** A double-spouted clay pot made to transfer the essence of a living being from one body to another

***The Book of Disruption:*** The first written magic and origin of

magic in the world, said to have been written by Feo, spirit
of fire, and broken into three pieces by the other elemental
spirits

**The Eshriki Empire:** A powerful witch empire three thousand
years ago whose rulers called themselves the Phars

**The Gethin:** An army of creatures brought into the world from
Kahge and given physical form by Marike, the first Eshriki
Phar

**Kahge:** A magic-infused reflection, shadow, or image imprint
of the natural world created when *The Book of Disruption* was
split into three

**The Lorian Uprising:** An unsuccessful revolution in Frayne
eighteen years ago aimed at replacing King Zey with his more
moderate brother, Roparzh

**The Ru:** The elite warriors who guard the Imperial Gardens

**The Shou-shu Monastery:** A monastery in Tianshi, capital city
of Yongguo, currently led by a monk named Gangzi

**The Sidhar Coven:** A Fraynish coven of witches—of which
Julia's mother, Ammi, was part—involved in the Lorian
Uprising

**The Xianren:** The immortal siblings, sometimes allies and
sometimes enemies, each charged with protecting a portion
of *The Book of Disruption:* Casimir (Lan Camshe), Gennady
(Zor Gen), and Mrs. Och (Och Farya)

# JULIA
# DEFIANT

$A$bove the wasted plains of the earth, after the battle was done, Haizea, goddess of vengeance, and Tisis, goddess of mercy, stood side by side and argued over which of them was needed.

"I will give the vanquished strength," said Haizea. "Look, down there, a young mother—her dress torn open, her husband dead. She kneels before the body of her murdered child. I will give her my whirlwind so that she might strike back at those who stole her joy."

"And then?" said Tisis. "Enslaved to the whirlwind, will she tear other children from their mothers, will she pillage and murder also? The enmity between these people cannot be brought to an end with vengeance. I will bring her my cup and let her drink. In mercy and forgiveness may she find peace, and give peace to future generations."

"Some things cannot be forgiven," said Haizea.

"Some things cannot be avenged," said Tisis.

"Then what good are we?" asked Haizea. "Why do they call for us and call for us, in times of war and in times of peace?"

The two goddesses went down to the plain, where the bodies of *the dead and the dying lay strewn. Tisis offered her cup to those who would drink, and to those who would strike back a hundredfold, Haizea gave her whirlwind. Then they came to the young mother they had argued over. She knelt in the dirt and looked up at them, her dark eyes reflecting their blazing glory. They told her: "Choose."*

# ONE

When did I first go over a wall that was meant to keep me out? I don't even remember. I've spent my life scaling walls. I've made a career out of what used to be just mischief— going where I am not supposed to go, seeing what I am not supposed to see, being someone I'm not. It has taken me farther from home than I'd ever imagined. This is a fine wall, tall and strong and tiled on top, and this is my third time going over it.

The sun set an hour ago, and the streets are already empty. I take a rope with a five-pronged hook at the end of it from my bag and step back a few paces, eyeing the wall and measuring the rope out. Then I give the hook a whirl and toss it up. It flies neatly, scraping against the stone on the other side and catching on the tiles at the top. I tug to make sure it's firm and then walk up the wall, hand over hand along the rope. Straddling the top of the wall, I coil the rope around the hooked head and tuck it back into my bag.

From here I can see the whole city, the broad, paved streets and peaked rooftops surrounding the Imperial Gardens at the center. This is Tianshi, capital of Yongguo, seat of the greatest empire the world has ever known. Within these walls, in the northwest of the city, lies the Shou-shu Monastery, famous for its bronze bells and long-lived monks. It is a maze of dark temples and alleys around the Main Hall— almost like a miniature version of the city itself.

If I look east, I can see all the way to the Dongshui Triangle, the slum where my brother is hiding out with my ex-lover. I ate supper with them last night, and Wyn was in a poor mood. He'd had too much to drink and called me unforgiving, which seemed funny at the time.

I shoulder the bag with the hook in it and slide both my legs over to the monastery side of the wall. I've thought a great deal about forgiveness and what is forgivable. Still, I've yet to tell him *I forgive you*, because even though I have, he wouldn't understand. When Wyn talks about forgiveness, he means having me back in his bed. It means something different to me. It means everything to me. It's why I'm here, ten thousand miles from home, dropping from this wall onto the gravel path below.

⤙

Getting here was no small matter. We crossed half the world in two months, by ship and by train, by horse and by camel, by riverboat and by donkey cart and on foot. We saw wonders I never knew existed: the white palace floating on the lake in Beru, built for the king's favorite concubine; the spiraling rock formations in the Loshi Desert; the Kastahor Mountains, cloaked in ice.

One evening, a few weeks into our journey, I found my brother, Benedek, sitting on the cooling desert sand, watching the sun setting behind the Eshriki Pyramids. Our tents and camels were just out of sight, over a dune. He smiled up at me and said something in Yongwen. This was Professor Baranyi's rule, that we speak only Yongwen on the journey, and if he ever tired of giving us lessons on steamships or in bedsits, he didn't show it. But I was having none of it here, alone with Benedek. To my chagrin, he'd proved a much more adept student than me.

"Can we just speak bleeding Fraynish for once?"

"You need the practice."

"Well, I don't want to practice with you."

It was always a relief to be alone with him—really, with any of my own crew, but with Dek in particular. It was the only time I could be at ease. The rest of them—well, we were careful with each other, and I was conscious every moment of trying to win their trust, if not their friendship, and conscious too that they could never really trust me. Not after what I'd done.

"I was saying that they're remarkable," said Dek, gesturing at the pyramids with his good arm. "You know, the part we see is just the very tip of the pyramid, poking above the sand. The rest, underneath the ground, is absolutely vast."

"Really?" I said, startled.

"No." He snorted. "Pea brain."

I punched him on the shoulder.

"Do you know what Mrs. Och said yesterday when she saw them?"

"What?"

"She said, 'I remember when they built those.'"

He laughed. The sun sank behind the pyramids, the golden light that suffused the clouds and the sand and the pyramids themselves deepening to crimson. He asked me, almost casually: "Do you suppose they'll forgive you if you find him?"

He didn't need to explain who he meant by *they* or by *him*. But the question took me aback all the same. He'd clearly been waiting for a moment alone with me to ask.

"I don't know," I said.

"Will you forgive yourself?"

"No."

"I wish you could."

"If wishes were horses," I said, shrugging it off, and he let it go. We watched the light fade in silence.

The truth is that the question of forgiveness fuels my days and plagues my nights. Goodness was not something I gave much thought to until I relinquished any possible claim to it. Am I evil, as Frederick once suggested? There is no way to remake the past. The very best I can strive for, the work of every day now, is to be a good person who once did an evil thing.

If atonement also happens to be fun, well, that is just good luck. I land on the path and set off at a light jog behind the monastery library. The monks retire to their sleeping quarters at sundown, so I don't need to worry about running into anybody. In my pocket, I have a wrinkled copy of the monastery map that Mrs. Och obtained for me. I've looked around enough to know it is inaccurate. Tonight's task is to fill in the gaps. If some parts of the monastery are secret, unmapped, it's a fair guess that that's where I ought to be looking.

I make my way through the southern end of the monastery, avoiding the Treasury, the only place where guards are posted both day and night—not monks either, but proper imperial guards. There are three hundred–plus monks here, and they all look much the same to me, with their crimson robes and shaved heads, their gaunt, hungry faces. I am looking for one man: Ko Dan. This is complicated, since I don't know what he looks like or anything else about him besides his name and the fact that a year and a half ago he worked a terrible magic that needs undoing. Perhaps most important, I don't know that he'll want to be found.

The monastery buildings are made of ancient wood from Yongguo's northern forests, where the trees are black as pitch and a hundred feet tall. The rooftops are bright blue tile, though in the dark, they look as black as the wood. I turn right at the west wall, passing the sleeping quarters, several minor temples, the broad road leading to the Main Hall, and the elaborate Garden of the Elements, behind which lies a well-tended vegetable plot and a small house with a light flickering inside.

Three nights in a row, when the rest of the monastery is dark, there has been this one light. Through the window I see the same old man sitting at his desk, writing. His face is wrinkled as a prune. He writes very quickly, as if agitated, page after page. He is wearing the crimson robe that all the monks wear, but he has a long braid down the back of his shaved head and a golden medallion on his chest.

When I told Mrs. Och and Frederick about the old man, they agreed it was probably Gangzi, elected leader of the Shou-shu Council. Anyone seeking to enter the monastery must obtain special permission from Gangzi, and my understanding is that this permission is so special it is never actually granted. Not even the emperor can come here unless Gangzi says so; the monastery is under Yongguo's protection but not its jurisdiction. Women are expressly forbidden to enter under any circumstances, and I admit that just sweetens the job, as far as I'm concerned. For all that, it is easy enough to get in. Just a wall, and no guards besides those at the Treasury. Only the wrath of the empire and magic-using monks to worry about if I get caught, and I never get caught. Well—hardly ever.

The prune-faced man folds the paper, addresses it, seals it with wax, and adds it to a bamboo basket nearly overflowing with letters. He dips his brush and sets about writing the next one. I'd like to get my hands on one of those letters and see what he's frantically writing about night after night, but I daren't enter the little house while he's there. I leave him to his work.

The Hall of Abnegation (Frederick's translation) stretches the entire length of the northernmost wall. I pause between the hall and the swallow coop, tilting the map in my hand so I can catch a little of the moonlight to see by, when the ground shifts right in front of me. I step back against the wall of the swallow coop, stifling my cry of surprise.

A flagstone rises up from the path and is eased aside soundlessly. A shadow emerges from the ground, fluid and swift. The shadow replaces the flagstone without a scrape or a clink and slips away from me, down the alley. Talk about luck. I follow, heart galloping now with the thrill of the chase, even though I don't know who or what I'm chasing yet.

We come to a wall about twice my height. Walls within walls within walls in this city. The shadow goes up and over it like a spider. I make a quick circuit of the wall. It forms a rectangle, fewer than two hundred paces right around, and there is a painted door facing south—locked. The wall is roughly made, the stones uneven enough that I can clamber up them easily, if not as smoothly as the shadow I'm stalking. I fling my leg over the top, lying flat to look down on the courtyard below.

At the center of the courtyard sits a modest house. Bamboo runs around the inside of the wall, thick and green. I see

9

no sign of the shadow I followed here, but two figures are seated at a table in the candlelit garden. They are playing Zhengfu, a strategy game with tiles, similar to the Fraynish game of Conquest. The larger of the two figures is singing softly as she plays. So much for no women in the monastery. The tune is familiar—and then I catch a snatch of it and am shocked to realize she is singing in Fraynish. I know the song from my own childhood. It's a depressing ditty about the weeping moon following the sun round and round, pulling her dark cape of stars behind her and longing for day. *Why so sad, Mistress Moon, why d'you cry?*

The other figure is so small I'd have guessed it was a child, except that she is smoking a pipe. She smacks down a tile, then scoops the singer's tiles off the board with a little bark of triumph. The singer laughs and they rise to their feet. By her voice and posture, I reckon the pipe smoker to be an old woman.

The singer blows out the candles, and they head toward the house, the old woman carrying something long and bulky I can't make out in the dark. I climb down the wall as fast as I dare, using the bamboo to steady myself, but the feathery tops of the stalks shake and rustle as I descend, and the singer looks back, calling out in Yongwen: "Is someone there?"

The old woman makes a beeline for me, and I realize she's holding an old-fashioned blunderbuss. She pries between the bamboo stalks with it, the tip of the muzzle just skimming my shoulder. Her face is only a foot from mine, peering this way and that. It is a stern face, if slightly blurred from my perspective, with great scraggly eyebrows. She looks right at me, but she doesn't see me, of course.

After checking the wall and the garden, she returns to the girl at the threshold of the house, and together they go inside, the girl casting a last look my way over her shoulder. I ease myself through the bamboo stalks and dash across the courtyard. They leave the door open to the chirping night insects, and so I slip in after them.

They pass through the main room to a smaller room sparsely furnished with a bed, a wardrobe, a dresser. There is a large wooden barrel to one side. The old woman takes the lid off, and steam pours upward from the hot water within. The girl is still humming her Fraynish tune, and by the lamplight, I can see her New Porian features, her fair skin and light-colored eyes. She cannot be much older than I am—eighteen or nineteen at most, I'd guess. She is thick-shouldered and plump, rather matronly in figure, but with a face ill suited for plumpness—too severe, with a small, pinched mouth and a long nose made comical by her round cheeks. She is dressed in a wide-sleeved robe of embroidered silk, like the upper-class ladies of Tianshi wear, her mousy brown hair held back with jade clasps.

The old woman says something I don't understand, and the girl laughs again, breaking off her song. In spite of my weeks of immersive study with Professor Baranyi, now that I am here, I find everybody speaking far too quickly and not following the linguistic rules of Yongwen as I've learned them at all. It is difficult to catch more than a snippet here and there.

The girl begins to undress. I've seen enough of the place, and it offends even my admittedly dinged sense of propriety to watch her take a bath, so I slip out to look for the shadow I followed here.

I find him outside, crouched on the roof, still as the night. I watch him for a few minutes but he doesn't move, and so I go over the wall, more slowly and quietly this time, and run back to the swallow coop. I reenter the visible world, so that everything pulls sharply into focus around me, and search for the flagstone the shadow came out from under. At first I'm just breaking my fingernails on stones that won't budge, but then I find the right cracks in the ground and pull it up.

Looking down the hole, I see nothing but darkness. I reach in and feel steel rungs—a ladder. I'm not going down there without knowing more, but I am curious to see what my spy will do if he thinks he's been discovered. So I leave the tunnel open, the flagstone lying there on the path, and I step back against the wall of the swallow coop, where the birds chirrup softly in their nests.

I vanish and wait.

# TWO

I don't hear the shadow coming—that's how good he is—
but I see him standing there, looking down at the open
tunnel, his face hidden by a hood. Then he bends quickly
to replace the flagstone and makes for the east wall of the
monastery.

My shadow-spy goes up the wall and over it, and the first
whisper of fear ghosts through me, cold in my veins. I've only
known one person who can go up a wall like that, and I don't
fancy meeting her like again. Me, I need my hook and rope
for this wall, and so I wait a minute or two, hoping he'll be
out of earshot but not yet out of sight. When I get to the
top of the wall, I scan the streets for a panicky second or
two before I spot the shadow heading toward the Xuanwu
Road. I drop down to the street and hurry after him, into
the Dongshui Triangle, still vanished in case the shadow
looks over his shoulder, which he doesn't.

This part of the city has a reputation for robbery, assault, opium, and illegal magic. The streets are mostly empty, but in an abandoned lot ahead, next to a collapsed wall, several figures are crouched around a bonfire. My spy keeps going, looking neither to the right nor to the left. A couple of the figures rise to watch him. One of them speaks, but my spy says nothing in return, does not even glance their way. I speed up, closing the gap between us somewhat. The rest of the men around the fire rise now, and there are more of them than I'd realized—eight or nine. They are climbing over the broken wall, streaming after my spy, shouting jeers. One of them smashes a bottle on the road. One of them draws a knife.

I can't decide if I should call out a warning about the knife, try to help. But it becomes clear very quickly that my spy, whoever he is, needs no warning, nor any other kind of help from me.

He tosses something casually over his shoulder and then bolts. It looks like a small pottery jar. It shatters on the road, and a buzzing swarm explodes up out of it. I fling myself up on the wall at the side of the road, and the men scatter, shouting and fleeing, a cloud of angry wasps in pursuit. I dash along the wall to the corner and see the shadow running south. Stars, but he's fast. I jump off the wall and go after him.

He slows down when he reaches the first tier of the Dongshui Triangle, the section closest to the Imperial Gardens. Iron tracks for electric trolleys run along the three tier roads, dividing the city's elegant neighborhoods from the shabbier ones, which are farther from the Imperial Gardens. I hang back but keep him in sight. This part of the city was burned sixty years ago when a group of old, wealthy families revolted against the meritocracy, and it has a haunted feel. The once great courtyard houses are collapsed, their walls broken, the charred buildings open to the night sky. A few homes survived the fire intact, but those are somehow the saddest of all, standing lonely and empty among their ruined neighbors.

My spy heads toward one of the undamaged houses. His hand on the door, he looks over his shoulder for the first time. The moon is out and I can see the shadow's face clear enough. He is just a boy, no older than me, with sharp cheekbones and a rather fierce expression. His eyes cut across the street, passing over me. Then he opens the door and disappears inside.

I stand in the road a minute, looking at the closed door. I'd hoped that the monastery's secret spaces would turn up Ko Dan, but I know from experience that sometimes the thing you hope to find does not look the way you expect it to at first. In any case, I have two things to report to Mrs. Och tonight. First, a Fraynish girl who stays up late playing Zhengfu. And second, that I am not the only spy with an interest in the Shou-shu Monastery.

# THREE

Since I'm in the neighborhood, I decide to drop in on Dek before going back to Mrs. Och's house. When we arrived in Tianshi, Mrs. Och split our group into three and sent us to different parts of the city. Her insistence that I live with her, Bianka, and Frederick came as a surprise—I'm not sure if I should take her wanting me close as a sign of how much she needs me or how little she trusts me. Perhaps a bit of both. Either way, I'm stuck living with the people who have the most reason to hate me.

Esme, my boss since I was a little pickpocket in Spira City, and her colleagues, Gregor and Csilla, are renting an elegant house in the first tier of the Xihuo Triangle, overlooking the canal. Gregor is posing as Lord Heriday, a visiting scholar, which is laughable. Professor Baranyi, our Yongguo expert, is acting as his official translator and, behind the scenes, his coach. I don't envy him the job of trying to teach a drunken ex-aristocrat con man how to fake an intellect, but the professor has been remarkably patient. Esme is acting as their manservant. We tried her out as a lady's maid, but in all her six-foot-tall fierce-browed splendor, she was predictably unconvincing. Gregor-as-Lord-Heriday is requesting permission to visit the Imperial Library. If Ko Dan does not turn up in the monastery, Mrs. Och reckons there will be records in the library to give us an idea of where he's gone.

Dek and Wyn, in the meantime, are meant to be digging up rumors—and, just in case, weapons—from the rogues and hustlers in the seedy Dongshui Triangle, but as far as I can tell, they are just going to lots of shady bars to get drunk and calling it reconnaissance. If I'm lucky, they'll have found some real coffee. I know Wyn has set finding coffee beans in this city of tea at a high priority.

The front door is ajar, and I go in without knocking. A lantern hangs from a hook on the wall, and the two of them are sitting at the table in their shirtsleeves—but not just the two of them. I freeze in the doorway, wondering if I should turn around and slip out before they see me.

There are two girls with them. One of the girls is playing cards with Wyn. She has cynical, low-lidded eyes, and her face paint has seen too many weary hours. Dek is practicing calligraphy, bent over a sheet of rice paper with a girl in an ancient-looking silk tunic a few sizes too big for her. Her gleaming blue-black hair is in an untidy knot on top of her head, and I can't see her face at first.

"Hullo, it's Julia," says Wyn, looking up at me. So much

for slipping away unseen. I step inside. I can smell bitter green tea, so I guess I am out of luck on the coffee.

Dek turns and breaks into a smile. His dark, curly hair is tied back. Usually he only does that when he's working, the rest of the time letting his hair fall over his face to hide the Scourge scars and blots around his missing eye. I'm a little surprised to see it tied back in the company of two girls.

"Working late?" he asks, nodding at my bag with the hook and rope inside. I shrug it off and put it down by the door. The girl next to him turns to face me now, looks me up and down. I can see right away that the two girls must be sisters, but this one is younger and prettier than the girl playing cards with Wyn.

"I didn't know you'd have visitors," I say.

"We're making friends in the neighborhood," says Wyn. He jerks a thumb at the older girl, who is resting her chin in her hand now, looking vaguely relieved to be abandoning the card game. "This one is Mia. Or Minnie. Or something."

"Mei," says Dek. "And her sister, Ling."

"It's hard to keep the names straight," says Wyn. "D'you want some tea, Julia? It's good to see you. Why can't you come live with us? We're lonely out here."

I refrain from saying that they don't look lonely.

"Mrs. Och wants me close," I say. "You haven't found coffee, then?"

"No such luck," Wyn sighs. "People just laugh at me when I ask for it."

One of Mrs. Och's tree pipits comes hopping across the

table and gives his knuckles a peck. We use them to send messages, birds being easier to enchant than most animals, according to Mrs. Och. Wyn was skeptical, muttering about how messenger birds are not uncommon and that instructing a bird by magic seemed simply lazy. The magic makes him uneasy, but he quite likes the birds themselves, which are only really tame with him, having fallen victim to his charms, as so many of us do.

The younger girl, Ling, brings me tea in a chipped cup, still staring at me with naked curiosity. The sleeves of her overlarge tunic nearly cover her hands, but when I take the cup from her, I notice her left hand is bandaged up to the knuckles. Her fingers are chapped and ink-stained, the nails bitten to the quick.

"We met them at a bar and brought them back here for their scintillating conversation and funny stories," says Wyn. He nods at glowering Mei. "This one has had us in stitches for hours."

"So you've been out this evening," I say, sitting down and looking at Dek's calligraphy. "What is the dark underbelly of Tianshi like?"

"Dark and underbellyish," says Dek, tousling my hair so some of the pins come loose. I swat his hand away.

Wyn adds: "Turns out these two lovelies have got an uncle who has some dealings with the monastery. Nice fellow."

I make myself meet his eyes, mainly so it's not obvious that I am always trying not to look at him. His eyes are a grayish green, the color of the sea after a storm. We've always guessed that his people were from North Arrekem or somewhere thereabouts, because of his dark skin, but who knows where he got those eyes. He doesn't know either, since his earliest memories are of the awful orphanage he ran away from. Csilla says his beauty is wasted on a man, and indeed there is something almost too pretty about his perfect lips and cheekbones, the arc of those dark eyebrows. It's not his beauty that slays me, though. It's the humor of his face I've always loved, the way he seems to be laughing at himself and the world, like he's in on a big joke, *the* big joke of human existence. Wyn radiates joy at being alive, and the feeling is contagious. Being with him was a joyful thing. Until I found him in bed with another girl, that is.

"He smuggles in tobacco and liquor for naughty monks," explains Wyn when I don't reply. Too busy getting lost in those eyes. Honestly, pull yourself together, Julia.

"Oh, so this is actually work, then, is it?" I ask.

Dek laughs.

"No harm in mixing business with pleasure," says Wyn. "What have you been up to?"

"The usual mischief," I say lightly. "Listen, can you find out who delivers mail to the monastery and who takes letters out? There ought to be a *lot* of letters going out every day."

"We'll look into it," says Dek.

Mei is rubbing her face like a sleepy cat, leaving black smudges around her eyes. Ling takes the brush from Dek, dips it in the inkpot, and writes something on his rice paper.

I don't know anything about calligraphy, but even I can see she's good at it. There is an easy flair to her characters that Dek's painstaking calligraphy lacks.

"What is that?" he asks in Yongwen. "A saying, a name?"

Ling tilts her head to one side, smiling as she answers him. No Fraynish girl has ever looked at Dek like that. In Spira City, Dek was an outcast, marked by Scourge. His scars, his missing eye, his withered arm and leg, were all sure signs of the illness that had terrorized Frayne. But Scourge never had such a strong foothold in Yongguo. There are cripples here, as there are cripples everywhere, and Dek is only one of them. His foreignness is more remarkable than the crutch he walks with or the puckered map of blots and scars on the right side of his face.

"It's a saying," says Dek, translating for Wyn and me: "Destiny must be hunted."

Mei, smudge-eyed and stifling a yawn, says, "Ling is very clever," and adds something about the Imperial Gardens that I can't understand.

"What did she say?" I ask Dek, annoyed that the conversation seems to be switching over to Yongwen.

"Ling has a tutor," says Dek. "She works as a dishwasher, but in her free time she studies literature and philosophy. Her family thinks she might pass the examinations and get them a place in the Imperial Gardens."

Ling stares at her own calligraphy, the expression on her face almost angry now, and I study her again. The system in Tianshi is peculiar in that the ruling class is not hereditary.

Power and prestige are not passed from one generation to the next but rather earned through a system of examinations. Anyone, even a peasant, may apply to take the Imperial Examinations. If they pass—showing a breadth of knowledge and also demonstrating excellence in at least one area of specialty—then both they and their entire family may live within the Imperial Gardens, that walled enclave of privilege at the center of the city. A family with a gifted child might pour all their resources into educating and preparing that child for the examinations. It is a huge gamble for a poor family, and naturally the wealthy have the significant advantage of money and time for tutors and study. But if Ling is truly exceptional, then even though she's a dishwasher from Dongshui and her uncle is a smuggler, her family might rise to the very top of Yongguo's society.

The most extraordinary contrast to Frayne here in Yongguo is that witchcraft is viewed simply as another kind of talent and can also earn you a place in the Imperial Gardens. While witchcraft is governed by strict laws, witches are highly respected, and a licensed witch may use her power in service of the empire. If my mother had been born here instead of in Frayne, she might have been a member of the Imperial Court. She would not have been drowned in the river like a rat.

Ling and Dek are leaning over the sheet of rice paper, heads almost touching, speaking Yongwen rapidly together. I understand the story of her hands now—the chapped skin and the ink and the close-bitten nails, hidden in her sleeves again. Mei has moved closer to Wyn and is resting her head on his shoulder. All at once, I feel very awkward.

"I should get back," I say, rising.

"You just got here," says Wyn.

"Mrs. Och will be wanting a report. Thanks for the tea."

"We'll find coffee in this blasted city, Brown Eyes. I swear it on my life!" he says dramatically. He doesn't call me Brown Eyes so often anymore.

"Good night," says Dek. "Be careful."

I give him a wave, shouldering my bag, and try to be happy for him that he's got a pretty girl to pass the evening with.

Halfway home, I am sure I'm being followed. I can't see anybody; it's just a feeling. It may be no more than jitters, but I go the rest of the way vanished anyway.

# FOUR

Even the animals are quiet when I return to the modest courtyard house in the Nanmu Triangle that serves, for now, as home to Mrs. Och, Bianka, Baby Theo, Frederick, and me. Spira City would be brilliant with gas lamps at this hour, but Tianshi is nearly pitch black. There is the odd flicker of a lantern here and there, the dim glow of a candle in a window; the rest is darkness. I think of home: the winding streets of the Twist, raucous laughter spilling out of the brothels, half-starved cats stalking rats, the smell of spice and snow and smoke. The sounds and smells are all different here: wet stone from the afternoon rain, which came down in a torrent while the bells of Shou-shu chimed their magic for it; lamp oil and chicken shit; the click of dice and low voices behind courtyard walls. Where Spira City comes alive at night, Tianshi nestles down close to the earth, the people withdraw, the lights go out.

A slight rustling and whispering greets my arrival, a hint

of smoke from the small folds of paper tucked into the cracks in the wall. Spells. If it were someone other than me coming through the door, the whole household would be woken by now. Ours is a simple three-sided courtyard house, though the front wall facing onto the street is thick enough to disguise it as a proper courtyard house with living quarters on all four sides. I pass through the gate and straight into the yard, where the cantankerous goat we bought for milk looks up at me curiously. The chickens are sleeping in their enclosures, the messenger tree pipit chirruping in its cage. The servants' quarters, kitchen, and washrooms along the sides of the courtyard are dark, but a lamp glimmers inside the main house.

"Can't sleep?"

He looks up, startled. Frederick always has a look about him like you've just jumped around a corner and shouted something obscene, but right now he is genuinely surprised. He was too deep in his book to hear me come in.

"I don't sleep much, to be honest," he says. "It always feels like such a colossal waste of time. Anything interesting?"

"Very," I say, leaving my bag in a corner and throwing myself into the chair next to him. "What do you make of a Fraynish girl, about my age, living in the monastery?"

He frowns. "Are you sure?"

"Of course I'm bleeding sure. It's not an easy mistake. I saw her, and I heard her singing a Fraynish song. There was somebody else spying on her too. He came up through a tunnel under the monastery. Lives in Dongshui."

Frederick raises his eyebrows and puts his book down on the table, a sign I've really got his attention. It's very irritating when he keeps hanging on to his book while you talk and you know he's just waiting for a chance to get back to it without seeming rude. Poor Frederick has been very book-deprived since we left Frayne. He bought a book he couldn't even read at a shop in Ishti, just because he wanted one to hold, I suspect, though he claims it was because he wanted to study classical Ishtan.

"Odd sort of coincidence. I wonder what Mrs. Och will make of it," he says. He hesitates a fraction of a second before adding: "You're sure the spy was a man?"

"A boy, I reckon. My height."

"But male."

"He was wearing trousers."

"So are you," he points out.

In Yongguo the peasant women often wear trousers, and I must say I've rather taken to it. I'd never given much thought to the impracticality of women's clothing until I started dressing like a boy. I am wearing black for nighttime creeping: a pair of cotton trousers that button at the waist and ankles, a loose tunic of the sort women in the countryside wear, and peasant boots, a shoe with a length of tough fabric that wraps to midway up the calf. I've got my knife tucked into the bindings, and I leave the bottoms of my trousers unbuttoned so I can reach it easily. My hair is pinned up on my head, but the pins pinch, so I loosen them now, letting my hair fall over my shoulders.

"Got a pen?" I say. "I should sketch the layout while it's fresh in my mind."

Frederick fetches me a cartridge pen from his box of writing supplies, and I lay out the wrinkled map next to a blank piece of paper. I draw a more complete map, marking the Fraynish girl's secret courtyard and the spy's tunnel by the swallow coop. I hand it to Frederick when I'm done.

"Impressive," he says.

"Gangzi, if it's him, is still writing loads of letters," I say, looking at my map over his shoulder. "I've asked Wyn and Dek to find out who takes out the mail. We might be able to nab a few and see what he's writing about. I'd like to get into the Treasury too. It's got a steel door and two guards on duty right through the night."

"We're here for a man, not Gangzi's correspondence or treasure," says Frederick.

"You never know where a clue might turn up. What sort of thing do magic-using monks stash in a treasury, anyway?"

"I've no idea."

I stretch my legs and get up. "Well, enjoy your book. I'm going to get some sleep. Unlike you, I find sleeping to be one of the absolute best uses of my time."

I am leaving the room when he says: "Julia."

Frederick met me as Ella—a compliant, illiterate house-maid. I was a spy in Mrs. Och's house, digging up secrets, and he was rather taken with that fictitious person. I know he will never be as fond of Julia as he was of Ella, but the way he says my name tells me he no longer sees her when he looks at me. If we are not exactly friends, crossing half the world together has afforded us a kind of ease with one another. He looks different now than he did back in Spira City. He was a gangly youth when I met him, all arms and legs, but the months of hard travel have added a layer of muscle that suits him well. His fair beard has grown long, and his face is sunburnt, which has the effect of making his eyes look even bluer behind his spectacles. I lean against the doorframe, waiting for him to say what I know he is going to say.

"You're sure . . . you aren't worried, then, about this spy?"

He doesn't say her name, but I know he's thinking of Pia. I know because I think about her all the time as well. The last time I saw her, she was broken on the ground, bleeding from the knife I'd stuck in her gut, but I know better than to believe that was the end of her. We all know that Casimir, her employer, isn't going to let us go with his prize. He'll be searching for us here.

"It wasn't her," I tell him.

He nods, looking relieved. "Good night, Julia," he says. "Well done."

I leave him to his book and tiptoe into the dark of the room I share with Bianka and Theo. I feel blindly for my nightgown hanging from a nail in the wall and change as quietly as I can. Little Theo stirs, and my eyes adjust to the darkness enough to see him lying on a mat, curled against Bianka. A sash around his waist is tied to her wrist. She has stitched a spell into the sash, writing with thread that it shall not be undone except by her hand, and she checks the needle she sewed it with every night to make sure it is unbroken and that the spell will hold. It is the only way she can let herself sleep; she will not risk having him stolen from her a second time. And yet she agreed to have me, who stole him first, share their room. If she hadn't, I would have had to bunk down with Mrs. Och, so I am doubly indebted.

I lie down gently on my own sleeping mat, barely two feet from Bianka, who once counted me her direst enemy, and Theo, who has never understood enough to blame me. He looks an ordinary boy, not even two years old yet, with corkscrewing dark curls and a smile to melt lead. But woven into his being is such magic as could undo or remake the world, if put to proper use. Marvel at *that* when he's spilling his milk or pulling your hair.

"Lala," he murmurs when I lie down, his eyelids fluttering.

"Shh," I whisper, reaching across the gap between our sleeping mats and giving him my finger to hold. He wraps his little fist around it and is back asleep in seconds.

Sleep takes longer for me. I stare at the softness, the absolute peace of his face at rest—no fear at all, tucked against his mother, no idea of how he is hunted across the world, no awareness of the magical fragment Ko Dan hid inside him, bound to his essence, and which we only hope Ko Dan can take back out. I watch him breathing in the dark, and I swear by all the holies, as I do every night, that I will keep him safe. I'll make it right.

# FIVE

"Good morning, Julia. You had an eventful night, I hear."

Mrs. Och is next to the hearth, a stone-lined pit in the center of the room, wearing a black Tianshi-style robe embroidered with golden birds. She is examining the map I drew last night. Her back is straight, her eyes bright and alert. There is an unusual vigor about her. I know what that means, even before I look at Frederick slumped over the table, his face a sickly gray. He raises one hand in greeting and lets it drop again.

"And you've had a busy morning already," I reply, unable to keep the bite out of my voice.

I know he agrees to this, but still it makes me angry—perhaps at myself, as much as at her, for refusing to give her any of my own life force. She is dying, though very slowly, her power waning—and Frederick, Professor Baranyi, and Bianka all volunteer their own strength when she needs it. Bianka weathers it best, of course, being a witch, but

Frederick has no unnatural powers. It is horrible to see her vivid and sprightly while he slouches there so diminished, without even the strength to read. He speaks of it very rationally, how we need Mrs. Och and she needs strength. But I remember what it felt like when she took mine by force—albeit to save our lives—and I cannot bring myself to give it to her willingly.

Either she doesn't notice my tone or she ignores it deliberately. She looks up at me, and I feel a sick little jolt at her still-unfamiliar face. For two weeks now she has appeared to be an elderly lady from Yongguo, her white hair knotted on top of her head, her accent matching whatever region we were passing through. Still, I can't get used to this changeability of hers.

"Describe to me the girl you saw in the monastery."

"My age. Brown hair. Fancy clothes." I fold my arms across my chest. "Do you know why she's there?"

I am good enough at reading faces, but I have never been able to read Mrs. Och's, no matter what she looks like.

"No," she says. "But you had better keep an eye on her."

"D'you think she has anything to do with Ko Dan?" I ask.

"I doubt it."

"Then why should we care about her?"

"I care about a great many things," she says mildly.

I bite back a sarcastic retort as Bianka comes in with an apron full of eggs and Theo at her heels. He is tugging at her skirt and begging, "Egg? Egg?"

"No, you may not hold one," she snaps, maintaining her

stride and half dragging him along with her. "Last time you broke them, d'you remember? And then you had to go without your breakfast."

He gives me a sly look and murmurs, "Lala umma egg."

I glare back warningly and am glad he can't really talk yet. In fact, I slipped him most of my breakfast that time. For such a little thing, he certainly has an appetite.

"Egg," he sighs again, in a very world-weary manner. Bianka kneels by the hearth and begins to crack them carelessly into a pan, not bothering about the bits of shell. I've had months to get used to Bianka's cooking.

Giving up all hope of holding and probably smashing an egg, Theo comes to me. I scoop him up and plant a kiss on his soft, golden cheek. Bianka shoots us a wary glance. I can't blame her, but I can't resist him either.

"We need more bread" is all she says.

"Julia will go to the market today," says Mrs. Och. She's quite fond of that construction, *Julia will*, and employs it freely. I give Theo another squeeze and pretend to take a bite of his fat neck while he chortles.

"At nightfall you will go back to the monastery. Enough mapping. I want Ko Dan."

"So do I!" I half shout, startling Theo, who wriggles free of my embrace, affronted. "What d'you think I'm doing there every night? There are three hundred of them, and I don't even know what he looks like! *You* told me not to be seen. What am I meant to do, go up to them one after another and say, *Hullo, which of you is Ko Dan?*"

"Do not be insolent."

She turns her cool gaze on me, and I quake. Most of the time she just looks like an old woman, even if her features vary. But I've seen her look like something else altogether, well beyond human, and there are moments when she looks at me and I feel the full force of her centuries upon centuries, her potential for transformation, the ancient, fading power hovering just behind the kindly face and still eyes.

"I just don't know what I'm supposed to do," I mutter.

"You are a resourceful girl, Julia. Find him. *How* is entirely up to you. I ask only that you remain unseen, particularly if there is another spy about."

Bianka stirs the eggs, not looking at me. Frederick's eyes are closed.

"I'll go get bread," I say curtly, and then, because I am angry and because I can do it, I vanish right in front of her. It wouldn't have worked, once—but I've learned a thing or two about what I can do since then.

Nothing changes in her expression—or nothing that I can see—but I hear Theo cry out, a muffled sound, and I feel a stab of regret. Bianka reaches for him, and I walk out, banging the door shut so they know I've gone.

We entered Tianshi on false papers, and we are all trying to stay out of sight as much as possible—easier for me than for the others. I follow the narrow road outside our gate to the Dongnan Canal and walk along it, toward the market.

To reach Tianshi from anywhere, you must cross either the desert or the sea, and its forbidding walls, famous the world round, are visible for miles, forming a rectangle around the great city. They call it the Heavenly City, and it is indeed a marvelous place. The bells of Shou-shu are chiming, a merry sound for fine weather. The sky is a distant, impossible blue, the sun pouring down on the brightly colored tile rooftops and the green leaves of the persimmon trees. The incantations on the bells were inscribed by long-ago witches; struck in a particular way, in a particular order, they can change the weather. That is why drought and other natural disasters so seldom strike Tianshi. The city and the forests and farmland surrounding it sit lush and green at the edge of the vast desert. The bells call and the rain comes. The bells warn, and the dust storm withdraws. So they say, in any case.

The smaller branches of the trees are wrapped in twists of paper, and some of these little slips are blowing along the street, having come loose from whatever branches they were fastened to, bearing somebody's dearest wish written out in elegant Yongwen characters. It's still odd to me, seeing customs long banned in Frayne flourishing out in the open in Yongguo—like the little shrines to the elements along the roads, or men walking about with tattoos visible on their hands, necks, even faces. I continue along the canal, which is full of narrow, painted boats, their gunwales hung with charms, everything slightly blurred by the haze of my vanishing, while the slender trees loose swirls of petals as well as wishes onto the breeze.

Not so long ago, my vanishing seemed a simple thing, a trick, a gift, and I never sought a reason for it. I thought of it like a pocket in the world, available only to me. A single step back into that space and I was hidden in plain view—from ordinary eyes, at least. There were exceptions: My friend Liddy, in Spira City, could still see me. Then Mrs. Och, and Theo too. But I've learned that the space I used to vanish into is merely the edge of somewhere else. And I've been practicing.

Another step back—my surroundings growing hazier, sound coming a bit muffled and distant—and not even the likes of Mrs. Och can see me. I tried it out on her on the steamer from Nim. "Tell me when you can't see me anymore," I said, and pulled away—carefully—one step, two steps. She didn't say anything, but I saw fear in her eyes when I returned to the world, and while I'm not exactly proud of it, I confess I felt a ripple of triumph. This power is all I've got, and with her I was always powerless. Not anymore.

Three steps back: My perspective begins to scramble, lose focus, and I feel a tingling, a loss of sensation that starts in my extremities. Four steps: I disappear into a dizzying vantage point from which my senses take in everything, from every direction, but I can't find or feel my own body—I don't *have* a body there. I've been practicing this too, because it's one way to get over a wall. From that unsettling nowhere, if I can focus in on a particular spot, I can return to my body there instead of where I started out. For example, on the other side of a wall. Still, I prefer the more traditional means of breaking and entering. Disappearing so completely leaves me feeling shaky and a bit sick. Always, I'm terrified I might not find my way back to my body.

And there is another place even beyond that. I have not dared return to it since I was in Casimir's fortress, where he broke my wrist and all the fingers on my left hand, told me how he watched my mother drown, threatened to cut me open and murder my friends before my eyes. Then, fueled by terror and pain and despair, I wanted only to escape my surroundings and my *self* entirely. And I did.

I still dream of those burning streets. I see my own hands, which were not human hands, and I remember how it felt, and I know that there is something in me I do not understand. The gift I've always taken pride in, *reveled* in, turns out to be the tip of something dark and vast and terrifying. I know it is there, at my back—that I must be something other than what I have believed, if I can enter there.

My desire to know what I can do—what I *am*—and my fear of knowing the same have been pressed up against each other for months. Now I have an idea—something that might lead me to Ko Dan. I've pretended to be many things I'm not. I try to tell myself this will be the same— a pretense—but my heart tightens in my chest just thinking about it. There's fear, yes, but something else too, something I can't quite name—a sort of quivering thrill, like that feeling when you stand at the edge of a high ledge and you almost think you might step off it just to see what it's like to fall.

# SIX

To pass the time on the ship that was carrying us along Ishti's great Mohasi River, Professor Baranyi told us the story of Haizea, Ishtan goddess of vengeance, and Tisis, goddess of mercy, arguing over a bereft mother after a battle. We asked him, "So what *did* she choose?" and he said, "Isn't that the whole of the human story? That choice?" This earned him a blank stare from Wyn, an eye roll from Bianka, and a chuckle from Frederick. I was struck less by the story than by the illustration he showed us in a book of the goddesses on their holy hill, watching the battle. Tisis was lovely, her hair like a river, stars on her skin, holding out a cup that overflowed with light. Haizea's hair coiled around her head like snakes, and her eyes were black caverns dripping blood. In one hand she held a whirlwind like a sword. Her hands and feet were clawed.

It was the hands that made me shiver, reminding me of the glimpse I'd had in that other place, high above the burning city, of a hand that was not my own at the end of my arm, holding the gun I would use on Casimir's witch, Shey. While Professor Baranyi pontificated on the parable of the goddesses, why they so often appear together in stories and in art, I stared at the picture of Haizea, looked into her bleeding eyes, and saw something I recognized. Today she will be my inspiration and my disguise.

There is a gap between the Hall of Abnegation and the monastery's north wall, where I've smelled tobacco early in the evening. I go there now and tuck myself against the wall, vanishing. Monks are not meant to smoke, of course. The Shou-shu monks practice something called selflessness, which is not exactly what it sounds like, but maybe that's just the poor translation. They strive to transcend the physical world, all of their bodily needs and worldly attachments. It is said that those who achieve selflessness live for hundreds of years, and that they do not eat or feel pain or desire—although *somebody* is eating those swallow's eggs and the vegetables in Gangzi's garden. In any case, the goal is immortality without the need for sustenance—the triumph of the spirit over the body. The greatest leader of Shou-shu was a man called Li Feizi, who is said to have lived a thousand years before one day walking out of the monastery to the holy mountain Tama-shan, where he perhaps remains to this day. Gangzi claims to be four hundred years old. I have my doubts, and anyway I can't imagine what the point of living forever would be if you're just going to stay shut up in a monastery not eating or feeling anything. I am not in the least surprised that out of three hundred monks, there are a few novices who are doing their time here for prestige, with no intention of taking the lifelong vows, and for whom a secret smoke break is a welcome reprieve from trying to transcend all desire and whatnot.

I hold the image of Haizea in my mind, half hoping that my smoking monk will not come tonight. But eventually he does, squeezing into the gap against the wall and trying to surreptitiously light his little pipe. He is young, and I suppose that can only make it easier. Then again, if he is too new, he may not know anything. I ease myself back into the world next to him, and his features come into focus. He gives a little squawk and drops his pipe.

"Oath breaker," I say in what I hope is passable Yongwen. I practiced it with Frederick this afternoon, once he'd recovered a bit from Mrs. Och's draining him. Even if I can deliver my lines, though, I can't be sure that I'll understand whatever this young monk might have to tell me.

He turns to flee, and I grab him by the shoulder. Here it is. I take a deep breath and yank him with me. One step—two—three—four—oh Nameless, help me—five: it feels like falling—back through the membrane of that edge-of-the-world space, back to the void in between, back to the place I swore I'd never revisit.

Kahge. That's what Mrs. Och's youngest brother, Gennady, called it—the hell of Rainist cosmology. But the idea of it is older than that. Whether he was right or not, it is *farther* than I remember. In Casimir's fortress, it felt as if that

39

place and the world were almost overlapping—I could see them both at once, could slip from one to the other and back again in an instant.

But this is different. I feel as if we are spinning in nothingness for a long time, the monastery and the city and the sky all around us at odd angles, and the monk screaming and then silenced, voiceless. For a horrible minute or two I think we are lost in the void, *lost*.

Then we are through. The boiling river is swollen, and Spira City, half formed and in flames, lies on either bank. Still Spira, no matter where *I* am—and I wonder why. We are standing on a boat that moves fast through the water, its ragged sails full even though there is no wind, only the still air steaming. The young monk falls to his knees, gibbering. My hand on his shoulder is a hooked, dark thing with black claws.

I am shaking with horror at the world transformed, *myself* transformed, but at the same time I feel a rush of something like triumph. Maybe just because I can do it. Not only by accident or in the madness of mortal terror but on purpose, with intent: I can pull another person right out of the world with me. Oh, what *am* I? And also, what power!

I spit the Yongwen words out, my voice hoarse and unfamiliar: *"Where is Ko Dan?"*

He stares at me, uncomprehending, and I think I've overdone it, terrified him beyond usefulness. I give him a shake, not too hard, but his bones in my grip feel absurdly fragile.

I am afraid I might snap him in two by accident. Easy, Julia. Focus. I repeat the question: *"Where is Ko Dan?"*

He stammers an answer that I can barely hear over the roar of flames sucking up the air, over the roar of my heart.

*"Again!"*

He is telling me he doesn't know. Hounds, what a waste this will be if he knows nothing at all. Now he is talking, but so fast that I don't understand.

*"Where? Where? Where?"*

He repeats his answer over and over, wringing his hands, and this much I do understand: Ko Dan is gone. Disappeared. My heart sinks. The monk is weeping, pouring sweat. I think he has pissed himself, and frankly I'm not far from doing the same. I manage the bit I memorized this afternoon, though:

*"I am Haizea, goddess of vengeance, and I will drown the world in blood and fire if you betray me. If you speak of this, the first blood will be yours. Do you hear me, human? Secret, secret, secret!"*

He promises, sobbing loudly. Even if he does tell, he'll be thought mad. When I look up, the boat is moving in slow circles. On the shore, a tall, cloaked figure with the face of a fox and enormous antlers reaches an arm toward me. Shadows gather behind him, monstrous shapes taking form through the smoke, tusks and snouts and curved teeth.

*"Lidari,"* crows the fox-faced figure, pointing right at me with his human hand. What the bleeding stars *are* these things? The other voices join in with awful screeches and roars: *"Lidari! Lidari!"*

I yank the whimpering monk back, away, spinning through emptiness and at last falling hard against the monastery's north wall, behind the Hall of Abnegation. The monk's knees give way instantly, and he sits, huddled and damp, staring up at me. I watch my hand pick up his pipe, stick it in his mouth, fetch his scattered matches, light it for him.

"Good man," I hear myself say in my own voice, putting a finger to my lips. "Not a word."

At first I think that I am all right. I can go to Kahge—or wherever it is—then come back to the world and be on my way. I'm just a little wobbly. But as I round the corner of the Hall of Abnegation, I start shaking so hard I can't walk anymore. I lean against the smooth wood of the hall, clenching and unclenching my fists, struggling to breathe. All I can hear is the rush and buzz of my blood.

My dirty fingernails bring me back to myself. I stare at my shaking hands—but they are just my hands, a girl's callused hands, broken fingernails. The image of those great hooked claws clutching the monk rises up in my mind, and my gorge rises too.

A basic rule of spying is to leave nothing behind—no sign that you have been there. But I leave the contents of my stomach on the path by the Hall of Abnegation before I can gather myself up and make my way home.

# SEVEN

"Stoy," says Theo, imperious in the way that surely only royalty and small children can be, pushing my breakfast off my lap and plunking himself down there instead.

"You're going to get me filthy!" I object, but I pull him close anyway, drawing comfort from the feel of his skin and my own—ordinary, human. And yet we have this in common, Theo and I: something inside us that is neither ordinary nor human at all.

In Theo's case, it is part of a book—*The Book of Disruption*. Mrs. Och says that long ago, when everything had a will and an essence of its own, the spirit of fire, called Feo in Fraynish lore, wrote magic into the world, disrupting the natural order by giving herself dominion. The original power grab, in other words. The other spirits joined together and subdued Feo. They couldn't completely destroy the book she'd made, but they managed to break it in three. Then they birthed the immortal Xianren—Mrs. Och, Casimir, and

Gennady, as I know them—and charged *them* with guarding the fragments of the Book, keeping them separate, and keeping order in a world now overflowing with magic. That's the story anyway. Millennia passed; the spirits dwindled and became part of the earth. The fragments of the Book changed shape too—Casimir's became a lake, Mrs. Och's a great tree, and Gennady's a shadow that clung to him. As their power faded, the Xianren had to reckon at last with the inevitability of death. Let's just say Casimir hasn't faced it gracefully. He decided to reassemble the Book, the source of magic in the world, turn it back into text, and harness its power. He already has two fragments: his own, and Mrs. Och's, which he stole.

He almost got the third, as well. Gennady, with the help of the monk Ko Dan, tried to hide his part of the Book from Casimir by binding it to his son's essence and then leaving Bianka and Theo behind so nobody would ever know. It was a ridiculous bit of overconfidence—secrets that big are hard to keep. When Casimir figured out what had happened, he hired me to kidnap Theo. I didn't know that was the job at first, but when it came down to it and Pia threatened my life and the lives of those I loved if I didn't obey Casimir, I proved myself a gutless pawn and did as I was told.

Every day, I wake up with that fact: I took Theo from his mother, and from safety, and I handed him over for silver. I nearly got him killed. Granted, I got him back too—but he's not yet safe. Not until we find Ko Dan and get the Book fragment out of Theo. Then it will be up to Mrs. Och to keep her brother from assembling the fragments. I intend to see Theo safely out of the whole business.

Now I hold him against me and rock back and forth a little. His legs are muddy, and he is wearing nothing but a dirty shirt that hangs to his knees. He looks quite the little urchin, except for how well fed he is, round-cheeked and dimpled at the knees and elbows. He goes about shoeless and perpetually underdressed, never seeming to feel the cold, but today the air is balmy and springlike and so I am having my breakfast on the steps outside. Or I'm trying to, anyway.

"Lala umma wap Teo," he says comfortably. "Stoy."

"Please," says Bianka, washing dishes by the pump.

"Pees," repeats Theo mechanically.

"All right," I say, laughing.

My mother used to tell us stories, Dek and I curled against her body in the bed for warmth. I hadn't thought about them in years, but now whenever Theo asks for a story, they return to me whole, emerging from the depths of my memory like glittering beasts rising up from the bottom of the sea, freighted with all the fears and wonders of my girlhood.

When I tell my mother's stories, I can't see her face, but I remember her intonation, her dark hair falling over her shoulders and brushing against my cheek. I remember her hands illustrating the story: clever brown fingers that became birds flying, soldiers marching, a spider pouncing, the breeze wafting, or the moonlight filtering down.

"Once upon a time," I say, and Theo sticks his thumb in

his mouth, "there was a fisherman called Tomas. He married a beautiful girl and they had a beautiful son."

"Sun!" cries Theo around his thumb, pointing at the sky with his other hand.

"Not that kind of sun," I say. "A boy, like you."

"Teo," he agrees, and goes back to sucking his thumb.

"Yes. So one day Tomas is out fishing when he feels a tug on the line, and he reels in a great big silver-blue fish, twisting about on the end of the hook." I mime reeling in a fishing rod, and Theo mimes along with one hand. "The fish lands on the rocks—*whap*—and says to the man, 'What do you want?' Well, the man is ever so surprised. Fish can't talk!"

Theo cackles. He's too young to understand the stories, but he seems to like them anyway.

"So he takes the fish home, fills a big pot with water from the well, and puts the fish in the pot. The fish swims in circles and asks him the same question again: 'What do you want?' It starts him thinking. At first Tomas thinks that maybe he already has everything he wants. He has his lovely wife, his lovely son, his lovely house on a lovely island. But the more he thinks about it, the more he thinks that none of that is what he wants most deeply. He doesn't want to waste his wish, and surely a fish that can talk is a fish that can grant wishes. So he tells his wife: 'Wife, this life is not the life for me. It does not fulfill my deepest wish. I must go and seek my heart's desire. Please take care of this fish until I come back.'"

Bianka has stopped washing the dishes and is watching

us with a complicated expression I can't interpret. Her hair, normally an unruly black cloud around her face, is tied back in a kerchief, and it makes her face look smaller, somehow diminished. She does not discourage Theo's affection for me, or mine for him, but I can only imagine how she feels seeing me with him. Still, she knows—I am sure she knows; I have told her and it was the truth and she believed it— that I would die before letting anyone harm him again. It's a strange thing to love a child so helplessly. It's different from every other love that I've known. When he laughs his beautiful, crescendoing laugh, I think my heart will crack right open. I could live on that laugh and nothing else.

"Go on," says Bianka. "What happens then?"

"Well, Tomas goes off and he travels the world. He has a great many fine adventures, but he keeps traveling to find his deepest desire. Years pass and he grows old. He is too tired to travel anymore. He goes home and finds his wife packing all her things. He asks her where the fish is. She tells him that she killed and ate it the night he left. Without Tomas to provide for them, they were very poor, but when their son was grown, he went to the city to seek his fortune. He was very clever and became a rich man. Now, she tells Tomas, she is going to live with him in his big house in the city so she can spend her old age in comfort. Tomas remains alone in the falling-down house on the island, and every day he thinks of that beautiful fish twisting in the air long ago and of the moment the fish spoke to him, when everything still seemed possible."

I stop, and Theo pulls his thumb out of his mouth.

"The end," I say lamely.

"Dee enn," he repeats, and slides off my lap, running to chase the chickens around the yard.

"Another of your mother's stories?" asks Bianka, staring at me.

"I don't know any others," I say, half apologetically.

They are odd stories to tell a child—they are odd stories in general—but Dek and I loved them when we were little. When my mother finished telling us that story, we were outraged, berating Tomas for his foolishness, for not seeing that he had everything he wanted already. But Ma said, "I think we are all like that." I can't say that I agree. I can think of times in my own life when I was so happy I only wished that nothing would ever change. Before Ma died, before Dek had Scourge. And then later, with Wyn, for a while. But I think my mother could relate to Tomas—his restless heart, his aimless longing.

Tiring quickly of the chickens, Theo goes and bangs on the gate with a stick.

"Mama!" he shouts. "Owwwwwd."

She shakes her head at him and sighs. "We're going to go mad if we have to stay cooped up in this courtyard much longer."

She looks so unhappy, squatting barefoot in the mud by the pump with the dirty dishes stacked next to her. She has been very low since I told her last night that Ko Dan was missing.

"I'll help wash up," I say. Theo gives up on the gate and comes over to splash under the water and get in the way. We laugh at him and wash up together and it almost feels natural, like we are friends—except, of course, it can never really feel that way.

Nearly clean now from the pump, shirt soaking, Theo runs squealing across the yard while we dry the dishes and carry them into the kitchen. Bianka heads back out ahead of me. From our makeshift scullery I hear her cry, "*Theo!*"

I run for the door, heart in my throat. She is bolting across the yard after him. Somehow he has gotten the latch of the gate open with his stick. He sees her coming and runs out into the road, shouting with glee. Before I can get across the yard, she has him, pulling him back in, slamming the gate. Her face is all twisted up and she is shouting at him: "Never run off! Never!" She whacks him on the backside. He squirms free of her and runs to me, grabbing my leg and howling with rage. Bianka stalks past us and then drops down on the steps, clutching her head in her hands and letting loose a ragged scream that dissolves into sobs.

Theo stops hollering and stares at her in shock. He can't understand any of it, of course—why he has to stay shut up in here or why his mother reacts with such ferocity when he tries to stray out of her sight. He can't feel that piece of *The Book of Disruption* fused to his flesh and blood and his innermost self. If anyone can take the text out of Theo without killing him, it will be the man who put it there. But if

Ko Dan has disappeared from Shou-shu, we are without leads or any idea of where to look for him.

"Theo, my darling," Bianka sobs, reaching for him. He lets go of me and dives into her arms. She pulls him close, covering his curly head with kisses; he buries his face in her neck. I leave them there, a horrible pit forming in my stomach, and go back into the main house.

"Ah, Julia," says Mrs. Och, smiling at me. A tree pipit is perched on her shoulder, and she is holding a rolled-up slip of paper. "We need to find you a dress."

"We do?"

"Yes. Gregor has been granted an appointment with the grand librarian."

# EIGHT

Later that afternoon I am at the elegant courtyard house in the Xihuo Triangle with Csilla's knee in my back while she pulls my corset on so tight I can hardly breathe. It's an item I rarely bothered with in Spira City and have not worn at all these past two months, traveling and dressing like a boy. I straighten my shoulders and grimace.

"Nice to see a waist on you again," says Csilla, pleased with her work.

"I don't know. I always wanted a brother," says Dek, who has come by with a sleek, nickel-plated pistol for Esme from a weapons dealer in Dongshui.

Esme laughs at my expression. Easy for her, dressed as a manservant. I'd begged to simply go along vanished, but Mrs. Och preferred to have a role for me just in case, reasoning that I could always vanish if need be but could not spring into existence if I started out vanished.

"I was getting used to breathing freely," I grumble. "I think

I might stick to men's clothes from now on. Take a leaf out of Esme's book."

"Oh, please no," says Csilla. She yanks my hair back so hard I yell and fastens it deftly on top of my head.

"A brother I could call Jules. We'd be a fearsome pair," continues Dek, carefully oiling the barrel of the pistol.

Csilla pinches my chin between her thumb and forefinger and frowns at my face, as if it isn't up to snuff. "Honestly, Julia, you're not bad-looking if you'd just put in a little effort."

"Well, we aren't aiming for beauty today," says Esme. "Plain as plain will do just fine. Julia ought not to attract too much attention."

No fear of that with Csilla nearby. She has been a great boon to the single New Porian dress shop in Tianshi. Today she is wearing a low-cut gown made of watered silk, with a ruffle of lace along the bust, her hair a fountain of white-gold curls. She is utterly contemptuous of the fashion in Tianshi. The women look like they are wearing drapes, she says. I thought so too when we first arrived, watching the ladies in their wide, stiff robes trotting around on dainty silk shoes. But the funny thing is that if you spend some time in a place, you start to see all its strangeness as natural, and I can imagine now how absurd and immodest Csilla's dress might appear to the dignified drape-women of Tianshi.

Csilla dresses me in a plainer gown than her own, a dark blue piece that buttons to my chin, the idea being to make me look as young, and therefore as harmless, as possible. It is still the most elegant dress I've ever worn, and I do not like it. I am meant to be Ella Heriday, Lord and Lady Heriday's daughter, an educated girl and my father's secretary. I look like a miserable governess. I try to take a deep breath, and think that the appearance of a trim waist is hardly worth this feeling of having my lungs locked up.

"I suppose if you've been off buying weapons, you haven't found out who collects the mail from the monastery yet," I say to Dek.

"I have, actually," says Dek. "Or Wyn has, I should say. A government employee brings the mail and takes it out twice a week, and there's a basket of letters bearing Gangzi's seal every time. Anything in particular you want?"

"I'd just like to know what he's writing about. Can you get me one?"

"I reckon we can buy one off the mail carrier," he says. "Mrs. Och gave us loads of money for bribes."

Gregor wanders in with a bottle, more than half empty, of the amber-colored persimmon wine *shijiu* in his hand, and Csilla spins me to face him.

"What do you think of your new daughter?" she asks. He looks me up and down, unimpressed.

"Don't know why you're taking so much trouble with her clothes. Nobody's going to look twice at her anyway."

I suppose I can't fault him for saying what I was just thinking myself.

"Put that bottle down," says Esme. "You can't turn up drunk."

She is the only one who can say it. Esme and Gregor have a long history, dating back to the so-called Lorian Uprising, in Frayne, the year before I was born. Esme's husband, Gustaf Moreau, was Gregor's best friend and a leader of the uprising. Gustaf was captured and hung, along with countless others, the uprising was crushed, and somehow the grief and failure has kept them bonded all these years after. Gregor's expression darkens, but he doesn't argue with her. He puts the *shijiu* on the lacquered side table, throws himself down on the settee, and then looks at the bottle.

"No point going in sober," he says. "I'm supposed to be a Fraynish aristocrat, remember? I grew up with the Fraynish aristocracy. They're drunk all the time."

"Maybe in *your* family," says Esme. "But you're supposed to be a scholarly nobleman, not the drunk, idle variety."

I try to catch Dek's eye, but he has gone back to polishing Esme's gun, studiously avoiding looking at me.

"Rotten stuff anyway, *shijiu*," says Gregor, still gazing at the bottle with a terrible longing. "Flaming Kahge, but I miss whiskey. What I'd do for a nice bottle of whiskey. Or rum. Give me rum. Anything but this fruity *shijiu* stuff. Barely taste it."

"Then stop bleeding drinking it," says Esme.

Csilla powders my face, her dark eyes bottomless and blank.

"Gregor's right, nobody's going to look at me," I say, but she keeps at me like I'm a painting she's working on.

54

Professor Baranyi comes in, and immediately the mood changes, becoming not exactly hostile, but guarded. When he sees me, the professor looks faintly surprised, as if he'd forgotten I'd be joining them. I wonder if he finds it as uncomfortable lodging with my gang as I do lodging with his. Probably slightly less so, since none of mine have any reason to want to murder him in his sleep; still, I reckon we'd both love to switch.

"Ah! Hello, Julia. Nice to see you," he says.

I doubt it is particularly nice to see me, but I say hello back politely.

"Is Mrs. Och well?"

"Much as usual," I reply.

"Well!" He looks around nervously, his eyes darting between Gregor and the near-empty bottle of *shijiu* a few times. "Are we ready?"

"Ready as we'll ever be!" declares Gregor, rising with a flourish but spoiling it by staggering a little and then giggling.

Even drunk, Gregor cuts a dashing figure. He is tall and broad and graying at the temples, and while his drink-ravaged face could not be called handsome anymore, he has a kind of charisma about him that can at times affect even those of us who know him and his weaknesses all too well. He makes a fine Fraynish aristocrat. Whether he can pose convincingly as a scholar is another question altogether, and I have my doubts, even though the professor has been coaching him for weeks.

Csilla slips her arm through his to steady him.

"You look *marvelous*," he tells her, and she softens against him.

When I was little, I thought Csilla impossibly glamorous, and she and Gregor struck me as very romantic in their moony-eyed devotion to one another—particularly compared to the endless quarreling I remember between my own parents. As I got older and lost some of my illusions, I came to see that drink has always been Gregor's one true love, and that Csilla's glamour is like lacquer painted over a brokenness I can barely fathom. Still, even knowing that they are bound above all by their shared disappointment— with life and with Gregor himself—when I see them gazing at each other this way, I envy them a little. I miss being in love and thinking it such a fine and unassailable thing.

# NINE

The Imperial Gardens are guarded by elite warriors called the Ru. Their lightweight, flexible armor covers all but their eyes. They stand with feet planted apart, eyes fixed straight ahead, gleaming weapons strapped to their chests and backs, double-pointed spears in their gloved fists. Wyn and I tried to make fun of them when we first arrived in Tianshi, but the truth is, there is something terrifying about them.

At the great Huanglong Gate, Gregor presents our invitation from the grand librarian to the Ru, and we pass under the twisting, gold-plated dragon that stretches over the top of the gate, its wide crimson mouth pointing down as if to gobble us up. The Imperial Gardens are reputed to be one of the wonders of the world, and indeed, stepping inside those grounds is like entering an enchanted fairyland. There are tiered waterfalls, ponds flashing with red-gold carp, walkways made of pale jade and lined with flowering trees, and brightly feathered birds that watch us from the branches above with an unsettling intelligence.

The Imperial Residences sit on a huge pedestal at the center of the gardens. Arranged around this pedestal, among the lakes and wooded paths and flower gardens, are the homes, studios, laboratories, and so on, of those citizens clever and talented enough to have earned a place here. The buildings are all white, which has a rather blinding effect, while the Imperial Residences are painted bright red, with gold-plated tiles on the sweeping rooftops.

A small troop of the Ru leads us up the steps to the Imperial Residences and an open-air pavilion overlooking the gardens. A tall, powerfully built man in an elegant silk robe, his long beard shot through with gray, is peering through a magnifying glass at a scroll spread across the table in front of him. He is holding what appears to be a needle. He looks up as we approach, then puts aside his instruments and, to all of our surprise, greets us in fluent Fraynish.

"Welcome to the Heavenly City, Lord Heriday," he says in a gravelly but pleasant voice. "I am Si Tan, the grand librarian of Yongguo."

Frederick explained to me that the grand librarian, officially head of the Imperial Library, functions almost as the prime minister does in Frayne—he is second only to the emperor. In fact, though, Yongguo's emperor is quite a young man, and it is said that the grand librarian and the empress dowager are the true powers behind the throne. Si Tan certainly looks like a man who is confident of his authority. He shakes Gregor's hand and raises Csilla's to his lips. She drops a deep curtsy.

"I thank you, I thank you!" booms Gregor. He claps Professor Baranyi on the shoulder, and the professor stumbles a bit. "I brought my translator, but it seems we have no need of him!"

I feel a flutter of anxiety at that. We'd all assumed that the professor would be the main communicator and Gregor merely a mouthpiece, a face. If the grand librarian speaks Fraynish, Gregor will have to bluff rather more effectively than we'd expected.

Si Tan looks at each of us in turn as Gregor introduces us. I do my best to appear unmemorable—the dull, bookish daughter—but still his eyes rest on me, drink me in. I feel as if I'm being memorized and explored. He is an intimidating size, and in spite of his scholarly beard, fine robe, and impeccable manners, there is something of a brute about him, I think. The way he moves like a giant cat, the way he flexes his large, powerful hands, the hardness around his eyes.

"Lovely place you've got here," says Gregor. He glances at the scroll on the table. "Doing a bit of writing, are you?"

"Come, I will show you," says Si Tan, waving him over. "I think miniaturism is not a popular art form in Frayne."

"Minia-whatsit?" says Gregor, bending over the long scroll. "Flaming Kahge, what's all this?"

I crane around him to look. The scroll is covered with beautiful rows of calligraphy, but there is a bright band of color all along its edges. Si Tan hands Gregor the magnifying glass. He peers through it and exclaims, "Hounds, how by the stars d'you do *that?*"

"A visiting artist from Piram introduced the form to Yongguo. We invited many artists from Piram to the city after that, to teach miniaturism." He offers the magnifying glass to each of us in turn. The colorful border is, in fact, a long and complicated illustration. There are boats on rivers, peasants crossing bridges, soldiers on horseback—all of it so tiny that to the naked eye it can hardly be made out at all, and yet I see with the magnifying glass that the soldiers are frowning, that the woman with the bucket of water on her head has a dreamy expression on her face.

"I am only an amateur, of course. It takes years to master the technique," says Si Tan.

"I should think so," blusters Gregor. "What's the bleeding point?"

If this is his impression of a scholar, I think he needs more practice.

"The point of art?" asks Si Tan, smiling faintly.

"It is tremendously clever," says Csilla quickly. "You're quite right that it hasn't reached Frayne. I have never seen anything like it."

"This is the story of a hero we call Muhan, who vanquished giants invading Yongguo from the north," says Si Tan.

"Giants?" says Csilla. She is holding Gregor's arm very tightly, like she's trying to restrain him. "Is it a true story?"

"A legend," he says. "But there is a kind of truth in such old stories, though your Fraynish king may not agree."

I can feel Professor Baranyi's agitation coming off him in

60

waves. He is like a cabriolet driver watching his vehicle roll down a hill without him to steer it.

"Very interesting," says Gregor, more subdued now. Perhaps Csilla has been pinching him.

"May I offer refreshment?" asks Si Tan, putting aside the scroll.

Gregor brightens immediately. "Splendid! Thank you, yes! It's thirsty weather, isn't it?"

The afternoon passes slowly, in awkward politeness and sipping tea, which has Gregor very glum and disappointed. I am glad now that I did not come vanished, as there is a tray of delicate wafers that melt to a sweet powder on the tongue. I help myself to as many as I can while the others make idle chat. Esme has to nudge me to get me to stop reaching for more, which seems unfair, since the tray is still half full and nobody else is eating any. I notice Si Tan looking over at Esme a number of times, trying to catch her eye, with the air of a boxer sussing out his opponent. He doesn't believe she's a servant, I think anxiously. This is a man who recognizes authority when he sees it, no matter how it's dressed.

Finally, wanting a drink very badly by now, Gregor runs out of patience and interrupts the conversation about architecture that Csilla is managing quite well to say, "Well now, my dear man, we are here to see if we might visit your famous library."

"Ah yes," says Si Tan, his eyes alert, the polite expression on his face shifting subtly. "You are interested in Shou-shu. Tell me."

"Well, yes, that's just it. The hierarchy is what I'm writing on. How monks rise in the ranks, how they keep their authority separate from the empire, that sort of thing."

Si Tan folds his big hands together in a gesture that to me seems full of menace, although I can't say why. "Most scholars want to know about the bells," he says. "Or the longevity of the monks."

"The organization of the place is my real interest," says Gregor. "Not the magic. I want to know how it functions on a, er, *human* level."

"Then why Shou-shu in particular?" asks Si Tan.

"Why? Because it is the most important sect, residing within the most powerful city in the world," says Gregor. He is not doing so badly, I think, even if it all sounds memorized. I am watching the professor out of the corner of my eye, but he is managing to keep his expression neutral. "They govern themselves, keep their numbers small, and have managed it for thousands of years without revolts, dissent, or trouble with the empire. Fascinating."

"You are interested in leadership?" Si Tan asks. "In Gangzi, head of the Shou-shu Council? Succession, perhaps?"

"Yes, yes," says Gregor enthusiastically. "How the leaders are chosen. How they wield their authority. What the rules are. That sort of thing."

"Your past work is largely on New Porian monks, I understand," says Si Tan. "They are subject to the state's authority, are they not?"

"Yes," says Gregor. "Very different system. We don't call

them monks in Frayne, but holies. They run the temples, but they answer to the Crown, yes."

"And it is the same in other New Porian countries?"

"Similar. They all answer to the heads of state, yes, all the holies."

"New Poria proclaims the ultimate authority of the Nameless One, and yet does not place its holies on equal footing with its kings and queens," remarks Si Tan.

"No, indeed, very true, bit of a contradiction, isn't it?" says Gregor, beginning to get nervous a good few minutes after the rest of us have started to sweat.

"You wrote a book on these . . . holies, you call them? The hierarchies within the Fraynish temples. Tell me about your findings."

Gregor blusters through some of what the professor has coached him on. Si Tan asks him one sharply pointed question after another, and with each answer Gregor seems to be floundering more. He does not sound like a man discussing his life's work. He sounds like a man terribly anxious to not say the wrong thing and being as vague as possible. I think I can feel us collectively beginning to panic. Since Esme isn't looking at me, I snatch three more wafers and stuff them into my mouth. I don't know what the penalty is for coming to the grand librarian under false pretenses. Si Tan grows more and more stern and specific. He asks for names. He asks for dates. Twice he corrects Gregor, showing us that he knows more than we'd reckoned about what the professor had hoped would be an obscure topic.

"The Holy Findis, two hundred years ago, wrote a dictum on the relationship between the king and the temple that was condemned, but he was not executed for treason after the trial. What was his defense?"

I have never heard of this case, and apparently neither has Gregor. Si Tan has stopped pretending this is a conversation. It is a test, and he wants us to know it.

"His defense?" says Gregor faintly.

Csilla is getting a wild look on her face.

The professor can't bear it anymore. "I remember taking notes on his trial defense for you, sir," he interjects. "You took a rather surprising position on it, as I remember. That he was not trying to save his life, but to offer a new way of looking at Crown and temple. He believed he *would* be executed for saying that the temple was the root of the tree and the Crown was the trunk, the people of Frayne the branches. But, in fact, the Crown rather liked the metaphor. Perhaps a poor understanding of botany allowed them to take it as a compliment . . ."

Si Tan turns his gaze slowly to the professor, who trails off a bit at the end. He has done Gregor no service here. We are all silent. Then Si Tan rises.

"It has been a pleasure meeting *all* of you," he says with chilling politeness.

He goes to his table, writes something on a scroll, and stamps it with his seal. We all just sit there, frozen. He rolls up the paper and, pointedly ignoring Gregor, hands it to Professor Baranyi.

"Here is my seal and permission," he says. "A man named Fan Ming will call on you tomorrow. He will be your guide and take you to the library. There are no restrictions—you may enter any part of the library and examine all the records you wish to see."

He bows to the professor and then to Esme while a stunned Gregor scrambles to his feet and bows back. I feel a little ill. He's figured us out completely, including who is really in charge here.

"Now, please, stay awhile, enjoy the view. I will ask someone to bring you dinner."

With that, he walks away from us, his elaborate robe trailing on the ground behind him. Esme shoots me a look from the corner of her eye. I pop one last wafer into my mouth and disappear in his wake, following him down the path and into the red building across the way. He walks down a corridor that opens into a room all hung with silk, so it looks like a bright cocoon. Reclined on something that is half seat, half bed, resting against a pile of cushions, is a tremendously large old woman, her white hair coiled snakelike upon her head. Her piles of thick, brilliantly colored clothing give an impression of utter shapelessness, as if there is no human form at all beneath them. Her face is powdered to a ghostly white. A hand with clawlike gold fingernails emerges from the mass of silk. She uses this hand to hold the long tube of a hookah to her lips, inhaling languorously and blowing out plumes of blue smoke that fill the room with their sweet smell.

Si Tan waves his hand in front of him to clear the smoke. He enters with no ceremony and sits himself down next to the woman. I follow him into the smoke of the room, willing myself not to cough. He leans close to her, murmuring in her ear. She smiles a little, like he is telling her something funny, and answers in a rasping voice, speaking out of one half of her mouth. The other half of her face is immobile.

I curse my terrible Yongwen. What good am I as a spy when I can't bleeding understand anything anybody says? Then, to my surprise, this powerful, elegant man lays his big head in her lap and closes his eyes. She strokes his hair distractedly and carries on smoking.

# TEN

I lie in bed listening to Bianka's breathing, Theo's breathing, the screech of cicadas in the trees outside. I try to relax, sleep, but my mind is galloping on and on so fast I can't bear to be still. I sit up before I've really thought it through, slip my nightdress off, and creep over to where my tunic and trousers are folded in the corner. I am halfway dressed when Bianka's voice comes out of the dark: "What are you doing?"

"Can't sleep," I whisper. "I'm going to go poke around the monastery."

I've had an idea. A bad idea, but I can't shake it.

Bianka sits up, watching me in the dark as I pull my boots on, wrap the straps around my calves, and fasten my knife to my right leg.

"Shouldn't you check in with Mrs. Och before you go running off?" she asks.

"She's asleep," I say, which may or may not be true and

is not really an answer to her question anyway. "I won't be long."

She doesn't argue with me. I shoulder my bag with the hook and rope and slip out into the main room. The house is dark except for a light under Mrs. Och's door. Surprised, I creep closer and press my ear to it. I hear the low murmur of a male voice. It sounds like Professor Baranyi, but I can't make out what he is saying. I stand there for a moment, bag over my shoulder, undecided. Then I go outside, sliding the door shut as quietly as I can behind me, and vanish—two steps back—by Mrs. Och's window. She keeps the paper blinds lowered, but they are uneven enough that I can peer through a crack at the bottom. Mrs. Och is at her table, hands folded in front of her. Frederick and Professor Baranyi are seated opposite her, leaning forward.

I take a shaky breath. I've been practicing vanishing, it's true, but still, there are things I am not confident of being able to do with any finesse. If I can see a place, I can move myself there by vanishing—kind of like jumping out of my body and jumping back into it somewhere else—but whether I can do it without alerting Mrs. Och is another question. It's risky, but that's never put me off before. I'd like to know what they're talking about so secretly in the middle of the night and why Bianka and I were not invited. I put down my bag and pull back, out of my body.

The courtyard scatters below me. I can hear the chickens breathing, can feel the warmth of the goat, his heart thudding comfortably behind sturdy ribs. I find the crack of light beneath the blinds, and the three people in the room. As soon as I focus on the opposite end of the room, the dark corner where the sliding door leads through to Mrs. Och's sleeping chamber, everything turns around and I am somewhere over the room—no, I am in the corner. I can never leave my body behind without terror, and the panic is so physical that it's difficult to stay vanished. I draw myself back against the wall, comforted as soon as I can feel my body again, the wild galloping of my heart—I'm still here, I'm still me, though vanished two steps from the world. They are blurred and their voices are muffled, but in the quiet of the room, I can just make out what they are saying.

"I'm honored." This from Frederick. "I've spent half my life dreaming of going to the Imperial Library!"

I stifle a laugh. I'll bet he has. Typical Frederick: when other boys were fantasizing about sailing the seas or joining the army, he was dreaming up library visits.

"We will need to tread very carefully," says Professor Baranyi. "Si Tan may have granted us permission only to see what we are really going to look for in the library. It might be best if Frederick and I go alone, acting as representatives of Lord Heriday."

"No," says Mrs. Och. "The permission is in Lord Heriday's name. Gregor needs to be there. You should take Esme and Julia as well, in case it is a trap."

"May I suggest that we tell Julia what *I* am doing there?" says Frederick. "She might be able to help. I should like to ask her questions."

"Not yet," says Mrs. Och. "Let us see what we find first."

"If I'm to research her power, surely she will want to know more about it as well, and she could provide useful details. . . ."

So that's it. I bite down on my lip hard, a stream of nasty names I'd like to shout at Mrs. Och running through my head.

She cuts him off: "Not yet. Do not make me repeat myself."

His mouth hangs open a moment, and then he closes it.

"The only recorded case of any creature crossing from Kahge to the world is that of the Gethin army," says Professor Baranyi, jumping in awkwardly. "We know that the first Eshriki Phar, Marike, brought the Gethin into the world three thousand years ago, but we do not know *how*. So you should begin your research with the Gethin and with Marike, but cast a wide net. Any texts dealing with Kahge—there will surely not be many—should be useful."

My knowledge of history is shaky at best, but even I know about the Eshriki Empire and Marike, the witch who founded it. It is a cautionary tale in Frayne of the evil days when witches ruled the civilized world. As for the Gethin, I know more about them than I'd like. In Spira City, I was hunted by the last of that tribe, and I shot him through the heart.

Frederick removes his spectacles and rubs his hand across his face. He looks exhausted.

"Are we sure that she disappears to *Kahge?*" he says.

"Whether the Gethin truly came from there is a matter of dispute, after all. Whether Kahge *exists* is a matter of dispute."

"If only we could ask Gennady precisely what he saw when she took him there," says Professor Baranyi.

"We could ask *Julia* what she sees," says Frederick, a note of impatience creeping into his voice. Oh, Frederick, I'm going to have to buy you a present or something.

"We will most certainly have a conversation with Julia when we know a little more," says Mrs. Och, not bothering to hide her irritation. "I have no doubt of Kahge's existence, nor do I doubt that Gennady would know it if he saw it. We—the Xianren—have always felt something beyond the world, something connected to our fragments of *The Book of Disruption*. I can feel the edge of things, and something beyond, but I cannot *go* there, as Julia claims she can."

I want to shout that I never claimed anything, but I keep quiet. I need to hear this.

"The only serious study of Kahge on record was conducted by Yongguo's philosopher-witches," says Mrs. Och, addressing herself mainly to Frederick now. "You will find these in the library. When *The Book of Disruption* was split into three, it was like an explosion of magic, too much for the world to contain and withstand. We think of the consequences in terms of the disruptions it left in the world—witches, magical creatures and objects—but the creation of Kahge was arguably the greatest consequence. The force of the Book's breaking created a kind of shadow—like an image imprint of the world—that we call Kahge. It lies apart from the world, and yet it is connected, and magic drains out of the world *through* Kahge, or so the philosopher-witches believed. I can say from my own experience that the world now is *less* magical than it was in the immediate aftermath of the Book's breaking, and I accept the theory that magic is draining slowly away—fading, just as the Xianren are fading. As for Kahge, the philosopher-witches claimed that life arose there but that they were half lives, like a reflection of life here, insubstantial. Still, somehow Marike is said to have brought the Gethin from Kahge, making an otherworldly and nearly immortal army to serve her empire, and the Gethin, whatever their powers, were certainly corporeal."

She pauses, and I wonder if, like me, they are all remembering that night in her house in Spira City, the Gethin's sad eyes, the way he felled us, one after another, and my lucky shot that brought him down.

She continues in a softer voice: "Witches and others have tried to reach Kahge since Marike's time, to access that overflow of magic, but none have succeeded. If Julia can truly move between the world and Kahge, I do not know what the implications are, for her or for the world. My inquiries about her mother before we left Frayne led nowhere. Everybody had a story about Ammi, but nothing to suggest that she was anything more than a clever and charismatic witch whose primary loyalty was to the Sidhar Coven. No, this is something unique to Julia herself, and I wish to know why."

I'm nearly choking on my fury now. That she is research-ing my abilities without telling me is bad enough, but inves-tigating my *mother* and keeping it a secret too?

"I will be looking for clues of Ko Dan's whereabouts in the library," the professor says to Frederick. "It will be up to you alone to see what you can find out about Kahge, any stories of creatures crossing over."

"I'll do my best."

"I trust you will be discreet," says Mrs. Och, her tone icy, and I know she means, *Don't tell Julia.* I stick my invisible tongue out at her.

He nods. I suppose I can't blame him—it's not as if he didn't try—but I'm annoyed anyway.

"Go home, my friend," she says to Professor Baranyi. "You will need to be well rested tomorrow."

Frederick and the professor bow to Mrs. Och and go out. I stay and watch her for a minute or two, but she just sits at her desk, not moving, hands folded in front of her. Lurking invisibly in her room is starting to give me the creeps, so I go over to the window and peer out at the shadowy figures of Frederick and Professor Baranyi in the courtyard. I fling myself out of my body again—oh hounds, but I hate this feeling—and the courtyard is expanding below me, if there *is* any me left, and yet I can hear Frederick's voice as if he were whispering in my ear:

"I do not like it. She should know about it, since it con-cerns her."

I return to myself by the corner where Theo likes to pee,

jarred back into my body, vanished only one step from the world.

"Mrs. Och is right," the professor says. "I understand your feelings, but there is no point working the poor girl up until we know more. There is always the possibility that what we discover will be dangerous."

"Dangerous how?" asks Frederick.

"I don't know," says Professor Baranyi wearily. "Let us see what we find, and then we will discuss it. Get some sleep, Frederick."

They bid each other good night, and Professor Baranyi goes clomping off down the road while Frederick goes back to the main house and lights a lamp. He'll be up all night reading, I reckon. As for me, I am in a righteous fury, and more than ready to stir up some trouble.

# ELEVEN

I start out at a jog, but soon I'm running full tilt down the empty streets, running so hard my legs and lungs ache. I am sick to death of reporting all my movements to Mrs. Och anyway, and if she's undertaking investigations without me, I am more than able to do the same. My chest fills with something like the exhilaration I used to get when out burgling or just roaming Spira City with Wyn. I felt so free back then.

The trolleys stop running at sunset, and so I have to cross the city on foot. I go over the monastery wall with my rope and hook and vanish next to the flagstone through which I saw the spy emerge two nights ago. I'm not in a waiting mood—far from it—and it's only a hunch that the boy is a regular visitor to the Fraynish girl's secret courtyard. But my hunch is right. It's less than an hour before he appears, quiet as a shadow, in the alley. As soon as he bends to lift the flagstone, I step into view, placing my foot over it. He leaps away and pulls from his belt a stick sharpened to a ferocious point. I hold up my hands to show I'm not armed. I won't deny I enjoy appearing this way, as if out of nowhere.

"I'd like a word with you," I say in Fraynish. I figure if he's spying on a Fraynish girl, he's likely enough to speak the language. But he doesn't answer. He bolts. *Blast.* I take off after him. If I can't catch him, this will have been fun but essentially pointless.

I catch up to him as he reaches the east wall of the monastery. I grab him by the shoulder, and he hits me in the face with his elbow, sending me reeling backward. He is nearly flying up the wall. I pull back, out of my body and over the wall, landing a little too hard, breathless and queasy, on the other side. I'm waiting for him there when he comes over. I hold my hands up like I'm surrendering.

"Hullo again," I say.

For a moment he just stares at me, his eyes round and terrified. Then he moves so fast that I don't have time to react; he spins me around and slams me into the wall. He's got me pinned, with the sharp stick pressed against my ribs. This is not exactly how I'd planned it. I'm realizing I hadn't planned it very well at all. All this disappearing and reappearing has got me feeling very queasy, but this isn't a position I care to linger in, so I pull away from the world again, vanishing out of his grip. He stumbles into the wall with a startled cry, and I return to myself a safe distance behind him.

"Over here," I say.

He spins around and draws in a sharp breath, putting

the stick in front of himself defensively. At least he hasn't thrown a jar of wasps at me yet. I rub my side where he jabbed me with the stick. He broke the skin, but it isn't serious.

The Yongwen words are clumsy in my mouth, and I hate to sound a fool at a moment like this, but I ask him: "Do you speak Fraynish?"

"Who you are?" The answer comes in strongly accented Fraynish, thank the Nameless.

"I'm sorry I frightened you," I say. "I just want to talk. Without you trying to kill me with a stick."

"Why?"

"I want to know who you are and what you're up to. And I'll bet that now you'd like to know the same about me. I thought we might be able to help each other out."

When he doesn't reply, I suggest: "We could get something to eat. I don't suppose you know where a girl can find coffee in this city?"

He lowers the stick slowly, and I try not to let my relief show.

"You walk in front," he says. "I tell you where to go."

There is no coffee. We sit on either side of a low table and drink tea from tiny, steaming cups. It is a hole-in-the-wall tea shop if ever there was one—just three tables, and a wizened old woman behind the counter. The place is empty, which is not surprising, as it's closing in on midnight now. The old woman brings us bowls of white rice and little dishes with bony fish and steamed eggplant in a sweet sauce.

The boy puts his pointed stick down on the table and lowers his hood. A long black braid hangs down his back, as is the fashion among young men in the city. His face is all sharp angles, his brows dark slashes over coal-black eyes, his full lips an incongruous softness in an otherwise rather severe countenance. He eats quickly with the two eating sticks they use in Yongguo, his eyes never leaving my face. I follow suit, somewhat clumsily. I'm hungry after all that jumping in and out of the world.

"What's your name?" I ask him.

He hesitates a fraction of a second before saying: "Huang."

I doubt that is his real name. He looks at me expectantly.

"I'm Ella," I say.

He finishes his meal, puts down the eating sticks, and stares at me, waiting.

"Who's the Fraynish girl you're watching?" I ask.

He blinks and says skeptically, "You do not know who is she?"

"If I knew, I wouldn't be asking you."

He shakes his head. "No. First you talk. Who you are? What you are doing here? How you can disappear?"

"The vanishing thing is just . . . something I can do. A trick. A bit of magic." Something that would get me killed in Frayne if I was found out but that I can admit to more freely here. "I'm looking for somebody in the monastery. Since you seem to spend a good bit of time there, I hoped you could help me."

"Who you are looking for?"

Well, here it is. Mrs. Och would be furious, but creeping about and speaking to nobody has gotten me exactly nowhere so far, and I don't know if it's just that he's armed with nothing more than a pointy stick, but I'm betting he doesn't work for Casimir.

"Ko Dan. D'you know him?"

He frowns at me. "He is not there."

"But you know who he is? You've seen him before?"

"He is important man there. Then he go away."

"When did he go away?"

"Year and half," he says.

Not long after putting Gennady's piece of *The Book of Disruption* into Theo, then. Gennady told us that Ko Dan put the fragment into Theo soon after he was born. The magic bound it to Theo's very essence so completely that it would live and die with him. According to Gennady, Ko Dan wanted to murder the baby immediately, thus destroying the text and putting an end to the whole business. But instead Gennady put Bianka and Theo on a train and disappeared from their lives, figuring nobody would ever find them. Only an unwed mother and her child, nobody important. As for Bianka, she didn't know at first what Gennady had done, that her child would forever be hunted by the world's immortals. Seems like the sort of thing you ought to tell a girl once you've knocked her up, if you ask me, but nobody has ever accused the Xianren of being overly considerate. If anyone has made worse choices than me in love, it's Bianka.

"Where is Ko Dan now?" I ask.

"I don't know. Why you want him?"

"I'm working for a Fraynish lady who needs his help," I say, which is more or less true. "You don't have any guesses where he might have run off to?"

He shakes his head. Blast. Well, I still want to know about the girl in the monastery.

"Now your turn," I say. "What are you up to?"

"I cannot tell you."

"I just told *you* what *I'm* doing."

He shrugs.

"Fine. Who do you work for?"

"I cannot tell you," he says again.

I give him an exasperated look, and he cracks the slightest smile, a dimple appearing in one cheek, which makes him look suddenly younger and less ferocious.

"Maybe your boss would like to meet me. Tell him you ran into a charming, witty, semi-attractive Fraynish girl with the ability to appear and disappear right before your eyes. That might interest him, don't you think?"

Incorrigible, I scold myself. He shows you a dimple and you start flirting.

He nods, pressing his lips together like he's trying not to laugh. "I think, maybe," he says.

"Does your boss speak Fraynish?"

He nods.

"All right. Tell him I want to meet him, and see what he says. How will I find you again?"

He gives me a wry look. "I think you know."

"I mean, perhaps you could leave me a message somewhere."

"Here." He nods toward the old woman behind the counter. "Old Thien can keep secret."

"All right. I'll check in with Old Thien soon."

He is drumming on the table very fast with his fingers, a restless tic. "You do not know who is the girl in Shou-shu?" he asks again, like he doesn't believe me.

"No," I say. "Why don't you tell me?"

He shakes his head. I laugh, and he cracks a small, cautious smile again, the dimple reemerging.

"How about the Treasury?" I ask. "Do you know what they keep in there?"

He shrugs, his eyes narrowing. "I am not thief."

"Neither am I," I assure him hurriedly. At least, not anymore. Still, whatever part of me drew me to thieving in the first place can't quite let go of that locked, guarded door.

"You are witch," he suggests.

"I'm not," I say.

He casts his eyes down for a second and then looks up at me, touching his fingers to his own jaw, to the same spot where he hit me with his elbow. Very seriously, he says, "I am sorry I hurt you."

Stars, this boy. Handsome, mysterious, quick on his feet, and now *sweet*. I struggle not to give him a melty look.

"No, it was . . . I shouldn't have approached you like that. I'm all right."

He knocks back the last of his tea and rises. I get up as well and pay Old Thien.

"Glad to meet you, Huang," I say once we're outside.

"Good night, Ella," he says.

Impulsively, maybe because I am hoping for another glimpse of that dimple, I say, "Oh hounds, look—it's Julia, actually."

This time he smiles for real—a luminous smile that changes his face completely. It's the kind of smile you can't help smiling back at. Two dimples, though the left one is deeper.

"I am Jun," he says.

# TWELVE

Our guide, Fan Ming, is a handsome man with a clear brow and intelligent eyes. He speaks Fraynish well, but formally and with great care, which makes him seem earnest and a little dull. When he switches to Yongwen to speak to the professor or Frederick, he is quite different, gesticulating and cracking jokes, making them laugh.

The Imperial Library is not in the city at all, to my surprise, but housed inside the holy mountain, Tama-shan, a day's journey north of the city on horseback through the forest. I'm relieved to find that our guide is such a pleasant, scholarly sort of fellow. It's obvious that Si Tan saw through Gregor's attempt to present himself as a scholar, but if we were being led off into the woods to have our throats cut, I don't think Fan Ming is the type of person they'd send to do the job. Then again, appearances can be deceiving, as I well know.

We leave the city through the Xuanwu Gate, under the

massive carved black turtle entwined with a snake. Outside the vast walls, makeshift markets and shantytowns have been built up close to the city. Sellers shout to us to come and try their goods, men sit in rows having their beards trimmed, old women pass us stooped double under heavy loads of firewood, and the stink of meat and fish hangs in the air, the lesser cuts and day-old catches being sold to those who can't afford the city's finer fare. We go to the stables just beyond the raucous market to rent our horses, then mount up and set out riding north. There are a few villages farther out, but we soon pass through all of these and travel the broad path through the forest until suppertime. I have never ridden a horse before. Thankfully, women in Yong-guo do not ride sidesaddle—an idiotic idea if ever there was one—but ride as men do, wearing trousers under a stiff, split robe that separates for the purpose of riding but falls to the ankles when one stands upright.

Even so, by the time we set up camp for the night, an hour's ride from the holy mountain itself, my tailbone feels as if it has been hammered up into my spine, and I can hardly walk. Tama-shan, rising out of the woods ahead of us, is crimson in the evening light, pointing like a finger at the sky. The spring nights are still cool, and so we build a fire, even though we've brought rice balls and dried fish with us and have no need to cook anything. The sky darkens, the stars come out, and we watch the mountain light up as the witches of Tama-shan lay their elaborate fires, writing out spells of safekeeping in flame.

As those distant fires appear on the mountainside, the temperature drops sharply. The trees around us tremble and shake their leaves. Our fire leaps upward, spitting sparks, and the river foams and rushes, as if trying to flee whatever is happening on the mountain. A foul wind sweeps over us, through us, and is gone as quickly as it came, but it leaves us all shivering and queasy, the trees and the grass bristling strangely, the rocks and the water bright even in the darkness.

"You feel that?" says Frederick, awed.

"The Tama-shan witches are strong," says Fan Ming, poking at the fire with a stick.

It's something I cannot get used to—that there are legitimate, important jobs for witches in this country. That one could discover in oneself such a power and find a way to use it profitably, openly, rather than hiding it.

When our fire begins to go down, Frederick heads in among the trees with a lantern to collect more wood, and I follow him.

"So Mrs. Och really thinks we'll be able to find out what's happened to Ko Dan at the library?" I ask him once we're out of Fan Ming's earshot.

"It's a fair bet," he says cheerfully. "Almost everything is a matter of public record in Yongguo—births, deaths, marriages, changes of domicile, all that. You can trace the movement of any registered citizen through library records, and copies of all the Shou-shu records are kept there as well. We should be able to find some hint, at the very least, and hopefully the professor will be able to disguise the real purpose of our research. Tremendously helpful that you found out how long ago he left."

I did not mention Jun last night but said I'd overheard that Ko Dan had gone missing a year and a half ago.

"And what will you be doing at the library?" I ask bluntly.

He gives me a startled look and says, "Why . . . helping." Then he bends over hurriedly to gather some branches. Frederick has always been an appalling liar.

"And you're feeling entirely better, then . . . after the other day when Mrs. Och took your strength?" I ask, letting him off the hook—for now.

"Oh, I'm fine."

We gather sticks in silence for a moment. I can tell he is trying to put some distance between us, but I follow him again.

"I wish you didn't let her do that to you," I say.

"I know," he sighs, finally looking right at me. "I choose to do it, Julia. To help her. And honestly, I'm quite recovered."

"It's horrible. She didn't used to do it in Spira City."

"She had more opportunities to rest and gather her strength then. This journey has been very hard on her."

"Or maybe she's developing a taste for it."

He shakes his head. "It's one way that I can be useful. I can't do what you can do, but I can give her the strength she needs when she needs it. She is a force for good, Julia. She has saved so many lives."

"She didn't save my mother."

It sounds absurd and childish as I say it. I don't know how to explain the revulsion I feel at this ancient immortal drinking up the energies of the young, or the uncomfortable mixture of fear, resentment, gratitude, and awe I feel for Mrs. Och. I bite my lip and wait for him to chide me, but he doesn't. When I look up to meet his eyes, they are all compassion and concern, none of which I deserve—not from him.

"Sorry," I say. "I'm being stupid."

"I wish you could trust her," he says. "She trusts *you*, you know. And with less reason, if I may say so."

I accept the rebuke. I can't answer it, after all, even if it stings. He's right—I don't trust her, and he knows perfectly well that she does not really trust me either. She may be a force for good, as he says, but she is mercilessly pragmatic, and I cannot forgive her for trying to keep from me knowledge of my own mother, of my *self*.

I follow him back to the camp. All evening, as we eat and talk, our fire leans in the direction of Tama-shan, ignoring the direction of the breeze and rising alarmingly high at times, the smoke streaming toward the fires on the mountain like it is being called that way. In the morning, the writing on the mountainside is black and smoldering, the spells still visible.

# THIRTEEN

Having risen at dawn, we reach the mountain before the morning dew has dried and tie our horses up at the edge of the forest. A middle-aged woman dressed in a peasant tunic sits on a stump by the cave that leads into the mountain. She is busy whittling something with a fierce-looking blade, but she looks up as Fan Ming approaches. He bows and shows her the letter of permission with Si Tan's seal. She glances at it, not stopping her whittling, and then looks over at us. The corners of her mouth turn down, but she nods curtly toward the cave, and in we go. Fan Ming leads the way, and Esme and I take up the rear.

Odd sort of library, if you ask me, though I'll grant you, I've never been to the regular kind either. The passageway slopes sharply downward, and then the tunnel turns into steps. They spiral around and around, deep underground, and the air gets colder.

"Suppose the punishment for trying to get into the library

under false pretenses is to be buried underneath it?" I whisper to Esme, but she shushes me. Then she stops and I run into her back, which is fairly like running into a solid wall. Fan Ming is exchanging greetings with someone else. Lanterns are lit, which is blinding for a few moments and then a relief. The tunnel walls look paler than I would have expected and are entirely smooth. The roof over us is high and vaulted. I think I see bats hanging up there.

We have reached the bottom of the stairs at last, and whoever is up ahead leads us along a straight passageway that opens into a painted cavern. The paint is so bright it looks wet in the lamplight. Demon gods glower down at us from the high ceiling; a sea dragon snaking along one wall attacks a ship manned by naked sailors; a giant octopus-like creature squats over a castle and appears to be shitting ink all over a bunch of squalling courtiers. I am gaping around at the walls when Esme nudges me. I hadn't gotten a good look at the figure who met us at the bottom of the stairs, but now I see her, hooded and kneeling on the floor, writing in a leather-bound book. There comes the smell of salt water—startling, so far from the sea—and a grinding sound from the stone walls. A door opens where there was no door before, the painted stone shifting aside.

Professor Baranyi holds up his lantern, peering into the darkness, and asks Fan Ming a question. Fan Ming says something about Shou-shu. Together they enter this second, smaller cavern, and they come out soon after, arms full of books bound in leather and flexible bamboo. These they set on a stone shelf at one end of the painted cavern. The professor has the sort of avid look on his face that I associate with gamblers off to the racetrack. He and Fan Ming are rather forgetting to pretend that Gregor—the supposed scholar—has anything to do with this at all.

Frederick says something to Fan Ming in Yongwen, and I recognize the word for Kahge. Fan Ming nods in agreement.

"If you are comfortable here," he says to the professor and Gregor, "I will take Frederick to the old part of the library. If you need anything, Bao Wei will help you."

Esme scowls at the witch, still kneeling on the floor with her legs tucked under her. Traveling with Bianka, and indeed traveling through Yongguo, has led my old crew to a new perspective on witches, so feared and reviled in Frayne, but still, I can see Esme does not want Fan Ming to leave them with *this* witch.

"Of course," says the professor. "Thank you very much."

"I'll come with you," I pipe up, joining Frederick over by Fan Ming. "I could help take notes."

Frederick and the professor exchange a stunned look, and then Frederick stammers, "Ah, no, thank you, Miss Heriday, that won't be necessary."

"I should like to," I say firmly. "It will be very good practice for me." Before he can protest again, I turn to Gregor. "What say you, Father?"

Gregor stares at me in confusion for a moment and then, because he doesn't know what to do, looks at Esme. She gives him a slight nod.

"Miss Heriday should stay with us," begins the professor, recovering from his surprise, but Gregor cuts him off.

"Not at all, it will be an interesting experience for her to explore the library a bit. Go on, my girl."

I smile, triumphant. "Thank you, Father."

Frederick and Professor Baranyi gape at each other but there is nothing they can do. Gregor is supposed to be the authority here, and they can hardly countermand his decision regarding his own daughter.

"Follow me, then," says Fan Ming. I shoot Esme a grateful look and she cocks an eyebrow at me. I'm going to have to explain this to her later.

The passageway we came along branches off into more tunnels and more painted caverns. After several turns I begin to worry I might not be able to find my way back to the others on my own. I do not at all like being this far underground. Frederick clears his throat a few times, glancing nervously at me, but I keep a brisk pace behind Fan Ming and do not look at him.

We reach a much smaller, plainer cavern, where a large woman, presumably one of the librarian-witches Frederick told me about, dozes in the corner. Simple shelves are carved into the walls, and these shelves are filled with bundles of slender bamboo strips nearly the length of my forearm. The woman's eyes snap open when we come in. Fan Ming bows low to her, speaking in very formal Yongwen. She nods and waves a hand toward the shelves, as if giving him permission.

"Many of the writings on Kahge are very old and must be handled carefully," says Fan Ming, taking out one of the bundles and untying the silk around it. The writing on the strips looks almost pictographic compared with the elegant modern Yongwen script I've grown used to seeing.

"May I?" asks Frederick, taking one of the strips in his hands like he's receiving a great treasure. I look at the paintings on the walls and my heart gives a jolt. At eye level there is a black-skinned woman clothed in gold holding a small bowl with two spouts; something white swirls out of the spouts. Next to her, a great many shadowy, white-eyed warriors, shining blades held aloft, are descending a hill topped by fire. The Gethin. I quiver a little inside. Encountering one of them was bad enough. I can barely imagine an army of them. No wonder the Eshriki Empire ruled half the world for so long.

"What is that?" I ask, pointing at the picture.

Fan Ming translates my question for the librarian-witch, then tells us her answer: "That is Marike bringing the Gethin into the world."

"The fire on the hilltop is meant to be Kahge?" asks Frederick, and Fan Ming nods.

I think about the Kahge I have seen—Spira City burning, and those revolting creatures alongside the steaming river, pointing at me.

"What does *lidari* mean?" I blurt out.

Frederick looks startled. "It is a name, is it not?" he says. "One of Marike's generals, or her advisor?"

Fan Ming asks the witch. She answers briefly, and he says, "Yes, Marike's prized general, one of the Gethin."

"So the Gethin *came* from Kahge," I say. "But could they go back and forth . . . between the world and Kahge?"

Again Fan Ming asks the librarian-witch. She shakes her head and answers at length, and then he says: "No, they were bound here by their bodies. A physical body cannot go over to Kahge, though it has been speculated that the *essence* of a Gethin might return to Kahge once its body was destroyed. There is no consensus on that, however."

But I *do* have a body in Kahge. I think of what Mrs. Och said: *If Julia can truly move between the world and Kahge, I do not know what the implications are, for her or for the world.* Thinking too closely about it makes me nauseous with fear.

"And that is the great question, is it not?" says Frederick. "Not only how Marike brought them across, but how she gave them their monstrous physical form?"

"Yes," Fan Ming translates. "It is a mystery none have been able to solve."

"This is older than any writing I've seen," says Frederick, returning to the bamboo strips. "Translating it will take more time than we have today. May I transcribe some of them?"

"Of course," says Fan Ming. "I will help you select those that seem most relevant." He pauses, as if struck by a thought. "The earliest recorded reference to Kahge is carved on a stele. Perhaps I could take Miss Heriday to make a rubbing while you start here."

"Very kind of you!" exclaims Frederick.

I try to catch his eye—I am not keen at all on being separated farther in this warren of tunnels and caverns beneath the mountain. But Frederick barely looks up from the bamboo strips, and I have no choice but to follow Fan Ming out of the cave. If he tries anything, he'll get more than he's bargained for, that's certain.

We climb a different stairway, winding upward until I am quite breathless, and come out into a vast cavern open to the light. The whole cavern is full of standing stones, tall and narrow like gravestones. I find myself blinking and squinting at the great oval view of the world through the opening at the far end of the cavern. We are facing south, and I can see over the forest we came through, the great walls of Tianshi off in the distance.

"The forest of stele," says Fan Ming, gesturing grandly at the standing stones.

He takes me in among them, most of the stones as tall as I am or taller, and I can see that they are all carved with text, some fresh and new, some ancient and worn. Before a very old stele, he sets down his basket and takes out a brush. He cleans the surface of the stone, then lays a sheet of rice paper over it.

"Please hold it still," he says, and I do. From his basket he takes what looks like a ball of dark wax and begins to carefully rub the surface of the rice paper with it, so that the inscription on the stone emerges pale amid the dark smudging on the sheet. When he is done and the text is clear on the paper, he rolls it up and hands it to me.

"There you are."

A cloaked figure calls to him from the entrance to the cavern.

"Excuse me a moment," he says to me. "There is something I must take care of, and then I will take you back to the others. Please—have a look around. There are many beautiful stones, and the air is fresher here than below."

"Thank you," I say, and watch him go. At first I am a little on edge, not sure of the meaning of his bringing me here and then leaving, but it's true it is more pleasant than in the claustrophobic tunnels underneath the mountain. I go to the edge of the cavern to look out over the forest, fingering the scroll he gave me. Perhaps this sheet of rice paper holds all the secrets to this power of mine, if it is a power and not a curse. I just need to make sure Frederick explains it to *me* before he tells Mrs. Och anything.

I feel as if I'm being watched. I turn around and nearly tumble off the ledge in my fright. Standing there is a woman—I think it is a woman—but she has no eyes, just a mass of dark stitching where eyes ought to be. Her head is smooth and hairless, every inch of her tattooed with writing. She wears a sleeveless tunic that hangs to her knees, and her arms and legs too are covered in black ink, the writing winding about her limbs. The air crackles as she moves through it.

"Fan Ming said I could rest here," I babble in Fraynish, forgetting every last word of Yongwen that I know.

"Show me your hand," she says in Yongwen. I don't dare

refuse, and so I hold out my hand to her. I see the little blade in her hand too late. She nicks my finger and pulls the blade away with a smear of blood on it. I cry out, trying to step around her so I'm not on the edge of the cliff. She snaps the fingers of her other hand, conjuring a little flame, perhaps with the characters tattooed on her fingertips, and holds the knife in the flame. My blood sizzles, and she says to me: "Your mother was a witch. Drowned."

That stills me. I clutch my bleeding finger and say, "Yes."

"Your father?" she asks.

"Just a man," I say in Fraynish. "Not much of one either."

She shakes her head, not understanding me, and barks: "Speak Yongwen."

I struggle for the words. All that study, and every last bit of it has flown.

"My father ... man," I manage in stuttering Yongwen. I cannot think of the word for *ordinary*, which would have been too much of a compliment anyway.

She sniffs the knife. The fingers of her free hand move in the air. It takes a minute to register what she's doing, and by the time I realize she's writing, it's too late. I've only ever seen one other witch who could work magic by simply writing in the air with her fingers. I try to move away from her but I cannot move at all. My thoughts have gone thick and slow as molasses, struggling to crawl along through a heavy, dark space. She raises my arm to her wrinkled lips, and then out comes a black tongue and she licks my wrist. Everything in me recoils, and I almost remember something—a way out, another place—but my mind is slowed and dim, and the thought slips away almost as soon as it comes.

The witch pads closer and puts her arms around me. Muttering to herself, she feels the knobs in my spine, lifts my hair to her face and sniffs it. I stare at the tiny, spidery writing running along her cheekbones, down the bridge of her nose, across her forehead, covering every bit of her. Even the stitching over her eyes, I realize, is not random but a mass of tiny threaded script. *Who are you?* I want to say, but I can't find a way to speak. She presses her thumb to my forehead and everything goes black.

# FOURTEEN

*I am kneeling on the pitching boat before Bianka while Theo traps a marble under a cup. My voice is thick with unshed tears: "I'd die before letting anything happen to him again. I swear to you, I'd die first." And she reaches for my hand.*

*Pia takes Theo from my arms, shuts the door in my face, and I am standing in the hall with a bag of silver.*

*I take the book off the shelf in Professor Baranyi's study—*Legends of the Xianren I*—and open the heavy tome in my lap.*

*I fire the gun and the Gethin falls. Mrs. Och is bleeding against the wall. I crawl over her wings to finish him off.*

*The fire is warm, the coffee is good, and Gregor says to me: "When the client wants to see you, I'll let you know."*

\*   \*   \*

A blur of images and memories rushes through me, spills out of me, like my life flashing before my eyes, slowing down for certain scenes and then speeding up, racing by. A flood of color, a bright burst of laughter, a scream, my heart racing— I think I will burst with feeling it all at once—my bare feet on the cobblestones, the moon rising over Mount Heriot, music pouring out of the temple, honey on my tongue, a hand on my cheek, waking with the morning light, all the lost moments returned to me and snatched away again in the space of half a breath.

And then it stops.

*I am sitting on the steps up to our flat above the laundry, eating an apple I've stolen. My mother was taken the night before, and I do not know what to do. I am horribly aware of my heart in my chest, its relentless thud-thud-thud. Dek and I had been to stare at the outer walls of the great prison, Hostorak, but we were just children—what could we do? My father stumbles down the stairs past me, a scarecrow in his raggedy clothes, his hair unkempt, his face ruined by opium. He looks back at me, but barely, half a glance over his shoulder, not meeting my eyes. "Forgive me," he mumbles, and then he is gone, and that is the last time I see him.*

Again the blur of sensation and emotion, my life speeding backward, and halting years earlier:

*I am shouting for my brother, and he comes, he always does. Two older boys have caught a cat and shut it in a box. They are looking for tinder to burn it, and the cat is howling in the box like it knows what they have in mind. When I tried to free the cat, one of them hit me right in the nose with his fist, and now my nose is bleeding all over my mouth and chin and pinafore. When Dek sees me, he is ablaze with fury. I tell him in a great sobbing jumble what is happening. Oh, the splendor of him striding down that street, the way he knocks those boys' heads together—never mind that they are both a year older than him—the way he sends them scurrying. He lets the cat out and tries to pat it, but it scratches him across the face. We come home bleeding but triumphant, and our mother looks at us and sighs. More laundry.*

And back, and back:

*They are quarreling, my ma and pa. He is searching the room, tearing it apart, and she is shouting at him, and Dek is shouting at both of them, but Pa is simply fixed on pulling open cupboards, looking in the kettle, pulling the mattress off the little bed, leaving our small home a ruin. He is looking for money. My mother grabs his arm and he shakes her off, and Dek lunges at him, roaring, and he gets knocked aside too. I am about two years old. I am crying, but nobody hears me, and then it is too awful for crying and I draw myself away from them. I hadn't known I could do it, but suddenly they are all a bit blurred, muted. I feel safe. My father goes storming off, and my mother and Dek are righting things about the flat when Dek says, "Where's Julia gone?" She looks around, her eyes moving right past me, and the same with him. They look and look but they do not see me sitting right there against the wall, still as a mouse, holding my* breath. *It seems obvious to me that they should not be able to see me. It seems like I have always known this hiding place in plain view was there for me and me alone. I watch them search for me, and my ma sends Dek running to look about the neighborhood, and then she looks so lost that I pity her, and I go and throw myself into her arms. I expect her to embrace me, to be relieved and happy, but she pulls me off her, holding me at arm's length and searching my face, her eyes wide and amazed, looking at me hard, like the answer might be there, and I am crying again—I just want her to hug me, to tell me it's all right, it's going to be all right.*

It is all wanting and terror and joy, the world huge and bright, and then a darkness unlike anything I've ever known, a rushing and roaring in my ears. I emerge again, but this is different:

*I am kneeling on the red earth with my mother, Ammi. But it is not me—I am not her child. A rocky crag looms over us, a little black house at the top of it. Far behind us and below us, the world is like a moving painting of itself, half real. She holds in her hands a small clay pot, almost like a teapot but with two spouts, one on either side of it.*

"*I have it,*" *she says to me.*

"*We are almost ready,*" *she says to me.*

"*Can I trust you?*" *she says to me.*

*Her dark eyes, her pretty mouth. I see her so clearly, and she seems to pulse with life. I envy it, I am hungry for it, and I will do anything, anything at all.*

*Her hand on my face. The warmth of her.*

*"You won't fail me."*

*It is a statement, not a question. She is fearless and lovely. Leaving me with my longing, she wades into a river of mud and disappears into the world. A gurgling voice above me says, "You need to go back. They are waiting for you."*

*And I wonder what I will tell them. I wonder if I will really betray them. But I know the answer to that. Her eyes, her skin, her beating heart, those little buildings far below, the whole story of human existence unfolding all at once, all the time—fear is nothing, loyalty nothing, next to my desire to be whole.*

I open my eyes and am vaguely surprised that I have eyes to open. I am sprawled numbly at the center of everything that has ever happened to me, all of it spread out to be examined by this witch's nimble fingers—except that last one, which is not my memory at all but someone else's, of somewhere I've never been or dreamed of. The witch is squatting on my chest and I can hardly breathe. Her tattooed hands work through the threads around me and all over me—or are those ribbons, or what are they?

Then I remember the thought that eluded me before: I can disappear. But the effort it would require feels quite beyond me. I watch the witch, so preoccupied with her task, and I notice the little knife strapped to her wrist.

I can't move my arm *in* the world, but I can pull it out of the world—just that part of me, just past the edge of things, far enough to be free of the spell paralyzing me. I vanish my arm, then swing it up and snatch her little knife. I stick the blade into her arm. She squawks. It's a stupid thing to do.

The knife is tiny, can make no more than a small puncture, and she has me immobile on the edge of a cliff.

She takes hold of a fistful of my hair and knocks my head against the rock. Suddenly I can hear a lot of talking, and it seems to me that maybe this noise has been going on for a long time. She gives my head another bang. Fan Ming is standing a few feet away, shouting. He is pressed against some invisible barrier in the air, trying to reach us, and there is Frederick behind him, also shouting. The witch ignores them and bends over my face. She bites my cheek, hard. The pain clears my head, and I pull my whole body back, blurring the world, freeing myself of whatever binds me. I shove her off me with all the strength I have. She sprawls on her back, grinning, my blood on her lips.

I make a desperate scramble toward Fan Ming and Frederick, feeling that surely this is all a dream, a nightmare. I find myself in Frederick's arms, and his voice, which is both too loud and oddly far away, is asking me if I am all right. Fan Ming is gesticulating wildly now, shouting at the witch. She raises her arms up above her head, fingers working. I whisper, "*Run,*" but none of us move, and then small winged shapes are diving down from the ceiling of the cavern, filling the air. *Bats.* Frederick shoves my head into his jacket and we are on the ground, me gasping for breath inside his coat, my face close to the rock. I feel a few vicious pinprick bites on my back, my legs. I thrash and yell in the darkness of Frederick's coat and then they are gone.

Frederick helps me to my feet. He is trembling and white-faced and the arm he shielded me with is bleeding. The witch is walking off among the standing stones. I try to make words, but my mouth feels thick and furry, my mind too heavy. I lean against Frederick and think about my mother, how clear she was in the memories the witch pulled out of me—a clearer picture than I've had in years—but that last one wasn't *my* memory, so whose was it? I'd half forgotten her face, its lively expression, the warmth of her gaze, the humor of her mouth. Ma, the luminous center of my world until she was gone—and it seems to me now that everything has been askew and all wrong ever since then, including me.

I wonder later if I fainted, but I'm too embarrassed to ask. Frederick carries me back to the painted cave below, where Professor Baranyi is standing at the shelf making notes and Gregor is pretending, not very convincingly, to be absorbed in a book.

Esme sees us first. Her face doesn't change, but the pistol Dek got her seems to leap from the holster at her side into her hand—she is pointing it straight at Fan Ming's forehead.

He blanches, raises his hands, and says in a rush: "A witch attacked Miss Heriday. Not one of the Tama-shan librarian-witches—I do not know who she is. I am sorry, but we must leave immediately. It is not safe, and I have no authority here."

"He's right," says Frederick. Esme lowers the gun slowly but does not holster it. I notice then, with some relief, that Fan Ming is holding the rolled-up stele rubbing he made for me. I thought I might have dropped it off the cliff when the witch appeared.

"A little more time—" begins Professor Baranyi, but Esme shuts him down.

"We're leaving now."

⌒

Professor Baranyi begged to prolong our stay, then asked for a private word with me, but Fan Ming and our witch escort, Bao Wei, were firm in ejecting us quickly from the library, and they flanked me the whole way out. With Esme on their side, the professor gave up, and now he looks very glum and unhappy on his horse.

As soon as we are back on the road in the forest, me slumped on a horse in front of Frederick, I feel better. When I sit up straighter, he says, "All right?"

"Yes," I say, relieved to find I can speak easily again. "I don't know what that blasted witch did to me."

His voice is low, close to my ear. "Fan Ming brought me up to the forest of stele, and you were . . . I don't know how to explain it . . . you were tied up on the ground, but the knots and bindings were not of any earthly matter. It was as if you were tied up by darkness, and all around you pieces of light and shadow were moving across the ground, and that witch was stirring through it all with her fingers."

I don't dare tell him what I saw, what I remembered. Not until I understand it a little better myself.

"Nameless only knows what she was doing. I hope you found *something* worth almost dying for in that place."

He gives a shaky laugh and says, "I think when all this

105

is over, I'm going to get a nice, quiet job at some obscure, second-rate university somewhere."

"You won't," I say. "You'll keep on doing horrifically dangerous and difficult things for Mrs. Och."

He laughs properly this time. "You're probably right," he says. And then, more gently: "What about you? What will you do when this is over?"

"I don't know," I say. "I reckon that depends."

"On what?"

"On how things turn out."

There is a heavy pause, full of all the terrible ways this *might* turn out. But even if we succeed, the truth is that the future terrifies me. Say we find Ko Dan. Say he fixes all this, and Theo is safe. Can I go back to Spira City? And if I can, then what? Back to a life of crime in the Twist? Or turn my back on that old life and become a barmaid, fending off desperate old coots night after night? I can't imagine a future for myself, a grown-up life I'd be glad to inhabit.

And beyond all that, it depends . . . it depends on what it means that I can disappear, that the world's edges are porous, but only to me.

"Why did you insist on coming with me in the library?" he asks.

I tell him the truth: "I overheard Mrs. Och asking you to research me. I want to know the answers too."

He is quiet for a bit. At last he says, "It is unusual for her to encounter something she cannot explain. I think it worries her."

"It worries me too," I say. "I thought it was all a great lark, a piece of brilliant luck, my vanishing trick, until I stumbled into Kahge. If that's what it is."

"Well, perhaps you can tell me . . . how it feels, what you see?" He's been dying to ask, I can tell—held back only by Mrs. Och wanting to keep me away from my own secrets.

I *do* trust Frederick, but it is hard to find words for how it feels. I tell him what I can—the steps of vanishing, the way it feels to lose contact with my body, how I am different in Kahge, Spira City aflame. And haltingly, I tell him about the creatures at the side of the river, screeching the name Lidari. Lidari, one of the Gethin, Marike's prize general thousands of years ago.

"I know that witch in the library said that the creatures in Kahge don't have bodies, but they *did*," I say. "They didn't look like the Gethin, though. What happened to Lidari, anyway?"

"He served Marike for centuries," replies Frederick. "Mrs. Och would be better able to tell you about her. Marike was the first real threat to the authority of the Xianren. Before that, every human empire had at least made a pretense of obedience to them. The Eshriki Empire was the beginning of the end of Xianren rule. Indeed, at one point, at the height of her power, she even imprisoned them and tried to reassemble *The Book of Disruption* herself."

"I remember reading about that in Professor Baranyi's study," I say. I hadn't understood what I was reading at the time. "She couldn't read the Book, though, could she?"

"No. Only the Xianren could read it and reassemble it. They outlived her empire, of course. The story is that Casimir hunted down Lidari, executed him, and sent his head to Marike. However, these legends are rarely the whole truth of the matter."

"So why would those . . . *creatures* in Kahge be shouting Lidari's name?"

"I've no idea," says Frederick, sounding ridiculously cheerful. He loves having baffling questions to dig into. "I hope that the transcriptions I made will be revealing once I translate them all."

I think again of the little pot my mother was holding in the vision I saw—like the little pot Marike held in the painting on the library wall. I don't dare ask about that—not yet.

"And you'll tell me what you find," I say. "No matter what Mrs. Och says."

A long pause, and then he says, "I'll tell you."

The cool forest passes by us, Tama-shan receding as the city walls approach. I try to take comfort in being myself, in my own body, safe among friends—more or less safe, more or less friends. But my skin is still crawling with residual fear as I think of what I saw in the cave, that other self, not me, whispering with my mother, plotting and longing . . . for what?

# FIFTEEN

We make it back to Tianshi just before the city gates close for the night. Fan Ming exchanges polite farewells with the professor and Frederick. Gregor has all but given up pretending to be Lord Heriday, since Fan Ming pays him no attention anyway. Then Fan Ming turns to me and says, "I am relieved you were not badly harmed, Miss Heriday. I am so sorry I could not prevent what must have been a very frightening experience."

Could not, would not, did not. I meet his eyes and thank him in my best polite Yongwen, but I'm thinking that if I'm ever alone in a dark tunnel with him again, things will go very differently. He promises us that he will report the "incident" to Si Tan, though I suspect that Si Tan orchestrated the whole thing.

We part ways with Gregor and Esme when we reach the second tier road, as we are going in different directions.

"Come see me in the morning," says Esme to me as we say our goodbyes, and I nod, wondering what on earth I will tell her to explain why I'm so interested in Frederick's research. Having people like Mrs. Och or Frederick know the awful depths of what I can do is one thing, but I'm afraid of how differently the people I love might look at me.

The moon is high and bright when the professor, Frederick, and I arrive at the house in Nanmu. Mrs. Och and Bianka are waiting up, and as soon as they see us, Bianka cries, "What happened to your *face?*"

I lift a hand to the scabby imprint of the witch's teeth on my cheek. "Somebody bit me," I say flatly, and then add: "A witch."

Mrs. Och raises her eyebrows.

"Julia was assaulted by a most powerful and unusual witch," says the professor. "Fan Ming seemed very shaken by it, but it is possible he was involved."

"Fan Ming took me to that cave and left me there," I say. "He knew."

"Come, sit by the fire," says Mrs. Och. "Describe to me what happened."

I feel very uncomfortable with all of them staring at me, but I tell them what the witch looked like, the way she sniffed and licked and bit me, the way she tumbled my memories about like she could pull them from me and examine them. I don't mention that last memory of my mother, the one that wasn't mine.

"Perhaps that is why we were granted access," says Mrs. Och when I am done. "Si Tan wanted to know who was prying around his library and for what. Now he will know not only what we are here for, but who you are and what you can do."

Who *am* I? What *can* I do?

"Julia wanted to assist me in my own, separate investigation," says Frederick cautiously, and Mrs. Och turns her most terrible gaze on him. He does not quite meet her eyes, but he carries on, stumbling only a little. Oh, Frederick—stalwart and true, you are. "We spoke of what she sees and experiences when she crosses over to Kahge. She saw some beings . . . creatures with physical form. They were calling out the name Lidari."

"Ah," says Mrs. Och. And that is all.

"Will you describe the creatures you saw, Julia?" says Professor Baranyi.

I do my best, though it makes me shudder to think of the misshapen beasts emerging from the mist, that antlered thing pointing at me with its human hand. I watch Mrs. Och as I talk, and I do not like the look on her face. The look of locking me out. Whatever she thinks about all this, she is not telling me.

"I'm sorry you've had a fright, Julia, but what about Ko Dan?" Bianka breaks in impatiently. "I thought this trip to the library was to find out where he's gone."

A look I can't interpret passes between the professor and Mrs. Och. Then he clears his throat and replies, "The Shou-shu records do indeed show Ko Dan taking a trip to Sirillia a year and a half ago, for the purpose of meeting with Zor Gen of the Xianren."

"We already know *that* from Gennady," snaps Bianka. Her nerves are clearly frayed. "They stuffed this magical book inside my son while I was sleeping."

"Indeed," says the professor. "Upon his return, Ko Dan was reprimanded—officially, for the misuse of a magical object. He was exiled to Tama-shan for meditative penance, the plan being that he would return to the monastery when he and Gangzi agreed he was ready. Now, I did find a new note in another record book suggesting that Ko Dan sent Gangzi an appeal requesting permission to return. There is no record of Gangzi's answer, but the appeal was registered only a few weeks ago. Of course, we have no way of knowing how accurate these records are. They might have cut his head off and put something rather prettier on the books. Given Si Tan's suspicion of us, we must also consider the possibility that the records were altered for our benefit and are intended to mislead us."

"But if it *is* true, then Ko Dan was *there* in Tama-shan?" cries Bianka.

My heart plunges into my stomach. To think we might have been so close to him and let the chance slip by! No wonder the professor didn't want to leave. I don't see how we'll get back inside the library. Si Tan isn't going to issue permission again, and while I am generally confident of my breaking-and-entering skills, a mountain aflame with protective spells is not something I want to take on.

"I tried to get us more time," says the professor helplessly.

"We need to confirm this version of events," says Mrs.

Och. "Dek and Wyn should press their contacts, find out what the rumors in the city are."

I hold back a snort, since their *contacts* seem to consist of a few barkeeps and two pretty girls.

"If we can be sure that Ko Dan is in the library, I will go there myself," says Mrs. Och to Bianka. "But we must be *sure*. Once I reveal myself, we will have only a short time to act. Now it's late. We will decide on a course of action in the morning."

And so we are dismissed. Frederick and Professor Baranyi go to make up a bed for the professor in the servants' quarters, as it's too late for him to go back to the house in Xihuo, and Mrs. Och retreats to her room, closing the door. Bianka looks at me and sighs.

"She didn't tell me the truth about Gennady or Theo until she had to," she says. "She likes to keep things to herself."

"I know," I say.

I stay awake for hours. Only when I'm sure there will be no secret whispered council about the True Nature of Julia—or anything else, for that matter—do I let myself sleep.

# SIXTEEN

I feel as if I've barely put my head down on the pillow when I'm woken by Theo's crying. He has pulled off his diaper and wet the bed, and Bianka is cursing a blue streak.

"Dipe umma *noooo!*" screams Theo when Bianka tries to pin a new diaper on him. He wriggles free of her. She sticks herself with one of the pins and begins cursing again. I leave them to it, wearily stripping the sheets off their mat and tossing them in a corner. I lay a spare blanket down to act as a sheet.

"We can wash those in the morning," I say. "No point trying to do it in the dark."

"*We?*" says Bianka. "Me, more likely. You'll be off doing whatever you do all day, intrigue and whatnot, and I'll be stuck here like always."

She is trying to hold Theo down, but he slams his head into her mouth and wriggles skillfully out of her grasp, fleeing across the room. She gasps with pain, raising a hand to her lip.

"Little rotter," she says, fighting back a sob. "Come here and put your diaper on."

"Dipe umma NO!" roars Theo. No doubt he's woken the whole household by now—not that Mrs. Och or Frederick is going to come to our aid.

"Look, how about I tell you a story while your mama fixes you up," I say.

Theo is standing in the corner of the room now, starkers, but he regards me warily, considering this.

"Yes," says Bianka with desperate enthusiasm. "Won't that be nice? You love Lala's stories, don't you, darling?"

"Stoy," he says, like it's his idea.

"I've got a good one you've never heard before," I say.

He comes plodding over, suspicious, still ready for a fight. I half want to laugh at how the powers of a witch and a vanishing spy combined are barely enough to get a tot into a diaper. But then, like always when I offer him a story, one comes up from the depths, all its details intact, every word that my own ma whispered to me all those years ago when we lay abed together in the dark nights.

I tell them about a princess so beautiful and so rich that noblemen the world over sought her hand in marriage. Her parents urged her toward various useful alliances, but she declared that she would only marry the man who brought her the Cup of Life, a magical cup said to grant its keeper immortality. Her parents were very angry, thinking this was a ploy of hers to never have to marry anyone. When they accused her of this, she admitted it freely, saying she preferred to stay unmarried and rule her own kingdom after they were gone. But one day something came to the palace—a creature half man, half dog, with a cloak made of darkness and ice—and he claimed to have in his possession the Cup of Life.

I pause. Like all my mother's stories, it is relentlessly grim. But Theo is quiet and diapered now, nestled against Bianka while she strokes his curls, so I carry on: "The princess quaked when she saw the thing that had come to see her. His dark boots seemed hardly to touch the ground, his cloak brought a terrible cold into the warm hall, and his face was that of a beast. He held in his clawed hands a simple cup of red clay, and she knew that to accept it and to accept him would indeed mean that she would live forever."

Theo's eyes are drooping closed, his breathing slowing down. I keep my voice to a soft monotone.

"Her parents pressed her to refuse and tried to cast the thing out, but their guards were frozen in time, unable to move. 'If you accept this,' said the beast, 'you will belong to me and you will never die. If you refuse, you will belong only to yourself, but soon your flesh will rot and your bones will turn to dust in the earth.' The princess shuddered to think of this fate. Better to live forever, whatever the cost. 'I accept,' she said, and she reached for the cup. The instant her fingertips touched the cup, it swallowed her up and she disappeared inside it. The beast tucked it back into his cloak and left the palace. Neither the princess nor the beast with the Cup of Life was ever seen again."

Oh, Ma, what *were* you thinking, telling us such tales? I lie there waiting for sleep to come, but then Bianka's voice comes instead, not sleepy in the slightest: "Such horrible stories you tell."

"They're the only ones I know."

I think again of the look on my mother's face in the vision or memory I had of her holding that double-spouted pot: *I have it.* Was it something so powerful she feared it might swallow her up? But she didn't seem afraid. She was never afraid. Even standing on the barge before the roaring crowd that day, her eyes roving over the people but never falling on me, held tight by Dek as I screamed and screamed, my world splintering around me. She must have been afraid, but she did not *look* afraid.

"My gran, who raised me, was not much one for stories," says Bianka. "Perhaps because all the good ones stink a little of folklore. She was a royalist, very taken with King Zey and his philosophy. She was too practical a woman to be telling me tales."

"What about your parents?" I ask.

"It's not a pretty story."

"That's all right. I mean, I don't mind. You needn't tell if it's . . . if you don't want to."

"No, it's not that," she says. "I never knew them, and so, while I think it sad, it is just another sad story about other people. My gran and granddad came to Frayne from

North Arrekem. They bought a dairy farm and my ma was a proper little milkmaid, but then a hired hand forced himself on her. He ran off afterward and left town. Nameless knows what became of him. My poor ma tried to get rid of me in the womb, but I held on, very stubborn. After I was born, she fell into a great sadness. She was unmarriageable now, and far too young to be caring for a babe, and some women, well, after having a baby, they can get awfully blue. That's how it was with her. She hung herself when I was a few weeks old. My gran and granddad raised me, and I loved them, but I never felt right in that little town that was all a-whisper about my ugly beginnings. My gran died of a fever when I was fourteen, and it was just impossible, me and my granddad alone and him such a quiet man. I still feel awful about it, but I left for Nim a year later, made my way as a dancer and cabaret singer. I never had the courage to go back and tell him I was sorry. I don't even know if he's still alive."

"When did you know that you were a witch?" I ask her.

A little laugh in the dark.

"Oh, first time I held a pen, I knew," she says. "Perhaps even before then. When I saw my granddad making notes in his ledger, keeping his accounts, I thought I *must* know how to do it. I told him I could keep the ledgers if he taught me to read and write a little, and so he did. And *then* I knew. I could feel it whenever the pen touched the page—how the paper became everything and the ink was my will and the world might bend to what I wrote. I didn't dare write anything to make it so, not until a calf I was fond of fell ill. Then I wrote on a scrap of paper *Missy don't die*. The whole house smelled of the magic, and I was terrified. I ate the paper I'd written on, and my gran and granddad never suspected, though they fussed and worried about the smell for a day."

"And Missy?" I ask.

"She got well again, but I was so feverish I couldn't get out of bed for a week. So I learned I could do it, and I learned what it cost me. It was too big a spell to start with—the saving of a life. I learned to hide it—how I couldn't burn, how strong I was—and I swore off writing anything. Too dangerous, too painful. I wanted to be a dancer, not a witch."

"If we find Ko Dan and he can help, might you stay here in Yongguo?" I ask. "Or somewhere else where witchcraft isn't punished?"

"No," she says. "Frayne is home, for all that it's no place for a witch. I'm a witch only by accident, not by choice. I've no true desire to write magic, never mind the way my fingers itch when they get hold of a pen. I want to go back to Nim."

"But what will you do?"

"I don't know. I'd rather keep myself than go back to being a rich man's mistress, though there's always money in that. If I could just get home, I'd find my feet. I have friends that would help us while I sort things out. If I save up enough, I could even open my own music hall by the sea. Oh, I don't know, I only want to have a life again, be done with this nightmare."

I think of all the women I've known. Scraping by in the

Twist, most of them, hawking their wares at market, scrubbing the privies of the rich, and so on. I used to swear, when I was little, that I would never be like them, nor even like Ma, her hands rough from washing, all those hours of rinsing and hanging and folding. Now I am surrounded by women who have forgone the well-trod path, the ordinary ways of being a woman in the world: Esme, with her criminal empire; Bianka, dancing and going about with rich men; Csilla, in the theater and Nameless knows what else before she left it all for Gregor. But I can't see among them any path that I might take.

"What about you?" she asks me, as if she's heard my thoughts.

"I want to go home too."

"And you'll have plenty of gold," she says, without cruelty. "You'll be all right."

It sounds foolish, trite, but I must say it anyway: "I'm not here for the gold."

"Oh, I know that," she says, and she reaches across the narrow gap between our sleeping mats, takes my hand, and draws it over Theo's chest, rising and falling, so that we are holding hands over him. "I wonder now if I can truly call the people I knew back in Nim my friends. They don't know what I am, and if they did know, I expect they'd turn me in."

"They might surprise you," I say, just to be kind. We both know how unlikely that is.

"I'm grateful to Mrs. Och," she continues. "I owe her my life, and Theo's. But I also know that, like Casimir and like

Gennady, she cares about something *in* Theo, not Theo himself—that bit of book they're all obsessed with. To me, he's not a bit of book, he's my darling boy." She squeezes my hand so hard my fingers hurt, the fingers Casimir broke, and her voice lowers a notch. "You took him from me, and I thought I wouldn't rest until I killed you myself. Even after you got him back, I thought about just ending you for what you did to him." Her grip tightens, and I bite my lip so as not to cry out. "There are moments, still, when I see you together and I think to myself, If she could do that, who knows what she could do? And yet—Mrs. Och has only ever helped me, but she doesn't love him. Everybody is here for something else—for money or adventure or their own purposes. You are the only one, besides me, who really loves him. You are the only one who came here for Theo."

She loosens her grip on my hand, and I let out a shuddering breath. "I do love him," I say.

I mean to go on, to say that I know she will never be able to trust me, to tell her how I despise myself for what I did, but I stop. It's all been said; there's no point saying it again. She is silent so long, eyes closed, that I think she has gone to sleep after all, her fingers slowly sliding from mine. When she speaks, her voice is thick and drowsing.

"I will *never* forgive you," she murmurs, slitting one eye open. "But you might be my only real friend. Isn't that funny?"

The eye drops closed again. I lie still until her breathing deepens, and then I slowly withdraw my hand. She does not stir, her hand resting alone now over Theo's heart. I lift myself on one elbow to look at them. The magicked sash is still around her waist, but she's forgotten to tie it to him. Careful not to wake him, I wind the other end of the sash around his fat little wrist and make it fast, binding him to her.

# SEVENTEEN

Wyn turns up in the morning with bad news in the form of a drawing. Not his. It is a sketch of Mrs. Och, Bianka, and me.

"This is plastered all over the city," he says, startling me at the henhouse, where I'm fetching eggs for breakfast. He looks altogether too good in Yongguo-style dress. His hair is getting a little wild, though. He hasn't had a haircut since the one I gave him months ago, bundled in our coats and perched on the roof outside his attic room—the spiky rooftops of the Twist around us, the autumn sky bright—back when we were happy, and I was just a girl who could vanish, and everything still seemed simple.

"Word is, you can ask for Shun Yi at the Hundred Lantern Hotel if you've seen any of these nefarious characters. Nice reward offered too."

I snatch the paper from him. There we are, the three of us in a row on the page.

"Not a good likeness of you," he adds. "Whoever did it botched your chin completely. And your expression—you've got quite a sappy look there."

It's not a flattering picture in the least, and, indeed, I'm looking uncharacteristically soulful, but it is me, without a doubt.

"Only the three of us. It's got to be Casimir. Where did you get it?"

"Snatched it off a wall. They're everywhere. But I reckon we don't need to worry too much. Mrs. Och doesn't even look Fraynish anymore, Bianka never leaves this courtyard, and you can be invisible. Who's going to identify any of you?"

"Si Tan, the grand librarian, saw me just the other day!" I snap at him. "Blast. I'd better show these to Mrs. Och. Are you staying for breakfast?"

"Of course! You've got eggs! Dek and I ought to get a chicken or two."

"You'd never remember to feed it," I say, taking up the basket.

The picture sets everyone on edge.

"It is Casimir," Mrs. Och agrees. "He would guess that we might come looking for Ko Dan. I would not be surprised to find his agents here."

"You don't think he might be behind Ko Dan's disappearance, do you?" I ask.

"Possible," says Mrs. Och. "But I think unlikely. Casimir holds no real sway here."

"It could be Agoston Horthy," I say, a bit desperately. The Fraynish prime minister frightens me less than Casimir does.

"I think not," she says. "Horthy does not know *you*. Besides, he would not pursue Theo so far beyond his borders. He does not know what he is."

"What he *is*?" says Bianka sharply. "He *is* a little boy. It's just that he's got something else stuffed inside him too."

Theo is sitting on the floor gnawing on something that looks like a rock but which I hope is a potato. He looks up, curious, aware that he is being discussed. I can't help feeling we ought to be more careful what we say around him now that he is picking up so many words.

"Only Casimir would go to the ends of the earth to find him," says Mrs. Och, ignoring Bianka. "We need to know who he has sent and how extensively he has infiltrated the city. Julia, you will investigate."

"I'll need money," I say.

Mrs. Och fetches me a chain of coins on a red string. In Yongguo the coins all have holes at their center and they are carried in clusters like this.

"Will this be enough?"

I nod, and slip the coins into my pocket.

"Come on," I say to Wyn. "I need your help this time."

Wyn finds a boy, aged ten or so, selling bunches of flowers from a little broken-down cart at the edge of the canal. Mrs. Och's coins are enough to buy the whole lot of flowers and more: an errand. Wyn's Yongwen is appalling, but he manages to convey the basic idea to the boy, showing him the picture and pointing out Mrs. Och as she used to appear back in Spira City. The boy is to say he saw a woman like her in the West Market. He should push for his reward, but not too hard. We don't want the fellow getting hurt; I just want a look at Shun Yi.

The boy does a happy jig and babbles very quickly, and Wyn says, "All right, all right then," clapping him on the shoulder. The boy wants to know where to find Wyn afterward, to report back, but Wyn tells him never mind that.

I am invisible, or all but, in that edge-of-the-world space. The boy darts off, and I am after him. He is a clever dodger, glancing over his shoulder often to check if he's being followed, taking back ways and crowded lanes. I slam into a woman carrying a basket of radishes, and that's it, I'm back in the world, everything pulling into focus, but I'm going to lose the kid if I don't run, so I run, leaving the woman shouting insults after me and collecting her radishes out of the gutter. I slip back to invisibility as we clear the alleyways, struggling to match the boy's pace while I'm vanished.

The Hundred Lantern Hotel is a many-storied building of gleaming yellow wood not far from the Imperial Gardens, its rear balconies overlooking the Dongnan Canal. It is easy to spot on the busy road because it really does have a hundred red lanterns hanging outside. I follow the boy into the main dining hall. The beefy barkeep makes to swat our boy away, but the kid dodges his hand, talking fast. The barkeep is halfway to cuffing him on the ear when he freezes at something the boy says. He lowers his hand uncertainly and beckons the boy to follow. He does, and so do I, vanished behind them.

The private eating rooms are along the side of the dining hall. The boy is bouncing on his toes, wriggling with the thrill of the coins in his pocket, the mystery of his assignment. The barkeep pulls back a curtain. The boy goes bouncing inside, with me close behind him, and then all his bounce and verve are gone.

I nearly run for it, but I'd have to move the curtain and then I'd be caught. I stay still against the wall, breath frozen in my throat.

There is Pia, those awful mechanical goggles emerging from her face where eyes should be. I smashed them with the hilt of my knife in Casimir's fortress, but somebody has repaired them since then. She is unchanged: ghastly pale, a helmet of black hair hanging to her jaw, long leather-clad limbs. I know, though, that underneath she must be different from the first time I laid eyes on her. There must be a scar on her belly where I stuck my knife. Or maybe not. What do I know about her, really? Maybe I left no mark. Maybe I could never really harm her.

The boy is speechless. We could have warned him, if only we'd known—and we should have known, but I didn't want to think it.

She speaks Yongwen, not well but competently, very formally—textbook Yongwen that even I can understand.

Fraynish is not her first language either. I don't know where she's from. It's impossible to imagine Pia as a little girl in a foreign country, speaking some language like it belongs to her.

"Sit down. I won't hurt you."

He is shaking all over. He has never seen anything like Pia, and now I'm sorry we collared him off the street.

"I *will* hurt you if you don't tell me what you're doing here," she says in her high, clipped voice, her too-correct Yongwen. "No games. The truth."

Wyn gave him money, with no threat of consequences for betrayal, and looked altogether nonthreatening compared to this. What fools we were.

The boy is speaking dialect and I do not understand him at all, but I know he's selling us out.

"Did you see this woman or not?" asks Pia, jabbing the picture of Mrs. Och with her finger.

"No," he tells her, head hanging.

"Describe the man who gave you money."

He babbles, presumably about Wyn. I daren't move, I daren't breathe.

"Fraynish?"

The boy doesn't know.

"Only a man?" asks Pia, frowning. "You did not see the girl in this picture? They did not ask you to come back to them afterward?"

"No," says the boy. He carries on, and I don't know what he's saying, but I know what Pia is thinking. I watch her thinking it, I watch the understanding click into place in her expression, the tension firing through her limbs. She looks around the small, curtained room, goggles whirring. The boy stops talking and stares at her. She stands up, hand on the long, curved knife at her hip. She draws it and the boy screams.

"Julia!" she calls, and I startle, jostling the curtain. She can't see me, but she turns sharply, fixing on the place where I am standing. "There you are," she hisses.

I run.

# EIGHTEEN

"Well. Blast."

It's not yet noon, but Wyn pours himself a glass of *shijiu* and offers me one. I shake my head, trying to steady myself. I fled straight back to their place in Dongshui from the Hundred Lantern Hotel and am still catching my breath.

"At least now we know," says Dek. "We're not really in a worse position than before."

"She knows we're here," I say. "She knows *I'm* here."

I'm thinking about how I knifed her and shut the trapdoor on her in Casimir's fortress. I'm thinking she's going to find me and cut me into pieces.

"She already knew that," says Dek. "Or she wouldn't be here. Tianshi is a big city. We can stay out of sight until we wrap things up."

"Now she knows what I look like," says Wyn. He's never even met her, but he's as shaken as I am.

Dek snorts. "What did the boy tell her? Foreign? Dark? Nobody is going to find you."

"That narrows it down a good deal," says Wyn. "I'm sure he mentioned devilishly handsome. That narrows it down even more."

"There are hundreds of foreigners in Tianshi," says Dek. "We'll keep a low profile."

"We *haven't* been keeping a low profile. I'm very memorable! A little asking around and she'll know where we're holed up. Hounds. We should talk to the girls. Let them know to keep their mouths shut."

"I doubt they need to be told," says Dek. "But we'll talk to them."

So Mei and Ling were not just one-time visitors.

"Maybe we should move," mutters Wyn.

Dek sips at his *shijiu*, makes a face, puts it down. "Julia— she can't really get to you, can she? I mean, you can just disappear if she gets close."

"Only if I see her coming," I admit.

I've explained to Dek a little about how I've learned to vanish farther, more completely, though I did not go so far as to tell him about Kahge, or whatever that place is. I told him mainly so he'd stop shadowing me so closely while we were traveling.

"You should take this."

He reaches under his sleeve, and I realize he's unfastening the wristlet filled with capsicum gas that I used to wear. One squirt temporarily blinds an attacker—and hurts like a demon too. I put a hand on his wrist to stop him.

"No, you keep it. I've got my knife, and I can vanish, like

you said. Besides, it's not much use against Pia. Those goggles protect her eyes. If she has eyes."

"We could get you a pistol," says Wyn. "Doesn't get much more effective than that."

I grimace. "I don't like them. And I don't want to put a hole in anybody anyway. I just want to make sure Pia doesn't find us before we find Ko Dan."

"Agreed," says Dek. "But look, I've been working on something else that might come in handy."

Dek is a wizard at designing weapons and other useful gadgets. He fetches a box full of finger-length darts with hollow ends and shows them to me.

"I got these from the circus. They use them for sedating animals. A bit of sleeping serum inside the hollow end, fasten the plunger back on, and then jab someone with the point while pressing the plunger. It'll knock them right out. A little tricky to gauge the right amount, but it should be a good, nonlethal way of dealing with a threat. Also, less noisy than the capsicum gas, which tends to lead to lots of screaming. I haven't tried it out yet—I wanted to use Wyn for a test run, but he objected, the coward. I'll give you a few just in case."

"Thanks." I watch him fill them carefully from a vial, one-handed, the open dart in the crook of his thumb, his other fingers managing the acrobatic feat of pouring without the thumb. I know better than to offer to help. Dek is very clever with the one hand he can use.

"By the way, we talked to the mail carrier yesterday and

made him a very generous offer," he says as he transfers the serum to the darts. "He was absolutely terrified. Wouldn't give me one of Gangzi's letters for love or money."

"I don't remember you offering *love*," says Wyn.

"Well, your Yongwen is terrible. How badly d'you want one, Julia? Now we've got this serum, we could knock him out and steal the whole basket."

"I don't even know if it's important," I say. "But if you can get one without hurting him, and without too much risk, I'd like to see what Gangzi's so busy writing."

"The mail goes out again the day after tomorrow," says Wyn. "I'll nick one for you, easy." Then, to Dek: "I *told* you we should have just stolen it, instead of trying to bribe him."

"I liked the novelty of bribery," sighs Dek. "But I suppose theft is where your talents lie."

He caps the last of the darts and makes a *ta-da* gesture with his good hand. Wyn picks one up and looks at it.

"All right, so if Pia turns up, we *might* be able to knock her out if we're tremendously lucky and she doesn't kill us first," he says. "But what are we going to tell Mrs. Och? Will she think we botched it, letting Pia know we're here?"

"I need to think," I say.

But there is nothing to think about. The only thing to do is to find Ko Dan and get out of Tianshi before Pia finds us, and while I know Mrs. Och might not like the way I'm going about it, I've got a contact now and I'm going to use it.

Old Thien has a note for me with an address on it. The note is written in Fraynish—not by Jun, I reckon, as the Fraynish is flawless and the handwriting that of an educated person—and explicitly instructs me to come alone. I can't say I like the sound of that. Dek and Wyn like it even less.

"The bleeding stars we're letting you go alone," says Wyn. "It could be a trap."

"We'll come armed and stay out of sight," says Dek. "Whistle if you need us."

I am unsure—it will annoy Jun if he discovers it—but in the end, I agree. He may have swoon-worthy cheekbones and dimples to die for, but that's no reason to trust him.

The address we arrive at isn't the house I saw Jun go into the other night. It is in the same part of Dongshui, though. The place is a wreck, a burnt-out shell. Nobody lives there, that much is obvious. The fellows settle behind a wall just up the road. I go vanished into the ruined house, through its courtyards and gutted rooms. Nobody. But when I go back outside, I see him, a blurry silhouette waiting in the bright, empty road. I suppose I'm showing off, but I get close to him before stepping back into the visible world, startling him. He pulls out the stick he jabbed me with before. I might have found his wielding a stick funny if my side didn't still hurt whenever I moved.

"That's unfriendly," I say. "I thought now we'd had tea, there wouldn't be any more of that."

"The note says come alone," he says. "You are not alone."

"You almost speared me with that stick the other night," I say. "That sort of thing makes a girl nervous."

His eyebrows go down in a scowl. No sympathy there. I shrug and whistle. Dek and Wyn emerge from behind the wall, pistols visible at their belts, and saunter over to us.

"I only want to meet your boss," I say. "But I think I'm allowed a bit of protection."

His mouth gives a mocking quirk. "That is not protection."

I don't have time to reply or ask him what he means by that. Very casually, he takes something from the pouch at his waist and tosses it into the road at Wyn's feet. I flinch, but it isn't a wasp nest like the one he threw the first night I followed him. We all stare at it—it looks like a grayish rock—and then a bolt of white flame shoots out of it, crackling. I leap back with a cry, momentarily blinded. There is a pistol shot, and Dek shouting, "Don't *shoot* him, you bleeding fool!" and then, "*Oi!*"

He is quick as anything, I'll give him that. He yanks Dek's crutch away from him and swings it at Wyn's head, landing such a blow that Wyn staggers and falls to one knee. Jun hits him again with the crutch and wrestles the gun away from him, then swings back toward Dek and shouts, "Drop gun!"

Dek is collapsed in the street anyway, has only just gotten his gun out. He lets it go.

"Stop it!" I shout.

Jun is breathing hard, his brow shining with sweat. Dek's

crutch is in one hand and Wyn's pistol is in the other, pointed at me.

"Don't move," he says, and the flare of white fire shrinks and vanishes. The thing in the street looks like a blob of black sludge now. Wyn groans, head in his hands. Dek is all right, though, and pulls himself to standing against the wall.

"That went well," he says to me.

"Shut up," I reply.

"Your friend shoot at me," Jun says accusingly.

"You set fire to the street," I say—realizing belatedly that the flame gave off no heat. "What *was* that?"

"I take *you* to meet boss," he says, ignoring my question. "Not them."

Wyn gets slowly to his feet. He looks rather sick. Jun tenses, but when Wyn makes no move, he tosses Dek's crutch back to him. Dek catches it awkwardly, says, "Thanks."

That's when I decide that I trust him—because he didn't hit Dek, and gave him back his crutch. Still pointing Wyn's gun at me, he snatches Dek's gun off the ground and tucks it into his belt.

"Now you go," he says to them.

I say, "It's all right. I'll be fine."

"I don't like this," says Dek, hitching his crutch back under his armpit.

But since Jun has both of their guns, there is really no argument to be had. They shuffle off, glancing over their shoulders anxiously. I give a jaunty wave to reassure them, and then they are out of sight. Jun lowers the pistol, and I relax a little.

"You know the house?" he asks.

"So do they," I tell him. I showed it to them on the way here, and if they try to stage a rescue, I'd rather he not be startled.

"Go," he says, and we do, to the house I remember from the night I followed him back.

# NINETEEN

We pass through the outer sections of the house and through an unkempt courtyard to the inner house, which is dark and decaying. The walls have holes in them. The floor is unswept. A mouse skitters out of sight as we enter. Jun dead-bolts each door behind him. I don't say that if Wyn and Dek turn up, locked doors won't keep them out. He knocks on a door at the end of a cobwebbed hall and calls out in Fraynish: "Boss, I bring the girl."

A singsonging male voice answers: "Bring her in, then, dove!"

This room is as poorly tended as the rest of the house, the once opulent furniture frayed and stained. At a desk by the window sits a Fraynish man in his fifties, or perhaps a little younger, but aged by debauchery. He wears a double-breasted waistcoat that, like the furniture, has seen better days, and he peers at me over a pair of crooked, gold-rimmed spectacles. The whole house, including its main occupant, gives the impression of past wealth and current decay.

"Julia, is it?" he says.

"Yes," I say.

"Real name?"

"Yes."

"I am Count Fournier."

He rises and comes around his desk toward me with springing steps, holding his hand out. I am startled to notice that he is in his stocking feet and his stockings have holes in them—a big knobby toe poking out the end of one. He is tall and bowlegged, with a gut that strains the buttons of his waistcoat. His features droop downward, as if the flesh of his face simply hasn't the energy to stay stuck up on his head any longer, and this gives him a rather sad expression. I take his sweaty hand, and he plants a kiss on my knuckles. I wonder if I am supposed to curtsy, but it seems silly in trousers.

"Charmed," he says. "Always a pleasure to meet someone from the homeland. May I offer you a drink?"

"No thank you."

"No? Very well. Do sit down."

I sit on one of the sofas, sinking deep into the ancient cushions, dust pluming up around me and making me cough. It smells like mold and cat piss, though I don't see any cats. Count Fournier sits across from me in a gigantic chaise, slinging one leg over the other. Jun stays standing by the door, pointing Dek's pistol at me as if I might suddenly attack the count. I wish he'd put it down.

"I'm going to tell you what I *know* about you first," Count Fournier says pleasantly. "And then I'll tell you what I *think*.

You may tell me how much I've got right. Won't that be fun?"

"Sounds like a barrel of laughs," I say.

"Let us begin. You are Fraynish. It is your native tongue. You are a witch of some kind. You have not been in Yong-guo long, and you speak the language only slightly. You have entered the Shou-shu Monastery secretly on multiple occasions. You are working for somebody with power and political interests rooted in Frayne. These things I know. Here is what I *think*. I think you are a low-class girl, prob-ably from Spira City, judging by your accent, and, in that case, probably from the Twist. I think you have been in-structed to find out what you can about the Fraynish girl in the monastery and about anybody involved with her. I think you know exactly who she is. I think you probably know a fair bit about me. I'd wager even odds that I will have to kill you shortly."

I decide, as he reaches the end of this little speech, that I do not like him much at all.

"What do you think of my guesses?" he asks.

"You're partly right," I reply. "But you've got it all wrong regarding the girl in the monastery and yourself. Also, I'm not a witch. Like I told Jun, I'm looking for the monk Ko Dan. I don't know anything about you or the Fraynish girl."

"That is a convenient story," he says. "But not very believable."

I see Wyn's face at the window for a second, waggling his

eyebrows at me, and I stiffen. I hope they don't come bursting in while Jun has the gun on me. I'd rather he not be startled with his finger on the trigger.

"Here's what I know about *you*," I say. "You're Fraynish nobility, but you're broke, and you've been stuck out here a long time. You're frightened because, whatever you're up to in the monastery with this Fraynish girl, you think I've found you out. But we've got different things going on, and we might even be able to help each other, if you could trust me."

He waves a hand at Jun, who lowers the pistol, looking relieved. "Go on, then," he says.

"I work for a Fraynish lady. . . . I can't tell you who she is, but she *is* very powerful, and finding Ko Dan is important to her. I reckon you've got connections in the city. I thought we could make a deal. If you'll do a bit of digging about Ko Dan and share with me whatever you find, I'll help you however you'd like. I'm sure you could think of something useful a girl who can vanish might do for you."

He takes this in.

"You really don't know who the girl in the monastery is?"

"Should I?"

He grins. His teeth are yellow. "I expect your employer knows—this powerful and important lady you work for."

"Maybe she does, but she didn't see fit to share it with me."

"What religion are you?" he asks, quite out of nowhere.

"I was raised Baltist, in the loosest sense," I reply.

"What does that mean, 'in the loosest sense'?"

"I was raised only in the loosest sense."

I feel Jun watching me closely. If I had to guess, I'd say he knows just what I mean.

"You are too young to remember the Lorian Uprising," says Count Fournier.

I'll bet an exiled count was on the wrong side of that rebellion, and I think I see the way to win him over.

"I was born the year after," I say. "But I heard stories of it. My parents and my employers were on the side of the revolutionaries back then."

He leans back, clasping his hands around one knee, and looks at me a long time, as if wondering whether to believe me.

"Have you heard of Gregor Chastain, or Esme and Gustaf Moreau?" I ask.

He looks properly surprised for the first time. "I knew Gustaf. Everybody knew Gustaf."

"If you lived in Spira City, then you know that after he was hung, his wife, Esme, took over the Twist. I worked for her, growing up. Now I work for someone else, and so do Esme and Gregor. It has nothing to do with your girl in the monastery."

"Gregor Chastain and Esme Moreau would know who she is," he says slyly.

"Well, I could bring them by, if you'd like," I say, a little too carelessly.

"*Could* you, now?" he asks, real interest in his eyes. "They are in Tianshi? How remarkable!"

"I just want to know about Ko Dan," I say, anxious that I've said too much. "I'll bring friends over, do a bit of spying for you, scare somebody you'd like scared, make you dinner, whatever you like, if you'll tell me what you know about Ko Dan."

"My dear girl, I do not know anything about Ko Dan."

I could kick myself for naming Esme and Gregor.

"So I'm wasting my bleeding time, am I?"

A click from the door. I leap to my feet as Jun spins around, raising the gun.

"Don't shoot!" I beg him, and the door swings wide, but there is nobody there. "Stop!" I call to Dek and Wyn, who are presumably in the hall. "Don't do anything!"

But then Wyn comes charging in with a sheet of scrap metal in front of him. Jun hesitates, which makes me think he's probably never fired a gun before. Dek appears in the doorway, pointing a little single-handed crossbow that used to belong to Professor Baranyi, and shoots him in the shoulder. Jun gives him a woozy look, tries to point the gun, then fumbles and drops it. He stares at the gun on the ground. "Faaa . . . ," he mutters, reaching for it, eyelids drooping, and then he falls, unconscious.

I skid to my knees next to him, feeling for a pulse. I can't breathe until I find it, steady in his wrist.

Wyn snatches up the pistol and points it at Count Fournier, tossing aside his scrap metal. The count sighs like somebody has just broken a teacup.

"Is Jun going to be all right?" he asks.

"I hope so." I shoot an evil look at Wyn and Dek. "I wasn't looking for a rescue."

"We couldn't be sure," says Wyn. "It didn't look entirely friendly in here."

He's got a darkly purpling bruise on his temple, but otherwise he seems to have recovered pretty well from being clocked on the head earlier. He helps me lift Jun onto the smelly sofa. Jun's head flops back, his mouth hanging open. He looks much younger this way, and I resist the urge to smooth back the strands of black hair that have fallen in his face.

"He'll be fine in an hour or so," says Dek, although he sounds less sure than I'd like. He told us himself that it's difficult to gauge the right dose with sleeping serum.

"He's not going to be happy with us when he wakes up," I say.

Wyn gives me an odd look. "Does it matter?"

I shrug. I'd been hoping for another of Jun's brilliant smiles, and instead it's been all scowls and pointing pistols. Of course, it shouldn't matter. We're not here to make friends.

"I suppose now you'd better answer some questions," I say to the count.

"I hope it's safe to assume that you two are not with the Fraynish delegation that arrived the other day," he says, looking Wyn and Dek over. "You don't look it."

He knows well enough that a Scourge survivor is an outcast in Frayne.

"They work with me. We don't know anything about any delegation," I say.

"We'd like to know, though," says Wyn, giving his pistol a little twirl.

"Somebody very high up, my contacts tell me," says Count Fournier. His voice is smooth, but I notice his fingers are trembling. "There have been delegations sent before, of course. They've been petitioning Gangzi and the emperor for permission to search the monastery for close to a year now."

"Why don't they just send somebody over the wall if they want to look around?" I ask. "It's hardly fortified."

"Because the Fraynish Crown fears Gangzi, and rightly so, but you never can be sure—they might fear the girl even more. That's why Jun has been spending so much time there. Keeping an eye."

"So she's someone important, this Fraynish girl?"

"Yes," chuckles the count. "She's important. King Zey has fallen ill. Have you heard?"

I hadn't. We haven't had news from Frayne since we left two months ago.

"He is an old man, and the doctors can do nothing more for him. A distant cousin has been named heir. But there are many who would agree that the girl in the monastery has a greater claim to the throne."

I stare at him blankly.

"She is King Zey's niece," he says. "Prince Roparzh's daughter. Her name is Zara."

It takes a minute for this to sink in. I remember the old story of a baby princeling smuggled out of Frayne when Prince Roparzh, King Zey's brother, was hung along with his wife and older children after the Lorian Uprising. I'd always assumed it was a wishful rumor. The revolutionaries had hoped to oust Zey and place his brother on the throne. Prince Roparzh was a Lorian by marriage, and certainly a more moderate man, without Zey's passion for stamping out every last glimmer of folklorish ways.

"Hounds," breathes Wyn. "That's a twist, isn't it? What in flaming Kahge is she doing *here*?"

"She has been raised, guarded, and educated in hiding, by witches and those allied with them," says Count Fournier. "There was a great network of us across the world working to keep her safe. Have you heard of the Sidhar Coven?"

"Yes," I say. Dek and I exchange a look. Our mother was a part of it.

"My aunt, Lady Laroche, is the head of that coven," he says eagerly, clearly proud of the association. "She brokered the deal with Gangzi a couple of years ago. We thought no place more secret, more secure than Shou-shu, which is protected by the empire but not answerable to any outside authority. But I have heard nothing from my aunt in over a year, have received no money, and I do not know if she is still alive." He speeds up, the floodgates open now: "This new Fraynish delegation will try to offer Gangzi something in exchange for the princess, make a deal, and if he believes his agreement with my aunt has expired, then perhaps they will succeed. If I had any connections left, I would get her out, but all my contacts have gone silent this past year. Many of the witches who organized the princess's escape in the first place have been hunted down by now. I am running out of money. Jun is the only employee I have left. I have no means with which to return home. . . ." He trails off. His hands are shaking badly now.

I gesture at Wyn to lower his pistol and he does.

"You see, you do need help," I say. "I'll talk to our employer. She has money and connections, no doubt about that. She might even know something about this Lady Laroche, your aunt. But I want you to ask around about Ko Dan. See if there are any rumors about where he went. If you can find something out for us, I'll bet my employer can help you and your princess. She's quite good at dodging the Fraynish Crown."

"You're really here for Ko Dan?" he asks wonderingly.

I nod.

"I confess I had some idea of who you worked for, though I couldn't be sure of her purpose." He slips from his pocket the picture of me, Bianka, and Mrs. Och that's plastered around the city. Of course. *Blast.*

"Jun recognized you from this picture," he says. "I don't know who this woman is." He points to Bianka, then slides his finger over to Mrs. Och. "But this—*this* is Och Farya of the Xianren." He looks up at us, eyes glinting.

I don't know whether to confirm or deny it, so I say nothing. Wyn and Dek follow my lead, their expressions blank.

"Her relationship with the Sidhar Coven has been . . . uneven," he says. "But overall she has been a friend to witches. Nobody told me . . . I assumed when I saw this that she had come for the princess. I couldn't be sure of her intentions—if she is working with or against the coven this time."

"Neither," I say. "She's here for Ko Dan."

"Well." He licks his lips. "That is a surprise. I remember Ko Dan, you know. When we were in talks with Gangzi about the princess, Ko Dan was always there too. He was Gangzi's right-hand man—his shadow, some of them used to call him. I will see what I can find out."

I look at Jun laid out on the sofa, his mouth soft.

"We're all right, then?" I ask. "There's been a bit of knocking each other about, but I think we ought to have a go at being friends."

"I couldn't agree more," he says. A different tune, now that the gun has changed hands, but never mind. I don't have to like him to believe what he's told me so far.

"I'm sorry about your boy here," says Dek, nodding at Jun. "We were worried about Julia."

"You don't have to worry about me," I say. "I can always disappear if things get bad, like you said before."

"I know," he says. "It's more than a bit ridiculous, me limping in to rescue you. But I do worry anyway. I can't help it. It's my vocation, I think—worrying about you."

The count watches us with interest, his spectacles sliding down his sweaty nose. "Jun told me how you disappear and reappear at will," he says.

"It comes in handy," I say shortly. "We'll be in touch soon."

"Won't you have a drink before you go?" he asks.

"No time," I say, ignoring the disappointed looks I get from Wyn and Dek. They've noticed the whiskey on the side table, of course. "Come on, fellows."

We all shake hands, very chummy now, and leave Count Fournier filling up a glass alone.

# TWENTY

Csilla greets us at the door of the elegant house in Xihuo and takes us through to a grand, open-air room overlooking the inner courtyard, with its flowering bushes and its small pond choked with water lilies. Professor Baranyi is next to a wan-looking Mrs. Och on the settee. Esme and Gregor are standing. We arranged the meeting by tree pipit, and everyone is here but Bianka and Theo—who are not to leave the house in Nanmu—and Frederick.

"Where's Frederick?" I ask, looking around for him.

"He did not want to leave Bianka and Theo unattended," says Professor Baranyi.

I refrain from rolling my eyes at the idea that Frederick might be any kind of protection for Bianka, and I say: "Well, we've got news. Good and bad."

"Start with the bad," says Gregor, sitting back with a glass of *shijiu*. "As is traditional."

"Pia is in Tianshi," I say. "And she knows we're here too."

"You saw her?" asks Mrs. Och sharply.

"Yes. She doesn't know where we're living, but she's here and she's looking for us. That's the bad news."

"You're all right, though?" asks Esme. She's looking at Wyn, his bruised, swollen face.

"That happened later," I say. "We're all right."

"*You're* all right," says Wyn, but he says it good-naturedly.

"The good news?" asks the professor faintly.

"We've found out who that girl in the monastery is. At least, I think we have." I pause for effect, but nobody says anything. "Well, according to my source, her name is Zara, and she's King Zey's niece. The rumors about a royal baby smuggled out of Frayne after the Lorian Uprising were true, seems like. She's here, and the Fraynish government already knows about it. There's a delegation trying to get permission to get into Shou-shu or have the princess turned out."

A short, stunned silence, and then they are all bursting with questions. I try to explain about Count Fournier and Jun. I can feel Mrs. Och's eyes on me, and I know she's probably furious that I've been doing all this behind her back, but I don't care. I feel quite important, bringing such monumental news. Esme and Gregor keep exchanging this wondering, peculiar look, like they've just remembered something about each other that's been buried a long time.

"I'd heard rumors about the princess in Yongguo," says Mrs. Och at last, her chilly voice breaking in and silencing the others. "I did not know for certain they were true.

Certainly, a baby girl was born to Zey's brother just before the uprising. We all knew what was coming, and I helped arrange for her to be taken out of Frayne. But I lost track of her years ago. I heard she died of a fever somewhere in Ishti more than a decade back, but then talk about her surfaced again in the Far East. If it is true, it is good news indeed."

"And King Zey is dying," repeats Esme. She looks at Gregor again—a helpless, resigned look this time. He is clutching the bottle of *shijiu* to his chest like a child clings to a favorite toy. "Who is left?" she says.

"There are many in Frayne who did not join the Lorian Uprising but who have no love of Agoston Horthy," he says fiercely. "Even among the aristocracy, there are those who would support a viable alternative to Zey and his ilk. And Princess Zara—if it is her—has a greater claim than some far-off cousin they've dug up."

"Does it really make such a difference?" asks Wyn. "This king or that queen, I mean."

Gregor pounds the table with his fist. "She is a Lorian princess!" he cries. "First of all, she has a *right* to the throne. Besides that, it would mean a sea change in Frayne, the change we fought for. Freedom of religion and thought! Imagine that! A Frayne that doesn't spend all its resources hunting down and drowning witches? That doesn't trample over its old traditions? Somebody who would flick off that murderous dog Agoston Horthy!"

"All right, all right," Csilla murmurs, patting his arm soothingly, but he is not soothed in the slightest.

"How can you say it makes no difference?" he cries, point‑ing at Wyn, who puts his hands up in mock surrender.

"This count thinks she's in danger, though," I break in. "He'd heard of Gustaf, by the way."

"Everybody who knew of the uprising knew Gustaf," says Esme calmly. She never speaks of her dead husband, or the child she lost to Scourge around the same time.

We are all quiet for a moment. Then Gregor stands up. He is flushed and trembling, but not from drink or lack of drink. There is something in his expression I don't recog‑nize, have never seen. Like he might weep—and not in a drunken, maudlin way, but tears of real, sober, great emo‑tion. He goes to the edge of the veranda and pours the whole bottle of *shijiu* out onto the ground. Then he comes back in and fetches three more bottles from the pantry and takes them and pours them out as well. Csilla begins to cry; she goes to him, and he folds her in his arms. They stand there weeping and clinging to each other, him rocking her in his embrace.

It's an affecting scene, I'll say that. I look at Esme, and her expression is odd, uncertain. Gregor has given up the drink before, many times. He always means it, and he always goes back to it in a matter of days. Csilla is the only one, besides Gregor, who ever believes it will last.

"And Ko Dan?" asks Mrs. Och, ignoring the dramatic scene. "Any word?"

I shake my head.

"This count Julia found has got connections," says Dek.

He can tell I'm on dangerous ground with Mrs. Och. "I bet he'll turn something up for us."

She nods. "Very well. You will pursue the matter with your new friends."

"What about the princess?" asks Esme.

Mrs. Och folds her hands in her lap. "The princess," she repeats, and then, unexpectedly, she smiles. "Why, we will take her back to Frayne and give her the throne."

# TWENTY-ONE

When at last our group breaks up, I try to slip out quickly with Dek and Wyn, but Esme calls me back: "Julia. I need to speak with you."

"Come for dinner after," says Dek to me, giving my shoulder a reassuring squeeze.

I nod and follow Esme reluctantly to the bamboo bench in the outer courtyard. We sit, and she says nothing, waiting. She used to do that when I'd done something bad as a kid, like breaking a window or stealing something I wasn't supposed to steal. She'd sit me down and look at me with that flinty gaze of hers, waiting for me to confess. I cracked every time, and I crack now. I tell her the truth. Just not all of it.

"Mrs. Och has got Frederick researching my . . . the vanishing thing. She wants to know why I can do it, but she's going about it behind my back. And I want to know too."

"Did he find anything?"

"Maybe. He's got to translate it all."

"I don't like it. This witch targeting you in the library too. Why you?"

"If Si Tan saw those pictures . . . I was the only one from the pictures that was there at the library."

"Julia." She puts her big hand on mine, and I stare at her scarred knuckles. Her gentleness is always vaguely surprising. I've seen those fists in action. "You are entitled to your secrets. But if you are in trouble, you must tell me. I have money. We can go home anytime. We don't owe Mrs. Och a thing."

"And the princess?" I say.

"I want to see it through. But I reckon we could manage it without Mrs. Och."

"You don't want to get on the wrong side of her."

"No, I don't. But if you're in danger, I'll do what needs doing. I can get you clear of all this."

"All right."

"Promise me you'll tell me if you need help."

"I'd better go," I say. She lets go of my hand.

I grew up with Esme's power and certainty at my back. The sorts of things that happened all too often to girls in the Twist never happened to me; no man would have dared to lay a finger on me. First I was Ammi's daughter, and then Esme's ward, and I felt safe and strong as a result. But we're beyond all that now. For all that her fists are like anvils and she's the fastest draw in the Twist and clever in ways you'd never suspect, in spite of all the folks who owe her favors and the money she's got stashed away—not even Esme can protect me from Casimir, or Mrs. Och, or the truth.

⌒

When I get to the little house in Dongshui, Mei and Ling are already there. I force a smile, biting back my annoyance. There is so much I want to talk over with Dek and Wyn, but we can hardly get into it in front of the girls, even if they don't speak Fraynish. Mei is ladling a sweet-smelling soup into bowls, and Ling is bent over a book, messy hair hanging in front of her face, while Dek strokes the back of her neck absentmindedly.

"Julia! Look, the girls have spent the day catching turtles and they've made a soup!" Wyn says this with false enthusiasm, fetching another bowl for me, and then pulls a horrified face behind Mei's back. Without turning around, she elbows him in the gut and he yelps. She says something in her dour voice, and Dek laughs.

"I'm not going to ask for the translation," says Wyn, sitting down.

Dek supplies it cheerfully anyway—"Barbarian"—as Mei puts the pot back on the stove.

"Quite a day," says Dek, raising his eyebrows at me meaningfully. I suppose that's as close as we're going to get to talking it over. But I'm starving, so I pull a chair up to the table and dig in with the others. I don't know what turtles are supposed to taste like, but the soup is hot and hearty, which is all I really need from a soup. I knock it back.

"Don't forget to breathe," Wyn says in mock horror. Mei says something approving, and Dek laughs again. Maybe I'm the opposite of a barbarian.

I look at my brother—relaxed, laughing, *happy*, one arm slung over Ling's shoulders—and an uncomfortable memory of our journey over the Kastahor Mountains comes back to me.

We took that route because Mrs. Och and Professor Baranyi feared those mountains less than trying to cross Xanuha, a mountainous country between Ishti and Yongguo. Xanuha is ruled by fierce warriors who overthrew a witch-led regime a hundred years ago, and they have defended themselves for centuries against the vast empire hulking on their northern border. They are apparently not welcoming to strangers, and even less so to magical strangers. But there was no beast that could carry us across the Kastahor Mountains, and Dek could not walk it. Bianka, being by far the strongest among us, had to carry him, like a child, on her back while the rest of us took turns carrying Theo. She never complained of the burden—she kept us all alive on that journey, conjuring the fire that kept us from freezing each night—but for Dek it was humiliating. I remember his face in the icy wind, tight and pale, thin-lipped. It was the hardest leg of the journey for all of us, and I was so preoccupied with my own suffering that I had little left over to think of him.

We set our camp one day at the base of a glacier that shone blue in the sunlight, and while we ate our meager supper, we watched half a mountain collapse, a day's journey or more away from us. The roar of it was deafening, the shape of the landscape changed, and we were still and somber because we were witnessing the ease with which this place could bury us. My awe at the beauty of the mountains had worn off quickly. Every inch of me hurt, and I was hungry all the time, worn down to a nub of the girl I'd started out as—that girl bent on atonement, with courage to spare for making right her wrongs.

"I hate this place," I said to Dek.

He rubbed his leg grimly and said nothing.

"Does it hurt?" I asked him.

"It always hurts," he grunted, the first words he'd spoken in days. "I'm used to hurting."

"Well, I'm not."

"Lucky you."

I don't know why I said it. I wish I could take it back. I said: "I don't feel lucky. I wish someone would carry *me*."

The white-lipped glare he gave me! I sobbed like an idiot, tears freezing on my face as soon as they fell, and he said nothing, returning to his silence.

But he changed when we reached Yongguo at last, as we crossed the grasslands and then the desert, stopping in settlements and cities where he was no more unusual than the rest of us. His money was accepted in the markets, nobody recoiled at his touch. I watched something open up in him, and somebody like my brother as he used to be reemerge. Somebody who laughs easily, somebody strong and self-assured.

I caught a moment alone with him when we were camping a few miles from the city walls and blurted without preamble: "I'm sorry about what I said." I didn't say *two weeks ago, in the mountains.* I didn't need to. He tucked my hair behind my ear and said, "You never need to say sorry to me."

Watching him now, I think I understand properly how terrible Spira City has been for him these past ten years. It didn't occur to either of us that there might be some other place he could go where things would be different, where he could go about freely, where a girl might look at him the way Ling looks at him. At least, it never occurred to *me*, and if it ever crossed his mind, he said nothing.

But Ling is not looking at him now. She is slurping her soup, eyes fixed on her book.

"The girl studies nonstop," says Wyn, noticing me looking at her.

Mei says something tart about hope and their family, and Dek translates: "She says all their hopes of a better life lie with Ling."

Ling slams the book shut at that, her face empty of expression. She takes a pair of peculiarly shaped dice from her pocket and tosses them onto the table, looking at me and saying something that sounds awfully like a challenge.

"*Look* at these!" exclaims Wyn, picking one up and rolling it. They are twelve-sided, white as bone, with black characters carved into each side.

Mei grunts disapprovingly as Ling takes a different book out of the pocket of her tunic and waves it at us—a fat little book that fits in her palm, with red binding and soft, worn pages. It looks well loved, all right.

"If we're going to play dice, we ought to drink," says Wyn. He brings a bottle of *shijiu* from the larder and pours us each a cup. Ling drinks hers down very quickly and explains the game to Dek. Best I can understand, it is some kind of fortune-telling game. She scoops up both dice with her bandaged hand and rolls them over to me.

"What happened to your hand?" I ask her. Whatever the damage, it's almost better, by the way she moves it. Dek gives me an irritated look, so I try again in Yongwen. "Your hand," I say, and then just tack "what?" onto the end of my nonsentence, which makes Dek roll his eyes. Ling pours herself another cup of *shijiu* and says curtly, "Broken."

The way she says it—bitter, guarded—makes me think of Casimir snapping my wrist, my fingers. I shake off the memory and the wave of nausea that accompanies it. Mei says something warningly to Ling about not drinking so much. Ling gives her a defiant look and knocks back her second cup.

"Stars, the girl can drink!" says Wyn, refilling her cup. Mei glares at him.

Ling wipes her mouth with her sleeve and leans across the table toward me, asking me a question.

"What is my ... what?" I ask, catching only half of it.

"Your destiny," says Dek, raising an eyebrow.

"How would I know?"

She slows her Yongwen down for me, like she's speaking

to a young, rather stupid child, so that I can understand her without Dek's translation: "What is your birthday?"

I can't remember the Yongwen names of the months, so I fumble out, "One month . . . later." I think that's what I say, anyway.

"How old will you be?"

At least I know numbers in Yongwen. "Seventeen."

She flips through the book furiously.

"The dominant constellation on the date of your birth, along with the dominant constellation right now, and the characters you roll combine to tell you your destiny today," Dek explains. "It's called *The Book of Ten Thousand Rooms*. It's actually a book of philosophy, but it's more commonly used for fortune-telling."

"Your destiny *today*?" says Wyn. "Does destiny change day to day? Not much of a destiny, then, is it?"

"Your destiny can change—indeed, it *does* change—depending on the choices you make," says Dek. "But in a larger sense, you keep heading in the same direction via different routes. No matter what, though, we're all trapped in the House of Ten Thousand Rooms."

"Why trapped?" I ask.

"Because no matter what we choose, we're within these rooms for the duration of our human lives," he says, and then flicks the book in Ling's hand. "Or within this book."

"So what's outside it?" I ask, and Dek translates this to Ling.

She looks at me, her eyes bright and her cheeks flushed

with the drink now. She licks her lips and says, in harshly accented Fraynish: "The beasts."

I can't explain it—I've not touched the *shijiu* myself— but a cold fear uncoils in my gut when she says this. I think of those things in Kahge pointing at me, shouting at me, emerging from the shadows. I think of how *I* am changed in that place.

"What beasts?" I whisper. Her lips part again as if she's about to speak, but suddenly she breaks out into peals of laughter instead. She says something scornful about witches.

"Ask the philosopher-witches," Dek translates, and then he says to her, "Take it easy on the drink or you'll get sick."

She gives him a look so coquettish I almost blush to see it, and she pours herself another cup. Mei mutters something under her breath.

"Roll," says Ling to me, so I roll the dice.

She examines the characters, flips madly through the book again, running her finger down the lines. Then she reads aloud.

Dek translates it, clearly amused: "Who dares defy his ruler has no honor."

I grin. "That's my fortune? Dishonor and defiance? Not bad."

Imperious now, Ling scoops up the dice and hands them to Wyn, demanding his birth date, flipping through the book when he rolls.

Dek translates again: "In the sight of the gods, a peasant and a king are the same."

Mei shakes her head like a disapproving mama from the Twist.

"Julia's and mine seem contradictory," says Wyn. "Hers is about not defying the ruler, and mine makes it sound like there ought not to be a ruler at all."

Mei explains this one, via Dek: "We have to abide by the rules of the world and submit properly to our role on earth. The gods don't view us according to our role but according to our submission. Our place in the world is only a costume we have to wear in order to become what we are, but we must *wear* it humbly."

Wyn shrugs. Mei cracks a rare smile and says something.

"She called you an idiot," says Dek cheerfully. A sharp exchange between Mei and Dek follows, and he amends it: "An affectionate word for an idiot, then. Someone who doesn't think deeply."

"Well, not about junk like this," grumbles Wyn.

Ling offers the dice to Mei, who shakes her head, scowling again. Ling laughs, jiggles the dice in her hand, and then rolls for herself. She finds the page and reads it in a high, mocking voice.

"Ambition is a mountain with no summit," translates Dek.

Ling shoves the dice at him, almost angrily. He rolls, and she finds the right page.

"'The thirsty man in the desert must learn to drink sand.'" Dek laughs a bit ruefully. "That works as a summary of the past, but I'd hoped it wouldn't be my future. I've drunk enough sand."

He pushes the book closed. Ling leans against his shoulder, the angry light in her eyes going out all at once. She looks almost wan.

I think Mei is scoffing that Ling cannot hold her liquor, but Dek doesn't translate, so I'm not sure. I'm thinking about Dek drinking sand. Suppose I'd been the one to get Scourge, left crippled and an outcast? I can't help thinking that Dek would have found another kind of life for me, even if it meant crossing the world, leaving our home behind. I'm thinking ten thousand rooms are not nearly enough, if every room requires submission.

"I don't believe in destiny," says Wyn, taking out a pack of cards and winking at me. I can't help my smile—it gives itself to him, whether I will it or not. "Chance rules the day, in the end. You play the hand you're dealt as best you can and that's the end of it. Isn't that right, Brown Eyes?"

"To chance, then," says Dek, raising his cup.

"To dishonor and defiance," I laugh.

"But no more sand," says Dek.

I meet his eyes and say: "No more sand."

Wyn shuffles and deals out.

# TWENTY-TWO

The following evening I am vanished near the entrance to a posh dining hall not far from the monastery, in Xishui's first tier. The dining area is arranged in a square around a pond full of water lilies so that those eating can look over the water. At the center of the pond, seated on a little stone island, one musician plucks at a stringed instrument and another plays on something like a flute. Huge rafters crisscross the ceiling, and the wood floors are polished to a deep shine.

Jun wasn't there when I spoke with Count Fournier earlier in the day. I asked after him, and the count told me he was quite recovered from the dart Dek shot into him. I didn't dare ask how angry he was. Now, at Count Fournier's request, I am waiting to see who is having dinner with the Fraynish ambassador tonight.

The hall is packed with the elegantly dressed members of Tianshi's elite, eating and drinking and listening to the music. Only one table by the water remains empty. When I see the two Fraynish men being escorted to it by the serving girl, my heart gives a sickening lurch in my chest.

I recognize the taller of the two men. He is unforgettable. The last time I saw him, I was crammed inside a cupboard in Mrs. Och's reading room and he stood next to Agoston Horthy, saying nothing while the prime minister sparred with Mrs. Och. I do not know what name he goes by, but I know that Bianka has met him too, and that he had an interest in Theo. He has a sweep of thick gray hair and a swarthy face that would be handsome except that his fine features are less noticeable than his one yellow eye and the patch he wears over the other eye.

The Fraynish ambassador is a heavyset man with thinning hair and a sunburnt face like an undercooked meatball. His waistcoat is adorned with medals of rank. The two men arrange themselves at the table, the fellow I recognize with his back to the water.

He wants a view of the place, I suppose. Here in the open, it would be impossible for anyone to lurk near enough to overhear a soft-spoken conversation. Unless, of course, that somebody happened to be invisible and standing right at the speaker's elbow.

The serving girl brings them rice wine and tray after tray of Tianshi's finest delicacies. The ambassador eats very fast, his eating sticks clacking against the ceramic dishes. He jams the food into his mouth, gives it a couple of chomps with those big jaws, and then gulps it down like some bulky but efficient eating machine.

"I'm afraid you will find that they are going to make us wait, Lord Skaal," says the ambassador nervously between enormous mouthfuls. "Si Tan likes to show foreign petitioners that they are of no importance, even when they are very important men like yourself. There is nothing to be done about it."

Lord Skaal is one of a rare type of man who has no tics or mannerisms. When he speaks, I am not expecting it because he does not lean forward or clear his throat or shift in any of the ways that most people do before they speak up. He has a pleasant voice, the tone of a friendly cabriolet driver meshing oddly with his upper-crust accent.

"We shall see how long we have to wait," he says. "I rather thought the grand librarian might be curious to meet me."

"Well, perhaps, perhaps," says the ambassador. "But you see, it's all about status here. They like to make you feel your lack of power."

"I did not come here to feel powerful," says Lord Skaal.

"Of course not," says the ambassador. "I only mean, it is a game, you see. He sometimes refuses to see me at all. It is most embarrassing."

"He will see me," says Lord Skaal, quite serenely. He glances over his shoulder at me—no, through me, though my heart leaps into my throat for a moment—and then he begins to ask the ambassador about Tianshi and the sights worth seeing. They talk for half an hour, no more, and leave together. I follow them back to the ambassador's house in the embassy section of the Beijin Triangle. Then I hop on a trolley to Dongshui.

Jun meets me at the door this time, his expression stony.

"Hullo," I say, heart sinking at the look on his face. "I've got news for your boss."

He nods and lets me in, leading me through the outer courtyard to the main house.

"Are you all right?" I ask, my voice stupidly bright. "I feel badly about yesterday. I never meant for any of that to happen."

"If your friends come here again, I shoot them," he says. "I ask Count Fournier to buy me a gun and he say yes. Look."

He shows me a sleek little pistol that fits in his palm. I'm rather sorry that meeting me and my crew has made him feel he needs more than his sharp stick and clever tricks.

"I'll pass that along," I say.

Count Fournier is asleep at his desk, and it takes a good few minutes for Jun to rouse him, but he livens up as I tell him what I've seen and heard tonight. He fixes himself a drink, not bothering to offer me one this time. When I'm done talking, he looks at Jun and asks: "Is that right?"

Jun nods.

I stare, uncomprehending for a moment, and then give a snort of exasperation. "Well, why'd you ask me to do the job if he was going to follow me anyway?"

"Not follow *you*," says Jun. "I cannot see you. I follow ambassador, check if you tell us the truth about what you see."

"What a waste of my evening." I am irritated, but my irritation gives way to curiosity. "Hang on—where were you in the restaurant, then? They had a view of the whole place."

The dimples come out in his cheeks and something flutters behind my rib cage.

"Ambassador is stupid to choose that place," he says, bouncing on his toes a bit in that restless way he has, like he might start turning cartwheels any moment. "There are big rafters on ceiling. I was on rafter, right over them."

I can't help laughing at that, and for a moment he seems to forget his grudge, and we just grin at each other—two spies appreciating a clever bit of spying.

I pull my eyes away and say to Count Fournier, "Have you heard of Lord Skaal before?"

"No," says the count. "But my contacts tell me that he is important, very close to Agoston Horthy."

"I saw them together once in Spira City," I say. "But why is he trying to meet with Si Tan? If he wants to get into the monastery, isn't it Gangzi he ought to be petitioning?"

"Si Tan is likely more open to negotiation," says the count. "And if there is anyone who holds some sway over Gangzi, it is Si Tan. In any case, it is bad news. I need to get the princess to safety as soon as possible. Will your people help us?"

He says *your people* with an avid sort of gleam in his eyes.

"That depends," I say. "Are you going to help *us* find Ko Dan, or do I have to jump through some more hoops?"

"No hoops, my dear," he says. "I've already put the word out. But I'm going to need money. For bribes, you understand."

"I'll bring you some," I say.

Count Fournier shoots Jun a pleased look, but Jun's gaze is snagging on mine again, another smile twitching at the corners of his mouth.

"Well," says Count Fournier, clearing his throat. "What I *do* know about Ko Dan is that he is a man-witch. Male witches are exceedingly rare, as I'm sure you know, and there was a lot of resistance, back in the day, regarding his joining the Shou-shu sect in the first place. Of course, they work a kind of magic with those bells, but the magic is *in* the bells, inscribed by witches a thousand years ago or more. He is the only one who can write magic himself. He was not born in Yongguo. He is from the Muyriki Islands, in the southern sea, but he came to Tianshi alone as a boy, bearing only a letter of recommendation from the Muyriki high holy, asking to apprentice with Gangzi. Gangzi made quite a pet of him. I don't know how or why he left the monastery. There are various stories. Some say he went mad, some say he was executed, and others say he became a secret advisor to the emperor. I never paid the rumors any mind, but I found him a curious fellow when I met him."

"What does he look like?"

"He is a young man, small, a gentle expression. He had a scar under his eye, shaped like a little star. Marked by magic, they said, or touched by the spirits. Who knows the truth of it?"

"D'you think they might have executed him?" I ask. I'd hate to think we came all this way looking for a dead man.

"It's possible, but I think Si Tan, in particular, would consider it a waste. They would want to make use of him somehow, I suspect. Still, if they considered him too dangerous or impossible to control, then yes, they would kill him. I do not know the nature of his crime. The penalty for misuse of magic that harms no one is ten years in prison."

"What are the penalties if someone *is* harmed?"

"It depends on who and how. Witches are drowned here too, you know."

"Witches who hurt people or use magic for their own gain," I say.

"Witches who are accused of that," he says, and then laughs at my expression. "I've been here too long, and I am a cynic. Witches may be useful to the empire or they may pose a threat. The empire keeps them close not because it loves witches but because it seeks to control them in the most efficient way. In Frayne, Horthy and the king drown witches indiscriminately, which is clumsy and brutal and stupid. There is more art to the managing of witches here, but don't imagine they are *not* managed. The penalty for not revealing yourself as a witch—by which I mean for *being* a witch without a license, even if you do not practice witchcraft—is death."

I am a little shaken by this. I suppose I'd imagined Yongguo as some kind of idyll for witches.

"A ruler cannot afford to ignore the fact that some small number of the population can alter nature itself merely by writing something down," he says.

"And what does your aunt, Lady Laroche, think about that?" I ask.

He smiles slyly. "Why, *she* believes witches cannot be ruled. It follows, then, that witches ought to rule. Now don't look so shocked, my dear! You've done very well. My contacts know everybody in this city. If you have money, I will find you Ko Dan."

# TWENTY-THREE

I am hoping to find Dek at home, but he isn't there. Wyn is asleep on a mat on the floor with Mei at his side, her arm flung back. An aching, dark space opens up inside me as I look down at them. I used to love to fall asleep in his arms, to wake up next to him.

But he's not mine anymore, never really was, and I have other things to do besides wallow in self-pity. I give him a sharp nudge with my foot.

"Ow," he mutters into the pillow. I nudge harder. He sits up and stares at me.

"Brown Eyes," he says blurrily, and then looks at Mei and back at me, uncertain.

"I need money," I say. "Where's Dek?"

"I don't bleeding know where he is," he grumbles. "It's the middle of the night. What do you need money for?"

"Dek said Mrs. Och gave you money for bribes. I need some."

"So she'd give some to you as well. Why d'you need to come waking me up?"

He gets up off the mat, careful not to disturb Mei. He is completely naked, all beautiful long limbs and . . . well. I look away.

"Aren't you precious," he scoffs, snatching his trousers from the floor and pulling them on. "Nothing you haven't seen before."

"I'd rather not wake Mrs. Och in the middle of the night," I say. "And I was hoping to see Dek."

The truth is, I want as little to do with Mrs. Och as possible. I want to find Ko Dan and get out of here. I follow Wyn into the other room, where he pulls up a floor plank and takes out a jar full of coins on strings and wads of paper money.

"How much?" he asks.

I help myself to most of the paper money, filling my pockets.

He gives a low whistle and asks, "D'you want me to come with you?"

"No."

"You're sure? It's not dangerous?"

"I'll be fine."

He sighs and rubs a sleepy hand over his face. "If you say so. You know if you ever need me . . . well, just say the word."

"You'd leave your poor girl alone in the bed?" There's more bite to my words than I really intended.

"Yes," he says.

We look at each other. He is all shadow, his bare chest a darkness I know so well. My loneliness opens wider and wider until I feel I am a small thing within it. I shake it off. I'm used to climbing out of this particular pit of regret and desire by now.

"Look, I'm sorry I woke you. I'll come by tomorrow if I get a chance. Tell Dek to stick around."

I can't really see his expression in the dark, and I am already turning away when he says, "I still love you, Julia."

He never told me that he loved me until I left him.

"I love you too," I say lightly, without turning around. Because I do, I always have, in a thousand different ways. I go out and close the door on him.

I don't go straight back to Count Fournier's with the money. I am restless, and my legs carry me, almost of their own volition, to the other side of the Imperial Gardens and the empty road outside the Hundred Lantern Hotel. My heart tightens in my chest as I look up at the lit windows. It is one of the few establishments still open this late. I should be keeping an eye on Pia. I could disappear and get into her room, if I knew which one, without her seeing me. But when I think about it, my breath catches in my throat and I am, quite simply, too frightened. Like a child closing their eyes and pretending the scary thing doesn't exist—if I don't see her, I don't have to think of her in Tianshi, hunting me, hunting Theo.

"What is here?"

I spin around, and there is Jun, just a few feet away.

"Are you following me?" I try to sound annoyed, in spite of a startling rush of gladness.

He jerks his chin at the hotel. "You look at this place like there is ghost inside."

I shake my head, start to turn away.

"Julia," he says, and I stop. There's something new in his expression, two parts mischief and one part uncertainty. "I can tell you what is here at Hundred Lantern Hotel."

"What?"

"Best red bean soup in Tianshi. Maybe in all Yongguo. Maybe in the world."

He arches an eyebrow invitingly, tilting his head toward the door. I can't help smiling, but I shake my head.

"I can't go in there."

He nods and says, "Come with me."

I don't ask where. He takes me across the Zhuque Road and through a maze of narrow streets to a small eatery with a single lantern hanging outside. I follow him down the steps into a candlelit cavern, where a girl of maybe twelve is serving drinks and filling pipes for old men. She sees Jun and waves, then points to a curtain at the back of the room. We sit down at a little booth behind the curtain. The girl brings us tea, and Jun signs at her with his fingers. She nods and disappears again, letting the curtain fall shut.

"What was that?"

"She is not hearing," he says. "She use signs. You know it?"

I shake my head.

"Can be useful if you are hearing or not," he says. "Maybe I will teach you one day."

I hope I'm not going to be in Tianshi much longer, but it gives me a warm feeling, the way he says this—as if he's taking it for granted that we are on the same side, that we will continue to know and help each other. And what *is* this? Why did he bring me here? I pull my hair out of my face, trying to comb through the tangles with my fingers. I would have washed my face and brushed my hair, at least, if I'd known I was going to end up in a candlelit booth with him.

He leans toward me across the table. "How you disappear?" he asks me.

"I just . . . do."

"Show me?"

Stars. He says it so sweetly.

"All right," I say. "There are . . . I mean, I can disappear just a little, or a lot. If I were to try and disappear just a little right now, it wouldn't work, because you're already looking at me. But I can go back farther. I won't move, so when I do it, grab my hand, all right?"

He nods, and I vanish. Two steps back. His eyes widen, and he reaches across the table for my hand. Everything pulls into focus as I'm yanked back into the world by the contact. I laugh at the stunned look on his face, and he gives his head a little shake. He's still holding my hand.

"If you disappear and I touch you, I can see you again. But before, you disappear while I am holding you."

178

"If I'm just vanished partway, a bump or something kind of . . . knocks me back," I say. "It's hard to explain it, but it's as if there are *layers* of vanishing." I don't know why I tell him this—it's dangerous territory—but I add: "I can even take you with me, if I try."

"Take me where?"

"I'll show you."

I hold his hand tightly, and I pull us back carefully, pull him with me. Two steps. The little room blurs around us, but he—he stays in focus.

"Nobody can see me now?" he whispers. His face is like a light in the faded nowhere, our own invisible cocoon just beyond the edges of the world.

"That's right," I say. My heart speeds up, and I let go of his hand. The room sharpens around us again. The girl from before pulls back the curtain and puts a plate of steaming pork buns in front of us. Jun thanks her with his fingers, and she lets the curtain fall shut again.

"You are afraid of somebody at Hundred Lantern Hotel," he says, splitting open one of the buns so steam pours out. It smells delicious, and my mouth starts watering immediately. I grab the other bun. "Is it same person who put up pictures of you and your boss?"

"Yes."

"This person is dangerous to you?"

"Very," I say.

"Why this person is looking for you?"

"It's complicated."

He nods, accepting this.

"This place is safe. Nobody will tell they see you."

We demolish our pork buns at the same lightning speed. He licks a finger to pick up the crumbs off the plate. I'm tempted to do the same but decide to make some effort at appearing ladylike.

"What about you?" I ask. "Where did you learn . . . well, the sorts of things you can do?"

He grins at me, the dimples reemerging. Blast ladylike—I lick a finger and help him finish the crumbs. From the pouch at his waist he takes out a grayish rock like the one that shot out a bolt of flame when he threw it at the ground. I recoil, and he laughs.

"Count Fournier buy me this," he says. "Touch."

I touch the rock with my fingertips, but it is not a rock at all. It is spongy and warm.

"It is just trick," he says. "The fire does not burn. But looks very hot and bright. If I throw it down, it can scare someone, give me a chance."

"It did scare us," I say. "I saw you leaving the monastery one night. You had a jar of wasps or something."

He grins at me again. Oh, I am utterly slain by this smiling, laughing, candlelit version of Jun.

"I learn that back home," he says. "Get nest at night when wasps are sleeping, trap in a jar, and you have like a bomb you can throw if someone is chasing you."

"So how long have you worked for Count Fournier?"

"Two years. Before that, I am acrobat in children's circus."

"An acrobat!" I'm impressed. "So did you run away with the circus as a kid?"

"Yes," he says. No more than that.

"What about your family?"

"They are not good," he says. His expression does not change, but I know how to recognize practiced nonchalance.

"Not good?"

"Not good." He says it firmly, and I let it go. "I love the circus. When I am getting bigger, I start training for the trapeze. I do dancing on horseback. It is so much fun." There is a longing in his face that twists my stomach into knots. "But the circus leader like young boys too much and I cannot stay with them. When I am thirteen, we come to Tianshi. This is great city with many chance, so I leave the circus. I do many kind of job here, but after one year Count Fournier hires me. He is best boss, so I stay with him. Good pay, safe place to live. He is not happy man, but he is good man."

We look at each other by the guttering candlelight.

"I was seven when my ma died," I offer. "She was a witch. They drowned her."

"I am sorry," he says. "You have father, or brothers?"

"A brother," I say. "You met him. The one with the crutch."

"He shoot me with sleep drug."

"I know. He was trying to help me."

"Maybe I forgive him, for you," he says slyly. And then changes the subject: "I love Tianshi. It is great city. Greatest in the world. You think so?"

"It's amazing," I say. "In Frayne, if you're born rich, you

181

stay that way, and same if you're born broke. Here, talent really counts for something."

Jun snorts. "Not so different here," he says dismissively.

"But the Imperial Examinations," I say. "I mean, a peasant can take them!"

"How can a peasant learn to read to take this exam?" he says. "And what is on this exam? Maybe I am great painter or great poet, but how can I know when I have no paints, no paper, no time? This exam is for people with money and people with time. If you can do rich person's thing, you can live in the Imperial Gardens. But they do not invite farmer who can make crops grow in a dry year, or goatherd who can deliver calf safely and keep his herd alive through winter, or fisherman who can catch most fish. Maybe if you take away the meat and rice and fish of the rich, they will think those talents are also important. But the men and women who feed this city are poor. I have great talent too, and I am more clever than many men who read poems all day, but I will never have my place in the Imperial Gardens either."

He says all this without rancor, but it stirs me.

"I reckon you're right," I say. "The deck is stacked no matter where you go."

"What does it mean?" he asks, and I try to explain the expression *stacked deck* to him.

"You play cards?" he asks me, eyes gleaming with mischief again.

"I'm all right," I say.

"I show you some trick next time," he says. I want to ask,

*Next time what?* but I'm afraid to spoil the moment. He is drumming rapidly on the table with his fingers again. I think I've never known someone who can be, at different moments, so restless and so still.

"What about Spira City?" he asks.

And so I tell him about home, all the things I miss. His eyes are black and shining, the angles of his face all the more dramatic in the flickering candlelight. I want to tell him I know what it's like trying to find a life large enough to fit who you are and what you can do. I want to ask him if he feels a pang whenever he sees children with their parents, children who are safe and loved. But instead I cast around for stories and descriptions that will make him laugh, and whenever he does, my heart belly flops all over the place. He tells me about the circus and traveling around Yongguo, and I try to imagine him as a slim young boy dancing on the back of a horse. The girl brings more tea, and we talk about our lives as they used to be—so much safer than talking about the here and now—until the candle burns down to a nub and goes out.

# TWENTY-FOUR

"Hey!" cries Frederick.

Cackling with glee, Theo tries to make off with his notebook, filled with the transcriptions of the bamboo strips from the Imperial Library, but Frederick gets it back and puts it on the table. "You mustn't touch these, Theo."

"Stoy!" Theo shouts.

"I'll tell you a story," I offer, looking sadly at my failed attempt at scallion pancakes, burnt to the pan.

"*Feyda* stoy," says Theo. "Buk!"

"I got him a book of fairy tales," explains Frederick. "They're in Yongwen, but I translate as I go. He likes the illustrations."

"Feyda umma *buk!*" insists Theo, trying to snatch the notebook again.

"We had better be careful of that," says Mrs. Och, watching him.

"Careful of what?" I ask.

"Theo learning language," she says. "No matter how it is bound, *The Book of Disruption* is a part of him."

"What do you mean?"

"I mean that his learning language might be dangerous. Oh, probably not so long as he cannot read or write. But even so, we should keep a close eye now that he is beginning to speak. Words have power, and his might have more than most."

That is an unsettling thought. I look at Frederick, who is stacking his notebooks and papers out of Theo's reach.

"Yes, yes," he's saying. "I'll read you a story."

"So nothing useful yet?" I ask him, gesturing at his notes.

"Nothing we don't know already," he says. "Although here is something interesting. Kahge might be described as an echo or reflection of the natural world, but it is not a perfect reflection. There are many reasons for this, one being that the elements in Kahge are not in balance. Because it is made of magic, fire is dominant. That might explain why what you see is like a reflection of the world on fire, or burning, or burnt. I am going to need a different dictionary to translate the pictographs on the rubbing—it is the oldest form of Yongwen I've seen. But there is a bookseller in the Beimu Triangle who has been very helpful. I'll go and see him today. *Yes*, Theo, all right!"

Theo has found the book of fairy tales and is waving it urgently at Frederick. Then he runs outside, and Frederick follows. I don't want to sit at the table with Mrs. Och, and so I take my burnt scallion pancakes out onto the steps, where

Bianka is sitting in the thin morning sunlight, carving a toy for Theo out of a block of wood.

She is carving much too fast. She is very jumpy about Lord Skaal being in the city, and I reckon carving is not the best activity for her at the moment, but I daren't say so. As soon as I sit down next to her, she says, "I don't care what Mrs. Och says. He's here for Theo."

"I think she's right that he's here for the princess," I say. "Casimir might know that we're here, but Agoston Horthy doesn't."

It is early, and the clouds in the east are gold-rimmed as the sun comes up. Frederick and Theo have settled on an empty crate by the pump, and Frederick is reading to him. Theo is riveted by the brilliantly colored illustrations that fill up most of the page, pointing out this and that. I doubt he'll be asking *me* for stories anymore.

"No," says Bianka. "I remember him. He was the first to come for Theo. We need to get out of Tianshi."

The knife in her hand is going still faster.

"Not yet," I say. "Count Fournier has put the word out. We need to sit tight. We'll know something about Ko Dan soon."

"I can't just sit in this courtyard and wait for them to appear and try to take Theo!" she cries. "Oh *blast*." She has whittled the wood away to nothing, her lap full of shavings. "I said I'd make him a toy. He has nothing to play with, and he torments the chickens."

"Mo! Mo!" cries Theo when Frederick reaches the end of the story. Frederick laughs and turns the page.

"You were wrong, you know," I tell Bianka, pointing at them. "When you said I was the only one besides you who loved Theo."

She looks at the two of them bent over the book together, almost cheek to cheek, Theo's chubby little hand fondling Frederick's beard, and her face softens.

"You're right," she says. "They adore each other."

I am about to reassure her again that Lord Skaal is surely here for the princess when a tree pipit flies over the wall and nearly crashes into my face. I give a yell, trying to fend it off. It drops a piece of paper in my lap and lands on the step next to me, cocking its head at me. I unroll the paper quickly. Dek's handwriting: *We've found him.*

The trolleys on the first tier road are always crowded in the morning, but I vanish and step onto the outer ledge, holding on to the window rail. I've seen people try to ride this way for free, though usually the driver spots them and shoos them off. The voices of merchants sing out from their shops and stalls along the side of the road, delicious smells waft up from the food stalls, and the peaked rooftops shimmer in the morning haze. I get off the trolley in Dongshui and buy sticky red rice wrapped in bamboo leaves so I can eat as I walk. I keep my hat down and my head low, hoping the seller doesn't look at me too closely and recognize the foreign girl whose picture is plastered on the walls of the city with a promised reward. Then I head in among the narrow dirt streets where the ramshackle houses practically lean up against each other, old men sitting outside playing Zhengfu and smoking while scrawny chickens run loose, shedding their feathers.

When I get to Dek's house, Mei and Ling are there again. Dek and Ling are at the table, flour-dusted to the elbows, making dumpling wrappings. Wyn and Mei are playing cards, and they both look bored out of their minds.

"These two seem to have moved in," I say.

"Julia!" Dek grins at me. His hair is braided Tianshi-style. "You got our message?"

"I hope by all the holies you mean you've found Ko Dan, or Bianka's going to have a fit and probably turn you into a toad."

"Ling told us. He was readmitted to the monastery at dawn. Apparently, word got out and there was quite a crowd gathered outside to watch him knock on the door and request entry, so for all that we've been pretending we've got the pulse of the city, we're obviously out of the loop. The girls went with their uncle and saw him themselves."

"You saw him go in?" I ask Ling in Fraynish. Dek translates, looking vaguely annoyed with me.

Ling nods, wiping her hands off and fetching me a rolled-up piece of paper. I unroll it and look at the drawing of a solemn, round-faced man with a star-shaped scar under his eye.

"Who drew this?"

"Ling did," says Wyn. "She's not bad, is she? Good technique."

"Can I ... um ... ownership?" I ask her in fumbling Yongwen.

Mei smirks a little at my bad Yongwen. Ling just shrugs, as if she doesn't care one way or the other, but when I fold it up to slip it into my pocket, her brow creases in an expression of surprise and hurt, and I wonder if it's some kind of insult to fold it. I've nowhere to put it rolled up, though.

"Where were you last night?" I ask Dek. "I wanted to talk to you."

"We went to the theater!" he says enthusiastically. "It costs almost nothing for standing room. All the rich people pay for balcony seats above and watch through their little binoculars, but we were right in front of the stage with the rabble. I've never seen anything like it—it was this kind of dance with masks. Ling was explaining it to me. Every movement means something; every mask has significance. Each animal is symbolic. What did we decide? Ling is a lynx, I'm a cormorant...."

"Panda," says Ling in Fraynish, pointing at Wyn, and I snort.

"What would I be?" I ask.

"Hmm, what do you think?" Dek asks Ling in Yongwen. He looks so happy. I can't remember seeing him look so happy. I should be glad to see it, but it makes my heart sink—that *this* place and this girl should be what makes him

189

happy. That there is no hope of freedom or love for him back home, the home I long for.

Ling studies me and then says, with the faintest smile: "Wolf."

I raise my eyebrows at her, not sure if I ought to be offended.

"Wolf?" says Dek, taken aback.

"Wolf," says Ling firmly.

"Are you going to the monastery now?" Wyn asks me, tired of the conversation and probably annoyed at having been declared a panda bear.

"No. Mrs. Och told me to report back to her after I'd spoken to you," I say. "I've got to report to her before I take a piss, apparently."

Dek laughs.

"Wait a bit if you're hungry," he says. "Ling is teaching me to make steamed dumplings."

"I *am* hungry," I say. "But Bianka's waiting too, and probably going mad. If it's really him, we'll be moving on soon, I reckon."

I look at Dek as I say this, but he shows no sign of having heard me, flattening the dough into perfect little circles.

"I'll walk you to the trolley," says Wyn.

"I don't need an escort."

"I'm not escorting you. I want to talk."

"Oh."

"Come back when you're done," says Dek. "We'll have dumplings ready!"

I don't know what to make of this happy, busy version of

my brother. I thank Ling for the picture again, and Wyn walks me out.

"Mail goes out from Shou-shu today," he says. "I was going to snatch one of Gangzi's letters if you still want it. Or should I not bother now that we've found Ko Dan?"

"Might as well get one just in case. Is that what you wanted to talk to me about?"

"No. Well, that was one thing." He clears his throat. "I'm just going to say it. I promise I'll drop it if you tell me that you don't feel anything for me anymore. But I think that you do, and I want you back, Brown Eyes. I want things to be like they used to be."

"That isn't going to happen," I say quickly, before I can say anything else. "Everything's changed. *We've* changed. Or I have, anyway."

We pass an old couple sharing a pipe outside. They look at us curiously, and I duck my head so that the brim of my hat hides my face.

"People don't change that much," says Wyn. "I'll own that I spoiled things. I was selfish and stupid. But it would be different if you'd give me another chance."

"You just finished telling me people don't change. Everybody knew what was happening except me. If I wasn't enough for you then, I don't see why I would be now."

"Because I wouldn't risk losing you again. But you should talk to more girls, Julia. The way you carry on, you'd think I was this roach among men for spending a night or two with Arly Winters."

"I don't carry on," I say, getting angry now. "*You* brought it up. I'd just as soon not talk about it at all. And if you *must* talk about it, don't lie to me and pretend it was only a night or two. What would your girl back at the house think about you telling me this?"

"This isn't about Mei."

"Of *course* it is! She thinks you're her fellow, and here you are trying to sweet-talk me back into bed with you. As far as I can tell, you want every girl you look at, especially the ones you haven't got."

"Don't be so bleeding naïve, Julia. All men are the same. Yes, if I see a pretty girl, I want her. Hounds, if I see an ugly girl, I want her. I wish you could understand how little it has to do with you, or with love. But that's what I'm trying to tell you: If it matters to you, I can just . . . resist all that. Be yours. Really yours. Haven't you been angry long enough?"

"I'm not angry," I say, deflated. "But things are different now."

"You haven't told me you don't feel anything for me anymore."

"Hounds, I'll always *feel* something for you. But not the same way I used to. I'm past it, all right?"

I hear myself saying it, and for the first time I almost think it might be true.

"Flaming Kahge, Julia—what do you want from a fellow?" He kicks a rock down the road, frightening a pair of chickens. "I'll own my mistake, but if you think there's a man out there who's any different, you're deluding yourself!"

I've heard enough.

"Fine, maybe men like you are common as dirt. That doesn't strike me as much to brag about. But I don't go around figuring everybody is just like me, and d'you know why not?"

He gives me an unhappy look.

"Because there is *nobody* like me," I tell him, and vanish, leaving him staring at the place where I was, where I'm not anymore.

# TWENTY-FIVE

"He's at the monastery," I tell Mrs. Och, showing her the picture Ling drew. She takes the paper from me and examines it. "Dek's girl saw him going up to the gate, said that everybody was talking about Ko Dan's return, and she drew this."

"What now?" whispers Bianka, watching the goat knock Theo over into the mud in the courtyard.

"I will go and see him myself," says Mrs. Och, rising and giving me back the picture. "Julia, you will come with me to make sure nothing is amiss and that I am not followed back. Frederick! I need strength."

He comes when she calls him. I can see the apprehension in his eyes even though he tries to hide it. He stretches out his hands. She reaches for him, and there is an awful hunger in her gaze. I can't watch. I turn away, leaving the room in a hurry, but I hear him gasp behind me, his knees hitting the floor.

"How are you going to get in?" I ask.

Mrs. Och is striding down the street, and I find myself half skipping to keep up with her, like a child whose long-legged parent won't slow down for them, taking two steps for every one of hers.

"I'll knock," she says.

"But doesn't that blow our cover? Then everybody knows we're here, what we're after."

"If Pia is in Tianshi, it is because Casimir already knows that we are here and what we want," says Mrs. Och. A fair point. "I expect that the grand librarian has a good idea as well. But if it is indeed Ko Dan in the monastery, and if he agrees to help us, then we will not need to hide much longer."

"What if it *isn't* him? What if he won't help us? What if he *can't* help us? Or what if he can't do it without hurting Theo?"

She gives me an impatient look. Her face is bright and alive with what she took from Frederick. I wonder, when I see her like this, if she takes only what she needs or perhaps more. How much she likes it. How much she does it just because she likes it.

"We did not come all this way to harm Theo," she says. "There is no point imagining a thousand possibilities before they come about. It is a drain on the mind."

"Fine. Say you get the text out of Theo. What will you do with it?"

"Perhaps destroy it."

"Destroy it? Really?"

"If it is possible, yes. The Book has been trying to unmake itself for centuries. The time of the Xianren is already past. Casimir is grasping at straws, but they are dangerous straws indeed, and best kept out of his reach forever. Julia, when the witch at the library searched your memories, did she uncover our purpose here? Does she know we are looking for Ko Dan?"

"I don't know," I say. "It was all moving very fast. She knows about Theo and the Book, I think, but the memories she seemed to stop over were from a long time ago. When I was little."

She frowns, dissatisfied with this answer, and boards a trolley at the second tier road. The other passengers make way for her instinctively. I go along vanished, no more chances for asking questions. We ride the trolley to the northwest part of the city and walk from there to the monastery.

"Behind me, Julia," she murmurs. "Unseen, if you please."

I do as she says. She pulls the bell at the main doors of Shou-shu. A panel is pulled back, and a face appears in the gap.

"Who are you?" the face asks in Yongwen.

She says "Och Farya," her Xianren name. No more hiding indeed.

"No woman may enter here," says the face.

A harsh laugh. The air hums. Her cloak billows, and she casts it to the ground. Fur ripples out of the back of her neck and along her outstretched arms, her hair moving and changing to match it. Bony spikes tear out of her back through the fabric of her robe and unfold into wings.

Her voice resonates when she speaks—making the point, presumably, that she is not exactly a woman, and not to be denied. Another face appears at the panel. The two faces deliberate, the panel is slammed, and we wait. The wings lie resting against her back like the wings of a great swan.

And then the doors creak open. The monks back away as she enters, with me vanished in her wake. The doors slam shut behind us.

# TWENTY-SIX

We are taken to the tiny, wooden Temple of Atonement behind the Treasury. There he is, kneeling before the many-armed statue of Gu'ama, West Arrekem goddess of repentance—the man from Ling's picture. Ko Dan. My letter-writing friend Prune Face—Gangzi—kneels next to him. They look up as we come in, and although his face is slightly blurred by my vanishing, I can make out the star-shaped scar under Ko Dan's left eye. He rises and bows to Mrs. Och. There is something loose and easy in the way he moves, as if he is more at peace inside his skin and bones than most. Gangzi rises rigidly, grimacing like his joints pain him, and gives a terse nod.

Mrs. Och remains in her startling Och Farya form, but the two men do not seem alarmed. They all greet each other politely in Yongwen, and then the three of them sit down right on the floor together, legs folded under them, which seems to cause Gangzi some difficulty, but he angrily brushes off Ko Dan's attempt to help him.

At first I try to follow their conversation, but it moves too quickly, so I give up and look around the temple instead. Painted on the wall behind them, lovely Tisis, goddess of mercy and forgiveness, is offering her golden cup. Behind her, a whirlwind in her fist, Haizea, goddess of vengeance, bares her teeth. Of course she is here too—she appears in nearly every story and illustration of Tisis. It's bewildering to me the way gods and goddesses from all over the world are welcome under the broad umbrella of the religion practiced in Yongguo, but Professor Baranyi says that they are all regarded as metaphors for the same essential truth. What that truth is, I couldn't say.

Ko Dan—if it is really him—is speaking at great length, low and urgent, illustrating something with his hands, and Mrs. Och is leaning forward, a greedy look in her eyes. I wonder about the purpose of this temple. Is it really possible to atone for one's misdeeds by just kneeling in this room and . . . what? Does he even know what he's atoning for? Does he know the consequences of what he did, the people who have died—people who had nothing at all to do with the Xianren or *The Book of Disruption* or any of this but whose lives were swept away by the storm he unleashed? The battle over that fragment of *The Book of Disruption* should have been between Gennady and Casimir. Instead, Bianka's life was turned upside down, Theo's life defined by this, my own life changed forever, and so many other lives upended or snuffed out. I'm thinking of the dead governess on the bridge in Spira City, dead by the mere accident of sharing a cabriolet with Bianka, and the other innocent victims of the Gethin. I'm thinking of the guard in Casimir's fortress, the one whose neck Bianka snapped because he was in her way, and she could think only of saving her son, and no other life meant anything to her. Is that her fault, or Ko Dan's, or Casimir's? Are we all unwittingly creating chaos we can't imagine, setting off chains of events whose brutal, bloody endings happen so far from us that we never even hear of them? Perhaps he's just doing what he's been told, finishing up his punishment, jumping through the final hoop before Gangzi lets him back.

My stomach rumbles, but nobody seems to hear it, thank the Nameless. I wish I'd asked Mrs. Och how long this was likely to take. Ko Dan stops speaking. Gangzi is looking at Mrs. Och with something like anger. She puts her hands together and seems to think very hard, and then she begins to speak and I hear *the witch* and *the child* and *Lan Camshe*. My heart speeds up.

When she is done, Ko Dan looks at Gangzi, who gives a single nod. Ko Dan says, in formal Yongwen, "I will try."

Mrs. Och walks south from the monastery. I watch the main doors awhile before running after her, vanished two steps back, the city blurred around me, my own footsteps muffled. I follow the silhouette of her cloaked figure. We pass along a street of silk shops in the Nanjin Triangle. A man smoking in a doorway tosses his cigarette aside and falls into step with me, though of course he does not see me. Mrs.

Och turns toward the Imperial Gardens and walks along its outer walls, and so does he. I gather she is going to walk the whole way back to Nanmu. I'm sure now that this fellow is tailing her, so I take one of Dek's darts from the pouch at my waist, unscrew the cap, and jab him in the arm.

It's effective, I'll say that. He stumbles sideways into the wall and goes down hard. A woman drops her basket of wish papers and runs to him, old wishes scattering in the gutter at the side of the road.

Mrs. Och keeps going, following the wall to the Dongnan Canal and crossing the bridge into Nanmu. I keep her in sight, but at a distance. When she is safely back home, I wait outside the courtyard for half an hour, vanished and thrumming with impatience, to be certain nobody else managed to follow us. Nobody comes and so I go in at last.

Frederick is slumped in a chair, still ghastly pale and weak from what she took from him. Bianka is leaning close to Mrs. Och at the table, her expression caught somewhere between terror and hope.

"Well?" Mrs. Och says to me when I come in.

"There was somebody following," I say. "I got rid of him." She nods briefly.

"So is it really him?" I ask. But I know the answer just from looking at her. Her eyes are fierce and bright, her lips parted in a near smile that is almost girlish in its excitement.

"I believe so," she says. "He was able to explain things about how the magic was done that have puzzled me for some time. They have . . . an item that I believed lost forever."

She shakes her head wonderingly, and then continues: "He believes that he can undo the binding of text to Theo without harming him. At least, he is willing to try, and Gangzi is willing to let him."

Theo looks up from the line of ants he is pursuing across the floor, interested because we are talking about him.

"He's willing to *try?*" says Bianka. "We need to be sure it isn't dangerous."

"Such magic does not come with guarantees," says Mrs. Och. "This is what we have come for. If you will not risk it, then it is only a matter of time before Theo is found and somebody else does the same thing without his well-being in mind."

Bianka stares at Mrs. Och, twisting her hands in her lap.

"All right. Yes. All right," she says rather mechanically.

"Good," says Mrs. Och. "Ready yourself and we will take him at once."

"Now?" Bianka whispers.

"Delaying will only increase the danger," answers Mrs. Och. "I want to get this done before Si Tan becomes involved."

Bianka looks at me, and suddenly I have to sit. I know exactly what she's feeling. Of course this is what we came here for, but it feels too sudden and too uncertain.

"Trust me a little further," says Mrs. Och softly. "You cannot hide him away forever, Bianka. Here is the chance to end it."

I wish she'd found another way to say that. Theo is

standing at Bianka's knee now and looking back and forth between us, aware that an important conversation about *him* is taking place, surely aware that his mother is afraid. I want to snatch him up and refuse to let them take him. But what am I thinking? We've crossed the world for this moment. I swore I'd make it right, and we've done it, we've found him.

"I'll come too," I say.

Mrs. Och gives me an impatient look. "No. We will need to move quickly once this is done. I want you to take a message to Count Fournier. We will meet with him first thing tomorrow morning."

She hands me a sealed letter addressed to the count, and I take it, but I repeat, "I want to come with you."

"Do what is *useful*, Julia, not what your guilt demands."

That lands like a blow, knocking the breath out of me.

"Bianka," says Mrs. Och sharply, and Bianka jumps. "You must decide now."

"Yes, all right," she whispers. She puts a trembling hand on Theo's curly head.

"Theo. Shall we take a walk, love?"

"Wawk?" His eyes go wide. He has not been allowed out of the courtyard since we got here.

Bianka nods at him, but her face is rigid as a mask, her smile desperate. "Let's get you into some trousers, shall we? Oh blast, where *are* his trousers?"

Theo begins a little jig, crowing, "Wawk! Wawk! Wawk!" Heart in my throat, I go digging through our things in the bedroom until I find a pair of his trousers. Once Theo figures out we're going to try and put him in clothes, he screams as if this is the greatest betrayal we could have enacted and puts up a tremendous fight, determined to maintain his mostly naked status. It takes both of us to wrestle his kicking legs and arching body into the little trousers. We got the fabric in Ishti, and Bianka sewed them, but already they are short on him, he is growing so quickly.

Bianka scrabbles in Frederick's writing box for a charcoal pencil, tucks it into her bodice, and gives me one more impossible look. I know I am mirroring all the terror and hope I see in her gaze right back at her. She puts on a large straw hat to hide her face and picks Theo up. Having completely forgotten the trouser battle within seconds of losing it, he waves to me cheerfully from her arms.

"Bah-bah, Lala!"

I walk them out and wave back from the gate as they round the corner to flag down a motor carriage. Turning the envelope in my hand, I half want to ignore Mrs. Och's instructions and follow them anyway. But she's right, of course—what good could I do, how could I help, when he has both his mother and Mrs. Och with him? *Do what is useful.* All right, then, I will be useful, since the Nameless knows I can't stay still another moment. I run for the second tier road and get a trolley to Count Fournier's house.

Count Fournier studies the letter from Mrs. Och, puffing his cheeks out.

"Thank the Nameless One," he says. "This Lord Skaal

you saw the other day has been granted a meeting with the grand librarian *and* Gangzi tomorrow! Ordinarily, Si Tan makes the Fraynish delegations wait for weeks, and Gangzi never agrees to meet with *anybody*. He must be seriously considering the Fraynish position. Nameless only knows what they are offering him! I won't put a reply in writing, better not, but tell your Mrs. Och we will expect her in the morning, as early as possible."

Jun brings me a cup of tea.

"An exciting time," he says, all dimples and shining eyes, but glad as I am to see him, I can barely smile back. My stomach is in knots.

"By the way, I've had some news about your monk," says Count Fournier, lighting a match and setting fire to Mrs. Och's letter. He drops the flaming, curling paper in an ashy bowl on the table apparently set there for the purpose of receiving burnt correspondence. "Very reliable source. This fellow has contacts all over the city, high and low. He claims Ko Dan has been imprisoned in Tianshi ever since his disappearance, on Si Tan's order. But not in an ordinary prison, he says. Somewhere secret in the Imperial Gardens."

I stare at him, not quite taking this in at first. Then I say, "No, he's back at the monastery. He got back yesterday."

Count Fournier shakes his head. "I heard there was some rumor to that effect, but no, this fellow is never wrong. I would believe him above any rumor in the streets."

"No," I say again, putting down my tea. "I *saw* him, at Shou-shu."

Count Fournier frowns and says, "How odd," and suddenly I go cold all over. I fumble in my pockets and find the picture Ling drew. I unfold it, my hands shaking as I do so, and shove it across the desk toward him.

The count peers at it through his spectacles and laughs. "But that's not him," he says.

"But the scar . . ." Panic rises hot and bitter in my throat.

He snorts. "Not hard to fake a scar. Well, look, it may just be a bad likeness. This looks nothing like him."

"It's a *very good* likeness of the man I saw," I say between my teeth.

"Then the man you saw was not Ko Dan," says the count. "Please stop looking at me like you're about to cut my throat, poppet. I am not trying to make you angry. I am telling you that this picture does not look like Ko Dan and that, according to my best informant, Ko Dan is in some kind of secret prison."

"Then why . . ." But I know why, of course. He says it anyway.

"Somebody has gone to a good deal of trouble to deceive you, my dear," he says, waving the paper at me. "This fellow is a fake, an impostor."

"They've taken Theo," I whisper.

"Who is Theo?" asks the count, annoyed.

Jun touches my elbow, his face full of concern. I am shaking all over, am back in the moment when I handed Theo over to Pia and my whole world collapsed. The thing I can never undo, the thing I am meant to make right, and Theo, dear little Theo, never again, I promised, *never again* would I let anybody harm him, and now . . .

"I have to go," I say. "Please—"

Jun nods. "I go with you."

# TWENTY-SEVEN

Jun keeps pace easily with my panicked sprint. In the Xi-shui Triangle, he pulls me down an alley and into a derelict hut, the roof half caved in, chicken dung everywhere. He moves a rusted pot from the hearth and then lifts the grate. There is a ladder leading down.

"This way," he says.

I start down the ladder, and he follows, pulling the grate back over the tunnel. My heart is crashing against my ribs like it's trying to break out, my mind just a roar of *TheoTheo-TheoTheo*. I see him frightened and alone, I see him cut open, I see him screaming, I see him dead and blank-eyed, and I hear myself sobbing loudly as I go slipping and scrambling down the narrow ladder. "More quiet!" Jun hisses down at me, but I can't control myself.

A voice from below calls up a question in Yongwen, startling me so badly I nearly fall, and Jun answers. There is the smell of lamp oil, and a light blazes up. A scrawny kid, maybe ten, hands the lantern to Jun when he reaches the bottom of the ladder. Jun presses a coin into his hand, says something or other about his mother, but I'm not paying attention.

"Come on," I urge him.

He starts down the tunnel at a swift jog and I follow. Little Theo, so excited to set out this afternoon, holding on to Bianka, his face bright and happy. Oh, Bianka. They won't get him from Bianka, she won't let them, she'll find a way, *TheoTheoTheoTheo.*

The tunnel forks a few times, and I stay right behind Jun. A couple of times I hear voices as we pass lit chambers dug out of the ground. In one of them, I glimpse a cluster of armed men dismembering something that I hope is not a body, but I think it is. We pass by fast.

"This is smugglers' route," says Jun over his shoulder, though I haven't asked. "Tunnels all under city. Tell me what you need."

"We need to save a little boy, get him out of the monastery, get them all out of there. My friends . . ." I break off, my voice shaking so much I don't know if I can make myself understood. Jun doesn't ask any more questions. We reach another ladder, and he snuffs out the lantern, leaving it there on the ground. He goes up the ladder, a fast-moving shadow, and I follow with sweaty palms and shaking knees. *I'll save him,* I think. I don't know how, but I'll save him.

Light pours down as Jun pushes aside the flagstone and slithers out. There is nobody on the path, but I hear chanting from the Hall of Abnegation.

"Where?" he asks me.

I head for the Temple of Atonement, the last place I saw Ko Dan—though if he is not Ko Dan, then who is he? Inevitably, we round a corner and run smack into a monk. I've got my knife out and pointed at his throat before he can open his mouth. Jun circles around behind him.

"Ask him if Gangzi has visitors," I say, not trusting my own Yongwen. Jun asks.

"The Main Hall," the monk tells us, wide-eyed.

"What are we going to do with him?" I ask Jun, pointing at the monk with my knife.

Jun looks at me like I'm deranged, and I don't know what I'm asking anyway. What are we supposed to do with him?

"Shouldn't we tie him up?" I suggest, rather ashamed of myself.

He shakes his head. "Only hurry," he says. "In, out. Come."

I am so grateful to have him with me. I slide my knife back into the fabric bands of my boot, and we leave the monk standing stunned in the path. The long alley to the Main Hall is walled on either side—easy for me to sneak up on, perhaps, but not for Jun. Two of the Ru are outside, armed with crossbows. I vanish. Jun is on top of the low wall in a flash, running along it. He throws a pale stone that goes rolling down the middle of the path toward the guards. They are aiming their weapons when there is a bang, and a burst of white smoke envelops them. An arrow wings its way by me, down the path. I run straight into the smoke, straight past the shouting guards, crashing through the door, tripping and tumbling to the wood floor.

There is Mrs. Och, but not as Mrs. Och—she is Och Farya, winged and terrible. Bianka is clutching Theo to her chest, stepping back, startled by the sudden noise. The false Ko Dan and Gangzi are with them, Ko Dan reaching for Theo.

They all freeze and look at me sprawled on the temple floor. One of the Ru from outside comes in after me and then falls forward, a wire twisting his ankles, thank you very much, Jun. I yell at Bianka, "He's not Ko Dan!"

I run for her as the second guard from outside charges into the hall. I can see Theo's mouth open in a wail, but I can't hear it over the roaring in my head, and everybody is in motion at once except Bianka. Her eyes are fixed on me, and I can see everything in her eyes in that moment. I know I am asking her to make an impossible decision in a split second, and she does.

She hands me Theo, and I vanish. An arrow strikes the wall right next to us. Ko Dan lunges for Bianka, and she hurls him across the hall, where he hits the wall and slumps to the ground.

Mrs. Och opens her mouth and lets out a roar that shakes the walls and knocks Gangzi off his feet. The guard that fired at me regains his footing quickly, aims his crossbow, and shoots her in the chest. She staggers and goes down on one knee, yanking the bloody arrow out. Bianka has the charcoal pencil she took from Frederick's writing box in her hand; she is writing something on the floor. Gangzi points at her and shouts a command as the smell of rotten flowers sweeps through the hall. The guard Jun tripped with wire shoots at her, but the arrow goes wide. He drops the bow and clutches his eyes.

Theo is crying into my neck, but there is so much noise and shouting now that I am not afraid of anybody hearing him, and I am ready to pull him all the way to Kahge if any more arrows start flying. The two guards, Ko Dan, and Gangzi are all grabbing at their eyes, and Gangzi is shouting something about magic. I see what Bianka has scribbled on the floor in charcoal: *blind.*

She drops the pencil, staggering a little. Her nose is bleeding, and Jun is next to her. I am weak with relief to see him unharmed.

"I am friend of Julia," he says. "Follow me!"

The two of them help Mrs. Och toward the door. There are three more of the Ru on the path ahead, running for the hall.

"Blast!" gasps Bianka. "I can't . . ."

Mrs. Och pulls herself upright, one hand clutched to her bleeding chest, and speaks in that awful, summoning voice. She raises a furred fist and pulls it down. A torrent of rain follows. We are soaked to the skin in seconds, the Ru briefly stunned, and then lightning blasts them. We run straight past the bodies, one of them scrabbling at the ground, the other two still.

Jun takes Mrs. Och and Bianka at a run to the flagstone by the swallow coop. Bianka is screaming, *"Julia!"* and Theo is thrashing in my arms, howling, "Mama, Mama!" I step back into the visible world full of people trying to kill us, everything so sharp and clear, the smell of blood and smoke and rain filling my nostrils. Theo practically leaps from me into Bianka's arms, and she pulls him close to her.

"Hurry!" says Jun. "Down ladder!"

Bianka goes first, with Theo in her arms, and Mrs. Och follows, looking up at me only once to say, "Get the impostor and bring him to me."

I've no idea how I'm going to manage that.

"I'll catch up," I say to Jun. "Thank you."

I want to say more, but it's all I can manage. He nods, and then he is gone too, the flagstone sliding into place over him. I stand still a moment to catch my breath. The storm has gone as quickly as it came, the sky clear and bright. I feel something sharp and stinging on my arm and look down to see a little red dart sticking into me. A sick feeling sweeps over me. Two of the black-clad Ru are striding toward me. One of them has a pistol-like contraption at his side. They blur into multitudes and then blackness spreads fast over everything, like ink spilled over a page.

# TWENTY-EIGHT

When I return to myself, I am lying in a comfortable bed like a convalescent. Sitting at my bedside is the witch from the Imperial Library, with her stitched-over eyes and her tattooed skin. She is bent over a little writing table, a sheet of rice paper and a pot of ink before her, and she is licking ink from the brush pensively, her tongue and lips quite black from it. She doesn't notice that I am awake. I keep very still and quiet, trying to figure out how I came to be here. It comes back to me slowly, the haze lifting bit by bit: the battle in the monastery, the dart in my arm. But they got away— Theo is all right. I remember that with a great rush of relief. Now I just have to get out of here, wherever *here* is.

The witch is so busy sucking on her brush that I figure I'll just vanish and walk out, but when I try to pull back, I find I can't. It's like being paralyzed, except that I *can* move my limbs, if only slightly. It is some deeper part of me that is fully immobilized—the part of me that pulls out of the world. That is when I notice the ribbons looped around my ankles, wrists, and waist—spools of red ribbon with untidy Yongwen script all over them. I must have made a small sound of dismay, for suddenly the witch's head shoots up and she points her awful face toward me.

She croons something at me in her scratchy voice and rings a little bell on the table. Then she goes springing over to the door and opens it. I lie helpless on the bed, looking around at the small, bare room with old-fashioned weapons displayed on the walls—double-edged axes, a scimitar, an ornate musket, a set of gleaming throwing knives. Hardly the most cheerful decor.

The witch returns to my bedside, and the oddest apparition comes rolling into the room. It is the old woman I saw the grand librarian whispering to after our first meeting with him. She is clothed in shapeless, beautiful silks and seated on a wheeled sort of platform, a pile of cushions supporting her bulk. Si Tan, the grand librarian, is pushing this contraption.

"A pleasure to see you again," he says congenially to me, in Fraynish. "How do you feel? Any headache or nausea?"

I nod. Bit of both.

"You look well, though. The young are so resilient." He adds something in Yongwen to the old woman, and she answers in her deep rasp.

"The empress dowager asks me to welcome you to the Imperial Residences," he says, bowing.

At least now I know where I am and who I'm dealing

with. Again, I find Si Tan's impeccable manners, his elegant clothing and long beard, somehow out of keeping with his physique, which suggests such brute power, the intensity and focus of a predator.

"You make it sound like I'm a guest," I say, struggling to sit up in spite of the ribbons looped carelessly over me.

Si Tan's smile is an awful baring of yellowed teeth. "So you are. But this is a city with laws, and the laws must be upheld. You have come here under an assumed identity, not declaring your true intentions or your abilities. Witches must be registered and licensed in Tianshi."

"I'm not a witch," I say.

The tattooed witch is hovering near Si Tan now, a quivering, hopeful look about her that I don't understand.

"That is a good place to start," says Si Tan. "Why don't you tell us who you are, and what?"

"My name is Julia," I say. I'll die before I tell him where Theo is, but he's welcome to my name. "I reckon your witch here has told you a bit about me already. She attacked me in the Imperial Library."

"Attacked? I am sorry. She can be difficult, this one, and what information she brought me about you was rather a jumble." He gives her a hard look, and she begins to weep, falling down before him and clutching the hem of his robe. The empress dowager looks disgusted and says something to Si Tan. He nods and speaks to the witch. I might be misunderstanding, but it sounds as if he is offering her a treat. She brightens, kissing his hand with her inky lips. He produces a little pipe from a pocket in his robe. She scurries to the corner with it, lighting it with a snap of her fingers. I recognize the sweet smell.

"Opium?"

"She is an interesting case," says Si Tan. "Her name is Cinzai. Her parents brought her to the Imperial Gardens when she was just four years old. They were farmers from the central provinces, very poor, and they had this girl, their seventh child, stronger than an ox and taking naps in the burning hearth. They were glad to be rid of her. She is an idiot, in fact, and it was a terrible task teaching her to read and write at all, but she is one of only a handful of witches in all the world who can write magic with symbols drawn in the air. Now, it is a difficult calculation that needs to be made with one so powerful. It is perhaps safer simply to drown her, and there were many on the Imperial Council in favor of that. They considered her too terrible a beast to master. If you are going to keep a witch such as this, you need a strong leash. Opium is a strong leash."

"That's revolting," I say.

"More humane than drowning, don't you think? Or perhaps not. What would *you* do with an insanely powerful woman with the intellect and impulses of a child?" He waits, as if he is seriously interested in my answer. When I say nothing, he continues placatingly: "I have the good of the empire to consider, you see, but I am open to suggestions. Now I want to talk about your business in Yongguo. I dangled Ko Dan in front of your friends and out came

Och Farya of the Xianren! The little boy she brought to the monastery is the receptacle for Zor Gen's fragment of *The Book of Disruption*. Is that right?"

"He's not a receptacle," I say.

Si Tan's smile this time is genuine—almost warm. "Pardon me. It was a poor choice of words. But the text is inside him, and Och Farya wants it removed. What does she intend to do with it?"

"I've no idea. Keep it away from her brother, for starters."

"That does seem prudent. I have met Lan Camshe, or Casimir, as he goes by now."

"So have I."

"What did you think of him?"

"He's a lunatic," I say.

"I agree with you. Not a man I should like to see with more power. Frayne is a well-placed pawn in a world that is changing, and the Xianren have been competing for control of it. We have kept them out of Yongguo's politics, but now they have brought their business to my doorstep and I cannot ignore it. We have rules about magic here. Och Farya should have come to me from the beginning."

"If you let me go, I'll tell her so," I say.

Si Tan gives a perfunctory smile, as if at a bad joke. The witch lets her pipe fall to the ground and slumps back against the wall in a happy daze. The empress dowager says something to Si Tan, and I hear the Yongwen word for Kahge. Something in his gaze sharpens, and my stomach turns over.

"At the library, Och Farya's friend the professor was

interested in Ko Dan, but another young man in your group transcribed a number of the philosopher-witch treatises on Kahge, on Marike, and on the Gethin. Why?"

"He's writing a book," I lie, not very convincingly.

Si Tan stares at me like he can rout the truth from me with his eyes. Then he says, "Have you heard of Ragg Rock?"

I shake my head slowly. But, in fact, I *have* heard of it. I rack my brain trying to remember where.

"I understand you asked a question about Lidari."

"A friend of Marike's, wasn't he?" I say, trying to sound merely curious. Fear is running cold through my veins now.

He seems to be thinking about my answer. He strokes his beard, watching me. The empress dowager mutters something to him, and he nods.

"Your mother was a member of the Sidhar Coven in Frayne," he says. "She was drowned, yes?"

I nod.

"Barbaric," he says softly—but if he's trying to win me over, he'd have done better not to dose his own witch with opium in front of me. I say nothing.

"I can see why Och Farya would value you," he says at last. "Don't we all wish that we could pass through the world invisible at times! It is a remarkable gift. I've heard of spells that hide a thing from view, but they work on the senses of the viewer, not the object itself, and as far as I know, they do not allow for movement. Besides, as with any magic affecting the senses, they are notoriously unreliable. *You* can travel freely, unseen, and yet it is not magic, or at least you do not use writing or language to do it. How *do* you do it? How does it feel?"

"I don't know how," I say. "It's just something I can do."

He turns and speaks to the empress dowager. She is watching me in a way that makes me anxious. Like I'm a snack. She replies to him in her gravelly voice.

"I understand your reticence," says Si Tan. "I am interested in you, Julia. I think we could be friends and help one another."

"Not sure I like how you treat your friends," I say, nodding at Cinzai in the corner.

His lips curl back in something that could be a grin or a snarl.

"She is not my friend," he says. "She is a weapon. Tell me, where can I find Och Farya? She and I need to have a conversation."

"No idea," I say. "She contacts me when she needs me, but I don't know where she hides out."

"If I keep you here, will she come for you, do you think?"

"Doubt it," I say. I have a feeling Mrs. Och would as soon let me rot.

"Well, we shall see," he says, and then there is a knock at the door. The empress dowager answers sharply. I think she is telling the knocker to go away, but the door opens and a young man in a splendid yellow robe comes in. He is maybe twenty-five or thirty, dark and very handsome, with the kind of simmering gaze that would turn my knees to jelly under somewhat different circumstances. He sees me on the bed, and his face registers astonishment. His eyes travel to the drugged witch in the corner, and his expression turns to one of distaste. He asks a question in Yongwen, and Si Tan answers, bowing deeply and calling him *Your Highness*. I realize with a jolt of surprise that this is the young emperor.

The emperor speaks to the dowager, ignoring Si Tan, his eyes straying to me a couple more times. She answers him curtly, flicking her long golden nails at him. He starts to reply, raising his voice, but the empress dowager cuts him off, ordering him out. The emperor gives me another long look, and I can't help thinking I'd enjoy this whole thing a good deal more if *he* were the one taking me prisoner.

"Are you . . . treated well?" he asks in halting Fraynish.

I look at the ribbons binding me. "I'm not sure. I'd like to go home."

The empress dowager lets out a stream of invective. The emperor scowls while Si Tan just stares off into the middle distance. Then the emperor bows to his mother, saying something between clenched teeth, and he goes out, slamming the door—sadly, without any more smoldering looks in my direction. I think to myself that if I make it out of here alive, I'll have quite a story to tell—watching the supreme head of the great Yongguo Empire being ordered out of a room like a dog by his mother.

In the silence that follows, Si Tan takes out the now familiar sketch of me, Mrs. Och, and Bianka. It seems everybody has got their hands on a copy.

"Somebody else is looking for you in Tianshi," he says. "Who is it?"

I shrug.

"Casimir's people?" he asks.

"Not sure *people* is the word I'd use," I reply.

"I was curious about you in particular when I saw these," he says. "I knew the moment I first laid eyes on you that you were not the educated, aristocratic girl you were pretending to be. I saw in you something far too shrewd for a girl who'd led a sheltered life."

"So you told your witch to chew on my face?" I ask.

"When you vanish, where do you go?"

The question is sudden, less considered than most of what he says, and there is something alert and hungry in his expression. It strikes me that nobody has ever asked me that before. It has never occurred to anybody else that I *go* somewhere.

"Nowhere," I say. "Just . . . nowhere."

He stares at me for a while and then says, "What is she like?"

"Who?" I ask stupidly.

"Och Farya. I have wanted to meet her for a long time. The eldest of the Xianren!"

"She's . . . I don't know. The more you get to know her, the scarier she is, I suppose."

He laughs politely, like I'm trying to be funny, which I'm not, and then a loud bell starts jangling somewhere outside the building.

The empress dowager grunts and draws a little pistol out from under a cushion. Si Tan hauls the drugged witch up by the arm and murmurs in her ear. She goes stumbling out, her jaw slack.

"Do you suppose it is Och Farya come to rescue her precious vanishing girl?" he asks me.

That doesn't seem terribly likely to me, but I am holding out some hope for it. I hear shots and shouts at a distance, then footsteps running nearby, more shouting, an awful scream, and still the bell clanging on and on. My heart is pounding, but I lie there bound in Cinzai's ribbons, unable to move.

The door swings open and the witch comes reeling back in, screaming. She's clutching her head, flailing and lurching around the room. There is something dark hanging from her left ear for a moment, and then it is gone—*inside* her ear. Si Tan sees it too and lets out a cry of rage. He snatches the scimitar from the wall and swings it. Her body goes limp and drops. Her head rolls toward me. A scream reaches my throat and gets stuck there. The black thing that vanished into her ear drops out of it and scuttles across the floor. It looks like a bug, a big centipede or something. Si Tan slices it neatly with the scimitar and it sparks and smokes and goes still. It is some piece of tiny machinery. Something small and red crawls out of the broken metal shell on threadlike legs. Si Tan's lips curl. He stomps on the thing, leaving a wet scarlet mark on the floor, and curses bitterly in Yongwen. We all look at the door then, and I see with a sinking heart who has come for me. It isn't Mrs. Och, of course. It's Pia.

# TWENTY-NINE

She stands in the doorway, cool as anything, with a carbine the length of her forearm pointed at the dowager in one hand and a short sword in the other. The dowager is pointing her little pistol at Pia, her chest rising and falling fast.

"Get up," says Pia to me.

"I can't," I say. "They've got me all tied up."

She jumps, kicking herself off the wall so that she ends up behind Si Tan, the muzzle of her carbine pressed against his jaw while the empress dowager's shot explodes against the wall. She shoves him closer to me with the gun, and then she cuts the ribbons around me with her short sword and tosses them aside. Si Tan watches me, expressionless, from the corner of his eye. My limbs feel heavy and slow, but I can move again. I get up off the bed unsteadily, trying not to look at Cinzai's head, her body bleeding blackly all over the floor, her tattooed fingers still twitching like they are trying to write something.

"Go get her gun," Pia orders me. To the dowager, she adds in Yongwen something to the effect that if she gives it over nicely, Si Tan might come back to her in one piece. Once I've got the gun, Pia tucks it into her belt and unloops a sort of harness on her back.

"Climb in here," she tells me. It is an awkward thing to attempt with my limbs still feeling so rubbery, but I manage it. The empress dowager watches us, her eyes little points of rage, her chins quivering.

"Casimir is bold," says Si Tan, very coldly, but Pia makes no reply. She yanks a strap on either side of her and the harness tightens around me, fastening me to her back so that I am like an overgrown child piggybacking on her psychotic mama. She shoves Si Tan's face with the carbine and instructs him to go down the hall ahead of us.

The bell is still clanging, and I hear what sounds like a great many footsteps approaching at a run, but Pia seems unconcerned. At the end of the hall, she takes a small cylinder from her belt and releases a blast at the ceiling, leaving a smoking hole above us. Then she swings her elbow, striking Si Tan in the face. He goes down like a log. Pia clambers up the wall with me on her back. I'm terrified I will throw off her balance, but as far as I can tell, my weight does not even slow her down. Broken wood and tile scrape against my back as she hauls us both through the hole in the roof. I bury my face in her shoulder to protect my head.

When I look up, she is running along the rooftop gable, and then she leaps a terrifying distance to the slanted edge of another roof. I am certain we will fall, but her footing never fails her, and she goes running up the side of that roof and over it. The Ru are milling in the streets below us, pointing crossbows. Something whizzes by us, but Pia is moving too fast to make an easy target. She flies from rooftop to rooftop and then suddenly down into the Imperial Gardens proper. Through gardens and galleries and residences—it is dizzying, and I have to close my eyes again. The clanging bell is receding in the distance now.

I open my eyes a crack when I feel that we are going straight up. She is climbing the outer wall. She reaches the top as the Ru are converging on us, but she is over the side before they reach us, dropping to the city below. I feel the impact when she lands jolt through me, but it doesn't slow her for even a second. I am bouncing on her back along the streets of Tianshi, people pointing and shouting as she sprints through the city, tireless. I think I'm going to be sick.

We reach the Hundred Lantern Hotel from the side. Up and through a window of a room, where a woman screams and ducks into the closet and a half-naked man leaps from the bed, scrambling for his pistol on the night table. Pia kicks the door wide and is down the hall, over the railing of the stairs to the floor below, and through another door. She closes the door and lets the harness loosen. I fall in an ungainly sprawl to the floor, scrambling out of the ridiculous contraption. I am gasping for breath even though she was the one running, my heart hammering. She is pointing the carbine at me now.

"I need to speak with you," she says. "Don't disappear."

I disappear.

⌒

The sun is getting low by the time I reach the house in Nanmu. I can hear Frederick's voice in the main room, loud and desperate: "You haven't the right! We must be allowed to discuss—"

"There will be no discussion of what I deem necessary," Mrs. Och is saying, pure ice, when I come in. She turns toward me, her expression unchanging. "Julia, where have you been?"

Bianka is crumpled on the floor like a rag doll. Her face has a sickly yellow tinge to it. Frederick looks a little better than when we left him this morning, but not much.

"The Imperial Gardens," I say. "Si Tan got hold of me."

"Are you hurt?" asks Frederick.

I shake my head, still trying to put together the picture before me and make sense of it. Mrs. Och is practically bursting with vitality and power. The table is covered with Frederick's notes, and the stele rubbing is spread out across it.

"Did you reveal our whereabouts?" Mrs. Och asks sharply. "Were you followed?"

I shake my head again, and her face relaxes.

"Tell me everything he said."

"He just wanted to know what we were up to. And he wants to meet you. He said we should have gone to him from the beginning."

She gives a short laugh at that. "I walked right into his trap," she says bitterly. "The impostor was most convincing. He knew things that he could only have heard from Ko Dan himself, wherever he is. There were details about the magic he worked with Gennady, and I was so eager to see . . . well, it doesn't matter now. I am glad you are safe, Julia. These two wanted to run off into the city to rescue you, but given your propensity to set off on your own little jaunts without informing anybody, I felt we ought to wait."

"I wanted to tell her brother," growls Bianka, trying to get up. "I knew she wouldn't stay away if she was all right . . . not without checking that we'd made it back safely."

"Well, she is here now," says Mrs. Och. "If you have all calmed down, we have a great deal to do. I must send a message to the professor immediately. Julia, you will take the message, and there is something else I need you to do."

"You're going to send her on an errand?" cries Bianka, managing to get up this time but looking rather like she wished she hadn't. "Look at her!"

"What do I look like?" I ask. And then my legs fold under me and I sit abruptly on the floor. "I could use something to eat," I say. I haven't eaten since breakfast.

"Get her some food," says Mrs. Och, and she sweeps off into her room to write her message.

"Where's Theo?" I ask.

"Sleeping," says Bianka. "Quite worn out from today's adventures."

"There's some stew," says Frederick. "I'll fix you a plate."

"I'll get some water," says Bianka, teetering a bit.

"You're worse off than me," I say. And then we get the giggles, all of us so utterly used up and pathetic we can hardly get a plate of food and a cup of water between us. It isn't really funny, of course—to be so helpless when we're being hunted. But I'm giddy with relief to have made it back safely, and touched beyond what I can say that Frederick and Bianka were so concerned about me, set to go and find me.

"What *happened?*" asks Bianka.

"As soon as you all went down the tunnel, I got shot with some kind of sleeping serum. I'm still woozy. I woke up and got interrogated by Si Tan and the empress dowager."

"The *empress!*" cries Bianka, impressed.

"You were amazing at the monastery," I tell her. "That spell!"

"Very quick thinking, to blind them," agrees Frederick admiringly.

"I dropped the bleeding pencil, though," she says. "I suppose they've broken it by now and undone the spell."

"Never mind. It held long enough for you to get out," I say.

Frederick goes tottering out to fetch some water, and when he brings me the cup, I empty it. I hadn't even realized how thirsty I was. He puts a plate of beef stew in front of me. The smell makes me queasy at first, but as soon as I have a bite, my hunger takes over. He offers some to Bianka, putting a tentative hand on her shoulder. She shakes her head, smiling up at him wearily.

"It was a clever trap, all right," I say. "Si Tan is keen to meet Mrs. Och."

"He can have her," mutters Bianka, but in a low voice.

"How did you get away?" asks Frederick. "They let you go?"

"No. I think they hoped Mrs. Och would come for me. But . . ."

Suddenly, I don't know why, but I don't want to tell them about Pia. I don't know what to make of her rescuing me— if that's what it was—and I am not ready to share it yet.

"Well, I got out, anyway," I finish lamely, and they don't question it. After all, haven't I always been able to get out of everything, out of everywhere, so far?

"I can't tell you how relieved I am," says Frederick with a warmth that startles me. "We've been worried sick."

"How did you know the man pretending to be Ko Dan was a fake?" asks Bianka. "It was just looking funny to me, with the guards there, but I was going to hand him over, Theo"—she shudders—"and then you turned up."

"Count Fournier," I reply. "I showed him the picture Ling drew, and he told me it wasn't Ko Dan."

"Thank the Nameless," says Bianka. "Your friend Jun was fantastic, got us all the way back to Nanmu underground before Mrs. Och sent him off. But then you didn't come back."

"We wanted to look for you," Frederick says, and then trails off.

"Thank you," I say. "Really." I point to his notes spread across the table and ask hopefully, "You've been working?"

"Professor Baranyi was kind enough to find me the dictionary I needed. The stele rubbing you brought back is about a place called Ragg Rock."

"Si Tan mentioned that," I say, frowning, and then I remember where I'd heard of it before. When I was a spy in Mrs. Och's house, I read about Ragg Rock in Professor Baranyi's study. One of his books claimed that the Xianren had joined forces to look for it but did not succeed.

"According to the stele rubbing, it is . . . I'm not sure how to translate it, exactly, but something like the way station at the edge of the world, just beyond what we might call our reality. It is a place that lies between the world and Kahge, and creatures from either place might be granted entry. They can go as far as Ragg Rock but no farther."

"Granted entry by who?" I ask.

"By . . . Ragg Rock," says Frederick. "That part is a bit confusing. I've been reading about Lidari too. I have seen him called a general of the Gethin army, but also Marike's son and, elsewhere, her lover. The references to him span centuries. He was an important figure, in any case, and closely connected to Marike. It's written that when the Eshriki Empire fell, Casimir hunted him down and killed him. You told me that the creatures you saw in Kahge were calling his name. If the essence of the Gethin do return to Kahge after their physical death in the world, he might have been among them. Did you see—were they directing it to one of their group?"

I glance at Mrs. Och's closed door. Feeling rather sick, I say: "They were pointing at me and saying it."

I can see that shocks him, which makes me feel even worse.

"I wonder if it could mean something more general, beyond the specific name. May I tell Mrs. Och and the professor this, Julia? They will have a better idea than I do of how to interpret it."

I grimace.

"I promise that I will keep you informed," he says gently. "But I don't think I can find out much more without their help."

"Fine. If you tell me everything they say."

He laughs a bit unhappily. It's an awkward position for him, I know.

"All right," he agrees.

Bianka puts her head in her hands and moans. "I feel awful."

"Did she take your strength?"

"Didn't even ask. Just grabbed my hands, and—yes," says Bianka.

"She was very weak when we got back—she'd been shot," says Frederick. "And she didn't want you running around the city when your likeness is all over the place and the Ru are out looking for you."

It's a bit halfhearted, I think, compared to his usual defense of Mrs. Och.

"I knew *you'd* never just leave one of us behind without going to look for us," says Bianka to me rather fiercely.

"And were the roles reversed, Julia might even have found

you and been able to assist you, and I would have agreed to let her try," says Mrs. Och, coming back into the main room with an envelope in her hand. "But the idea that the two of you would be able to find her, let alone *rescue* her, was simply ludicrous. Julia is more than capable of taking care of herself—and here she is."

I want to tell her that today I was not so capable of taking care of myself . . . except I don't want to tell her about Pia.

"Count Fournier thinks Ko Dan is imprisoned somewhere in the city, possibly in the Imperial Gardens," I say. "We could still get him out."

"Perhaps," says Mrs. Och. "But if Si Tan is aware of our presence and our designs, then we are running out of time. When it was only Pia, I thought we could hold out awhile. She hunts us alone, in a city unfamiliar to her, a city where she has no allies. Si Tan controls this city completely. We cannot stay hidden here if *he* is looking for us—not for long. However, I still intend to meet with your count first thing in the morning. He may have more information about Ko Dan, and I would like to get Princess Zara to Frayne as soon as possible."

"Do we have . . . *time* for that?" asks Bianka uneasily, and I can see she is worried that, having failed to find Ko Dan, Mrs. Och is shifting her interest to the princess.

"Princess Zara is the key to a Frayne that will be safe for you," says Mrs. Och. "Removing Agoston Horthy from power will diminish Casimir's influence in Frayne as well. It will turn the tide in our favor. These are matters far more important than . . ." She stops, and for an awful moment I think she is going to say *Theo's life*. But she doesn't say that. "Mere trivialities," she finishes.

It hits me like a thunderbolt, and then I feel a true idiot. "You *knew* Princess Zara was in the monastery," I say. "We didn't come all this way just for Theo. You came for *her*."

Horror breaks across Bianka's face. Mrs. Och doesn't bother to deny it.

"If all goes well, we will return to Frayne with the heir to the throne, *The Book of Disruption* safe from Casimir, and Theo safe too," she says.

I have a horrible feeling she may be listing these goals in order of priority.

Mrs. Och holds out a piece of paper to me. I try to hide my shock when I see it. She has drawn a picture of the double-spouted pot—the one I saw my mother holding when the witch was sorting through my memories, the one painted on the wall in the Imperial Library.

Her eyes narrow. "You recognize it?"

"I saw a picture of it in the library," I say, taking the paper and showing it to Frederick. "Do you remember?"

He nods.

"It is called the Ankh-nu," says Mrs. Och. "It dates back to the beginning of the Eshriki Empire—you see the hiero-glyph on its side, the symbol for life. There are a few physical objects in the world that have magic written deeply into them, like the bells of Shou-shu. The Ankh-nu is far beyond any of them."

"What does it do?" asks Frederick, examining the picture.

"*This* is what Ko Dan used to put Gennady's fragment of *The Book of Disruption* into Theo. At least, that is what the impostor told me, and I believe it must be true, for there is no other way it could have been done. It is for transferring a living essence from one physical vessel to another. The essence is what some might call the soul, the spark of life, whatever it is that animates the mind, holds the memory, makes us who we *are*. The Ankh-nu can lift the essence of self from its physical bindings and put it into another body, another vessel. It is said that Marike created it for the purpose of bringing the Gethin from Kahge into the world, although where their *bodies* came from is still a mystery. There are even stories that she extended her own life to near immortality by means of the Ankh-nu."

"How would it make someone immortal?" asks Bianka.

"The essence is bound to the body," says Mrs. Och. "It lives and dies with the body, but it is the *body* that grows old and decays. If the essence can be transferred to another body, it will continue to live in that one. And so as one body began to age and die, Marike would choose another. She would *switch*, in other words, leaving her victim inside the body she was leaving behind and taking possession of the new body. It is said that until the Sirillian emperor captured and executed Marike, she had changed bodies more than three hundred times. Indeed, there are those who believe that she lives still, that she was never caught."

"But it's not really possible, is it?" exclaims Frederick.

"I have never seen the Ankh-nu myself," says Mrs. Och. "They say the greatest witches in Eshrik gave their blood and their lives to assist Marike in its making."

"Why would they do that?" cries Bianka.

"It may be only a story," says Mrs. Och. "But Marike was very good at persuading others to do things for her, even to give their lives for her. I remember her. She was . . ." Her mouth tightens suddenly. "It was not that she was so power-ful, even, for a witch, but she was clever, charismatic, and she knew how to manipulate people."

"But if the Ankh-nu is for the transferring of a living essence— Ah, I see, *The Book of Disruption is* alive, in a sense, isn't it?" says Frederick.

"Yes," says Mrs. Och. "The Book has an essence of its own. In the beginning, it was text, but certainly alive. Later, after the Eshriki Phars tried and failed to read it, the Book began to change form, trying to unmake itself and become part of the world, part of nature, as the spirits had done. I hid my own fragment underground. It took root and grew into a huge cherry tree. Casimir lived then in a great castle in the foothills of the Parnese Mountains. His fragment be-came a brilliant green lake that swallowed the castle. Gen-nady traveled the world, carrying his fragment with him, and it became an implike shadow, clinging to his back—it rooted itself in *him*, since he would not let it root itself in the earth. But Casimir's witch Shey has been able to return Casimir's fragment and mine to their original form, I be-lieve. Ko Dan—the *real* Ko Dan—used the Ankh-nu to transfer Gennady's fragment to Theo's body and bind it to his essence, to live and die with him. He made the fragment *mortal.*"

"While I slept," Bianka mutters, and her eyes narrow dangerously. I think that it would be much better for Gennady if he never sees her again.

Frederick asks Mrs. Och: "How did Ko Dan come to have the Ankh-nu?"

"They claim it has been in the monastery for centuries," says Mrs. Och. "I don't know. The Shou-shu monks have acquired some remarkable treasures, but this . . . well."

How did my *mother* come to have it? What was she doing with it? The vision of my mother with the Ankh-nu, those creatures in Kahge pointing at me and hissing *"Lidari"* . . . My heart is thundering in my chest now, a terrible thought beginning to take shape. I need to see Dek. Oh hounds, I need my brother. My hands begin to shake.

"If the true Ko Dan is to take the text fragment out of Theo without harming him, he will need the Ankh-nu again, I believe," says Mrs. Och.

And perhaps it is a sign of how much of a natural thief is left in me, but I feel something close to relief break through my panic when I realize what she's saying.

"You want me to steal it," I say. "It'll be in the Treasury."

I'll have a reason to break in there after all.

"Yes," says Mrs. Och. "I want the Ankh-nu, and I want the princess, and I want Ko Dan, and we have very little time in which to find all three."

I shovel the last few bites of food into my mouth and get up. "All right," I say. "I'm feeling better."

A faint smile plays around the edges of her mouth.

"I am glad. First you will take this letter to Professor Baranyi. I would like him to attend the meeting with Count Fournier tomorrow morning. Esme should come as well."

"Your tree pipit could deliver a letter," protests Bianka.

"This is important. I must know it has reached his hands."

"At least you trust me more than a bird," I say, too exhausted and wound up to watch my mouth. I put the drawing of the Ankh-nu in my pocket and take the letter as well.

"I too was worried for you," Mrs. Och says stiffly. "I must choose the most prudent course, but I hope you do not see it as a lack of concern for your safety."

"Oh, it's all right," I say, surprised by this little pronouncement. I rather *do* see it as a lack of concern for my safety—I have never thought Mrs. Och was particularly concerned for my safety—but I don't say that.

"Be careful," says Frederick. "If I have to worry anymore, I might turn into a mother hen."

"You're quite close as it is," teases Bianka. "Those red feathers."

She tousles his hair. He laughs and takes her hand, their fingers twining together. At first I'm startled, but then I feel foolish not to have seen it before—how close they were becoming. Of course, they're shut up in this courtyard much of every day together. I feel a little pang—not jealousy, not really, only everybody seems to have a hand to hold but me. Stupid thought at a time like this.

"I'll be back soon," I say, fetching my bag with the rope and hook. I put a small lantern in it, and matches, and hurry out into the evening. As soon as I'm away from the house, I open Mrs. Och's letter. She has written it in some foreign language I can't read—not even in Yongwen, for which I might have found someone to translate. My heart sinks. There is no reason for her to write to Professor Baranyi in a language I can't read—unless she doesn't want *me* to know what she's written.

# THIRTY

I deliver Mrs. Och's letter but don't stay long to chat with Esme, though I can tell she wants me to come in. In the doorway, I fill her in quickly on the false Ko Dan and on Mrs. Och's plans. When I ask after Gregor, she tells me he is still having tremors and is quite ill from lack of drink but has not asked for it once.

The trolleys stop at sundown, and the sky is already a rich orange in the west, so I say goodbye and run for the second tier road. It is dark by the time I get to Dek's place. Mei is making supper, and Wyn has set up an easel and is working on a Yongguo-style ink-brush painting. No sign of Dek, though the trays and bowls and flour from the dumpling making are still all over the table, attracting flies.

"Bleeding hounds, where does he *go* all the time?"

"Enjoying the freedom he has here," says Wyn, shrugging, but I think there is something else in his expression.

"Why do you look that way?"

"I think I look the way I always look. Don't I? How do I look, darling?" he calls to Mei.

She answers in Yongwen, and he shrugs cheerfully.

"How do you even talk to each other?" I ask.

"We don't," he says. "It's beautiful. I should have found a girl I couldn't talk to ages ago."

I raise my eyebrows.

"I don't mean that," he says quickly. "Look, Dek is going a little wild, but then, he won't be able to do this when he's back in Spira City, will he?"

"If *you're* worried he's overdoing it, he must be on a terrible binge."

He laughs. "Well—it's not the booze and roaming around that worries me. It's this girl and how attached he's getting right before we're planning to clear out. But I reckon he knows what he's doing. Look, Brown Eyes, I'm sorry about this morning. I was out of line. Friends?"

"Of course," I say, relieved.

"So how did it go today? Have you got Ko Dan?"

"It wasn't him. Things are a bit of a mess right now."

"Maybe this will help."

With a flourish, he hands me a piece of paper shut with a red wax seal. I'd almost forgotten about Gangzi's letters, but I am very glad to have one in my hands now, when we desperately need a lead. I break the seal open and look at the letter, but I can't read it, of course. I fold it up and slip it into my pocket.

"Thanks. I'll show this to Frederick." I point at his

painting, which is a fair imitation of a landscape, with a mountain furred with trees, and say, "This is new for you."

He grins. "Watch this."

With a few deft strokes, he paints an enormous frog peering over the mountain. The perspective shifts, and it is not a mountain at all but a mossy rock. I laugh out loud. "That's clever."

"How's this for a character reversal?" he says. "Dek's off carousing, and here I am at home studying art. Informally. You know, if I lived here, it wouldn't matter about my being an orphan or a crook. If I could show I had talent, they'd give me a grand house in the Imperial Gardens and I'd live like a king, drawing pictures all day long. It doesn't matter what you come from here, it matters what you can *do*."

I think of what Jun said—how the most downtrodden have no time to pursue things like painting and poetry, how their skills are not prized by Tianshi's elite.

"You don't want to stay, do you?" I ask Wyn.

"Not bleeding likely. I miss Spira City. Don't you?"

I nod.

"I think about it all the time, what I'll do when we get back." He puts down his brush. "We'll go to Reveille and hear who's playing. I miss Ma Fole's hot cakes, Fraynish coffee at the riverside cafés. Hounds, I even miss my drafty little room and feeding pigeons on the roof. If we're back by summertime, we'll go dancing at the village festivals and drink good Fraynish wine—no more of this *shijiu* rot."

Tentatively, like probing a nearly healed wound, I think

about how it used to be when we did those things together, coming back after midnight and falling laughing into bed, his hands unlacing my dress, his breath hot on my neck. I've never been happier. Mei comes in from the kitchen with plates of overcooked meat and vegetables, nodding at me with a stony expression. There is hardly space on the table, but she shoves some of the clutter aside and puts the plates down at one end.

"D'you want some?" asks Wyn.

I shake my head. "I've just eaten. You won't believe the day I've had, Wyn—"

The door bangs open, and Dek and Ling come in.

"Lost my crutch," he rasps. He is leaning hard against Ling, who looks like she's going to topple over from the weight of him. I jump to my feet to help. They both smell of liquor. Mei says something sharp to Ling—she's speaking dialect, and I doubt even Dek understands her—but Ling doesn't answer. The two of them collapse into chairs at the filthy table. He looks greasy and unwashed. His hair is still tied back.

"Where've you been?" I ask crossly.

"Gambling," Dek says, and laughs. "You ought to come next time, Wyn. It was the strangest place. I've lost all our money, I'm afraid! Oh! Did you find Ko Dan?"

"It wasn't him," I say.

"No? Stars. Too bad." He shoves at a dirty tray so that he can put his elbows on the table. "What a mess. We'll have to fire the housekeeper."

He winks at Ling, who is chewing ferociously at a finger-nail on her bandaged hand. The bandage is looking grubby and frayed.

"You used to be so good about cleaning up," I say. It occurs to me only now that I never really helped with the cleaning, that Dek always kept our room spotless.

"I used to be trapped in a flat all day," he replies.

Mei stacks the dirty trays and bowls from the morning with a good deal of angry clanging and banging, staring hard at Ling. Ling keeps working at her fingernail, her eyes cast down until Mei goes back into the kitchen. Then she smiles at Dek. It's a luminous smile, and he smiles back like he can't help it and puts a hand to her cheek. She leans into him, sighing. They look happy as anything, if a bit drunk and worn out. She's bitten her nail so badly it's bleeding.

"I need to talk to you." I'm trying to sound measured but it comes out like I'm yelling. "Things are very bad right now."

"What's going on?"

"We need to talk in *private*. But first you need to wash. You stink."

Wyn and Dek exchange a look, and Wyn goes back to his painting.

"All right," says Dek, getting up. "But the well water is freezing. I want you to know I'll be cursing your name the whole time."

"That's fine," I tell him. "Curse away."

# THIRTY-ONE

Half an hour later, we are climbing the narrow steps up the city wall. There is a walkway along the top of the wall, and the view over the city is spectacular. Bats swoop among the trees, and the rooftops make a sea of dark tiles, pointed like waves, around the walls of the Imperial Gardens. Behind us, the fires on distant Tama-shan are coming out. Without his crutch, Dek has to hang on to my shoulder and sort of hop and shuffle along, something that would have wounded his pride terribly not so long ago, but now he doesn't seem to mind.

We perch on the ledge of the wall, legs dangling over the city below. Before leaving the house, I told them about the false Ko Dan and my confrontation with Si Tan and the empress dowager. I didn't want to ask the obvious question in front of the girls, but now I do: "Listen. Ling and Mei told you about the fake Ko Dan, and Ling gave you that picture. There's no way they could have known, is there?"

"No," says Dek firmly. "It was general gossip. Ling drew

the fellow she saw, but there was a whole crowd watching him return to the city and go up to the monastery, people following the whole way. Everybody believed it was him. Besides, the girls aren't connected. They're nobodies in this city."

"All right," I say. "You haven't told her anything, have you? About Mrs. Och or Theo?"

"Of course not," he says, shocked, and then adds: "Not because I don't trust her. But I don't want her to know anything that could be dangerous to *her*."

"And she hasn't asked any questions?"

"Julia, stop it," he says, irritated. "Of course she's asked questions. About you, mostly, because you come banging in and out in a foul mood all the time, and she wonders why we're here. But they are normal, curious sorts of questions, and I've put her off. She doesn't push."

"She doesn't know about the house in Nanmu?"

"No!" He gives me an exasperated look.

And then—I can't help it—I blurt out: "Since when do you go to *gambling* dens?"

His face changes, and he laughs at my expression. He is handsome, my brother—even with the Scourge scars and blots, his right eyelid stitched shut over the missing eye. I am so used to him keeping his hair over his face, but when he ties it back, and when he looks happy, the disfigurement barely matters.

"I'm trying new things, Julia. Don't worry, I won't make a habit of it."

"It's just . . . it's not like you. I never know where you are anymore."

"What's not like me?" he says lightly. "Not like me, I suppose, to have a girl, to have a good time, to go anywhere or do anything. Does it really bother you?"

"That's not what I mean," I say, but I'm not sure, maybe it is.

"I never know where *you* are," he says. "But I had to get used to that a long time ago. Tianshi is a city of wonders, and I want to see all of it, try everything!"

I am afraid of his answer, but I ask him, "Will you be sorry to go back home?"

The silence stretches on so long my stomach drops.

"What if we didn't go back?" he says at last. "Once we get paid, we'll have plenty to live on here—for years, even, if we live modestly."

"I barely speak Yongwen," I manage to say.

"You'd learn if we stayed," he says. "Esme's already said she's going to retire, and I know you don't want to take over from her. I can't go back to living in a dark room, people spitting at me or running away whenever I show my face. We've seen a bit of the world now. I want more."

"But what by the holies would we *do* here?"

"What are we going to do back in Spira City?"

"I just . . . I don't know . . . it's *home.*"

"Not to me. Oh, don't look that way. If you want to go back, we'll go back." He says this so lightly, but I feel as if my heart is breaking. The idea of living in Tianshi feels

247

impossible, but who am I to drag him back to a city where he can never have this kind of freedom? No more drinking sand, we said.

"I'd have to get used to the idea," I say, hating how broken my voice sounds. What a spoiled child I've always been with my brother.

"Never mind it, Julia. I'm not going to insist on staying if it makes you unhappy."

But how long have we both put my happiness ahead of his?

"Are you in love with Ling?" I ask.

"I don't know," he says, suddenly vague. "She makes me happy."

"She looks at me funny."

"You're an unusual girl—always running around on secret errands—you're about her age, and you're my sister. She's curious about you." He sighs. "When I mention Frayne to her, she talks about it like it's this terrible, backward place. She says she's heard it's dirty and full of sickness and rats, not to mention the indiscriminate drowning of witches."

"Maybe things will be different. Esme and Gregor seem pretty fixed that there's going to be a revolution. We're meeting with Count Fournier in the morning to see about getting the princess out."

"The last revolution was a bloodbath. Half the revolutionaries were slaughtered before the thing even began. I wouldn't bet on another one going any better. I hope Esme and Gregor come to their senses before getting involved."

"Gregor's still not drinking," I say. "I think . . . I mean, Esme says he's really trying."

"Good luck to him." He sounds unconvinced, and I can hardly blame him. Then he puts his arm around me and says, "Don't worry, Julia. If you're really fixed on going back to Spira City, we'll set up again, just like old times. Maybe you'll meet some handsome fellow and settle down."

I roll my eyes at him.

"Go on—wouldn't that be grand? Little dark-haired tots running around calling me Uncle Dek? And it turns out you like children more than you thought, isn't that right?"

"I like *one* child," I say. "Not *children*."

He's laughing, but I can't laugh along.

"Oh, come on," he says. "What's the matter?"

My heart twists itself into a dark, painful knot. I take out the picture of the Ankh-nu and show it to him. "Mrs. Och thinks this thing is in the monastery Treasury. She wants me to steal it."

"What is it?"

"She says it's what Ko Dan used to put Gennady's bit of *The Book of Disruption* inside Theo. The story is that Marike made it, and it's for separating a person's essence—or the essence of anything alive—from the physical parts and putting it into . . . well, into another body."

"And *The Book of Disruption* has an essence?"

"Apparently. So Ko Dan used *this* to bind the Book fragment's essence to Theo. And apparently, *Marike* used it to stay alive by switching bodies whenever the body she'd been using got too old."

Dek makes a sound halfway between a laugh and a cry of horror. "And what happened to whoever's body it was she was hopping into?"

"I don't know. I suppose they got stuffed into the previous body and died of old age or whatever she was about to die of before she switched with them."

"How revolting!" He shakes his head, and I can tell he doesn't believe it.

I take a deep breath and tell him: "When I was in the Imperial Library and the witch there was looking through my memories, there was one memory . . . I saw our ma. She had the Ankh-nu, and she was talking to somebody, telling them she had it and that she was ready or something."

"You remember this from when you were little?" he asks carefully.

"No . . . it was somebody else's memory, or that's what it felt like. I'm not sure. But there's more." I can't look at him while I say this. I stare at my hands and get it out in a rush. "When I disappear . . . if I pull back as far as possible, I end up . . . somewhere else. It's like Spira City, but burning and made of shadows. I pulled Gennady there by accident when we were in Casimir's fortress, and he said it was Kahge. Now Mrs. Och has got Frederick *researching* me. And in the memory I saw, there was Ma, making some kind of deal with . . . I think it might have been a creature from Kahge. It wanted to go to the world. I felt that—how much it wanted to go to the world. What if she used the Ankh-nu and put the creature in *me* and that's why I can disappear?"

I don't know if I feel better or worse now that I've said it out loud. My heart is thundering in my ears.

"Hounds, Julia—don't go jumping to wild conclusions!" he cries.

I make myself keep going: "Frederick says Kahge isn't like Rainists make it out to be, under the earth and the Dark Ones. He says it's like a . . . a shadow of the world, but made of magic."

"And how does Frederick know that?"

"Well, that's the old idea of Kahge. It doesn't really matter what it's called, the point is that I go *somewhere*, and it's not of this earth, I can tell you that."

"Then stop," he says firmly. "Whatever magic you've got . . . if it takes you somewhere else, don't go there. Stay close. Stay here."

"But why *can* I . . . what does it mean?"

"I've no idea. But look, this memory you're talking about could just as well have been *planted* by the witch at the Imperial Library. You don't know that it's real at all. I don't know why you can vanish, and Nameless knows I don't know a thing about Kahge, but it doesn't mean Ma *did* something to you. Maybe it's good to have Mrs. Och looking into it. Wouldn't it be better to find out the truth?"

I nod, though honestly, I think that depends on what the truth is.

"Just don't leap to conclusions yet," he says. "All right?"

I nod again, because I can't say anything around the lump in my throat. He pulls me to him, and we hold each other there on the edge of the wall, the dark city below us, for a while.

"I feel like I can never quite forgive her," I admit at last. He doesn't ask who. He knows.

"Forgive her for what?"

"Oh, for . . . I don't know, going after Casimir, being part of the Sidhar Coven, getting involved. Sometimes I think that if she'd loved us more, she wouldn't have risked her life that way. She wouldn't have risked leaving us behind."

"It wasn't lack of love, Julia. She tried to be a mother and a revolutionary both, and she died trying."

"I know."

"What about our pa, then?"

"What about him?"

"Do you forgive *him*?"

That gives me pause. "I don't think about him much," I say at last. "I reckon I loved him when I was very little, because he was there, and Ma loved him and you loved him. But mostly I remember him like a stranger who stumbled around and took up space and upset everybody, and then he was gone, and I never missed him."

"I was hard on him when he was around."

"Well, somebody had to be."

"It didn't help," he says. "Being hard on him didn't help, and being soft on him didn't help. There was nothing any of us could ever do for him. But the thing is, I remember him before. You were too little. By the time you were three or four, he was an opium eater through and through. But before that, he and I would go to the track together. I remember his pipe smoke back when he just smoked tobacco. I remember sitting in his lap, and he'd pretend I was riding a horse, his knees galloping along. Before you were born, Ma would go away a lot—hounds, I don't remember, for days, sometimes longer, seemed like weeks—and it would just be me and Pa. We'd do everything together, eat from the same plate, I'd sleep right next to him. After you were born, she was around more, and he had that fall and broke his hip. When he started to disappear, bit by bit, I hated him for it. Hounds, I hated him. He left us years and years before he walked out."

"I know." I'd never thought how much harder it must have been for Dek, who remembered him as something else.

"He was an athlete, very physical, like you. He didn't know how to be a cripple. He didn't know how to be a man with a bad leg looking for work, or a father who couldn't chase after his kids. I still wonder why Ma didn't do something for him. You know, help him with his hip or the pain somehow."

"With magic?"

"Yes. If she could save my life . . ."

"But it took so much from her. She was never the same after that. And people would have suspected."

He looks miserable, and I stop. It's unkind to remind him how she destroyed herself saving him. That last year of her life, she was a shadow of who she'd been before. "Why are we talking about Pa anyway?"

"Because we're talking about forgiveness. Isn't it always our parents we have to forgive? Either for not being there, or for what they did when they *were* there?"

I laugh at the way he puts it, but I reckon he's probably right. "You're the one I couldn't have lived without," I say. "You still are."

"Well, you won't have to," he says, mussing my hair.

"We'll stay together," I say. "Wherever we go."

"Of course. Hounds, Julia. Of *course*."

"If you don't want to go home, we'll stay here."

I make myself say it, and I make myself mean it. I can't imagine a life for myself outside of Spira City, being a foreigner forever in this strange city—but it's my turn to think about Dek's happiness now.

He kisses the top of my head. "Let's get this job done first," he says. "Then we'll talk about what's next."

I fold up the picture of the Ankh-nu and put it back in my pocket. I'd like to stay here with Dek, looking over the city and feeling like I am myself, just a girl, just his sister. But I've got some thieving to do.

# THIRTY-TWO

There are two guards outside the Treasury, as always. The squat, steel-doored building is separated from the Temple of Atonement by a row of bushes. Jun crouches behind the bushes, a silent shadow, while I stand next to one of the guards, vanished, and count in my head. When I reach twenty, Jun tosses a handful of gravel at the roof of the Treasury. It skitters along the tiles; both guards startle and look up. Jun aims the little handheld crossbow I got from Dek and shoots one guard with a dart while I stab a dart into the neck of the fellow next to me. They sway and fall together. Neither has time to raise the alarm. I reappear, grinning like crazy.

"That is easy part," says Jun, but he's smiling too, his dimples showing. How he can go from looking so fierce to looking so sweet in less than half a second astounds me. I could watch the change all day. "How we can open this door?"

"*That's* the easy part," I tell him, producing Dek's magnetic pick with a flourish. I am showing off, I admit, and while either one of us could have managed this job alone, doing it together is more fun. I was touched by how relieved he was to see me when I turned up at Count Fournier's. When I described the job to him, assuring him that it was not common thieving but necessary to save Theo's life, his eyes lit up. He is a boy after my own heart, all right.

Dek's pick gets the door open in a jiff, and once we are inside, I take out the lantern and light it. Jun gives a low whistle, carrying the lantern along the shelves. I have never seen such a sight myself. Paintings, ancient scrolls, crowns, weaponry, pottery, jade sculpture, gem-studded goblets, a diamond the size of my fist, and chest after chest filled with bricks of gold—the Shou-shu Monastery is wealthy beyond anything I've ever imagined.

"Why they have all this?" says Jun. "They are monks! What they need gold for?"

"Everybody likes gold," I say. "I don't see it, though. How often does the guard change?"

"Three hours," says Jun.

"All right. We should be able to check every inch of this place in three hours."

And we do. We empty every chest, feel every stone and beam for hidden panels. Jun climbs along the rafters of the ceiling with the lantern, then comes swinging down, landing in front of me. The lantern flickers, making his face go dark and then light as he holds it up and looks around the room again.

"Your treasure is not here," he says. "I think they guard ordinary treasure in ordinary way—locks and guards. But if they have magical treasure, they would guard in a magical way. We cannot find it like this."

"I reckon you're right," I agree. I'd hoped at least *something* might come easily.

"Guard will change before too long," he says.

So we leave, locking the door behind us and giggling at the idea of the guards waking up and how confused they will be, with nothing missing from the Treasury. Still, going back to Mrs. Och empty-handed when she has made it clear that we are out of time leaves me with a pit in my stomach.

We walk slowly through the Xishui Triangle. I'm trying to think of something to say that will make him smile at me again when he grabs my hand and pulls me up a quiet road toward an ancient-looking tree, gnarled and twisted, its branches a darker black against the night sky. Only when we are right under its branches do I see the twists of paper, as numerous as the leaves.

"Look," says Jun, squatting by the thick trunk. I kneel on the ground to see what he is showing me. It is a little wooden box nestled between the tree roots, and inside it there is a pot of ink, a brush, and hundreds of blank strips of paper.

"Do you ever write wish?" he asks me.

"No," I say. "I don't understand why people do it. If you're not a witch, writing something down isn't going to do anything."

"The magic does not come from witch," says Jun. "You don't know that? The magic come from *writing*. From words. Some people—witches—they can bring that magic out. But there is power in any writing. If I write, I cannot make magic happen, but still the writing has some magic in it. Maybe it can change some small thing. Give me some luck, or some chance."

From what I've seen of witches and magic and luck, I'm not sure I believe this. But Jun is already unscrewing the cap of the inkpot, dipping the brush. He writes something in swift characters on a slip of paper, then gives me a mischievous look and goes scampering up the tree, looking for a good spot.

"I like to put my wish near top," he says from above. I cannot even make out the shape of him among the dark leaves.

"Why?"

"I don't know. Feels more lucky."

I pick up the brush, dip it, and pause. I have the overwhelming urge to write *Forgive me* on the paper and tie it to the tree. I think it, brush poised: Forgive me. Forgive me. But who am I asking for forgiveness? Frederick would say that in the eyes of the Nameless I am already forgiven, that we are all forgiven for our mortal errors, and that every moment of our lives is a clean slate, starting over. And what does it matter if I am forgiven by those I've wronged? If I forgive myself? What does it change? Not what I did, nor what I mean to do.

And so I write, *Keep Theo safe*, and I climb up the tree after Jun, twisting my wish onto a twig with no other wishes.

"Come here!" he calls, and I climb higher, to where he sits astride a branch, his head poking above the leaves at the top of the tree. The branches are thick and sturdy even this high up. He reaches for me and pulls me onto the branch next to him, so we are facing each other. My back is against the trunk, and he is balanced out on the branch, seeming entirely at ease way up here. It is a clear night, and the moon is just a sliver, the sky strung with stars. I look straight up, thinking of the map of the planets Frederick showed me once, how tiny the world looked in the endless sea of space, and I try to hope that what I've written has some power.

"I am sorry we cannot find your magic treasure," says Jun. "But I am glad you ask me for help." He smooths my hair back from my face with soft fingers, and that touch ripples right through me, setting my skin alight. He is looking at me very seriously.

"What you wish for?" he asks.

"Doesn't it spoil the wish if I tell you? Make it not come true?"

He looks puzzled. "Writing wish is not like that," he says.

Looking at him in the moonlight, the dark leaves around his face, I almost want to tell him everything, open my heart like a box and take my secrets out one by one to lay before him. I can't, of course—I can't tell him my secrets. But I can tell him my wish, and so I do: "I wished for Theo to be safe."

He smiles. "You are good person."

That brings me all at once to the edge of weeping. "Not really."

"You are," he says, nodding. "I make selfish wish."

"All right, what was yours?"

He smiles that wicked smile again, the dimples coming out, and I hold on harder to the branch beneath me. "Every night since I meet you, I do not sleep enough. Do you know why?"

"Why?"

"Because instead of sleeping, I am lying in my bed and wondering, What it is like to kiss Julia? I am trying to imagine it, and not sleeping, just imagining. So I wish for a kiss from Julia. Maybe if I know, I can sleep again."

"Waste of a wish," I tell him, laughing, and the sky seems to tilt dangerously overhead. "You could have had that anytime."

I lean in to kiss him. He kisses me back with the softest mouth. I think of Wyn, but fleetingly. Jun's kisses don't allow my mind to wander far from the feeling of his mouth on mine. I pull him closer, fit my legs over his thighs, leaning back against the trunk.

"You are strange girl," he murmurs, which isn't exactly the most romantic thing anybody's ever said to me, but I don't care. I'll pretend he meant *dazzling* and it got lost in translation.

"Hush. Get your wish's worth."

He smiles that irresistible smile, leaning in so his lips catch mine again, his hand sliding round to the back of my neck, pulling me deeper into his kiss. The image of that antlered, fox-faced beast pointing at me across the steaming river in Kahge flashes through my mind. *Lidari.* But none of it can be true, not with Jun kissing me this way, not with everything I'm feeling right now. My longing expands, filling up with something else, something like defiance. I put my hands under his tunic and yank it roughly over his head, this hunger opening wider and wider. I surrender to it, let it root me in my body, my *self.* There is a tattoo over his heart, a Yongwen symbol. I run my fingers over it.

"What is that?" I ask.

"It means *luck,*" he whispers, and I almost want to cry. Instead, I move his hands away to untie my own tunic. He lifts it over my head, and we let the tunics drop and tangle on the branches below, his eyes fixed on mine. I feel lighter and lighter—more and more real. His skin is brilliant in the moonlight, and he pulls me up against the length of his smooth torso, whispering to me in Yongwen.

"I don't know what you're saying!" I laugh.

It feels desperate and effortless at the same time, and I'm drinking in the sound of his laughter, the warmth of his skin. For a little while I am only Julia, and I think of nothing else.

# THIRTY-THREE

"What are you doing still up?" I ask.

Bianka is sitting at the table, sewing by candlelight. She speaks softly, as if she doesn't want to be heard: "Shut the door. Quietly."

I do as she says, put down my bag with the hook and lantern in it, and slide into the chair next to her. My legs are still wobbly, like I've got water in my knees. She's making a new pair of trousers for Theo.

"Any luck tonight?" she asks me. She's still whispering, and so I whisper in reply.

"I've just searched the entire Treasury. No Ankh-nu, no Ko Dan. It's not looking good."

"Are *you* all right?" she asks.

"Oh, fine."

I'm thinking that this has been the longest, strangest, worst, best, most terrifying, most remarkable day and night of my life, but I don't say that, of course. Still, from the hope of finding Ko Dan this morning and then the rescue of Theo and the others from the monastery, to my encounter with Si Tan, then charging across the city with Pia, breaking into the Treasury, and making love in a treetop with beautiful Jun, I desperately need to get some sleep and then have a minute or two just to breathe and think.

I lay my head on my arm. My skin is cool from the night air and my sleeve smells of sweat, and I can still feel everywhere Jun touched me and kissed me. I'm worn out but still hungry for him, his fingers and his mouth, and if I feel all this, then how can I be anything but a girl, the girl I've always been? A shudder of pleasure runs through me, but at the same moment my mind throws images back in answer—of my clawed hands in that burning city, those impossible beasts hissing *"Lidari"* at me. I squeeze my eyes shut.

"I'm awake because I'm waiting for you," says Bianka in an odd voice.

I sit up and look at her.

"Professor Baranyi is here," she whispers. "Frederick is with them. Mrs. Och asked me to tell her when you got back." She pauses, and adds, "I'm just going to finish this row of stitches, and then I'd better let them know you're here."

My blood cools rapidly. "Thank you," I murmur, and she nods, bending over her sewing again.

I go outside. The crack under the blinds is just enough. I am more confident, having done this before. I vanish, and aim myself for the dark corner near Mrs. Och's bedroom door.

Frederick looks downcast. His head is bowed, and he is silent.

"You will find Silver Moya here," Mrs. Och is saying to the professor, the two of them bending over a map at her desk. The professor looks very flustered.

"Yes, yes," he mutters.

"If you are granted entry, you must ask in particular about Lidari," she says. "We need to know for certain what became of him."

"Yes," he says again. "Of course, yes. Do you think . . . ? Well, we shall go at once."

Frederick looks up. "I'm to go with him?" he asks. He looks as if he's been arguing for a while and is exhausted from it. "Is it dangerous?"

"To be turned away is not dangerous," she says. "But if you are granted entry, I do not know! I gave up on Ragg Rock a very long time ago. You should hurry. I want to know what we are dealing with before daybreak, if possible. I am trusting Julia with a great deal at the moment, and I do not like risk."

If Jun's touch seemed to draw the rage and fear away from me, it comes back now in a rush, a metallic taste on my tongue, a bitterness in my throat.

"I am sure she can be trusted," says Frederick, but in a weary, halfhearted way, as if he doesn't expect to be listened to. "She's frightened. She's . . . stars, you only have to talk to her for five minutes to see who she *is*."

"I seem to remember you vouching for her trustworthiness

when she was posing as Ella the housemaid as well," says Mrs. Och bitingly, and Frederick's shoulders slump. "Your confidence does not reassure me in the slightest. It may be that she has simply traded one disguise for another, and I need to be sure."

Professor Baranyi is putting on his coat. He and Frederick go out together, past Bianka stitching by the fire. Frederick says good night to her, but she does not look up. Mrs. Och watches them go, and I go with them, vanished.

They go to a little clock shop in the third tier of the Beimu Triangle, near the east gate. The shop is shuttered and closed for the night, but the professor knocks anyway, and at length an old man with a candle opens the door for them. They exchange a few words and are ushered inside. The clock shop looks quite ordinary. Through a door behind the counter is a workshop, dark and empty. The old man lights a lamp, and a tired-looking woman comes through the door, wrapping a robe around herself and nodding greetings. She asks something in Yongwen, and the professor answers very formally. She asks Frederick then. He confirms whatever it is she has said, and she indicates that they should sit at the broad worktable.

Carefully, deliberately, she takes out a scroll of rice paper, a pot of ink, a small bowl, and a brush and lays them all out. Then she scatters some seeds across the table and fetches a bird from a cage hanging near the ceiling. Cages with sleeping birds inside hang all around the room. This one wakes up and begins pecking at the seed. The woman unscrews the back of her ink brush to reveal a little blade, then reaches for Professor Baranyi's hand. She slices his finger and squeezes some blood into the tiny bowl. She pours some ink from the pot into the bowl, mixing it with the blood, dips the brush, and writes something on the page.

They sit there silently for a bit. She smiles apologetically, raising her shoulders in a shrug, and asks Frederick if he is willing. He does not look as if he wants to try, but he offers his hand and lets her slice his finger. She does the same as before with a fresh bowl, and again they all sit there awkwardly. Then she gets up, puts away the writing implements, and takes the little bird back to its cage. I don't know what I've just seen. Professor Baranyi and Frederick look rather relieved, I think.

The professor asks something politely, taking a piece of paper out of his coat pocket. He unfolds it and shows it to the woman. She looks at it and shakes her head. I look over her shoulder and give a start. It is the picture of me, Mrs. Och, and Bianka that has been circulating, and he is pointing at my picture, asking her if she's seen me before. Frederick looks quite miserable. Professor Baranyi tucks the picture back into his pocket, thanking the woman, and we all go back to Mrs. Och's house, where Bianka is still sewing by the fire, looking like she's about to fall asleep over her needlework.

Mrs. Och is in her room, a candle burnt down to nearly nothing on her desk, her back rigid.

"It didn't work," says Professor Baranyi.

"Frederick, make the professor a bed in the servants' quarters so he does not have to go back to Xihuo tonight," she says, sounding angry. "I am going to bed. We will visit the count in the morning."

"And Julia?" asks Professor Baranyi. "Silver Moya claimed not to have seen her."

Mrs. Och hesitates. "We will have to trust her for now," she says at last. "We can't do it without her. Not without attracting a good deal of attention, anyway. I hope you are right about her, Frederick."

Frederick and the professor go to the servants' quarters, and when Mrs. Och closes her door, I reappear, startling Bianka.

"Well?" she asks me.

"They're suspicious of me, but I don't know why," I say, and I tell her what I saw. She is as baffled as I am, and for a few minutes we say nothing, puzzling it over.

"I'd better tell her you're back," she says at last. She goes and knocks on Mrs. Och's door.

"Julia is here," she says when Mrs. Och opens it.

"Ah. The Ankh-nu?" she asks me eagerly, swinging the door wide.

I shake my head, trying not to let my anger show on my face.

"Worse and worse," she mutters, and gives me a long look, like she's not sure she should believe me. "Go to bed. We will speak in the morning."

"I'm going to sleep as well," says Bianka. She squeezes my hand. "Coming?"

"In a minute," I say.

She nods and goes into the room we share with Theo. I find Frederick in his room in the servants' quarters, sitting on the edge of his narrow cot with his face in his hands.

"Did you find it?" he asks me, looking up.

"No."

"Well, we will have to hope that your Count Fournier has some leads for us tomorrow. Oh stars, it nearly *is* tomorrow." He hesitates, and I can see he is trying to decide what to tell me, who to betray.

I spare him the struggle and say: "Why has she got you going to some witch in the middle of the night? What was that about? Who's Silver Moya?"

He gapes at me and then lets out an unhappy laugh.

"I wish she would agree to talk to you directly," he says. "There's obviously no point trying to keep anything from you."

"Don't tell her, please," I say, suddenly frightened at the thought of what she might do if she knew I'd been spying on *her*.

He sighs. "I won't," he says. "Only because she'd be furious. But I'd be very glad if my life contained less *Don't tell hers*, on both sides."

"I need to know what's going on. It isn't fair to keep it from me."

"Silver Moya is a witch," he says. "Or, a kind of witch.

There are hundreds of her particular sort around the world. There is one in Spira City, as a matter of fact. They are called in adolescence—I am not sure of the details, but my understanding is that they begin to have visions of Ragg Rock and may then choose to accept the role and the name of Silver Moya. Only they can make a request of Ragg Rock. As for Ragg Rock—well, I am not sure if it is a place or a creature . . . or what exactly. We know only that a number of witches throughout history *claim* to have had entry to some in-between place via a Silver Moya. She did not ask us for money, only a bit of blood."

"I saw," I say.

"You were there?" He looks torn between amusement and annoyance. "Well then, you know that nothing happened."

"But what does Mrs. Och want? She told you to find out about Lidari."

"I told her about those things in Kahge calling you Lidari, as you said," he tells me. "She was disturbed."

"She thinks I'm connected to them," I say.

"I don't know what she thinks. She has not shared any theories with me. I'm not sure she has any."

"And she thought I might be . . . what, visiting Ragg Rock myself?"

"Perhaps. Mainly she wanted to know about Lidari. What had become of him."

"Frederick—did *you* know that Mrs. Och wanted to come to Yongguo for the princess?"

"No. She doesn't take me that far into her confidence."

"The professor must have known."

"I imagine they spoke of it. But you mustn't think Theo's safety is not important to her."

"Oh, I believe *The Book of Disruption* is important to her," I say, not very nicely. He looks unhappy but doesn't argue. Suddenly I remember that I've got Gangzi's letter in my pocket. I take it out and hand it to him. "Look, Wyn got hold of this today. It's a letter from Gangzi to . . . somebody."

He reads it and raises his eyebrows. "It's addressed to some minor official in Gumao—a city bordering Rossha, in the north. I'll show this to Mrs. Och in the morning. She'll be glad to have a clue, at least."

"What does it say?"

"See this symbol?"

He shows me the letter. I hadn't picked it out among the Yongwen characters, but there is the Eshriki symbol for life—the *ankh*. "He is asking this official to conduct a search of the city. He describes a double-spouted pot with the hieroglyph on each side."

"So the Ankh-nu is in Gumao?" I say, confused.

"See if you can get a few more of these," says Frederick.

I rest my head against the doorframe and feel myself drifting toward sleep, everything that has happened today a tangle in my mind: the stars, Jun's hands on me, the taut muscles of his arms and chest, Si Tan's horrible smile, Cinzai's head coming off—I raise my head with a jolt. Frederick looks concerned.

"Are you all right?"

"Exhausted," I say, which isn't the half of it.

He hesitates and then says, as if he's been trying to work out the phrasing and hasn't quite got it: "Whatever we find out . . . about Kahge and all that . . . it doesn't really change who you are, Julia. You must believe that."

"I do," I say. But I'm lying.

# THIRTY-FOUR

A tugging at my scalp wakes me up. Theo is busy with my hair, knotting and matting it.

"Oh, Theo, what a mess!" I cry, feeling my head. It is sticky and smells of honey. I must have been sleeping like a log.

"Lala umma ebby ebby sump," he says cheerfully.

The early-morning sun is filtering through the curtains. I pick him up and hurry outside, still in my nightdress. Bianka is washing her face at the pump. Mrs. Och sits on the steps, looking bent and ancient.

"Did Frederick show you Gangzi's letter?" I ask her.

She nods.

"Well, what do you think? He's lost the Ankh-nu, hasn't he?"

"I don't know. I've sent a pipit instructing your brother to get some more of the letters," she says. "How are you feeling?"

"Better," I say, and it's true. I don't know how long I slept, but it was a deep sleep, and now I'm hungry. I put Theo down, and he runs to Bianka, who scoops him up and kisses him.

"Good," she says. "Eat something, and we will go see your Count Fournier."

She retreats to her room, and I boil myself an egg, glad to see there is still bread as well, a little stale, but we have some butter that will make it edible. The honeypot is nearly empty and full of small, dirty fingerprints. I bring my breakfast outside to eat in the sun.

"You were talking in your sleep," says Bianka, coming and sitting with me on the steps. Theo clambers up onto her shoulders, singing to himself a gibberish song.

"I'm sorry." I dread to think what I might have been saying. I think of Jun and fight my smile. Oh Nameless, the look on his face! Only an acrobat could manage the things we did in a treetop. Just thinking of it makes me shiver.

"Sounded like you were fighting all night," she says. "I'm surprised to see you so well rested, to be honest."

"I'm on edge. I just hope the count has something useful to tell us."

She avoids the subject and says instead: "What on earth has happened to your hair?"

"Your son," I say dryly. "I don't think it's going to comb out."

She tries to work her fingers through the sticky tangles. "Hounds, is that *honey*? Oh, Theo!"

Theo scrambles off her shoulders to examine his handiwork with pride and then goes to dig a hole at the bottom of the steps with a stick.

"Ow," I say as she pulls at my hair.

"Well, if you ever brushed it in the first place, he might not have been able to make such a mess of it," she says, laughing. "But you're right, it'll have to be cut. I can cut it to your chin if you like—some girls make that look very stylish and modern."

I think of Pia, the sharp line of hair ending at her jaw.

"No," I say quickly. "Just cut it like a boy's. I've been dressing like one anyway. Given the way things are, the less I look like me, the better, I reckon."

"All right." She fetches her sewing scissors and settles behind me on the steps, snipping away. I watch the long hanks of matted hair falling to the ground and listen to Bianka humming—an unexpectedly happy sound.

"So. You and Frederick," I say.

"Yes." I hear the smile in her voice.

"I had no idea you felt that way about him."

There is a pause, and then she says, "Well, proximity changes things. And he's good to Theo. I want to be with someone I can count on for a change."

I think that that's not terribly fair to Frederick, but I don't say so. It's not really any of my business.

"Listen," she says, lowering her voice. "I wanted to tell you—just in case. You know the bag I've got hanging from a hook in the bedroom?"

"Yes."

"Have you ever looked inside it?"

"No," I say, hurt she had to ask.

She hears my tone and says placatingly, "Well, you *are* a spy. And I wouldn't have minded. Anyway, there's some dry food in it—just emergency rations—a fair bit of money, a few diapers, and a change of clothes for Theo."

"All right," I say. We are quiet for a moment, just listening to the *snip snip snip* of the scissors around my ears and neck. "And?"

"If something happens to me and . . . I don't know, if you need to run, you take Theo and you take that bag."

"Nothing's going to happen to you," I say.

"One has to think about these things," she says, and then Frederick and Professor Baranyi come through the gate. Frederick is carrying a basket laden with fruit and vegetables from the market in one hand and a stick with something shaggy at the end of it in the other. The professor glances at me nervously and asks, "Is Mrs. Och inside?"

I nod coldly, and he goes in. Frederick joins Bianka and me on the steps, putting down his basket.

"What on earth are you doing?"

"Theo made a mess of Julia's hair, so I'm cutting it off," says Bianka.

"I'm going to look like a boy in a minute," I say.

"Feyda!" cheers Theo.

"Hullo, monkey," says Frederick. "Look what I've got you! It's a horse!"

He presents Theo with the stick, and I realize that the shaggy bit at the end is meant to be a horse's head, its mane made of rags. I grab a hard little apple out of the basket and take a bite. Frederick shows Theo how to ride the toy horse, and Theo goes galloping around the courtyard, shouting with glee.

"That was nice of you," says Bianka.

"I thought he might like something to play with besides chickens and rocks," says Frederick.

Bianka brushes the stray hairs off my shoulders and says, "There—you look absolutely terrible."

"Good thing we haven't got a mirror." I touch a hand to my shorn head. It feels so strange, the weight of my hair gone.

"It's not so bad, actually," says Frederick kindly. "It's a bad haircut, but it brings out your eyes."

A strange humming feeling washes over me all of a sudden, the courtyard somehow too bright, the sky too high, everything too much, not right. Theo has stopped galloping around on his horse and is squatting with a stick, drawing something in the dirt.

"What's happening?" asks Bianka, alarmed. Her voice sounds echoey and unreal.

Something rises up out of the dirt. It is huge, with the head of a goat and a great furred body staggering on enormous chicken legs. *Kahge*—that is my first thought. Theo laughs in delight at the thing looming over him. The look on his face is one of amazed recognition.

"Theo!" Bianka leaps toward him.

"The stick!" cries Mrs. Och from the doorway, and I realize what has happened the instant she says it. Bianka snatches Theo away from the lumbering creature, and I dive for the stick he has dropped in the dirt, lying next to his clumsy drawing. Hairy arms grab at me, catch me around the waist, but I've got the stick, and I snap it in two. The thing crumbles to nothing, to dirt, and the air and the courtyard return to normal. I sit panting in the dirt, Bianka clutching Theo to her, Frederick wielding the sewing scissors next to me like he is going to take down a magicked monster with them.

"Well," says Mrs. Och, coming over to look at Theo's picture. It just looks like a scribble in the dirt, although there is something resembling a head and a body, I suppose. "I was afraid of that."

"Afraid of what? What was that thing?" shouts Bianka.

"Teo stoy!" crows Theo, delighted with himself, trying to wriggle out of her arms.

"It's *The Book of Disruption*," says Frederick. "He's not a witch, but still, a part of the most powerful text on earth is inside him. He can write magic . . . in a way."

"He can't *write*—he's just a baby! Those aren't even words—it hardly looks like *anything*!" cries Bianka.

"The earliest writing was pictographic," says Mrs. Och. "Until we can get the text out of him, we must keep him from making pictures. His imagination combined with the act of writing is much too strong."

"Oh hell," says Bianka.

"Teo tick," says Theo, picking up half of the broken stick and looking at me indignantly.

"Put that down at once," says Mrs. Och, snatching it away from him so hard he topples over. He gapes at her and begins to cry.

"Keep a close eye," she says to Bianka and Frederick. Then she turns to me. "Julia, come. We are leaving."

# THIRTY-FIVE

"Oh, your lovely hair!" cries Csilla when I arrive at Count Fournier's house with Mrs. Och and the professor. Mrs. Och looks vaguely annoyed that Csilla and Gregor are there as well.

"Pish," says Esme. "What use has Julia for lovely hair?"

Which I might have found insulting if I didn't have so much else on my mind.

"Ah, well," says Csilla forlornly. "It'll grow back."

Jun is standing by the door. I am absurdly nervous to look at him, but I do. He makes an O of surprise with his mouth and then grins, and my stomach somersaults wildly. I smile back and then can't wipe the smile off my face, so I look down to try and hide my ridiculous expression. Hounds, I'm an idiot. I want to drag him into the hall with me, away from the others.

Count Fournier looks overwhelmed to have us all in his dilapidated parlor: Gregor, gray-faced but upright, his mouth a line of grim endurance; Esme, long-limbed, benign, and genderless; and Csilla, who always looks set for a night at the opera, though her face paint is a little brighter and more careless than usual. Professor Baranyi helps Mrs. Och to the smelly sofa, where I was held at gunpoint just a few days ago. It's so strange now to think of Jun pointing a gun at me. Count Fournier seems uncertain about kissing Mrs. Och's hand, and in the end just clasps it loosely and then goes springing over to his liquor cabinet. He is wearing shoes for the first time since I've met him.

"Thank you all for coming! Och Farya, it is a great honor. I never imagined I might host one of the Xianren! May I . . . Brandy, anyone? Or whiskey?"

He is already pouring a glass, which he then holds toward Gregor, beaming.

"No!" says Gregor hoarsely, and stuffs his trembling hands into his pockets. Csilla rushes to take his arm.

"Please put it away," she begs the count. "We don't want any!"

He looks confused, but he puts the glass down. "Well then," he says, a bit sadly.

I sneak another look at Jun. He winks, and a wave of heat goes through me, thinking of his hands slipping under my tunic, his ragged breath in my ear.

"Do you have word of Ko Dan?" asks Mrs. Och sharply. Nothing to kill a pleasant fantasy like the sound of her voice.

Count Fournier shakes his head nervously. "There are a hundred different rumors. The source I trust the most believes him to be imprisoned in the Imperial Gardens by order of Si Tan, but even that I cannot confirm beyond doubt, and nobody can tell me exactly where."

"And you say that Old Zey is ill?" says Mrs. Och, leaving the question of Ko Dan behind rather quicker than I like.

"Dying," says the count. "The Sidhar Coven has been reassembling."

"What little is left of it," says Mrs. Och dismissively.

"I have no money, no means of returning, but if you take me back with you, I have contacts all over Frayne—the names of well-connected people who are waiting for a revolution."

"Witches and a few Lorians might be ready to rise up, but are the people?" asks Esme. "It cannot be a revolution of witches. That is not a revolution. That is a coup, and the people will not support it."

"The people will be ready if they have a princess," says Gregor. "I am sure of it."

"We have met with one impostor recently," says Mrs. Och. "Are you certain this is Zara, daughter of Prince Roparzh? What proofs does she have of her identity?"

"She has in her possession the family's royal seal, her father's ring, and a certificate signed by a holy at her birth. These will be contested, of course, but it will be enough to convince the people. More important . . . well, you will see when you meet her. She is obviously of royal blood. She has been educated broadly and has lived in many countries, sometimes under very difficult conditions. She is intelligent and thoughtful and wise well beyond her years. She will be a fine queen, you can be sure of that. But we have to act quickly—Si Tan and Gangzi are meeting today with the Fraynish ambassador and Lord Skaal."

"Meeting where?" asks Mrs. Och.

"The Imperial Gardens, I assume," says Count Fournier. "That is where Si Tan receives guests."

"We will take Princess Zara to Frayne immediately," says Mrs. Och.

I understand now why she wanted to bring all of us on this journey to Tianshi. She knew Gregor and Esme were involved in the Lorian Uprising, that they would be perfect for this task. She did not bring them here for Theo at all.

"I have no money," says the count again, humbly. "But Zara trusts me, and I have connections. I have been involved for years. I wish to help."

"Julia will go now to fetch her," says Mrs. Och, ignoring his plea. "How can we ensure that the princess goes with her willingly?"

The count has a frantic look, like he realizes he is being left behind, cut out of the whole business.

"She will know," he says. "She has a sense of these things, of whom she can trust. I cannot get in myself, but Jun could manage it unseen and he knows the monastery. . . ."

My heart leaps, and Jun and I grin at each other like lunatics. Esme's eyes narrow a bit, looking at us, but I don't care.

"Julia will go alone," says Mrs. Och. "She does not need help."

Jun's smile falls away, and he looks from Mrs. Och back to me.

"He helped tremendously the other day," I say. "In a pinch, I'd like him with me. If he's willing," I add, looking at Jun. He begins to smile again, but Mrs. Och puts an end to it.

"No. Julia will get the princess and bring her to my house. Julia alone. Thank you, Count Fournier. I will be happy to pay your passage home if you wish to return to Frayne."

We all stand there uncertainly as Mrs. Och rises to her feet, Professor Baranyi taking her arm to help her.

I look at Jun. He says, "You cannot take tunnels. They are flooding them. Everybody running like rats."

"Who is flooding them?" I ask.

"I don't know. Somebody. Not much places to hide in Tianshi today. Ru are out searching homes. Maybe they are looking for you?"

"Julia!" Mrs. Och says sharply. "There is no time to waste. Fetch the princess and take her to my house. Do not let anybody see you."

So I leave them all there: Jun, helplessly watching me go; Mrs. Och, counting paper money out onto Count Fournier's desk; and Gregor, looking at everything except the brandy on the side table, Csilla on his arm like an anchor straining against a storm.

# THIRTY-SIX

The monastery is surrounded by the Ru. There is no chance of going over the wall with my hook. The only way to do it is to vanish farther than I like—back through the foggy space at the edge of the world to that reeling nowhere where I must angle my perspective to make sure I don't lose the wall completely. My aim is off; I land on a temple rooftop and slide down, grunting.

The old woman meets me at the door of the little house, pointing the blunderbuss at me with a look in her eye that says, *Yes, this thing will break my arm if I fire it, but don't think I won't.* Princess Zara, stout in a brilliantly patterned silk robe, her frizzy hair pinned up with jade combs, is holding a pistol, but her eyes are clear and unafraid. She says something to the old woman. The old woman just grunts and keeps pointing the blunderbuss at me.

"Count Fournier sent me," I say, my hands raised and visible. "You're not safe here anymore. King Zey is dying, and we mean to take you back to Frayne to, um, claim the throne."

She receives my news with an equanimity I find hard to believe, just nods her head and tucks her pistol away inside her wide sleeve.

"I'll need my bag," she says, and fetches a battered valise from under her bed. Then she speaks to the old woman in Yongwen. Slowly the blunderbuss lowers. The old woman's chin crumples and wobbles. Tears pour down her wrinkled cheeks. Princess Zara embraces her. They cling to each other for a long moment while I stand there feeling increasingly awkward. When at last they pull apart, Princess Zara presses a clinking bag of coins into the old woman's hand.

"The thing is," I say, "the monastery is surrounded, and so to get you out . . . it's going to be a little strange. You'll have to hang on to me. Just close your eyes and don't let go."

"Are we going to fly out?" she asks, her eyes twinkling, as if I'm joking.

"Not exactly," I say. "You might be scared, or startled, but please hang on."

She says simply, "I trust you"—which, under the circumstances, is one of the strangest things she could possibly say, but I'm not complaining. She kisses the old woman one more time.

"Well," I say awkwardly, "just put your arms around me."

As if we are going to dance, she puts one arm around my waist and the other across my shoulders, the valise in her hand bumping against my hip. For a moment, I think I don't know how to do this and the whole thing feels utterly absurd and embarrassing, showing up here and telling her to hold me. I grab the princess around the waist and yank back. For a horrible split second, I'm afraid we're just going to fall over on the ground, but then we're through. I can feel her heartbeat quickening as the world fades around us and I pull up, up, and everything is spinning under us. Too high, I feel like we are soaring way over the city, like a balloon whose string has been cut, like we are going to get lost in the sky. I panic, and we are zooming in close, too close, and then I'm afraid I am going to dash us to bits in the street. I come back to myself right outside a shop selling painted silk fans. I hear somebody scream. The princess is struggling to get out of my grip, so I grab on to her, pull us out of the world again, trying to control it better. A few streets at a time. I vanish far enough that it seems as if we are hanging over the city but not too far above it, then pick a spot farther along, reappear there, stop and breathe, ignore the shouts, pull back again. In this way we cross the city—leapfrogging in and out of the world.

Once, I pull back too far—or it feels as if something is pulling *me*. I hear a whispering sort of hum behind me—the city gone, a rising roar—but no, here it is, the street, the trees swaying in the breeze, blossoms and wishes floating down, a beautiful day, and the princess's breath hoarse in my ear, her arms tight around me, hanging on for dear life. I find the house in Nanmu and put us in the courtyard, startling Bianka, Theo, and Frederick. Not bad, I think, quite pleased with myself. Faster than a trolley.

I let go of the princess, and she staggers a little, her face very pale, but she composes herself quickly. No shrieking from the walls, so I suppose they must have gotten rid of all the protective warning spells in preparation for her arrival.

"Thank you," she says, and puts down her valise.

"This is Princess Zara," I say to Frederick and Bianka, trying to look steadier than I feel after leap-vanishing across the city.

Bianka drops a curtsy. Frederick bows hastily as well.

"Oh, don't bother," says the princess, laughing. She recovers fast, I'll say that for her. "Well, that was ... different. Might I ask for a cup of tea?"

# THIRTY-SEVEN

The others return soon after we've made tea. The house feels smaller than usual as they all come pouring into the main room and greet the princess with bows and curtsies and noisy exclamations of concern. Princess Zara, for her part, is all smiles and graciousness, as if quite in her element. More tea is made, and maps are rolled out across the table. Theo is delighted by the hubbub, getting in everyone's way and shrieking with excitement. Bianka hovers close to him, watching his hands anxiously.

"I mean, what do I do if he draws something with his finger? I can't break his *finger*," she whispers to me. "I'm going to go mad watching him like this!"

After greeting the princess, Mrs. Och goes immediately to her room, indicating that Professor Baranyi and I are to follow her.

"Well done," she tells me, sinking into her chair. I can see the morning has taken a lot out of her, but I'm not much inclined to sympathy.

"All very well to have the princess," I say. "But what about Ko Dan? Or the Ankh-nu?"

"I will visit Si Tan tomorrow," she says.

For a moment I'm speechless, and then I splutter: "You'll *visit* him? Why am I sneaking around getting assaulted and kidnapped when you're just going to go sauntering into the monastery or the Imperial Gardens for a chat? Why didn't you do that to begin with?"

"It is a last resort, Julia," Mrs. Och says wearily. "Perhaps I can persuade him to help us. If not, we will have to leave immediately."

I want to kick my chair over and storm out of there, but not as much as I want to hear what she's going to say next, so I stay put.

"I need to know what passes between Gangzi and Lord Skaal today. We may have even less time than we think. You will go to the Imperial Gardens now and report straight back to me."

"Fine, I'll go," I say. "But d'you really think you can just go have a chat with Si Tan and he'll say, *Oh, I understand completely, look, I've got Ko Dan stashed in this cupboard, you can borrow him whenever you like, and here is the Ankh-nu as well?*"

She stares at me unsmilingly. "No, I do not anticipate that. But I will see what I can get from him."

I can tell I've been dismissed, so I get up. I'm almost out the door when she says, "You are doing well, Julia. You really are . . . most remarkable."

"Thank you," I say, a bit taken aback by this. She looks

terribly tired. Professor Baranyi helps her toward her bed, and I go out, closing the door behind me.

Spira City will be only beginning to shake off winter's clutches, but today feels almost like summer in Tianshi. The air is warm, and the Imperial Gardens are full of the smell of flowering trees, pollen drifting on the breeze. For all that it frightens me to think about what I am, what might be *in* me that enables me to walk the edge of the world, unseen, I can't deny that at times like these I enjoy it tremendously— walking right past the Ru, slipping through the gate and making my way through this forbidden sanctuary and up the steps toward the pavilion.

It seems that I am just in time. Si Tan is there with Gangzi at his side, exchanging elaborate greetings with the ambassador and Lord Skaal, who is dressed unprepossessingly in a long black coat and riding clothes. A servant comes with drinks and little cakes, and Si Tan begs his visitors to sit. His tone is gracious, as always, but his eyes are like flint. He is an intimidating figure, but Lord Skaal does not appear to be intimidated in the slightest.

Once the servant is gone, Si Tan breaks the brief silence: "Lord Skaal, I am pleased to meet you. I have heard some interesting things about you. They say you are Agoston Horthy's most prized official and that you have almost single-handedly eliminated magic from Frayne. Which seems surprising, given the rumors I have heard of your own background."

"People love to invent stories, and I'm sure my exploits have been exaggerated," says Lord Skaal coolly.

"Your prime minister is lucky to have you," says Si Tan.

"It is I who am lucky to serve under him," Lord Skaal returns. "Please, thank Gangzi for agreeing to speak with me. I am most grateful to have you here as a translator, Lord Grand Librarian. I'm afraid I speak no Yongwen at all."

Si Tan smiles thinly. "If you mean to take up this matter of visiting the monastery, I am afraid you will have no more luck than your predecessors in persuading Gangzi to go against his honor."

"Indeed, you have refused all that the good ambassador here has offered you thus far in exchange for the girl pretending to be the traitor Roparzh's daughter," says Lord Skaal. "I wonder if there is any inducement we *can* offer."

He doesn't pose it as a question, but he pauses. Si Tan murmurs to Gangzi in Yongwen, and Gangzi, in a cracked, angry voice, responds at length. Si Tan seems to do some editing in his translation, which is briefer:

"There is nothing, no threat or reward, that your tiny kingdom can realistically offer to tempt or compel Gangzi. He is not interested in anything more you have to say. However, I would be glad to give you a tour of the Imperial Gardens."

"I do hope you appreciate the fact that we haven't just gone and snatched her," says Lord Skaal.

Si Tan raises his eyebrows. "If you made an assault on the monastery, Lord Skaal, Yongguo would crush Frayne utterly in swift and justified vengeance."

The ambassador's jaw drops. He would be a terrible poker player. But Lord Skaal is unfazed.

"To be sure. As a matter of fact, I didn't come here only to plead for entry to the monastery. I have some news, as well. Agoston Horthy wanted me to inform you in person that Lady Laroche has been captured, charged with witchcraft and treason, found guilty, and sentenced to death."

Lady Laroche. Count Fournier called her his aunt, said she was the head of the Sidhar Coven in Frayne. No wonder he hasn't heard from her in a while. I'm not going to enjoy delivering that news to him.

Si Tan doesn't miss a beat. "The penalty in Frayne for treason is hanging, and the penalty for witchcraft is drowning. Which did you choose? Or did you attempt both?"

"The prime minister's intent, after getting whatever information from her he could, was to behead her first, before casting her body into the river Syne, so that the head could be sent to you as proof. I understand your reluctance to break your agreement with such a lady, but now that the lady herself has expired, surely we can come to our own agreement."

Si Tan translates this to Gangzi, who rises and does a fair bit of shouting and spitting and finger waving before hunching back into his seat.

"He doesn't seem happy," remarks Lord Skaal. "Was he fond of the lady?"

"He is expressing disgust at your barbarism," says Si Tan. "You are such backward fools, he says, with your heads in the sand, imagining you can eradicate something as elemental

292

as magic. Might as well try to fight the air we breathe, et cetera, et cetera."

"Perhaps he is right," says Lord Skaal. "Nevertheless, the lady is dead by now, as are most of her associates. There is no reason for you to keep hanging on to the girl. What use is she to you?"

Si Tan translates. Gangzi creases his face and mutters something in reply.

"Gangzi does not intend to do anything for you because he does not like you," says Si Tan. "Shou-shu is peaceful and independent. The monks have no quarrel with outsiders, and outsiders have always given them the respect due to them. The monastery stood unguarded for centuries because it had no need of guards. If you desecrate that place by breaching its walls without Gangzi's permission, I have promised him that Yongguo will destroy Frayne. Shou-shu is a jewel in our country, and it is under our protection. Any defilement of the monastery will mean the annihilation of your little kingdom."

"Frayne is rather a distance," remarks Lord Skaal. "An awful lot of mountains to cross in one direction, and an awful lot of ocean in the other. Can't think it would be worth your while invading us for a girl that means nothing to you."

"I say nothing of a girl. I am talking about respect," says Si Tan. While his voice remains calm and polite, it seems to me that his entire body thrums with violence. "You have no knowledge of magic, only your fear of it. You have no idea what our empire can do."

The ambassador has gone quite white. He bursts in: "No need to talk of war, my friends! We have come here openly and honestly. There will be no desecration of the monastery."

"No, of course not," says Lord Skaal smoothly. "I just thought the threat of invasion rather out of proportion."

Si Tan says nothing, and I'm thinking that our snatching the princess might have repercussions we hadn't imagined, since surely the Fraynish delegation will be blamed for it.

"Well then, it appears we have gotten nowhere," says Lord Skaal. "If I can persuade this fellow to like me, might he give me the girl? Is that really what all this hinges on? Shall I buy him a drink or let him beat me at cards? What do monks like to do, anyway?"

"I do not think he can be persuaded to like you," says Si Tan, smiling slightly.

"Pity. In spite of all my charm. It causes me to doubt myself." Lord Skaal rises, and the ambassador scrambles to his feet as well. They both bow to their hosts. Si Tan stands up, taller than both of them, and bows in return, but Gangzi just turns his head aside, staring through me, his face crinkled with contempt.

"If you wish to extend your stay in Yongguo, come and see me again," says Si Tan to Lord Skaal meaningfully. "I could find you a position here, if you wanted one."

The ambassador gapes again, but Lord Skaal only says, "That is very kind of you, but I am happy with my current position."

I follow closely as the two men are escorted to the gate by

the Ru. The ambassador's entourage is waiting outside with a small battalion of motor cabs.

"The prime minister will not be pleased. What are we going to do?" says the ambassador in a low voice.

Lord Skaal shrugs. "Lady Laroche is dead. The girl is no use to them; they're just being disagreeable. They'll turn her out eventually, and we'll be on hand when they do. The main thing is that we know where she is and that we find out who is supporting her here. Clear *them* out of the way and the girl will be hung out to dry. Cheaper than the alternatives, honestly. Don't worry, my good fellow."

"Well, you seem to have it in hand," says the ambassador uncertainly.

Lord Skaal laughs—the same pleasant laugh I remember.

"I'd like to think so," he says. "But nothing ever goes as one expects. Especially when dealing with people like these. We will speak again later. I have some other business I need to attend to in the city. I'll go on foot."

"Alone?" asks the ambassador, shocked.

"Yes."

"We'll dine at six?"

"I look forward to it."

Lord Skaal shakes the ambassador's hand and sets off into the city with me at his heels. I am still so preoccupied with the fear of what our kidnapping of the princess might mean for Frayne that I don't notice where we are going until we are right at the door of the Hundred Lantern Hotel.

# THIRTY-EIGHT

The girl behind the counter is rubbing her eyes with the heels of her palms. Lord Skaal approaches and drops a string of heavy coins on the counter, startling her. She gives him a wary look.

"Looking for a foreign woman," he says in Fraynish. He makes circles with his fingers, holding them up to his face like goggles and mimicking a whirring sound. "You know who I mean. Which room?"

She shakes her head. He drops another string of coins in front of her, then draws back his coat to show her the pistol at his hip. "Go on," he says. "It only gets worse from here."

She looks at the coins for a half second, then sweeps them off the counter into the pocket of her apron. She makes for the stairs, beckoning him to follow. Suddenly I have the feeling that we are being watched. I turn around, scanning the dining hall, but I see nobody, and Lord Skaal and the girl are already halfway up the stairs, so I run after them. In the hallway, the girl is pointing to a door. Lord Skaal mimes un-locking it, but she shakes her head vigorously and he shoos her away. My heart is in my throat as he knocks. No answer. He sniffs at the door, gives an impatient sigh, then backs up and kicks it down.

"Sorry, were you sleeping?" he calls out, backing away from the door. He knows quite well who is behind it and what she is capable of. Still no reply. He approaches the bro-ken door cautiously.

"I came to say hello, since we both happen to be here in Tianshi. Thought I could buy you a drink."

He inches into the room, and I go after him.

"Ah. There you are."

She is standing by the window, her curved knife in her hand. I find myself fixating on it, unable to look away from the bright blade. Hello, Pia's knife edge, old friend.

"You broke my door down because you want to buy me a drink?" she asks dryly.

"Sorry—bit extreme, perhaps. Only I'm short on time and you weren't opening up. Shall we call a truce and go down to the bar?"

"No," says Pia. "Tell me why I should not kill you."

"Because my mother would weep for me," he says lightly. "Come, there is no reason for either of us to be killing the other. Though I'd feel better if you'd put that knife away."

She sheathes the knife and says, "I don't need a knife to kill you."

"I'm sure you don't," he says. "But I really did come here to chat. After all, we're very nearly allies, aren't we? The prime minister thinks of Lord Casimir almost as a brother."

"A brother?" Her lip curls.

"A mentor, perhaps," says Lord Skaal.

"A benefactor," suggests Pia. "And too fearful an enemy to risk provoking."

"Well, that describes my relationship to my own brother quite well," says Lord Skaal. "You see, it is as I said."

"Why are you in Tianshi?" she asks.

"Do we have to do this standing across the room from each other? Can we at least sit down?"

But there is nowhere to sit. The room is bare except for a bed that looks as if it has never been slept in and a nightstand.

"No," says Pia.

"Very well, we'll be uncomfortable if that is what you prefer. You know, I've been curious to meet you for a long time." He looks around, looks at *me* with that one yellow eye, as if perturbed. For a moment my heart stalls, but no, he is only looking through me.

"Why are you in Tianshi?" she asks again.

"For Princess Zara, or whoever she is," he says. "You know Lady Laroche?"

"I know the lady," says Pia, all ice.

He looks in my direction again and says, "Somebody else is here."

Horror threads its way up my spine. Pia's goggles whir. He steps toward me, and I pull back farther, far enough that I can barely make out his features and he is just a blurred silhouette, my fingers and toes tingling, that nothing-nowhere right at my back, ready for me to fall into it.

I hear his voice only faintly, as if from very far away: "It is gone. Almost."

And Pia's voice: "There is nobody here. Why are you asking me about Lady Laroche?"

"She cut a deal with the Shou-shu monks a few years back and they took in Prince Roparzh's daughter, or someone pretending to be his daughter. The ambassador tried to get her handed over as soon as he learned of it, but there was no budging Gangzi. We set about cutting off the princess's organization at the roots, drowning the witches who made the deal and supported her. Capturing Lady Laroche was the final blow to the girl's support system, and once it was done, I was sent here to try again to get hold of the girl and identify her."

I feel faint, so far back from the world. I ease a little closer so that I can feel my fingers and toes again. Their voices come clearer, though I still cannot make out the expressions on their faces.

"You captured Lady Laroche?" asks Pia.

"Personally," says Lord Skaal with a bow. "I hope she was not a friend."

"No," says Pia. There is something odd in her voice. "She was not that. Is she dead?"

"Yes."

"I do not believe it."

"I assure you, it was quite the operation, and Agoston

Horthy's greatest triumph since he crushed the Lorian Uprising. What remains of the Sidhar Coven topples with her."

Pia is quiet.

"Anyway, that's what *I* am doing in Tianshi. Casimir supports Agoston Horthy's efforts to get rid of this girl, particularly now that King Zey is so ill, but I doubt his interest in the matter is strong enough to send *you*, and I received no word. So what *are* you doing here?"

"I am here for something else," she says.

"Yes, that's what I was just implying," he says, sardonic. "Is *Casimir* in Tianshi?"

"No."

"His sister? Mrs. Och?"

Pia's goggles whir.

"I am only curious. My orders concern the princess, that's all." He looks toward me, through me, again. "There it is again. This scent has been with me since I met with the grand librarian. I assumed—"

"There is nobody here," says Pia again.

He gives a sniff. "Somebody *is* here," he murmurs very softly, like a threatening purr. He can't see me, I tell myself. He can't see me.

"I am tired of this game," says Pia sharply. "It is time for you to leave."

He is uneasy now. "I have a very keen sense of smell, you know. I trust it over my eyesight. There *is* somebody else in this room with us."

"This is my room. It is not your concern."

"Then you know who it is?"

She pauses and then says, "Yes."

I am torn between panicking and laughing. So they both know I'm here, but neither of them can actually *see* me.

"You've been having me followed?" he asks, and when she doesn't reply, he says, "Well, that seems unfriendly, but I'll let it slide. Are you here because of that same old matter with the little boy? That has been bothering me a long time."

"Why should it bother you?"

"I saw him once, you know. Obtained some samples—blood, tissue, hair. His pretty witch mother did not like me much. What *is* he?"

"I don't know."

"Really? You don't know?"

"Nor do I care."

"Would you be interested to know what I found out about him when I ran my tests?"

"No."

"What an incurious creature you are!" He glances toward me again. Since they know I am here anyway, I have allowed myself to draw a little closer. "You and I both know that there are a great many variations on the human. Some of us are born a little different, or become so later on. This boy, however—he is woven through and through with something potent, something incomprehensible. He is not touched by magic, he is *made of* magic, as far as I could tell. And the Xianren covet him. What could he be? How can you not wonder?"

"I am done with all manner of wondering."

"But you *are* here for him?"

Silence.

"I'm not going to try to find him myself," Lord Skaal assures her. "I haven't the manpower here, and those are not my instructions. To be honest, I have wondered about you quite as often as I've wondered about him. I hoped we might find we had things to talk about."

"I am done talking to you."

He nods, looking almost relieved. "It's lonely being different, don't you find? Sometimes I think I want to talk with somebody else who is . . . well, also *different*. But the trouble with people who are *different* in the manner that you and I are different is that they are so often such flaming arseholes. Well, if you change your mind, you can find me at the ambassador's house. I'll be staying there awhile. My apologies for the door."

He looks in my direction as he goes out and bares his teeth at me. Even though I know he can't see me, I flinch. I stay in the corner of the room, watching Pia, waiting to see what she will do next. She looks out the window for a few minutes, perhaps watching Lord Skaal depart on the street below, and then she says, almost gently: "Julia. Show yourself."

*Run*, I tell myself. *Go home, you stupid girl. Too risky.* But a dangerous mix of curiosity, fear, and longing is pulling at me, outweighing all my reason and better judgment. I step back into the world, and Pia's face comes into focus.

# THIRTY-NINE

"You've cut your hair," she says, looking me over. Back in the world, closer to her, I feel the broken-ice pitch of her voice grating against my eardrums.

"It was getting in the way."

"You have been following Lord Skaal?"

"Yes." No point lying—she knows I have been.

"Then Mrs. Och is here for the princess too. I suppose that is not surprising. What do you make of him? Keen sense of smell!" She starts to laugh. It is not a pleasant sound. "I am glad you have come, Julia, even if only because you were led here. It was not kind of you to run away after I rescued you from Si Tan. I have been thinking of how to draw you out, and none of the ideas I had were pleasant. But I need to speak to you. It is not about the boy."

"All right. Here I am. What is it about?"

"I am instructed to tell you that Casimir's offer of employment stands. Should you become disillusioned with your

Mrs. Och—or should you decide you want more gold and more freedom than she can give you—well, in that case, it appears that you know where to find me."

"I'd have thought it was clear by now what I think of Casimir and his offer."

Pia grins, wolflike. "I told him you would say as much. But why, then, have you yoked yourself to Mrs. Och?"

"If you can't see the difference between Mrs. Och and Casimir, then we're not alike at all," I tell her, and instantly regret it.

"You are deluded if you think the difference between your master and mine is such a great one," she says. "And you are a fool to imagine that the outcome of their conflict really matters for the likes of us. I am Casimir's creature, as you are Mrs. Och's. We are very alike indeed."

"I'm not her creature."

"Then what are you?"

"I'm just . . . me." As if that answers anything at all. And anyway, maybe I'm not.

"I am to ask you what you want. Casimir is willing to give you whatever you ask if you will accept his contract."

"Safety for Theo," I say immediately, without really thinking about what I'll do if she agrees.

"Except that," she says. "But anything else. Anything you desire."

"No."

She tilts her head at me, the goggles whirring in and out again.

"You fight so hard for this boy, sacrifice so much. But what is he to you, after all?"

I just shake my head. There's no explaining love to Pia.

"And when I find him? You will weep, I assume, and then you will carry on with your life. Or will you be bent on revenge? Will you come looking for me?"

"You won't find him. But if you did, I'd come looking for you."

A vivid image of Haizea and her whirlwind rises up in my mind: her bleeding eyes, her fist clenching the storm.

"Then we are sure to meet again," she says. "Even once this business with the boy is ended, however it ends, Casimir will not give up on you. He longs to understand and harness this power of yours."

I feel a chill closing around my heart. "Casimir's contract—it's not a piece of paper, is it?"

She grins, but there is no joy or even humor in her expression.

"Can I see it?" I ask.

She pulls off her leather glove, and I walk over to her at the window. She turns the inside of her wrist to me, and I see the silvery disk, which I know to be scalding hot, nested in folds of shiny scar flesh. My stomach curls.

"How does it work?"

"It is a living contract. The surest way to allow it to take hold is to insert it at the wrist—a minor operation—and allow it some days to grow toward the brain. It is less likely to kill you if introduced in this way. It can also be inserted via the ear, which is faster but much riskier—it results in death about half the time, and even if the person survives, it leaves them deaf in one ear and a little mad. Once it enters your brain, your will is bound to his, inextricably. I could not disobey him even if I wished to."

"That's what you put in Cinzai's ear," I say, remembering the witch flailing and screaming, the thing that crawled into her ear. "That's why Si Tan killed her."

"In a matter of minutes she would either have belonged to Casimir or she would have been dead," says Pia. "In her case, the gamble was worth it, the loss nothing to him. But Casimir wants *you* undamaged, as much as possible."

"Does it hurt?"

"Not anymore."

"Why would you let him do that to you?"

Her face is so white, her lips a thin line, those goggles masking any expression I might have been able to read if she'd had eyes.

"I was broken," she says—her voice suddenly losing that shattering, high edge. "He said that he could piece me back together. Make me whole. Oh, there was gold too, plenty of gold. What difference did it make to me? Every servitude looked alike, and this one came with more money."

"Did he make you whole?" I can't stop myself from asking.

"If you are broken the way I was broken, there is no way to be whole again."

"Broken how?"

We are standing so close together, heads bent toward each

other, and she answers me as if we were friends, as if we trusted one another.

"Casimir destroyed me bodily and put me back together, but before that . . . you heard Lord Skaal speak of Lady Laroche and the Sidhar Coven? I belonged to them for a time, and they broke my body and my spirit in a thousand ways, but I came to them broken, as well. When did it begin?" The goggles whir—out, in. "There was a man, a long time ago. My first memories are of being frightened of him." Then she shrugs. "But there is always a man; there is always a dark corner and people who pretend not to see. That is a common story. It seemed at the time that I was broken already, born broken, and that my brokenness summoned him to me, thick-fingered and stinking, out of the dark. It was all so long ago, and I have no memory further back, no memory of being whole."

I feel sick. I hear myself saying, "I'm sorry. . . ."

The goggles give a sharp whir, and she snaps her chin up. "But why?"

I don't know how to answer that. She studies my face. I can't imagine what she sees there.

"My mother was part of the Sidhar Coven," I say.

"Yes. Did Casimir not tell you?"

"Tell me what?"

"Before they sent Ammi, your mother, to bind him in stone and bury him in the sea, I was sent to kill him. I was the coven's pet assassin, their little attack dog. I did not succeed, of course. He smashed me to pieces. He shattered my bones. He put out my eyes. He did all manner of things to me, and still I did not die, I did not die. Casimir is not one for a quick kill. He likes to see what he's dealing with. Pain and fear, in their most extreme forms, reveal so much. He saw I was a resilient sort of dog, and that I had no will of my own. How convenient, how ideal! And so he did not kill me. He repaired me, more or less. What you see"—she spreads her hands—"is the work of his mechanic. His greatest work, so he says. He had me put back together, he offered gold, and he put his contract into me. I submitted to all of this. I could not go back to the coven, for they had made it clear what the result of failure would be."

I want to ask, but I can't. She answers anyway.

"I did not know Ammi. I knew *of* her, of course. But she moved in higher circles than I did."

"But you're not a witch," I say.

"No—and so I was never part of the coven. Only their dog, as I say."

"You didn't have family?"

"None that cared to be so. I was a stray dog for some time, and that is a hard life. I was glad of a leash. I didn't mind being beaten if it meant I had a hearth to curl up on. They were cruel to me, the witches who took charge of me. Casimir destroyed me, yes, but once I submitted to him, he was a good master. Plenty of gold—not that I care so much for gold, but I enjoy a comfortable bed, a fine meal. More than gold, he gave me honesty, and he was the first to do so. Casimir does not pretend to be other than what he is, nor does he pretend I am other than what I am. There is something to be said for that. It is more than you receive from your Mrs. Och, I think."

My mouth is dry. "What do you mean?"

"I mean that you are her dog," she says, "but neither of you will call it what it is."

"I'm not her dog, and she'd be a fool to think me so," I say.

"You are so young—it would break my heart, if there were anything left to break. You do not understand what is happening. You think it is about a little boy. It is not about the little boy. It is about power. The world is terrible, has always been terrible, and the striving and seeking and suffering of powerless mortals is a great waste of effort. I do as I am told and that is all. Casimir never needed to put his contract in me. I would be his, regardless. Do you understand what I am telling you?"

"No! I really *don't* understand what you're on about. Why don't you tell it to me straight?"

"I am trying to explain." She sounds more agitated than I have ever heard her. "If I cannot make you understand, then there will come a time, soon, when I must hurt you or kill you. I do not wish it, but I will do it."

"I'm leaving," I say, backing away from her.

"Wait! Please wait." She puts up a hand, entreating. "Let me explain something you cannot fail to understand. The strong think that they cannot be broken. I've seen it a thousand times—that unfounded confidence before the fact. The truth of the matter is that everyone can be broken.

Everyone. Any person who has known real pain knows this to be true. I can take you to a place, Julia, where you will no longer care what becomes of that boy, or anything, or anyone. A place where all that matters to you is that the pain should stop. There is a place even beyond that where you would worship me as the god who brings you pain or relief from pain. It is a very nasty and time-consuming business, but I have done it before, and if I must, I will do it again. I wanted to speak to you first, to tell you of my own life, my own history, because I hope it will not be necessary for you to endure what I did or become what I have become."

"You can't lay a hand on me," I say. "You know it." But my voice quavers a little. I feel the emptiness at my back; I am ready to fall into it, to leap out of the world and away from her whirring goggles, her dead white face.

She goes over to the nightstand by her bed. From the drawer she takes the ribbons Cinzai, Si Tan's witch, bound me in.

"You are not invulnerable," she says. "I have seen you rendered helpless, tied to the world by that poor brute's magic—and Casimir employs a far more powerful witch than her. Think on it, Julia. I would rather we find another way to bring you to Casimir's side."

Panic comes in a great wave. Stupidly, blindly, I reach for the knife in my boot. She moves faster than I can think. Something strikes my chin—her foot, perhaps—and I am scrabbling on the floor, stunned. Then the sound of glass shattering, the thunk of something landing on the floor, a figure running toward me, and a bolt of white flame in the middle of the room, shooting up to the ceiling. Pia snarls, raising one arm to shield her goggles from the glare. I see him first, Jun, right next to me, aiming his pistol. Pia is moving toward us, knife in her hand now. He fires the gun, but she doesn't stop. I grab him as her knife flashes toward him, and in my terror, I pull him straight through that invisible space—through and through and through to the other side, to the gray street, whirling with ash, and the burning air.

# FORTY

The street shimmers. There is a man walking toward us. Not a man—it is the top hat that makes me think so, but he is transparent, I can see the street right through him, through the fixed grin on his skeletal face. A girl creeps up behind him, reaches deftly into his pocket, and pulls out a snake. She looks at us and winks, and I hear a horrible noise in my throat because it is *me* as a little girl, but with pooling black eyes and a chalk-white face. No—something shifts, and it is little Pia with goggles for eyes. My own scream startles me—not a human sound. Jun is struggling against me. My hooked hands grip his shoulders, holding him fast.

I hear hoofbeats. Or perhaps it is just my heart beating. The street has gone whirling away from us. I am running with him, and I am so much stronger than he is here—he seems to weigh nothing—and then we are outside the little flat I grew up in, the laundry shop at street level. I've run home. In the doorway stands the antlered, fox-faced creature I saw before. He has a curved blade in his mottled, half-decayed human hand, a blade with a jagged, strangely glittering edge. His teeth are bared in a stiff snarl.

"Lidari," he says.

"Who are you?" I cry in a not-mine voice.

There are more of them in the street now. A crocodile head is snapping atop the rangy, rotting body of a lion, ribs showing through the torn flesh. Some apelike thing with a starved panther face is loping toward us. Another one looks human but *dead*, with the bright yellow eyes of some other creature rolling about in its head. They are closing in on me, holding long, narrow stalks with hooks at the end. Everything feels horribly slowed down. Fox Face's blade comes swinging toward me. I move, but not fast enough. The blade catches me on the arm, though for the moment I feel nothing but heat where it strikes me. My legs buckle and I fall down on the street, Jun shouting something, the gun going off, cries of triumph from this mob of patched-together beasts. The blade goes up again, up into the burning sky. I am fixed on it. It comes down. I grab Jun and pull back hard, right through the street. I hear something like rushing water, the long, anguished hiss, *"Lidariiii."* We are above Pia's room, broken glass all over the floor, Pia crouched, knife in hand, listening for us. There is shouting from the hall.

I aim for the window, trying to catch sight of the road below. We end up on the opposite rooftop, jarred back into ourselves and the world. The sun is low in the sky, and there is hardly anyone in the road. I can still see Pia through her broken window.

A click. Jun has pressed the muzzle of his pistol to my head. He speaks through clenched teeth.

"What. Are. You?"

I swallow. My throat feels burnt dry from the terrible air of that place. I gulp in a breath of Tianshi's fragrant springtime air, with its hint of warmth and honey.

"I'm sorry," I manage to get out.

He slides down the other side of the roof and drops into the alley behind. I follow. He backs away from me, pistol pointed at my chest, his face closed and tight and pale.

"You are monster," he says, and his voice shakes.

"I didn't mean to," I say. I feel so weak, like I can barely stand up. "Jun, please. When we were there . . . what did I look like?"

"Like *monster!*" He screams this last word at me and gives the pistol a threatening jerk, breathing hard.

I put a finger to my lips. Pia is only one street over, may be out looking for us now.

"Stop pointing that thing at me," I say, trying to sound reasonable and halfway calm. "We need to get out of here."

"Stay away or I shoot," he says. The gun is shaking in his hands.

"Please lower that thing," I beg him. "She would have killed you. I was trying to save us, and I . . . I didn't mean to go there. I'm scared to death myself. I'm sorry."

"Go where? What is that place?"

I say, "I don't know," because I can't tell him, not when

314

he is looking at me that way, scared out of his wits already. Saying *Kahge* isn't going to calm him down. I'm terrified he's going to put a hole in me just from nerves.

"Please . . ." I don't know what to say to him. "Look, *you* followed *me*."

But then I realize he couldn't have. He must have been following Lord Skaal.

"Stay away," he says, backing down the alley. Then he ducks around a corner and is gone. My arm gives a dull throb, and that's when I notice I'm standing in a puddle of my own blood. My knees give out under me.

Later it feels like a dream: I can't say for sure that any of it happened, nor can I think of an alternate theory for how I got home. Lying there bleeding in the road. Her boots beside me. She crouches next to me, and if I didn't know her better, I would say her voice sounds sad.

"This is not the day for you to die, Julia."

Lying in her bed as she binds my arm. Her face looms over me, taking up my whole view of the world. Those awful goggles.

"If you could tell me where you live, I'd take you home," she says. A brittle laugh. "Here, this will give you strength. Think of what I said and come back to me tomorrow, or I will have to find you. One more chance. I want you to choose. I want to give you that much."

Her fingers in my mouth, a bitter pill dissolving on my tongue. Then everything is sharp and clear. I am running, the evening air cooling around me, my heart hammering with something like joy. I could run forever. Blood rushes and pulses in my arm, the bandage soaked through in no time, but there is no pain, no feeling at all except for the speed of my limbs, almost like flying, because I barely feel my feet hitting the ground. The wind is roaring in my ears—or maybe the roaring is inside my head, I can't tell. I vanish when I reach Nanmu, as is my habit, and something tugs at my arm, hard. Blood flows out into the air, flows straight out and away, out of the world.

I vault over the courtyard wall, everything coming into terrible focus, the hard planes and edges of the world, Frederick's voice banging about inside my skull: "What's happened? Are you all right?" And I am on the ground—how did I get on the ground? I feel as if my heart is going to explode from my chest. They are all in a knot around me, and I hear Princess Zara saying, "Give her space," Esme saying, "Her arm—she's hurt."

Bianka lifts me in her arms. We are indoors, the ceiling swinging over me, the floor buckling under me. She holds me and tells me, "It's all right, it's going to be all right."

"I need to clean and stitch this *now*," says Esme.

Something wet and burning on my arm. I let out a strangled yell. It sounds like a dog barking; the world narrows down to Frederick's anxious face peering over Bianka's shoulder, Bianka holding me fast, and then Esme's needle biting my arm again and again.

# FORTY-ONE

Professor Baranyi holds a little vial under my nose. It burns my nostrils, burns my mind clear. Mrs. Och's room settles around me with a jolt, my heart thudding back to sudden slowness. Mrs. Och is at her desk, hands folded before her, and I am seated opposite her.

"Better?" asks the professor, corking the vial.

I nod and finger the bandage on my throbbing arm. I'm relieved to see Frederick is here too. They won't do anything to me with him here. But then I wonder why I think they might do anything to me.

"What happened?" asks Mrs. Och.

"May I have some water?"

I'm only partly stalling, trying to remember what happened and what I can tell her. My mouth is dry as dust. She nods at Frederick, and he goes out.

"I went to the Imperial Gardens, like you said," I tell her, my mind groping back through the day.

"Did Si Tan mention us to Lord Skaal?"

"No," I say. "But he threatened to invade Frayne if they tried to make off with the princess, and surely he'll think it *was* them."

Frederick comes back in with a cup of water, which I drink gratefully. Mrs. Och waves my concern aside. "I will tell him tomorrow that it was me," she says. "Once the princess is out of the city."

"They said Lady Laroche is dead," I add, remembering how casually Lord Skaal talked of sending Si Tan her head. The leader of the Sidhar Coven. She must have known my mother.

"Lady Laroche?" cries Professor Baranyi. "That is a blow indeed, if we hope for a revolution."

"Perhaps not," says Mrs. Och. "Go on, Julia. How were you injured?"

"The meeting didn't go very well, and then Lord Skaal headed off into the city, so I followed him, and he went to the Hundred Lantern Hotel. He wanted to talk to Pia."

This is where it all gets difficult to explain, but I tell her as much of their conversation as I remember, and how he seemed able to smell me, which makes her chuckle for some reason. Not particularly funny from my perspective. Her face reveals nothing when I tell her about Pia's offer and her threats, how she said Casimir would give me *anything,* and how Jun appeared, crashing through the window. If he was following Lord Skaal, watching through the window, I can only imagine his surprise at suddenly seeing *me* in the room with Pia. But he broke his cover to try and help me, and what must he think now? I think of his face when he screamed *Monster!* at me in the alley, and my stomach curls with misery. I refrain from mentioning Pia's remarks about Mrs. Och: *You are her dog, but neither of you will call it what it is.*

"Pia cut your arm?" suggests Professor Baranyi when I stop.

"No," I say.

Now the hard part. I stare at my hands in my lap—my ordinary hands—and I tell them about what happened after: Kahge, the nightmare quality of it, my home and my childhood distorted and horrifying, those revolting creatures, the bright blade cutting my arm.

I look up at her. There is no point hiding it—Frederick has already told her—so I say, "When those creatures in Kahge shout at me, I think they are calling *me* Lidari. Why?"

Professor Baranyi gives her an anxious look, but she keeps her gaze trained on me, unmoving and revealing nothing.

"Lidari was Marike's associate," says Mrs. Och. "I never met him, of course. Marike was the first ruler to defy the Xianren. We suffered our first true defeat at her hands. Casimir claimed to have had Lidari killed . . . oh, a thousand years ago or more. Why the creatures in Kahge call *you* Lidari, I cannot fathom." Suddenly she laughs—an odd and humorless sound. "Are you sure of your parentage, Julia?"

My heart goes cold and heavy at that. Well, I asked, and now I may be getting the answer I dread more than anything—the half thought that sits at the back of my mind like a grinning goblin, taunting me: *You are not what you think you are.*

"What do you mean?" My voice shakes, and I hate myself for it.

"Only that your mother, being a witch, might have sought some connection with Kahge," says Mrs. Och. "The fact that she was able to bind Casimir—she must have had some very great magic to assist her, and you were born shortly after that. Could your birth be the result of some deal made with the half beings of Kahge?"

She is halfway there herself, without knowing the memory or vision I had of my mother with the Ankh-nu. And how casually she suggests my deepest buried fear, that I may not be of this world, not human at all, not *myself.* I begin to shake. No, no, I am Julia, I have always been Julia, this is a mistake, they are all mistaken. Frederick comes to my side quickly, putting his hands on my shoulders.

"I look like my mother," I whisper. "I look like *Dek.*"

"Oh, indeed," says Mrs. Och, watching me very carefully. "I did not mean to upset you." She smiles a strange, false smile. "Julia, I want you to work for me."

"I do work for you," I say.

"You work for me now because of Theo. But soon I will return to Frayne. There may be a revolution, and if there is not, there will still be the work of trying to get witches out

320

of the country and protect those that remain. You would be a tremendous asset, and you would be well compensated. It is dangerous work, of course, but it is important, and I would be glad to have you working alongside the professor and Frederick and myself. I would also help you to untangle this mystery of your unusual gift. It would serve us all well to understand why you can go to Kahge."

Frederick lets go of my shoulders, as if he's just noticed how tightly he was hanging on to me.

For a moment I am speechless. Is it that easy? Can I join Mrs. Och's inner circle, working to destroy Agoston Horthy and save women like my mother? Isn't that a dream come true—to put my skills and strengths to work, not for theft and blackmail but for helping those who need it, righting the wrongs that have shaped my own life? Surely it beats mopping floors for a pittance. It seems like the answer to all my uncertainties and fears about the future. And to have her help me find out why I can vanish as I do—when surely she is the only one who *can* help me— should be irresistible. Still, the idea of working for Mrs. Och does not sit right with me. Pia has planted her poison in my ear.

And Dek doesn't want to go back.

I lick my lips and say, "Thank you," because what else am I to say? And what does Pia know about Mrs. Och *or* me?

"Good," says Mrs. Och. "Tonight some of our party will take the princess out of the city. They will wait two days for the rest of us to join them at a farm a half day's journey from here. I will meet with Si Tan in the morning and hope we can come to some agreement regarding Ko Dan. If we cannot—well, I fear we shouldn't stay in this city much longer."

I look at my hands again, my dirty fingernails—or is that blood? They are trembling, and I ball them into fists to make them still.

"Perhaps we should let Julia rest a bit," says Frederick gently.

"Indeed," says Mrs. Och. "But, Julia, next time you must consult me before you do something reckless like visit Pia. I can only captain this ship through the storm if all members of my crew keep to their posts."

"I didn't exactly mean to *visit* her."

"How is your arm?" she asks.

"It hurts, but I reckon I'll be all right. Esme knows how to patch a body up."

"She is quite formidable, your Esme," says Mrs. Och. "We will speak again in the morning."

Frederick and I go out. He looks like he wants to say something to me, but Theo catapults into me as soon as we emerge from Mrs. Och's room. I twist sideways, trying to protect my hurt arm, and a hush falls over the table. The main door is open to the cool evening air, cicadas screeching in the trees outside the courtyard.

"Come," says Esme, breaking the silence and pulling out a chair for me. "Eat something."

I sit down in the chair she offers, across from Princess Zara, and they all watch me carefully, their faces yellowish in the candlelight. The plates are cluttered among the dripping candles—strips of mottled beef, black mushrooms, bowls of steaming rice, stewed duck, figs, persimmons, and bamboo tips. I am too tired to be hungry, but I let Csilla fill my plate anyway.

"I hope you weren't injured on my account," says the princess.

Of course—I turned up raving and bleeding and generally behaving like a lunatic. No doubt they'd like to know why. I give them a much-altered abbreviated version of what I've just told Mrs. Och, leaving out Kahge and blaming my injury on Pia. Frederick, sitting down at the other end of the table and filling his own plate, doesn't correct me or even look at me.

"I'm grieved to hear of Lady Laroche's passing," says Princess Zara. "I owe her a great deal."

She doesn't look particularly grieved, but I suppose it's a lot to take in all at once.

Theo makes a circuit of the table, crawling onto laps and eating everyone's bamboo tips, all of us keeping a nervous eye on his every gesture lest he start drawing. Soon the conversation picks up again. Gregor, Esme, Csilla, the professor, and Princess Zara are leaving tonight, via a smugglers' tunnel that will take them to the other side of the city wall. It is not part of the regular tunnel circuit—which is flooded anyway—and I am given to understand that the use of it has cost Mrs. Och dearly. They will wait two days at a farm we used on our way to Tianshi and then carry on to Frayne without us if we have not joined them by then. Now they are discussing an alternate route that would avoid the Kastahor Mountains—hiding on a cargo train to the southern border and then passing through the kingdom of Xanuha to the Parnese states.

"We didn't come that way because we understood the Xanuha warriors to be ruthless about their territory, and it is a mountainous region also," says the professor.

"But nothing like the Kastahor Mountains," says the princess. "I have ties to that kingdom, I stayed with them for some months when I was younger. I'm sure the queen of Xanuha will grant us safe passage and guides. I am amazed that you survived the journey through the Kastahor Mountains."

"Barely," says Esme. "I would prefer to take almost any route but that one."

"I would still rather brave a sea voyage," says Csilla.

"No," says the princess. "Not unless we can find a *very* well-armed vessel. The pirates off the coast here rule the seas, and about half of them are in Casimir's pay."

"How did you know to trust me?" I interrupt.

They all go quiet and stare at me again.

"I have a sense of such things," says the princess, with an easy smile.

"What kind of sense?"

She folds her napkin, suddenly brisk, and says, "It is a

small gift compared to your own. But I can sense the intentions and emotions of everyone nearby. I can tell if they mean me well or ill, if they are at ease or afraid, lying to me or telling the truth. These things are as clear to me as the color of a person's eyes to you."

"Stars," says Csilla. "That must be useful."

"It has kept me safe a great many times," the princess acknowledges. "There is a wealth of goodwill and noble intent here. I am grateful to have such friends."

"Do you *want* to be queen?" I blurt. Perhaps it's a stupid question, but she is not much older than me and has spent her entire life running around the world hiding from people who want to kill her. I wouldn't wonder if she just wanted to go live a peaceful, quiet life somewhere, if that were possible. Be free.

"It isn't a matter of wanting," she replies. "Although I have never wanted anything else. My family was executed unjustly. My father was murdered by his own brother, and that man still occupies the throne and allows his prime minister to devastate Frayne through his fanatical vendetta against magic and folklore and the traditions of our people. I believe in the Nameless One, but I believe in the spirits too, and I know magic can be a force of good as well as a force of evil. I believe I have the power and the purpose to change Frayne for the better, to lead New Poria toward a more tolerant age. I believe it is my destiny."

She says all of this calmly and evenly. Only upon the word *murdered* does an edge come to her voice. We are all quiet, and into the silence, the bells of Shou-shu chime the closing of the city gates and nightfall. The princess rises and begins to stack the dishes to take out and wash at the pump. Theo is dozing in Bianka's lap now, full of bamboo tips. Bianka watches Princess Zara go out with the dishes, a rapt expression on her face. I wonder how many princesses share in the washing up after meals. I think I am falling under her spell myself, imagining what Frayne might be if this strange girl ruled it.

While the others are cleaning up and packing their belongings, I go out for some air and find Gregor smoking on the steps.

"Quite something, isn't she?" he says.

"Yes."

There is a cup full of some dark liquid beside him. An unexpected anger wells up inside me.

"What's this?" I ask, picking up the cup.

"Tea," he says.

I give him a scathing look and sniff it. It is tea. I put it back down on the step and sit next to him. "Stars. I'm sorry, Gregor."

He waves my apology aside. "You're quite within your rights to be suspicious."

"It's none of my business. I shouldn't be sniffing your tea."

"You think I'll fail," he says flatly. When I don't answer,

he looks down at his trembling fingers, takes another savage draw on his smoke. "You've told me enough times that people don't change."

"That's true, I have." But I have a good deal at stake in believing otherwise now. I need to believe that we *can* choose or change our paths, ourselves, that we are not trapped like flies in amber, held by our pointless or terrible destinies.

I examine his face, full of a younger man's anger. It's the kind of righteous anger you would need, I suppose, to try and overthrow a tyrant, to believe it is possible to change a world that remains so stubbornly cruel from one dynasty to the next.

"You've seen this before, I know," he says. "You've seen me fail, just like you saw your old man fail. You've seen it a hundred times."

"Yes," I say.

"It's different this time," he tells me, stabbing his cigarette out on the step.

It's true, I *have* seen it a hundred times. This failure of a man to change, to love the people who need him more than the drug that feeds him, is something I broke my heart on when I was still cutting teeth. I don't know why it's so hard for me to say it, and I don't know if I mean it or not, but I want to mean it, and so I say: "You'll do all right this time, Gregor. I'm sure of it."

His face is like dawn breaking, the way it brightens, and I think, it hurt only a little to give him that.

"It *will* be different. *I* will be. It's all going to be different," he whispers.

"I know it will, I know it," I say, the last part a wheeze as he crushes me in a hug. I put my uninjured arm around his big shoulders. The booze has had Gregor on a leash for so long I don't really believe he knows how to walk the world without it, but by all the holies, I am going to let myself hope for him just a little this time.

The goodbyes are brief and hushed. Esme has gone out and returned driving a horse cart with a hollow bottom for the princess and the others to hide inside until they get to the tunnel, after which they will go on foot.

I hear the professor murmuring to Frederick, "You *will* take care of her, won't you?" and Frederick offering reassurances. I am surprised that Frederick is staying and Professor Baranyi is going, but nobody questions Mrs. Och's decisions. I suspect that she is not willing to let my crew carry off the princess without one of her own going along too. She might admire Esme, but she does not want to cede control to her.

I wish them luck, half asleep on my feet by now, dread closing like a dark fist around my heart. Csilla tells me again that my hair will grow out, and Esme gets down from the cart to plant a kiss on my forehead. Gregor, Csilla, the professor, and the princess climb one by one into the false bottom of the cart and lie flat. Esme lays the planks back over them, and I am queasily reminded of a coffin being shut. I have an awful feeling that this is the last I will see of them, but I banish the thought, bury it deep. Esme gets back onto the front of the cart, gives the reins a jerk, waves at us, and they are gone into the night.

# FORTY-TWO

We are still at our breakfast the following morning when Mrs. Och strides out of her room and says, "I will go to Si Tan now. Bianka, I need strength."

Bianka's expression darkens. "I might need it myself. I've a little boy to take care of."

"Teo," says Theo placidly from Frederick's lap, and I think again that he understands so much now and we need to watch what we say.

"Julia and Frederick can tend to Theo," says Mrs. Och.

"That's not what I mean," says Bianka through gritted teeth.

"Take mine," offers Frederick.

"I need more than that," says Mrs. Och. "I need Bianka." She looks at me. "Or perhaps Julia would do."

"No," I say.

"She's hurt," says Bianka. Mrs. Och swings her eyes back to Bianka, and Bianka breaks her gaze first.

"This is our last attempt to find Ko Dan," says Mrs. Och. "You have seen what Theo will be capable of. We need to remove the text from him not only to protect *him* but to protect the world from a child with such terrible power. I do not know what to expect from Si Tan. I need strength."

Bianka curses under her breath.

"I'll take Theo outside," says Frederick.

"Coward," mutters Bianka, which is unkind, but I think she's right that he does not want to watch. They both look at me then, as if they are expecting me to leave. I stand my ground and stare at Mrs. Och. If she is not ashamed, let her do it in front of me.

Her eyes were blue in Spira City and now they are nearly black, but her piercing glare is the same. She takes Bianka's hands in hers. Bianka's limbs go loose at once, and she sinks to her knees, the deep brown of her complexion dimming, her eyes rolling back, broken sobs shaking loose from her throat—while Mrs. Och's back straightens, power flowing into her, making her seem instantly younger and stronger. It lasts only a minute. Mrs. Och releases her and Bianka crumples to the floor, gasping.

Mrs. Och turns to me, her expression bright and fierce, almost exultant. "Fetch me my cloak," she says.

"Fetch it yourself."

For a moment, I think she will strike me, and if she does, I don't know what I might do. But instead she lets out a little bark of laughter.

"Such children," she scoffs, and strides to her room.

Bianka recovers faster than Frederick or I would, that much is true. Her face is grim and faded, but she gets back up again. I try to help her, but she pushes my arm aside. Mrs. Och sweeps past us with her cloak over her shoulders, out into the sunshine, where Frederick is reading to Theo from the book of fairy tales. In the doorway, Bianka plucks my sleeve. I look at her, our eyes locking—like in the Main Hall at Shou-shu, that moment when she handed Theo to me and let me vanish with him. *I trust you,* her eyes are saying. *I trust* only *you.* I know what she is asking me.

"Shall I come with you?" I call after Mrs. Och. "I could keep an eye out."

"No," says Mrs. Och, already at the gate now, brimming with Bianka's youth and power. "Wait here."

But I go anyway.

⌒

I ignore the sharp twinge deep inside my arm when I vanish. Mrs. Och hails a motor carriage, and my heart sinks. I can't run behind the carriage vanished, certainly not with my arm throbbing under its bandage, the pain jarring me with every step. I manage to hold on to the back of the carriage with my uninjured arm, and I thank the stars for the smooth, paved roads of Tianshi.

She gets out, paying the boy at the Huanglong Gate, and announces herself to the Ru. In no time she is being marched along the broad streets within the compound. I follow, vanished two steps back, everything a muffled blur around me. Something still tugs at my stitches, insistent.

This time we do not go up the steps to the Imperial Residences but stop at one of the sprawling white courtyard houses at the foot of it. We pass through a leafy outer courtyard, through an archway, and into an attractive outdoor pavilion in one of the inner courtyards. A woman dressed in silk, with black hair hanging straight down her back, brings delicate wafers and green tea. She speaks sharply to the Ru, who remove themselves by several feet but do not go away. She seems too young to be Si Tan's wife but too elegant to be a servant, and who knows which is more plausible—that he should have a very young wife or a very elegant servant.

Mrs. Och seats herself on a pillowed bench in the pavilion, and I position myself slightly behind her. We do not have to wait long before Si Tan emerges from the main house in a gorgeous embroidered robe. The woman in silk has disappeared. He comes toward Mrs. Och, bowing, his manner quite different from every other time I've seen him. There is a tension and an eagerness about him now. He almost seems nervous.

"Och Farya," he says in his flawless Fraynish. "It is an honor to meet you."

She nods, and gestures for him to sit down, as if this is her place. I want to see her face, but even vanished two steps back, I feel safer out of her line of sight. The stitches in my arm are straining, something pulling at them.

"You tried to trick me," she says.

"I beg your pardon. I did not know for certain *whom* I was tricking. I met an unusual group of foreigners in my city, lying to my face and seeking Ko Dan, and I wanted to find out why."

"You know what the boy is."

"Gennady's son, and vessel to one-third of *The Book of Disruption*," he says placidly.

"What does the grand librarian of Yongguo want with a fragment of *The Book of Disruption?* Surely you do not intend to put it in your library."

"I want what your brother Gennady wanted, but sooner."

"The text fragment destroyed," she says. "*The Book of Disruption* rendered forever incomplete, unreadable."

"Yes. The world belongs to human empires now, and I do not like to think what kind of world Casimir would make. But my understanding was that you were against the idea of the Book's destruction."

"I was," says Mrs. Och. "But Casimir has lost his senses. I see no other way to keep him from reassembling the Book now."

"If the fragment is destroyed, *The Book of Disruption* will be broken forever. The spirits have faded already. Witches here and there will be all that is left of magic in the world. You are at peace with that?"

"No," she says. "Not at peace. But it is inevitable."

"I am glad we agree," says Si Tan, though he looks more wary than relieved.

"Where is Ko Dan?" asks Mrs. Och.

"You do not need Ko Dan to destroy the text, Och Farya. If the text is bound to the boy, it will perish with him."

"I know that," she says impatiently. "I want Ko Dan to take the text *out* of the child. Then we will destroy it."

"It cannot be done."

"I would like to ask Ko Dan himself whether it can be done."

"That is impossible."

"Where is he?"

"It is not your concern. Is that really why you have come all this way? For the child's sake?"

"Yes—for the child's sake," says Mrs. Och. "But not only for the child."

"The princess," he says.

"She is gone," says Mrs. Och. "My people are taking her to Frayne."

A long silence stretches between them. "You took her from Shou-shu," he says slowly.

She nods once. Si Tan steeples his fingers.

"Och Farya, you are making things very difficult for me. If you had come to me from the beginning, we could have worked out this business with the princess together with Gangzi. She was still under his protection, and he is not a man who takes lightly his honor being slighted. What am I to tell him?"

"You may tell him that the princess left the monastery and is returning to Frayne to claim her throne," says Mrs.

Och. "She left of her own accord with her own people. She was never a prisoner, surely."

"Were you responsible for the raid on the Shou-shu Treasury?" he asks.

She inclines her head.

"But nothing was taken. What were you looking for?"

"The Ankh-nu."

He gives a gruff bark of laughter. "You come here brazenly, with no respect for Shou-shu, no respect for me, and admit that you are trying to steal one of the world's great treasures from us? Your lack of grace surprises me, Och Farya."

"Does it? But I do not respect you or that ridiculous sect of monks pretending they can live forever. Why should I? I am not interested in the rules you've invented or the games you play with ancient objects and people whose power runs deeper than your own. I have my own goals."

His expression hardens. "I am sorry to disappoint you, but you will not find the Ankh-nu in the monastery."

"You have lost it, then. I am afraid of who might have it. Did you really hope to use it as Marike did?"

"It's true, then?" he asks her, something greedy and avid coming into his expression. He leans forward. "Did she really live for hundreds of years, using the Ankh-nu to move her essence from one body to another?"

"I believe it is true," says Mrs. Och. "But no one else besides Marike has managed to use the Ankh-nu in that way. Nobody else has been able to coax any magic from it at all . . . except Ko Dan."

Si Tan looks horrified for a moment, like she has struck him. Then he returns to himself and says curtly, "Indeed, Ko Dan *was* able to use it. If he could transfer the essence of the Book into a living body, I dared hope perhaps he could learn to do more than that."

"I suppose it is more likely than your monks learning to live forever by way of asceticism and force of will or some such nonsense."

"The human body fails us all," says Si Tan. "But the *essence*, our inner selves, our intelligence, the *truth* of what we are . . . all of that needs only a vehicle to live on! You cannot understand it. You are not bound as we are to some mortal sack, a frail and aging cage of meat and bone. Surely the spirit of a great man is larger than his fleshly prison and should be able to live beyond it. I will not let all that I am be snuffed out by oblivion. I am *bigger* than that."

"All mortals feel so," says Mrs. Och dismissively. "But they die all the same. I have no wish to lay claim to the Ankh-nu. I only want Ko Dan to use it once. He may be able to save a child's life, destroy the text fragment, and thereby keep the world safe from Casimir. Is it not all to the good?"

"What you ask is impossible."

"Then Ko Dan is dead?"

He lifts his chin, eyes flashing with sudden anger. "You have come to my city without announcing your presence, and every act you have taken has been one of subterfuge or sacrilege. You admit freely that you have no respect for me. What right do you have to demand information, let alone help?"

"Yongguo is the greatest empire in the world, which makes you one of the most powerful men in the world, if not *the* most powerful. I use the word *power* here in the sense of authority, of course. You have no *true* power, nothing that cannot be taken from you. The balance will shift if Casimir reassembles *The Book of Disruption*. Kahge was created by the splitting of the Book, but if the fragments are bound together again, Kahge will be pulled back into the world, everything will be changed, and the order you so cherish will be shattered. We have a shared interest in keeping the Book from my brother. If you fear him, you should help me."

"How can I trust anything you say? How do I know you do not wish to make use of the Book yourself, or that you are not allied with Casimir, as in the past? You ask so much of me, and you have offered me nothing."

"Ah. You want me to offer you something. Do you have any suggestions?"

"Your vanishing girl," he says without hesitating, and I go cold all over.

"No," says Mrs. Och. "She is mine."

I see his lips moving, but I can't hear him anymore. My ears are full of a distant roar, and my arm is bleeding freely, the stitches split wide. The blood is not running down my arm but seeping through the sleeve and out into the air in crimson threads, then vanishing. The pavilion keeps blurring and then brightening, fading in and out of view, and something is pulling, pulling, pulling at my arm, at my blood, the roaring sound rising and drowning them out, then receding again. I need to get out of here. I need to get back to the house. Esme will fix my arm. No, Esme has left already. I need to tell Bianka.

Si Tan is on his feet now, his voice barely controlled: "One single life! For the sake of a hundred thousand lives or more, for the sake of a world that, for all its ills, can still be changed for the better, I beg you to destroy the child and with him *The Book of Disruption.*"

My heart gives a horrible jolt. I need to see her face. I try to move closer, but the twinge and tug at my arm becomes a yank, the roar drowning out whatever else they are saying. Blood gushing. I see the pavilion from every angle for a single blurred second—Mrs. Och's face, her lips moving, her yellow teeth—and then I am nowhere, and I can't get back.

I land in the steaming courtyard outside Esme's old building—a gutted wreck here. The statue in the fountain is all tentacles reaching, blood-dark water boiling inside it. From every side of the square, those patchwork creatures are coming.

Some of them have human faces, some of them have wings and are swooping overhead, and many of them are holding those peculiar hooked stalks to their mouths. Everything is pouring out of my arm—all thought and breath and strength—and *he* is bounding toward me with something close to grace, the fox-faced beast with his majestic antlers. In his gray rotting hand he has the jagged, glittering blade that sliced my arm open.

I try to pull away, back to the world, but I can't feel the edge of things. I can't find my way out of here. As if this is everywhere. As if the world I know is gone. The antlered beast is closing on me fast, and I jump.

It is almost like flying. I feel like Pia. I go right over his head, landing on the other side of him, and stagger, amazed at myself. More and more of them are swarming. A jackal-faced thing comes at me, and the hook on his stalk bites my shoulder. I grab the creature by the neck and toss him aside, pull the hook out of me. Oh, I am strong here, *strong*. Even dizzy and bleeding, I am stronger and faster than they are.

Still, there are too many of them. Another hook bites at me, and another. Talons rake across my back. I hurl another off me—this one knots of muscle without skin, wielding something that looks like a common garden hoe. A boar-headed monster with a spear charges me. I dodge and grab the spear, yanking it from its owner, and his half-rotten arm comes away with it.

Then something pulls at my very heart, an awful lurching, like when Mrs. Och took my life force to save us from Casimir—something deep and fundamental being grabbed, stolen. A hook has got me on the arm, and the stalk seems to have come alive, turning a fleshy pink, bending and swirling.

A bat-faced thing sucks on the other end of it, poised on several hairy legs. I can barely feel my hands to move them, but I pull the hook out of me with fumbling fingers, and immediately I feel my strength returning.

They are closing in around me, shuffling, monstrous, and now I know to fear the hooks, to get them out of me before they sap my strength. Shouts of *"Lidari! Lidari!"* rise up. I feel a sharp burn and push in my side. The antlered fox-beast is looming over me, making to swing his blade again. I tear the hooks out of my skin and bound away from them as fast as I can. Now a bright, hot pain is radiating out from my side, and I can feel blood running out of the wound.

I flee, and they follow, screeching *"Lidari!"* Near the river, with a little distance from the mob, I can feel it again, the space around me. I pull away so fast, thinking of nothing but escape, and I land, hard—right between Mrs. Och and Si Tan in the pavilion.

In seconds, the Ru have closed around the pavilion, bows drawn. Mrs. Och throws off her cloak, wings tearing out of her back, her face blooming into its half-animal self. She stretches out her arms as if to ward off the Ru, and in a voice that echoes like a hundred voices, she cries: "She is mine!"

Si Tan's face is truly fearful for the first time. He is shouting at her in Yongwen. I stagger to my feet. My tunic is sticking to me, blood on my arm, on my side, everywhere.

"I'm sorry," I sob at Mrs. Och. Throwing myself on her mercy. The Ru are waiting for Si Tan's command. She scoops me into her arms like I'm a child and cries: "Make way!"

Si Tan makes an angry gesture at the Ru and they fall back. Mrs. Och carries me through the Imperial Gardens to the Huanglong Gate, but I pass out before we reach it.

# FORTY-THREE

A light rain is falling when I wake. My side and arm are clumsily bandaged. I scramble out of the bedroom. Frederick is in the main room, scribbling in his little notebook, but he drops it as soon as he sees me. The front doors are open, and I can see Bianka washing diapers outside, Theo galloping around her on his toy horse.

"Bianka," Frederick calls to her in a low voice. She leaves the diapers and comes running up the steps. Theo drops the horse, darts past her, and throws his arms around my leg.

I cry out with the impact, my side exploding with pain. Bianka pulls him off me.

"Ouch?" he says in surprise.

"What happened?" whispers Bianka.

"Si Tan's not going to help us," I gasp, fighting my nausea.

"I know that. But what happened to *you?*"

"It's complicated. How angry is she?"

"Difficult to say. She hasn't come out of her room."

I touch the bandage wrapped around my middle. "Who fixed me up?"

"I did," says Frederick. "Stitches too. Sorry—I'm not very good at it."

"Hounds. Well, thanks. Have I been out long?"

"Not so very long," Bianka begins, and then Mrs. Och emerges from her room.

"Julia." Her voice would freeze live flame. "Explain yourself."

"I followed you." No point lying now. "I'm sorry. I was . . . I don't know what happened. I was *pulled* into Kahge. I was vanished, just like normal, but they pulled me right through and . . . they were trying to kill me—but I got out. They can *pull* me there!"

"Why did you follow me?"

Her face is terrible. I've never seen her in such a rage, but I realize suddenly that she is *afraid*. But of what? Of *me*?

I look at Bianka. She says nothing, holding on to Theo and staring at the ground. I suppose that's only fair. She depends on Mrs. Och far more than I do. She can't come out and say, after everything, that she doesn't trust her. So it's on me.

"I wanted to know what passed between you," I say, lifting my chin.

Her face twists. She grabs my shoulders and pulls me close to her, peering into my eyes, searching for something. I gasp with pain, my arm and my side crying out.

"Lidari?" she whispers, so close to me I can taste her stale breath. I shake free of her, staggering back.

"No!" I yelp. "It's me, Julia!"

She straightens and says stiffly: "Yesterday I made you an offer of permanent employment. I withdraw that offer now. You no longer work for me. Not in the future and not now. I gave you a second chance after you betrayed me, and you have betrayed me again. I am done with you. Leave my house now and do not return."

All the air goes out of me.

Bianka's hand flies to her heart. Theo has wriggled out of her arms, and now he is hanging on to my leg, staring up at us with big, frightened eyes. He knows something important is happening.

"Promise me you won't do what he said," I say. "You won't harm Theo. Promise me that. Promise Bianka."

Bianka picks Theo up and takes a step back.

"I did not cross the world in the evening of my life to do him harm," says Mrs. Och evenly. She has recovered and is quite in control of herself again. "I shall do everything within my power to protect him, as I have done since I knew of his existence. But it is no business of yours any longer. Now go."

"I need help!" I beg her. "Those creatures *pulled* me into Kahge and tried to kill me!"

"You'll have no help from me."

Frederick's head is bowed. If he won't speak up for me, I really am done here. I force my voice to be steady. "I reckon you owe me some of that gold, then."

"I owe you nothing," says Mrs. Och, her voice rising again. "You will leave now, or I will destroy you where you stand."

"You can't!" cries Bianka. "This is Julia!"

"Julia, who was a spy and our enemy, who kidnapped your son, who has proved herself untrustworthy yet again, and who may not be who she claims to be at all," says Mrs. Och. "She is lucky I am willing to let her go."

I am trying to think of some response—*may not be who she claims to be?*—but she cuts me off before I can find words: "Your brother will be paid in full and dismissed. You may return to Frayne or wherever you like with him, but do not let me see you again."

"Lala!" says Theo urgently, reaching for me. I look at Bianka, who has pressed a hand to her mouth, her eyes filling.

"You'll be all right," I say to her, which is completely senseless, of course. I ought to say something more, but I can't bear to say goodbye to them, and I can't bear Mrs. Och's eyes on me anymore. So I just go.

# FORTY-FOUR

Even without vanishing, I can feel it—the tug at my stitches, under my bandages. Suddenly it is like a hook to the wound in my side. The street blurs and slides sideways, and I am hanging above it all, my perspective widening, wheeling outward. I fling myself back into my body in the road, and as I do so, I feel the stitches tearing again. Panic pours through me, fast and cold. *They can reach me here where I stand, here in my body, in the world.* The wounds are straining under the bandages, blood seeping out of the lesser scratches on my shoulders, neck, and forearm. I break into a run. At first I think I am going to Dek's, but I change my mind halfway. I go to Count Fournier's house and bang on the outer door. Nobody answers.

"Jun!" I shout. I go down on one knee and pick the lock, go through the outer courtyard, and bang on the next door, then pick that lock as well. When I get the door open, there he is, pointing his gun at me.

"Get out," he says.

"I need your help," I beg. "Please. I'm hurt."

The gun doesn't scare me as much as it should. I am as sure as I can be that Jun isn't going to shoot me. I lift my tunic so he can see the blood-drenched bandage around my middle. "Look," I say.

He stares at the bandage and then at my face, bouncing lightly on his toes. It breaks my heart a little. How quickly I've come to love that coiled restlessness in him, the way he looks like he might, at any moment, break into a sprint or start turning cartwheels. Just the other night he kissed me in the tree until I didn't know up from down anymore, and now here we are.

I grope for words to persuade him. "It's just me. Julia." Is that the truth? Oh Nameless, please let it be the truth! "What happened before—it was an accident. I need help or I'm going to bleed out."

I feel faint, but I can't tell if it's from blood loss or if I am being pulled out of the world again. I grab the doorframe like I'm clinging to this place, this moment, gripping so hard that the wood digs into my hand. That brings me back to myself a little. *"Please."* I'm weeping openly now. "It's me, it's just me."

He tucks the gun into his belt.

"Come."

I follow him through the inner courtyard to a narrow room at the back of the house, the roof collapsed. It is all boxes and clutter and bits of broken tile everywhere, half open to the sky. He picks his way through the wreckage, never turning his back on me for more than an instant, and finds somewhere a metal box with antiseptic, bandages, and such.

"Hullo."

I hadn't seen Count Fournier, and I jump at his voice. He is sprawled in a corner, an empty bottle of brandy next to him. As I turn toward him, everything blurs again, that dizzying pull at my wounds coming from nowhere. I fall to my knees, press my hands to the floor, breathing hard. I need to concentrate just to stay here, in this place, in this body.

I try to focus on him leaning against the wall, legs loose on the floor, head bobbing, a silly grin on his face. It's so oddly familiar. I used to come home to find my father like this.

"Jun says you are some kind of monster," he says, sounding entirely happy.

"I'm not." But maybe I am. I don't know what I am.

"Sit here," says Jun, finding an unbroken chair. I pull myself into it. He removes my tunic—an unhappy echo of the other night—and unwraps the bandage. I hoped then that he thought I was pretty, that he liked my body. Now I only hope not to terrify or disgust him. With my unhurt arm, I hold my bloody, torn tunic over my chest, because even in this state I feel self-conscious sitting half naked in front of Count Fournier, drunk as he is.

"What happen?" asks Jun, touching my side with such soft fingers. "These stiches are rip right open."

"Something's after me," I say between clenched teeth. There it is again—pulling, pulling. Jun backs away, eyes widening in horror. The blood does not run down my side. It flows outward, away from me, into the air, and disappears. Wisps of blood are escaping from the lesser scratches and floating away from me too.

"Make it stop," I whisper. I'm so afraid he's going to run away and leave me. I watch him get a handle on himself, make a decision.

"I give you some whiskey."

"I may have drunk it all," drawls the count.

"I'll manage without," I say.

Jun stares at me a second and then gives a short nod. He kneels next to me, setting straight to work. He is not as fast or as steady as Esme, but he stitches my side back up. Maybe it's pointless—they will just rip me open again. But the hot, sharp pain of the needle focuses me. I try not to jerk away, to hang on to the pain that keeps me in my body. The blurring and the sense of slipping out of myself stops.

"You're not a monster," says Count Fournier, watching me. "I've known a few. Believe me."

"Thanks," I manage to grind out between my teeth.

"How is the princess?" he asks.

"Gone. They left last night."

"Good."

Jun breaks off the thread and sets about stitching up my arm. I squeeze my eyes shut, but that's worse. I need to see

350

the world and feel the pain as much as possible. I stare at the sky through the gaps in the roof and grind my teeth.

"I get you clean bandages," he says when he's done. I turn toward him, and a deep tremor goes through me, looking at his face up close—close enough to kiss. The slant of his cheekbones, the line of his jaw, those full lips and black eyes—I think of his mouth against mine, his hands moving over me. How I can still want him in this condition, I don't know, but I do.

"Can I have the needle?" I ask.

He looks at me, his eyebrows going down.

"It helps," I say. "Pain helps . . . keep me here."

He hands me the blood-slicked needle wordlessly and goes rooting around for bandages.

"What will you do?" I ask the count, trying to ignore my blood battering against the new stitches. My arm and my side are burning, but I'll take the pain gladly over the other-worldly pull. "Don't you want to go home?"

"This is home, as much as anywhere, by now," he says, waving a hand around the broken, cluttered room. "But as for what I will *do*—who knows? I worry about Jun. He'll have to find other employment."

"I like his prospects better than yours," I say frankly.

He chuckles at that. "Well, I'm an old toad now. I've stopped caring much what becomes of me. Oh, I would like to see Princess Zara on the throne in Frayne. To see my childhood home again. To feel I had something to give. But the distance from here to there is . . ." He holds up the empty bottle and examines it. "Unmanageable," he says at last. His eyes fall closed for a long moment, and I think he might be asleep, but then they flick open again and he smiles at me.

Because I think I have to, I tell him: "I heard that Lady Laroche, your aunt, has been executed. I'm sorry."

"I feared it might be so," he says. "You know, when I was little—hounds, I was afraid of her." He laughs. "But she won me over. She wins everyone over, given a chance. I can't quite imagine . . . I've never known anybody so alive. It is hard to imagine her dead."

Jun wraps my side and my arm firmly with the clean bandages and helps me pull the bloody tunic back on. Whenever I feel the edges of things starting to blur, that tug, I stab myself in the thigh with the needle, which jolts me right back to myself. That is something, at least. Jun backs away, watching me, and the wariness in his gaze hurts almost as much as my stitched-up wounds.

"What you will do now?" he asks me.

"Have you heard of a witch called Silver Moya?"

"Everybody know Silver Moya," he says.

"Silver Moya!" cries Count Fournier. "The plot thickens!" He begins to giggle.

"She is unlicensed witch," says Jun. "But she never get arrested. Just small things. Luck charms, bone casting, illegal potion."

"I need to go see her," I say. "Later . . . I'll explain everything. Or I'll try, anyway."

"Explain," he says, his voice hardening.

"I will."

"Now."

The pull, the drift, the slide. I see his eyes widen, and I think I must be fading. I drive the needle into my leg a bit too hard and yell with pain. He flinches as I return to myself.

"Explain now," he says. "Or do not come back here."

I roll the needle between my fingers. I can get through this, I tell myself. Deep breaths and needle jabs. I can confess the whole bewildering, ugly thing to the only person I've known who seems so much *like me*, except for one enormous difference—that I might not be a person at all.

So I tell him.

When I was a child, my parents never talked about witches or magic or the Lorian Uprising. We saw the wreckage of the old ways around us for a few years, and then even those last hints of the way things once were disappeared as well. I remember the smashed shrines in the woods outside Forrestal, the old folks sitting on their stoops and muttering to one another, many of them with scars and burn marks, and, of course, the Cleansings, where women, young and old, quaked on the big government barge and were tossed into the river Syne to drown.

One of the stories my mother told us was about a bear and a girl who switched bodies. They woke up one morning, each in their own home, but in the wrong body. They had to flee their families and homes, for the bear-in-girl's-body would have been eaten, and the girl-in-bear's-body would have been shot and killed. They were not safe anymore among their own kind, having ceased to *be* their own kind. The bear-in-girl's-body ended up begging in the city. She did not speak any human language, and she was friendless and alone and confused. The girl-in-bear's-body had to learn to hunt in the forest, and she was shunned by other bears, who sensed that something was amiss. But as the years went by, they learned how to be what they had become. The bear-in-girl's-body learned language and how to use it, she learned the rules of the human world, and she even fell in love. Likewise, the girl-in-bear's-body learned how to be a bear—how to catch fish in the river, gather berries, and be with other bears. Still, they both thought often of their old lives, their true families.

One evening, when the moon was full, the bear-turned-girl crept into the forest. She wanted to wade in the stream, dig in the earth, feel her old world around her. That same night, the girl-turned-bear crept into the city. She wanted so badly to see a human face, to smell bread baking, to hear speech and laughter and song.

Well, this being one of my mother's stories, you can imagine how it ended. The bear-turned-girl romped through the woods, happy as can be, until a pack of wolves set upon her and tore her to pieces. When she died, her body turned back into the body of a bear. The girl-turned-bear was spotted in the city and shot. The bullet did not kill her, but the moment the bear-turned-girl in the woods was killed by wolves, the spell lifted. The girl-bear turned back into a young woman, bleeding from the gunshot wound in her side. The people thought she must be a witch, and they threw her into the river. She was bleeding heavily, and they would not let her swim to shore, and so she drowned.

My mother stroked my hair as I wept and said, "Oh, come now, it's only a story," but I know she didn't believe that, and she would not have told me such a terrible story only for my entertainment. Now I wonder what she thought the story meant. Wonder if it means that magic is random and brutal, that we cannot choose it, and it can change us, take us from ourselves and from the lives we might have wished for if we had not been somehow chosen. Or if the point is that you can never stop being who you are and loving what you love, no matter how you change on the outside.

Or perhaps it means that you will never stop longing for who you *thought* you were before you became something else.

I think of that old story again as I am telling Jun about who I used to be—a pleasure-loving girl with a skill that set her apart and with no moral compass to speak of—and who I am now, the big question mark. I tell him about the Xianren, and Kahge, and *The Book of Disruption*. I tell him about Pia and Si Tan. I tell him how afraid I am of what I might be, of why I can vanish. I tell him about Theo, and I tell him the awful thing I did. I tell him everything.

When I'm done, he meets my eyes for a long moment, and

he looks more thoughtful than afraid. I want so much to touch his face, but I don't dare.

"I forgive you what you did to me," he says gravely. "Do not do that again."

"I promise."

"Good. I go with you to Silver Moya."

# FORTY-FIVE

We enter the clock shop Professor Baranyi and Frederick went to the other night. The benign-looking old man who opened the door to them is at the counter. When Jun asks him for Silver Moya, he waves a hand at the curtain behind him. In the workshop behind the curtain, the same woman, dressed in simple peasant garb, is sitting cross-legged on the dirty floor, tinkering with a clock. She has a wide, sweet face—the kind of face you trust instinctively. She puts down the clock and the screwdriver when we come in and pushes back her dirty hair.

"You talk," says Jun to me.

"I want see . . . ," I start in hesitant Yongwen, but then I don't know how to say it, and so I finish in Fraynish: "Ragg Rock."

The woman rises and puts away her clock, clearing the worktable behind her. She climbs up on a stepladder at the back of the room and takes a little bird from one of the cages onto her crooked finger, brings it over to the table, and gestures at me to sit. The tabletop is sticky, and the stool is so high that it leaves my legs dangling like a child's.

In a very businesslike manner, as if she's about to take an order for a custom-made clock, Silver Moya scatters a bit of seed on the table, then unrolls a piece of rice paper, opens her inkpot, pours a little ink into a bowl, and takes out her brush with the sharp blade on one end. The sparrow hops around, pecking at the seed. Silver Moya reaches for my hand, her face smiling and kind.

"I need a little blood," she says in careful Yongwen. "May I?"

I offer my hand, still holding the needle Jun gave me in the hand of my hurt arm. She slices the soft pad of my thumb and then holds it over the inky bowl, squeezing out a few thick, scarlet drops. I'm relieved that this blood, at least, does not float away and disappear. She releases my hand, then bunches her mouth up and dips the brush.

I see everything up close for a moment—the bristles of the brush emerging from the bowl, heavy and dripping with darkness. The brush comes down on the page, and I feel the jolt of it, the potency of this magic, all natural law crushed between the ink-black brush and the empty page. Dark, wet lines move across the paper, and everything shifts. I smell rain. Lightheaded, I fumble the needle and it slips between my fingers. Sound is amplified—the needle hits the floor with an awful crash—and then the final stroke of the brush sweeps everything aside, leaves the world changed.

The sparrow hops around on the table, chirping. The room has gone shadowy and still. The little bird is the only thing properly in focus. It is bright and moving, every feather twitching with life and color. It cocks its head and chirps at me. Silver Moya is still as a statue—Jun, likewise, motionless, a silhouette. The bird takes off from the table, flying out an open door I had not seen, a bright door leading into the world. The bird's movement is like a hook inside me, and I twist after it, nearly falling off the stool in my hurry to follow. I want to say something to Jun, but words are far-off, sticky things, and I am light as air, flowing after the bird.

Outside, the city is like a painting, one-dimensional, unmoving. Only the bird and I are alive, in motion. The bird shoots down the street, dipping and rising, and I run after it, light on my feet. Like the bird, I am real, I am alive, fluid and shining. I pass people in the streets, but their faces are blank and wooden, their expressions painted on. The road curves, and I follow the bird up stone steps that wind and twist up a craggy hill that has never been in this city before. Tianshi seethes below, falling farther and farther behind us. The air turns sharp, acrid. The bird falls like a stone and lies smoking at my feet, its feathers singed.

Before me, there is a crumbled archway—or what must have been an archway once, but now the top is broken and so it is two curved pillars in the road, crusted with lichen. My blood hums, and I step through it, over the scorched bird.

The road runs straight into a muddy swamp. A mist lies over the swamp, obscuring whatever is beyond it. Behind me, the stone stairs are crumbling down toward the painted city. I can go back or I can go forward. I step into the mud and instantly sink up to my thigh. I wade a bit, and it gets deeper, rising over the wound in my side. What am I to do? Then the ground is gone and I am flailing, looking for something to hang on to, but there is nothing. I swim through the thick muck and into the mist, where I can see nothing at all.

# FORTY-SIX

My hand touches slippery rock. Weak with relief at finding something solid, I clamber up onto the shore, my clothes heavy with mud. The fog around me lifts, and there is—I want to say a woman, but she is not quite that—a creature shaped like a woman on the path before me, pointing a bow, with arrow drawn, at me, but the bow and the arrow are made of fire. I blink, but the apparition is still there.

"Hold on, don't shoot." I scramble to my feet. A rope of mud bursts out of the ground and wraps itself around my ankle. I scream and try to kick it off, thinking it a snake or some creature living in the mud, but then another one bursts forth and grabs my other ankle. The mud vines give a yank, and I am flat on my belly, winded, on the ground before the woman-thing and her fiery bow and arrow.

"Please . . . ," I begin, but I can't decide—please, *what?*

She is naked, a reddish brown color, and there is something odd about her skin—something claylike about its consistency.

Her face too appears to be made of wet clay and is not holding its shape very well. Her eyebrows are mossy clumps, her hair a shag of weeds and reeds, her eyes black stones, shiny and unmoving. When she bares her teeth at me, they look to have been stuck haphazardly into her gums—each one sharpened to a point. She is a terrible thing to behold.

"Raaaa," she gurgles at me—a thick, muddy sound.

"Is this Ragg Rock?" I cry.

She jerks her head at me, as if to say, *Go on.* Or maybe *Go away*—who can tell?

"I'm in trouble. I need help. . . ." I realize suddenly that I don't feel it here—that tug from Kahge. My arm and my side hurt badly, but it is an ordinary pain, the kind of thing you would expect to feel after being whacked with a sword and then stitched up without anesthetic. "There's a little boy, a happy, gorgeous fellow, but he's got part of *The Book of Disruption* stuck in him, and he's going to end up killed or worse if we can't get it out of him."

I'm babbling. Slow down, Julia. Figure out what's going on here. What this thing is. Where you are.

"Raaaa," she says again. Then, gurglingly: "Hel-lo."

"Hello," I pant.

"Raaaaaaggh. Tell me . . . more."

"Is this Ragg Rock?" I ask again.

"I am," she says. Her voice sounds a bit less liquid. She folds the flaming bow and arrow into a sphere between her hands and extinguishes it. The tentacles, or whatever they are, fall away from my feet, crumbling into mud. I rise slowly.

"Do not . . . *hurt* me," she says.

The mud around my feet curls up like a wave, threatening, as if to back her up.

"Of course I won't," I say. "I didn't come here to hurt anybody."

She really is made of mud and clay, I realize—like somebody tried to build the semblance of a woman out of earth and moss and stone. There are cracks in the dry clay of her legs, and yet she moves quite as well as I do. Rather better, at the moment.

"Come," she says, beckoning me along the path, up the hill—a craggy, damp rock covered in moss and brambles. The sky is an evening color, a deep blue-gray, with shreds of cloud moving fast over it, but no sun or moon or stars that I can see. Muddy rivulets run down the hill to the swamp below, which surrounds the rock like a moat. A black hut stands at the top of the hill—black, as though it has been burnt, though it stands firm enough—and all at once I recognize this place from the vision of my mother with the Ankh-nu. She was *here*—my mother was here—and the memory comes back vividly, the way I felt looking at her, that awful longing, but it wasn't *me*, please Nameless, it wasn't me.

I climb after Ragg Rock. When I look behind me, I can see Tianshi tumbling at the bottom of the hill, beyond the swamp, a little bit askew. The green rice fields and the forests stream out from the city and its tilting walls. There is Tama-shan, poking up like a red finger, and beyond it, the desert. As I look, I feel the world rushing toward me, or my perspective soaring out over it, over the desert. There are walled cities, the rivers and railroads that zig and zag between them, miles of terraced rice fields cut out of the hills, old fortresses where warlords sit glowering in heavy robes. I put out a hand to steady myself as it all goes zooming past me. A woman drinking from a jeweled cup, out her window the yellow sand whipped by the wind. The grasslands becoming foothills becoming mountains. It is moving too fast—the swaying ocean, palaces, and villages, wild beasts hunkered down in their dark places, old women whispering around fires, children playing on muddy riverbanks. It is like seeing everything up close and from a great distance all at once—an exaggerated version of how I see when I am midway between the world and Kahge. I yank my gaze from the wide world and stagger on the path behind Ragg Rock. Dizzy, I hurry after her, leaving the world reeling and unspooling behind me.

When we reach the little hut, she does not take me inside but, instead, takes me around to the back of it, to the other side of the hill.

Far below us, a ghostly, smoking Spira City forms and dissolves along with other places I have seen, and places I've never laid eyes on too. Cities and forests rise up, take shape, then undulate and collapse, becoming something else. Beyond this shifting, burning no place, black cliffs and mountains spit fire, and beyond those, that giant whorl of purplish green cloud, spinning and roaring.

"Kahge," I say, and Ragg Rock croaks, "Kahge."

"What is that?" I ask, pointing at the roaring storm of cloud in the far distance.

"That? I wonder. Maybe it is the edge of . . . something, or everything."

"*Maybe?* Don't you know?"

"Why would I know?"

She looks right at me, and that is unsettling. Can she really *see* me with those black stones stuck unevenly in the mud of her face?

"Speak more," she says. "Tell me . . ." She thinks for a moment. "Tell me a story."

Oh, for heaven's sake. Now I'm to tell fairy tales to Ragg Rock, whatever she is, wherever this is, and who knows what is happening back at Mrs. Och's. But I don't know what to do except obey. I tell her the story of the girl-bear and the bear-girl that I thought of at Count Fournier's house. She nods avidly while I speak. When it's finished, I say, "It's not a very nice story, is it?"

"It's a very good story," she says, speaking more easily now. One of her teeth has come loose and is hanging lopsidedly from her gums, which are the same red-brown mud as the rest of her. "Come inside—I want to show you something."

I follow her into the hut. There is nothing much here, nowhere to sit, just a cauldron boiling with, as far as I can tell, more red mud, and a hutch made of wire and wood.

"Look," she says, squatting by the hutch. I crouch next to her. Inside it, a thin brown rabbit is sniffing despondently at a pile of grass. Ragg Rock reaches one of her clay hands into the hutch and strokes the rabbit's back.

"This is my bunny," she croons. "He's so soft. I can't decide what to name him."

I have no idea what to say. She looks at me with those pebble eyes. Her voice is much less garbled now. "Do you want to pet him?"

I don't particularly, but I reach in and stroke the soft fur. He is warm, and breathing fast.

"So there are animals here?" I say.

"No—he is from the world. Tianshi's Silver Moya brought him to me as a present. Wasn't that nice? She thought I'd like a pet."

Is that the key to magical, otherworldly assistance? Bring a fluffy bunny to the made-of-mud creature at the edge of the world? Wouldn't Mrs. Och be surprised to hear it.

"He's lovely," I say. It comes out sarcastic. Hounds, be nice to the mad mud woman, Julia. Try not to get killed.

"What should I name him?"

"Oh, I don't know. What about George? He looks like a George."

"Does he?" She turns her gaze back to the rabbit, stroking his back rhythmically. "That's what I'll call him. I like him. I like to touch him. I'm lonely."

"I'm not surprised." It is hard to imagine a more desolate place, and surely there can be no place more isolated.

"You've come to ask me for help, haven't you?"

"I suppose so." It seems foolish now—given that I don't

really know where this is, what she is, what her allegiances might be, if any.

A rumble in her throat, like a growl. She rises, making an impatient gesture for me to follow.

"People want things," she says, striding out of the hut and around to the side of it. "The shadows in Kahge want things too: *Make us whole. Make us alive.* How am I to do *that?* Mothers from the world come, begging me to return their dead children or some such impossible thing, and I can't, and I don't want to watch anybody else drown themselves in the mud. Witches come, and they say they will give me things, but they *do not have* things I want. Sometimes they try to hurt me because I cannot help them. They think they can *make* me do things. They think they can take something from me, from this place. I don't like that. I don't let the strong ones come here, the ones who might hurt me, not them, I don't let them in, never."

So that's why the Xianren could never reach her. Quite right of her to fear them too. I'm confused by her sudden fluency, the casual tone, why she speaks Fraynish when she seemed not to use language at all mere minutes ago.

"I won't hurt you," I say.

She looks at me, and her muddy lips form a smile. "I know. *You* cannot hurt me. But I need more food for the rabbit."

"What kind of food?"

"Silver Moya gave me apples and lettuce, but he ate them all, and now I have just grass and corn for him. He doesn't care for grass and corn so much. The corn isn't right, anyway.

She hasn't come back. She brought me the rabbit because I asked her to live here with me. She's afraid I won't let her leave if she comes again. But I only want food for the rabbit, *nice* things that he likes."

She looks as desperately unhappy as someone with a face made of mud could possibly look.

"I could bring you apples and lettuce," I say. "Where did you get him corn? I don't see any corn here."

She pats the big boulder we've stopped at, and I realize it is not a boulder but a massive dial. The black face of the rock is shot through with streaks of copper and silver and iron. Characters that look vaguely like the old pictorial Yongwen characters I saw in the Imperial Library are carved all around the edges of the rock face. The dial at the center points to a character very like the Yongwen character for *earth* that I've seen at small shrines by the road.

Ragg Rock grabs the dial and twists it to the right with an awful grinding sound that I feel in my teeth and bones. The rock shudders under my feet. A thick blanket of moss crawls over the ground, and trees shoot up like spikes out of the moat at the bottom of the little hill, branches spreading outward and bursting into green. They grow up and up, obscuring the view of the city below, creeping up the hill toward us. Dusky, skeletal butterflies the size of my head come winging out of the sudden woods, spiraling around the hut behind us and into the evening-colored sky, and there are other flickering shapes among the trees, like animals, but not fixed, colorless.

"I can find some things," says Ragg Rock. "The bugs are the most real, but my rabbit does not like bugs. I can find grass and grain." She twists the dial again, and the woods collapse into a cornfield, tall and yellow. I stagger as the moss under my feet recedes.

"Water," she says with another twist, and water pours out of the rock, the cornfield tumbling into a proper moat now, like a river circling the hill, bright and fresh and moving. "Animals must have water, you know. I can keep him *alive*, but he liked the apples and the lettuce best, the things from the world. I've found some trees that bear fruit, but not apple trees. I've found crops, but not lettuce." She yanks the dial again. The ground heaves. I think I'm going to throw up. I grab the boulder to keep myself steady, and the water turns back into mud. She turns a horrible, sharp-toothed grin toward me.

"I liked your story about the girl and the bear. I can tell someone has hurt you. If you bring me some apples and lettuce, you can stay here as long as you like. This is a good place to hide. Nobody would find you. Nobody can come if I don't let them in, and I can tell when somebody asks to come—the blood tells me things—what they fear and what they want, how strong they are."

"I'll bring you apples and lettuce," I manage to say, cautiously letting go of the rock now that she seems to be done changing the landscape. "But I can't stay. I wanted ... I thought maybe you would know what I am."

"Why would I know?" she asks, impatience creeping into

her voice. "Everybody thinks I will just *know* things. I know *some* things. I have this view"—she sweeps her hand in a circle, taking in both open doorways of the hut, the world at one side and Kahge at the other—"and I've been watching things happen for . . . oh, a *very* long time. But I don't know *you*. You look like a girl. Aren't you a girl?"

I realize with a horrible start that she is sounding more and more like *me*. Not just the way she speaks—her casual, low-class Fraynish, which sprang up after her initial gurgles and foreign-sounding hello—but her *voice*. After several minutes with me, she has learned to mimic me perfectly, borrowing my language and my *sound*.

"Maybe I am," I say. "You said those shadows in Kahge ask you for things."

"They want to come into the world, be real, be whole. This is the closest any of them get. They can see the world from here, if I let them. I don't anymore. Not since one of them got out. I made a mistake. I get lonely sometimes, and I make mistakes."

*One of them got out.* I feel sick.

"I've been to Kahge," I say. "I can go there."

She looks at me with those pebble eyes and says, "How?"

"I don't know. I just can. And some of the shadows are not really very shadowy. They have bodies. I mean, their bodies are like a mix of animals from the world."

"Oh, *them*," she says, almost sheepishly, if it's possible for a mud woman to look sheepish. "I know the ones you mean. That was a mistake too."

"What are they?"

"Just shadows, like the others. But a witch came to me . . . oh, nearly half a century ago now. I should never have let her in. Too strong. But so much grief that it pushed out everything else I might have seen, and I was curious what she meant to do with all the body parts."

"Body parts?" I say faintly.

"She made a deal with them. She met them here and brought them parts from the world. She fastened those parts onto them with magic so they would have bodies. And she gave them other things too. They can love and feel pain, they can sleep and even eat. I wanted to see if it would work."

"Why did she do it? What did they do for her?"

"They each gave her some essence. A tiny bit. Enough for a terrible spell, to bring life back to someone she'd lost. But I don't think it went how she wanted. She tried to come back here again, and there was so much rage it frightened me. I didn't let her. She tries, and I never let her. And those shadows with the body parts are angry too and trying to get into the world, and I don't let them come here either anymore. Too much trouble. The whole thing was a mistake."

I reckon I can guess what they want with *me*. I think about those hooks biting into me, the sucking tubes, the way it felt like my core was being pulled loose. Perhaps they think they can take from me whatever enables me to cross over. Perhaps they can.

But that doesn't explain why they call me Lidari. So I tell

her: "I saw them in Kahge. They tried to kill me. And . . . they called me Lidari."

The mossy eyebrows go up. Something guarded comes into her expression.

"Lidari was their leader," she says, and then adds after a long pause: "But he's gone now."

"Gone where?" I ask, thinking, Please *not* inside my skin and bones.

"I don't know."

"You said one of them got out. Did you mean Lidari?"

She nods slowly. She is not relaxed anymore. She has gone very wary.

"When?"

"The last time . . . maybe seventeen years ago. The others were so angry that he'd left them behind."

My heart is thundering in my ears now. I steady myself on the rock.

"And a witch helped him, didn't she?"

"I just let them come here to meet. Lidari had always been interesting. He'd been in the world before, and it made him more . . . *human* than the rest of them. After so long in the world, his essence had changed. He had a sort of body of his own even in Kahge—he didn't want the animal parts. And I liked the witch too. I thought she was my friend. I got muddled."

"I think that witch was my mother," I say. I feel as if the pieces are all there before me, but I can't quite assemble them into a picture that makes sense. Not yet. "Her name was Ammi."

"Yes," says Ragg Rock, even more wary. "Ammi. That's right."

"Could my mother and Lidari have . . . *had* me? I mean, could I be Lidari's child?"

I've never longed to claim my father, but I would rather have a pathetic opium eater as a father than some otherworldly half-alive monster.

"No," says Ragg Rock, laughing—an eerie echo of my own laugh. "Shadows from Kahge can't procreate any more than they can die—they aren't alive enough for either. Only the living can make life, and even among the living it is complicated. If a woman mates with a dog or a horse, she doesn't give birth to a little half-dog or half-horse baby. A baby comes from two living humans. I know *that* much."

The hollow fear that has been crawling through me for days now is spreading, widening, opening up like a dark, poisonous flower. I think of Theo, the text that was woven into him as a baby—and my mother with the Ankh-nu, which is for transferring an essence from one being to another. The memory I had that was not mine. Perhaps Lidari's memory.

"Then could Lidari's essence have been put *inside* me somehow?" I force myself to ask. I don't want to believe that I might be carrying around something else, *someone* else, inside me, but I can't shake the idea either.

"I've no idea," she says. "I mean, I think you would *know*. He's not the sort to sit silent."

"I'm different in Kahge," I say. "I look like something else."

"What do you look like?"

"I don't know exactly. Monstrous."

"Well, it *would* be a distorted reflection," she says, shrugging, just the way I shrug.

"One of them cut me with a sword, and now it seems like they can pull me to them, right out of the world. Like my blood is a rope crossing the world to Kahge." I don't know how to express it. "They had these hooks and tubes, they were trying to take something from me."

"Solanze's sword?" she says.

"I don't know. Is that the fox-faced one with the antlers?"

"Yes. He's been leading the rest of them since Lidari disappeared," she says. "That was another present from the witch who gave them bodies. It was forged partly in the world and partly in Kahge. It can steal your blood, and blood is important for magic. I'm not surprised he can call you if he got some of your blood with that sword. If that's their bridge to you, you could take it from him, take it out of Kahge. Then they couldn't call you there."

"How would I do that?" The last thing I want is to ever go back there.

She shifts a bit, and suddenly her ankle crumbles, the leg angling down and hitting the ground, separating completely from the dried-out foot. "Blasted hounds!" she curses, falling. Horrified, I don't move fast enough to catch her, and she lands hard, her arm breaking off at the elbow.

"Oh, oh, oh!" she sobs, though it's all sound and a contorted face—no tears from her black pebble eyes.

"What can I do?" I ask desperately. It is horrible watching somebody go literally to pieces before you.

"Get my foot," she whimpers. She grabs her broken-off arm in her other hand and pulls herself up the path to the little hut. I pick up the clay foot—it is surprisingly heavy—and follow her.

Inside the hut, she shifts herself to a sitting position and scoots over to the pot of mud boiling on the hearth. I help her fit the broken foot back to the stump of her leg. With her one hand, she reaches into the mud and scoops out a bubbling handful.

"I hadn't noticed I was getting so dry," she mutters. She slathers the hot, wet mud over her ankle and foot, working it into the cracks. Soon her leg is red and moist and supple and she does not need me to hold it in place. She twists and flexes it, wiggles her toes as she moistens the mud between them, giving them a bit of extra length. She does her arm next, sealing it back together at the elbow and covering the whole thing with another layer of mud. More relaxed now, she keeps steadily wiping the mud over her shoulders, her breasts and belly, between her thighs and then up her neck and cheeks, with gentle dabs.

"Do my back?" she asks lazily.

"It's too hot," I say, looking at the bubbling pot.

"Oh, it cools fast." She scoops up some mud and holds it out to me. It *is* hot, but it doesn't burn me. I take some in my hands and spread it over her back. She rolls her shoulders so the shoulder blades flex as I work.

"I just thought of something better than getting Solanze's sword!" she cries. "We'll stop your wounds up with my mud!

Then they won't be able to reach your blood. Not even with the sword—not with *this* stuff in the way."

I want to say no, but then I think of that tug, tug, tug, and I think I'm willing to do anything to stop those things from pulling me out of the world. If I don't have to go back to Kahge and try to make off with a magical sword, all the better. So I take off my tunic and let her unwind the bandage on my arm. She pulls a pointed tooth right out of her gum and uses it to slice open Jun's stitches.

"Ow!" I shout, tears springing to my eyes.

"Don't be a baby. This will *work*." She scoops some mud out of the pot and fills the wound in my arm. The pain is blinding for an instant, the scalding mud inside me, and I let loose a scream, but almost as quickly as it comes, the pain is replaced by an odd, thick numbness. She goes to work on my side next. I clench my teeth and let her do it, looking at the hardening clay-red streak in my arm where the wound was just moments ago. She dabs a blob of mud on each of the scratches the hooks made.

"They won't be able to get at your blood through that!" she says cheerfully.

"I'm not Lidari," I say, pleading. "Am I? I don't want to be."

"You don't seem like him," she says. "Too jumpy and anxious, for one thing. Lidari always knew what he was about. Your blood when it called me was ordinary, human. Just stay away from Kahge. Those animal bodies are coming apart, and when they do, they won't be able to wield that sword anymore. They'll just be what they were. And they won't be able to call your blood through this mud."

376

That is a relief to hear but doesn't explain away my thousand questions.

"Who *was* Lidari, exactly?"

She looks cross at first, and I think she isn't going to answer, but then she says: "I reckon he was always a little more alive than the others. A little more gumption, a little more *wanting*. Marike saw something in him, anyway. She brought him over—that whole business with the Gethin." Her mouth points down suddenly.

"So the Eshriki Phars really brought the Gethin from Kahge?"

"Oh yes."

"How?"

"It was Marike." She looks angry now. "She and Lidari made that little pot of hers. They used some of her essence, some of his, some of my clay, and the blood of a hundred witches. I don't know how they made the Gethin bodies. I should have paid more attention. It seemed like it hadn't worked—like her pot just swallowed the essences. But then later there was this army. It's my fault. I didn't know what she meant to do. Marike . . ."

She breaks off and rocks back on her heels, a faraway look on her face. I bend and flex my arm. The wound is entirely sealed up by the strip of red mud. It doesn't even hurt anymore.

"Marike what?" I prompt her.

"The whole of the Arrekem continent was hers, and the Parnese armies were all that stood between her and conquest of the kingdoms to the north. Old Poria didn't even exist then, it was just clusters of warring tribes, some witch-led and some not. I admired Marike. Is that stupid? The Xianren were always trying to get at me, and I was scared of them, and I liked watching her defy them. Anyway, Lidari was Gethin first, but then she put his *essence* in the Parnese emperor's body. She *switched* them and killed the Gethin body with the emperor inside it. So Lidari pretended to be the emperor, wearing his body, and married Marike, and then half the world was hers. For a while, anyway. The two of them . . . they planned to live forever, jumping from one body to another. It worked for centuries, until Lan Camshe captured Lidari and executed the body he was in. His essence came back to Kahge—I don't know how. It didn't happen to the rest of them."

"What happened to Marike?" I whisper.

"She was captured and drowned when the Sirillian Empire rose. Well, there are some who said she switched bodies and lived on."

"She never came back for Lidari?"

"I didn't let her back, nor any of her underlings. Not after what she did with the Gethin. I was afraid of her."

I look down the hill at Tianshi, tumbling below.

"How do I get back?"

"I've been very nice to you," says Ragg Rock, her voice caught now between anger and wheedling. "I've told you all kinds of things, *and* I've helped you. You *said* you'd bring me some food for George. Something from the world that he'll like. I don't want him to be unhappy here."

"Yes," I promise. "I'll come back. I'll bring apples and lettuce."

"Good." She smiles again. "Then just swim back across the moat and go down the hill. Go to Silver Moya when you want to come back. I'll recognize your blood. Come back soon."

"I'll come as soon as I can. But first I have to help a little boy. He's got part of *The Book of Disruption* stuck in him. Do you know about that?"

"Oh yes. Zor Gen's son. That's the Xianren's business. You should stay out of it."

"I can't," I say.

"Why not?"

"I love him."

"Oh," she says, nodding. "Love. Yes. I hear about that all the time. But don't forget what you promised me."

# FORTY-SEVEN

The little house in Dongshui is dark, but I knock anyway, knowing better by now than to go barging in. Quite right too. A moment or two, and the door opens, a candle flickering in Wyn's hand. With his other hand, he's tucking his shirt into his trousers.

"Holy stars, what's happened to you?" he cries when he sees me. "Your clothes! Your *hair*."

"Can I come in?"

"Of course." He pulls the door wide and steps back. Mei comes out of the bedroom, tying a robe loosely around her waist. She gives me a startled glare as she lights the lamp. I must look a fright.

"Is Dek here?"

"No. Oh, don't look at me that way. What am I supposed to do, give him a curfew? Mrs. Och sent a pipit. We're supposed to be leaving the city in the morning. Why are you covered in mud?"

"Things have gotten complicated."

"Complicated how?"

"I've been sacked."

"And then Mrs. Och tried to drown you in a mud puddle?"

"Not exactly. Have you got anything to eat?"

He has some cold dumplings left in the larder. I fill him in on what happened with Mrs. Och and Si Tan while I eat, every bite making me feel more rooted in my body and the world. I don't talk about Kahge or Ragg Rock, because I've never told him the whole truth about vanishing to Kahge and I don't know how to tell him now. So I tell him I got muddy going through the tunnels, and he just raises his eyebrows, like he knows I'm lying but isn't going to push it. Mei slouches in a chair for a bit while I talk and then goes back to bed without saying anything to either of us.

"I don't think she likes me," I say.

"You aren't very friendly to her," he remarks. I consider this. I suppose I'm not.

"Does she know you're leaving?" I ask.

"Yes. I doubt she'll miss me. I'm not leading her on, Julia. It's not like Ling and Dek—some great connection. Look, I've got something to cheer you up. It might even get you back in Mrs. Och's good graces."

He goes into the bedroom and returns with a bamboo basket full of letters, all closed with Gangzi's wax seal. I rifle through them. "How did you get these?"

"I had to pull a pistol on the mail carrier. I'll be a wanted man now, so good thing we're leaving."

"You shot him?" I ask faintly.

"No, of course I didn't shoot him! Hounds, Julia. I just threatened to. Anyway, here are your letters."

A soft *tap-tap* at the door. I start up, thinking it must be Dek. Wyn opens the door and manages to look relieved and annoyed at the same time. It's Frederick.

"I'd hoped to find you here," he says, rushing past Wyn. "Holies, what's happened? Are you all right?"

I hesitate. I want to tell him, but I don't want Wyn to hear. I can't bear for Wyn to think me less than human, but Frederick knows so much already, and I need to tell somebody.

"Can we take a walk?" I ask.

"Of course," says Frederick.

I can see the hurt on Wyn's face. "It's not safe around here," he says.

"We won't go far."

I feel more able to speak freely out in the dark street. I don't look at Frederick as I tell him everything. I roll up my filthy sleeve to show him the scar of red mud on my arm. It gives me a chill to see it there, this strip of mud flesh, like a part of Ragg Rock. He touches it lightly with his fingertips, but I feel nothing there at all. A blank spot on my arm, nerveless.

"You mustn't vanish again until we know more," he says to me. "It's terrifying to think that they can reach you now that they've shed your blood."

"I won't," I say. "What's happening back at the house?"

"I'm to get supplies first thing in the morning. We're leaving the city and meeting the others at the farm."

"So Mrs. Och has given up on Ko Dan?"

"He is either dead or locked up, and Si Tan is set against us. The Ru are out searching the city. I shouldn't even have come here, but I had to see you. Bianka and I have both tried to persuade Mrs. Och to reconsider, but she insists she can't trust you."

"I don't trust *her*," I say.

"Do you trust anyone?"

It stings to be asked that. Is that really what he thinks? That I trust nobody?

"Yes," I say. "Quite a few people. Including you. I trust you completely, as a matter of fact."

Silence at that. I don't dare look at him. I carry on in a rush, the words coming out of my mouth before I've thought them through.

"I've just found out that before I was born . . . I mean, *just* before I was born, my mother went to Ragg Rock and made some kind of deal, or I think she did, with Lidari. To bring him into the world using the Ankh-nu. And since she went to try to kill Casimir right after, I suppose she got some power or magic from him in return. I think . . . I'm afraid *that* is what I am—just some monster from Kahge. What if that's true, and everything I think I am is false, and being Julia is a . . . a disguise?" He tries to stop me, but I can't stop now, my worst nightmares fully taking shape in words for the first time and pouring out of me. "What if the *thing* inside me decides to shrug off this disguise, and everything I think I am is gone, just sloughed off, and I'm something else, something horrible? Maybe that would explain it—why I kidnapped Theo, why I have to try so hard—I mean, it feels like such hard *work* just to be decent and to do what is right, and perhaps I'm wrong anyway, about what is right. . . ."

"All of that sounds very human indeed," says Frederick, gripping my hands. "I don't know the truth of it, Julia. But suppose you discovered for certain that your origins were not what you thought? That, in fact, you are somehow from Kahge?" Seeing my face, he holds up a hand. "I don't believe that is true. But I am asking you, if it were—what would change? Would you stop caring about Theo? Abandon your attempt to help him?"

"You don't understand," I cry. "I'm afraid I might not be in control of my feelings. That they could change, if I'm so changeable. That I could be . . . I don't know, overthrown from within."

"You have crossed over to *somewhere*—whether it is Kahge or not, I can't say. You have been something else and yet still who you are, unchanged within, and you have returned. Whatever your powers, whatever else may be inside you, you are and have been Julia, with Julia's feelings and hopes and tremendous courage, with Julia's *goodness*, all along."

"My goodness and a couple of pennies would buy you a cup of coffee," I say—a feeble old joke of my father's. Funny I remember it now.

Frederick shakes his head. "That's not true. You need to forgive yourself."

"I'm trying to earn it."

"Saving Theo won't change what you did," he says. "You

have earned Bianka's friendship, and mine, in *spite* of what you did, by being the brave and selfless person you've chosen to be, minute after minute and day after day."

I feel something collapse inside me, and I practically fall into his arms. He holds me close against his chest, so I can hear his steady heartbeat against my ear. Standing here in the dark road, terrified and exhausted and caked with dried mud, I want so badly to believe that he's right. How could I feel so much, if I am not Julia? Then it occurs to me that I'm getting him very muddy, and I pull away, suddenly awkward.

"I should get back," I say. "I need to speak to Dek when he comes home."

"I'll take up your case again with Mrs. Och," he says. "But she is not easy to sway once she's made up her mind."

We go back to the house, where Wyn is dozing in his chair, and I give Frederick the basket of letters.

"Take these to Mrs. Och," I say. "Maybe there will be a clue about the Ankh-nu, if we're lucky."

"I'll go through them all tonight," he promises.

We say our goodbyes, and I close the door behind him.

Wyn's head jerks up. "Frederick gone home?" he asks. "Is all forgiven?"

What a question.

"I don't think Mrs. Och is going to change her mind," I say.

A pause, and then he says, looking at the ceiling, "I wouldn't have guessed he was your type."

If I were not quite so wrung out, I might have laughed.

"I don't think I've got a type," I say, and leave it at that. I'm hardly going to tell Wyn about Jun. And anyway, Jun thinks I'm a monster now.

"Look, I don't even know if Dek's coming back tonight," says Wyn. "I'd offer you my bed, but Mei's in it right now. You could take Dek's, or we could lay a blanket on the floor. I wish we could put you up in better style."

"I can't go to sleep," I say. "I've got to find Ko Dan before Mrs. Och leaves the city."

"What, tonight? How?"

"I don't know."

Another knock at the door, but it isn't Dek this time either. It is a ragged scamp with a message for *me*, written in Fraynish, a fast scrawl: *Help me please. Come to Old Thien's. Jun.*

# FORTY-EIGHT

I leave Wyn at the little house, refusing his offers to come with me. For all that Jun helped me and said he forgave me, I can't forget the look of terror on his face in the alley after I dragged him with me into Kahge. The way he said the word *monster*. It sits like poison in my chest, how frightened of me he was once he'd seen the truth about me with his own eyes. I want so badly to believe that he trusts me, that he would turn to me for help, that there could still be something between us. So I don't stop to ask myself how likely it really is—not until I burst into Old Thien's and see Pia, her booted feet up on the table.

She swings her legs down to the floor and gestures with a gloved hand at the seat across from her.

I don't dare vanish, and so I sit down opposite her. Blast, blast, *blast*. If she knows about this place . . . if she knows about Jun . . . she's been following me. I should have known she wouldn't just be sitting around in that hotel. Thank the

Nameless I always vanish in Nanmu. At least she can't know where Mrs. Och's house is—where Theo is.

"Have you made up your mind?" she asks.

"What?"

"I know you aren't going to give up the boy, of course. But you could still give yourself up. Then Casimir would go on chasing Mrs. Och around the world, and there's no guessing who might prevail, but it wouldn't be your problem anymore. You'd have gold, adventure, freedom of a kind. Better than being broken. I'm hoping you've thought it through."

"I've had a fair bit going on since I last saw you," I say.

"So it would seem," she says, looking me over. "I wasn't sure you'd make it back at all last night, the way you were bleeding. And yet here you are, walking in as if you'd never been harmed. Remarkable."

"I'm not going to work for Casimir," I say.

The goggles whir but her expression does not change.

"I'm not working for Mrs. Och anymore either, as it happens," I add. "I was a bit too independent for her liking. I've been sacked. So I reckon I'm out of this business altogether."

She gives a shattering little laugh—it sounds like thin glass hit with a stick.

"You'll never be out of it. Not now that Casimir has seen what you can do." She leans across the table toward me. "What happened to you? You disappeared, and you came back bleeding. I thought it was a kind of visual trick, the disappearing. But you *went* somewhere and something hurt you, isn't that right?"

"Yes."

I half want to tell her. She wouldn't stare at me in disbelief or horror. She would not be frightened, appalled, sickened. But I keep my mouth shut.

"Shey could help you, if you need help," she says.

I shudder, remembering the sad-faced, hunchbacked witch. "I shot her a few times."

"She wouldn't hold it against you."

"Like you don't hold it against me, the way I stuck a knife in you and left you for dead?"

She smiles.

"I am not interested in vengeance, Julia. I am done with the whirlwind."

The image of Haizea, bleeding-eyed, her teeth bared, rises up in my mind.

"Done with it?"

My head is spinning, but she sits back, suddenly chatty and relaxed. "I had my chance with it. Casimir understands vengeance, and he can be generous. He indulged me, gave me a part to play in the destruction of the Sidhar Coven. There was a satisfaction in it, I won't deny. I made my keepers crawl. Some of them I left for dead, and some of them I left with pain and nightmares. But it is an ugly sort of work. The whirlwind has no end."

Casimir. If I had the chance, if I had the power, what would I do to him? Casimir, who drowned my mother. Casimir, who broke my hand and nose. Casimir, who took Theo. But it was me who took Theo. That was me.

"Those who terrorize the weak so rarely imagine the day when their victim might grow to be strong. I even found the man who came to me when I was small, the one I told you about, who took from me things I didn't yet know that I had. He loomed so large in my memories of him, and yet when I found him again, he was an ordinary-size man, getting on in years, with bad teeth, ill health, and a wife who despised him. He was puny and cowering. I let the whirlwind rise. I let it tear him limb from limb and scatter the pieces of him far and wide. There is no right or wrong in the eye of that storm, only the power of it, only the certainty of what it will do, that nothing in its path can stop it. But it is a powerful thing to contain within oneself. If it does not tear you apart, at least it leaves you changed. It empties you out as it does its work. I would say that, yes, there is satisfaction in it, even a kind of joy, but less than you would think, and afterward, well ... the landscape is changed. Everything that used to matter has been blown apart. There is so much vacant space and nothing to replace the fury."

I don't want to sit here chatting with Pia about what a lunatic she is, and yet I find myself riveted all the same.

"Do you regret it?"

"No. But I have had my fill of it. I have had my fill of strife and rage and even hope. This, here"—she folds up the bottom of her glove and flashes the disk of hot metal on her inner wrist at me—"this is the closest I have come to knowing peace. The freedom from choice. You might find it a relief."

I shake my head, my insides shriveling. "I'd die before I let him take me like that."

"You know as well as I do . . . no, not quite as well as I do, but even so, you *know* that there are a great many things worse than death, and that you will submit to Casimir rather than undergo them."

The silence stretches between us.

"What do you intend now that you are no longer in Mrs. Och's employ?" she asks.

"I'll figure something out."

"Last chance, Julia. Please consider carefully. Am I to tell Casimir that your answer is no?"

"You can tell him whatever you bleeding like," I say, getting up.

I am at the door when she says, in a sort of drawl, "Before you came to Tianshi, I'd almost forgotten that you had a brother."

I freeze.

"The cripple," she says. "Was it Scourge?"

I turn toward her slowly. Her hand is on her knife, ready for me.

"What have you done to him?"

"Nothing. I expect he's out having a good time with his girl. Pretty, isn't she?"

"Stay away from him." But my voice shakes badly when I say it.

She shrugs. "Your friend Jun, though . . . he is easier to follow than you are. You have this irritating habit of suddenly disappearing. I gave Count Fournier's address to Lord Skaal as a gesture of cooperation. He's been looking for anyone who helped the princess. So if you happen to find that either of them has been harmed, it was not by me. Not directly, in any case."

I pull the door wide and run.

# FORTY-NINE

The house in Dongshui is empty except for Mei sleeping in Wyn's bed. Wyn is gone. No sign of Dek. I stand there in the dark, listening to my own breathing, but I have no idea where they might have gone, no way to find either of them. I leave a scrawled note on the table: *Not safe here.* Then I wake up a very cross Mei, hustling her into her clothes and out of there. She lets me take her home—a sad little place under the shadow of the north wall—and she closes the door in my face without saying good night.

Count Fournier's house is dark and unchanged from the outside, but inside it has been torn to pieces. I find the count's body on the floor behind his desk, full of bloody holes. His expression is one of frozen dismay. I kneel next to him, and even though his dead eyes are staring up at the ceiling, I say his name, as if he might answer: "Count Fournier!"

I understand now why people close the eyes of the dead. It is too horrible to leave them staring at nothing, their death most apparent in the eyes, which are not windows to anything anymore. His eyelids still feel warm and soft under my fingers when I close them. I leave him there, my heart thundering in my ears, and search the rest of the house.

Jun is slumped against a wall in the broken room at the back of the house, fumbling with the box of bandages he used on me earlier. Tears slip out the corners of his eyes when he sees me. His right side is dark with blood.

"Let me look," I say.

"Bullet is here," he says thickly, pointing to his right shoulder. "I go down, play dead. There are so many—too many."

"I'm so sorry."

"He is dead."

"I know. You need a doctor. Tell me where to go."

His eyes close, and I feel like the ground is falling away underneath me.

"Jun, pay attention! Where can I find a doctor?"

He heaves a sigh. "First I need sleep."

"*Don't* go to sleep. I'm going to get help!"

He gives me a blurry look and shuts his eyes again.

I'm afraid to vanish, but I'm not strong enough to carry him any other way. I pull him to me—he smells like blood and sweat—and back to the edge of that bodiless place, where the room scatters beneath me, all its angles up close and far away at once. Immediately I feel the tumult of my blood under the mud of Ragg Rock, the reaching and tugging from something just beyond the void. I aim for the window and we land in the inner courtyard, hitting the ground too hard, Jun's head lolling back in my arms. A sob catches in my throat. I pull back again, out over Tianshi, the swooping tiles of the rooftops gleaming dark below me, around me the canals rippling black and silent through the city, the stars coming out, and the moon gazing down at it all like a blank, unhappy eye. The sky is full of winged shapes, which confuses and frightens me. I take us down into Nanmu, returning to myself next to a small shrine to the spirit of the earth, piled around with fruit and wine and cups of rice. Ragg Rock was right: for all that the beings in Kahge might pull at my blood, the mud is a total barrier, more effective than my flesh, which melts away and reforms itself too easily between the world and its shadow. I look up with my own eyes; those winged shapes are still coasting over the city, huge birds swooping lower. I take a breath and pull back again.

I carry Jun to Mrs. Och's house in staggering leaps in and out of the world. I hear a hiss behind me, faint but persistent: *"Lidari."*

*Shey could help you,* said Pia. The only tempting part of her offer, now that Mrs. Och is done with me. I kick open the gate, and the spells in the courtyard walls start to screech like an army of cicadas.

"It's me!" I shout, trying to drag Jun across the courtyard. "I need help!"

Frederick reaches me first, helps me carry Jun inside.

"He's been shot," I say.

Jun is barely conscious now, mumbling deliriously. I am

so focused on him that I don't see her coming. Mrs. Och descends on me and sweeps me outside, depositing me at the bottom of the steps in a startled jumble. Bianka comes running out after us.

"Go inside," Mrs. Och commands her. "And make that racket from the walls stop immediately!"

"You shan't hurt her," says Bianka, her voice shaking, stepping between us. "I won't let you."

"It's all right," I say to Bianka, getting to my feet. "She can't touch me." I direct this to Mrs. Och, who stares me down.

"Go help Frederick," I beg Bianka. "Help Jun. I need to speak to Mrs. Och."

"Call if you need me," she says, going back inside but leaving the door open. Mrs. Och and I face each other in the courtyard. The screeching from the walls goes suddenly quiet, and the night lies heavy all around us. I can hear anxious voices from the neighboring courtyards. The sky is dark, but the darker shadows of hundreds of birds still fill the sky.

"What's going on?" I ask.

"Si Tan is looking for us," says Mrs. Och. "We have to leave. I told you never to set foot in my house again. Why are you here?"

"Jun's been shot," I say. "I didn't know where else to take him. He saved you that time in the monastery. Count Fournier's dead, Jun's got no one now, and he *helped* us. Will you help him?"

"I am not going to throw him bleeding into the street, if that's what you are asking," she says crisply. "But it seems that if I want to be done with you, I must take more extreme measures than simply telling you so."

"Wait," I say. "I've been to Ragg Rock. Look."

I pull up my tunic so she can see the long strip of mud in my side—and then I have the surely rare experience of seeing her stunned and speechless. She reaches out a trembling hand and runs her index finger along the clay scar.

"What did Gangzi's letters say?" I ask her.

She stares at me for a long moment, and then she says, "He is writing to every warlord, every minor official, every town leader and police chief and influential family across the empire. He is enlisting them all in a search for the Ankh-nu. It could be anywhere."

"Then we've as good a chance of finding it as they have," I say.

She smiles mockingly, and I force the question around the lump rising in my throat: "You think I might be Lidari. Don't you?"

"I do not know what you are."

"Well, neither do I!"

"What do you want from me, Julia?"

"One more chance," I say. "Not for my sake—for Theo and Bianka. I don't expect you to pay me. When it's done, you'll never hear from me again unless you ask for me, and if ever you ask for me, I'll come. Let me find Ko Dan and bring him to you."

"How?"

"I don't know yet. But I will. Maybe *he* can help us find the Ankh-nu."

She touches the mud scar again, presses on it. I step away from her, pulling my tunic back down.

"We cannot stay here," she says, and gestures at the sky, the low-swooping birds.

"Just wait a few hours," I plead. "I'll bring you Ko Dan."

"You are confident, Julia."

No, only desperate. I wait while she looks into me, like she's struggling to see straight through to the center of me. Whatever might be there, I can't say. Then she says, "You have until morning, but I will wait no longer than that."

"I'll find him," I say with a certainty I am far from feeling. "But . . . if I don't?"

"Yes?"

"You'd never do what Si Tan wants, would you? I need to know. I need to be sure that you'll never hurt Theo."

"If it came to a choice between his life and a thousand lives or more, what would you do? Would you still want to save him, at any cost to the world?"

"It hasn't come to that," I say. Because I don't want to say that, yes, I would choose Theo. I would choose Theo no matter what.

"I have lived a long time," she says. "Casimir would say that the details do not matter. A life here, a life there. What can it mean, in the great oblivion of time, in this small corner of space, all of it just a brief flare in the emptiness? Casimir tries to make his gestures great ones, his goals, his thoughts, all of them large, so that his life might matter, signify *something* in the great void of time and space. In my opinion, any attempt at largeness is futile. It is easy enough to believe that none of it matters, that life and love are meaningless, that there is nothing worth caring about. But here we are all the same. If I can bring relief to those who suffer, if I can offer help to those who think they are beyond it, if I can act on the side of right in this tiny play, then I shall do so, for I *must* act, whether for good or for ill. Call it an attention to detail. We are here, and we must make our choices. What Gennady did was wrong—creating a living vessel for his fragment of the Book. But now Theo *is* alive, he *is* a child, and if I can give him a chance at life, I shall do so." She passes a hand over her face suddenly, as if she is moved, and I am shocked to see it. But her voice is clear and cool when she continues, changing direction slightly. "Regrets pile up as the years pass. You know it yourself, as young as you are. Live for centuries and the regrets and sorrows and losses can become too much to bear. I will do what is *right*. I will protect Theo as long as it is *right* to do so."

"So where is the tipping point? When is it no longer right to protect him, according to you?"

"Find me Ko Dan by morning," she says, "and you will not need to wonder."

The birds are swooping lower and lower over the city. One of them comes diving straight into the courtyard, right over our heads, so that we both duck instinctively and cover our heads with our arms. It is as big as a swan, and black. It swoops right around the courtyard and drops a scroll of paper on the ground between us before shooting up over the wall and away again.

We dive for the paper at the same time. I get it first, scrambling away from her and unrolling it while she advances on me, her face pure murder, her hand out, demanding it.

"It's blank," I say. I let her take it from me. Her eyes move across the page as if she is reading, and my heart plunges.

"It's *blank*," I say again. "Do you see something? Are you reading it?"

She raises her eyes to me, and the paper crumbles to nothing in her hands.

"What was that?" I shout.

"A warning from Si Tan," she says.

"What kind of warning? What did it say?"

"We are out of time."

We stare at each other for a beat, and then I swing around and go back inside, grabbing my bag and stuffing a coil of rope into it. Bianka is writing magic next to Jun, who appears to be sleeping peacefully now, his bloody shoulder neatly bandaged.

"He lost quite a lot of blood," says Frederick.

"It's fine," Bianka says through gritted teeth. The tip of her pen breaks. "Blast. Get me another, will you?"

Mrs. Och comes in behind me. I can feel her watching me. I turn around, hoisting the bag over my shoulder.

"I'm going to get him right now," I say, heading for the door.

"Julia," says Mrs. Och—a low, threatening hum.

"Wait for me here," I tell her without turning around. "I'll be back with Ko Dan."

I vanish and make my way through the city, where the birds fill the sky, diving at houses. I find the same blank scrolls of paper in the streets, in the gutters, and each one, after I've looked at it, dissolves into air, and none of them show me anything. I break into a run.

I'm thinking of those little hooks the beasts in Kahge had, made to pull something out of me, whatever I had that they wanted; I'm thinking of Casimir offering me anything I desired if I'd bind myself to him, let him harness my power; of Si Tan asking Mrs. Och to give me to him, like I was a head of cattle, and Mrs. Och answering, *She is mine.* Pia's voice: *You are her dog.*

But I am no one's dog, and whatever lies within me, whether Lidari or something else lurks inside Julia's skin and bones, there will be no harnessing of this power by anyone else, and no hooks will draw me out. Those who would make use of me, who want to take possession of me, they've known all along what I am only just beginning to understand: I am stronger than they are. Whatever its source, this power is terrible, unstoppable—and *mine.*

# FIFTY

I find Si Tan in the cocoon-like room hung with silk, bent over a map of Yongguo with the empress dowager, both of them smoking fragrant black cigarettes and murmuring to each other. The dowager sees me first as I appear before them. She reaches into her robe for her pistol, and Si Tan leaps to his feet, his face registering shock, and puts out a hand to stop me.

I grab him by the neck. I need less than a moment—less time than it takes for him to throw me off, less time than it takes for the dowager to aim her pistol. I dig my hand into the flesh of his neck and pull.

We cross that boundary of nothingness, the world and our selves receding, and we land in the black husk of the city I grew up in. I pull in a breath of burnt air. My hands like claws, my arms darkly scaled. This is what I am, then—this monster. This too.

Si Tan's eyes are wild, the whites visible all around the quivering irises. I drag him toward the boiling river, and he stumbles along with me. For all his physical power in the world, *here* I am stronger than him—much stronger.

Those patchwork beasts come almost immediately, with their hooks and tubes and rusted weapons.

"Do you know what this place is?" I ask.

"Some illusion," gasps Si Tan.

"No," I say. "This is Kahge. I'm going to leave you here and let these creatures eat you unless you help me."

"Help you do *what?*"

"Is Ko Dan alive?"

"Yes," he cries.

"Then take me to him."

His face contorts, fury and fear together. "Och Farya has sent you to threaten me."

"Not her," I say. "Forget her. Look at *me*. I could leave you here to die and I'd feel *nothing*. Next the empress dowager. The emperor himself. His heir. I can pull you all out of the world one by one, end the imperial line as quick as you please. You can't see me, and you can't stop me, and now you know how quick and easy I can do it. Take me to Ko Dan."

"It will not matter," he gasps. "Ko Dan cannot help you."

And now those awful monsters are upon us. But I am ready for this. I am ready for a fight I can win. I let go of Si Tan, who cries out, reaching for me, and I leap for the fox-faced creature, the one Ragg Rock called Solanze. His sword is about the length of my forearm, bright and curved, the jagged edge glinting and winking at me. I get hold of that arm before he can swing the sword.

We struggle soundlessly for a moment, my face right next

to his snarling muzzle. Something close to joy is rising in my chest—but it isn't joy, it is too bitter for that, too swollen with fury. Trying to wrest the sword from him, I break his arm right off and stagger backward, stunned. A stinking smoke pours from the bloodless shoulder socket. I pry the sword from the dead hand and drop the arm, my stomach heaving with disgust. Their bodies just costumes indeed. Something catches against my back, stinging—those little hooks. I whirl in a circle, cutting the tubes and pulling out the hooks, and then I swing Solanze's sword at the creatures.

They recoil and flee now that I have the sword, ignoring Si Tan as he huddles on the ground and shouts something at me. But I can't hear him over the roar in the air, the buzz of my own blood, the cries of these shadow-monsters. Solanze grabs me from behind with his one arm, pulling me toward him. I break free of him easily and spin to face him. He has got one of those hooks now. It catches me on the cheek, right below my eye, and scrapes a gash down to my lip as I pull away from it. I swing the sword; he raises his arm as if to defend himself with it, and I cut his remaining hand clean off. More foul gray smoke. He goes down on one knee, scrabbling for the hand, screaming words I don't understand, except for *Lidari*.

For a moment, I see myself reflected in a window, standing over Solanze, sword aloft. My hair is moving around my head in smoky tendrils, my eyes are black pools, and there is a crimson line down the side of my face, which is both my face and yet not.

"Take me back!" Si Tan is slowly scrambling toward me,

404

like he's moving underwater, his face a mask of terror. With the hand not holding Solanze's sword, I drag him to the river's edge and then let go of him, pointing at the boiling river with my clawed finger.

"Take me to Ko Dan. If you don't, I'll bring you back and drop you in there. Then I'll go see if the emperor can be more helpful."

"I'll take you," he gasps. "It won't help. You will see."

I haven't really got the stomach for any of this. I'll take what I can get. We go back. I am this monster, and then I am nothing, and then I am Julia.

Si Tan leads me through the dark to his own house, where he met with Mrs. Och. I have a firm grip on his arm, and I keep us both vanished two steps back, so it is like walking through a hazy tunnel together, the world a blur on either side. I am ready to pull him back to Kahge at the slightest sound or unexpected movement. My cheek is burning, and I have Solanze's sword in my hand.

In the central courtyard, next to a flowering hibiscus bush, is a neatly swept stairway with a door at the bottom.

"Here," he murmurs, and opens the door.

The room is mostly bare. There is a bed, a table, two chairs, a basin, an electric lamp. And there is a young man sitting in one of the chairs, his hands loose in his lap. He looks up at us, his expression bleak. He has a star-shaped scar under his eye. Suddenly I am wild with hope.

"Ko Dan," I breathe. "Just . . . here? In your house?"

"Yes," says Si Tan.

Ko Dan looks me over. "Who is this?" he asks in Yongwen, his voice a low rasp.

"I need you to come with me." I give Si Tan's arm a shake. "Blast. Does he speak Fraynish?"

Ko Dan frowns. "*Who* is this?" he asks Si Tan again.

Si Tan speaks to him in Yongwen. I hear *Och Farya* and *Zor Gen*. The way he talks, and the despairing look on Ko Dan's face, make me think Ko Dan is afraid of him.

Then Si Tan says to me: "You may find Och Farya has changed her mind when you return."

"The birds," I say. "That was you. But the papers were blank."

"A message for her," he replies. "For her eyes only. The city gates are locked. There is no way out of Tianshi for her or for the boy. I have offered her an alliance. For all that she scoffs, she cannot deny the might of our empire. And I have told her the truth: there is no way to remove the text from the child. The Ankh-nu is missing, and Ko Dan remembers nothing. The only way to keep the Book from Casimir is to destroy the vessel—the boy."

"What do you mean, remembers nothing?"

"*He* did not put the fragment of *The Book of Disruption* into Gennady's son."

My heart is plunging and plunging. Here, my moment of triumph, when I've found Ko Dan at last. I hear Si Tan's words, but I can't make sense of what he is telling me.

"Then who *did* it? Gennady said . . . he *said* it was Ko Dan."

Si Tan lets a bitter little laugh out.

"Do you really not know?" he asks. "I thought perhaps you did. That you might be in league with her."

"With who?" I am going to throttle him in a moment. "Start at the beginning."

"Your mother," he says. "Marike."

Ko Dan watches with vague interest as my knees turn to water. I have to balance myself against the wall. Something comes alive in Si Tan's face, and I see the danger in it.

"Sit in that chair," I tell him, pointing with the sword. Solanze's sword does not look so impressive here—the jagged edge rough, not glittering anymore, just a damaged, rather rusty old weapon. "I can still take you to Kahge and leave you there."

He sits. My cheek is throbbing. I touch my hand to it, and my fingers come away wet and red with blood.

"What," I say very carefully. I can't find words. "Tell me. Explain."

"I have been trying to piece it together myself," says Si Tan. "I have spent my life searching for the Ankh-nu. Two years ago, Ko Dan received a letter from a witch claiming to have it. She was offering it to us—for the monastery to keep safe. I sent Ko Dan to meet this witch—with an armed escort, of course. The escort was murdered and Ko Dan disappeared for weeks. When he returned, he claimed that he had been kidnapped and taken many miles away to a mountain cave, where a masked witch came and performed some magic on him, using the Ankh-nu. Afterward, he remained for weeks in the cave. Armed witches gave him food and water and kept him there. But—and here is where it gets really interesting—his body was not his body anymore. There was no mirror for him to see his own face, but his body was older, different, and entirely unfamiliar, until the masked witch returned with the Ankh-nu and gave him back his own body. Then he was set loose and found his way back to Tianshi. I had Cinzai search his memory to try to find the truth, and it was as he told us. More than this—his body has been touched by another essence. The traces are still upon him."

My mind is reeling. I can't untangle this on my own.

"What about my *mother*?"

"Cinzai found the Ankh-nu in one of your memories," says Si Tan coolly. "She relayed it all to us. Your mother used it. But only Marike can use the Ankh-nu. Only Marike and Lidari, in all of human history, have been able to borrow the body of another by means of the Ankh-nu."

"So you mean . . ." But I stop. I can't put it together.

"*Marike* borrowed Ko Dan's body. If alive, of course, she would have feared the possibility of Casimir assembling *The Book of Disruption*. But she would have known too that Gennady would never deal directly with her. She had made enemies of all the Xianren. He would not have trusted her. So she used Ko Dan's body as a disguise to approach Gennady. Young as he is, Ko Dan is well known and respected, even by the Xianren. *Marike* put the text in the little boy, presumably intending to destroy him and thus the text, but she failed in that. And then she returned Ko Dan to his own body once she was finished with it. The question is only how willing he was. I have not been able to discern *that* from his memories—whether he was her prisoner or her accomplice. We are trying to separate out the traces her essence left upon his body. It is a difficult magic, and it has taken its toll on him, as you can see. But I believe that if we *can* isolate those traces, we may be able to use them to find Marike and the Ankh-nu as well." A rather mad laugh, and then he pauses, the avid look in his eyes sharpening, focusing in on me. "But perhaps there is an easier way. Perhaps *you* know where she is."

"Why would I know? Why would you think my *mother* is Marike just because she had the Ankh-nu? My mother drowned years ago."

"Who but Marike could use the Ankh-nu? Who but Marike could defeat Casimir, even temporarily? Who but Marike would dare to *try?* Who but Marike would want to bring Lidari back to the world? She is still alive, playing her games, borrowing bodies. The question is—who are *you?*"

Those creatures hissing *"Lidari,"* Mrs. Och searching my face for something—*someone*—else. No. No. No.

"I'm not . . ." I say, but I don't know how to finish the sentence. I need somebody to help me figure this out. If it's true . . . but I can't think it yet.

Si Tan rises, and his eyes are dangerous. I push myself off the wall and stand unsteadily. The sword feels so heavy suddenly.

"Sit in that chair or we go back to Kahge," I tell him. He sits. I take out my rope.

"You will not get out of the city," he says.

"Don't be an idiot," I say. "You aren't going to stop me. You *can't* stop me."

Ko Dan just watches, expressionless, while I bind Si Tan to the chair. I gather he hasn't been treated particularly well. Si Tan curses at me coarsely, dropping his accent, and I realize that he does not come from the upper classes at all, that his accent and manners have been carefully learned.

I stand up, and Ko Dan stiffens, fearful.

"He is *mine*," hisses Si Tan, but I ignore him.

"You're coming with me," I say to Ko Dan, who stares at me uncomprehendingly. I grab his arm and pull him out of the world.

# FIFTY-ONE

I am getting the hang of carrying another person with me between the world and its shadow. When we hang bodiless over the streets, I focus on the farthest point I can, taking us there at the speed of my own gaze, then return to the world for a split second before pulling back out, throwing my perspective wide again and finding the next point, and the next. In this way, we reach the courtyard of the house in Nanmu within minutes.

The first gray glimmers of dawn are lightening the sky. Frederick is in the courtyard arguing with Ling in rapid Yongwen, and she is crying. Wyn is standing helplessly by.

"What's going on?" I ask sharply, reappearing. "What is *she* doing here?"

They all stop and stare at me, then at Ko Dan, who has pulled free of me and backed against the courtyard wall. He looks down at his own body, and at his hands, flexing them—I suppose not an unnatural reaction for a man who had his body stolen from him once before.

"What happened to you?" cries Wyn. "Your face . . ."

"I'm fine," I say.

"Is this . . . ?" Frederick takes a step toward Ko Dan and says something to him in Yongwen that Ko Dan appears to find reassuring. He nods, relaxing a little. Ling is still sobbing.

"*Where is Dek?*" I shout.

"He's all right. He and Ling were at a play, and Pia found them," says Frederick quickly. "They got away, and he told Ling this address, sent her here in a motor carriage. He's gone to fetch Mei and bring her back here too. Ling is worried about her, and I was just saying Mrs. Och won't allow it, but—"

Ling bursts out, shouting something at Wyn, jabbing her finger in his face. He looks sheepish. "My *sister!*" she finishes in Fraynish.

"I'm sorry!" says Wyn. And then, to me, he says: "I was sleeping at home after you left, and the pipit came with a message from Mrs. Och, telling Dek and me to go to the farm to meet up with the others. I didn't want to leave without you, and I didn't know where Dek was, so I came here. I had no idea the girls were in any danger or I would never have left Mei alone."

"*I* took Mei home!" I say to Ling. "She's fine!"

Ling puts her face in her hands, and her shoulders shake as Frederick translates this for her.

"I think we should all just stay here and wait for Dek," says Wyn. "What *happened* to your face, Brown Eyes? Where'd you get that sword?"

"Fighting monsters," I say. "Come on, let's introduce Ko Dan to Mrs. Och."

Frederick speaks to him in Yongwen again, and Ko Dan goes to him, giving me a wide berth like I'm a mad dog. Ling takes her hands away from her face and looks at me, her face blotchy from crying.

"Come inside, then," I say. "It can't matter. We won't be here much longer."

So we all go in together. Mrs. Och and Bianka are poring over a map of Yongguo. Bianka is holding Theo tight. The sash he sleeps with is wrapped around his waist, tying him to her.

"Here is Ko Dan," I announce, but the moment feels hollow because I know it's no use.

Bianka leaps to her feet. Mrs. Och rises more slowly, looking from my bleeding face to Ko Dan.

"Dare I ask you how you have done this?" she says.

"Probably better not."

Mrs. Och speaks to Ko Dan in Yongwen, and he bows and answers.

"Can he do it?" Bianka cries. "Without harming Theo?"

"Teo," says Theo, trying to squirm free of her, but she squeezes him closer.

Mrs. Och holds up a hand, giving Bianka a stern glare. Then her eyes fall on Ling.

"Who is this?" she asks, acid-voiced.

"Dek's girl," I say.

"Pia came across them, and Dek sent her here," says Wyn. "He's gone to get her sister too."

Mrs. Och waves this aside and turns back to Ko Dan. Frederick manages to persuade him to sit down.

"We ought to see to that gash on your cheek," says Bianka to me. "It looks very nasty."

I put down Solanze's ugly sword, and we sit around the hearth while Mrs. Och batters Ko Dan with questions, her voice rising sharply. Ling glances at them in horror a few times, and I can only imagine what she's hearing. I can't follow the rapid conversation around the table, so I just sit and let Bianka wash my cheek, Theo still bound to her, tugging at the sash but cowed by the tension in the room.

"I ought to stitch it," she says. "Not sure I'm up for another spell."

"Please don't. I'm so sick of being sewn up."

"Well, it's going to be a whopping scar," she says, and Wyn says, "It'll suit you, very piratical."

I can't bring myself to care at the moment. Wyn fetches me a clean cloth, which I hold to the wound. Mrs. Och bangs on the table with a fist, her voice turning angry.

"Is he going to help?" Bianka asks me in a low voice. "*Can he help?*"

I don't know what to say. "It's a little complicated," I mutter.

Even though I've done what I set out to do, I know it's a flop; the way to help Theo has slipped away from us. We crossed the world to find this man, and for nothing. The things Si Tan said keep turning and turning in my mind. Marike took Ko Dan's body. Marike, wearing the monk's body, made the deal with Gennady, put the Book into Theo, and disappeared again with the Ankh-nu. Years before that, Marike-as-Ammi went to Ragg Rock and brought Lidari across to the world with the Ankh-nu. Somehow she then defeated Casimir and had a child—me. And the creatures in Kahge sensed Lidari's essence in me.

Suppose it's all true. Suppose my mother is Marike. Then she did not drown, it was not her on that boat at all, but someone else in another discarded body, for if my mother is Marike, she was in Sirillia working a terrible magic less than two years ago. And if we're to save Theo, somehow we have to find her.

I feel dizzy. I don't know if it's joy or fear making me tremble. I don't know if I should believe anything Si Tan said. I need to talk to Dek.

"Why is he taking so long?" I say without explaining who I mean, but Wyn nods at me, his forehead creased with concern. Ling plays peekaboo with a restless Theo. She seems calmer now. And then Jun emerges from Mrs. Och's room, taking in the crowd of us.

I leap up, my cheek throbbing. He is a little pale, but upright and moving and still beautiful, his arm and shoulder wrapped in a sling. Whereas, I—well, if ever he thought I was a little bit pretty, I am not now. My chopped hair, my eyes swollen with tears shed and unshed, my face still streaked with mud and now with a great ugly gash across it—I must look a horror, and I see the shock register in his eyes.

"Are you all right?" I ask stupidly.

He nods, easing himself into a chair by the hearth, and doesn't ask me if *I* am all right.

The conversation in Yongwen is carrying on more calmly now, and so Bianka boils eggs and butters bread for breakfast, poor Theo complaining bitterly about the sash. Ling puts on a kettle for tea, as if she's at home.

At last, Mrs. Och says in Fraynish, "No matter what, we cannot stay in the city. But Bianka, Theo, Frederick, and I will not go back to Frayne quite yet." She looks at me. "You will go your own way now, Julia. Wyn should join the others at the farm immediately. They will leave by nightfall, and they will be safer if he is with them."

I wonder if she knows—if Ko Dan understood what Si Tan said about my mother.

"What about Dek?" asks Wyn.

"If he's not here soon, I'll go find him," I say. Trying to push down the fear.

"We'll stick together, you and me," Wyn says to me. But I shake my head.

"You should go. Gregor and Esme can shoot straight, at least, but Mrs. Och is right—it'll be better if you're with them. Get the princess back to Frayne in one piece."

"I want to help *you*," says Wyn. "I want to get you and Dek back to Frayne in one piece."

"This is how you help," I say. "I'm going to get Dek out of here. I'll take him by vanishing, and it'll be easier if it's just him. The others could use you."

He looks downcast, but he nods. I don't want to say good-bye to Wyn, but I want him safely out of here, and I need to save my strength for Dek. I don't reckon we're going back to Frayne yet either. Mrs. Och may think she can shrug me off now, but if she is about to go off looking for my mother, she's not doing it without me.

"How are we going to get out of the city, if the gates are locked and the Ru are everywhere?" asks Wyn.

"You'll need my help," I say to Mrs. Och, but she shakes her head at me.

Jun pushes his plate away. He keeps looking everywhere except at me. "I take you," he says to Wyn. "I know some way out. Secret way."

"Good," says Mrs. Och. "But leave quickly. More and more routes will be shut to you the longer we wait."

This sets us all in motion. Bianka fills gourds with water from the pump, and I pack them some bread and dried fruit. Wyn just sits there looking stricken until Jun takes his pistol, which Wyn has left on the table, and tucks it into his belt.

"Hey, that's mine!" says Wyn, coming to life.

"I should have gun, not you," says Jun. "In case we meet trouble."

"I was thinking that *I* should have the gun in case we meet trouble," says Wyn.

"You are not good shot."

Wyn's mouth quirks a little. "I'm a very good shot," he says.

"You miss when you shoot at me."

"Oh, that. Well, that was more of a warning shot."

Jun pats the pistol at his belt, as if making a final argument. Wyn looks torn between anger and amusement, but he shrugs, then shoulders the bag of food and water.

"Take care of them," I say to Wyn. "Get them home."

"I will," he says. "Don't do anything foolish, Julia. Come home safely."

He pulls me into his embrace. I let my arms go around his too-familiar frame, his heartbeat against my ear, my dear, beautiful boy. But my own heart feels like a stone in my chest. Jun stands in the doorway, watching us with no expression on his face.

"Let's go," says Jun. "Before too light."

"Wait."

I follow him out onto the steps.

"What will you do?" I ask him. "I mean, after."

"I am not decided yet," he says.

"You could come with us," I say, knowing as I say it how stupid it is.

He lifts an eyebrow. "This is my home. Greatest city in the world."

"I know," I say. "It's just . . ." Don't be such a coward, Julia, just say it. "One night with you doesn't feel like enough."

Something in his expression softens a little. "I do not understand many thing about you, Julia," he says. "It is too much for me to not know. I cannot love girl who changes into monster. But I am wishing luck for you."

He touches a hand lightly to his chest, where the tattoo for luck is hidden beneath his shirt.

"I'm so sorry ... about Count Fournier," I manage. "It's my fault."

"Not your fault," he says, and then he leans forward and kisses my cheek, under the gash, and I nearly crumble right there. He turns and walks away across the courtyard.

"Hold up," says Wyn, behind me. "Did you and he ... ?"

"Go on, hurry," I say, giving him a shove. He gives me a cockeyed look that might have made me laugh under different circumstances, but he goes after Jun, waving from the gate. And then they are gone. I feel something ease in me. The more people I love who get out of here, the better.

I go back into the main room, where Ling is offering around tea. Mrs. Och waves her away impatiently, but Ko Dan takes a cup and raises it to his lips, nodding gratefully at her.

"We part ways here, Julia," says Mrs. Och to me. Something awful in her expression. So much we are not saying. Marike's name, for starters.

"Dek is meeting us back here," I say. "I'll leave with him, and not before that."

But where is he, where is he, where is he?

She scowls and turns back to Ko Dan, directing a sharp question at him in Yongwen. He puts his cup down, and fear flashes across his face. He looks at Frederick, his mouth open but no sound coming out.

"What is it?" asks Frederick, leaning forward.

Ko Dan touches a hand to his chest. His eyes go wide, and he begins to shake. It happens so fast. Foam on his lips, veins bulging at his temples, eyes turning crimson as the blood vessels explode. He falls sideways, rigid and shaking, Frederick and Bianka at his side, shouting. I can't move. Mrs. Och says in a cold, tight voice: "Poison."

It takes only a few seconds, though time feels slowed down horribly: his purpling face, his body convulsing and then falling still. My heart is thumping so loudly in my chest that Bianka's screams seem distant, and my thoughts are moving slowly, like underwater thoughts: Doctor. Too late. Poison. The teacup on the ground—green tea spilling onto the floor.

*Ling.*

I whirl around, but she is gone. The gate is swinging in the courtyard. I snatch up Solanze's sword and go over the wall. She is running down the road, around the corner. I catch her easily and slam her into the wall. She gives a little cry, like a kitten mewing. I pull her back and slam her into the wall again. I don't know what I'm doing. It's too late, of course. I grab her wrists, pinning her to the wall, screaming *"Why?"* at her—but my question is answered for me. The dirty bandage on her wrist. Even through the fabric, I can feel the heat. I tear it off her.

She has gone limp against the wall, sobbing. There, in her wrist, that little disk of metal, the burnt skin peeled back around it. Casimir's contract.

"You work for Casimir," I breathe.

Of course she and Dek didn't just *get away* from Pia. But he told her Mrs. Och's address. How long do we have? I hold the sword to her throat. "Where is Dek?" I grind out.

She tilts her head back a little, as if daring me to cut her throat, and says in Fraynish: "Safe." Then she asks me a question in Yongwen. It takes me a minute to understand that she's asking if Ko Dan is dead.

"Yes!" I shout. "Of course he's dead. You're a liar and a murderer! We'll all be killed now!"

Hounds, the look on her face. I lower the sword and step away.

"My sister," she says in Yongwen, and her voice cracks. She tries to grab the sword from me, but I yank it away. She lets out a laugh that sounds more like the yelp of an animal caught in a trap. Then she starts biting at her wrist until she gets that metal disk between her teeth. It must be burning her lips, but she doesn't stop. She pulls it loose, her face contorted and gray. A silvery thread follows. She pulls and pulls with the fingers of her other hand now, the bright thread spooling out of her, slick with her blood.

I don't want to watch, but I can't tear my eyes away either. One more sharp tug, and something like a bloody jewel the size of a baby's tooth comes slipping out of her wrist. She drops it with a shuddering cry. Behind it stream countless tendrils, several inches long. They move and flail, then find the ground like hundreds of tiny legs. The little jewel comes crawling toward me, gathering speed. It skitters for my leg, and I jump away, shouting inarticulately. Quick as anything, Ling grabs a loose stone from the ground and brings it smashing down on the thing. The tendrils go limp. She raises the rock cautiously. Whatever it was, it is just a wet red blob on the street now.

"His contract," I say.

Ling looks up at me, and words start pouring out of her, about Dek and Mei and a rich man and the Imperial Gardens, but I can't follow, and her wrist is bleeding badly, her face turning a disconcerting ashen color.

"You need to see to that," I say, picking up the dirty bandage I tore off her.

I wrap it around her bleeding wrist. She stares at me with such a defeated expression, but she lets me bind it. I may not understand her fast Yongwen, but I can read the whole story in her face—I *know* this story, because it was my story too. A talented girl in a big city, stuck, and then something comes along that could really change things. A big chance. In my case, a heap of silver. In hers, maybe the promise of a way to the Imperial Gardens. For both of us, it was a poisoned promise, but how were we to know? By the time we knew for sure that we were working for the wrong side, it was too late. She's killed a man, and I don't think it's really sunk in yet, just like it took a while to hit me that I'd kidnapped a child.

I ask her in Fraynish because, honestly, I can't think straight enough to even try in Yongwen: "They threatened Mei, didn't they?"

I don't know how much Fraynish she understands, but I think she can see in my face everything that I can see in hers. We crouch there in the road together, and she nods. The bandage is already turning dark with blood. I've done a lousy job, but I don't have time to take care of Ling, and I reckon she knows how to take care of herself.

"Does Pia know where the house is?" I ask her. She looks at me blankly, so I point down the road, and put my fingers in goggle shapes around my eyes. She nods again. I need to get back there right away. I start to rise, and she catches hold of my sleeve. She is saying something about Dek, her eyes gone hard and bright. I only understand the word *sorry*.

"I'll tell him," I say. "Get your sister safe. Hide."

Go where Casimir can't find you, can't reach you. I see my own story written so starkly in her miserable expression that it makes me feel ill. We both look at the little blob in the road; then she locks eyes with me one more time, gives a small nod, turns, and starts running. I dash back to the house.

The gate is wide open. Frederick is alone, slumped on the floor next to Ko Dan's dead body. He is chalk-white and limp, his eyes half-lidded. I skid to my knees beside him and grab his shoulders.

"What happened?"

"They left." It is barely a whisper.

"*What?*" I scream.

"She said . . . there was no time."

"She—who?"

"Mrs. Och."

"Mrs. Och," I repeat. "Mrs. Och took Bianka and Theo. *Where?*"

"Leaving . . . the city."

Without Frederick. Without *me*. She wanted to get out of here without me. But there is no way out of the city, Si Tan said.

"Bianka?" I manage to ask.

"She took my . . . force and . . . Bianka's too. Left her just enough to . . . walk. So fast. She said—no time."

Maybe she means to get them away safe, but I don't believe it. *Where is the tipping point?* I asked her, and she told me to bring her Ko Dan. But now he is dead, was not the right man anyway, and if there is no way to get the text out of Theo, then the surest way to keep the Book from Casimir is to destroy it. To kill Theo, who is himself becoming dangerous. Ally herself with the most powerful empire in the world.

My panic is rising fast. I squash it down, trying to clear my mind, trying to think where they would go, how I can find them. They can't have gone far; it has been only a minute or two. If I go now, I can still catch them.

A voice from the doorway: "Is it your blood or someone else's you're covered with this time?"

I look up, and there is Pia.

# FIFTY-TWO

Frederick is struggling to get up. I pull back, out of sight, but Pia is ready for that. She yanks Frederick to his feet, her curved knife at his throat.

"Stay where I can see you," she snarls. "And drop that sword."

I reappear and do as she says. She drags Frederick with her from room to room. He almost looks like he's asleep, except that he's so pale.

"Where is the boy?" she calls to me.

"I *don't know*. Mrs. Och has taken him, and I've no idea where. I told you—I don't work for her anymore."

"And yet here you are."

"She left us behind."

"Who is the corpse?" she asks, jerking her head at Ko Dan. My stomach clenches. I found him for this. To be killed within the hour.

"Ko Dan," I say.

"Ah," says Pia. "Then you found him."

"I thought . . . he was a witch. But she poisoned him."

"There are poisons that work well on witches," she says. "Or well enough. The girl succeeded in that, at least. We weren't sure if you had him or not."

"Ling was working for you all along."

"For Casimir," she corrects me.

"For how long?"

"Since you arrived in Tianshi. But this house was harder to find than we'd expected. Your brother didn't give Ling the address until today, and I had to pretend to capture her and threaten her life to pry it from him. She was supposed to get the little boy and bring him to me."

My heart stutters, thinking of Ling playing peekaboo with Theo. But Bianka had him tied to her. Oh, Bianka.

"You threatened her sister if she didn't go along with it, didn't you?" I say.

"Her sister, her grandmother, her uncle, her little cousin," says Pia casually.

"She took the contract out," I say. "That . . . thing. She pulled it right out of her wrist."

"Ah," says Pia, and her goggles whir. "It hadn't fully attached yet. If it had, I wouldn't have needed to threaten the sister. It takes some time. Where has she gone?"

"No idea," I say, relieved that it's true. "Will they be all right?"

"They are no longer useful," says Pia. "We are done with them. But the contract must have been quite far along. Pulling it out at this stage . . . I can't say what the damage will be."

426

She was able to run, I tell myself. If she could run, she must be all right. I wonder what rejecting Casimir's contract will mean for Ling's dreams of the Imperial Gardens. But I don't have time to think of that—of what she might have lost. There's no winning any game with Casimir, whichever side you're on.

"You really don't know where Mrs. Och has taken the little boy?" asks Pia.

"No."

"Disappointing. I was going to offer you a trade. The little boy for your brother."

It takes everything I've got not to snatch up the sword and try to stick another hole in her. My voice shakes badly, but I manage to ask her: "Where is he?"

Pia lets go of Frederick, and he slides to the floor, gasping. She spreads her hands—I've seen her make that gesture before, a Lorian gesture, the acceptance of mystery.

"I passed him along to my contact as soon as he gave us this address and Ling was on her way here. She was awfully fond of your brother. I had to swear up and down no harm would come to him. Of course, my word is worth less than nothing, and I do not know where they have gone now."

"Did you hurt him?"

"No more than was necessary to subdue him. He will be taken to Casimir, and Casimir will decide what to do with him. It won't be pretty. Unless, of course, you have something to offer in exchange. A little boy, for example."

I feel as if my veins are full of sand, everything slowing

down, everything inside me grinding to a halt, my heart struggling to beat against the terrible pressure of so much weight.

"I can't," I whisper. "I told you, I don't know where he is."

"Casimir might accept another trade," says Pia. "After all, he is very keen on *you*, as well. Then your brother could go home with a nice bag of gold for good measure."

I think of that tentacled little blob Ling pulled out of her. Something starts to beat inside me, something deeper and stronger than my stuttering heartbeat. Like a drum calling forth a different kind of strength. Like the pulse of some other, terrible Julia.

"Give me the day to look for Theo," I say. "If I can't find him, I'll turn myself over to Casimir in exchange for Dek's life. Wait for me at the Hundred Lantern Hotel."

"Wait for you?" Pia's goggles whir. "I don't think I ought to let you out of my sight."

"I'll come," I say. "You know I will, for Dek."

She nods, once. "Very well."

I go and kneel next to Frederick.

"I have to go."

"I know."

"I'll be back."

"You don't . . . have to come back," he says.

His face is pinched and tight, his eyes faded, all the color drained out of him. How much did she take?

"Will you be all right?"

He says, "She wouldn't . . . she wouldn't . . ." But who

428

knows what she would do. His eyes slide toward me, find mine. "I can't move."

"You don't need to move right now. But don't die. Please."

"I'll try . . . not to," he says, almost smiling.

Pia stands on the steps, looking out at the dawn.

"If you hurt him, I *will* kill you," I say. It sounds so hollow.

"I have no interest in him," she tells me. "Not yet. But do not make me wait too long, Julia. Nightfall, or I will work my way through everyone you care for and leave you a trail of corpses by which to find me."

# FIFTY-THREE

I run out into the lane with Solanze's sword. They can't have gone far, but I can't risk going in the wrong direction. I vanish and pull back—four steps—hanging over the courtyard, where Pia is sheathing her knife and heading for the gate. I pull myself back a little farther, the city spinning beneath me—too far. I focus again on the area around the house. The streets are quiet. I feel the new core of me beating, beating, beating. Over the rooftops my vanished gaze skims, over the courtyards, the alleys, the main roads.

I find them on the canal. A boy of no more than thirteen or fourteen is punting them along. Theo is sitting in the bottom of the boat at Bianka's feet, and Bianka is slumped over like she has barely the strength to hold herself upright. My heart contracts. Mrs. Och doesn't mean to take them out of the city. She wants them on the water. She's made Bianka weak, and she has taken her—a witch!—out on the water.

I pulled my perspective too far out and I come out of it too fast, forgetting to focus on a destination point. I am plunging through the sky.

Mrs. Och looks up.

For a moment, my heart stalls with panic. I am falling fast. I pull back, vanishing again. Then I am everywhere, nowhere, I can feel myself scattering, the city spreading wide beneath me. I narrow my focus, hurl myself toward the boat.

I miss by a few inches and hit the water. I emerge gasping at the front of the boat, clutching the gunwale. The boy has dropped his pole, is screaming and pointing at me. Mrs. Och moves quickly. She grabs Bianka by the arm—Bianka, still tied to Theo by the magicked sash—and heaves her like a rag doll over the side of the boat into the canal, Theo pulled along after.

Oh, I remember it, it lives inside me—the low path by the river Syne, my screams like those of an animal in a trap, and how my mother fell and the water closed over her and she was gone and I did nothing, I did nothing. But I am not that powerless girl, not anymore. This time, I go after her.

Letting go of the sword, I grab Theo, I grab Bianka's hand, and now I know why witches cannot swim or float. She pulls us both under, fast, like something beneath is sucking her down—something stronger than me, stronger than her, stronger than anything. Trying to pull her toward the surface is utterly futile. I try to pull them out of the world, but something in the water has her and will not release her. We rush downward, my lungs bursting, the seconds drawn out to eternity. I can barely make out her face, but she is yanking her hand from mine. She is tearing at the sash, Theo's body struggling against me. The sash comes free and she is gone so quickly, disappearing into the darkness below, and I am holding Theo and kicking madly for the surface, bright and wavering above us.

I break through it, surging out of the water and nearly capsizing the boat, gasping in a desperate lungful of air. Theo is flailing, making horrible choking sounds, and then he vomits water all over my neck. Mrs. Och is standing in the boat with a long knife in her hand—not Mrs. Och but Och Farya now, winged and terrible. She does not hesitate—her eyes fixed on Theo, still retching in my arms, she dives straight for him with the knife. I let go of the boat and swing my arm for her wrist. As soon as I've got a hand on her, I yank hard, hurling myself back, pulling all three of us out of the world and straight through to Kahge.

We land in another boat, a charred boat with ragged sails moving fast through a river of lava. Both sides of the river are lined with her Spira City house, over and over again, windows ablaze like eyes, and giant white spiderish things are crawling out the doors toward the fiery river.

I shove her away from me, away from Theo. He lets loose a howl that at least means he's able to breathe, followed by more choking and retching.

"I did everything I could for them!" cries Mrs. Och. Her voice sounds strange and thin here. And then she lunges at us with the knife.

I let Theo slide to the bottom of the boat, and I grab her

arm, twisting it with both hands. I can see she is taken aback by my strength here, but she is no patchwork half creature coming apart at the seams. She hurls me off, and the knife flashes toward me. I roll aside and then throw myself at her again, grabbing her around the waist, bringing her down with me. For a surreal moment, it is like the grappling sort of fights I had as a kid in the streets of the Twist. The kind of fight Dek had to pull me out of, dragging me home with a busted lip and raw knuckles, blood humming, defiant. But this is not the Twist, I am not a child, and nobody is getting me out of this. She chucks me against the gunwale and staggers back to her feet, making for Theo, who is screaming on the deck. I dive after her. I snap her wrist back, and this time I manage to wrench the knife out of her grasp. I position myself in front of Theo again. She pauses for half a second.

"Lidari—if you are Lidari—"

"I'm Julia!" I howl at her. "I'm Julia!"

And then she comes at me. I thrust with the knife, my mind full of Bianka disappearing into the canal, tearing off the enchanted sash—handing me Theo once more and for the last time. *Oh, Bianka, Bianka.* The knife goes into Och Farya, right up to the hilt, and she doubles over it, her face livid.

My only thought is to *stop* her. I know a knife wound is not enough to stop her. I keep driving her back with the knife in her gut. I push her right over the gunwale, and she topples into the lava. A high and terrible sound comes from her throat, fading to a hiss. Hanging over the gunwale and holding her under with the knife, I can feel the heat from the river going to the very core of me, the way I felt the ice in me when we crossed the Kastahor Mountains, back when I still hoped I might be a girl with a monster inside her, instead of a monster with a girl on the outside. The fire rolls over her and over her. My throat hurts, and my ears are full of an awful sound, and then I realize I'm screaming. I pull the knife out of her and drop it there on the boat. I pick up Theo, who is shuddering and gasping, canal water seeping out of his eyes and nose and ears, while a terrible form hauls itself out of the lava and back over the gunwale.

I mean to leave her there, leave her behind. I leap up, up into the hot sky, out of this place, feeling too late the hand that clamps around my ankle. When I land back in the boat on the canal in Tianshi, what is left of Mrs. Och has come with us: bones and blackened flesh, a smoking, hissing carcass. Still some noise comes from between her teeth. It sounds like *"Lidariii."*

The punters on their approaching vessels scream when we appear. I see a boat full of the Ru, armed with crossbows, bearing down on us. Arrows fly. I kick loose of Mrs. Och's grip and pull Theo away from it all—into the air, the nothingness, where I can't even feel his arms around my neck, his breath in my ear, his hot tears against my cheek. I leave Bianka and Solanze's sword at the bottom of the canal. I leave Mrs. Och for dead, or as close as she can come to that, her burnt corpse floating down the canal on the boat.

I am so far from pity, so far from mercy—I have forgotten how to feel such things.

Frederick hasn't moved, but he opens his eyes. I grab Bianka's bag, the one she told me about, hanging from a hook in the wall in what was our room—*If something happens to me, you take Theo and you take that bag.* I add the book of Yongwen fairy tales, sling the bag over my shoulder. Then I crouch next to Frederick.

"Hold on to me," I say. Theo between us, I take them to Silver Moya's, coasting over the city, and though I am carrying them in and out of the world and themselves, they hold on to me like I can save them, and they are not afraid of me. Trusting me. Not asking me why, not even when I stop to steal apples and lettuce from the market.

It is so hard to tell Frederick. I'm afraid that he won't believe me, that he will doubt what I saw or what I say, that he will tell me I did not have to do what I did. He weeps silently, his face in his hands. I hold him, Theo still between us. Neither of us can stop holding on to Theo. As if we can keep him safe from what has already happened, what he has already lost, motherless now and unprotected, except by us.

She mixes my blood and Frederick's and Theo's into the little bowl with some ink. Theo roars with outrage when we slice his finger, and I can't bear it, can't bear to hurt him even this tiny bit. But I don't know what else to do. Silver Moya's brush flattens the world and makes way for the hill to Ragg Rock. The paper city is full of paper people who do not see us, and we follow the bird, bright and so alive, so terribly alive, but not for long, everything peeling away as we climb.

From Ragg Rock, the city looks farther away than it did before, faded. The same is true of Kahge, the far-off storm steaming and swirling through a thick haze. I squint, trying to take my gaze to the city gates, the roads beyond, but it all remains a distant blur.

"I can't see anything."

"You've taken a part of *The Book of Disruption* out of the world," says Ragg Rock. "Everything is farther apart now."

I remember what Mrs. Och said—that reassembling *The Book of Disruption* would pull Kahge into the world. The world and Kahge were close, I suppose, when Theo was in Casimir's fortress with the other two text fragments— which might explain why it was so easy for me to pass from one place to the other then. Now both seem impossibly distant.

Ragg Rock's pebble eyes are fixed on Theo. Head-to-toe muddy, he is exploring the mossy crags between the world and the nonworld, as if he has forgotten what he saw—his mother disappearing into the dark of the canal.

I try to scour the city for Dek, but from this distance it has become impossible.

Ragg Rock uses a flint knife to slice off strips of apple, and Theo feeds them to the rabbit, fascinated. Frederick is lying in the corner of the hut. I try to explain to him about the stone dial, so he knows there will be food and water for them, in spite of how barren it looks.

"Wabbit," Theo tells Frederick urgently, tugging at his sleeve. "Dat wabbit, Feyda!"

I don't know that he's ever made such a perfect sentence before. I press the heels of my palms against my eyes, inhaling, pushing down my grief and fear, down, down, down, out of my way.

"How long can they stay?" I ask Ragg Rock when I can speak again.

"Forever, if they are nice," she says. "But it will change a person." And she grins at us with her stone teeth and muddy gums.

"I'll bring more food for the rabbit when I can," I say. "But you can't let anybody else come . . . not if they are coming for Theo. Not even me."

"You won't come back?"

"I will. I'll try. But I mean . . . you said you can tell *why* somebody is coming, didn't you? What they want? I'll come to see them. But if I'm coming to take Theo, you can't let me in." I'm choking on my own words. "Only Frederick can take Theo from here. Not me, nor anyone else. That's important. Only Frederick."

She nods slowly.

"Do you promise?" I plead. "You won't let me . . . if I try?"

"I promise," she says. But she says it flatly, and I don't know how I can trust her. I don't really know what she is, how she feels—this bunny-loving mud woman, old as time. And Frederick is still so weak.

Theo tires of the rabbit and wanders out onto the hill, past the stone dial, chasing after one of the giant skeletal butterflies that came out of the now vanished woods. I want to tell her, *Don't let him get too near the mud moat; he could drown.* I want to tell her, *You will need to watch him; he is still so little, he is not as resilient as a rabbit, even.* He runs down the hill, his little legs so much steadier than when I first met him. He is so much more like a boy than a baby already, but Bianka won't see this, won't hear him learning to speak, watch him learning to run. Ragg Rock watches him with no expression on her clay face, and I know I am being ridiculous—she is no child's nursemaid—but I have no choice anyway, can only hope Frederick finds his strength returning soon. This is the only place that is out of Casimir's reach.

"You mustn't let him draw anything," I say. "He can make things real if he imagines them and draws them."

Ragg Rock smiles, like I've told her something charming about him.

"Mama!" barks Theo, running back into the hut, commanding us.

"Mama's not here. You need to stay with Frederick," I tell him, my voice strangled.

"Mama!" he roars, and then he throws his arms around my leg. "Lala umma beppo stoy."

"Frederick will read you a story when he's a little better. Something with a happy ending."

I try to kiss him, but he pulls away from me, cross, and goes back to the rabbit.

"What will you do?" asks Frederick.

"I'm going to kill Casimir."

He doesn't say, *Don't be a fool.* Or *Stay.* Or *Let's go, we'll hide, together we'll hide—there's another way, there must be another way.*

"I'll be praying for you," he says. "Every minute."

And for all that I don't know if I believe in the power of prayer, I find some comfort in that.

I leave them with Ragg Rock and return to the world, the bright and lovely springtime day in Tianshi. I'm not holding out much hope, but I soar over the city in vanishing leaps, pulling back and in again, searching for Dek. I don't find him. When the bells of Shou-shu chime for the setting sun, I make my way, defeated, to the Hundred Lantern Hotel, and there I offer myself up to Pia.

# FIFTY-FOUR

It takes two days to reach the coast. Pia secures us a first-class cabin on a luxury steamer. She is not concerned about the notorious pirates off the coast of Yongguo—most of whom belong to Casimir, if Princess Zara was right. Nor does she appear worried that I might try to cut her throat in the night, though I lie in my comfortable berth and think of little else. I suppose she knows I won't risk it, not with Dek in Casimir's hands. Or perhaps she doesn't care if I do. I am beginning to understand her.

She takes me up on deck at sunset one evening. I am dressed like her, because the only clothes she has for me are her own and I could not get the stink of blood out of mine. The other passengers avoid us, and who can blame them? I see islands on the horizon. Dolphins are leaping near the prow, the pink sky full of seabirds wheeling, rainbow-colored fish flying. We stand side by side at the railing, looking at the sea.

It's beautiful, but I don't care about beauty. The drum-beat at my center has summoned a storm, a howling wind within. It is spinning higher and higher, whipping itself into a frenzy, a terrible force gathering. The sun dips to touch the horizon and spills bloody across the water, like a murder.

All right, Dek: I forgive myself. It's past time, isn't it, now that I am barely who I was? I forgive myself for being such a stupid child, for being callow and cowardly when I took Theo from Mrs. Och's house, a lifetime and many selves ago. I was afraid, and I was a fool, and I can forgive myself for that.

I can even forgive myself for the rest. For failing Bianka—just moments too slow. For failing to save Ko Dan or Count Fournier, for the murder of Mrs. Och, for the many blunders that have led us to this pass. I'm putting it all behind me. You are the only one with whom there was never any need for explanations or forgiveness.

And perhaps it doesn't matter—what I've done, what I am. We choose each moment, Frederick says. I've seen Casimir's contract skittering on its little legs, but in the grip of this fury, I don't believe he has any magic strong enough to put a leash around me. At this moment, I believe that I could gather Kahge in my fist like the edge of a tablecloth and hurl all the might of hell at my enemies. I believe I could tear down the world to save you, level cities and leave empires in ruins behind me—and I'll do it, if that's what it takes.

Pia turns away from the sunset to look at me, and I look back, unflinching. I see myself reflected in her goggles, the new scar a black slash down the side of my face.

"I'm sorry, Julia," she says, and her voice is soft, as I've never heard it before.

But my own voice is like a knife when I answer her: "Don't be."

No more trying to hold on to the girl I hoped I was. I'm finished with the business of atonement. I'm coming for you, Dek, and I am bringing the whirlwind with me.

# ACKNOWLEDGMENTS

Sitting down to write this makes me feel lucky, just like sitting down to write every morning makes me feel lucky. It takes a little book-loving army to turn a story into a book that works and isn't riddled with errors and inconsistencies, to make it look beautiful and enticing (and readable!), to get it out into the world and try to persuade readers to give it a try. I know just how tremendously lucky I am to be working with such kind, brilliant, dedicated people. Thank you a million times over to my agent, Steve Malk; to my editor, Nancy Siscoe; to Amy Black in Canada; and to everyone at Knopf and Doubleday Books for giving Julia a home and taking such good care of her. I am beyond grateful.

Thank you also to my generous and insightful beta readers—Dana Alison Levy, Kip Wilson Rechea, and Samantha Cohoe. I owe you all the chocolate in the world.

I dread to imagine where my stories and I would be without my band of stalwarts. Thank you to my beloved brothers; my inspiring grandmother; the people who didn't start out as family but became so—Jon, Giles, Mick; and my parents, who gave me calm waters, a blank map, and bright horizons to start off with, and built my heart into an unsinkable ship fit for the stormiest seas.

# ABOUT THE AUTHOR

CATHERINE EGAN grew up in Vancouver, Canada. Since then, she has lived on a volcanic island in Japan (which erupted while she was there and sent her hurtling straight into the arms of her now husband), in Tokyo, Kyoto, and Beijing, on an oil rig in the middle of Bohai Bay, then in New Jersey, and now in New Haven, Connecticut.

She is currently occupied with writing books and fighting dragon armies with her warrior children. You can read more about her at catherineegan.com and follow her on Twitter at @ByCatherineEgan.

# The Brazilian State

# BILDNER WESTERN HEMISPHERE STUDIES

### Series Editor: Mauricio A. Font
The Graduate Center and Queens College
City University of New York

This series represents a joint publication initiative of the Bildner Center for Western Hemisphere Studies at the City University of New York Graduate Center and Lexington Books. The books published in this series endeavor to support the Center's mission of generating greater comprehension of contemporary issues in the Americas, creating an international dialogue on policy issues, and producing research on a range of topics that are both country and theme specific.

# The Brazilian State

*Debate and Agenda*

Edited by Mauricio A. Font and Laura Randall

with the assistance of Janaina Saad

LEXINGTON BOOKS
*Lanham • Boulder • New York • Toronto • Plymouth, UK*

Published by Lexington Books
A wholly owned subsidiary of The Rowman & Littlefield Publishing Group, Inc.
4501 Forbes Boulevard, Suite 200, Lanham, Maryland 20706
http://www.lexingtonbooks.com

Estover Road, Plymouth PL6 7PY, United Kingdom

British Library Cataloguing in Publication Information Available

**Library of Congress Cataloging-in-Publication Data**

The Brazilian state : debate and agenda / edited by Mauricio Font and Laura Randall.
    p. cm.
  Includes bibliographical references and index.
  ISBN 978-0-7391-6731-1 (hardback) — ISBN 978-0-7391-6889-9 (electronic)
  1. Brazil—Politics and government—1985–2002—Congresses. 2. Brazil—Politics and
government—2003—Congresses. 3. Brazil—Economic policy—Congresses 4. Brazil—
Economic conditions—1985—Congresses. 5. Brazil—Social conditions—1985—
Congresses. I. Font, Mauricio A. (Mauricio Augusto) II. Randall, Laura.
  F2538.3.B7524 2011
  981.06'4—dc23                                              2011021149

Printed in the United States of America

# Contents

# Tables

# Figures

# Acknowledgments

The Bildner Center for Western Hemisphere Studies is grateful to the many individuals who were involved with this book and with the International Symposium "The Brazilian State: Paths and Prospects of Dirigisme and Liberalization" held at The Graduate Center, City University of New York, on November 9-10, 2009. We thank all contributors and participants for their papers and comments, as well as for their patience throughout the process of publishing this book. As co-editor, Laura Randall provided essential guidance on the papers as well as in the overall organization of the book. The Bildner Center staff played a significant role in the entire production process of this book. Janaina Saad helped edit the papers, arrange texts and graphics, and organize the conference. We also thank Carlos Ruiz and Ben Guttmann for their assistance with formatting and structuring the book. We greatly appreciate the efforts of professors Desmond Arias, Amy Chazkel, John Collins, and Kenneth Erickson in providing continued guidance to participants. Jackie Slater, John Arias, and Jacqueline Ha provided greatly helped in the preparation and logistics of the conference. Dr. Brian Schwartz and The Graduate Center must be thanked for their support of the Bildner Center.

As part of the *Bildner Western Hemisphere Studies* series, this volume advances the Bildner Center's mission of generating greater comprehension, dialogue, and debate about contemporary issues in the Americas. In particular, the Center's Brazil Project focuses on issues of state and society in Brazil. Naturally, authors are responsible for their own views and their positions do not necessarily represent those of the Bildner Center. Our hope is that by exposing different approaches and ideas, this series will shed light on contemporary issues in the Americas.We salute Justin Race and Lexington Books as we expand the list of exciting titles in this series.

*Mauricio A. Font*
*Director, Bildner Center for Western Hemisphere Studies*

# Part I
# Approaches, Actors, and Dynamics

# 1

# INTRODUCTION

*Mauricio A. Font*

In the late 1990s and then again in 2005, Brazil faced economic and political adversities that seemed to confirm chronic institutional and political blocks to development. Very shortly after, however, news about the country focused on its achievements in economic performance, social development, and enhanced international standing. Increasingly after 2005, perceptions and realities stood old Brazilian clichés on their heads—the "sleeping giant" had awakened, the "country of the future" had arrived (e.g., Nóbrega 2005).

Success has many fathers. The reforms of the 1990s, the policies of the Lula presidency, the commodities boom driven by Asian demand, and yet other factors have been singled out as providing the main impetus for change. The role of the state in the new phase of Brazilian development is the main concern of this volume. On a practical level, it addresses the question of the extent to which state actions have reduced bottlenecks to the country's sustained development and global standing.

## REFORM, RECOVERY, AND DEVELOPMENT

The disastrous stagnation and hyperinflation in the 1980s and early 1990s provides the background to understanding the Brazilian economy and polity since the mid-1990s. The debt crisis of the 1980s and the increasing public deficit had undermined the government's traditional role in promoting development and indicated the exhaustion of the statist economic model that had been in place for decades. Several emergency economic plans attempted to control hyperinflation but failed miserably. Pessimism grew about the ability of policy makers to manage fiscal affairs and stabilize the economy.[1] In 1993-94, the Real Plan (*Plano Real*) and the related reforms that followed ended high inflation, made public administration more fiscally responsible, ushered in a new era in the organization of the state and its development roles, and began to reposition Brazil in the world scene. As Brazilian prices stabilized so did politics. The economy began to grow. Optimism and faith in democracy gradually returned. Still, vulnerability remained. The hard-achieved results were endangered by the global financial meltdown related to the Asian crisis of 1997–1998 and the disruption it brought to ongoing reform processes in emergent countries, including neighboring Chile and Argentina. Argentina's catastrophic meltdown in 2001 had a major impact on the region. To prevent a comparable financial collapse, Brazilian authorities adopted a floating exchange rate. The Brazilian *real*—introduced in 1994—lost value, but inflation did not return. Confidence gradually returned and so did economic growth. The new fiscal approach had obviously made a major difference.

Policymakers were relieved. Still, the lingering effects of the crisis contributed to the 2002 electoral defeat of the original reformist coalition that had been put together by outgoing president Fernando Henrique Cardoso. Luiz Inácio Lula da Silva's election as president of Brazil fueled fears of a return to past populist practices. Many observers braced for the rejection of policies that leftist Lula and his associates in the Workers' Party had attacked as part of neoliberal "damned legacy,"[2] but the new authorities largely maintained the previous government's policies of economic stabilization and fiscal responsibility after taking office in early 2003.

---

1. My own account of this period is found in Font (2002), from which I draw my discussion of conditions from the 1990s through 2002. For the earlier collapse of public finances, see Baer (2008), Galle and Bertolli (2004).

2. The "damned legacy" (*"herança maldita"*) became a political cliché of the Brazilian left, implying the excise of the fiscal adjustment and much of the reform effort of the 1990s.

Brazil seemed to have entered a new era of stabilization, fiscal responsibility, and related liberalization policies—even as many voices within the Workers' Party and aligned intellectuals continued to press hard for a return to and a larger development role for the state and policies associated with "developmentalism" of past decades.

As growth gathered speed after 2006, it did so in the framework of continuity as well as new initiatives in economic policy. Economic momentum and continuity strengthened Brazil's defenses against international shocks. A test of this ability came sooner than expected. When the global financial crisis of 2008 wreaked havoc to the world economy, its local impact was relatively mild.[3] Together with the impact of social policies, the optimistic economic scenario decisively contributed to the election of Dilma Rousseff as President in 2010. Like Lula da Silva's, her campaign had sent reassuring signs that the economic model would not change.

Current Brazilian policymakers are the first to argue that monetary and fiscal policies have been and remain pillars of sustained recovery. But other factors stand out. The seemingly insatiable Asian demand for soy, minerals, and other commodities remains very important. Together with the opening of the soy frontier in the central plateau, Brazil's energy sector had a bonanza with the expanded prospects for biofuels and then the discovery of huge new oil fields. In fact, the economy found itself in a veritable boom. In addition to natural resource endowment and private entrepreneurship, other socio-economic factors would also need to be taken into account in a full understanding of the new dynamism.

Debate continues about institutional modernization and the precise role of the state in the economy. Some actors and analysts still view the reforms and related state policies since the 1990s in the context of the arrival of a new liberal order either imposed by international agencies or brought about by the diffusion of ideas and practices.[4] Others emphasize endogenous factors centering on coalitional shifts or the impact of institutions. Sallum (1996) provides a careful analysis of the role of social classes and interest groups. Font (2002: chapter 9) presents a structural realignment perspective linking political actors to the rise of a new paradigm. Some authors

---

3. In 2009, the Brazilian economy contracted by only 0.18 percent in 2009, while the US economy shrank by 2.4 percent. Meanwhile, Brazil's unemployment rate continued to decline—from 9.6 percent in 2007 to 7.9 percent in 2009 (see Appendix and World Bank, 2009).

4. Various works by Bresser-Pereira illustrate this view. A full discussion of the broader intellectual debate is beyond the reach of this introduction.

focus on single dimensions of the shift. For example, João Paulo Peixoto notes the rise of pragmatism.

Either catastrophic or highly optimistic scenarios are often found in the debate about consequences. The focus in this volume is on empirically grounded attempts to isolate the impact of policies, while acknowledging that politicization adds to the challenge of assessing the impact of policies.

Arguments about continuity between recent governments can place rather different emphases. For instance, Renato Boschi's chapter emphasizes the survival of the statist tradition and the emergence of a new developmental economic model. Various other works view the Cardoso and Lula governments as part of the same era of reform (Font 2002).

A significant number of Brazilian intellectuals support the idea of a new developmentalist economic model. For instance, several essays in *São Paulo em Perspectiva* (20 [3], 2006) argue for a new statism or developmentalism while addressing the debate about continuity or convergence between liberalization and development policy. These articles generally tend to share a critical reading of the liberalizing reforms as well as an equally emphatic defense of developmentalism, both old and new. The older version of developmentalism is seen as responsible for much of Brazilian development from 1930 through 1980, while the second is put forth as alternative to the liberalization model of the 1990s. The opening essay by Bresser-Pereira (2006) argues that conventional economic orthodoxy—"neoliberal policies and reforms"—have failed in Brazil as well as throughout Latin America, creating conditions for the rise of national development strategies sharing a "new developmentalism." Like its older version, the new developmentalism is nationalist and rejects "pressures from the North," but accepts such basic principles as export-orientation, rejection of protectionism, and support for fiscal discipline and public saving. The new Brazilian developmentalism rejects FDI-directed growth strategies, open capital accounts, unregulated exchange rates, and monetarism.[5]

## THIS VOLUME

The chapters in this volume present historical, theoretical-interpretive, and substantive perspectives on the above set of issues. Part I dwells on actors, con-

---

5. Besides Bresser-Pereira, this issue contains essays by economists Luiz Fernando de Paula, Ricardo Carneiro, José Eli da Veiga, and others. The article by Armando Castelar Pinheiro and Fabio Giambiagi ("Sem clima para crescer") deviates from the main emphasis of this publication and presents arguments critical of the state and the dysfunctions of the development state.

texts, institutions, and ideas. João Paulo Peixoto reviews the changing role of the state in the trajectory from the Vargas years (including his return as president in 1950) to the Cardoso years, discussing implications for modernization of the state and development strategies. Over time, he argues, the debate between different ideologies and institution-building efforts converged on the rise of pragmatism as well as a reaffirmation of the need for administrative modernization.

Renato Boschi explores what he sees as the revival of state developmentalism in the wake of the market-oriented reforms from 1990 to 2002. He emphasizes continuity in regard to the role of the state. The expansion of state capabilities from the 1930s to the 1970s, together with the social priorities of the Lula government, opened up the internal market as a major way of promoting growth and employment. In this view, economic stabilization and the regulation of the banking and financial industries achieved in the 1990s did not represent a sharp break from the previous state-sponsored model. Brazil preserved strategic bureaucratic nuclei and patterns of business-state relations facilitating the country's search for a new model in the era of globalization.

Glauco Arbix and Scott Martin cover the same ground and reach only partly similar conclusions. Their review of the Brazilian debate about developmentalism focuses on the rise of new state capacities in fiscal and competitiveness policies (including trade, industry, science and technology, and social policy) since the mid-1990s. These capabilities are leading to a new model of economic expansion based on pro-market intervention with an emphasis on social policy. Brazil has thus defined and brought into existence the tools for a new development model, even if this experience with the neo-activist state has yet to be fully conceptualized and understood.

Political scientist Eiiti Sato shares an optimistic assessment of the short-term prospects for economic expansion and vitality, and goes on to highlight the structural investments still needed for sustained long-term growth, arguing that the federal government has in fact performed poorly in the area of competitiveness. Economic policy has been too cautious in relation to international capital flows, limiting the country's ability to benefit from the cycle of growth in the world economy but also has helped to insulate the nation against shocks. Sato is hence more skeptical than the authors of the previous two chapters.

Other authors in this volume illuminate policy-making processes and further highlight the need for a sustained reform process. Maria Rita Loureiro et al. shed light on the role of the bureaucracy relative to political parties and interest groups, providing a deeper understanding of Brazilian political dynamics. They identify important political actors and review major studies of the Brazilian polity. David Fleischer reviews the successful and unsuccessful attempts at political reform during the Cardoso and Lula presidencies, showing that much of the reform agenda has yet to be accomplished: from the 1997 constitutional amendment allowing reelection, to aspects of the system of proportional representation (PR) lists, the adoption of electronic voting machines, and the disposition of blank ballots. Probing the failure of proposals to change election rules (in 2003, 2007 and 2009), he thus provides a full map of the country's political reform agenda.

The chapter by J. Ricardo Tranjan discusses different participatory budgeting programs in Porto Alegre and concludes that the coexistence of such programs has had a positive impact on local democratic practices. He advances the term "constructive confluence" as challenge to other views of a "perverse confluence" detrimental to democratization. Tranjan argues that despite their different views of the scale and scope of civil society engagement, both the *participatory budgeting* practices and the *local solidarity governance* initiatives attempt to surmount traditional statist and free-market models. In Porto Alegre, the confluence of civil society discourses and participatory practices is augmenting democratization and creating new spaces for citizens' participation.

Part II of this volume deepens the focus on social and cultural policy. The first two chapters discuss how the changing Brazilian state responds to demands from different social groups. José Roberto Savoia's study of pensions identifies significant imbalances in Brazil's social security system. Distortions include the disparity between contributions and disbursements as well as unequal benefits or rights and a large informal sector. Savoia discusses the effects of reform efforts by the Lula government and argues for further reform to improve the nation's pension laws and system.

Lia Zanotta Machado concentrates on the Brazilian feminist movement and its interactions with the federal government. Growing out of the confrontation against the military regime in the seventies, the feminist movement shifted to a strategy of negotiation beginning in the twenty-first century. Throughout this change, the logic of addressing the state has always been present. During the Lula years, government-supported initiatives such as the National Council of Women's Rights and the proposal of National Conferences for Women's Policies showed a proactive state response not only to the demands of feminist movements but also efforts at coalition formation. Divergence within the government in how to respond to political pressures and key proposals on women's rights has resulted in cleavages between political positions of the government and feminist groups. In the context of increased public space for dialogue and institutionalization of the feminist movement, Lia Zanotta Machado concludes that the women's movement must build on its momentum and engage in new alliances.

Anthropologist John Collins sheds light on the also proactive presence of the state in the cultural sphere. Cultural policy has not received adequate attention in the past. Collins links policies of cultural patrimony to efforts at state consolidation, placing the state at the center of the analysis of culture and federal institutions on cultural heritage, analyzing two distinct approaches to heritage planning in different historical periods. The concern with monuments and buildings overlaps with that of people's everyday habits. His position is that understanding the role of cultural heritage in Brazilian citizenship and political economy depends on tracking this relationship between buildings and quotidian habits.

Part III shifts the focus to Brazil's financial sector, responses to the global financial crisis of 2008, and shifts in capital market dynamics. Fernando Sotelino, Monica Arruda de Almeida, and Elaine da Silveira Leite comment on the trends and performance of economic and financial policies. Sotelino's analysis of the structure of Brazil's financial industry underlines its particularities. He highlights the balance between private and public sector banks as well as between domestic and foreign banks. Brazil's financial market remains one of the world's best capitalized and supervised. Sotelino reviews the prospects for the consolidation of a sustainable credit market in Brazil, noting that public sector banks finance much of new investments.

Monica Arruda de Almeida studies Brazil's adherence to the main international efforts to combat money laundering and financial terrorism in order to improve the reputation of its financial institutions and their capacity to attract foreign capital. Though these measures have resulted in enhanced international credibility, the improvement in Brazil's international reputation is largely due to the country's more effective management of its debt portfolio and the stability of its monetary and fiscal policies.

The last chapter in this section on finances is Elaine Leite's examination of how the Brazilian financial system encourages savings and investment by constituents previously unfamiliar with, or even marginalized by, the financial system. Although the new process of "financialization" involves traditional state and non-state actors, she brings out the role of emergent financial intermediaries popularly known as "gurus" in promoting ideas of self-help that legitimate personal finance and directly contribute to this recent trend in Brazilian society. The new "moral entrepreneurs" of finance educate the broad public on ways to invest to achieve economic security. While pointing to state incentives and efforts at establishing a conducive legal and institutional framework, she argues that a new culture of investment blending notions of success, happiness, and wealth is emerging in Brazil.

Part IV gives attention to Brazil's shifting global relations, particularly its strategic economic and political relations with the transatlantic community and its regional energy policy agenda. Thomas Trebat's discussion of Brazil's evolving global economic and political role highlights areas of cooperation and conflict with the transatlantic community. Though Brazil's economic and political development policies have been broadly in tune with the American and European agenda, noteworthy areas of conflict and disagreements are also present. Brazil's aspirations of becoming a regional and global power-broker have resulted in divergences with members of the transatlantic community. Trebat makes the case for an agenda for future cooperation between Brazil and the United States that aims at greater global and economic stability while respecting Brazil's autonomy in global affairs.

Christine Gustafson and Leslie Elliott Armijo discuss the Brazilian state's approach to regional energy policy from 1990 to 2009. Comparing its vision of energy cooperation in the Americas with those of the United States and Venezuela, all of which represent different patterns of regional integration, the authors argue that the Brazilian approach may be the most likely to be implemented.

Together, the papers in this volume illuminate the lineaments of state action and critical details of the debates on the role of the state in Brazil. They shed light on the impact of political institutional processes on social change in this large and dynamic country. Together with the increasingly rich studies of other large emerging countries, the focus on newly dynamic Brazil enriches the comparative discussion of development processes and the role that political actors and institutions play in them. Brazilian society, the Brazilian polity, and internal debate are still in flux. The essays in this volume serve as invitation to an exciting, diverse, and dynamic field of inquiry.

# 2

# THE BRAZILIAN STATE
# SINCE VARGAS

*João Paulo M. Peixoto*

*Abstract: This paper discusses the scope and profile of the state in Brazil since the Vargas Era (1930-1945 and 1951-1954) through the Cardoso (1995-2002) and Lula (2003-2010) administrations. It addresses issues about the changing role of the state and its implications for economic development and political modernization. This period of time encompasses the diverse ideologies and institution-building efforts implemented during these years.*

Structural reforms, as changes in the political and economic roles of the state, must be analyzed in light of simultaneous changes in the political and economic spheres. This is regardless of which happens first—whether economic reform, as in Chile, or political change, as in Brazil, or both at the same time, as was the case in Russia.

From this perspective, the state reform process is yet another variation of timeless ideological dispute between liberals and statists; between liberalism and socialism; between market economy and state economy; between capitalism and socialism; and in the end, a new version of the classic "battle" between right and left. Still, regardless of political regime or ideology, the search for an efficient state has been among the top priorities of politicians in almost every country in the world.

11

State reform in Brazil has been a goal pursued by dictators, authoritarians, and liberals alike. Since at least the 1930s, the country has experienced a continuous process of state modernization. This process characterized the 1930s, 1960s, and 1990s, regardless of the type of political regime.

In Latin America in the 1990s, a set of liberal economic policy prescriptions known as the "Washington Consensus" constituted a new "light" for state reform and economic restructuring. Brazil was not an exception (Williamson, 1990; Evans, 1992 and1995; Haggard and Kaufman, 1992). State sponsorship of economic development in Latin America had been present prior to the advent of neo-liberalism and was most heavily entrenched during the 20th century. In Brazil, State existed until the breakdown of its economic policy of Import Substitution Industrialization during the debt crisis of the 1980s. These experiences lead to a greater role for the state in policy and decision-making and a far smaller one for civil society.

The shift towards a less interventionist or "neoliberal" state occurred most significantly under the Fernando Henrique Cardoso administration (1995-2002). The administration accomplished this transformation without losing sight of the proper role of government as prioritizing basic "public goods" such as education and health. Under Luis Inácio Lula da Silva (2003-2010), however, the pendulum seems to have returned to the previous model, in which the state is viewed as a paramount for economic development. This shift is very reminiscent of the ideological perspective in place under Getúlio Dornelles Vargas (1930-1945) and the authoritarian regime (1964-1985).

TABLE 2-1. The Brazilian State Since 1822

| | Type of State | Political Regime | Constitution | Form of Government |
|---|---|---|---|---|
| 1822-1889 | Unitary | Limited Democracy | Pre-Constitutional 1822 to 1824 and Constitutional 1824 to 1889 | Monarchy |
| 1889-1937 | Federal | Limited Democracy | Provisory Government 1889-1891; Constitutional 1891-1930; Provisory Government 1930-1934; Constitutional 1934-1937 | Republic |
| 1937- 1945 | Unitary in practice, federal in theory | Dictatorship | Dictatorship | Republic |
| 1946-1964 | Federal | Democracy | Constitutional | Republic |
| 1964-1985 | Federal | Authoritarian | Constitutional | Republic |
| 1985- Present | Federal | Democracy | Constitutional | Republic |

*Source*: Peixoto, 2009.

This article addresses the phases of the Brazilian state mainly concerning its political, economic, and administrative functions over contrasting administrations since 1930.

## HISTORICAL CONTEXT

Since its founding, the Brazilian state has gone through multiple political structures (see Table 2-1) and has been tied to ever-changing economic priorities (see Table 2-2). Its functions are seen as the maintenance of internal peace; the conquest, unity, and expansion of territory; and sovereignty. Since political survival and internal peace are more easily defined in economic terms, states have shifted responsibility to economic transformation. The Liberal, the Socialist, and the Welfare State were the three predominant forms of the state throughout the 20th century. The crises of the state during the 1990s impacted all three political ideologies. Soviet Communism disappeared; liberalism became more embedded in social matters; and social democracy embraced an open market economy under the "third wave" of revisionism.

The changing role of the state continues to be affected by mutations of the international political system. As a result of this process, the interventionist state has emerged as a distinct and modernized institution that is able to impose its priorities upon society. A strictly non-interventionist state has never existed and probably never will, the recurring dilemma is not whether the state should intervene in economic sectors. Rather its the limits and scope of such actions. As the twentieth century progressed in Brazil, reform became a basic theme for public administrations.

The first initial attempt to modernize the public sector occurred during the first Vargas presidency with the creation of the nation's first civil service apparatus DASP Departamento Administrativo do Serviço Público (The Public Service Management Department) in 1936. This reformation also included the implementation of administrative reforms designed to eliminate nepotism and clientelism.

The standardization of civil service employment through merit-based exams was a cornerstone for the modernization of Brazil's public sector. This merit system was introduced aiming at establishing a new era of government efficiency in the tropics, replacing a system based on spoils, clientelism, and nepotism. Unfortunately, even today merit-based requirements have not been fully implemented in Brazil. This is despite a new wave of professionalization that came along with the military regime's administrative provisions for the public sector. Entrance by examination, promotion by merit, and the unification of administrative functions formed the foundation for this initial phase of Brazil's modernization in the spirit of the Northcote-Trevelyan Report (1854) in the United Kingdom.[1] From the developmental state of the 1960s to the contemporary regulatory state, the role of government and the proper model for a public administration were at the center of this field of literature, especially after the passage of the 1988 Constitution. During the 1960s and 1980s, the actions of government and public administrations alternately were acclaimed and denigrated.

Due to globalization and the subsequent change the international system, state reform, and public sector modernization has once again captured the attention of governments. It is viewed not only as a mechanism to encourage changes in government but also as a way to improve public sector efficiency and to adapt to the cultural, economic, and political forces of modernization.

## Cycles of the Brazilian Government

The reformist agenda that Brazil adopted in recent years is only one of the various models that has defined the role of government since the founding of the First Republic. In total there are five distinct phases of Brazil's political evolution.

The first phase occurred soon after the proclamation of the Republic in 1889, when the country established its first Republican Constitution (1891) and ended with the Revolution of October 1930. During this period, Brazil was a predominantly rural and oligarchic society.

The second phase, often seen as the rise of *modern Brazil*, came about during the Getúlio Vargas era (1930 to 1945).[2] Vargas incorporated into the government's agenda the imperative for change and the quest for modernity, drawing from the ideals espoused by the revolutionary movement that brought him to power. When looking at these early years of Vargas' rule, it is important to focus upon the period 1937-1945. During this phase of his dictatorship, also known as the "New State" (*Estado Novo*) political parties were

---

1. *Report on the Organization of the Permanent Civil Service*, 1853. London, House of Commons.
2. The Vargas Era means a specific political and economic model used in the two different periods that President Getúlio Vargas governed Brazil (1930-1945 and 1951-1954). The first was essentially characterized by authoritarianism and modernization, and the second was characterized by nationalism and populism. Both profoundly marked the Brazilian political and economic development, and levied long after President Vargas' death in 1954.

TABLE 2-2. Cycles of the Brazilian Government, 1930-2011

| Period | President | Features |
|---|---|---|
| Nov. 1930–Oct. 1945 | Getúlio Vargas | Industrialization, Modernization of the Public Sector, State Intervention in the Economy |
| Jan. 1946–Jan. 1951 | General Eurico Gaspar Dutra | Economic Liberalization Redemocratization, Exchange Rate Crises |
| Jan. 1951–Aug. 1954 | Getúlio Vargas | Nationalism, Populism, State Intervention in the Economy |
| Jan. 1956–Jan. 1961 | Juscelino Kubitschek | Developmentalism, New Capital of Brasilia, Inflation, Industrialization |
| Jan. 1961–Aug. 1961 and Sep. 1961–Mar. 1964, respectively | Jânio Quadros and João Goulart | Right and Left Wing Populism, Parliamentary |
| Mar. 1964–Mar. 1985 | Humberto de Alencar Castelo Branco, Artur da Costa e Silva, Emílio Garrastazu Médici, Ernesto Geisel, João Batista de Oliveira Figueiredo | Nationalism; State Modernization; Economic Reforms; National Security and Development Doctrine; Debt Crisis |
| Mar. 1985–Mar. 1990 | José Sarney | New Republic, Constitution of 1988, Economic Nationalism, High Inflation, and Cruzado Plan |
| Mar. 1990–Dec. 1992 | Fernando Collor | Economic Reforms, Neoliberalism, Administrative Reform, Impeachment, Privatization |
| Dec. 1992–Jan. 1995 | Itamar Franco | Real Plan, Statism, Economic Nationalism |
| Jan. 1995–Jan. 2002 | Fernando Henrique Cardoso | Real Plan, Economic Stabilization, State Reform, Privatization, Reelection, Pragmatism |
| Jan. 2003–Jan. 2011 | Luis Inácio Lula da Silva | Pragmatism, Economic Stability, Populism, Statism, Democratic Left, Extensive Social Policies |

*Source*: Own elaboration, Peixoto (2009).

abolished, the Congress was closed, interventors (federally appointed Governors also vested with legislative powers) were nominated in the states, and a rigorous censorship of the press was established. Vargas seized the opportunity to introduce substantial changes to public administration in Brazil. He institutionalized the centralization of power at the federal level of government, making the president and the state omnipresent figures in Brazilian politics. During the *Estado Novo*, Vargas practically abolished the Federation, ruling Brazil as if it were a unitary state rather than a federal one.

The third phase of Brazil's political evolution immediately followed Vargas' first period in office (1930-1945). Eurico Gaspar Dutra (1946-1951) worked to return Brazil to normal conditions and democracy. He called a Constituent Assembly, which wrote a new constitution on September 18,

1946. Politically, it was characterized by a new liberal constitution that attempted to re-democratize Brazil and its political institutions. Investment focused on infrastructure, per capita income grew a little more than 3.5%, and inflation was roughly 12% (Goldsmith, 1986: 221). Juscelino Kubitschek's administration (1956-1960) emphasized economic development despite its very high inflationary cost and the sharp rise of the public sector deficit. After Jânio Quadros' brief presidential rule (December 1960 to August 1961), João Goulart adopted a populist, leftist style of government that ended in a political and economic collapse of the administration, opening the political arena for the military intervention in 1964.

The fourth phase began with the 1964 military regime and lasted up to its end in 1985. During these twenty-one years, successive military presidents ruled Brazil, motivated basically by a two-fold ideology: national security and development. Modernization, development, and economic and political stability were the signposts of the regime. But the use of a bureaucratic authoritarian to achieve these goals led to unavoidably elevated political and social costs.

The fifth and final stage of Brazil's political evolution began with the so-called "New Republic" (1985-1989) which ushered in the first civilian president (Tancredo Neves) after two decades of military rule. However, Neves never took office after falling victim to a fatal illness. His vice-president José Sarney was installed instead and governed the country from 1985 to 1989. Sarney's administration was marked by an open, full-fledged democracy. The 1988 Constitution incorporated the return of economic nationalism and a pro-state orientation for policies. During his administration, Brazil experienced high inflation (80 percent a month in his final days) and worsening levels of public service, despite achieving social progress. However, the circumstances in which President Sarney's administration ended (high inflation, political erosion due to weak presidential leadership, and society's despising of an entire generation of old politicians), gave birth to a new style of leadership. The inauguration of President Fernando Collor de Mello on 15 March 1990 represented a turning point. He introduced a vigorous program of structural reforms based on center-right, neo-liberal economic policies to cope with the crisis caused by Brazil's Vargas-era economic and political institutions. His first act was to implant a form of market-oriented liberalism that was to be politically tempered by social democrat precepts.

The sharpest contrast between Collor and his predecessors was his determination to push ahead with the privatization of state-owned enterprises and to attack inflation. Collor assumed power with a radical and vigorous economic plan (Provisional Measure 155, 15 March 1990) to fight the legacy of economic disorder left by the Sarney administration. President Collor had to confront inflation rates of over 70 percent per month, plummeting exports, an overvalued currency, an unsustainable budget deficit, low investment levels, and an inefficient and oversized bureaucracy. Most bank deposits were frozen, as were wages and prices, and economic activity was immediately and adversely affected. Evasions of these economic restrictions soon occurred and additional reforms stalled. As a result, price restrictions were released, and inflation returned but this time at a much higher annual rate because of the government's loose monetary policy. The Collor administration responded with Collor Plan II, a feeble attempt to regain control of spiraling inflation. Its primary contribution was to recognize that if a tight fiscal policy would be sustained, prices of public goods that had been held constant would have to be raised.

In the months following Collor's impeachment under accusations of corruption in 1992, the economy continued on its path of extreme turbulence. His successor, Itamar Franco (Collor's vice president) had four finance ministers in a period of 8 months until he finally appointed Fernando Henrique Cardoso, often referred to as FHC (June 1993). Cardoso was the creator of the Real (Brazilian monetary unit) Plan—*Plano Real* which officially took effect on July 1st, 1994. Although some of its measures had been gradually introduced after he first became finance minister (1993-1994), the Real Plan changed both the political and economic future of the country.

Following his success as finance minister, Cardoso won a landslide victory in his bid for the presidency of Brazil. His party, the PSDB (Partido da Social Democracia Brasileira), formed a pragmatic political alliance with the PFL (Partido da Frente Liberal, now Democratas) to garner broader support in the elections. Upon his inauguration (1 January 1995), he pledged to continue the fight against inflation and upheld the Real Plan as his main political objective.

It is also important to point out that the 1990s saw the inauguration of the first directly-elected president of the Republic after more than two decades of military rule, as well as the first impeachment of a president (Fernando Collor de Mello) in Brazilian history. Additionally significant a constitutional change in 1997 allowed the nation to re-elect a president for the first time in its history as a Republic. These years of structural reforms and upheavals produced a politically and economically transformed Brazil.

Political modernization and economic stabilization are probably the lasting legacy of FHC's administration to Brazilian democracy and capitalism. President Cardoso eliminated several state monopolies, as discussed below, followed by a vigorous program of privatization. Along with these measures he tried to introduce a program of reforms (tax, social security, and labor) in the economic sphere, but his efforts were unsuccessful in Congress.

When President Lula took over the presidency of the Republic in January 2003, he wanted to complete the unfinished reform agenda and also to implement a program of microeconomic reforms intended to sustain growth in the long run. This was elaborated by economist Marcos Lisboa as Under Secretary for Economic Policy at the Ministry of Finance. Micro reform measures included improving the quality of the taxation system; policies for social inclusion anchored in widening credit opportunities for public servants and the retired population as a whole; and bureaucratic simplification in order to attract private investments.

There also was an incomplete Social Security reform. Despite Lula's union experience, labor reforms were abandoned. This was due to the large number of union leaders holding governmental positions, political obstacles in Congress, and pressure exercised by the PT. Another Cardoso policy Lula discontinued was the privatization of state owned companies because of the PT's ideological views about the role of the state.

## State and Development in Brazil

Throughout its almost two hundred years of existence, the Brazilian state has witnessed major changes.[3] The Revolution of 1930 initiated the period of Brazil's great industrialization[4] (Baer, 1995: 39). The commitment towards modernization was expressed by political, economic, and public institutions within Brazil. In the political sphere, a new ruling class replaced the old rural (coffee) oligarchy, their leaders, and values. This group was identified by the revolutionary military officers called lieutenants or *tenentes,* and the civilian "liberal constitutionalists," who applied ideals of reform

---

3. At first Brazil was a monarchy and later adopted republicanism in 1889—it used to be a unitary state and now is a federation. Since the republic, a presidentialist system has been adopted, but it did have a parliamentary system of government for 17 months. Democracy has been the reigning political regime for most of the time, but Brazil had a dictatorship from 1937 to 1945 and recently, there was an authoritarian regime of 21 years.

4. Werner Baer (1995) argues that, differently from industrial growth, "industrialization is present when industry becomes the leading growth sector of the economy and causes pronounced structural changes."

and modernization to Brazil's institutions. According to Brazilian political economist Celso Furtado, they proposed an industrialization of the country through "import substitution," a term that denotes the state's actions to lead to the creation of key, basic industries (Furtado, 1976: 117).

As a result of adopting this policy, Brazil experienced its first wave of uninterrupted industrialization from 1930 to 1945. The breakdown of orthodox economic policies, in the wake of the 1929 international economic crisis, led the administration of President Vargas to expand the state's role in the nation's industrial development. Through direct and indirect interventions, the state enlarged its activities in the promotion of Brazil's economic development.[5] Heightened nationalism and the need for industrialization resulted in calls for centralized planning, the development of a national steel industry, and state-funded technological research—in manufacturing, transportation, and heavy industry. These measures were in accordance with Keynesian and neo-Keynesian policies that governments must stimulate economic activity. This policy recommendation contrasted sharply with previous assumptions and the practice of policymakers of favoring balanced budgets.

Keynes' theories justified the implementation of social welfare reforms by capitalist democracies and authoritarian regimes alike. In the case of Brazil, economic initiatives included: the establishment of Petrobras (Petróleo Brasileiro S/A) in 1953; the opening of Brazil's first steelworks (Companhia Siderúrgica Nacional, founded on April 9, 1941, and whose operations began in 1946) at Volta Redonda; and the body of labor laws issued in 1943 condensed as CLT (Consolidação das Leis do Trabalho).

The adoption of the Keynesian economic model by Brazil coincided with the need for government social policies to alleviate the effects from the massive economic and social tragedies that had occurred in the decades following the stock market crash in October 1929. The convergence of the Great Depression, industrialization, urbanization, industrial worker militancy, and of the accession of an activist to the presidency all worked to expand the state's sphere of influence in Brazil (Topik, 1989: 100). Growing state intervention in the economy marked the Vargas years[6] and continued to be

---

5. Industrialization during the First Republic did not include capital goods or basic industries. For a detailed account of that period, see Steven Topik (1987). In this article we follow the standard assumption that expanded state interventionism has its origins in the centralized, authoritarian, nationalist, intrusive, Vargas Regime.

6. Getúlio Vargas was the head and the heart of the system. As such, he dominated the political life of Brazil, whether as a president, or in *absentia*. He continued to exercise political power for 24 years, one-fourth of the first hundred years of the Republic.

characteristic of Brazilian development from the early 1930s until the end
of the 1980s.

It was this interventionist state—the New State (*Estado Novo*)—that
became broadly associated with the Vargas tenure in office (1930-1945;
1951-1954). It was characterized by economic policies that sought to mitigate consequences of the crisis of the 1920s. These policies changed in a
more liberal direction during the years of President Dutra (1946-1951). In
economic matters, contrary to the Cooke Mission's recommendations
(1943),[7] the Vargas administration initiated policies that promoted the
nationalization of industries and increased state interventionism. The Vargas government began to draw Brazil into a wave of economic nationalism
that was legally endorsed by the Constitutions of 1934 and 1937. Restrictions were applied to the commercial activities of foreign-owned interests in
banking, insurance, media (newspapers and magazines), and other industrial sectors. For example, foreigners in the agricultural sector could not
own land until they had established permanent residency as farmers or had
worked in agriculture in Brazil for at least one year. Restrictions were levied
upon the labor market as well. Foreigners were not allowed to constitute
more than one-third of a company's employees or to receive more than one-
third of the wage salaries in any industrial, commercial, or public enterprise,
except under special circumstances permitted by the government (Hill,
1947: 303-04). As in other Latin American countries that nationalized
industries, statism and nationalism in Brazil went together. Vargas' *Estado
Novo* followed such a pattern by issuing several nationalist decrees. In official dictums, President Vargas declared that "at least twenty percent of all
the coal bought by factories must be Brazilian coal. Some alcohol from Brazilian sugar must be mixed with all gasoline. Manioc flour must be mixed
with wheat flour. In those ways the government lent a helping hand to
struggling Brazilian industries" (MacDonald, 1954: 152).

Protectionism favored the industrialization program of the country and
extended the state's activities further into the spheres of business. The Vargas administration established new governmental standards, centralizing
the powers of the federal government in political, economic, and administrative matters. These actions were implemented towards the strengthening
of the nation-state. President Vargas expanded the government's "machine"
with the creation of a series of new ministries (Ministry of Labor, Ministry

---

7. The Cooke mission recommended that the task of industrialization should be left to the private sector, while the government should concentrate on general industrial planning, developing
industrial credit facilities, and providing technical education. See Werner Baer (1995: 43).

of Industry and Commerce, Ministry of Education and Health) and nationalizations that allowed the federal bureaucracy to grow. In this manner, there was an institutionalization and formalization of the centralist (political, economic, and administrative) tendencies that had existed for decades alongside alternating periods of decentralization.

It is fair to credit President Vargas with the shaping of almost all state and government institutions that now characterize modern Brazil. Some of these institutions have even proven resilient to the current wave of reforms of the 1990s and are still in place in almost an unaltered state it points out to the fact that because no one prior to Vargas—or after him—has amassed a greater power in ruling Brazil.

## REFORMS AFTER VARGAS (1954-2009)

Successive administrations pursued the goal of transforming Brazil into a modern, independent, and industrialized nation capable of playing an important role in the international scene. Brazilian political elites viewed industrial development as a hallmark of a modern economy. Development became a national goal despite the lack of consensus among politicians and planners on the methods to achieve it. The dispute lay between the nationalist, state-led model, and the free-market ideologies of classical economics. In the administration of President Juscelino Kubitschek de Oliveira (1955-1960), the role of the state was significantly enlarged to promote industrialization, build infrastructure, and encourage foreign investments in Brazil. During this period, nationalism lost ground to a wave of "developmentalism" that was anchored in the *Plano de Metas* (1955-1960). The economic results were impressive. Between 1955 and 1961, industrial production grew 80 percent (steel production, 100 percent) while mechanical industry, electricity, telecommunication, and transportation materials expanded 125 percent, 380 percent, and 600 percent, respectively. Industrial growth was channeled into increases in national and personal income. From 1957 to 1961, GNP grew seven percent and per capita income increased four percent. By the end of the 1950s, the growth of the Gross Domestic Product (GDP) in Brazil had outpaced the rest of Latin America by three-fold. However, the cost of these advances, including the cost of building the nation's new capital of Brasília, was a growing public debt and rising inflation. Eventually, Brazil was forced to break from its membership in the IMF (International Monetary Fund) in a political maneuver intended to protect its national sovereignty against foreign pressures to reform (Fausto, 2001: 239-40).

Getúlio's development model initiated in the 1930s, prove to be decisive for Brazil, as it emphasized industrialization and social inclusion. This economic model persisted for decades and shaped Brazil's economy, in part because of a competent bureaucracy in high levels of state apparatus. Vargas' development model gradually lost its strength beginning in 1979, with the start of the last administration of the military regime, which had begun in 1964, led by President João Batista de Oliveira Figueiredo, until the end of the President José Sarney administration in 1989.

The fall of communism in Eastern Europe on November 9, 1989 was paradigmatic for Brazil. The Soviet Union imploded, ruined by economic deterioration and by Michael S. Gorbachev's renunciation of force to hold it together. The unprecedented event launched a new wave of structural reforms around the world.

At the same moment, a "third wave" of globalization was gaining force and spreading at an incredible velocity. Models that combined free market policies with democratic structures became the accepted form for political and economic organization under globalization. State reform programs around the world adopted these models under the almost universal assumption that a democracy was the only acceptable form of government. Such a political system was considered the best means to ensure a framework of liberties that would provide lasting solutions for the political, economic, and social problems, which many nations faced.

Whichever the country, structural reforms have not led to a cessation of state intervention in the economy, as opponents have proclaimed. Instead, these policies have placed limits on the state, allowing domestic economic structures to adjust to the new realities that globalization has brought. There is clear evidence that pragmatism has been upheld as an important variable to implement changes regardless of ideological constraints. The Brazilian case will be considered from this perspective.

In Brazil, structural pressures-such as the fiscal crisis of the 1980s, along with excessive intervention by the state in the economy and the paradigmatic changes in the international political and economic orders-legitimized the reform policies implemented during the nineties.

One of President Cardoso's main objectives was to pass the constitutional amendments to eliminate the state monopolies, such as oil and telecommunications. Such action had not been possible during the Constitutional revision process in 1993.

Immediately after his inauguration, Cardoso began to concentrate on his economic reform agenda. Continuous amendments to the economic chapter of the 1988 Constitution were necessary to ensure the success of the anti-inflation program. The underlying reason for the successful stabilization plans is that Cardoso's government improved fiscal responsibility by decreasing public expenditures.

Economic reforms advanced rapidly because of the effective coalition that was constructed among Cardoso's political allies. No political force in Congress could oppose the government's voting bloc composed of more than 370 out of 513 Deputies and 60 out of 81 Senators. However, the lack of cohesiveness and discipline endemic to Brazilian politics led to the constant need to guarantee that political allies perpetually cast their votes in favor of the government proposal.

Four major political parties vigorously opposed the reforms of the Cardoso administration (1995–2002). Strong opposition came from the left-wing political parties that included the Partido dos Trabalhadores (PT) and the Partido Democrático Trabalhista (PDT). Luiz Inácio Lula da Silva was the leader of the PT while former Rio de Janeiro Governor Leonel Brizola commanded the PDT. Both men had been presidential candidates in 1989 and 1994, and were defeated by President Cardoso. Other smaller political parties formed part of that opposition forces such as the PCdoB and a far left splinter group of the PT, the PSTU (Partido Socialista dos Trabalhadores Unificado). Both of these parties' representatives originally had refused to sign the 1988 Constitution but became very keen at defending its "social advances" against Cardoso's recommendations for reform.

Outside the official legislative debate, most trade unions and many civil society organizations opposed the reforms. The most militant of the trade was CUT (Central Única dos Trabalhadores/Unified Worker's Union), which had close political ties with the PT. Both the leadership and the rank-and-file of this union were strongly antagonistic to privatization of state industries, as well as to social security, and administrative reforms. Employees' associations of state-owned enterprises were also active in the anti-reform movement. The most vocal employees' groups included those for the Petrobras, the TELEBRÁS (Telecomunicações Brasileiras S/A), and the Banco do Brasil. These companies' employee associations went as far as to pay for advertisements on television that attacked the reform program.

They argued that the reforms were designed to "sell out the wealth of the Brazilian people" and compromise their "national patrimony."

Another source of opposition came from many civil society organizations in Brazil and included such diverse groups as OAB (Ordem dos Advogados do Brasil) Brazilian Bar Association, the ABI (Associação Brasileira de Imprensa) Brazilian Bar Association, and the CNBB (Conferência Nacional dos Bispos do Brasil) National Conference of Brazilian Bishops. Their main argument was that the reforms would seriously jeopardize the social and economic rights included in the 1988 Constitution. They also argued that the reforms would challenge to national interest. Among trade unions, one important exception to the anti-reform stance was Força Sindical, an organization that was largely composed of metalworkers from the city of São Paulo, and was CUT's main competitor.

Although many of the center and center-left parties were divided on the issue of reform, almost all of them eventually came out in favor of it. The most important supporters were the three political parties that had comprised the coalition to elect President Fernando Henrique Cardoso in 1994. President Cardoso was also able to organize a viable legislative coalition that was formed with the PMDB (Partido do Movimento Democrático Brasileiro). The PMDB adopted a hegemonic attitude during the constitution's drafting in 1987 but it had begun to show serious concern over about the wisdom of many of the provisions by 1995. On the right, the PPB (Partido Progressista Brasileiro) [formerly ARENA (Aliança Renovadora Nacional) and currently PP (Partido Progressista-the party that had given legislative support to the military regime-came out in favor of the reforms, attracted to the platform of economic liberalism. Though the PPB clearly was convinced that the reform drive could give the Cardoso administration a political advantage, it fought hard in Congress to prevent the debate from being sidetracked by left-wing pressure. After May 1996, the PPB became increasingly involved in governance and officially joined the governing coalition. One of its members of parliament, Deputy Francisco Dornelles, was appointed to the President's Cabinet as Minister of Industry and Commerce. Pratini de Morais, another member of the PPB, was selected to serve in the Cabinet as the Minister of Agriculture. All the political parties that became allied with the Cardoso government chose to implement a pragmatic strategy to reflect the country's economic reality and address changes in the national and international arena.

Apart from political parties, trade associations, and related organizations assisted the reform efforts because they were extremely concerned with some of the key issues on the agenda such as privatization, tax reform, foreign investments, and the end of state monopolies. FIESP (Federação das Indústrias do Estado de São Paulo) and its national counterpart CNI (Confederação Nacional da Indústria) lobbied the legislature in favor of the reform's passage. In the case of the privatization of the national telecommunication company, a special interest group was organized precisely to argue the case for liberalizing the constitutional provisions that blocked its sale. It was financed by major private enterprises directly involved in the sector. Some workers' organizations like the São Paulo metalworkers' union and its national affiliate Força Sindical championed such reforms.

The political battle over reform divided combatants into two distinct groups: the ideologists versus the pragmatists. The pragmatic nature of Brazil's electorate was best surmised by the Minister of Social Security Roberto Brant when he stated "I never changed my ideology, but voters don't link ideology to political parties. [The] PMDB, PFL, and PSDB could be one (and the) same thing."

Economic Reforms After 1988. Economic liberalization, state modernization, and privatization were introduced into the Brazilian political agenda in an incisive, continuous, and socially legitimate way that had never been seen before. The withdrawal of the state ("desestatização") had actually started during the government of President João Batista Figueiredo (1979-1985), when the state abandoned the statist economic policies. But the big push for reform came through post-1988 structural reforms that included the sale of the telecommunications, oil, and electric energy companies.

Reform defined the 1989 campaign, and it became government priority after the inauguration of President Fernando Collor de Mello. The polarized 1989 presidential election between Fernando Collor de Mello (PRN, Partido da Reconstrução Nacional) and Luiz Inácio Lula da Silva (PT) was a trailer for the struggle that would arise for the implementation of structural changes in Brazil. President Collor was not a militant liberal. On the contrary, his policies were more identifiable with authoritarianism than with neo-liberalism. He practiced economic liberalism during his two years in office because there was a real wish for change in several aspects of national life. These economic measures led to one of the two most important aspects of the Collor administration: the introduction of neoliberalism, and his impeachment for corruption charges. His successor President Itamar Franco, characterized for his reserved stance on these and other national issues, was not a reformer and allowed the agenda for structural reforms to stagnate during his administration (1992-1995). He even tried, without success, to block the privatization of CSN (National Steel Company) as well as the sale of other state companies that occurred during his tenure. The next president to give priority to structural reform was Fernando Henrique Cardoso, whose 1994 campaign was strongly based on the need to implement deep institutional changes in Brazil. Although the Collor government's reform program (the "Big Project") had been largely forgotten,[8] its basic principles were carried over into President Fernando Henrique's administration. Some of the "Big Project's" creators had held top jobs in the economic areas of both Presidents Collor's and FHC's administrations.

## Constitutional Way: Changing the Economic Order

Legal frameworks significantly affect the economic performance. In the case of Brazil, the 1988 Constitution favored state capitalism and economic nationalism over a liberalized and internationalized free-market economy. The constitutions set out general principals, and also specific provisions that define national life in ways that most nations address with specific laws, rather than of Constitutional provisions.

After President Cardoso assumed power in 1995, he asked the National Congress to rewrite all the sections in the Constitution pertaining to taxation, foreign investment, energy, telecommunications, mining, social security, labor relations, and the provision of public services. There are five paradigmatic points that were incorporated into the 1988 Constitution that Cardoso's reforms attempted to redress. These were: the constitutional perpetuation of state monopolies in telecommunications; in oil monopolies; the preservation of state enterprises; the limited participation of foreign companies in the country's mineral sector, and the government's continued monopoly of the commercialization of piped gas. It is important to note that Congressional approval to amend the constitution for each of these provisions-during the first six months of President Fernando Henrique's government lead to the economic liberalization, and policies of state reform that today are evident in Brazil.

---

8. The "Big Project" had been inaugurated in Brazil following the fall of the Berlin Wall in 1989 and is associated with the neo-liberal phase of the economy.

*The State Monopoly in Telecommunications (Art. 21, XI).* This provision established the state's monopoly of the telecommunications sector as defined in 1988 Constitution. Given the legal weight of its text, the maximum the government could do to liberalize the sector was to allow for its use by firms whose majority control was held by state-owned companies. The constitution legitimized the practices that were already existent in the sector. Since their creation under the military regime, the state telecom holdings of TELEBRAS Telecomunicações Brasileiras S/A (Brazilian Telephone Company) and EMBRATEL Empresa Brasileira de Telecomunicações Brazilian (Telecom Company) allowed the federal government, and certain states, (e.g. Rio Grande do Sul) to be the country's only telephone operators and to assume the role of the private sector.[9]

With the passage of the 1988 Constitution, it became known that Brazil did not intend to open its telecommunications market to private operators because such a move would require a constitutional amendment.

It did not take long for the impact of this stipulation upon national and foreign investors to materialize. A state telecommunications monopoly was seen as the only option, permanent, and inviolable. Paradoxically, this pronouncement occurred at the same time the decrease in state investments. The drop reduced the quality of the services and a technological backlog that state companies could not hide with any amount of publicity.

*The State's Monopoly of the Oil Sector (Art. 177).* One of the most sensitive issues of the reform agenda was defining, on a constitutional level, the degree of monopoly power that could be exerted by the state oil company Petrobras. From the creation of Petrobras in 1953 until the promulgation of the 1988 Constitution, the state's monopoly in the sector was defined by law. After 1988, it became a constitutional matter that complicated the prospects for any changes. The constitution even stipulated the royalties that Petrobras was to pay oil producing states and municipalities. In some case, access to foreign know-how was possible through the use of foreign state owned enterprises.

*The Definition of a State Enterprise (Art. 171).* As a symbolic issue, the redefinition of what constituted a state enterprise or national company was another extremely important constitutional change. Unfortunately, the

---

9. There were some telephone companies where TELEBRAS participated on a minority basis, the main example being *Companhia Telefônica Central do Brasil* (CTBC), which provided services in the Minas Gerais region.

Constitution of 1988 as a legal framework functioned as an obstacle for the efforts to attract foreign capital. Certain aspects of the Brazilian economy, like high interest rates, did encourage the entrance of foreign capital but it was directed to the financial market and not toward productive investments.

The specific rules governing foreign investment created an extended debate in the constitutional assembly. The difference in treatment between foreign and national companies had been limited to a few sectors of the economy that were considered strategic, such as computer sciences (Baaklini and Rego, 1988). The constitutional assembly in 1987 imported the exact stipulations of the computer science law and used them to regulate foreign investment in all sectors.

*Participation of Foreign Companies in Mining (Art. 176, paragraph 1).* The constitutional prohibition against foreign companies investing in Brazil's mining industry was as important as the laws established for telecommunications and oil. According to the Constitution, all mineral resources belonged to the nation, and their exploration could only be done by domestically-owned companies or Brazilian citizens.

Geologists and mining engineers actively defended its approval and the result was the flight of foreign capital from the Brazilian mining sector. Mining production was negatively affected by this decision to restrict foreign investment. At a time when all Latin American countries were going through the process of an economic opening, the new constitution excluded Brazil from the lucrative opportunities with foreign investors.

*State Monopoly on Piped Gas.* Another important constitutional change that was proposed ended the monopoly held by the states over the commercialization of piped gas. The 1988 Constitution had passed control of this sector to the governments of the Brazil's 26 states.

With the passage of Cardoso's amendments in 1995, private companies were granted permission to operate in this sector. These changes followed the same legislative trend that other developing countries had taken in the 1990s. Such stipulations included a decrease (or elimination) in the restrictions placed on foreign participation in the sector and a reduction in the power of state monopolies.

The constitutional reform process in Brazil during the 1990s reveals that it was dominated by the classic questions of "who won what, when, and how much." The first and frustrated attempt at a constitutional revision in 1993 was commonly considered a "well succeeded failure." However, it allowed then-presidential candidate Fernando Henrique Cardoso to adopt these incomplete institutional reforms as one of his main platforms in a campaign that eventually would take him to the presidency.

The Cardoso presidency abolished the state oil and telecommunications monopolies, opened commercialization of piped gas to private companies, removed significant legal obstacles to national and foreign companies, and opened the mining sector to international investors. These developments were not reversed under President Lula.

**Pragmatism as a Method for State Reform.** Despite these reforms, the Brazilian economy is far from having fully liberalized institutions or neo-liberal structures, and the Brazilian state lacks key attributes of a liberal state. There are three basic points that can help explain why reforms have not achieved these ends. First, Brazil is not nor has ever been a liberal society, either economically or politically. Second, the structural reforms instituted during the 1990s were designed as short-term measures to cope with the grave fiscal crisis and to attend to the new, non-ideological scenario enforced by globalization. Lastly, a radical center in the political spectrum has emerged to offset the complete adoption of neo-liberal policies.

The pragmatic character of Brazil's state reform, and the prevalence of liberal ideas among influential political leaders in the Cardoso administration, created the impression of economic and political liberalism. However, the country's economic crisis needed a fiscal adjustment aimed at reducing the public deficit to bearable levels and at allowing the government to recover its investment capacity and ability to manage national accounts. The president, state governors, and party leadership in Congress did not act on these questions of reform with ideological intentions but instead responded to them according to the demands of the grave fiscal crisis.

## Reforming the State: A Summary

Modern-day Brazil had experienced four major reforms in its state apparatus in the 1930s, 1964, 1990, and in 1995. The pioneering reform during "Estado Novo" set the basis for an administrative and interventionist state; the reform related to the authoritarian modernization period during the

1964 regime; the "Collor shock" in 1990; and the Bresser-Pereira reform in 1995.

The first reform was characterized by administrative centralization, by state intervention on a number of sectors of national life, and notably by the creation of DASP to eliminate nepotism. At that time President Getúlio Vargas wanted universities to be autonomous and to have administrative freedom under certain national parameters.

The second reform had its major feature in "administration for development," which coincided with the golden period of public administration in Brazil, and the world, that was in force mainly during the 1960s and 1970s. The administrative reform provided for by Law Decree 200 (February 25,

TABLE 2-3. Four Approaches to Administrative Reform, 1930-2009

| 1930–1945 | Administrative reform to implement bureaucracy: DASP |
| 1964–1985 | Modernization of authoritarian regime: Law decree 200 |
| 1995–2002 | Managerial (Incomplete) FHC/MARE (Ministério da Administração Federal e Reforma do Estado) |
| 2002–2009 | Governance: More government effectiveness |

*Source*: Peixoto, 2009.

1967) at the end of the President Humberto de Alencar Castelo Branco (1964-1967) administration in March 15, 1967 introduced twice as many modernization elements and, as the first reform, the simplification of the federal administrative machine such as the five basic principles stated in Law Decree 200: Planning; Coordination; Delegation and Deconcentration of Powers; and Controlling. All are based on the idea that the state should be removed from instances where it is a hindrance to private initiative; on the belief in professionalization; on privatization; and on the modernization and debureaucratization of public service. The administrative reform of 1967 contains new administrative mechanisms, and was based on strong political and philosophical principles. It was initiated under President Castelo Branco by Helio Beltrão, who served as a key policy maker for public sector reorganization. The reform depended on the presumption of trust (to trust people and their judgement); detachment from the fetishism of document (to believe in people more than in documents); and the decision to pay a price for simplification and for stimulation, therefore eliminating expensive contrasts. He summarized these ideas saying that "those who decide have a right to a certain margin of error; it is better to run the risks of decentralization than of stagnation." The effort for change and state modernization was followed by other administrations regardless of the political regime, as had already happened in the pre-1964 period.

The other reform thread in the FHC era was the reorganization of the state apparatus, which rested on three fronts: institutional-legal, cultural, and managerial. The first aimed at removing legal hindrances to modernizing public administration. The second involved a cultural change in order to allow a transition from bureaucracy to management, as part of the changing environment in the field of public administration with the adoption of the NPM (New Public Management).[10] The aim of that change was to move from bureaucratic administrations (more focused on processes, controls, and hierarchy) to a more market oriented form of public sector management. In Brazil the NPM principles were part of the Plano de Reforma do Aparelho do Estado (Plan for the Reform of the State Apparatus), launched during the FHC presidency by Luiz Carlos Bresser-Pereira, who served as Minister of State Reform and Public Administration. Finally, public management would deal with administration improvement through modernizing organizational structure and management methods. It must be pointed out that the first reforms were intended to prepare the government to formulate, rather than implement, public policies.

## LULA AND THE UNFINISHED AGENDA

On January 1, 2003 Luiz Inácio Lula da Silva became the first metalworker in Brazil and Latin America's history to be sworn in to the presidency. Lula, succeeded the sociologist and PhD Fernando Henrique Cardoso, the first president to be reelected in the Republican era in Brazil. Both are from leftist parties: the PT and the PSDB, respectively; a fact that is new in Brazilian politics over the last 40 years. Both FHC and Lula come from a neo-Marxist background: the first in his intellectual formation, and the second from his union activities, aligned with PT's socialist proposals. Both of them, committed to economic rationality, undertook an agenda of structural reform that changed the face of the Brazilian state.

This agenda was taken up despite resistance from within their own parties. Playing the moderator's role, both presidents move pragmatically in their quest to neutralize ideological positions seeking to shape the reform agenda. They rapidly aligned themselves with the international economic architecture

10. The NPM is a management philosophy used by governments throughout the world since 1980s to modernize the public sector.

and the multilateral finance agencies, notably the IMF and the World Bank, perplexing the orthodox left. President Cardoso's legacy in the field of state reform include structural changes such as public sector modernization, economics, and social security reform. His administration was also responsible for deepening democracy and the market economy, as well as for strengthening the international presence of Brazil through presidential diplomacy and macroeconomic stability, probably its more successful aspect.

Eight years of social democracy improved and enhanced the reform agenda inaugurated in the early 1990's. While Collor's presidency had been dedicated to reintroducing the principles of economic liberalism according to ideas from the Washington Consensus, the expectations created about the new left-wing presidency of Lula da Silva were oriented to immediately reverse such economic policies. To the despair of the radical left within the PT, this did not happen. On the contrary, the new administration deepened the implementation of orthodox economic policies, announcing its intentions during the electoral campaign of 2002, when it launched the "Carta ao Povo Brasileiro" (Letter to the Brazilian People) in which Lula stated that his government would honor the country's financial contracts and obligations. He also stressed his disposition to "preserve whatever primary budget surplus would be necessary in order to prevent an increase in the internal debt that would destroy confidence in the capacity of the government to honoring its commitments." The markets interpreted Lula's promise as a commitment to continuity by enacting market-friendly policies, such as honoring the country's external debt and upholding fiscal discipline. The letter was widely perceived as a turning point in the relationships between the PT's candidate and the markets, which slowly but surely began to change their perceptions of the threat to their interests represented by a possible Lula victory (Panizza, 2006), and continued to have a favorable reaction to the Lula presidency.

Facing an incomplete agenda of state reform, Lula encountered a complex set of challenges as he became president:

- Govern efficiently at the federal level,
- Maintain economic stability,
- Implement the long term promise of implementing a "truly" social agenda,
- Control the PT's radicals while retaining its ideology,
- Carry on the agenda of state reform,
- Promote sustainable economic development, and

- Make a difference against the PSDB by appearing as the "real" leftist political party in Brazil.

Moreover, during his electoral campaign president Lula promised to continue to push reforms in favor of state modernization. Accordingly, he announced a set of institutional reforms: social security, tax/fiscal, trade unions, labor, political, and agrarian reforms. At the end of his mandate, however, the results shown by his administration have been modest in this regard. Out of the proposals, only three (judiciary, social security, and tax/fiscal) were partially implemented. Although strongly demanded by many sectors in Brazil, a strong agenda of state reform is still waiting for a better political moment, probably after the inauguration in 2011 of a new President. The lack of political will by President Lula da Silva to move ahead with a state reform agenda can be explained mainly by his own and his party's vision about the role of the state, which differs sharply from the one defended by President Cardoso and the PSDB.

This statist ideology prevailed on different occasions since the beginning of his administration in 2003. One of the first targets to be attacked was the model of regulatory agencies, such as Agência Nacional do Petróleo (ANP, National Petroleum Agency). The ANP was responsible for regulating the oil sector, and put in place during the Cardoso presidency-commanded by former Chief of Staff Dilma Rousseff. The government sent to Congress a new law regulating the agencies, changing their responsibilities, and diminishing their autonomy. When Congress did not fully approve the new legislation, they sought another way to diminish the power of the regulatory agencies. That was the case with the vitally important ANP, whose new head was former Deputy Haroldo de Lima, a member of the Partido Comunista do Brasil. This appointment suggested that the liberal approach to the public sector may be reaching its end. Another front was to enlarge and widen the scope of the public sector by increasing the number of ministers to thirty-seven, an unprecedented number of cabinet level positions.

Instead of being a reformist government, Lula's two terms have been governments of programs rather than governments of reform. The inability of the Lula-PT years to greatly advance the state reform agenda might have been due to ideological constraints regarding the role of the state.

## CONCLUSION

Deep structural changes have taken place in Brazil since 1990. Through policy measures, laws, and institutional changes, several administrations have gradually reduced or, in some cases, even extinguished the power of state monopolies and have promoted structural reforms in the economic realm, social security, administration, and fiscal matters. In the implementation of these policies, fiscal crises and the unavoidable economic reality imposed by the process of globalization have forced ideological sophistication to be abandoned in the name of pragmatism. The aggregation of these internal and external pressures has prompted Brazil to minimize its pro-state tendencies and enter a new era of pragmatic, liberal-inspired economic policies.

However, these changes have not completely altered the statist model of the twentieth-century. Brazil's leaders remain uncomfortable with pure neoliberalism and prefer what could be called social democratic approach, though not necessarily the one proposed by PSDB.

*Reform Agenda for 2010.* Brazil will have to continue its search for public sector modernization in the coming years. A new round of structural reform will be crucial to achieve it. The following sectors deserve priority for the reform agenda:

- *Administrative reform* to lower the costs of bureaucracy for ordinary citizens as well as for businesses,[11] reduce the size of the state, eliminate waste of resources in the public sector, and restrain the number of politically appointed positions in government.

- *Judiciary reform* to speed the judiciary system, reduce costs, and enhance social confidence in the institutions of the judiciary.

- *Fiscal and tax reform* to diminish the level of tied revenues in the federal budget; improve the efficiency and make less complicated the tax revenue machinery; and reduce the number of indirect taxes via the consolidation of state and federal taxes into more efficient national value-added tax structure.

- *Labor and trade union reform* to introduce direct negotiation between companies and unions through the labor collective agreements and

---

11. According to the World Bank reports on bureaucracy (2009) among different countries in the world, Brazil appears in a bad position. Industrialized countries are permanently in search of new measures in order to be more attractive to businesses. They are champions in bureaucratic simplification. The richest countries in the world—USA, Japan, China, Canada, Switzerland, Norway, Denmark, United Kingdom, and Singapore are at the same time the easiest in which to do business. In general it is twice more difficult to open and close down new companies in poor countries than in the rich countries. In the globalized world we are living in, bureaucratic simplification is necessary for survival.

diminishing the level of intervention in those disputes by Labor courts and to alleviate part of the tax incidence over the payroll which almost doubles the cost of legal employees due to this high tax burden. The main laws regulating labor were created more than 60 years ago during the Vargas era and need urgent change.[12]

- *Social security reform* to continue and improve measures seeking to attack fraud and corruption, and reduce payments of undue benefits; to increase inspection in order to inhibit tax evasion and informality in the labor market, enlarging the size of the contributors base; and to regulate the changes in the system approved by Congress in 2003, spreading its new regulations to states and municipalities, as some of those changes require passing and implementing new legislation.

- *Political reform* to improve campaign financing, party loyalty, the electoral system, and the party system.

Finally, it should be noted that reforms have been oriented to enhance the government's capacity to design public policies rather than implementing them. The country needs to reverse this pattern, dedicating efforts on both sides of the coin at the same time: not only designing good policies, but—more important—efficiently implementing and managing them.

From institution building under Vargas, through succeeding policies the leftist 'reformas de base' proposed, but never introduced by João Goulart; the conservative modernization implemented during the military regime; the adoption of neoliberalism forced by globalization put in place by Fernando Collor's administration; the quasi-liberalism adopted during the Cardoso and Lula presidencies—Brazil's state reforms have followed a traditional zigzag path observed in other areas of public policy. Even by flirting with the left, or right, and never getting a determined and continuous course of action in government policies, pragmatism alone cannot ensure lasting success. Principles and values need to be firmly attached to government actions to achieve truly enduring results. The state reform agenda continues to be central to enhancing the development and modernization of Brazil's political and economic institutions.

---

12. In part due to such an outdated legislation almost half of the labor force is outside the legal system, working in the informality apart from the legislation with no access to social security and other benefits.

# 3

# STATE DEVELOPMENTALISM: CONTINUITY & UNCERTAINTY

*Renato Boschi*

*Abstract: This chapter focuses on the revival of state developmentalism in Brazil in the wake of market-oriented reforms (1990–2002). The main argument is that more so than the anticyclical policies adopted to face the crisis of 2008, state capacities dating back to the ISI developmental period (1930–1980) together with the emphasis of the Lula government (2003–2010) on social inclusion opened up the internal market alternative to circumvent bottlenecks of growth and employment. The timing and intensity of these reforms was such that lines of continuity dating back to the previous state-sponsored model were maintained, preserving strategic bureaucratic nuclei and patterns of business-state relations, which constitute comparative institutional advantages in the era of post neoliberal globalization.*

In contrast with other crises that have recently struck the worldwide capitalist system, the recession that began in the end of 2008 as a result of the deregulation of financial markets did not originate in the periphery of the system. Nor did it drastically affect many of the emerging economies, particularly those in Latin America including Brazil. Furthermore, evidence of recovery has also appeared quicker in Brazil, in contrast to the recession that still looms over the United States and Europe.[1]

Employment rates have surged along with positive and considerable[2] gross domestic product (GDP) growth predictions. The adoption of emergency anticyclical policies by several countries including Brazil is evidence of a possible revival of a more active and interventionist role of the State. This time some emerging economies in Latin America and, specifically, Brazil, pioneered interventionist and developmentalist policies in the wake of the unsuccessful market-oriented reforms guided by the Washington Consensus. In Brazil, Chile, and Argentina center-left governments implemented policies reviving the role of the state, signaling a return to certain principles of developmentalism more typical of the period that preceded market-oriented reforms yet redefined and readapted to new times (Boschi, 2008; Boschi and Gaitán, 2008; 2008a; 2009). In Argentina, the drastic measures adopted to deal with previous crises, such as in 2002, were an early sign of the need to break with neoliberal orthodoxy at the macro-economic level. It was a crucial step for the reactivation of growth along the lines of a neo-developmentalist model (Bresser-Pereira, 2009). In other countries, as was the case in Bolivia, Venezuela, and Ecuador, leftist governments reenacted their own versions of national revolutions and adopted radical measures that resulted in renationalization or reprivatization.

In this context, one must question the role of previous trajectories and the institutional characteristics of the different production regimes relative to the different responses to the crisis. This, in turn, would require an analysis of what role the state might play in various capitalist systems that are currently being reshaped and redesigned, especially in peripheral and in emerging countries (Boschi, 2009). The role of the state in these cases is a lot more central and strategic than it is in advanced countries. (Hall, 2007; Amable, 2003). While recent analyses do not go as far as to deny the importance of dimensions operating at the level of the private sector, they treat the state as a crucial element due to its powerful allocative and regulative capacities (Weiss, 2010). In the Brazilian case, the positive role of state intervention in the configuring of a modality of capitalism that has proven itself to be more coordinated and articulated over the course of time. Beginning with the

---

1. According to the IBGE the Brazilian economy outperformed other economies. In the second quarter of 2009 compared to the previous quarter, in twelve selected OECD economies, those that had positive GDP growth rates were South Korea (2.6%), Australia (0.6%), Japan (0.6%), France (0.3%), and Germany (0.3%). In this subgroup, only South Korea had a higher growth rate than Brazil (1.9%). At the opposite end, one must remember the scale of the economic retraction faced by Holland (-2.0%) and Mexico (-1.1%). Canada (-0.9%), the United Kingdom (-0.7%), Italy (-0.5%), and the United States (-0.3%) complete the list of selected countries that registered a shrinking GDP (Carta IEDI n. 370, "Produção Industrial em Maio de 2009: Recuperação Gradual." Available at: www.iedi.org.br).

2. A 1.9% GDP growth rate recorded between the first and second quarters indicates that the economy is on an upward trajectory. The unemployment rate has dropped in the last four consecutive months as well. In March it was at 9% and in July it had dropped to 8.1%—rates that are considerably low for a recession ("PIB cresceu 1,9%: a crise era um V," 14/09/2009. Data available at: http://www.ipea.gov.br/003/00301009.jsp?ttCD_CHAVE=12005).

modernizing revolution implemented by Vargas in the 1930s, followed by the brand of developmentalism of the Kubitschek era in the 1950s—which promoted industrialization based on the import substitution model (ISI)—and completed by the enhancement of the State-led economic model and its expansion in the productive sphere during the years of military rule. Rather than solely focusing on the State in general terms—strengthened as it was during this process of industrial revolutionizing throughout the twentieth century—one must pay close attention to the Executive branch, regardless of the nature of the political regime in power. It has been shown to fulfill various roles: the articulator of Weberian bureaucracies that constituted themselves over time (Kohli, 2004; Boschi and Lima, 2002); the shaping force behind work/labor relations; and the articulator of the private and public sectors by means of the creation of a corporative structure of interest representation (Diniz and Boschi, 2004).

The forms of social protection implemented at different points in time are no less important in the consideration of the role of the State. They have evolved from modest yet important social policies aimed at wage-earning workers and those in the formal labor market. They were gradually redesigned and expanded in time and eventually complemented by (also modest) health and pension reforms. These reforms took place in the context of the neoliberal policies of the 1990s to what can be called the "expansion of social frontier" by means of a set of targeted policies aimed at eradicating poverty and reducing inequalities structural inequality is a defining trait in the configuration of Brazilian capitalism. Accentuated by policies that resulted in income concentration throughout the developmentalist period, especially under military governments. This is the result of several factors including a top-down model of transition, which neglected agrarian reform; rapid urbanization due to rural emigration; social exclusion due to the aforementioned social incorporation via labor corporatism. Thus, poverty reduction policies are preconditions to interrupt vicious circles or "negative complementarities." These unsavory results are repeatedly pointed out with respect to the organization of the Brazilian productive regime from the perspective of how corporations carry out their activities (Schneider, 2008). Solving this problem implies the fulfillment of basic conditions necessary to incorporate a vast segment of the population into the consumer market.

In considering the process of development its crucial to keep in mind that the outcome of policies can only be adequately assessed within a long-range time frame. If without a doubt not all the effects of policies are known or

even consciously expected when they are first enacted. Recently, the importance of time has been reintroduced systematically in analyses (Pierson,
2004). The decisions concerning policies in this field, in most cases, involve
the accumulation of experiences. The production of new ideas capable of
asserting themselves, of being assimilated by institutions, and, finally, of
being leveraged by support coalitions, thus determining the correction of
previous trajectories. Ideas, interests and institutions follow different timings and are interwoven in distinct ways. Understanding this complex articulation has been at the core of discussions within the different
contemporary strands of institutional analysis, and, more specifically in
those focusing on the comparative analysis of the transformations of global
capitalism. In contrast to the emphasis placed on "path dependency," the
most recent debates have stressed the importance of correction of previous
trajectories. These corrections have been marked by changes in the elites'
frames of reference, combined with the timing and capability of certain
institutions to make a difference. Central elements in this respect are the
patterns of organization of the private sector and its articulations with the
state—as one of the dimensions of the production regime—in addition to
the patterns of financing, capital/labor conflict resolution; education and
skilled labor training policies; and incentives for technology generation
(Amable, 2003; Boyer, 2005; Campbell and Pedersen, 2007; Crouch and
Farrell, 2004; Crouch, 2005; Deeg, 2005; Deeg and Jackson, 2007; Hall,
2007; Jackson and Deeg, 2006; Thelen, 2004).

In the specific case of the revival of the state and of neo-interventionism
as a protection against systemic crises, long term considerations are fundamental in order to grasp the continuity of trajectories in the context of the
substantial changes in the international scenario. With the emergence of
China as a power, consequent opportunities and restrictions redefine the
relative positions of different countries. In the newly defined scenario in
which markets must yield to the logic of politics, the possibility of new
autonomous national projects (even if they aim at strategies that will allow
them to compete in a globalized marketplace) are increasingly linked to
how political institutions can process conflict. In this scenario, political
institutions play a decisive role since they constitute the filter through
which new agendas are produced and implemented in a national context.
Thus, policies in these areas will fundamentally depend on how they are
conducted, the political interplay between actors in charge of implementing
them, the nature of the government coalitions that are forged to support a

developmentalist platform, and on previous trajectories—both in terms of the developmentalist model as well as in terms of the timing and manner in which market-oriented reforms took course.

Chile, for example, carried out these reforms earlier, in a more favorable international context and under a military regime whose transition to democracy was gradual and negotiated. At the same time, Brazil intensified the process of industrialization through import substitution, carried out an equally controlled transition, albeit one that more quickly expanded the political universe without restrictions and which was marked by the presence of expressive and organized social forces. In contrast, over time Argentina did not accumulate capacities in line with state developmentalism; it implemented radical reform, underwent a strong productive downturn, became extremely vulnerable to foreign shocks. Recently, it seems to have entered a less tortuous path, showing strong signs of recovery after resorting to unorthodox economic instruments to strengthen the state. In sum, it is a matter of legacies, trajectories, and different timings that today configure different modalities of capitalist development, as well as possibilities for the recovery of growth in the context of post neoliberal globalization. The timing of market-oriented reforms and how they were implemented were more drastic in the cases of Chile and Argentina; its later implementation in Brazil and the social resistance it faced served to preserve elements of its developmentalist past, especially in terms of state capacities. Brazil, despite its tradition of strong interventionism, has operated under conditions of intense competition. The capitalist model, adapted to the functioning of financial markets, and progressively based on publicly-traded stock companies, tends towards internationalization and, most importantly, maintains a macro-economic policy that has rigidly kept intact the foundations of stabilization. The maneuvering space left for development policies thus becomes more geared towards long-term time frames, the creation of institutions capable of assuring the interlocution between the business sector and the state, and the implementation of anticyclical and industrial policies.

In this sense, the main argument of this paper is precisely that the market-oriented reforms implemented in the 1990s were not able to wipe out, as intended, the legacy of the Vargas era. In fact it remains alive in more than one fundamental aspect for the current configuration of Brazilian capitalism. These aspects mainly have to do with the persistence of an institutional matrix established by Vargas, which proved itself capable of articulating the interests of the private sector. It was also able to inaugurate forms of interlocution between these and the state on one hand, and on the other, the prevalence of labor laws that have withstood flexibilization and are still responsible for several rights of unionized sectors of the formal economy. The continuity of this path expresses itself as well in the active presence of agencies created during Vargas' second term, such as the Banco Nacional de Desenvolvimento (BNDES, National Bank for Development). BNDES has played a crucial role in the fostering of productive activity and in the development of the country, and has recently expanded its actions into the regional sphere.

In innovative fashion and, in this sense, in contrast to the concentrating tendencies of the latter-day developmentalist matrix, the social inclusion policies based on combating poverty and reducing social inequality implemented since the Lula government are a watershed, offering a development alternative that is geared towards the domestic market. The ensemble of anticyclical measures have been put in place in the wake of these processes as a follow-up to stabilization—which, in turn, is based on the regulation of the financial system established during the presidency of Fernando Henrique Cardoso.

The first section of this paper focuses on the continuity of the developmentalist paths in terms of the patterns of interaction between the state and the private sector while recognizing the significant role of the BNDES as a development agency. In the second section, I point out the main measures adopted by the current government to face the financial crisis and emphasize within these measures the importance of social inclusion by looking at more immediate consequences. Finally, I will highlight the expansion of the social frontier as the trademark of state interventionism in recent years, and as the main factor in the configuration of Brazilian productive regime—one that simultaneously combines an inward expansion with an outward thrust to compete globally.

## BUSINESS INTERESTS AND DEVELOPMENT AGENCIES

The corporatist structure of business interest representation, set up during the first Vargas administration, constitutes, along with the Labor Legislation, one of the most expressive continuities within the institutional trajectory of Brazilian capitalism. On a positive note, it is possible to show that they established the foundations for organized collective action of the business sector as well as for conflict regulation between capital and labor. This institutional architecture was very controversial and received substantial criticism when it was first implemented. This was due to its potential control of the labor sector, the creation of a weak and dependent business class, and, according to some more recent evaluations, to the fact that this approach is reminiscent of the authoritarian principles of the Estado Novo, and its potential to create obstacles for the flexibilization of the labor market. However, specifically in the case of the organization of business interests as the main mechanism of articulation between the business sector and the state, the structure has changed and adapted to modern times demonstrating its flexibility and propensity to change. Despite competitive or complementary formats of business collective action organization created throughout the years—fragmentation and the specialization of this structure discussed in previous works (Diniz and Boschi, 2004; 2007), a possibly inferior performance if compared to mediation structures in other contexts (Pedersen, 2008; Schneider, 1995; 2004)—its centrality in the organization of the productive Brazilian regime is undeniable.

Generally speaking, which characteristics within the realm of the private sector could provide responses in favor of developmentalism? We could say that pragmatism and adaptive capacity led the entrepreneurs to act extremely fast as they confronted the changes that took place in the institutional framework with the transition of the 1990s. This transition—characterized by an extensive variety of institutional frameworks as the result of the combination of more centralized modalities of coordination with a coordination conducted by the market after the economic reforms—led to a rapid adaptation of business organizations to the new market conditions. With redemocratization, Congress played a prominent role in the formulation of legislation pertinent to business. In this way, the Congress became a target for the collective action of the business sector, through the utilization of lobbies. Business organizations—anchored in a dual structure with compulsory and voluntary modalities of collective action that adapted since the beginning of the industrialization led by the state in the 1930s—was characterized, at that moment, as very complex, combining segmentation with centralization. Again, in a quick adaptive effort, this structure revealed itself to be suited to play a central role in terms of coordination activities in the new productive regime.

Organizations that bring together more traditional developmentalists, such as the *Instituto de Estudo para o Desenvolvimento Industrial* (IEDI, Institute for the Study of Industrial Development) have been producing studies and documents that systematically analyze the situation of the industry; it publishes IEDI Newsletters, current industrial outlook bulletins on the Internet, and systematically advocate for the establishment of partnerships with the government to encourage industrial development. FIESP (Federation of Industries of the State of São Paulo, the most important among regional industry entities) has broken its long tradition of unity around a single candidacy for its leadership and, for the first time, there was internal competition for it. It has moved towards relative autonomy vis-à-vis the state, but still in the direction of the establishment of linkages. CNI (National Confederation of Industry, the highest entity of the business sector in Brazil) went through a process of significant modernization, and created a coordination office for legislative affairs—COAL—which follows up on demands made by the industry to Congress (Mancuso, 2004; 2007). CNI engaged in elaborating productivity and technological application studies and has taken charge of labor relations. A series of sector associations and others organized by productive chains such as ONIP (National Organization of Industry and Petroleum), have also proven themselves to be very effective in the defense of their interests through coordination activities. To sum up, there is evidence, in the associative sphere of the private sector, of an adaptation to modern times. This is especially true from the point of view of the articulation of firms in the productive regime that was established after the market-oriented reforms in Brazil (Diniz and Boschi, 2004).

In the context of creating comparative institutional advantages in terms of the articulation between the state and the private sector, the CDES (Council of Economic and Social Development) was created as a state initiative out of the necessity of more wide-randing modalities of interlocution with civil society as a whole in the new developmentalist model. Far from replicating old formulas and the supposedly authoritarian characteristics of the period when the official corporatist structure was established, this nucleus has functioned as a consulting body whose goal is to formulate directives for development policies. The CDES, a consulting agency at the service of the president created in 2003, is composed of 103 members—90 of them are members of civil society, 13 ministers, and the president. Like other agencies that are part of a network of institutions, the CDES differs from the corporatist councils of the developmentalist period that made them an essential modality of economic regulation for that period (Boschi and Lima 2002)—in the sense that it is not a representative organ of specific categories and, much less, focused on the definition of policies tailored to the needs of different sectors or on the solution of capital/business conflicts. The CDES focuses on the creation of consensus and the establishment of directives for development, providing guiding principles for the different spheres of government. The forum has actually proved itself to perform this function effectively. It can be said that it has been positively accepted within the government despite being a very recent experiment, therefore, making it hard to reach definite conclusions on the subject (Costa, 2006). The emphasis placed on the social dimension is an all-encompassing concern of the CDES. It is in line with the perspective of the Lula government of framing development in terms of equality—as opposed to the developmentalism approach of the 20th century. While the dominant concept during that period was to foster growth and only thereafter distribute wealth, the CDES has as its main principle the reduction of inequality, hoping to reduce the GINI coefficient from 0.569 in 2004 to 0.400 in 2022. Equality should be a guiding principle for all the decisions of the public sector. The goal is to double the share of the national wealth received by the poorest 20% in this time period. In order to achieve this goal, education is a strategic priority in the transition to a new model of development, side by side with the public health system (Sistema Único de Saúde), and the appreciation in value of the minimum wage to follow inflation targets.

Besides the CDES, the National Council of Industrial Development (CNDI) was created in April 2004, and charged with the implementation of the Development Agenda's main objectives. The CNDI is presented as a consultative agency responsible for defining the directives for the industrial development of the country. It subsidizes the formulation of public policies focused on industrial development, infrastructure activities, normalization of measures that allow for greater competitiveness of enterprises, and financing of entrepreneurial activities. Linked to the Presidency, the Council is composed of 13 ministers, the president of BNDES, 14 members of the private sector, and workers. Among the CNDI's development coordination activities there is a plan for investment and systemic innovation in the durable consumer goods industries, and the establishment of links between governmental agencies, universities, and research institutions for partnerships utilizing the sectoral funds from the Ministry of Science and Technology. Finally, in December of 2004, an executive agency was created—ABDI (Brazilian Agency of Industrial Development)—whose objective is to implement industrial development policies. The Agency seeks to "execute and articulate actions and strategies of industrial policy by supporting the processes of innovation and development to the competitiveness of the productive sector" (ABDI).

In addition to the initiatives to support the private sector, it is possible to highlight the concern with creating institutional conditions in the long run—especially those concerning the establishment of relations with the private sector. One can observe the revival in the post-reform scenario of a specific trajectory of development based on a modality of state interventionism that innovates, but that also continues the state developmentalism of the twentieth century. In short, the transition seems to have consolidated itself in terms of a flexible institutional arrangement with regards to the state/private sector relation, with new forums for cooperation and a more modern associative structure, based on the corporatist structures of the developmentalist period. One can also note the engenderment of institutional competitiveness with the creation, on one hand, of an apparatus to encourage development on the industrial policy front, and, on the other, through stimuli to exports and promotion of continental integration, on the foreign policy front.

The state reform implemented during the Fernando Henrique Cardoso government preserves certain nuclei of technical and bureaucratic excellence and maintains development institutions, such as the BNDES. During that administration, while it was in charge of implementing privatizations, BNDES clearly demonstrated that it was playing a role as prominent as during the developmentalism phase. Despite an apparent interruption in the agency's mission—it was responsible for carrying out neoliberal privatization—the continuity of its trajectory is explained by the strict adherence to the constitutional precepts defined when it was created during the second Vargas government, namely the support of projects that encourage job creation. The BNDES then equipped itself and broadened its scope, especially once Lula took office, and more recently its strategic mission has veered towards the regional level, so as to include all of South America.

As pointed out earlier, the economic policy of the Lula government had as a starting point the commitment to maintain the stability achieved with the implementation of the Real Plan during Fernando Henrique's Cardoso first term. The PT government came into power in an extremely restrictive context of strong inflationary tendencies, high levels of foreign debt, and an ill-equipped state apparatus resulting from an unfinished administrative reform, and an intense privatization process. Considering such a scenario, the reorientation of public expenditure was remarkable, with the adoption of a selective modality of interventionism focused on industrial policy, export incentives, and specific support programs for small and medium businesses, among other national initiatives. These were complemented with an extremely incisive initiative in the foreign policy front directed at regional integration. Behind this result, we can find the government's determination to give the BNDES a prominent role, rendering it the nucleus of an institutional network that coordinated development activities. The Lula government sought to redefine the BNDES's role, to turn it into a promoter of stimulus for the private sector without parallel in Latin America, in terms of significance, size, and diversity of functions. This redefinition sought the implementation of an industrial, technological, and trade policy (PITCE). It included a series of new credit lines available to small and medium enterprises and the increase of support to export activities (Boschi, 2008).

The BNDES's function is determined by its provision of credit for long-term investments with lower annual interest rates (9.7%), mainly to small and medium businesses. Three main directives guided the BNDES's actions in the last few years, especially starting in 2005: enhanced agility, with improvements in management routines and procedures; reduction in loan costs; and democratization of credit access. The BNDES's disbursements—the amounts that were actually transferred to businesses—reached R$47 billion that year, a record figure for project financing, 17.5% higher than the R$40 billion in 2004. In the industrial sector, BNDES financing reached R$23.4 billion, growing 48% in relation to the previous year (R$15.8 billion). In the first three years of Lula's government, the BNDES disbursed R$122 billion, R$66 billion (54%) of which were allocated to the capital goods sector, an important barometer of the investment rhythm in Brazilian production (Boschi, 2008).

A recent study investigates the BNDES's role as a development agency, emphasizing the points that support Brazil's inclusion in the small club of advanced countries (Almeida, forthcoming). The objective of the study is not to defend that it is up to Lula's government to make Brazil gain entry to this club, but rather to identify the impact of domestic decisions on the country's recent material progress. According to this author's analysis, the BNDES developed a series of strategies to complement its macroeconomic stabilization efforts and offer coordination mechanisms. BNDES has played an important role in the promotion of a national industrial, technological, and trade policy. Highlighting its role would mean questioning the current idea that the trade and capital market dynamics explain, by themselves, the country's recent economic performance.

In a similar direction, another recent work (Santana, forthcoming) shows the role of the BNDES and of the pension funds, of both public banks and state companies, that have been crucial for the stabilization of macroeconomic variables affecting the labor market and important sectors of the Brazilian industry. In turn, these actors secure an advantage in the capacity to innovate and compete in the global market and establish a space in which their interests can be intermediated and guided towards the formation of new productive coalitions. The BNDES, in addition to establishing itself as the main long-term financing source for the transformation and infra-structure industries, plays a strategic role as a provider of credit lines precisely at times of cyclical variations due to international financial crises. The BNDES is thus able to provide the economy with adjustment mechanisms helping to stave off the harmful effects of crises on investment rates, employment, and growth.[3] According to the data presented in Santana's analysis the BNDES backed credit lines accounted for 20% of the total of credit offered by Banks to the private sector. In 2009 the sum of the credit offered by the BNDES and by other public banks was equivalent to the total value of private banks, that is, about 18% of the Gross Domestic Product (GDP). In all, public federal banks accounted for 38% of the total credit offered by the banking system. The BNDES has maintained its disbursements at a steady rising rate. From 1999 to 2002 it nearly doubled the volume of disbursements. From 2003 to 2008 they increased by 175%. Santana concludes that these state-owned investment and credit institutions constitute one of the institutional legacies that have become the object of a new political interpretation of development. It also runs counter to the hegemonic assessment of the independent role of market forces in the Brazil's recent cycle of economic expansion.

## CRISIS, RESPONSE AND SOCIAL INCLUSION

In a piece written in 1997 comparing the trajectories of Brazil and Mexico in terms of their wealth accumulation and political regimes, Marques

---

3. On October 7, 2008, just after the beginning of the crisis, the BNDES announced the expansion of its export credit lines to counteract the scarcity of credit in the market. An additional 5 billion reais were offered given the need to finance pre-shipping operations. These resources could be used to acquire capital assets and consumer goods ("BNDES amplia linhas de financiamento à exportação para suprir escassez de crédito no mercado," 07/10/2008).

Pereira and Théret (2009) shows that the policies adopted by these two countries—which were originally based on a rather similar developmentalist tradition during the initial period of industrialization through import substitution[4] divergered directions in the 1970s, and the aftereffects are seen in the ensuing patterns of economic performance. In line with the arguments advanced in this paper, these authors emphasize the importance of the political dimension as a determining factor of economic development, and of the trajectories that are estabilshed in each case: whereas in Brazil the military government furthered the ISI model in order to acquire capital assets, thereby concentrating income, in Mexico the PRI favored a strategy of demanding expansion without rearranging its productive structure. The legacies of the institutional forms of regulation at the time of the ISI model therefore shaped the reactions of each country to the challenges of financial globalization and liberalization: clientelistic salary negotiations, a structuralist approach in managing monetary and financial policies, and economic nationalism aptly describe the Brazilian trajectory. This contrasts with the corporatism, monetarism, and political nationalism of the Mexican case. Building upon this differentiation regarding the processes of political intervention of the state, the forms of social protection, and the nature of the political regime, the authors depict a scenario to understand the current state of affairs: the importance of the political democratic option coupled, with the possibility of growth sustained by the domestic market, accompanied by a perspective of income redistribution as a possible route of development in the Brazilian case, in contrast with Mexico which followed the path of later democratization and externally oriented growth.[5]

The option for targeted policies aimed at the reduction of poverty and social inequality, although an item on the Fernando Henrique Cardoso agenda, had to wait until the Lula government before it became a development priority. This shift epitomizes the strategy of development based on social incorporation and expansion of the domestic market. They comprise an array of policies centered around, yet not limited to, the Bolsa Família, a means-tested income support program created by the Lula government for poor families to keep their children in school. These are complemented by other initiatives aimed at expanding access to citizenship, and to the con-

---

4. That is, accumulation regimes identical at the macro-economic level, albeit installed by different types of political regimes and contrasting institutional forms of regulation.

5. "The conclusion that must be spelled out at the normative level of this comparative analysis of the long-term interplay of mediating regulatory institutions is that the reduction of social and regional inequalities constitute, in both cases, a fundamental condition of development" (Marques Pereira and Théret, 2009: 42).

sumer market, the most recent of which is access to the banking system as a doorway to micro-credit lines.

Some effects of this policy redirection can be assessed based on the data of the 2007 Household Sample National Survey—PNAD (IBGE, 2007). According to an IPEA report (2008) which analyzes the data produced by the survey, the degree of inequality in Brazil dropped sharply and constantly since the beginning of this century. The exact figure is 7%, meaning that the GINI coefficient dropped from 0.593 in 2001 to 0.552 in 2007, at an annual rate of 1.2%, as shown in Figure 3-1 below.

FIGURE 3-1. Gini Coefficient 1977-2007

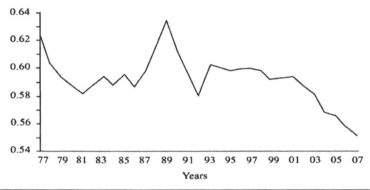

Years

*Source*: Data produced on the basis of PNAD (National Sample of Household Research).

The above mentioned survey employed other indicators as well: the ratio between the average income of the richest 10% and of the poorest 40%, and that of the richest 20% and the poorest 20%. In both cases, the indicators show a considerable decline in the inequality in income distribution from 2001 to 2007: the first ratio declined 5.2%. (IPEA, 2008). In addition, the study shows that this drop, which has been observed since 2001, is the longest lasting one in the last three decades. There have been six continuous years of declining rates of inequality. From 2001 to 2007, the income of those in the lowest income bracket has increased significantly, which in turn lowered the levels of poverty and extreme poverty. The analysis estimates that the recent decline in extreme poverty occurred at a rate three times faster than it would be necessary in order to achieve the Millennium Development Goal, set for 2015, which in fact was reached in 2006 (IPEA, 2008).

Regarding social mobility, the 2007 survey shows that only 27.4% fall in the lowest income bracket (less than R$545.66 net family income per month) (IPEA, 2008). This corresponds to 13.8 million people moving up the social ladder, out of which 10.8 million crossed the threshold separating group 1 from group 2 (intermediate net family incomes between R$545.66 to R$1,350.82 per month); and 3.6 million advanced from group 2 to group 3 (the higher income bracket above R$ 1,350.82). The highest increase in social mobility occured in the transition from group 1 to group 2, representing 74% of those which were able to ascend socially. Mostly, this mobility took place in the Northeast, North and Central-West regions— 5.3 million, or 52%, whereas the transition from group 2 to group 3 occured in the Southeast and South regions—2.7 million or 69.9%.

Some of the data concerning the reduction of poverty are also revealing. In this sense, one should note the reduction in the number of people below the poverty line, especially after 2003 (see Table 3-1).

TABLE 3-1. Percent of Population with Net Family Income Below the Poverty Line, 1995–2007

| 1995 | 4.0 | 2002 | 3.0 |
|------|-----|------|-----|
| 1996 | 5.0 | 2003 | 4.0 |
| 1997 | 4.0 | 2004 | 2.0 |
| 1998 | 4.0 | 2005 | 1.0 |
| 1999 | 4.0 | 2006 | 9.0 |
| 2000 | 6.0 | 2007 | 8.0 |
| 2001 | 4.0 |      |     |

*Source*: IPEADATA, 2009.

According to PNAD (2007) data, employment increased 1.6% from 89.3 million workers in 2006 to 90.8 million in 2007. Furthermore, the real average income of those employed increased 3.2%, reaching its highest level since 1996. The unemployment rate decreased marginally and is now at 8.2%, the lowest level of this decade. There has been an overall increase in the number of so-called formal or protected job positions and a reduction of those attached to the informal market. As a result of job expansion, the degree of informality decreased significantly from 55.1% in 2006 to 54.1% in 2007. Considering only the most reliable forms of employment relationships (paid wages, autonomous labor, employers), informality has dropped from 49.7% to 48.9% in this same period. A result in this reduction of informality has been the increase of the percentage of workers that contribute to the social pension system (this figure has climbed from 48.8% in 2006 to 50.7% in 2007) considering that the number of those contributing has dovetailed with remained the increase of the number of protected workers (IPEA 2008).

The graphs below (Figure 3-2) exemplify the above mentioned tendencies, which were, already in progress before the onset of the crisis.

FIGURE 3-2. Employment Data, 2001-2007

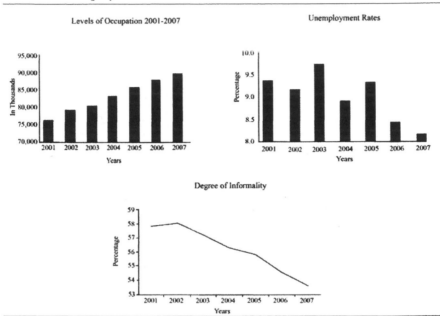

*Source*: IPEA, 2008a.

It is in the wake of these previous policies and the establishment of an institutional framework through time that it is possible to understand the effect of anti-cyclical policies adopted to weather the crisis. These policies aim to secure and expand excluded sectors in the consumer market, and the industrial sector's production of durable goods oriented towards (but not exclusively to) the domestic market, while at the same time maintaining levels of employment through concessions of fiscal incentives as shown below.

The financial market crisis certainly had an impact on the Brazilian economy, and in certain regards, it influenced aforementioned positive results. When the crisis struck, the country was on a roll in terms of employment compared to the last 30 years, with an unemployment rate of approximately 6%. Still, the burst of the real estate bubble caused by the subprime market caused Brazil 800,000 formal job losses in the span of only three months.

The newly instituted Bolsa Família program helped to prevent people from losing jobs and falling back into poverty. On average, from October 2008 to June 2009, the poverty rate decreased 2.8% compared to the same period the previous year. In this period, 503,000 people were removed from poverty and inequality dropped 0.4%. According to the IPEA, this is why that one year after the peak of the crisis, poverty and inequality rates remained at almost the same level as before 2008. Thus, the real outcome of the crisis can be said to have been a sudden slowdown in the reduction of poverty and inequality, something that had been occurring quite rapidly in the last years, with an average of 5 million people moving out of poverty each year.[6]

Among the main anticyclical policies adopted I would like to highlight the following:

A minimum wage real (above-inflation) increase of over 6% effective March 2010 note that 2/3 of all pension benefits are equal to one minimum wage;

All benefits beyond the minimum wage were adjusted according to past inflation with no loss in purchase power from 2008 to 2009;

Expansion of directed credit, especially of credit lines offered by public financial institutions, such as the BNDES, Caixa Econômica, and Banco do Brasil;

Creation of two new taxes on individuals, increasing available government funds;

The addition of 1.3 million people in the Bolsa Familia program;

Increased efforts in the implementation of investment projects established by the Growth Acceleration Program *(Programa de Aceleração do Crescimento*, PAC);

Reduction of the annual primary budget surplus target, previously established at 4.3% and reduced to 2.5%;

Launching of the Minha Casa, Minha Vida (My House, my Life) housing program which includes the construction of 1 million homes for people with incomes below 10 minimum wages. This program will require investments amounting to R$34 billion and will try to keep the housing sector moving at a strong pace. According to estimates made by the Caixa Econômica Federal, 800 thousand jobs will be created this year.

Maintenance/expansion of public expenditure with employees, social programs, and direct activities of the state and,

---

6. "Políticas anticíclicas protegem base da pirâmide," 09/09/2009 (http://www.ipea.gov.br/003/00301009.jsp?ttCD_CHAVE=11914).

Reduction of the Tax on Industrialized Products (Imposto sobre Produtos indus-trializados-IPI) in several sectors, among them, the automobile industry.[7]

In the realm of economic policies, the reduction of the IPI in sectors such as home appliances, construction, and automobile industry was responsible for preserving, directly and indirectly, up to 60,000 jobs and for 13.4% of car sales in the first semester, which translates to sales of 191,000 cars.[8] As a result, these numbers show that the anticyclical policies worked effectively—they stimulated spending, increased sales, energized the economy and made the consumer spend savings at a time when the uncertainties provoked by the crisis made it difficult to do so suggested otherwise. Therefore, the IPI reduction in these sectors was especially important in energizing the economy.

The anti-cyclical policies taken by the government also had a positive impact concerning employment, insofar as more than half of the jobs lost were recovered, which provided families with greater purchasing power as well as stimulus for growth. Last May, the rate of unemployment dropped to approximately 9% in the six main metropolitan regions of Brazil—São Paulo, Rio de Janeiro, Belo Horizonte, Salvador, Recife, and Porto Alegre. Large companies such as Vale and Embraer announced significant cuts in personnel and output. But, to the surprise of many analysts, the job market turned out to be the life line of the Brazilian economy.

The social programs supported by the government, such as the Bolsa Familia, the above-inflation increases of the minimum wage, and the PAC (even if slow in its implementation), have rescued Brazil from recession while protecting a fraction of the population that would have otherwise been excluded from the formal economy.

Given Brazil's quick recovery from the international financial crisis, on September 22, 2009, Moody's credit rating agency promoted Brazil to investment grade. To date, Brazil has achieved investment grade according to three credit rating agencies: Standard and Poor's, the Canadian agency Dominion Bond Rating Service, and the Japanese agencies Rating and Investment Information, and Japan Credit Rating Agency. It's important to realize the fact that Brazil was the only country to receive the rating upgrade during the crisis.[9]

---

7. "PIB cresceu 1,9%: a crise era um V," 14/09/2009 (http://www.ipea.gov.br/003/00301009.jsp?ttCD_CHAVE=12005).

8. "A mão visível do governo," 02/09/2009 (http://jbonline.terra.com.br/pextra/2009/09/02/e020927895.asp).

Concerning industrial performance, IEDI's newsletter n° 371, "Industrial Production and Jobs: More Positive Signs with Distinct Regional and Sector Characteristics," had predicted a significant improvement of industrial production, pointing out that, if the external scenario remained favorable as it has in the previous months, recovery could come and the level of the production reached before the crisis accentuated. The recent evolution of production, although it has shown a less robust growth rate and rather negative levels in the last five months, indicates, nevertheless, a marginally positive tendency. However, differentiated regional performances still persist.

In fact, production in some states has started to improve, as is the case of São Paulo. Comparing the months of March and April, industrial production in this state increased 2.4% (with seasonal variations accounted for) after growing 1.1% in April. Evidently, this does not mean that industries in São Paulo have returned to pre-crisis levels of production. Compared to May 2008, there has been an 11.6% decrease in production, and in the accumulated index for the first five months of 2009, industrial output in the state of São Paulo decreased 14.6%. However the 2.4% increase in May might be the first indication of industrial recovery in São Paulo. It's an important development, with implications for the rest of the Brazilian industry, since the state's industrial complex accounts for a good portion of the demand for products from other regions of the country. IEDI's preliminary assessment, based on output patterns for May 2009, indicates the industry's positive reaction to the crisis. This reaction is buttressed by improved credit conditions, the fiscal unburdening provided by the IPI cuts, and by the domestic market's enhanced demand capacity. Therefore the anticyclical policies announced by the government—postponement of tax reductions for automobiles, motorcycles, home appliances, construction material, trucks, wheat flour for bread, and tax cuts for capital assets, and, most important, the reduction of credit costs provided by the BNDES for the acquisition of machinery, and equipment—should favor the industry's response.[10]

---

9. According to Moody's, "the chances that Brazil's rating continues to improve are reasonably high" since "economic conditions seem favorable to constant reductions of public debt indicators, given the perspective of growth in the short term and the probability that macroeconomic conditions will continue warranting one-digit interest rates, a condition that fundamentally changes the dynamics behind the debt." Moody's positive outlook adds that "the absence of fundamental macroeconomic inbalances in the Brazilian economy is a favorable condition given that it places the country in good standing in relation to other sovereign creditors in the same rating category yet with greater fiscal and foreign challenges." Brasil torna-se Grau de investimento pela Moody's. Available at: http://www.fazenda.gov.br/portugues/documentos/2009/Nota-Moodys-220909.pdf

10. Carta IEDI n. 370—Produção Industrial em Maio de 2009: Recuperação Gradual (www.iedi.org.br).

Industrial output, after the 20% drop between September and December 2008, already shows a positive growth rate of 7.9%, between December 2008 and June 2009, according to data that includes control for seasonal variations produced by the PIM/IBGE (Constanzi, 2009) (See Figure 3-3).

FIGURE 3-3. Industrial Output, 2007-2010 (2002=100)

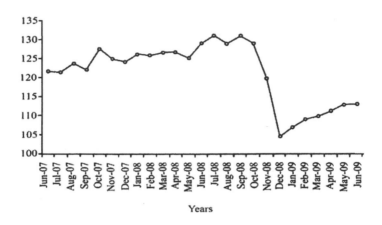

*Source*: Monthly Industrial Survey *(Pesquisa Industrial Mensal, Produção Física)*, IBGE, 2009.

## CONCLUSION: ESTABLISH A VIRTUOUS CIRCLE?

Development involves long-term processes that are best analyzed in hindsight, since there are uncertainties about the impact and direction of change. In certain aspects, especially those pertaining to structural dimensions, we can speak of path dependency in terms of institutional choices taken at the outset of any process. This includes, those which begin to generate increasing returns for the federal institutes, bureaucracies, and political institutions capable of ensuring governability, and enhancing the executive's effectiveness. In other aspects, as in the case of the types of social security associated with a certain productive regime, it would be more appropriate to speak of a trajectory that is influenced by changes or reorientations in policies, even in a radical fashion, according to changes in the elites' reference points. We can affirm that, depending on context, a single factor can be an obstacle or a stimulus for development.

In the Brazilian case, as I have attempted to show, the long-term analysis indicates, on one hand, the path dependency of state institutions in terms of their role as the coordinator of economic activities, and on the other, the continuation of a trajectory that has undergone adjustments over time in terms of social and inclusion policies. Finally, a factor such as the size of the population can shift from being considered an obstacle to development, as was the case not too long ago, to becoming a facilitator for development within a new outlook, as it seems to be the case now. The late buildup process of the state apparatus in the 1930s—actually the result of a political rupture with the oligarchic agro-exporting model—continuing with the progressive import-substitution industrialization, was combined, however, with a process of social exclusion and income concentration. Under authoritarian governments and democratic interregnums, this logic was pushed forward by the ruling elites in an outlook of growing foreign debt, and high inflation that ended up exhausting this type of development predominant until the end of the 1970s. Concurrently to the political regime, there is the transition to a competitive and pluralist democracy, characterized by the expansion of the political spectrum. The neoliberal turn led to a resizing of the state and of state interventions, which combined market regulation and orthodox macroeconomic policies. The financial system, which had undergone reforms in the 1970s, was improved and regulated during the implementation of the Real Plan. However, structures and models from the previous model—especially those relating to the articulation of the state with the private sector, as well as those related to development and productive activities—remained in place.

A party with roots in the labor movement emerges democratically in the political scene and, after reaching the presidency, implemented developmentalist policies while maintaining the principles of monetary stability established by the previous government. It did this through the administration of the interest rate, exchange rate, and public spending. The main difference between the two governments is the latter's prioritization of poverty reduction and social policies. Utilizing this framework, we can evaluate the impact of the international crisis and the emergency policies adopted to manage the economic slowdown. What can be called the "expansion of the social frontier," besides a striking feature of the new outlook, is the doorway to a new development model based on the possibility of domestic market expansion. This is without overlooking the insertion in foreign markets, ensured by an extremely diversified and complex export portfolio, of which primary goods and agro-exports are but a few of its components. Combining these tendencies with a foreign policy characterized by a strong orientation towards regional integration, it is possible to foresee the establishment of a positive context for development in Brazil. The rich energetic potential that opens up with the exploration of the pré-sal and ecological resources demands action in the realm of regulation and implementation of strategies for sustainability. This scenario not only further empowers the comeback of the state as the central actor in a new development model, but also makes it the nucleus of the productive regime. Problems will certainly exist, especially in governing the intense conflict among traditional oligarchies, big rural landowners, and conservative sectors in general. It is precisely in this scenario that politics can make a difference, playing an open game that simultaneously articulates uncertainties and possibilities.

# 4

# NEW DIRECTIONS IN PUBLIC POLICY AND STATE-SOCIETY RELATIONS

*Glauco Arbix and Scott B. Martin*

*Abstract:* This chapter takes as its point of departure the notion that an incipient new development model is taking shape in Brazil. This model recovers the state as a focal point, but in a manner quite distinct from the heavy-handed, often dirigiste role of the developmentalist state of what some have insightfully termed the period of the state-centered matrix. The visible outlines of this new model, though incipient, suggest its compatibility with political democracy and open economies. A central argument of this chapter emphasizes the new synergies that have emerged, to some extent by design, and to some extent by virtuous accident, across economic and social policy—traditionally two very distinct spheres of public policy in Brazil in terms of aims and institutions.

This decade's rapid growth of many large developing countries, and the critique and political backlash against neoliberalism, have begun to reinvigorate age-old debates about the prospects and "state of the state."[1] Debates about the declining state—until recently common in the literature about globalization—have shifted. Without a doubt, states in many developing countries have altered dramatically their real policy capacities and institutions as well as relationships with civil society. In part this was done in

---

1. This paper draws on ideas first presented in Arbix and Miranda (2009).

response to globalization, but also in reaction to changes in national political systems. Since the 1990s, in Brazil as in many developing countries, states no longer seem to wear the straitjacket suggested by neo-classical orthodoxy. In fact, it could be argued that states have never really been in retreat anywhere in the world, even in their weakest moment. Still, they have definitely undergone major transformations that make them quite distinct from the pre-neoliberal, pre-globalization "states of old," with their statism and dirigisme.

We propose to explore the shifting roles and forms of intervention of the contemporary Brazilian state, with a focus on theorizing and re-conceptualizing evolving approaches to economic and social policy that are captured neither by the market fundamentalist/neoliberal or old (or revived) "developmental state" or *desenvolvimentista* paradigms. A more synergistic, two-way pattern of state-market relations seems to be emerging in Brazil, centered on state roles of promotion of competitiveness and innovation. At the same time, the state has assumed a heightened role in social policy oriented toward combating poverty, making inroads against inequality, and promoting market incorporation of underprivileged citizens. Thus far, the response to the global crisis that began in 2008 suggests a deepening of these trends as well as the resiliency of emerging practices and institutions.

In the next section, we will briefly situate our discussion within the context of (1) recent debates about the state concerning impacts of globalization and the apparent decline of the neoliberal paradigm as well as, (2) recent efforts to characterize these patterns or promote alternatives to neoliberalism using the conceptual apparatus of developmentalism. Following that, the heart of the paper will explore the emergence and evolution since the mid-1990s of what we identify as new state capacities in the areas of fiscal policy, competitiveness policy (toward trade, industry, and science and technology), and social policy, including reform and expansion of traditional entitlements together with expanded targeted social assistance. Along the way, we discuss the synergies across these revived and re-oriented state roles; how they diverge from developmentalist practices and concepts (particularly under the military regime); how they emerge out of the democratization process and policy learning; and how together with other developments they seem to have helped produce a new model of income-redistributing and equity-enhancing growth. Toward the end, we discuss why the enticing alternative label of "social democratic," quite often applied to the Lula government, may be misleading or incomplete given divergence from what that concept has meant, including in recent influential research on "peripheral social democracy." We conclude with a call for recognizing that Brazil's recent evolution is not well captured by any of these labels, and the need for a conceptual apparatus that will enable us to analyze and explain the emergence and possible consolidation of a "neo-activist" state form (to borrow Weiss's term) that does not yet have a ready-made conceptual paradigm among social scientists. This state takes on an enabling position of moderate, pro-market intervention via an active competitiveness policy, joined closely with a much stronger role in providing social services and benefits. It is also increasingly linked to fostering market inclusion for the previously underserved and excluded, in addition to transferring income in targeted fashion to increasingly broad segments of the poor and extremely poor.

## GLOBALIZATION, STATES, AND DEVELOPMENT: FROM NEOLIBERALISM TO NEODEVELOPMENTALISM?

If much of the decade of the nineties was marked by considerable preoccupation about globalization-induced "convergence" toward a narrow minimalist neoliberal or market fundamentalist state, the past decade or so has been marked by powerful empirical and theoretical refutations of such determinism. This has been applied to both advanced and developing countries[2] as well as interesting discussions about varieties of capitalism in the North (Hall and Soskice eds., 2001), and alternatives or successors to neoliberal versions of capitalism for Latin America and the global South (e.g., Huber ed., 2002). The sense of a palpable (if not necessarily definitive) decline of neoliberal policy and doctrines, and the associated Washington Consensus is widespread, in part given the backlash generated against those policies at the national and international levels. Within that general intellectual and policy milieu, some scholars (e.g., Weiss ed., 2004; Weiss forthcoming), have begun to creatively explore how states seemingly are carving out new roles, and development strategies that are both post-neoliberal and post-developmental. Meanwhile, some analysts in Brazil (Bresser-Pereira, 2004 and 2006; Sicsú and Renaut eds., 2004), reflecting the tremendous hold that developmentalist thinking still has in certain intellectual quarters, have begun to discuss—in part as pro-

---

2. Restricting the focus to studies centering mostly on the global South, we can cite Weiss ed. (2004) regarding states in general, and with regard to social welfare polices in particular, Glatzer and Rueschemeyer, eds. (2005) and Haggard and Kaufman (2008).

posed doctrine and in part as description of the emerging empirical reality they seek to analyze and promote—a "novo desenvolvimentismo" with roots in the "old developmentalism." For his part, the current Finance Minister, Guido Mantega, spoke in September 2007 of a "social-desenvolvimentismo" that he believed was emerging under Lula.[3]

The problem with attempts to revive or re-orient the developmental state concept, in our view, is that it conflates very distinct experiences, across time and disparate countries. By associating state behavior narrowly with economic performance, especially growth of Gross Domestic Product (GDP), it tends to obscure the real debate that needs to occur about recent transformations. It reduces the diverse dimensions of state action and capacity— their roots in society and in institutional relations—to the simple movement of the economy, in particular the macroeconomy. Thus, the new profile of the state would be narrowly defined by its capacity (in reality, its success) to deliver better economic performance.

The debt crisis of the early 1980s, which resulted in the corrosion and collapse of the economy of Latin America, and Brazil in particular, was the first great blow to the developmentalist edifice constructed over the 1950s and 1960s and still operating—albeit with greater difficulties—in the 1970s. During the nineties, economic opening and privatization processes were key turning points that ended a long cycle of protectionism. Also affected was the direct presence of the state as a producer of goods and services, and as heavy-handed regulator creator of private firms and entire sectors. The structural changes promoted during the course of the 1990s took place within a process of global integration, marked particularly by the newly founded World Trade Organization and international financial liberalization. In terms of the structural characteristics of the national state, these global changes produced a point of no return, in Brazil and elsewhere. At the same time, the transformations produced new configurations that by no means approximated the most orthodox pro-market models or prescriptions. They were based on the idea of an inert state, responsible only for setting basic rules and broad regulations for private markets, and notable reactive in character. In fact, we argue—for the Brazilian case, though the argument could be extended to many other countries— that the state never did withdraw altogether, even though various foundational elements were irreversibly altered, and in due course, new elements were added, such that

---

3. Interview with Radiobrás, September 12, 2007, reported in Edla Lula and Daniel Lima, "Brasil entrou no novo ciclo econômico do social-desenvolvimentismo," Agência Brasil, September 23, 2007.

in its current form it bears little resemblance to either orthodox market fundamentalism or the developmental state.

## STATE CAPACITY AND SOCIAL POLICY: CONTRASTS WITH THE OLD DEVELOPMENTALISM

We argue that the contemporary Brazilian state has evolved, within the broad context of economic opening and political democratization. Even as old forms of state capacity associated with the country's particular version of "developmentalism"—particularly but not only in its late, military regime phase—have been undermined by market reforms and by economic opening, new forms of state capacity have emerged and taken shape. This has not been a "neat" or coherent or linear process, but nonetheless, when one steps back from the process of change (a subject we tackle in the following section) to focus on its concrete manifestations today, it is difficult to understate the extent of the transformations. State capacity has, in short, been transformed and adapted, rather than simply declining. Additionally it has taken on new characteristics not captured by the developmentalist or neoliberal paradigms (or that of populism, however that contested concept might be applied).

It is rather easy to quickly relate the process by which the main developmental capacities of the old military-developmentalist state were dismantled, or suffered serious decline, in the 1980s and, particularly 1990s. Emerging in the broader context of fiscal crisis, continuous stabilization crises, and extremely high levels of inflations amidst the exhaustion of the ISI model, extensive privatization of state-owned enterprises under Collor (1990–1992) and, particularly, Cardoso (1995–2002) undermined the state capacity to shape productive investment in steel, petrochemicals, and mining. The power deriving from a centralization of fiscal authority in the federal government was undermined not only by the general atmosphere of crisis, but also by the fuzzy fiscal federalism of the 1988 Constitution. Furthermore, there were successive financial crises and initial difficulties in working out the rules of fiscal federalism, such as the "fiscal war," over state-level incentives to attract investment. Rapid and indiscriminate trade liberalization from the Collor government onward, in the broader context of privatization and persistent fiscal crisis, weakened the once considerable ability of Brasília to promote—through sectoral industrial policies involving subsidies, protection, and investment incentives—domestically owned firms as either "national champions" or important firms that could work in close alliance with multinationals (e.g. auto parts).

Of course, the coercive capacity of the military-developmentalist state—one of the main attributes of the state in that era—was debilitated by democratization and a shift in the balance of relations between civil and military authorities, as well as other processes of a more socio-structural nature.

The fiscal sector was one of the first of the key areas in which state capacity has been reconstructed over the past two presidencies. Numerous elements beyond the starting point of macroeconomic stabilization under the Real Plan—a de facto renegotiation of the fiscal pact between federation and states, incremental tax and social security reforms, administrative reforms, tight-fisted monetary policies including primary fiscal surpluses—have contributed to this process of restoring the state's key capacity to tax, spend, and invest. It is well known that Brazil has one of the highest tax to GDP ratios in the developing world; scholars have also noted how crucial fiscal health and fiscal capacity are in offering either a more permissive or a more restrictive environment for social policy (Haggard and Kaufman, 2008). With the Real Plan, not simply did the state gain a better handle on management of various large fiscal burdens such as social security and management of subnational sovereign debt, but it was also able to maintain a large tax base ("revenue extraction capacity," if one wishes to be more abstract), through periodic—typically incremental—tax reforms, even amidst persistent cycles of crisis, stabilization, and recovery including the late 1990s recession. As finances improved and growth picked up, this extractive capacity has restored the state's ability to undertake key investments in infrastructure, social services, and science and technology. Policy orientations placed these as high priorities.

A second key area of renewed and transformed state capacity combined with a substantive reorientation in substance is in trade policy (broadly conceived) that is tied to the general theme of competitiveness policy which is a key element of the new market-friendly Brazilian state activism. While extensive protection has been left behind since the trade liberalization of the early 1990s, and indeed the World Trade Organization (WTO) and other international trade commitments create further general constrains, the federal government has taken on and steadily expanded its role in trade promotion in the Cardoso and particularly the Lula governments. This primarily takes the form of an aggressive promotion of these very bilateral and multilateral free trade agreements within and beyond the Americas (and opposition to those, such as the now defunct Free Trade of the America proposal of the 1990s and early 2000s) as well as energetic defense of perceived Brazilian interests within multilateral trade negotiations. Of note is, that unlike the more straightforward economic nationalism of developmentalism's yesteryear, this involves an ambitious and elaborate effort to cultivate foreign market access for Brazilian goods as well as increasingly for foreign direct investment (FDI) abroad by Brazilian firms [where for instance Brazilian firms were responsible for 14 mergers and acquisitions in 2008 (Arbix and Miranda, 2009)]. One result of this policy has been a very strong and healthy diversification of Brazil's foreign trading relationships over the past decade or so, in particular in terms of a relative diminution in its trade dependence vis-à-vis traditional Northern partners among the OECD powers and relative increase in its ties with the global South, most notably China but also sub-Saharan Africa and other regions outside the Americas. This has been closely related to a diversification in the range of exports in terms of sectors, degrees of value added, and types, which include not just simple commodities, but also value-added commodities such as ethanol as well as manufactured goods across an increasingly diverse range.

Moreover, while the country has perhaps not been as aggressive as some East Asian countries in trying to use all the remaining tools of permissible selective protection at its disposal within a post-WTO world,[4] Brasília has not shied away from a sometimes aggressive defense of measures such as the automotive regime of the mid to late 1990s (forcing multinationals to invest directly in the country if they wished to receive lower tariffs on imports) or successfully challenging US cotton subsidies within WTO mechanisms (Evans, 2005b).

In all these cases, whether pursuing multilateral or bilateral trade disputes, or negotiating new trade deals (e.g., taking a much greater role in the Doha round than in the previous Uruguay round of global trade talks), or channeling lines of credit through the BNDES, trade promotion involves increasingly closer relationships of consultation with firms and sectors who can benefit quite tangibly and directly from specific expanded market opportunities.

In sum, even within a context of openness that policy elites across the last two presidencies have not just accepted but actively embraced in a historic shift for Brazil—the state has not taken this a simple cue to retreat into a

---

4. For a good analysis of what "policy space" might remain within WTO rules for competitiveness and other policies on the part of developing countries, see Gallagher ed., 2005, in particular the essays by Alice Amsden and Peter Evans.

passive "laissez faire" position of accepting Brazil's inherited comparative advantage or current structure of imports, exports, and trading partners.

Besides trade policy understood broadly, competitiveness policy has two other key, closely related dimensions—industrial policy and science and technology, or national innovation, policy. In both these areas, one finds an increasingly pro-active role of the state, mainly within the Lula government but to some extent building on some institutional innovations from the Cardoso administration, with respect to (1) strategic policy formulation and related creation of new institutions for such purposes; and (2) development finance.

In 1999 the Ministry of Development, Industry, and Commerce was created. This was a step that would loom as more significant after Lula took office in 2003, and began to place greater emphasis on formulating an active competitiveness policy. Yet the initial institutional move placed significant responsibility for both trade policy and policy toward industry, commerce, and services into a single cabinet-level agency.

It is difficult to trace a fully coherent and rational arc in the process of creation of policy designs and institutionalities for industrial policy under Lula. Rather, the process seems in part an experimental one of trial and error—and thus arguably of policy learning among cabinet and mid-level officials—in which, over time, the degree of coordination among agencies and of explicitness in goals (through a more "results-based" approach) as well as ambition of goals have all tended to increase. In the early years of the first Lula government, when concerns about macroeconomic stability and structural reforms that would cement the government's credibility with the international financial community prevailed, the Conselho Nacional de Desenvolvimento Econômico e Social (CNDES) was established in 2003. Its role has been primarily consultative, rather than becoming a kind of national negotiating forum that extends nationally the principles of the sectoral chambers or regional chamber of the greater ABC region comprising Santo André, São Bernardo do Campo and São Caetano do Sul (which some at the time might have hoped or, depending on their perspective, feared). Nonetheless, in bringing in not only business associations but also labor unions and other civil society organizations into a broader debate about national development priorities, the CNDES at least set an important early tone of dialogue and societal, particularly business, participation in a process of promoting a public-private alliance for development, which has remained and grown in subsequent years.

Created in late 2004 and early 2005, the Agência Brasileira de Desenvolvimento Industrial (ABDI) is a networked institution, formally under the Ministry of Development, Industry, and Trade, that brings together in its governing deliberative council federal ministries and funding agencies, private sector representatives from inside and outside the official corporatist business structure, labor (CUT, *Central Única dos Trabalhadores*), and universities to promote technological and economic development in sectors of Brazilian industry. ABDI has played a leading role in seeking to develop an industrial policy and helps identify and guide investment decisions in technological research, innovation, and industrial development. The comprehensive framework that the ABDI has developed under its *Política de Desenvolvimento Produtivo* (PDP, Policy of Productive Development) stresses the importance of public investment and support to build capability in infrastructure, capital goods, exports, and technology firms (Trubek, 2008). One interesting aspect of the PDP is that it set in 2007 a series of concrete measurable benchmarks, or "macrometas," for 2010 in terms of desired improvements in the country's ratios of fixed investments, share of global exports, share of private R&D in total GDP, and number of exporting micro and small enterprises.

Another new institution, also created in January 2005, is the Conselho Nacional de Desenvolvimento Industrial (CNDI, National Council for Industrial Development); an inter-ministerial body comprised of all the main ministries with responsibilities for economic, social, and environmental policy, other development-related agencies [including the IPEA (Institute for Applied Economic Research) with its advisory function and BNDES as national development bank] along with 14 representatives from civil society. Its primary function is to "propose to the President national policies and specific measures to promote Brazil's industrial development."[5] The Council plays important roles of agenda-setting as well as coordination and mediation of disputes among ministries that may bring to the table different bureaucratic, partisan, or other types of interests as well as potential competing ideas and priorities.

Along with the creation of new institutions, traditional institutions have been strengthened. Of note, particularly with regard to science and technology, or national innovation, policy is the strengthening of (1) the Ministry of Science and Technology's funding agency for public, private, and mixed

---

5. Ministério do Desenvolvimento, Indústria e Comércio Exterior, http://www.mdic.gov.br/sitio/interna/interna.php?area=1&menu=558.

projects of applied and basic research, FINEP (Financiadora de Estudos e Projetos) and (2) state-level foundations and technology institutes that play similar roles at the subnational level. With promotion of firm-level innovation now articulated as a major policy goal under the 2005 National Innovation Law, the FINEP's funding has increased substantially and also its emphasis on lending directly to firms has been enhanced significantly. In addition, funding for the federal university system has increased generally and in terms of support for dynamic high-tech sectors in particular, including the creation of new universities such as the Federal University of the Greater ABC Region, and there is much evidence of heightened university-firm linkages in terms of fostering innovation. In addition, the long-standing national development bank dating from the advent of developmentalism in the 1950s, the BNDES, has recently enjoyed a higher profile, revamped role for which even the liberal *The Economist*[6]—usually no fan of industrial policy—has delivered grudging praise. The Bank's assets stood at US$120bn as of end-2008, according to the magazine, and its annual lending portfolio is now larger than that of the World Bank (Trubek, 2008), at around US$100bn. Noting that "[I]n the past its funds were sometimes handed out according to political expediency, to dying companies and in pursuit of a patchily successful industrial policy," *The Economist* notes the BNDES' recently expanded role as a venture capitalist and direct provider of trade finance during the recent credit crunch as well as its "slim" administration comprised of "career civil servants" that has engaged in "less political lending of late."[7] All of the areas of improvement noted by the article relate to problems that have plagued the BNDES, a quintessential institution from the developmentalist era, and that seem to have been overcome or at least been addressed in large measure.

The BNDES' heightened role as a venture capitalist is of particular importance because it reflects not just a new policy instrument but also a strategic shift toward greater emphasis on promoting innovation in nascent or promising new sectors as well as traditional lending to established firms and sectors. And while this role no doubt grew in the context of the quite agile stimulative and anti-crisis posture that the Brazilian state in general has displayed with respect to limiting the impacts of the global recession on the country's growth

---

6. "Central Planning: Rediscovering the Charms of BNDES," *The Economist*, April 16, 2009.

7. The magazine's only two caveats are that "the government still has a thing about helping to create big companies that can conquer rivals abroad" that is reflected in BNDES policies (a debatable point in terms of wisdom of policy priorities) and that its enhanced role as trade financier and venture capitalist has to do with wider capital market inefficiencies and insufficiencies in Brazil.

(a topic to which we turn below), this evolution has been underway for a number of years under the Lula presidency. We reproduce the following summary from Trubek that builds on the work of several Brazilian specialists:

> BNDESPAR is the investment bank arms of BNDES whose goals include support for technological innovation, small business, and start-ups producing innovative and competitive products; the creation of a seed money and venture capital market; and support for the acquisition of foreign assets by Brazilian firms. BNDESPAR both operates like a private equity fund and venture capitalist and supports other institutions that perform these roles. BNDESPAR can make direct investment in start-ups and unlisted companies; participate in their management; and affect corporate strategy and governance. In some cases, BNDESPAR requires that firms receiving its support submit innovation plans. It also encourages the firms it supports to secure private capital through IPOs. But the bank also supports closed investment funds that provide private equity and venture capital especially for small and medium size firms. BNDESPAR invests in privately managed closed funds that are targeted at specific sectors and attract substantial private funding: currently these funds have raised $4 for every $1 committed by the Bank.

This novel role for the BNDES in terms of close public-private collaboration in support of private entrepreneurship and innovation is characterized by Mattos and Coutinho (2008) as a new "model of risk-taking" that the Brazilian state is arguably taking on. The authors insightfully contrast this new type of state role in industrial policy with the states' industrial policy role as "owner of state-owned enterprises" and "picking winners" under developmentalism as well as the neoliberal model of "privatization."

A fourth area where state capacity was weakly developed under military (and earlier, pre-1964 versions of) *desenvolvimentismo* and has become much more so since the 1990s is in social policy. Despite some modest expansions of social security benefits, health care access, and local educational spending requirements under the military regime,[8] Brazil's welfare regime remained highly segmented and (like the economic model itself) regressive in its impact on income distribution during this period. Newly created programs such as FUNRURAL as well as terms of access for newly incorporated groups in the social security system were riddled with patron-

---

8. This discussion draws on Haggard and Kaufman (2008: 100-03). The notable extensions of coverage included: the extension of noncontributory pensions to some peasants and rural poor under the newly created *Fundo de Assistência ao Trabalhador Rural* (FUNRURAL) in 1971; the 1979 expansion of rural clinics in the Northeast under the Programa de Interiorizacão das Acões de Saúde e Saneamento (PIASS), and extension of access to emergency heath-care for all citizens; and a 1983 constitutional amendment mandating that states spend at least 15% of all federal transfer on education.

age for the official ARENA (*Aliança Renovadora Nacional*) party, and "cash benefits to the rural and urban informal sectors—about one-half the minimum wage . . . remained minimal compared to those going to the civil service, other formal sector workers, and (of course) the military itself" (Haggard and Kaufman, 2008: 101-02). Filgueira and Filgueira (2002: 138-39) characterize Brazil's welfare regime through the end of the 1970s as "dual . . . with an almost universal development of primary education and a significant though stratified degree of health coverage . . . [exacerbated by] the problem of territorial heterogeneity. . . . [S]ocial protection systems [such as this] cushion social segmentation only for those sectors incorporated into modern frameworks of protection. These systems exacerbate stratification between the latter and those not fortunate enough to be part of such frameworks." In addition, of course, the military regime heightened the coercive elements of the state-corporatist structure of labor organization and labor relations (which was extended to agricultural wage-laborers), which helped allow for a model of de facto flexible external and internal labor markets.

The process has been uneven across policy spheres, and full of its fits and starts, but gradually under Brazil's nearly quarter century as a "new democracy" a system of social protection has taken shape and expanded, with particularly decisive strides made since the late 1990s and under the current government. One of the most notable elements of the initial period of the Nova República (under Sarney, Collor, and Franco) was the relative absence or failure of concrete social reform despite the rhetorical emphasis on social inclusion, as documented and analyzed at length by Weyland (1996). Yet there were important constitutional provisions in the 1988 document, inserted through active pressure from civil society, the labor movement, and politicians seeking to cater to these interests, that expanded general, if vaguely defined, rights in access to education, health care, and social security. In addition, specific benefits were created or extended in the Constitution (or in subsequent legislation by the Sarney government), such as sick leave, maternity leave, and unemployment insurance. These principles became important as they established normative goals as well as in some cases institutional templates (in particular, devolution of resources and responsibility to subnational governments) that influenced concretely subsequent reform efforts. Meanwhile, there was contradictory movement in regulation of labor markets and labor relations, as expanded worker benefits, as well as rights to strike and freedom of association created in the 1988 Constitution, were limited in practice by the absence of subsequent implementing legislation or subsequent legislation that interpreted them narrowly. Meanwhile, the labor market reforms of the Cardoso era were "flexibilizing" in nature (i.e, seeking to create more market- and employer-friendly labor norms), even if the government did not achieve as much as it sought due to opposition from unions and their political allies in the opposition.

While the Cardoso government chipped away at some of the social and labor market protections of formal-sector (mostly private-sector) workers in terms of individual labor and social security, it also pursued or furthered important health and education reforms that expanded access to previously uncovered or underserved groups at the same time. There was considerable pressure from below from the *sanitarista* movement on health care, building on the 1988 constitutional provisions and ordinary legislation adopted in 1990 implementing decentralization to municipalities as well as strengthening the Ministry of Health and weakening INAMPS. Responding to this pressure and through a series of executive decree, the Ministry of Health oversaw a large-scale reorganization of the health care system over the course of the 1990s: "By 2002, almost all of Brazil's 5560 municipalities had met the regulatory standards for primary-care services, and about 560 of these receive funding for all services in their jurisdiction" (Haggard and Kaufman, 2008: 285, citing Arretche, 2004).

In education, there was a modest "reallocat[ion] of resources within the primary-education sector and recasting [of] the regulatory and oversight function of the ministry of education" (Haggard and Kaufman, 2008: 285-86; see also Draibe). At the same time, proposals to impose fees and cut wages in higher education were beaten back by political and labor opposition. Meanwhile, the government managed to gain passage from Congress of legislation expanding, under the military-created FUNDEF (*Fundo de Manutenção e Desenvolvimento do Ensino Fundamental*), federal transfers to primary education—which is a state and local responsibility—with mandated shares for teaching pay. Of note about both of these modest but significant health and education reforms was that not only did they expand services to previously excluded or underserved regions and populations, but they also did so *without* focusing on a "neoliberal" social policy orientation centered on privatization, private care or insurance, vouchers, and the like.

Much the same could be said about the two-stage social security reform during the Cardoso and Lula governments. It was, as Haggard and Kaufman (2008) underline, "gradual and parametric," focusing not on privatization and individual accounts (*à la* the then quite internationally and widely diffused "Chilean model" of pension reform) or even "multi-pillar," creating parallel private systems. Instead, reform focused on shoring up and rationalizing the public system, equalizing benefits across the public and private sectors, and avoiding anomalies that allowed for multiple pensions for certain occupational groupings. To be sure, even these limited reforms were contentious, and in particular the more ambitious and draconian 1995 proposals by the Cardoso government had to be scaled back considerably to secure passage by 1998, given the strenuous opposition of well organized pensioners and unionists as well as from the political opposition led by the PT.

The most notable innovation in social policy, of course, has been in terms of targeted social assistance to the poor. This began to occur on a significant scale through the conditional cash transfer scheme known as Bolsa Escola, adopted in 1997 and building on experiences in subnational governments from both the PT (Workers Party) and PSDB (Brazilian Social Democratic Party) as well as on parallel experience with other smaller-scale conditional cash transfers at the federal level (Soares et al., 2007). The program, which is based on various human development conditionalities tied to school attendance, vaccinations, nutritional monitoring, and pre and post-natal tests, has subsequently been extended enormously by the Lula government, from the 4.5 million families it reached by 2002 to a total of 11.6 million in 2005 (and from 0.15 percent of GDP in 2002 to 0.4-0.5 percent as of early 2009);[9] as a response to the global recession, it was announced in early 2009 that the program would be extended to an additional 1.3 million families (ILO, 2009). Studies have found that is has had positive impacts on reducing dropout rates and on raising family income (Morley and Coady 2003, cited in Haggard and Kaufman 2008: 287) as well as on reducing poverty (see below) and inequality (Soares et al. 2007).[10]

Of particular importance from a state capacity-building perspective is the degree of institutional innovation and efficiency of this scheme in terms of its careful and highly progressive targeting (even better than that of CCTs, or Conditional Cash Transfers, in other countries according to research by Soares et al. 2007), its decentralized implementation through municipali-

---

9. 2002 data are reported in Haggard and Kaufman (2008: 287), 2005 data by IPEA, and the new expansion announced in 2009 reported in International Labour Organization (2009). Percentages of expenditures on cash transfers in GDP are estimated by ILO (2009) and Soares (2007), respectively, and do not reflect the most recent expansions.

10. By breaking the fall in the Gini over the 1995-2004 into factor components, the authors reach the conclusion that conditional cash transfer schemes (centralized in the Bolsa Família from 2003) accounted for 21% of the total drop.

ties, and its minimization of leakages and overhead costs (82% of spending reaches beneficiaries' pockets, it has been estimated (IPEA, 2006).

Another important development is the expansion of coverage of the social security system, which has steadily grown from 54.4% of the economically active population in 2002 to 59.6% in 2008, according to IPEA. Unlike some previous expansions that took place by bringing in non-contributors through the Seguro Especial or "special public pension" for non-contributory rural workers (and thus contributing to the fiscal problems of the *Previdência* or Social Security system), this expansion has occurred almost entirely through bringing in new contributors to the system or already covered individuals shifting to contributory status.

Moreover, health and education spending as a share of GDP have grown considerably in recent years, magnifying impacts of institutional reforms instituted in the latter 1990s. After gradual expansions that began in 2000 and brought spending up to approximately 1.8 to 1.9 percent each in 2002, outlays have approximately doubled to 3.65 and 4.05 percent, respectively, by 2008. While it is difficult to quantify evolution over time, spending on job training and labor market assistance reached 9.38 million families as of 2008; micro-credit benefited 2 million families under the PROGER (Program for Employment and Income Generation) as of 2007, while unemployment insurance was received by 6.9 million families in 2008. Total social spending, at the federal, state, and local levels, as a share of GDP, has grown considerably from the 1980s to 1990s and then into the current decade (see Table 4-1).

TABLE 4-1. Public Social Spending as Share of GDP, 1980–2005

| Year | Share of GDP (%) |
|------|------------------|
| 1980 | 13.9 |
| 1985 | 13.3 |
| 1990 | 19.0 |
| 1995 | 19.2 |
| 2005 | 21.9 |

*Source*: Based on data from Médici and Maciel (1996), and IPEA.

The combined impact of institutional reforms in existing entitlements coupled with institutional innovations in the form of cash transfers, together with fiscally sustainable increases in spending for both types of programs, is the creation of a considerable network of social protection that has not existed previously in Brazil. And while Brazil's "welfare state" still has segmented qualities, benefiting the better organized and remunerated in the formal and public sectors disproportionately, this segmentation is now much less acute than it has been for decades, and perhaps since the creation of the country's first social benefits many decades ago.

While it is related to economic policy more than social policy, we also must not forget the impact of the successive annual increases in the minimum wage, which have raised its purchasing power considerably after many years of real decline. Combined with formal-sector job creation (which has occurred despite these measures and standard neoclassical economists' views about the job-destroying impacts of minimum wage rises), this measure has contributed significantly to income gains at the lower end of the income spectrum.

As a result of the acceleration of economic growth—under conditions of low inflation, a real increase in the minimum wage, and strong social policies—the decline in poverty and inequality has been substantial. The Fundação Getulio Vargas (FGV) calculates a widely cited index in Brazil that measures evolution of income distribution based on "consumption potential," through a division of people into classes A-E, with classes D and E referring, respectively, to the poor and the extremely poor.[11] Based on this methodology, in 2003 the number of Brazilians in poverty and extreme poverty was 54.85 million. By 2008, the number had fallen to 40.37 million. By 2009, at the height of the financial crisis, overall poverty had risen only slightly 41.64 million, while the numbers of absolute poor (Class E) had continued to fall, from 16.02 to 15.32 million (Neri, 2010:12).

Altogether this means that between 2003 and 2009 around 29 million Brazilians escaped poverty and moved into class C, which is generally referred to as the "new middle class" by the FGV. Taken altogether, the top three income strata—classes A, B, and C—grew by 35.7 million from 2003 to 2009, while classes D and F together fell from 96.2 to 73.2 million over the same period. That "new middle class" found in Class C represents slightly over half (50.5%) of the Brazilian population (Neri 2010: 38). The social, economic, and political consequences of Brazil's "becoming a middle-class-majority country" remain to be studied and analyzed.

Overall, the country's Gini coefficient has been declining sharply from its historically extremely high levels since 2001. Inequality began to drop in

---

11. Monthly household income classes are defined in US$ as E (0-316), D (316-569), C (569-2,843), B (2,843-3,707), A1 (3,707-5,496), A2 (5,496 and above). FGV methodology. Cf. Neri 2010: 44); US$1= R$1.7 (Average, November 2010).

1998 but then rose again over the period when Brazil felt the worst impacts of a financial crisis in 1999-2000, then began its steady downward path.

What seems to be taking shape in contemporary Brazil is a new development model of "growth with equity" that relies not just on export demand but also increases in domestic consumption that build on more buoyant incomes, labor markets, and government income transfers. This more balanced relationship between internal and external demand stimulus would seem to be at least one of the factors that has contributed to Brazil's more rapid recovery from the global recession than that of its Latin American neighbors. Another factor relates to our point about expanding and re-oriented state capacities; in response to the global recession, the government has taken a number of measures—increase trade financing via BNDES and expanding Bolsa Família coverage, as noted above, as well as expanding consumer access to credit for purchases of white goods and consumer durables—to blunt the impact of global trends and bring the country quickly out of what proved to be a very brief and mild recession. In addition, the newly expanded network of social protection had its own automatic counter-cyclical or cushioning impact.

The combined impact of short-term measures and the benefits of longer-term changes in social policy—together with the country's high level of reserves and other policies of macroeconomic stability—clearly demonstrates a capacity for crisis management that the Brazilian state has historically lacked in response to external shocks, such as the oil shocks of the 1970s, debt crisis of the 1980s, or even (in terms of rapidity of adjustment) the financial crisis of the late 2000s. It will be important, of course, to see if the trends of steady, significant decline in poverty and inequality continue unabated or instead experience at least a "pause" given the brief recession and decline in annual growth projections in 2009, when such numbers become available. But there are certainly strong grounds for optimism that social impacts have been much more limited than was initially feared.

What stands out, in a state capacity-building perspective, in the creation or expansion of these key equity-enhancing social programs and policies is the degree to which they have been largely free from the widespread fraud, corruption, and clientelism of Brazil's notoriously patrimonial state, even amidst high-level scandals touching deep into the halls of power in both the current and previous administrations. De-centralization has much to do with that, and the bases for decentralization were initially set by the much-maligned 1988 Constitution, though careful program design and monitoring are required to avoid traditional local patronage from siphoning off resources. While this dimension of the reforms has perhaps not been as fully analyzed and explored as it might, there is a notable degree of transparency, administrative competence, and even-handedness that was lacking historically in the provision of Brazil's social services.

Brazil's developmentalist-era state was known for promoting an income-concentrating economic model and for promoting a pattern of limited transfers almost exclusively to key organized constituencies that left out the bulk of the truly needy and was largely regressive in its distributive impact. In the current decade we bear witness to an economic model that has broadened employment, promoted wage growth, and expanded consumption in the bottom half of the income spectrum. It is reinforced by an emerging new pattern of social spending that has greatly improved positive impacts on income poverty (and arguable other aspects of poverty); together, the two have helped lower inequality, as measured by the Gini, considerably. Moreover, while some may attribute Brazil's economic success up to the current crisis primarily to the global commodity boom[12] our discussion above of the diversified sectoral profile of Brazilian innovation and exports paints a different picture. On the more narrow but significant question of the impact of commodity prices on drops in inequality and poverty—an issue sometimes raised by skeptics about the durability or uniqueness of Brazil's recent social gains—Huber (2002) finds statistical evidence from regression analysis that the positive impacts of public spending on inequality and poverty (including absolute poverty) of the Lula government and other governments she similarly categorizes as "social democratic" in Latin America (Bachelet and Lagos in Chile and Vásquez in Uruguay) are robust even when controlling for the commodity boom.

Beyond the politically charged issue of who should take the most credit among the past two governing parties and presidents in Brazil, we wish instead to emphasize the importance of institutional continuity and deepening from the late 1990s to the present. There has been a cumulative impact of economic and social reforms that were begun at an earlier moment under a different economic environment and that have been carried forward, in some cases re-oriented (as with a greater emphasis on competitiveness policy and

---

12. Huber also finds that "new left" governments of all types, including populists such as Kirchner in Argentina and Chávez in Venezuela, evidence superior performance on poverty and inequality reduction—measured cross-nationally or within-country—than center-right governments. Of additional note is her finding that, when one controls for the commodity boom, social democratic governments tend to produce greater declines on poverty and inequality, raising the prospect that these gains may be more "fiscally sustainable" (Huber, 2002).

aggressive trade diplomacy), and backed by greater resources in a global and domestic environment that has been more permissive (at least until September 2008). The cumulative impact has been to rebuild a state whose Leviathan-like role in economic life and social affairs under developmentalism had deteriorated to an incapacitated position of extreme weakness by the late 1980s and early 1990s, riddled with conflicts and inefficiencies and incapable of mediating conflicts between contending social and political forces and of building consensus toward a new development model looking forward that was compatible with the country's still-nascent democracy. Surely problems of corruption and malfeasance continue to plague governments at all levels. Yet by the historical yardstick of where the country was in the quite recent past, the progress that has been achieved in rebuilding the state since the mid-1990s is remarkable. There are significant evident synergies between historic progress in fiscal stability, a competitiveness policy that promotes innovation and diversified sectoral transformation, and policies of greater inclusion through transfer payment as well as services that expand human capital.

Of particular note, we stress, is the degree to which the emerging development model reflects a much more mature relationship with organized interests and the citizenry. This relationship involves a new state role of channeling conflict, building consensus, creating spaces of negotiation and consultation around key issues, and seeking finally to join the vibrancy of a dynamic civil society and electoral competition evident for several decades with major strides toward much-delayed social inclusion in more recent years.

## A "SOCIAL DEMOCRATIC" BREAKTHROUGH?

If we find the major analytical categories that authors apply to contemporary Brazil's development trajectory all wanting—the developmental state or developmentalism (in whatever "neo" guise) or neoliberalism—the question remains, how then can we best categorize and conceptualize this trajectory? In this concluding section, we will consider yet another category or label that analysts sometimes apply to Brazil, particularly under Lula, which is that of "social democracy" or "social democratic" (e.g., Lustig 2009; Sandbrook et al. 2007: 238-42; Castañeda, 2006). Is Brazil experiencing a "social democratic breakthrough?" While it is tempting to make that argument, and the country's recent trajectory bears some important resemblance to hallmarks of social democracy, particularly in its manifestations in the global South (Sandbrook et al., 2007), ultimately we believe that considerable caution must be exercised in applying this concept too readily.

It is important to make some conceptual distinctions here. First, social democracy as a concept (with a small 's' and small 'd') for characterizing a particular model of development or mode of state-society-market relations needs to be distinguished from Social Democratic (with a capital "S" and capital "D") parties, the Socialist International, and other political forces that seek to embrace explicitly that partisan and ideological label and all its historical associations. Objectively, many "social democracies" are not based on the political predominance of parties that use, or even accept, the "Social Democratic" label, or have membership in the Socialist International. In Brazil, the matter is complicated, because the PSDB has claimed that mantle (particular in its "Social Democracy lite," "Third Way" variant à la Tony Blair's New Labour in the UK) despite its lack of organized links to unions or other forces in civil society (long seen as intrinsic to social democracy), and because it has positioned itself in government and opposition more toward the center as opposed to the PT's more center-left stance. While it has long espoused some ill-defined version of "democratic socialism," the PT, for its part, has never accepted the social democratic label and has tried to distinguish itself from both Stalinism and classic, pre-Third Way, European-style Social Democracy, which its sympathizers and militants seem to associate narrowly with a distasteful top-down, bureaucratic, and reformist style of governance. Nonetheless, in terms of the Lula government's orientations in office, and the party's experience in government at subnational levels (e.g., Nylen, 2003), it would seem that the party's efforts to pursue social reforms that advance equality and participation within a framework of democratic capitalism suggest more similarity with what some might see as a "classically social democratic orientation" (in its early phases of deep, broad social reforms) than they themselves recognize or admit.

Moreover, it is also important to make an analytical distinction between party and president, given the tensions that have been evident between party and the executive at times, not to mention PT defections from dissident elements to Lula's left. The party itself still maintains references to socialism as an important unifying ideological element, without many practical translations into programmatic/policy prescriptions, however. Indeed, one might argue, at an analytical level and among Brazilian and perhaps also Brazilianist scholars, the category as a useful, long-standing approach to social scientific inquiry (e.g, Przeworksi, 1985; Esping-Andersen, 1985;

Huber, 2002; Rueschemeyer, Stephens and Stephens, 1992) has unfortunately been spoiled by how the term has been appropriated (or misappropriated) in political praxis, where it is bandied about readily as a simple "label" devoid of deeper analytical content.

Second, it is widely noted that Brazil and other countries in the region and developing world more generally seem to lack the structural prerequisites of social democratic governance—namely, a large industrial working class, organized into strong peak labor confederations (e.g., Roberts, 1998). This makes, it is argued, structurally impossible the links to a programmatic left party (or parties) dedicated to social transformation through economic, social, and political reforms, not to mention the kind of peak bargaining of organization of labor and capital with the state, that used to be quintessential to European social democracy (e.g., Esping-Andersen, 1985; Przeworski, 1985). However, contrasting with these views is the concept of a specific version of social democracy arising historically in certain countries or locations of the global South—peripheral social democracy (Sandbrook et al., 2007). This analytical approach emphasizes the key role that is played, instead, by associations of rural laborers, the urban poor, and other non-industrial proletarians in terms of providing a social base as well as organized sources of continual pressure on reformist and left parties seeking and holding political power and to use the state as a lever for reform. It is in this sense that Sandbrook et al. (2007) argue that Lula's government is "social democratic" (while a "social democratic regime" has not yet emerged, in their view). Of interest in their analysis is the fact that in all the countries or territories to which they apply this label over the course of decades of development, there were *at least two* competing parties who attempted to appeal to an organized, mobilized civil society (typically *none* of which called itself "social democratic") and to occupy what we have called above the "reform space" within the national political universe.

We see important similarities but more fundamental differences between Brazil's recent development and the model of peripheral social democracy on three fronts—its social welfare model, its patterns of interest intermediation and of governing parties' relations with core constituencies. In terms of social policy, the rapidity, depth, and scope of the expansion of social services and benefits, discussed in previous sections, reminds one of periods of rapid inclusionary social reforms in earlier historical moments in the cases discussed by Sandbrook and co-authors, with the attendant rapid increases in performance on social indicators that the authors underline. However, the social programs of today's Brazil are still far from universalistic in coverage or in terms of their underlying principles and indeed ethos of access. They are, for the most part, targeted and means-tested programs, directed at poverty as carefully measured and below certain income thresholds, albeit expanding to larger segments of the poor over time. In this sense, they respond to the critique (not unique to neoliberalism but strongly associated with it) about "welfare state" approaches to social policy that has guided the social policy orientations of international financial institutions and developing country governments across the political spectrum. Institutionally as well as in the political imaginary, Bolsa Familia is a "program for the poor," and not part of some more broadly institutionally comprehensive set of goods and services that near-poor or even middle-class Brazilians can access. This is true even if more poor Brazilians in the rural sector or urban-informal economies have been brought into the social security system and other programs (as discussed above) that were traditionally limited to formal-sector workers. Indeed, what seems to be distinctive about Brazil's conditional cash transfer scheme from other modalities of the same concept of targeted transfers tied to behavioral modification conditionalities for recipients pursued in a range of different countries in the Americas is mostly the generosity and scope of the program as well as its high level of cost-effectiveness.

So, to be sure, there have been gains in universalism as well as coverage and generosity, particularly compared to the highly segmented and stratified social welfare model of the previous era, but Brazil's "welfare state" still remains segmented. This is significant insofar as it potentially undermines social solidarity in the sense that, in a future downturn or under a future government of a different political orientation, citizens from various social classes will not necessarily perceive "a cut in my benefits as a cut in all our benefits." This political logic, key to the underlying social consensus or social contract that tends to underlie a social democratic version of social policy and a welfare state, is still quite lacking in Brazil. There formal-sector entitlement programs and those for the poor are perceived and experienced (because they are administratively structured and politically "packaged") as separate. It is still too early to say, particularly vis-à-vis fickle middle-class Brazilians where Lula's support has waned or among business elites who accept social transfers as long as they do not impact on state finances or growth, that an "inclusionary social contract" has emerged and been consolidated in Brazil.

The differences are also more striking than the similarities with respect to social democratic patterns of interest intermediation, based on mechanisms of inter-group and cross-class consensus building and negotiation and an ethos of class compromise. As noted above, channels for participation of unions, civil society organizations, and business associations in dialogues, and in some cases negotiations, about aspects of economic and social policy have grown under the Lula government. As examples we would cite the Council on Food Security and National Council on Education, Science and Technology. However, tripartite mechanisms of concertation regarding incomes policy, wages, and the like have not been forthcoming, and efforts at labor relations and labor markets—initiated with much fanfare in the first Lula government through extensive tripartite consultation in the National Labor Forum (a tripartite labor-business-government body operating in 1993 and 1994)—proved stillborn as the government backed off them in response to opposition from both within and outside the governing coalition. Those who expected greater high-level negotiation and reform with respect to labor issues have been disappointed. State interaction with organized civil society, while exhibiting the gains in access, transparency, and frequency noted earlier, still reflects a more diffuse pattern of interest intermediation, with multiple and competing channels and points of access and more arms' length pressure, than we would expect from the stronger, more sustained, and more authoritative channels of access to decision-making under social democracy, as characterized by Sandbrook et al. As a national governing party (or more precisely lead force in a multi-party alliance), the PT has become more of a "state party"—and to some extent more of a "catch-all" party and become more distant from its social movement and labor movement roots (see Keck, 1992). This evolution is fed by several converging "streams"—the weakening of its urban-industrial base in the Southeast and perhaps South, the strengthening of its (or rather Lula's) base in the Northeast and North that have disproportionately benefited from its anti-poverty policies mainly because of their greater objective level of poverty, and the tendency for many from the party's "movement base"—labor leaders, activists from urban movements, etc.—to move into executive positions (leading to concerns among some about "loss of cadres" and "subordination of party to state") as well a tendency for many of the groups and associations to face a difficult choice between a certain political subordination to the PT/state or moving into a position of open opposition, dissidence, or splitting off. Some of this is a natural by-product of a party closely tied to organized civil society moving into national power for the first time, yet to some extent it may be questioned whether there has been enough maturity on both sides to maintain an arms-length relationship of mutual respect (which historically the PT and movements managed to maintain through careful institutional separation of roles as the party developed out of movements, rather than vice versa) and respect for the right to combine political support with principled opposition issue by issue.

In sum, Brazil's development trajectory seems to occupy some kind of intermediate space, where perhaps it is appropriate to speak of hybrid categories, but not of it exhibiting, or moving clearly towards, broadly encompassing "models" such as neo-developmentalism or neoliberalism. This does not mean that we adopt a theoretical position that "Brazil can't be compared" because it is so *sui generis*, either generally or contemporarily. Nor should it understate the extent to which we see the emergence and some steps toward the possible consolidation of a new type of state, which takes on an enabling position of moderate, pro-market intervention via competitiveness policy and a much stronger role in providing social services and benefits that is increasingly linked to fostering market inclusion for the previously underserved and excluded and not simply transferring income in targeted fashion to the poor.

Whatever precise terminology might be most appropriate—a debate we seek to open without attempting to resolve here—the final question that calls out for greater analysis are the conditions under which this emerging model can be consolidated or not. Brazil has had two strong presidents with outsized personalities over the past 15 years who have left a big impact, and between the two there are complex patterns of continuity and change, but above all key underlying reform continuities that are frequently not appreciated by analysts or, in particular, political actors. The policies they pursued in office have not necessarily represented uniform, consensual positions within their respective parties, and their policies have reflected complex relations both between executive and governing party as well as between executive and coalition partners within the cabinet and congressional base. This is likely to continue to be the case, and thus much will depend on whether current directions and recent institutional innovations in both economic and social policy will survive electoral succession—whichever party's candidate emerges victorious. The candidates of the two major parties may each have motives for wanting to distance themselves in office from their predecessors of whatever party, and coalitional politics in the next government could become more complex on the left with the existence of opposition candidacies on the PT's left flank. This is all not simply a matter of politics of the state, but also—as we have tried to argue in this essay—politicians' interplay with key constituencies and organizations as well as the electorate and civil society more generally in a more open, democratic context.

# 5

# CRISIS AND BEYOND: RESPONSES AND PROSPECTS

*Eiiti Sato*

*Abstract: This chapter argues that prospects of a successful Brazilian economy are good in the short term, but in the long run there are some structural problems to overcome. The main reason is that short term conditions have not been accompanied by long term structural investments. Investments in infrastructure as well as in some key areas of technological development depend on government initiatives. Furthermore, Brazilian economic policy has been remarkably anti-globalization—i. e., against integration to global markets. The chapter explores these structural problems, and concludes that the current world crisis will not greatly change Brazil's chances to benefit from an emerging cycle of growth in the international economic order.*

## SETTING THE PROBLEM

The Brazilian government has been optimistic regarding the overall situation of the Brazilian economy. Even analysts from other countries and international organizations have been quite optimistic about the Brazilian capacity to handle the current imbalances and challenges brought about by the world economic crisis. The present analysis argues that the current optimism regarding the Brazilian economy is reasonable only in the short term. In the long run, the perspectives associated with a new cycle of growth do not seem very bright for the Brazilian economy. The main reason for this contrast is that important aspects of the macroeconomic conditions of the Brazilian economy are relatively well balanced, but weaknesses remain in important structural aspects amid increasing international competition. Compared to leading industrial economies as well as to other emerging countries during the last two decades, Brazil did not make the investments in key areas needed to keep up with technological advancements.

Keynesian economic policies can be adequate to manage business cycle variations, and consequently to cope with crises such as the ones that the world economy has been going through since 2008. Nevertheless, a Schumpeterian approach seems to be much more appropriate to understand the overall possibilities for an economy to be successful in the aftermath of a crisis, because history shows that every systemic crisis has been associated with structural changes in the world economy. Keynesian theory is important—even fundamental—to understand the problem of economic equilibrium, but Schumpeter's views are essential to understand the process of economic growth and the succession of long term economic cycles based on structural changes in the world economy.

Peter Drucker summarizes the main differences between these two approaches: the Keynesian view is based on the idea that money and credit (the symbolic economy) are independent and even determine the production and distribution of goods and services (the real economy). The Schumpeterian approach is based on the view that growth and change form an essential dimension of economic life, and as a consequence technological innovation, economic disequilibrium, and crises should be considered as intrinsic components of the economic process (Drucker, 1986: 104).

According to Drucker, in such a process the capacities for innovation and entrepreneurship inevitably produce changes that from time to time appear as a deep crisis. This indicates that a new long cycle of growth based on new patterns of technology is about to start or has already started. In this way Drucker argues that Keynes' approach is really essential to cope with unemployment, inflation, and stagnation or recession—but crises cannot be seen only as momentary imbalances and misbehavior of some economic variables such as inflation, unemployment, or shortage of liquidity. When crises such as the one that affected the world economy in 2008 are deep, anticyclical measures are not enough. It is necessary to look at structural factors related to technological changes and at the mechanisms and institutions through which economic activities are conducted.

Schumpeter says that economic growth is basically a turbulent process (Schumpeter, 1982). Schumpeter's best-known phrase is "creative destruction." As new economic activities are created, they often replace older ones; for example, automobiles replaced horse and carriage transport. The gain represented by new automobile output and the new businesses associated with, as well as the wealth embodied in new homes built in automobile producing areas, is offset by the loss of the horse industry, and its associated businesses and homes. Currently, the difference in environmental impact also would be taken into account in a Schumpeterian accounting of the net gain or loss to an economy from economic growth. Thus, if economic figures show that within a period of time the world GDP has increased by 100%, one cannot simply conclude that the size of the world production has doubled without considering the fact that probably the structure of the world economy has changed too, including products, firms, institutions, and patterns of trade and investments. The economic system should be seen as a dynamic process characterized by the constant interplay of two contradictory forces: on one side most actors are strongly engaged in promoting growth and change, while on the other side, other actors demand order, stability, and the demand for security.

The positive aspects which assure a comfortable position for the Brazilian economy regarding the current problems in the world economy are basically those related to macroeconomic variables: the low rates of inflation, the large amount of foreign reserves, the absence of any significant pressures on the economy generated by foreign debt, and the sense of realism which has prevailed among those who had to manage the Brazilian monetary system during the last decade. Since 1994, when the Real Plan was launched under President Itamar Franco, monetary stabilization has been the most important aspect of economic policy in Brazil, bringing about the many benefits deriving from a more stable and predictable economic environment.[1]

There are very few reasons to think that the immediate aftermath of the world financial crisis will be expressive for Brazil compared to other economies. Nevertheless, in the long run one cannot be so optimistic. Some structural problems regarding the relationship between the government sector and private business still persist, and some of these problems actually have

---

1. The Real Plan was issued in February of 1994 by president Itamar Franco. It established the real as the Brazilian national currency. The law that established the Real Plan was designed to bring down the high rates of persistent inflation. The Plan included also other measures to assure fiscal balance, a more effective role for the Central Bank in managing liquidity in domestic markets, and the gradual opening of the economy to foreign trade. See http://portalexame.abril.com.br/economia/15-anos-plano-real-seus-protagonistas-481015.html.

been aggravated during the years since the Real Plan was issued and implemented.

This chapter explores these structural problems and shows that the current world crisis will not greatly change the prospects for Brazil no matter how the current crisis affects the international economic order. It indicates the three basic developments that make it difficult for the Brazilian government to issue long term policies: (1) the "fiscal trap," (2) the dominance of political disputes in determining public investments, and (3) the lack of a long term industrial development policy coherent with world trends for goods and services. These problems were made more difficult by anti-globalization sentiments among policy makers.

First, the "fiscal trap" is understood as the imbalance between the rising demand for increasing public expenditure and the insufficiently increasing revenues that therefore do not pay for this expenditure. The demand for increased public expenditure is facilitated by political and judicial systems that drain a great deal of the scarce resources, which should be invested in the modernization of public services. A great deal of expenditures with pensions, and refunds based on alleged unfairness derived from government measures often depends on dubious interpretation of the law. Judicial decisions can also produce unexpected problems in the public revenues by granting tax exemptions also based on dubious legal interpretations. An instructive example is the amount of welfare grants and pensions paid to retired workers and individuals entitled to receive a variety of welfare benefits. This produces a deficit, which is increasing yearly. In 2008, the deficit between the contribution paid by individuals, firms, and other organizations and the pensions and other forms of social welfare disbursement attained R\$42.9 billion (almost US\$24 billion).[2] For those workers who have retired from public service, figures are even worse. According to Brazilian laws there are several cases in which a retired public officer earns a pension which is higher than the salary paid to an officer in similar position but who is not yet retired.[3]

Second, the dominance of political disputes in determining public investments increased when political power moved from military to civilian hands, and investments in economic development dwindled dramatically.[4] The Military administration's main concern was national economic devel-

---

2. See http://www.estadao.com.br./estadaodehoje/2010020/no.
3. Figures released by the Ministry of Welfare show that by the end of 2008 there were 6 million people regularly working for the Brazilian state (Federal, State, and Municipal levels), and 3 million retirees and pensioners (Ministério da Previdência Social, 2008: 45).

opment and improvement of social conditions to avoid communism and social unrest. They emphasized investments in infrastructure. The military left power in 1985. Politically, the process of transferring the power from military hands to civilian hands was called "democratization," but, under civilian administrations, political disputes over privileges and preferences of political parties regarding electoral and individual interests rather than the modernization and efficiency of public services determined the allocation of public investment.[5] Public investments dwindled sharply, making harbors, roads, energy plants, and research institutions increasingly inadequate to match the highly dynamic demands of competition in world markets.

Third, the lack of a long-term industrial development policy coherent with world trends for products and services reflects the fact that since the 1980s, the Brazilian government virtually has abandoned investments in technological development. Here the term technological development does not mean R&D (Research and Development) to create new products and new industrial processes. Investments in this area of technological innovation are mainly financed by industrial corporations and by private capital.

In this paper, "technological development" refers to public investments in universities, laboratories, and the many scientific and technical institutions that provide support for industrial activities.[6] It also refers to investments in areas that the government wishes to develop, but in which private capital hardly can play a significant role, such as the development of alternative sources of energy, the improvement of defense industry, and the exploration of outer space technology. Furthermore, biased policies and initiatives can be damaging to industrial development. In 1984, the Brazilian Congress, stimulated by nationalistic sentiments, approved a law by which the import of computers and related products was prohibited for seven years. Exceptions were to be examined by a Special Secretariat attached to the President's Cabinet. Nevertheless, the national computer industry did not develop as much as expected by the government authorities and Brazilian

---

4. The military seized power in 1964 and remained until 1985. Every military administration—from Castello Branco (1964-67) to João Figueiredo (1979-85)—had issued a "development plan" defining priorities, resources, and strategies to attain development goals.

5. Since 2009, Brazil has 37 Ministries which are distributed basically among Senators and Deputies from political parties which support the president: PT (Political party of the president) holds 17 Ministries; PMDB holds 7; PSB holds 2; PP (Progressive Party), PV (Green Party), PCdoB (Communist Party), PDT (Democratic Labor Party), and PR have one Ministry each. Only seven positions which have Ministry status are held by people who are not clearly engaged in political parties.

6. There is a set of institutions that form a sort of "technological infrastructure" in modern economies. These institutions provide essential services such as preparation of skilled manpower, metrology, protection of intellectual property, laboratories to support scientific and technological cooperation, international certification, participation in joint research programs, etc.

industry was severely affected, becoming outdated, and the economy as a whole lost competitiveness.[7] Restrictive policies such as the one implemented in the mid 1980s prohibiting the importation of products like computers in order to develop a national industry have been abandoned since the 1990s.

These three problems together created a social and economic environment that became more likely to foster stagnation instead of creativity and innovation. Even in areas like the production and use of ethanol and other biofuels, Brazil is a follower rather than a leader. Furthermore, the technology used to produce bio-fuels is an old technology, and is not a new alternative for the future, because the technology is essentially the same as the one used in engines powered by gasoline or diesel from petroleum. The main research centers worldwide are now developing new concepts of engines, and also are under pressure to develop new technologies more adequate to large populations, particularly in countries like China and India, which are facing the challenge of providing large scale increases in their consumption without damaging the environment too much.[8] The anti-globalization sentiments among policy makers had mixed effects on the Brazilian economy. Brazil had less integration into global financial markets than many other nations not only because of its longstanding inflationary experience, state oriented views of the bureaucracy, and nationalism, but also because monetary authorities in Brazil have constructed a domestic financial regime favoring control rather than free flow of capital. Consequently, Brazil did not get many of the benefits derived from the soaring financial markets of the fifteen years previous to the crisis. On the other hand, Brazil did not suffer many consequences of the 2008 crisis when the falling prices of financial assets hit the more globalized economies, because to a large extent the country had stayed relatively apart from the global financial competition.

## Macroeconomic Variables and Keynesian Policies

When 2009 was ending, the worst moment of the world financial crisis seemed to have already passed, and stabilization and growth was slowly

---

7. See the analysis of the Brazilian computer industry in mid 1980s presented by C. Frischtak in Rushing, Francis W. and Brown ed. (1986: 31-69).

8. Analysts say that the Conference of Copenhagen was a failure because no significant agreement was attained, but it showed largely enough that environment has moved to the forefront of the issues the world is concerned with. The United Nations Climate Change Conference (COP-15, Dec. 7-18th, 2009) brought to Copenhagen presidents and prime ministers from more than a hundred countries and registered more than 25,000 participants from almost every country in the world.

becoming a prospect even for the US, Japan, and large European economies. Nevertheless, it was not yet clear whether such a prospect of stabilization and growth was part of a new emerging long cycle of growth, or was a simple succession of random growth bubbles derived from Keynesian policies implemented by governments to cope with falling markets and unemployment.

Brazil was one of the economies least affected by the consequences of the financial crisis. Growth halted and unemployment increased but not as much as in countries like the US, Japan, Germany, and most emerging economies. In the first quarter of 2009 among emerging market economies, only China, India, and Indonesia did not suffer a reduction in their GDP. Brazilian GDP fell by 1.8%, but the figure was pretty small when compared to Japan (-8.8%), Germany (-6.9%), France (-3.2%), the US (-2.6%), Mexico (-8.6%), and South Korea (-4.3%)(UNCTAD, 2009). In former crises the overall situation was the reverse, i.e., Brazil usually suffered the consequences of any turbulence that was taking place in the world economy much more than did major economies. Two main reasons can be pointed out to explain the relatively good condition of the Brazilian economy on the eve of the 2008 financial crisis: the soundness of the main macroeconomic variables, and the relatively low level of integration to the world economy.

Since the oil crisis in the 1970s, the Brazilian economy went through a long period of persistent inflation and economic instability. Only the implementation of the Real Plan in 1994 created the basic conditions for a stable monetary system necessary to produce an economic environment more appropriate to foster business, investments, and foreign trade. By the end of 2002 when Mr. Lula da Silva was about to start his first term as president of Brazil, there was a great concern that his administration would abandon the Real Plan and monetary stability as a crucial part of the economic policy for the country. Fortunately this did not happen and when the 2008 financial crisis came about, the Brazilian economy had already accumulated some important assets. A persistent balance of payments surplus has permitted an increase in foreign reserves to more than US$200 billion, which meant that the level of reserves was higher than the total foreign liabilities. Furthermore the largest part of such liabilities already had been well negotiated during the late years of the Cardoso administration, which ended in 2002. The negotiations established a very comfortable schedule that virtually eliminated the pressures represented by foreign debt.[9]

---

9. According to official figures provided by Brazilian Central Bank in December 2008, the Brazilian reserves were around US$205 billion while foreign debt totaled US$195.8 billion from which only 22% referred to short-term bonds.

Another important reason for the good condition of the Brazilian economy in 2008 is that since the Real Plan was issued in 1994, monetary policy has given a strong support to the banking system. Except for the turbulences of a few months associated with the 1999 reform of the Real Plan, the Brazilian economy had already enjoyed a period of stability for almost 15 years.[10]

Historically, the Brazilian banking system has been essentially private and even the state owned banks have been bound to follow the same rules applied to private banks: both suffered little influence and pressure from the government authorities. The main privileges assigned to public banks have been the current accounts of government agencies and funds owned by public companies that are allocated to public banks.

The Brazilian monetary crisis of 1999 shook the national financial system by severely reducing the value of bonds, stocks, and other financial assets. Nevertheless, the government response was quite effective. A large program of mergers and acquisitions was produced under the sponsorship of the Federal Government. It provided enough funds, and new rules were issued to make the banking system safer and less vulnerable to variations in the business cycle. The reform of the banking system of 1999 avoided panic, financial assets very quickly regained the confidence of the public, and profits of banks continued high. It is possible to say that banks and other financial institutions actually did not suffer any critical harm from the 1999 Brazilian monetary crisis, but rather gained maturity and increased their importance to the national economy as a whole. The overall result was that the Brazilian economy became more stable and inflation went down consistently to a level of one digit per year.[11]

During these years the interest rate in the Brazilian financial market remained much higher than in any other stable economy, attracting domestic and foreign capital. By December 2005, the interest rate managed by Brazilian Central Bank was 18.0% while the inflation rate was only 5.69%. When the world financial crisis broke out in mid 2008, the interest rate in Brazil was still very high (12.92%).[12] A considerable part of the assets of the banking system was composed of Brazilian Treasury bonds issued to finance

10. When the Real Plan was issued in 1994 the exchange rate was fixed (R$1.00 = US$1.00), and was allowed to oscillate within a narrow band. The exchange rate was considered as the "anchor" to keep economic stability. By the Real Plan reform in 1999, the Central Bank abandoned the system to the US dollar, adopted a floating exchange rate system, and the interest rate managed by the National Monetary Committee became the basic instrument to cope with inflationary pressures.

11. From 1990 to 1994 (included) the inflation rate in Brazil was very high (764.0% per year). The *Real* Plan brought the inflation down to the level of 8.6% (average 1995-2000), and in 2005 inflation registered was 5.69% (*O Globo*, 2006: 27).

12. Figures are released by Brazilian Central Bank (http://www.bcb.gov.br/?copomjuros).

public debt. These bonds were very safe assets, especially when compared to the US sub-prime market. Under such a circumstance the interest rate put some pressure on the public debt, but at the same time it acted as a sort of guarantee for the banks by providing a good profit within a stable and safe environment for financial assets. As a result, one can say that for almost a decade before the 2008 financial crisis the Brazilian banking system earned enough profit to be able to meet the turbulences and downturns of business cycles without great concern. Furthermore, the high interest rates could be reduced considerably, thus serving as an additional and effective instrument of monetary policy to offset the recession produced by the world crisis.

The evolution of foreign trade also was favorable to the Brazilian economy. The two decades of persistent growth of the world economy have permitted an increase of exports to both traditional and emerging markets. Traditional markets such as the US and Europe were joined by emerging markets from Asia and from other regions, substantially increasing the demand for industrial goods as well as for commodities. In such an environment of growing demand, the size and diversification of the Brazilian economy allowed the nation to benefit from world economic growth. On the other hand, the Brazilian economy had a long tradition of restricting imports by taxation and by exchange rate mechanisms. The relatively low level of imports combined with an increasing demand for the nation's exports gave the Brazilian economy a consistent trade surplus, increasing foreign reserves to a level that made its foreign debt almost irrelevant. Even the soaring prices of oil in world markets in the years previous to the 2008 crisis did not represent a substantial pressure on Brazil's balance of payments, because in recent years domestic oil production has increased enough to meet domestic consumption.

Despite the fact that foreign trade increased substantially during the last decade, it did not lead to a strong dependence on trade to promote stability and growth. Foreign trade still represents only 1/5 of the Brazilian GDP.[13] Particularly since president Lula da Silva inaugurated his first term in 2003, most critics of the Brazilian economic policy have been arguing that the sluggish performance of the Brazilian economy, when compared to other emerging countries, was due to a hesitant attitude regarding integration to world markets. Their argument is that Brazilian economic growth strategy has been too much inward looking, despising the dynamism of world mar-

---

13. World trade figures show that Brazilian participation in world merchandise exports remained roughly at the same level since the 1980s (1.2% in 1983, 1.0% in 1993; and 1.3% in 2008) just following the rate of growth of the world trade (*WTO Statistics 2009*, Table I.6).

kets.[14] Critics also say that politics and ideology have been inappropriately dominant in commercial policy that gives too much importance to trade agreements with poor economies rather than to the main world markets. Generally trading with poor economies is difficult, expensive, and produces small results when compared to large world markets. Nevertheless expectations are that these countries give their support to Brazilian government demand for a permanent seat in the United Nations Security Council. In fact fiscal mechanisms protected Brazilian domestic markets from other economies which were much more productive and competitive. Consequently, Brazil was not forced to increase its productivity to meet efficient competitors from these economies, and trading with poor countries reduces the need for productivity and competitiveness.

During the last two decades the rates of growth of other emerging economies—particularly from Asia—were substantially higher than that of Brazil. Countries like South Korea, Chile, and Mexico, frequently are mentioned as good examples of countries that have adopted a desirable strategy of economic growth with a strong integration into the world economy. Their economies have been severely impacted by the 2008 financial crisis. Ironically such a low level of integration to the world economy became an asset for Brazil: in the short run, the Brazilian domestic market was large enough to reduce the effect of the world recession. In this regard, the case of the car industry can be instructive. Due to the relatively low level of dependence on world markets, Brazil's simple tax reduction on vehicles and auto parts avoided a recession in this quite influential industrial sector.[15] In other sectors that are more dependent on exports such as mining, shoes, and commodities, the effects of the world recession could not be avoided.

Despite Brazil's success in mitigating the short-term effects of the 2008 financial crisis, in the long run the nation's prospects are not so positive. Brazil probably will not become a leading economy in the near future. Important investments in economic infrastructure as well as in science and technology are essential to raise productivity and competitiveness; they

---

14. In 1983, China's share of the world exports was similar to Brazil's share (1.2%) but in 2008 China's share of the world exports had attained 9.1% and South Korea's share increased from 0.5% to 2.6% (*idem*).

15. The figures released by the Brazilian Association of Producers of Cars and other Vehicles (ANFAVEA) show that in the first four months of 2009 the exports of cars, other vehicles, and auto parts have dropped by almost 50% when compared with the same period of 2008. Nevertheless exports represent only about 20% of the total sales of the car industry in Brazil. This fact explains why a tax reduction was a measure enough to stimulate domestic demand to fairly offset the decrease in foreign demand (http://www.anfavea.com.br/tabelas.html).

have been neglected systematically for more than a score of years. In the past public investments were essential, for example, to establish the steel industry and to create a national airplane industry. Even in agriculture public investments were essential to develop varieties of crops well fitted to Brazilian climate and soil; and to combat plagues to make Brazilian agriculture efficient and competitive.[16]

## CRISIS: THE LONG-TERM PROSPECTS

History shows that in modern times Schumpeter's analysis is correct: after every deep crisis the dynamism in the world economy reappears based on new technological patterns. It is not the case that war and crises are the best stimuli for innovation, but just simply an observation that after deep crises and great wars lots of innovations have appeared. This happened after the great depression of the 1930s, and it occurred also after the oil crisis of the 1970s that brought about the third world debt crisis of the early 1980s but also stimulated competition and innovation particularly in information, transport, and communication technologies. There is no reason to suppose that the aftermath of the current crisis of globalization will be different in general, but specific new trends are increasingly apparent. These are: (1) the relative weight of the economies that were small when international economic rules were established in the 1940s and 1950s is likely to be better represented in the world regimes and institutions; (2) international regimes probably will be more robust and binding, particularly regarding world financial transactions; (3) the new economy which has been emerging since the end of the last century is going green, i.e. more technologies are being created or transformed fostered by concerns with environmental impacts. These trends are particularly important to a country such as Brazil whose interests are various and worldwide.

### Economies in World Regimes

There is a widespread consensus regarding the fact that institutions and practices, which were designed after the 1930s crisis and World War II, pro-

---

16. The CSN (Companhia Siderúrgica Nacional), the first steel industry in Brazil, and the CTA (Technological Center of the Brazilian Air Force), essential to the national airplane industry, were established in the aftermath of the World War II. The EMBRAPA (State Company for Research in Agriculture) was established in 1972 under the military regime. Simon Schwartzman gives a comprehensive view of the main facts and investments in science and technology in Brazil in the 20th century (S. Schwartzman, 2001).

duced a long period of a relatively peaceful world as well as of economic growth without parallel in the history of modern times. To a large extent these achievements were products of an international economic order that reflected a particular hierarchy among nations. While traditional European powers dwindled economically, politically the overwhelming power of the US was central to molding the emerging new world. The Cold war represented a remarkable feature of the world politics for decades, and in many aspects the cold war bipolarity reinforced the primacy of the US's economic power. The Soviet Union, while competing with the US in ideological and strategic terms, left free room for the US's predominance in the world economy. Even the process of European integration was fueled by the US capacity to finance trade and reconstruction. For example, in the late 1940s and early 1950s the Marshall Plan had played an important role in this process. Available figures show that in early 1950s the GNP of the US was bigger than the GNP of the other six great powers altogether, and the two Conferences which have settled the basis of the peace after the end of the war were attended by the "Big Three" referring to the US, Britain, and the Soviet Union.[17] The establishment of the main post-war institutions largely reflected that particular distribution of wealth and power.[18]

Nevertheless, the world scene has changed substantially. The cold war is gone, and due to the fact that economic growth is essentially an uneven process in the long run, the world distribution of wealth and power also has changed substantially.[19] As a consequence, similarly to Britain's economic history in the late nineteenth century, after the 1960s the US economy continued to grow, but its rates of growth were much lower than in other regions.

At the time of the Bretton Woods Conference in 1944[20] the US Treasury possessed more than 70% of the world gold reserves, and the arrangements that were settled at the Conference reflected these figures.[21] Benefited by the US views on world security and economic strategies, Western European

---

17. According to Paul Kennedy, in 1950 the GNP of the US was US$381 billion while the GNP of Britain, France, Italy, West Germany, Japan, and the USSR together totaled only US$356 billion (Kennedy, 1988: 475).

18. The United Nations dates from 1945; the Bretton Woods institutions, 1944; the GATT, 1947; the NATO, 1949. Other institutions created in the 1950s even at the regional level in Europe and elsewhere were also strongly influenced by the world economic and political scene in which the leadership of the US was an essential factor.

19. In the late 1950s "development theories" became an increasingly popular issue among economists and one of the more influential though criticized book was The Stages of Growth written by W. W. Rostow who argued that the US was the only economy which had at that time attained the 5th stage (mass consumption economy) but any other country could follow the track and attain the same level of industrial production of the US (W. W. Rostow, 1960).

20. Henry Nau gives a large account of the central role played by the US in the post-war era (Nau, 1990).

countries regained momentum and were followed by Japan. In twenty years time they reconstructed their economies and modernized their industries and became serious competitors with the US in terms of economic efficiency. Later other economies, particularly in Asia, followed the same path. Even in Latin America some poles of growth and modernization showed up. It is very symbolic that by the end of the 1950s the US gold reserves had dropped to less than 50% of the world gold reserves.

Many other facts and figures show the many changes that took place in the patterns of distribution of wealth and power. Currently most of the international regimes in both political and economic matters no longer reflect the weight of countries and regions in the world scenario. As a consequence, the agenda of international organizations frequently is outdated or simply does not fit the interests of governments and societies. Another consequence is that many important international issues have been negotiated and managed outside of the institutions created by the Bretton Woods agreement. Initiatives such as the G-8, the G-20, and the Global Economic Forum, as well as bilateral talks and meetings for specific purposes, became more frequent and more effective in world diplomacy. The OAS and the World Bank lost momentum, and the IMF and the GATT substantially changed their purposes and modes of operation.

The interaction between political and economic conditions led Brazil to attempt to play a more significant role in the regional and world politics and economy. Particularly in South America, the size and the weight of Brazil became increasingly important in shaping the process of regional integration. Nonetheless, Brazil is aware that it has frontier lines with every South American country except Ecuador and Chile, and potentially populist leaderships always tend to elect a foreign country as the enemy to be blamed for any failure in domestic politics. Since the 19th century in various circumstances, Brazil was identified as a regional imperial power to be checked by Spanish speaking neighbors.[22]

21. In early 1960s Robert Triffin wrote a thoughtful paper raising the problem of the stability of the Bretton Woods dollar based monetary system in an environment of declining gold reserves of the US Treasury (Triffin, 1960).

22. A permanent concern of Rio Branco, who commanded Brazilian foreign policy between 1902 and 1912, was largely focused on how to avoid an imperialist label for the country. Even before 1902 Rio Branco had occasion to show that discretion and low profile politics should be more adequate to live peacefully in the region. After his victorious performance in the territorial arbitration process in Washington between Brazil and Argentina in 1894, Rio Branco decided not to go to Rio de Janeiro on his way to London where he occupied a diplomatic position. He knew that his countrymen had prepared a big celebration for him: "He did not accept the invitation to come to Brazil to be honored by his countrymen. For him such an homage looked like an unnecessary public exhibition and a discourtesy to Zeballos (the Argentinian negotiator) and to Argentina," wrote Álvaro Lins (Lins, 1962: 213).

At the global level the scenario for Brazilian diplomacy is also blurred and the issue of reform of the United Nations (UN) is very instructive: the possibility of Brazil becoming a really influential power in the world system has to be seen against an unpredictable interplay of ambiguous and rather contradictory forces. Domestically most critics of Brazilian diplomacy argue that the country has been wasting too much time and energy by fighting for a permanent seat in the UN Security Council and by trying to be a leader of the developing world. Furthermore resources available for foreign policy are too scarce to support large and expensive commitments in the international arena, and it is not clear yet to what extent such an involvement with world politics will effectively help the promotion of Brazilian interests.

## A World of Robust International Regimes

To a large extent the recent world financial crisis can be understood as another product of the mismatch between the existing regimes and the new actors and new technological patterns which have substantially changed the ways of doing business in the world economy. The succession of trade cycles and crises in the 20th century has shown that freedom to create opportunities for gains must be balanced by international norms to prevent predatory competition. With respect to this phenomenon it seems instructive to look at history to assess current concerns regarding the international financial regime that present some parallels relative to what had happened in the post-war years.

The Bretton Woods Conference is generally associated with post-war reconstruction. The participants of the Conference were concerned with what to do when the war came to an end. The main concerns underpinning the Bretton Woods negotiations had their origins in the 1920s hyperinflation and the 1930s economic downfall; reconstruction and growth were not the prime concern.[23]

Basically the 1929 collapse was an unprecedented experience. The bitter memories left by the 1930s crisis included the perception that the volatility of the financial system exacerbated the falling markets instead of dampening their causes and effects. Governments and economists were still completely lacking in experience, monetary authorities did not have any instrument to address financial crises before this time, and the pre-Keynesian theories did not include any role for the government. The fact is that the

---

23. See de Vries (1972). Particularly regarding US/UK negotiations within the Conference see Gardner (1956) (Kindleberger, 1987: 117-96).

widespread view among economic authorities and analysts at the time of Bretton Woods Conference was that the "herd behavior" of the financial agents was crucial to the process by which the 1930s crisis virtually went out of control. In their view the "herd behavior" derived essentially from the unregulated markets of stocks, bonds, and other financial assets. Charles P. Kindleberger gives a detailed account of the process by which the 1929 crash turned into a depression showing that a succession of "panics" in different areas and different moments shrinking bank deposits and credits, cutting the prices of commodities, and reducing confidence in financial assets had led finally to the generalized crisis through the 1930s.

## Purposes and Goals

The Bretton Woods Conference took place in July 1944, but did not become operative until 1959, when all the European currencies became convertible. Under this system, the IMF and the IBRD were established. The IMF was developed as a permanent international body. The summary of agreements states, "The nations should consult and agree on international monetary changes which affect each other. They should outlaw practices which are agreed to be harmful to world prosperity, and they should assist each other to overcome short-term exchange difficulties."

Against such a background it seems easy to understand why the establishment of a stable monetary system was associated with mechanisms to control the flow of capital. The Bretton Woods arrangements established that governments could manage large capital flows among countries. International private capital flow should be restricted to direct investments and to bonds issued under the supervision of governments and institutions such as the World Bank. In short, what Bretton Woods did regarding financial flows was replace the free flow of capital regime for a regime based on regulation and control.

Similarly one can say that today the free flow of capital regime is about to be replaced by mechanisms designed to limit and to control the flow of money among financial markets. Even in the heyday of the Bretton Woods system there were leakages in the international financial flow regime, such as the Eurodollar market that started to grow in the 1950s. All European currencies became convertible in 1959. During the 1970s, the financial regime established following the Bretton Woods agreements became unsustainable and started to be changed dramatically. Two landmarks in such a process are the abandonment of the convertibility of the US dollar to gold, and the formation of a huge petrodollar market. The deregulation of the financial system was fuelled not only by savings from oil markets but also by new technologies that created opportunities for business and gains based on the increasing world wide integration of financial markets.

The 1980s are called "the lost decade" because of its slow economic growth and financial crises. Although none of these crises produced a systemic impact on the world economy because they did not threaten central economies to an extent that would force them to change their institutions and practices (Stiglitz, 2003).[24]

The title of Joseph Stiglitz' book—*The Roaring Nineties: a New History of the World's Most Prosperous Decade*—reveals the widespread perception regarding the remarkable performance of the world economy. Actually, looking back now it seems quite clear that there were many fragilities in the financial markets, but no one can deny that in an environment in which fortunes were mushrooming any critical comment would sound really awkward. Alan Greenspan was one of those who had made critical comments regarding financial markets, but obviously due to his position as president —or even as former president—of the US Federal Reserve System he could not say too much without provoking a "herd behavior" reaction in the market.[25] In such an environment in which a great deal of individuals, firms, and nations were getting richer, one can hardly think that anyone would propose any kind of change for the financial regime, especially to limit and to control the flow of funds.

The 2008 financial crisis brought about a radical change in the perceptions of opportunities and financial flows. The dominant new perception was that together with emergency rescue measures, governments and international organizations should produce mechanisms to limit and control the size and reduce the volatility of capital flows by providing a set of rules and norms with the necessary means to assure the compliance of individuals, firms, and governments. These norms and rules should fall not only on the process of issuing bonds, stocks, and other forms of financial assets which are traded, but also on the institutions and their procedures, particularly on stock exchanges, banks, and monetary institutions.[26]

---

24. From 1990 to 2005 world trade increased by a consistent rate of 6% yearly and the world production around 2.5% a year (statistics from WTO reports). From 2003 to 2007 the average increase of the world production was 3.3% a year, and the world exports were increasing by a rate of 7.6% per year (UNCTAD, 2009).

25. Alan Greenspan was the president of the Federal Reserve System from 1987 to 2006.

For a long time the world financial market included a relatively small number of financial centers—basically the US, main European economies, and Japan—but globalization from the 1980s onwards brought into the world market tens of emerging economies in which bonds and stocks could be issued, bought, and sold. As a consequence, opportunities have increased but risks and sources of instability also increased, and the world financial market became more anarchical.

Before the crisis broke out some isolated measures to control the flow of capital were taken by countries as Chile and Brazil, but isolated measures in an anarchical environment tend to produce very limited effects, particularly on small economies.

Banks and financial institutions operating in countries where authorities permit individuals and firms to keep secret accounts under the argument of privacy are a target of more regulation and control. These financial institutions, known as "fiscal havens," as well as the governments which shelter them, have been under siege since terrorism went to the forefront of the international political agenda. The fiscal havens also have been used to facilitate drug-dealing, corruption, smuggling, and to all sorts of illicit practices. They are essential instruments for transferring funds and keeping laundered money. The 2008 financial crisis gave an additional push to tighten the siege on "fiscal havens" because the amount of illicit money was soaring and regulation hardly can separate money from legal and illegal origins. Both can influence financial markets. Even countries such as Switzerland, where the banking system had a longstanding tradition of keeping secret accounts are changing their laws.

Currently, initiatives of cooperation to create mechanisms of regulation of the financial markets are on the way in most international organizations. These negotiations reflect the increasing multipolarity of the world economy. In the last decades, the emergence of Asia is only a highlight of a more complex and profound change in the structure of the international economic order.[27]

---

26. The *Pittsburgh Summit of the G-20* (Sept. 24-25/2009) produced a statement in which the necessity of a more robust international regime for banking and financial operations is stressed several times. Various measures were suggested ranging from regular meetings of the G-20 to the establishment of international bodies such as the Financial Stability Board (FSB) to enhance the grip capacity of the international economic cooperation framework.

27. In the early 1980s, US exports represented 12% of the world exports, Germany's 9%, and China's only 1%; in 2005, the US exports reduced their participation to 8.9%, Germany's increased to 10.5%, and China's increased to 7.5%, becoming the third largest exporter. South Korea is another instructive case: from almost negligible participation in the world exports in the early 1980s, the nation increased its participation to more than 2.5% overtaking by far countries such as Brazil and Mexico (WTO, 2007).

Earlier attempts to change the trade aspects of the international economic order suggest that when coordination in the international level becomes difficult a more binding regime tends to appear. When the GATT was created in the late 1940s the US economy was largely dominant. To foster international trade the first initiative was to create an International Trade Organization (ITO). It was to be an organization rather similar to the World Trade Organization (WTO) of our times. William Diebold in an essay published in the early 1950s—just after the decision taken by the US authorities to abandon the ITO—showed that the ITO seemed too binding to the US interests, who replaced it by the GATT (Diebold, 1952). It is interesting to note that the 52 countries other than the US which signed the Havana Charter establishing the ITO in 1948 did not say anything or take any initiative when the ITO was buried.

Forty years later the US largely had lost its predominance over other economies, and during the Uruguay Round (1986-94) trade negotiations had reached a complete deadlock. The US, the European powers, and even some emerging economies had different views about several issues regarding trade. In the end the stalemate was broken on January 1, 1995 by creating the World Trade Organization (WTO) which was weaker than the former ITO. The WTO was called "the GATT with teeth" meaning that the trade regime became more binding. This, and other developments making requirements for economic and financial reporting similar among nations, suggests that globalization is progressing by establishing binding regimes based on cooperation and compliance.

Another reason why Brazil did not suffer much from the 2008 crisis is because to a large extent the country had stayed relatively apart from global financial competition. For many reasons monetary authorities in Brazil have constructed a domestic financial regime favoring control rather than free flow of capital. Brazil's long inflationary experience, its tradition of state oriented views of the bureaucracy, and its nationalism are among the more important reasons. In this way it seems that a more binding regime with norms and rules can fit the Brazilian experience much better than the free market regime.

## CLEAN TECHNOLOGIES: THE EMERGING PATTERN FOR INDUSTRY AND ENERGY

Economists interpret technological changes as cyclical, i.e. when some remarkable technological innovation occurs, industry and many forms of economic activity also change, creating new products and processes, and defining new patterns for markets and opportunities.[28] The first stages of the industrial revolution created the necessary conditions for the European and the US expansion in the 19th century based on a largely liberal economy. Actually the US had considerable intervention in the economy at the State level, and there was Federal action to provide infrastructure, such as railroads, and intermittent Federal and State granting of charters and regulation of banking. Nevertheless these interventions differed from actions taken after the 1930s crisis and World War II. It seems enough to mention the fact that in the 1930s government revenues in the US represented only 4.5% of the GDP, and that after the New Deal experience government revenues increased consistently and continuously to achieve nowadays 1/4 of the GDP.[29] Furthermore, the nature of government intervention in the economy during the New Deal included the creation of various agencies and financial mechanisms to give the population widespread instruments of welfare, incentives to industrial innovation, investments in urban development, etc.

The New Deal focused on domestic needs. US policy increasingly dealt with international needs, beginning in the 1940s. In 1970, the US became a net importer of oil, and the soaring prices of oil in the 1970s led to the transfer of huge amounts of savings amassed by oil exporting economies to private financial markets. Banks and other private financial institutions had their safe boxes full of money—notably petrodollars—and governments, particularly from indebted third world countries, started to borrow heavily from private banks. Deregulation of capital flow emerged as a natural solution.

The difficulties derived from the oil crisis led to the adoption of new strategies of economic development by individuals, corporations, and state owned organizations. These led to new technologies for computers, information flow, and transport.

---

28. The classical author regarding this view is obviously Joseph Schumpeter (1911) who inspired most approaches which give importance to technology as a factor of development and economic growth. Among such authors are Peter Drucker and Michael Porter. See Schumpeter, 1982.

29. Statistical figures available in the page of the Executive Office of the President of the United States. GPO Access. See http://gpoaccess.gov/eop/tables08.html.

Capital markets also flourished not only based on petrodollars but also on the possibilities opened by new information technology that permitted integration of the main world stock markets in real time. These developments benefitted Asian nations more than Brazil and other Latin American nations that did not actively take part in the globalization process.[30]

A new aspect of international trade is the search for new patterns for products and production processes that have less damaging effects on the environment. These are needed because the patterns of consumption currently existing in affluent societies cannot be extended to hundreds of millions of people without provoking an exhaustion of essential raw materials and serious environmental problems. For example, if only in China and India every year 2% of their population are integrated to the global standard of middle class, every year there will be some additional 20 million cars running (equivalent to almost the automobile fleet of a country like Brazil), consuming fuels, discarding used tires and other auto parts, and discharging a quantity of pollutant gas into the atmosphere. The same kind of argument can be applied to other aspects which compose the standard of living in terms of desirable comforts: food, clothing, air transportation, personal hygiene, education, leisure, etc. More than half of the world population still has a standard of living well below that of a typical middle class Western nation. For example, the carbon dioxide ($CO_2$) per capita emissions in industrial societies are at least five times higher than the average of developing economies.[31] Nevertheless, there is a widespread consensus that it is a legitimate demand of any society for individuals to have access to all goods and facilities which are available to people living in modern societies.

Another source of pressure to change technology is the desire for economic security. To a large extent a modern standard of living still relies on oil and other non-renewable natural resources that are unevenly distributed among regions and countries. While wealthy industrial societies such as Germany and Japan are lacking in some essential raw materials, other economies—such as most members of OPEC—have large reserves of natural resources but do not have the economic infrastructure needed to produce industrial goods from these resources. Since the 1970s the perspectives of

---

30. In 1983, South and Central America represented 4.4% of the world merchandise exports, and in 2007 the share of South and Central America dropped to only 3.7%. In the same period Asia (Japan not included) more than doubled its share of the world merchandise exports from 11.1% in 1983 to 22.7% (*WTO Statistics 2008*, Table I.6).

31. According to UNCTAD, in 2006 the per capita carbon dioxide discharged into atmosphere every year in industrialized countries was equivalent to 10.9 tons while in India the individual carbon dioxide emission was only 1.1 tons (UNCTAD, 2009: 136).

natural resources shortage, particularly petroleum, have been haunting the world economy, and the fears of shortage of an essential commodity such as oil recently worsened due to an increasing nationalism and religious fundamentalism in the Middle East. In such an environment industrial countries have been strongly stimulated to develop products and forms of energy less dependent on petroleum coming from unstable states easily influenced by political forces resistant to international integration.

Against this political and economic background, large and well-funded research programs in the field of production and use of energy have been developed for wind, solar, and all forms of alternative energy, as well as for all means to reduce the consumption and to increase the efficiency of industrial plants, equipment, and even architectural design. The leading countries in such efforts have been the US, Japan, and Western European countries. They are investing heavily in developing the use of solar energy despite the fact that they are geographically situated in regions poorly gifted with sunlight, while China is dramatically increasing its investments in clean energy.[32]

The same concern regarding energy production and consumption can be seen in terms of reducing the waste by recycling and management of industrial by-products and discarded objects and materials. In the long run the life in large cities will be virtually unbearable unless some changes are introduced in the current patterns of consumption.

In many ways international regimes already reflect these concerns. Trade regimes have introduced environmental clauses basically derived from commercial controversies involving fishing, forest products, and from various forms of waste production and discard. Allegations of protectionism hidden behind environmental arguments should be considered as effective in some specific cases, but the dominant view in the international community is that by any means environment protection at large should be included in the every day life of the world population. Environmental clauses are already included in trade regimes and it seems likely to expect that other international regimes will also move in the same direction. Brazil, however, has kept a predominantly defensive attitude in most negotiation forums, arguing that allegations regarding environmental requirements and intellectual property rights are hidden forms of protectionism of industrial countries.

---

32. China, which has been pointed out as a leading economy for the next decades, is also increasing dramatically investments in clean energy. F. Zakary states that today China has the largest investment program in clean energy mainly solar technology (Zakaria, 2008).

Domestically, the volume of R&D investments in most areas of alternative sources of energy have been small in both private and public organizations, suggesting that in the emerging cycle of growth Brazil is bound to lag behind other nations.

In the next pages this essay concludes by attempting to capture some of the trends in the Brazilian economy vis-à-vis the perspectives that seem to be emerging from a new cycle of growth in the world economy.

## BRAZIL AND THE NEW CYCLE OF GROWTH IN THE WORLD ECONOMY

## Brazil and the Management of Short-term Problems

As discussed in the early pages of this essay, Brazil went through the 2008 crisis much better than most countries. Inflationary pressures were low and the domestic financial market did not depend heavily on international bonds and stocks that were turning sour. Domestic public debt was relatively high (around 50% of the GDP) but for years it had been quite well managed in financial terms, and it has been an important support for the banking system to go through the crisis. Moreover, unlike banks in many other nations, Brazilian banks had a great part of their assets in very safe Federal Treasury bonds.

This supports the predominantly positive views of Brazilian economic policy that are held even by those who criticize president Lula da Silva's administration. Those who are more optimistic tend to see the crisis as a threshold of a new era in which Brazil will play a role as an important power in the world scene. Nevertheless, when we look at structural conditions instead of focusing on macroeconomic variables of the Brazilian economy, the outlook for the near future indicates only a limited benefit for Brazil in a new cycle of economic growth, because of its limited investment in technology and modernization.

### Bad Management: Inadequate Infrastructure

There are visible deficits in almost every sector of Brazil's economic infrastructure. Transportation systems are not only insufficient; the poor quality of roads, services, and equipment can be observed everywhere. In a large country like Brazil, transportation of goods and people is essential to link regions, markets, and the different phases of the production process. For example, in a large city like São Paulo public transportation is very precarious and instead, people use their own cars. As a consequence, the everyday life of the population is plagued by horrific traffic jams in which hundreds of thousands of people waste their time, and tons of unnecessarily burned fuel are discharged into the atmosphere. In this way a comparison between Greater London and São Paulo is instructive. The area of both cities is approximately 1,550 km², but the population of São Paulo is substantially larger: São Paulo has a population of 11 million inhabitants while Greater London has a population of 7.5 million inhabitants. São Paulo has the best metro system among Brazilian cities, nevertheless when compared to London the differences are dramatic. By the end of 2009, the São Paulo metro system had only 61.3 km of rails uniting 55 metro stations while the London underground system was around 400 km long and had 270 stations so that, unlike São Paulo, in London people can go everywhere in the city without using their own car.[33]

A more accurate account of the high costs of the losses derived from the poor infrastructure of a city like São Paulo includes other effects that are the result of precarious infrastructure, such as frequent floods even when the rains are not so heavy, and car crashes in numbers far above the figures of industrial countries with a proportionally greater number of vehicles. Obviously the list is too long to be presented, but it seems enough to say that inadequate infrastructure leads to waste, environmental damages, additional costs, and low productivity. In fact, since the 1970s any significant investment has been done only to cope with some kind of imminent collapse.

## *Technological Development in the Emerging Cycle of Growth*

The sources and uses of energy in Brazil may define its ability to control its economic growth. Brazil imports electricity and natural gas. The need to secure these resources influences government loans to supplying nations, adjustments in prices for their products, and explains Petrobras' investments abroad. Furthermore, the technological development in energy alternatives is worth discussing because energy systems are critical in defining products and processes. The US has invested in the production of energy from alternative sources, while in Brazil investments have been made in technologies from the past. Public policy in this regard is basically oriented

---

33. Figures available in official pages of the cities of São Paulo and London: http://www.capital.sp.gov.br/portalpmsp/homec.jsp (Sao Paulo); http://www.london.gov.uk/thelondonplan.jsp (London).

to constructing large energy plants based on traditional forms of energy (hydroelectric, nuclear, and gas or carbon powered plants).

Perhaps the Brazilian government should pay more attention to uncertainties of the market that can worsen if a significant technological breakthrough occurs.

## Modern Society, Obsolete State

The case of insufficient investment in infrastructure, energy, and technology for the future shows that the greatest liability of the Brazilian nation continues to be the malfunction of the state. Every aspect ranging from needs of the every day life to harbors, public education, and technological innovation that depend on some kind of government initiative simply do not work properly. Modern life depends on many systems—generally interconnected—most of them funded and managed by public authorities. Private companies can provide buses to transport people in a big city, but some kind of public authority will be needed to organize and to manage the whole system. Private firms usually make roads, but the money to build the roads comes from official agencies established by the municipalities, states or federal government. Education at any level can be provided by public schools and universities or by private institutions, but in either case government authorities will be always playing an essential role by establishing and enforcing rules and requirements, and in most cases providing funds to assure the quality and even the access to education for the poor. A great deal of the modern technological development depends directly on government initiative either because there are implications for defense and other strategic aspects and/or because the amount of money as well as the time needed cannot be provided by private sources through allocation by an unregulated market.

Sound macroeconomic conditions though essential are not enough. In Brazil civil society and the market are quite active and strong, but the state is obsolete and has been working very badly in most areas. To make things worse, the judiciary system has a longstanding tradition of being completely self-centered and most of the time dedicated to protecting those who in some way have done something wrong to individuals, firms, and institutions. Not only corrupt politicians and dishonest businessmen tend to feel safe under the judiciary institutions, but generally the laws are largely lenient even with those who commit crimes such as drug-dealing, robbery or smuggling.

When individuals and organizations are oriented to misbehavior, and innovation and creativity are not properly rewarded, society declines inevitably. Unfortunately it seems that in many aspects this is what is happening in Brazil.

# 6

# BUREAUCRATS, PARTIES, AND INTEREST GROUPS

*Maria Rita Loureiro, Cecília Olivieri,*
and *Ana Cristina Braga Martes*

*Abstract:* The chapter discusses the relationship between politics and bureaucracy in Brazil. Based on studies on the emergence and consolidation of the bureaucracy developed in the context of the wider debate on the relationship between state and society, the text examines the ties built between the government bureaucracy, political parties, and interest groups. The chapter emphasizes the significance of understanding the nature and scope of the power of bureaucrats in the general structure of the state, especially those coming from the functions of the Executive and Legislative, the relationship between them and their links with political parties and interest groups. Understanding the bureaucracy in Brazil is therefore inseparable from debates about the hypertrophy of the executive over the legislature and the weakness of the governing function of political parties, not only in authoritarian times, but also in democratic periods. The text takes up issues such as patronage, bureaucratic insulation, corporatism, and meritocracy, seeking to understand them in the logic of the political system and its challenges to the democratic order.

Politicians make decisions and bureaucrats merely administer. This view, which bears the stamp of common sense, is to be found in various public administration texts. However, in one of the most insightful studies into the role reserved for these two groups of players in contemporary democracies, Aberbach, Putnam, and Rockman (1981) show that, in all seven of the developed countries studied, the public bureaucracy is an integral part of the decision-making processes of the Executive branch, and furthermore that the Legislative branch wields power over the bureaucracy.

Bureaucrats have played an active part in decision-making processes in contemporary democracies.[1] Even when only prioritizing procedures or even the technical dimensions of problems, bureaucrats make relevant contributions because the state acts in different areas and deals with ever more complex issues. Contemporary authors have highlighted the bureaucratization of politics and the politicization of bureaucracy. Both adopt hybrid action strategies: politicians base their decisions on technical criteria while bureaucrats reinforce their political roles by mediating the interests of specific clientele groups and the signals sent out by the politicians.

Studies on pluralist democracies have paid considerable attention to the participation of bureaucrats in the decision-making process. Charles Lindblom emphasizes the way they operate, particularly when public policies are being implemented. According to the author, such policies are generally approved by the legislature in a general and vague way that requires the intervention of the bureaucrats in working out details and specifications. The involvement of bureaucrats with the decision making, which is seen by Lindblom as inevitable or even sometimes desirable in the contemporary world, occurs because those who are governing lack time and are not closely familiar with the specialized subjects that characterize most governmental action (Lindblom and Woodhouse, 1993).

In Brazil, bureaucracy not only forms part of the decision-making process, but is in fact one of the most important players. It has played a prominent role in the definition and conduct of public policies in authoritarian as well as democratic periods when parties and organized social groups recovered their capacity to influence or participate in government. In an influential analysis of Brazil's party system, Campello de Souza (1976) indicates how the roots of the crucial problems of Brazilian political parties—enormous institutional fragility, an inability to participate effectively in the preparation of public policies and the generalized persistence of clientelistic practices—lie in the type of relation that has been established between them and the government.

Bureaucratic power is never exercised on the basis of its own resources alone. The power of the bureaucrats depends on the backing of or delegation by some strategic political player seeking to sustain positions as policymakers. In other words, bureaucracy only plays a directing role in govern-

---

1. As Woodrow Wilson stated, "The administration is outside the political sphere. Administrative issues are not political issues" ("The study of administration," *Political Science Quarterly* June, 1887).

ment based on the granting of power by other political players or, in extreme situations, based on the usurpation of this power (Martins, 1974).

Stating that bureaucrats are relevant when it comes to government decisions does not mean ignoring their institutional dependence on political authority, or denying that the ultimate responsibility for decisions belongs to the politicians, as Max Weber pointed out. But affirming the institutional dependence of the power of the bureaucrats on politicians does not mean reducing bureaucracy to being a mere instrument of the executive branch. The assumption that there is separation between the administrative area and the political area is a legal formula that helps us understand the roles and responsibilities of each of these players, but which does not detract from the political nature of the role and activities of bureaucrats (Miliband, 1983: 143).

Brazil and the United States share such political institutions as a presidential system, a federative structure, and an administration open to lateral entries.[2] But relations between bureaucracy, the Executive, and the Legislative branch are very different in the two countries. In the United States, despite the fact that the bureaucratic apparatus is under the functional responsibility and within the structure of the executive, its main "master" is the Congress. In other words, delegation of power to the bureaucracy, and consequently its backing, comes mainly from the legislative branch, albeit not exclusively. This is what gives rise to distinctive aspects of the relation between politics and bureaucracy in the United States: members of Congress have the means of controlling the actions of the bureaucrats, and political parties have exercised both their representative and governmental functions, regardless of the expansion of the functions of the Executive and of its bureaucratic apparatus.[3]

To better specify the relations between politics and bureaucracy in Brazil, this chapter reviews major studies on the emergence and consolidation of the bureaucracy as a relevant player in the decision-making process and the links that have been established historically between it, the Executive, political parties, and interest groups. It looks at the broader debate about rela-

---

2. Bureaucracies that are more permeable to lateral entries are those in which some of the top echelon positions can be filled by professionals who have not necessarily had a public career, i.e., they did not climb the respective rungs of the hierarchical ladder, but were indicated for the position as a result of their previous activities outside the public sector.

3. From the theoretical point of view it is necessary to differentiate two essential functions of the parties in a democratic order: the representative function, in other words, representing the various different interests of society, and the government function, i.e., the capacity to determine or influence government decisions through the formulation of projects for the country, imposing direction on public policies (Campello De Souza, 1976).

tions between state and society by focusing on the processes that led to a strengthening of the decision-making role of the bureaucracy vis-à-vis other political players, and hence its impact on democratic order. This perspective cannot be disassociated from the issue of hypertrophy of the Executive relative to the legislature, the weakness of the governmental function of political parties, and the problem of the state's relations with interest groups—both in the sense of the attempt made by private groups to take over governmental organs and, in the opposite sense, of the cooptation of these groups by state agents.[4]

Generally, the literature about bureaucracy in Brazil is not very extensive when compared with the literature in the United States. It consists, above all, of case studies of government agencies and works on two of the few more consolidated public careers in the country; the armed forces and the diplomatic service. Furthermore, this literature refers above all to the authoritarian periods, since the blocking of the democratic paths of political participation redirected political activity to within the state's bureaucratic apparatus. Also, unlike the North-American literature, the main focus of which is on the effectiveness of the democratic controls over bureaucracy (Wood and Waterman, 1994), studies in Brazil have favored an analysis of the relationship between state and society. In other words, the focus on the bureaucracy in Brazil has been a by-product of the concern with the central role played by the state in Brazilian society.

Despite nuances and variations in emphasis, two main analytical strands dominate in these studies. The first approaches bureaucracy from the point of view of the class-driven nature of government—and it emphasizes the macro-structural transformation processes which Brazilian society experienced after the 1930s, which led to centralization of power in the federal executive and expansion of the state apparatus and public bureaucracy. The second strand favors the study of bureaucracy from the prism of its links with political institutions. Its central theme can be summarized as a discussion about the dilemmas between bureaucratic insulation versus clientelism and patronage.[5]

---

4. We use the expression "governmental capacity," as used by Campello de Souza (1976: XXII): "the capacity to formulate and implement a broad spectrum of public policies."

5. As José Murilo de Carvalho indicates, "the concept of clientelism was always used in a loose way." Generally speaking, it indicates a type of relation between political players that involves the granting of public benefits in the form of jobs, tax benefits, and exemptions, in exchange for political support, above all by way of the vote. In turn, patronage in Brazil refers, above all, to the distribution of public jobs for political convenience purposes, especially too for votes. For more details about the difference between these political relations, including "coronelismo" and "mandonismo," see Carvalho (1997).

Three caveats are in order. First, this essay does not ignore the discussion in today's democratic theory relating to the crisis in representative institutions and to the decline in political parties. The latter have been considered incapable of expressing all the splits that exist in contemporary societies. They are also losing space within the context of growing media communication or the return of charismatic leaders (Przeworski, Stokes, and Manin, 1999; Novaro, 2000; Lavalle, Houtzager, and Castello, 2006). However, parties are still the mediation institutions *par excellence,* between society and the state. In Brazil, for example, analyses of post-1985 governments underline the centrality of parties in the organization and functioning of the Executive and its relations with the legislature (Meneguello, 1998). Furthermore, theoretical works effectively argue that representative democracy is firmly founded on parties (Urbinati, 2006).

The second clarification refers to the concept of bureaucracy. The political player we highlight—which we call "bureaucracy"—comprises incumbents of the top echelon, or the directors of the direct and indirect administrative bodies of the Executive. These people may be both career civil servants (who comprise the stable body of government) and professionals from outside the public sector (recruited from private companies, non-state entities, such as universities or research centers and from trade unions and civil society organizations) who temporarily undertake activities as directors in governmental bodies.[6] Therefore, when we refer to bureaucracy we are talking about the individual players or "informal groups" who occupy top echelon positions, and we refer to state agencies or organs as the bureaucratic apparatus.[7]

Finally, the literature discussed in this work refers exclusively to the economic policy decision-making process. This restriction is justified by the fact that most of the studies about the expansion of the central state bureaucracy in Brazil concentrate on the way the developmental national state is assembled and, therefore, on the agencies charged with regulation, funding and economic planning. Despite this limitation we believe that questioning the links between bureaucracy and politics is also pertinent to other public policy areas.

---

6. Although not extensive, there is some literature in Brazil that analyzes the recruitment process of those who come from outside the state to occupy positions in the public policy decision-making organs (see Schneider, 1994; Loureiro, 1997; Olivieri, 2007; D'Araujo, 2007).

7. Examples of informal groups that took part in the top echelon of public bureaucracy at different times in our history are the members of the Vargas Economic Assistance group in the 1950s; they were the originators of groups formed with nationalist and developmental ideas (D'Araújo, 1982). Also the economic team that prepared the Real Plan in 1993-94 comprised groups of former colleagues from the Economics schools in Rio de Janeiro (Loureiro, 1997).

CAPITALIST STATE, SOCIAL CLASSES, AND BUREAUCRACY

A series of studies carried out predominantly throughout the 1970s and 1980s and growing out of the Marxist tradition, share a class-based approach to the state. Often influenced by the interpretative current expounded by Italian theoretician Antônio Gramsci, this strand of analysis starts by highlighting the absence of hegemony in the bourgeoisie in Brazil and the latter's inability to prepare a political project for the nation. They try to understand how, given this absence, the state assumes the function of the promoter of development through industrialization. That is, the focus is on the central role assumed by the state after the 1930s in constructing the national developmental project within a context that is marked by an absence of hegemony in the entrepreneurial class and by social fragmentation. Notwithstanding their internal differences, some authors in this strand more clearly express the analytical characteristics of the strand as a whole.[8]

Draibe (1985) analyzes the role of the state in the industrialization process and the "metamorphoses" which the bureaucratic apparatus underwent throughout this process, noting the "courses" adopted by its directorial nucleus under the influence of different political forces. Emphasizing social class differences, on the one hand, and the formation of the bureaucratic structures of the state on the other, the action of bureaucrats is seen from the point of view of the degree of autonomy of the state relative to social classes. The autonomy is not viewed as full or absolute, but is founded on the unstable field of inter-class relations and decisively rooted in the multiplicity and heterogeneity of political forces. This heterogeneity and the incapacity of the bourgeoisie to exercise hegemony allow the state to act with a certain degree of autonomy, according to this author. Put another way, the relations between the classes not only marks out the limits but also the direction of the state's autonomous action.

Economic conflicts impinging on decision-making bodies intensify the political dimension of supposedly technical resolutions. Top echelon technicians act politically when they arbitrate or negotiate interests in localized confrontations and constitute one of the many forces that seek to make their points of view prevail in public policy decisions. The force of the tech-

---

8. There are countless pieces of work on the expansion of the bureaucratic apparatus of the national developmental state in Brazil (its regulatory agencies and economic planning) after the 1930s, such as Dalland, 1968; Cohn, 1968; Ianni, 1971; Wirth, 1970; Lafer, 1970; Singer, 1974; Benevides, 1976; Bresser Pereira, 1977. Our intention here is not to review all this literature but to highlight those studies that raise the question of the links between politics and bureaucrats or, in other words, the role of the bureaucratic elite within the political system.

nician derives from the incapacity of the economic interests to impose themselves to the same extent as the market's regulatory forces. Brought directly within the sphere of government, the different interests face each other in public sector arenas, and the alliances they help establish within each organ are ephemeral because they were built around isolated projects or one-off measures. This is the more independent and politicized action space of bureaucracy. Given the inter-penetration of policies and their growing degree of complexity, the special knowledge of the technician and his domination of the content of decisions enable him to operate as the pivot in the alliances between interest groups and inter-bureaucratic articulation (Draibe, 1985: 43).

Examining the subsequent period, Martins (1985) focuses on class structure to understand the expansion of the capitalist state and the transformations in bureaucracy arising from this expansion. For Martins, the nature of the role of the state and its fragmentation into various organizations with different degrees of autonomy come from social disarticulation, from the nature of the class structure in continuous transformation, and from the presence of international players controlling parts of the production system. Therefore, what allows the state to convert itself into an historic agent of transformation is not its relative autonomy vis-à-vis the dominant class, but "the autonomy of the political dimension vis-à-vis other instances of the social structure." The autonomy of the politician precedes and conditions the autonomy of the state and refers to a given way of development, which in the case of Brazil is characterized by social disarticulation.

Although the analysis of bureaucracy only acquires a fuller meaning when it is referred to the state's class dimension, it is not only by identifying the classes that directly benefit from the state that the top rung on the ladder of power can be found or that the nature of the relations between state bureaucracy and the owners of capital can be clarified. This is why Martins analyzes the expansion of the state as a concrete way of evaluating the development of capitalism in Brazil. To do so, he emphasizes two dimensions of state action; its extractive capacity and the expansion of its corporate activities. He concentrates on three agencies—Banco Nacional de Desenvolvimento Econômico (BNDE) *[National Economic Development Bank]*, Conselho de Desenvolvimento Industrial (CDI) *[Industrial Development Council]*, and Carteira de Comércio Exterior (CACEX) *[Foreign Trade Portfolio]*. These agencies operate in strategic areas: public funding, encouraging industrial investment, and the promotion of foreign trade.

The way in which each of these agencies is involved in the state apparatus (on the fringe, at the core, or in specific sectors of government) marks in a decisive way the functioning conditions, nature, and volume of funds that they handle, as well as the reach of their action. For Martins, it is not delegation of the attributions of political power that confers degrees of importance on each agency, but the power resources they manage to bring together and maximize via their actions and the choices conferred by the nature of their respective involvement with the state apparatus. Through their placement in or out of the government sector these agencies develop behaviors that are more or less autonomous and innovative.

These examples thus illustrate that pluralism in Brazil does not happen at the level of society, but within the scope of the state, as the actions of the agencies end up substituting the political parties. In other words, interests in society are so dispersed and disorganized that they are only structured by the organization provided by state institutions. According to the author, this situation partly explains the differences in the logic that exists in the state apparatus and, on the other hand, tends to accentuate its segmentation even more and disorganizes it internally.

Also focused on the post-1964 authoritarian regime, Werneck Vianna (1987) carried out a case study of the National Monetary Council (CMN), and from the transformations in this decision-making agency this author points to the character and role of the Brazilian state coordinating the direction of capitalist expansion by planning and organizing it.

Two theoretical perspectives allow this author to understand the CMN as an intermediation body for segmented corporate interests: that of state corporativism, which in the words of Schmitter (1971) is linked to highly centralized, bureaucratic political regimes that have weak parties; and the analyses of O'Donnell (1975) of the so-called bureaucratic-authoritarian state. This theoretical reference point also leads to interpreting the institutional transformations in the CMN between 1964-74, from a monetary regulatory body (as it was intended to be when it was created in 1964 and, therefore, a corporate chamber for accommodating the specific interests of the financial sector) to a national coordination body that centralized all economic policies between 1969-74 under Minister Delfim Neto.

As the CMN started to filter and select demands from groups, its actions were not mere bureaucratic routine but political acts by means of which interests were negotiated and channeled to within the state. Different bureaucracies attended the various clienteles, thereby helping to segment claims and make the state capable of dealing with different pressures and even with opposing demands. The bureaucracy does not just act as an intermediary of interests. It also selects them and organizes them politically.

In short, the group of texts selected as expressing the first analytical strand assumes that the structural characteristics of the bureaucratic apparatus (heterogeneity, the disarticulation of organizational structures and public policies) come from a lack of hegemony of the dominant class and the consequent absence of a unifying political direction. In other words, the state internalizes the diversity of the political conflicts in its various organs, institutes, government corporations, and companies. Bureaucracy becomes hostage to a set of interests. But, at the same time it emerges as beneficiary, when through them it promotes its own specific forms of power (for example, issuing regulations, deciding about financing, and the like) and thereby gains some degree of action autonomy. In other words, the structure, organization, growth, and directions of the state can be explained to a considerable extent as a function of the forms of expression of the conflicts between the classes. In the last analysis, the autonomy of the state and the bureaucrats comes from the cracks in this disarticulated set of organs, given the weakness of the classes to impose a single and coordinated direction on the state as a whole.

The majority of these works refers to the authoritarian period, when the tendency to transfer the political struggle to within the bureaucracy and thus to the executive branch expanded. But it is interesting to note that the same movement occurred in the democratic period between 1946 and 1964, which was analyzed by Draibe. The author shows that even under democratic rules, the executive maintained the extent of the power of the bureaucracy, its role as the promoter of industrialization and the heterogeneous and autonomous action of its bureaucrats, with parliamentarians being relegated to a position of spectators.

## AUTHORITARIANISM AND BUREAUCRATIC RINGS

Cardoso (1975) discusses the ways in which the interests of the dominant classes are articulated within the government apparatus, building on a critique of the above analytical perspective. This author marks the transition from the first to the second interpretative strand. Focused on the relations between the state and society in the context of the post-64 authoritarian regime, Cardoso formulates the concept of bureaucratic rings because he considers that the concept of the bourgeois state is not enough to explain the policies implemented by the state of the "Revolution of 64." In other words, to the extent that political conflict and power struggles cannot be deduced from the abstract determinations of class, they must be analyzed in their concrete forms of expression. Not only the parties, but state organizations are used by groups as means to the exercise of power.

This leads to rethinking the political system in terms of rings that cut horizontally through the public and the private realms. The relation between state and society is mediated by bureaucratic organizations. The interests of civil society thus gain space within the state. The bureaucratization of the axes of power and the correlated politicization of bureaucracies leads in turn to rethinking democracy in the sense of creating counterweights to the tendencies that arise from the nature of large bureaucratic organizations—manipulation, absence of transparency, lack of responsibility, and even a perverse form of authoritarianism (Cardoso, 1975: 182-85).

The rings are circles of information and pressure (therefore, of power) constituted as mechanisms to allow articulation between sectors of the state and sectors of the social classes. Under the protection of the political society, they ensure at the same time a cooptation mechanism to integrate within the decision-making positions of leadership members of the employee, businesspeople, and military classes who become participants of the political arena, but they join it *qua personae* and not as "representatives" of their class corporations. They are called "bureaucratic" precisely in order to underline where their headquarters need to be located in the state apparatus. This does not differ greatly from how the military regime allowed private interests to participate in the emergence of instruments of political and bureaucratic struggle within the state apparatus. According to Cardoso, the idea of corporativism is unsuitable for characterizing the relation between state and class because it presupposes something that does not exist in the rings, the organization of the classes and their representation, even though this takes place under state control (Cardoso, 1975: 208-09).

## PARTIES, BUREAUCRACY, AND THE POLITICAL SYSTEM

This second analytical strand considers bureaucracy to be a central player in the decision processes of economic policies in Brazil and approaches the bureaucratic phenomenon from its links with the structure of government, the party system, and clientelism. According to Campello de Souza (1976), the main author dealing with this problem, the dominant presence of bureaucrats in the decision-making arenas of public policies comes from the historical incapacity of political parties to assume their governmental attributions. In turn, this is related to the preponderant role the state exercised in the Brazilian political system from the 1930s and even in the 1946-1964 democratic period.

The centralization of the power of the authoritarian state in the period from 1930 to 1945, along with the creation of ways of representing society interests via state corporativism, meant that the corporate structures reduced the governmental function of the parties, while the growth in power of the bureaucratic apparatus responded to the logic of centralization. In other words, incapable of exercising their governmental functions and restricting themselves to the representative function, the parties were left to defend short term or particularistic interests that were concerned only with paying for the support they received and guaranteeing their power (Campello de Souza, 1976).

So, clientelism is not a specific characteristic of the Brazilian political system, or even a stage in its development, as often argued, but a way of controlling the political resources to be used by the parties, which are trying in this way to generate power for themselves and consolidate their position as institutions. Given the extent of clientelism in Brazil's political system, the essential thing is to explain the degree by which the Brazilian parties feed indiscriminately on clientelism, making it a strategy for acquiring and consolidating power.

In other words, as the parties were unable to consolidate their governmental function of preparing and defending government projects, the bureaucrats performed the role in the decision arenas that the parties did not. In turn, the exercise of the governmental function by the bureaucracy relieves the parties of this process, increasingly relegating them to the function of representatives of particularistic clienteles or groups in society and reinforcing their practice of merely reproducing positions of power—reelection and the raising of the necessary funds. As a result, a vicious circle keeps the parties further and further away from discussions about government programs and projects for the nation, making the bureaucracies the most important channels for transmitting the interests of society to within the state.

The most crucial political implication of this process, in which bureaucrats assume decision-making functions in the vacuum left by the parties, is the maintenance of the fragility of democratic institutions. As that author so lucidly stated, the development of a democracy depends on the institutionalization of a party system that is capable of "guaranteeing both the stability and effectiveness of the function of governing and the strength and authenticity of the function of representing various different interests" (Campello de Souza, 1976: 50).

Other authors had already presented elements that stated the argument of Campello de Souza. Examining the developmental economic policy in Brazil in the democratic period from 1947 to 1964, Nathaniel Leff, for example, observes a considerable autonomy of the government agencies and states the importance of the technicians vis-à-vis parties that were not there to aggregate interests and formulate broader projects for the country. Not only did Congress refuse to become involved in more complex subjects, but the technicians also had a monopoly on the formulation of economic policy, the context of which increasingly focused on problems like inflation, the balance of payments, and the need for public investment (Leff, 1977: 132-33).

Writing subsequently, Sola (1998) also shares the perception of Campello de Souza. When analyzing the weight of economic ideas on political decisions in the 1946-1964 period of democracy she emphasizes the role that technicians played in the state apparatus, despite the divergences or controversies that existed between their main representatives. Examining the role of nationalist technicians in the political system, that author also shows that they were not articulated via the parties but by other institutions (such as clubs, research centers, professional or corporate associations), which served also as recruitment channels for public sector employment positions.

The economic assistance office in the second Vargas government illustrates not only the role performed by the bureaucracy in the democratic period, but equally the way it functioned, insulated from Congress and party pressures. Responsible for preparing the most important projects of this government—Petrobras, Eletrobrás, the National Coal Plan, CAPES, the National Immigration Institute, the National Agrarian Policy Committee, the Industrial Development Commission, Banco do Nordeste do Brasil, and many others—the Assistance Office consisted of technicians of a nationalist orientation working under Rômulo Almeida, all of whom opposed the actions of the Brazil and United States Mixed Commission, which were taken to represent the interests of North-American companies, at the very heart of the Vargas government (D'Araújo, 1982: 136).

Therefore, here we reiterate not only the exclusion of Congress and the parties from major national decisions, but also their deligitimization in a period of democracy. Below, we examine the other authors of the strand that favors links between parties and the bureaucracy. We are grouping them into two different sub-groups, since they do not view this relationship in the same way. The first indicates bureaucratic insulation as a possible way of overcoming clientelism and avoiding interest groups taking over the bureaucracy, without raising the problem of its implications for democratic order. The second group, in contrast, emphasizes the problems that the insulation solution poses for democracy.

## Clientelism vs. Bureaucratic Insulation

Given the high degree of clientelism and patronage in the Brazilian political system, some authors hold or assume that to govern in a rational and efficient way it is necessary to delegate decisions to the bureaucrats and technicians. Concerned with characterizing what she defined as the dilemma of politics in Latin America, Geddes (1996) shows that from the point of view of the politicians, the insulation of the agencies to protect them against clientelistic pressures generates a dilemma. If, on the one hand, it makes it possible to achieve greater effectiveness in public policies, on the other it may lead to the government losing support in Congress. In other words, if a government is only guided by the logic of drumming up support in its recruitment for public administration, it may weaken its own capacity for shaping policies—or, at the opposite extreme, giving too much power to its technocrats may lead to its decision-making capacity being obstructed because of a lack of support in Congress.

Gouveia (1994) analyzes the power and the action logic of public bureaucrats in Brazil, taking as subject the group of technicians who took part in the Commission for Reorganizing Public Finance at the beginning of the 1980s. The author's hypothesis is that these bureaucrats, unlike the groups that propagate corporate interests, knew how to construct a self-protection system that was permanent, regardless of any party political changes. They fully identified with their situation as employees as well as with the ethos of public interest. As many entered the career after 1964, at a time when there was a depoliticization of society and an absence of public debate, they developed no strong ties with the parties. So this group, which was involved with the reform of the public financial institutions, was characterized by great external isolation, by strong internal loyalty, and by points of view formed in their professional practice.

Similarly, although using a rational choice theory approach, Geddes concludes that insulated agencies improve the performance and increase the capacity of the state. Insulation, or the constitution of "pockets of efficiency," was a necessary political resource for guaranteeing and maintaining political commitments, bearing in mind the economic development projects.

## Insulation and Democratic Deficit

Unlike Geddes and Gouveia, who do not discuss the power bases of the insulated bureaucracy and thus assume it is neutral, and imply advocacy of insulation as a strategy for increasing the efficiency of state action, Nunes (1997) and Diniz (1997) question the consequences and the extent of insulation. They argue that if insulation helps avoid personalism and patronage in the name of a more technical approach, it also reduces the scope for formulating policies, which means the exclusion of political parties, Congress, and popular demands.

Nunes shows that the introduction of modern capitalism in Brazil interacted with the creation of a syncretic institutional system, in which several different principles for structuring relations between society and political institutions operate—clientelism, corporativism, universalism of procedures, and bureaucratic insulation. The institutionalization of these four, he says, progressed gradually throughout the twentieth century, as state institutions were constituted, particularly those dedicated to social and economic intervention and the modern relations of citizenship.

Bureaucratic insulation was developed in the 1950s to promote national development, so that the administration of economic policies and strategic decisions ended up being carried out outside the parties. The culmination of this process came in the government of Juscelino Kubitschek (JK) with the creation of two main agencies linked to planning and carrying out the Targets' Plan: Executive Groups and The Development Council. Both agencies forged an alternative path to that of traditional bureaucracy and the universalism of procedures. Created by decree, the Executive Groups totally ignored the parties and Congress. Kubitschek insulated these agencies, while at the same time using clientelism and the promise of employment. He prevented the DASP from holding civil service public entrance exams, encouraged hiring people who had not passed these exams, and made clientelistic nominations.[9]

Diniz, referring to the work of Nunes, also deals with the concept of bureaucratic insulation and attributes a role to the parties that is similar to the one emphasized by Campello de Souza. Heavily involved with a political system marked by centralization and by a "bureaucratic monopoly over decisions, political parties became tributaries of state power, deprived as they were of governmental functions and therefore of the effective capacity to have an influence over the decision-making process" (Diniz, 1997: 19).

Diniz questions the impact of bureaucratic insulation on the basis of an analysis of the responses of the first two governments of the New Republic to the crises of the 1980s and 1990s—foreign debt crisis, inflation, redemocratization. Because of the high levels of voluntarism in the state elite, principally in the economic area, insulation not only creates a democratic problem (relieving Congress and the political parties of the main government decisions), but also a problem of governmental effectiveness. The capacity of the government to take decisions unilaterally does not coincide with its capacity to articulate and negotiate the costs and gains of the measures taken towards economic restructuring and state reform.

Analyzing the democratic transition in Brazil under the New Republic, Sola (1998) also emphasizes the confinement of the decision-making arenas when faced with the pressures of competitive politics, the growing opacity of interests there represented and the high level of decision-making autonomy enjoyed by the economists in power. Referring also to the democratic period, Loureiro (1997) reinforces this perception, showing the monopoly that certain bureaucratic segments had over decisions in the area of macroeconomic policy. This monopoly refers not only to the career employees working in the ministries of Finance and Planning and the Central Bank, but above all to the group of economists who were renowned in university circles and the financial markets who were recruited temporarily for commissioned posts in the top echelon of the federal Executive.

In short, the economic bureaucracies in democratic governments also acted as policymakers in decision-making arenas that were restricted and insulated from the participation of the parties and Congress and therefore

---

9. Also in the JK government the way the executive or parallel administration groups functioned is marked by the undisputed hegemony of the technicians vis-à-vis other political players and their autonomy vis-à-vis Congress. Hence the observations of Luciano Martins about them: "Kubitschek himself declares that the technicians had (during his government) absolute freedom to prepare the plan. The available data seem to indicate that technocracy not only represented the most important role in the preparation and performance of the Targets' Plan but that it managed to have the political controls to which it had been previously submitted relaxed" (Martins, 1974: 427).

"protected" (by presidential backing or by a strong minister) from broader interests in the political spectrum.[10]

## FINAL CONSIDERATIONS

The arguments and authors discussed above point out the importance of bureaucracy as a fundamental player in the decision-making process in Brazil even when the authors differ in regard to the source of bureaucratic power. If, in the first strand, the power of the bureaucracy comes from the socio-economic interests it represents within the state apparatus, in the second its power derives above all from the strategic decision of the heads of the Executive to choose bureaucrats to fill management positions in the public service, with the fundamental objective of guaranteeing that they direct and control the administrative apparatus. In both cases the bureaucrats are elevated to positions of great political and administrative power— and this situation generates the two situations indicated by the literature we analyzed: the taking over of sectors of the state by the socio-economic interests that the bureaucracy "represents" and the potential the bureaucrats have of becoming autonomous, relative to the politicians that named them and to interest groups themselves.

So, this analysis refers back to discussions about the role that the bureaucracy plays in the Brazilian government. Generally speaking, debates about the functioning of our political system indicate that its main characteristics—presidentialism, a multiparty state, and federalism—form part of what has been appropriately called coalition-based presidentialism (Abranches, 1988: 21-22).

In addition to the proportional representation electoral system, the fragmented nature of the Brazilian multiparty system has created a situation in which the political party of the President never manages to obtain, in isolation, a majority of seats in Congress, thus demanding alliances with several other parties in order to govern.

---

10. A report by a journalist who was behind the scenes when the Cruzado Plan was prepared in the Sarney government in 1986 reveals just how far the parties and members of Congress were from the decision-making arenas of economic policies: "Various circumstances suggested to Ulisses Guimarães (then president of the PMDB, the main party supporting the government) that it would be convenient to adopt an attitude of prudence and caution. Although there were many members of the PMDB among the "fathers of reform" the truth is that until the night before there was no party articulation supporting their actions within government. All the party agencies and organs were left on the sidelines; how could they assume a ready-made proposal that had been set up under these circumstances and that, because of its technical level and nature of something new, was difficult to understand and evaluate" (Sardenberg, 1987: 289).

If the view of coalition-based presidentialism is practically consensual, the same is not true with regard to the effects of these institutional features on the dynamic of the political system. For some authors, this combination is problematic or even "explosive" and generates enormous difficulties for the president when it comes to governing—in other words, a serious state of ungovernability (Abranches, 1988; Mainwaring, 1993). Other authors reach an opposite interpretation. Coalition-based presidentialism in Brazil provides the president with institutional resources—the authority to legislate by means of provisional measures and to control the budget—which allow him to concentrate power and thus guarantee governability. Following the latter interpretation, the regulatory norms of Congress, by emphasizing the role of party leaders, are also guided by the same logic of concentrating power (Figueiredo and Limongi, 1999). Other authors argue in favor of the governability theory of the Brazilian political system, not because of the concentration of power, but due to the continuous negotiations between the executive and legislative branches, which include negotiations about occupying key positions in the federal bureaucracy.[11]

The view that the current institutional characteristics of the Brazilian political system do not prevent governability, provided the Executive and Congress have the capacity to negotiate with each other in order to construct coalitions, helps our understanding of the articulation between bureaucracy and politics. The bureaucratic apparatus performs a decisive role in the functioning of politics since it constitutes the material basis for the exercise of government, not just in the formulation and performance of public policies (as in any contemporary society), but also because its positions are used as exchange currency for guaranteeing congressional support.

However, as has already been pointed out by Geddes (1996), the use of a large number of the administration positions as exchange currency by the government to obtain support in Congress creates a crucial dilemma for the President. Granting positions to coalition parties leads to decreased control over part of the administrative apparatus, but this control is necessary for carrying out government policies and programs. If, on the contrary, the President favors a strategy of non-negotiation or the insulation of bureau-

---

11. With regard to the debate about how the Brazilian political system functions, see the important work on systematization by Vicente Palermo, who provides four different interpretations: a) the theory of "ungovernability" by concentrating power; b) the theory of governability by fragmenting power; c) the theory of governability by concentrating power; and d) the theory of governability by negotiation, with which he identifies (Palermo, 2000).

cratic positions under pressure from the parties, this may result in a decision-paralysis situation caused by congressional non-collaboration.

Historically, democratic governments in Brazil have tried to get around this dilemma by using different strategies. In the 1950s, Vargas and Kubitschek segmented the bureaucratic apparatus by separation, having on one side the ministries and positions that were open to negotiation and on the other the "protected" or insulated areas—such as the economic development agencies, which became known as "islands of excellence" (D'Araújo, 1982; Benevides, 1976; Lafer, 1970).

In more recent times, the Cardoso government, in addition to segmentation of the bureaucracy, also used the strategy of naming, for those ministries granted to parties from his support base in Congress, an executive secretary (or vice-minister) he trusted or who was loyal to the central nucleus of government constituted by the ministry of finance. The mission of this top employee, also known in the slang of the time in the esplanade of ministries in Brasília as "the president's man," was to monitor the decisions taken by the ministers who were indicated as a result of the party coalition agreements, thereby guaranteeing that they did not move too far away from the direction established by the governmental nucleus (Loureiro and Abrucio, 1999). In the Lula government the activities of internal control, put into effect in the different ministries under the command of the Federal Control Department of the Office of the Comptroller General, can be understood as being another type of mechanism. Through this office the President can get around the risk of his government projects becoming unviable because of the negotiation of positions in the bureaucratic apparatus in order to obtain political support (Olivieri, 2010b).

The above analysis suggests new lines of research on the theme of relations between politics and the bureaucracy in Brazil.

First, the power of the bureaucracy has never been usurped from politicians, who granted it even in authoritarian regimes. In other words, politicians, however much they reinforce the decision power of specific bureaucratic agencies, always make bureaucracy dependent on political authority. Therefore, we cannot talk about technocracy in the strict sense of the word; it is enough to say a type of power that derives exclusively from technical competence or from specialized knowledge.[12]

The fundamental point is to understand the nature and the reach of the power of the bureaucrats in the general structure of the state, especially that coming from the main functions of the Executive Branch or the Legislative

Branch, from the relationship between both and their links with the parties and the interest groups. In short, understanding bureaucracy in Brazil as the policymaker is inseparable from debates about the hypertrophy of the Executive relative to the Legislature and the weakness of the governmental function of the political parties.

Studies that analyze the relationship between bureaucracy and the political system in democratic periods, especially post-1988, are rare. The literature is generally full of material indicating how politics becomes confined within the state in authoritarian regimes, in other words, disputes for power projects become internalized within the bureaucratic apparatus and bureaucrats play a predominant role in defining and implementing such projects. So, in asking for more research in this area, one of the inferences that can be drawn from this analysis is the following: in the post-1988 democracy period also, fundamental decisions about public policies are in the hands of the executive branch and the bureaucracy is still its main policymaker, since the central characteristic of Brazilian political parties still seems to be an incapacity to exercise the functions of government.

Another topic that merits additional studies refers to the possible connivance, even in democratic times, of Congress, the parties and organized society with the expansion of the power of the bureaucracy. It is perhaps even possible to talk of the existence of an inclination in favor of the power of the bureaucracy on the part of political players, either because of their weakness (their institutional and/or political incapacity to oppose the decisions of the Executive) or because of their interest in creating particularistic, clientelist or corporativist ways of influencing the decisions of the bureaucracy and the executive branch of government.

Finally, but no less relevant, the time is ripe for new research into the power of the bureaucracy and its relations with politics in Brazil to be carried out in other areas of public policy, especially in the social policy area.

---

12. For the discussion about technocracy see the classic study by Meynaud (1964) and on the role of technicians in the decision-making process in Brazil in the 1946-64 democratic period, see Sola (1998). Bresser-Pereira (1972) considers techno-bureaucracy or technocracy as the new dominant social class in the new way of producing that would succeed capitalism, characterized by the predominance of technique and by statism.

# 7

# POLITICAL REFORM:
# A "NEVER-ENDING STORY"

## David Fleischer

*Abstract: After analyzing the attempts at political reform during the presidency of Fernando Henrique Car-
doso (1995-2002), the further attempts at adopting such reforms during the term of President Luiz Inácio
Lula da Silva (2003-2010) are examined. The reforms adopted during the Cardoso period were: a constitutional amendment in 1997 allowing one consecutive reelection of the president, governors, and mayors; a 30%
quota for women candidates on the PR lists for deputy; the adoption of electronic voting machines; and blank
ballots being counted as null votes in elections as of 1998. Two examples of judicialization of politics were
examined where the Supreme Electoral Court (TSE) and Supreme Federal Court (STF) imposed changes in
election rules. In March 2002, the judiciary determined that election coalitions be verticalized. In 2007,
"party loyalty" was imposed that prohibited politicians from switching parties after they had been elected. Traditionally, these reform "packages" are presented in odd years because the long election recess in even years
reduces the congressional calendar. Thus, it is possible that yet another attempt at political reform might be
attempted in 2011.*

In May 2001, the Bildner Center convened a symposium to examine Brazil's
reforms since the mid 1990s. The papers presented at this meeting were collected in a volume published in 2004 (Font and Spanakos, 2004). My chapter
in that volume examined Brazil's progress on "political reform" that I then
defined as [President] Cardoso's "missing link"—indicating that he had not
been able to implement certain reforms with the result that he was unable to
obtain the approval of some of his other proposals (Fleischer, 2004a).

Now, eight and a half years after my analysis in 2001, I propose to address this question again—that is, what, if any, political reforms have been achieved during President Luiz Inácio Lula da Silva's (Lula) nearly seven years in office (2003-2009)? The answer is "not much progress achieved"— thus the subtitle of this paper—"A never-ending story."

This paper will address "political reforms" of Brazil's election and political party legislation, but will not deal with the broader topic of "reform of the State" (Abranches, 1996; Seixas and Proença, 2005)—that involves the relations among the three powers of government (Vianna, 2002); institutional reforms, such as the Judiciary Reform approved in 2004 (Renault and Bottini, 2005; Sadek, 2002 and 2004; Tavares Filho, 2005); federalism relations; tax and fiscal reforms; reform of labor laws; among others.

## POLITICAL REFORMS, 1995-2002

In my 2004 book chapter (Fleischer, 2004a), I catalogued several political reforms that had been enacted during the Presidency of Fernando Henrique Cardoso (1995-2002). The first and perhaps the most important change (the Reelection Amendment) was approved in 1997 and allowed Cardoso and the 27 governors (elected in 1994) to stand for immediate reelection in 1998 (Fleischer, 1998). In sequence, this change allowed the Mayors elected in 1996 to stand for reelection in 2000 (Fleischer, 2002; Viana and Coelho, 2008).

In 1995, Congress approved a 20% quota for women candidates on party lists for Brazil's open list proportional elections (for federal and state deputy, and city council). Because of Brazil's open-list PR system this change had very little impact on the number of women elected to the Chamber of Deputies. Actually, in 1998, fewer women were elected deputy than in 1994. Since then, this quota was increased to 30%, but with negligible results (Araujo, 2001).

In the 1996 municipal elections, the TSE (Tribunal Superior Eleitoral - Supreme Electoral Court) used a new system of electronic voting machines instead of traditional paper ballots for the first time in about 40 towns and cities. The result was considered successful and was expanded in the 1998 general elections to include about 60% of the electorate and was used exclusively in five states—Brasília, Rio de Janeiro, Alagoas, Roraima, and Amapá (Silva, 2002).

In August 1997, Congress decided that blank votes for deputy would be considered "null" [not included in the total of "valid" votes], as in majority elections (President, Governors, Senators, and Mayors). Since 1946, blank ballots had been included in the total of "valid votes" and thus "inflated" the vote total for the calculation of the election quotient. Analyzing the results of the 1994 elections, most party leaders decided that this change would have little impact in 1998, and might even facilitate the reelection of their deputies, because they figured that without the blank votes, the total "valid" vote would be less and thus the election quotient in each state would be smaller. The election quotient in each state is determined by dividing the total "valid" vote by the number of seats (deputies) representing that state. If the total valid vote were reduced (by excluding the blank ballots), the smaller total would produce a smaller quotient.

However, these "projections" did not take into consideration two important factors: (1) from one election to another (four years), Brazil's electorate expands by about 10%; and (2) because of extensive use of the new electronic voting machines in 1998, the number of blank and null votes declined significantly (Table 7-1). The result was a larger valid vote total in 1998 than in 1994, and thus larger elections quotients in all states.

The results of the 1998 elections for the five states that used the new electronic voting machines exclusively were compared to those in 1994 (paper ballots). This comparison clearly showed the impact of these machines. As seen in Table 7-1, the proportion of null and blank ballots was reduced considerably and as a result the valid vote and the election quotients were much larger.

The increase in the total valid vote varied between 21.87% in Alagoas to 53.20% in Roraima. The latter was a federal territory transformed into a state by the 1988 Constitution and received considerable migration in the 1990s. The more typical states—Rio de Janeiro and Brasília—had increases of 32.95% and 37.49%, respectively. As a result, the election quotients in all of the five states (with the same number of seats in 1994 and 1998) increased, instead of decreasing, as predicted by party analysts in 1997. The total null and blank votes in these five states was 3,950,199 in 1994, but was reduced to 1,061,832 in 1998. With the electronic voting machines in 1998, it became easier to vote for candidates rather than to vote null or blank—because the voter received no instructions regarding null or blank votes. In 1994, with paper ballots it was "easy" to scribble the ballot (null), or just deposit it in the ballot box (blank).

Each electronic voting machine was outfitted with a small color TV screen and a keyboard based on a touch-tone phone. Once the voter's ID was verified by the poll workers, the system was opened for him/her to vote, office by

TABLE 7-1. Impact of Electronic Voting on Elections, 1994 versus 1998

| Year | Amapá | Roraima | Alagoas | Rio | Brasília |
|---|---|---|---|---|---|
| 1994 | | | | | |
| Electorate | 197,171 | 119,888 | 1,156,990 | 9,129,373 | 1,064,247 |
| Abstention | 54,790 | 26,554 | 177,923 | 1,674,130 | 147,504 |
| Votes Cast | 142,281 | 93,334 | 979067 | 7,455,243 | 916,743 |
| Nulls | 22, 829 | 10,913 | 274,862 | 2,106,195 | 190,140 |
| Blanks | 20,599 | 7,641 | 206,617 | 1,009,518 | 100,885 |
| Valid Vote* | 119, 552 | 82,421 | 704,205 | 5,349,048 | 726,603 |
| Seats | 08 | 08 | 09 | 46 | 08 |
| PR Quotient | 14,944 | 10,302.6 | 78,245 | 116,283.7 | 90,825.4 |
| 1998 | | | | | |
| Electorate | 213,289 | 170,620 | 1,383,600 | 9,971,830 | 1,267,925 |
| Abstention | 28,941 | 36,897 | 390,465 | 2,017,061 | 196,417 |
| Votes Cast | 184,348 | 133,723 | 993,135 | 7,954,769 | 1,071,508 |
| Nulls | 3,844 | 4,097 | 65,099 | 420,245 | 31,078 |
| Blanks | 3,102 | 3,345 | 69,792 | 423,225 | 41,447 |
| Valid Vote# | 177,402 | 126,272 | 858,244 | 7,11,298 | 998,983 |
| Seats | 08 | 08 | 09 | 46 | 08 |
| PR Quotient | 22,175 | 15,784 | 95,350.4 | 154,593.3 | 124,872.9 |

*Valid vote in 1994= Votes cast minus Nulls

# Valid Vote in 1998= Votes cast minus Nulls minus Blanks

Differences 1994/1998

| | | | | | |
|---|---|---|---|---|---|
| Electorate | +08.17% | +42.32% | +16.38% | +09.23% | +19.14% |
| Abstention | -47.18% | +38.95% | +119.46% | +20.48% | +33.16 |
| Votes Cast | +29.48% | +43.27% | +01.44% | +06.70% | +16.88 |
| Nulls | -83.16% | -62.46% | -76.32% | -80.05% | -83.66% |
| Blanks | -84.94% | -56.11% | -66.22% | -58.08% | -58.92% |
| Valid Vote | +48.39% | +53.20% | +21.87% | +32.95% | +37.49% |
| PR Quotient | +7,231 | +5,481.4 | +17,115.4 | +38,309.6 | +34,047.5 |

1994: Total Nulls + Blanks = 3,950,199          1998: Total Nulls + Blanks = 1,061,832

*Nationwide:* 61,111,922 (57.6%) voters used electronic voting machines in 1998.

Source: Fleischer, 2006.

office. Once the voter keyed in the four- or five-digit code for a candidate, his/her photo popped up on the screen together with the candidate's name and party label, and the machine asked "Do you wish to vote for this candidate?" If this candidate was the voter's choice, he/she would push the green "Confirm" button and then proceed to the next office. Usually, voters take a "crib sheet" along with the code numbers for their pre-selected candidates.

These electronic voting machines were used exclusively in the 2000 municipal elections which were the first immediate reelection opportunity for Mayors. Of the 3,448 Mayors who ran for reelection, 2,006 were returned to office (58.2%). In 1998, 22 of the 27 governors ran for reelection and 15

(68.2%) were successful. Three of the latter who were victorious on the second round runoff reversed the first round result (Fleischer, 1998).

## POLITICAL REFORMS, 2002-09

Several publications have focused on "political reform" during the Lula period, since 2003 (Avelar and Cintra, 2007; Avritzer and Anastásia, 2006; Benevides, Vannuchi, and Kerche, 2003; Rennó, 2007; Soares and Rennó, 2006; Teixeira, 2009; Viana and Nascimento, 2008).

### Judicialization

This period witnessed several "reforms" in the rules regarding Brazil's elections that were determined [decided] by the Judiciary—changes not enacted by Congress—and thus are called the "Judicialization of Politics" (Ferraz Junior, 2008; Taylor and da Ros, 2008; Vianna, 1999; Vianna, Baumann, and Salles, 2007).

### *Verticalization*

The first of these measures imposed by the Judiciary, was TSE Resolution 21002 in February 26, 2002 that verticalized election coalitions. The Supreme Electoral Court decided that coalitions among political parties in Brazil were *exdrúxulas* [odd, extravagant, unusual]—or "incongruent" comparing the composition of presidential and state-level party coalitions. That is to say, parties in a certain presidential coalition might oppose each other in some states, while parties in opposite presidential coalitions might be united in the same state-level coalition. This TSE Resolution obliged the presidential coalitions to be replicated in each of the 27 states, with no "incongruent" party alliances.

Although Congress attempted to approve a Constitutional Amendment reversing this decision, this was only possible in 2006 and so will only take effect for the 2010 general elections. Thus, this rule applied to both the 2002 and 2006 elections.

As seen in Table 7-2, the most visible effect of this verticalization was that the number of coalitions at the state level doubled—from 72 and 79 in 1994 and 1998 to 140 in 2002 and 2006 (Fleischer, 2006). However, this "new rule" did not inhibit Lula's victory in the presidential election nor the PT (Worker's Party) electing the largest number of federal deputies (91 versus 59

TABLE 7-2. Profile of State-Level Coalitions in 1994, 1998, 2002, and 2006

|  | 1994 | 1998 | 2002 | 2006 |
|---|---|---|---|---|
| Coalitions | 72 | 79 | 140 | 140 |
| Coalitions per state |  |  |  |  |
| 2 | 15 | 11* | 0 | 0 |
| 3 | 8 | 11 | 0 | 1 |
| 4 | 2 | 3 | 8 | 7 |
| 5 | 2 | 1 | 11 | 10 |
| More than 5 | 0 | 1 | 8** | 9** |
| Average | 2.97 | 2.93 | 5.19 | 5.19 |

*Notes:*\*In 1998, Acre had only one coalition, and the PFL, PPB, and PMDB ran separate slates. \*\*The Rio de Janeiro had eight coalitions in 2002, and nine in 2006.
*Source*: Fleischer, 2006.

in 1998). On the other hand, the PSDB (Brazilian Social Democratic Party) was reduced from 99 to 65 deputies and the PFL (Partido da Frente Liberal, Liberal Front Party) from 105 to 76 (Fleischer, 2007a: 310-11).

The PFL had been allied with the PSDB in the victorious Cardoso coalitions in 1994 and 1998, but broke with the PSDB in 2002 and did not participate in any presidential coalition, and thus was free to join the most advantageous coalitions at the state level. However, in 2006, the PSDB and PFL again formed a presidential coalition and were subject to the verticalization rules. In 2006, several political parties that had participated in presidential coalitions in 2002, decided to abstain in order to enhance their results at the state level—PMDB (Brazilian Democratic Movement Party), PSB (Brazilian Socialist Party), PTB (Labor Party), PL (Liberal Party), PP (Progressive Party), and PPS (Socialist People's Party). The smaller and medium sized parties were fearful of falling below the 5% threshold barrier that was in effect in 2006 (Castro, 2006; Fleischer, 2007a: 334-36).

Table 7-3 below shows how some of these parties maintained their state level alliances without participating in presidential coalitions. In 2006, the PSDB-PFL presidential coalition was replicated in only 13 states, while the PT (Worker's Party)-PCdoB (Communist Party) presidential coalition was replicated in all but two states. The traditional Lula coalition partner (PSB) did not participate in any presidential coalition, but joined in 15 PT-PCdoB coalitions at the state level. The former PCB (Brazilian Communist Party) changed its name to PPS as well as its political posture in 1991 and formed coalitions on the Right with the PSDB-PFL in 11 states, but did not join its former "comrades" (PT-PCdoB) in any states. Finally, the PMDB "went alone" in 2006, and was thus "free" to join any coalition at the state level in 2006—PSDB-PFL in 7 states, PT-PCdoB in 5 states, and "alone" in the other 15 states.

TABLE 7-3. Configuration of Presidential and State-Level Coalitions in 2006

| Presidential Coalitions | State-Level Coalitions |
|---|---|
| PSDB + PFL | in 13 states |
| PT + PCdoB | in 25 states |
| "Independent" Parties | |
| PSB + PT + PCdoB | in 15 states |
| PPS + PT +PCdoB | in zero states |
| PMDB + PSDB +PFL | in 7 states |
| PMDB + PT + PCdoB | in 5 states |
| PMDB "alone" | in 15 states |

*Source*: Fleischer, 2006.

## Party Loyalty

A second exercise in "Judicialization of Politics" was imposed by the Judiciary in March 2007 regarding "party loyalty." Brazil has used the worst variant of proportional representation since 1945—the open list. The parties (and coalitions) organize their lists of candidates for deputy state by state in no predetermined order. The voters have two alternatives, either vote for the party or vote for one name on one of these lists—and usually some 95% choose to vote for a name. This system produces some aberrations and is very conducive to bloc voting by segments—religions, ethnic groups, labor unions, and other corporative groups that instruct "their" voters to concentrate their votes on one or two names in each state. The open-list PR system produces a weak party system (Nicolau, 2006b; A.M. Santos, 2006a; Viana and Coelho, 2008).

Traditionally, this system has been subject to frequent party switching by deputies as the President attracts politicians into his government support bloc in Congress (Melo, 2004; Reis, 2007; A.M. Santos, 2006b; F. Santos, 2006; Santos Filho and Miguel, 2008). This "party migration" following both the October 2002 and 2006 elections deprived the PFL of a simple majority over the PMDB in the Senate resulting from the elections—and also deprived it of the prerogative of electing the president of the Upper House.

As seen in Table 7-4, following the October 6, 2002 election, the PMDB declined from 23 to 19 senators, while the PFL delegation expanded from 18 to 20. However, as of February 1, 2003, the PMDB gained one senator and the PFL lost two. Thus, the PMDB elected Senator José Sarney (PMDB-Amapá) President of the Senate for a second time.

TABLE 7-4. Senate and Chamber "Party Migration," 2002-03 and 2006-07

| Party | Sequence 2002->2003 | | | Sequence 2006 -> 2007 | | |
|---|---|---|---|---|---|---|
| | August | Elected in October | Sworn in February | August | Elected in October | Sworn in February |
| **Senate** | | | | | | |
| PMDB | 23 | 19 | 20 | 20 | 15 | 20 |
| PFL | 18 | 20 | 18 | 16 | 18 | 17 |
| PSDB | 14 | 11 | 12 | 16 | 15 | 13 |
| PT | 8 | 14 | 14 | 12 | 11 | 11 |
| PTB | 4 | 3 | 4 | 4 | 4 | 5 |
| PDT | 5 | 5 | 4 | 4 | 5 | 4 |
| PSB | 3 | 3 | 3 | 2 | 3 | 3 |
| PPB/PP* | 2 | 1 | 0 | 0 | 1 | 1 |
| Other | 3 | 5 | 6 | 7 | 9 | 7 |
| TOTAL | 81 | 81 | 81 | 81 | 81 | 81 |
| **Chamber** | | | | | | |
| PMDB | 87 | 74 | 69 | 78 | 89 | 91 |
| PFL | 97 | 84 | 76 | 64 | 65 | 62 |
| PSDB | 95 | 71 | 65 | 59 | 66 | 63 |
| PT | 58 | 91 | 91 | 81 | 83 | 82 |
| PTB | 33 | 26 | 45 | 53 | 22 | 20 |
| PDT | 16 | 21 | 17 | 20 | 24 | 23 |
| PPB/PP* | 53 | 49 | 44 | 50 | 41 | 42 |
| PL/PR** | 27 | 27 | 29 | 37 | 23 | 34 |
| PSB | 17 | 22 | 19 | 27 | 27 | 27 |
| PPS | 12 | 15 | 18 | 15 | 22 | 16 |
| PCdoB | 10 | 12 | 12 | 12 | 13 | 13 |
| Other | 8 | 21 | 18 | 27 | 38 | 40 |
| TOTAL | 513 | 513 | 513 | 513 | 513 | 513 |

*Notes:* *At the end of 2006, the PPB changed its name to PP. **At the end of 2006, the PL incorporated Prona and changed its name to PR.
*Source:* Fleischer, 2007a.

After the October 1, 2006 election, the PMDB was reduced from 20 to 15 senators, while the PFL increased from 16 to 18. Thus, in theory, the PFL should have elected the Senate President on February 1, 2007. However, in the interim between the election and the seating of the new senators, the PFL lost one senator and was reduced to 17, while the PMDB gained five "migrants," and its delegation again reached 20 senators and was able to reelect the Senate President—Sen. Renan Calheiros (PMDB-Alagoas).

Greatly dissatisfied at having "lost" the presidency of the Upper House twice (in 2003 and 2007) due to "party migrations," in late February 2007, the PFL filed a brief at the TSE regarding the problem of party switching—if the mandate of those elected "belonged" to the party that elected them, or whether the mandate was "personal"—the deputy or senator would be free to migrate and take their respective mandate with them to the new party.

The TSE responded quite quickly (by a 6-to-1 decision) to the PFL "complaint" on March 27, 2007 via Resolution 22610/2007—that, "yes" the mandate belonged to the party that had elected the deputy or senator and that those who switched parties after they were elected would lose their respective mandate. This new jurisprudence "regulating" the problem of "party infidelity" would be adjudicated by the TSE.

It took six months for this TSE decision to be confirmed by the Supreme Court (STF) on October 25, 2007. In the meantime, Congress could have approved legislation regulating the question of "party loyalty," but was unwilling or unable to do so. The only modification imposed by the STF was that the TSE resolution could not be retroactive, i.e. this decision would only apply for those who changed parties after March 27, 2007, and should not be applied for those who switched after the October 2006 elections and before that date. In the suits filed by parties who lost mandates through party "migration," as of October 2009, only one deputy lost his mandate via TSE decision.

However, the election law deadline stated that any person planning to run for office in the October 3, 2010 elections must confirm his/her party membership one year prior to the election—or by October 3, 2009. Because many politicians planning to run for reelection (or other offices) in 2010 traditionally seek a new party that offers more "advantages" just prior to this deadline—in September 2009, four senators and 32 federal deputies changed parties, and in the process "demoralized" this TSE attempt at "judicialization of politics" to regulate the question of "party loyalty" (Bragon and Cabral, 2009).

## Reform Attempts in the Chamber

During the Lula government (2003-2010), three attempts were made to approve changes in Brazil's election laws—in 2003, 2007, and 2009 (Barreto and Fleischer, 2008; Caiado, 2007; Câmara dos Deputados, 2007; Fleischer, 2004b and 2004c; Klein, 2007; Teixeira, 2009).

In 1995, the Senate took the lead and established a temporary committee to study the question of "political reform" and produce concrete suggestions to this end. This committee produced several bills and proposed several constitutional amendments, some of which were actually approved by the Senate. The committee report organized by its reporter, Senator Sérgio Machado (PSDB-Ceará), was released in 1998 (Machado, S., 1998).

In early 2003, it was the Chamber of Deputies' turn to initiate a reform proposal and a special committee was constituted, with Deputy Alexandre Cardoso (PSB-Rio de Janeiro) as Chair and Deputy Ronaldo Caiado (PFL-Goiás) as Reporter. After many sessions and hearings—plus an international seminar organized by the Brazilian Political Science Association and the Chamber of Deputies on June 3-5, 2003—this committee finally voted out its report on December 3, 2003 in the form of *Projeto de Lei* (PL, legislative bill) 2679/03.

This PL was perhaps the best of the three proposals produced in the Chamber (Santos, E.C., 2004a), and had five components:

*Election System.* Brazil's election system would continue to use proportional representation, but with a closed list. Each party or coalition of parties would have to elaborate its list of candidates state-by-state in a predetermined rank order, and the voter would then vote for a party list, and no longer be able to select an individual candidate. The manner by which each party would elaborate its respective list was not detailed in this proposal—party executive committee, state party convention, or by a primary among its registered voters (Nicolau, 2006b and 2007). However, the proposal detailed the "preference order" (by individual vote totals in 2002) for inclusion on this pre-ordered list: first, candidates who had been elected in 2002; second, alternates who had become permanent deputies; third, alternates who served at least six months; and fourth, candidates who were elected in 2002 but switched parties. This fourth criterion was rejected by both the PTB and the PL; they had received the largest number of "migrants" after the 2002 elections.

*Party "Federations."* This quite "novel" idea would have replaced party election coalitions that were always dissolved immediately after each election. A "federation of parties" would be formed to elect deputies, but after the election, the federation would be required to remain together for three years (after the 2006 elections) and only be dissolved in September 2009, one year prior to the next (2010) election. This measure would have resolved three "problems:" it (a) would not have required the prohibition of coalitions in the PR elections; (b) would have preserved the identity of the small and micro parties within each federation; and (c) would have eliminated the problem of "migration" of deputies after each election.

*Party Loyalty*, as a result of the proposed reform, party loyalty would not be as rigid as during the military regime, but "migration" of deputies would be limited by the effects of the closed-list and party federations.

*Exclusion Clause.* This proposal set the "exclusion barrier" at 2% of the valid vote and the election of at least one deputy in five states. This would not have been a "rigid" barrier (as the 5% barrier in Germany), but parties not surpassing this barrier would not be allowed to "function" within the Chamber (could not have a leadership position, nor assign deputies to committees). The intent was to force mergers of these excluded parties with larger parties. In 2006, nine parties were not able to surpass this 2% barrier.

*Campaign Finance.* The proposed reform would have made campaign finance exclusively "public" and private campaign contributions would have been prohibited, both by persons and firms (Fleischer, 2004c). The total amount to be distributed among the parties would have been R$966 million (US$322 million)—R$7.00 (US$2.33) for each of the 138 million registered voters. The distribution would have been as follows:

1. 1% divided equally among all parties registered at the TSE
1% of R$966 million = R$9.66 million

2. 14% divided equally among the parties represented in the Chamber
14% of R$966 million = R$135.14 million

3. 85% proportionate to the size of each party delegation of deputies elected in October 2002
85% of R$966 million = R$821.1 million

This mechanism would have penalized the "small" and micro parties, and especially the middle sized parties, such as the PTB and the PL that had benefited from the "migration" of deputies after the October 2002 elections.

As an example, this calculation is applied to a "micro" party (PSD) and the largest party (PT) in the 2002 elections—considering that 30 parties might exist in 2006 and that by then 15 parties might be represented in the Chamber.

PSD (elected 4 federal deputies in 2002)
1/30 of R$9.66 million = R$322,000.00
1/15 of R$135.24 million = R$9,016,000.00
4/513 of R$821.10 million = R$6,402,000.00
                    TOTAL = R$15,740,000.00

PT (elected 91 federal deputies in 2002)
1/30 of R$9.66 million = R$322,000.00
1/15 of R$135.24 million = R$9,016,000.00
91/513 of R$821.10 million = R$145,653,000.00

$$TOTAL = R\$154,911,000.00$$

The total for each party would be allocated as follows:

- 30% for the national administration of the party if it were in a presidential coalition,

- 20% for the national administration of the party if it were not involved in a presidential coalition,

- The rest (70% or 80%) would go to the state sections of each party, with 50% proportionate to the number of voters (in each state) and 50% proportionate to the size of the party's delegation in the respective state legislature.

This distribution would have funded the party's campaign in each of the 27 states (governor, senator, and state/federal deputies).

The vote by this 38-member committee that approved PL 2679/03 was 26 favorable, 11 against, and one abstaining. One PFL and one PMDB deputy voted against this proposal as well as the three deputies (each) representing the PTB, PP, and PL. The single PPS deputy abstained. The PSDB, PT, PMDB, and PFL deputies were cohesive in favor of this reform—but those from the PTB, PP, and PL felt "threatened." In 2004, the leaders of these three government bloc parties plus the PDT (Democratic Labor Party) refused to sign the "urgency" request for the deliberation of this proposal and threatened to adopt obstruction tactics if the PT leadership insisted on its deliberation. Because these three parties had 151 deputies in the government bloc, PL 2679/03 was never brought to the floor of the Chamber for deliberation. In July 2003, there were "signs" that the bloc of evangelical deputies was not favorable to this reform (Braga, 2003; Cruvinel, 2003).

Jairo Nicolau (2004) remembered that "public campaign finance with fiscal monitoring and penalties is the best way to reduce scandals" and misuse of campaign funds. On the other hand, Wanderley Guilherme dos Santos assumed a radical position against this reform, especially the "closed list" that he felt would limit the freedom of the voter to choose his/her [individual] candidate:

> The closed list imprisons the voter, who today—with the open list system—can vote for the party list (the party or individual candidate). This proposal does not allow the voter to choose his/her representative, allowing the usurpers to decide the candidates that this vote will elect. They say that this will elevate the moral paragon of Brazil's democracy (W. G. Santos, 2004).

Following the municipal elections in 2004, discussions regarding political reforms should have returned to the agenda of the Chamber. However the Lower House became preoccupied with its own internal scandals—the so-called mensalão involving a "monthly allowance" in return for deputies' votes, and the scandal that forced the resignation of the then Chamber President, Deputy Severino Cavalcanti (PP-Pernambuco) in September 2007.

*Threshold Barrier.* Because the Chamber was "distracted" in 2005, the "threshold barrier" that had been part of the election legislation since 1995 was not postponed [again] and went into effect for the 2006 elections. This added to the "anxiety" of some middle sized political parties that had already decided not to join any presidential coalition in 2006, in order to have more freedom to join diverse state-level coalitions—with the objective of surpassing the "stiff" 5% barrier.

Of the 21 parties that elected at least one deputy in 2006, only seven parties were able to surpass the 5% threshold barrier, twelve parties polled more than 2% of the valid vote, and seven had less than 1%. Had the "rigid" German threshold barrier been applied to these election results, the seven parties that surpassed the barrier could elect 395 deputies and the other 118 seats, "elected" by the other 14 parties, would have been redistributed among the seven parties (Fleischer, 2007b). Thus, many analysts thought that with seven parties in the Chamber, the governability of the Lula government in 2007 would have been enhanced.

In a desperate effort to surpass the 5% barrier ex post facto in October-November 2006, the PL merged with Prona (Party of the Reconstruction of the National Order) to form the new PR (Republican Party) and the PTB incorporated PAN (National Agrarian Party). Two other mergers were being contemplated: (1) PV (Green Party) + PSoL (Socialism and Freedom Party); and (2) PPS + PMN (National Mobilization Party) + PHS (Humanistic Solidarity Party) to form MD (Democratic Movement).

In December 2006, the STF ruled that this "make believe" barrier was unconstitutional, because it created first class and second class deputies. The "second class" deputies elected by the 14 parties that had not surpassed the 5% barrier would have been prohibited from having a leadership office in the Chamber and their 118 deputies would not have received committee assignments. The "intent" of this barrier was to force these deputies to "migrate" to the "first class" parties. With good reason, the Supreme Court decided that this was not constitutional. Probably, if the barrier had been "rigid" and just simply excluded those 14 parties from the Chamber altogether, the STF would have upheld this measure as constitutional.

In the "new" Chamber in 2007, after nearly a 50% turnover in the 2006 elections, another proposal (quite similar to PL 2679/03) was voted on in June. All the proposals were roundly defeated.

Two years later, in early 2009, the Lula government decided that, different from 2003 and 2007, the Executive Branch would get into the act to propose a political reform package and pressure for its approval by Congress. This "package" with seven proposals was elaborated by SAL/MJ (Secretariat for Legislative Affairs/Ministry of Justice) and delivered to Congress on February 10, 2009 (Guerreiro, 2009).The seven items that repeated some of the items in PL 2679/03 included in this "package" were:

1. A "rigid" threshold barrier of 1% of the valid vote and at least 0.5% in nine states. In 2006, this would have seated 14 parties and eliminated 7. Only 12 seats would have been redistributed.

2. A "closed list" in PR to "strengthen and institutionalize Brazil's political parties."

3. Establishment of exclusive public campaign finance, to reduce the dependence of parties and candidates on private campaign finance and make campaign spending more "transparent."

4. Prohibition of coalitions for PR elections, but allowing them for majority elections (President, Senator, Governor, and Mayor). The 2003 idea of "party federations" was not resuscitated.

5. Extension of ineligibility for running for office to include persons convicted of crimes at the first level of the Judiciary (by a federal or state judge). These persons would be ineligible for three years after their conviction. Those deputies and candidates with criminal records are nicknamed *fichas sujas* (dirty records).

6. Criminalization of vote buying, to reinforce the 1999 law in terms of ineligibility.

7. Reinforcement of party loyalty by establishing regulations to administer the 2007 TSE/STF decision that a deputy or senator who leaves or is expelled from the party that elected him/her would lose their mandate and be replaced by their respective alternate (*suplente*).

This package was defeated *in toto* in the Chamber of Deputies in June 2009. The main obstacles to its adoption were: (1) some 200 deputies have already been convicted of crimes at the first level of the Judiciary; and (2) many groups, corporative segments, evangelical church groups and the private sector use the open list PR system to elect "their" deputies.

Finally, regarding the *fichas sujas*, in September 2009 a massive, grassroots petition campaign—popular initiative—delivered petitions with over one and a half million signatures of registered voters proposing that Congress approve legislation making all persons with "dirty" criminal records [convicted at the first level] ineligible forever. This is similar to the prohibitions placed on felons by many states in the US. Congress approved this popular initiative on June 4, 2010 and the TSE confirmed that it would operate retroactively for the 2010 elections. However, the final version of this law prohibited candidacies of those convicted of crimes (election law violations, corruption, etc.) by second level court (a state supreme court or a regional federal court). Also, those who resigned their mandates to escape expulsion were also considered ineligible. In August 2010, the TSE received 1,253 cases from the state election courts requesting the ineligibility of *fichas sujas*.

In July 2006, the TRE-RJ (Tribunal Regional Eleitoral - Rio de Janeiro Regional Electoral Court) took the "novel" initiative to cancel the candidacies of all *fichas sujas* and it took the TSE some 30 days to overturn this decision. In the meantime, the TV networks in Rio de Janeiro aired this list of fichas sujas every day on their news programs with photos, names, and party affiliation of these "purged" candidates. After the October 2006 election, the TRE-RJ president had the satisfaction of announcing that none of these fichas sujas had been elected or reelected.

## CONCLUSIONS

This "never-ending" story probably will continue in 2011 with the new Congress elected in October 2010. Traditionally, large reform packages are deliberated in odd years (as seen above) because of a more complete legislative calendar. In even years, Brazil has either municipal or general elections that occasion long "recess" periods, usually from late June to early November during the campaign period, when deputies and senators "disappear" to work on their own campaigns or those of their municipal allies.

In order to accommodate the heavy pressures to retain the open list PR system, it is possible that a mixed election system might be proposed in 2011 that would combine a single-member district system with the open-list PR system on a 50% /50% division of seats (Cintra, 2008).

Probably the topics from the 2003, 2007, and 2009 reform attempts would reemerge, such as: prohibition of coalitions in PR elections, campaign finance, a relatively "low" (rigid) threshold barrier, and party loyalty.

On the other hand, other topics might be deliberated, such as the elimination of the obligatory vote, but retaining the obligation of voter registration (Ribeiro, 2003; Santos, E.C., 2004b; P.H. Soares, 2004a).

# 8

# CIVIL SOCIETY DISCOURSES AND PRACTICES IN PORTO ALEGRE

*J. Ricardo Tranjan*

*Abstract: An influential thesis put forward by Evelina Dagnino suggests that in Brazil those advocating participatory democracy and those holding neo-liberal views of the state use the terms civil society, democracy, and citizenship in sharply different ways. In Dagnino's view, this is a "perverse confluence" that has detrimental impact on democratization. In this chapter I test this argument in Porto Alegre, a city wherein two participatory programs and civil society discourse coexist. Participatory Budgeting (OP) is grounded on a discourse of radical democratization of the state and allows for popular participation in public administration. The Local Solidarity Governance (GSL) uses liberal terms such as social capital and social responsibility and encourages civil society to participate in public-private partnerships. I argue that this seemingly archetypical case of perverse confluence is not in fact perverse.*

The various models of the state espoused by different political groups intrinsically include an ideal of civil society. In Brazil, those advocating participatory democracy and those holding neoliberal views of the state held sharply contrasting opinions about the meaning of civil society, democracy, and citizenship.[1] When these views lead to concerted political actions grounded in "a set of beliefs, interests, worldviews, and representations of what ought to be societal life," these views and actions are called "a political project." In the past two

---

1. Political projects here refer to concerted political actions grounded in "a set of beliefs, interests, worldviews, and representations of what ought to be societal life" (Dagnino, Olvera, and Panfichi, 2006: 38).

decades, however, the neo-liberal and participatory democracy views were modified and the differences between them decreased, providing an example of "perverse confluence" of political projects. Evelina Dagnino (2004: 96) argues that a democratizing and participatory political project emerged in the early 1980s, found expression in the debates leading to the adoption of the 1988 Constitution, and then continued to work for the deepening of democracy, the expansion of citizenship, and the "creation of spaces where the power of the State can be shared with society." In the 1990s, a neo-liberal political project promoted civil society and participation as part of a strategy to reduce the state's regulatory role. Since civil society, citizenship, and participation were notions already established in political discourse, the task of the neo-liberal project is to make their meanings more congruent with an international ideology that imposes severe restrictions on the social responsibility of the state. Dagnino (2007: 550) argues that the "perverse nature of the confluence between the participatory and the neo-liberal projects lies in the fact that both not only require a vibrant and proactive civil society, but also share several core notions, such as citizenship, participation, and civil society, albeit used with very different meanings."[2]

In this paper I test Dagninos' hypothesis of "perverse confluence" in Porto Alegre, a Brazilian city known for its active citizenry and participatory programs. Porto Alegre is one of the first state capitals to elect a mayor from the *Partido dos Trabalhadores* (PT, Workers Party) and in 1989, the city became known as the world-capital of participatory democracy. Porto Alegre's now-famous *Orçamento Participativo* (OP, Participatory Budgeting) was widely documented and influenced similar experiments in numerous cities in Brazil, Latin America, and the world.[3] In 2004, the PT lost the first municipal election in 16 years to a heterogeneous political coalition. The opposition had learned that in order to defeat PT it had to promise to keep the participatory budgeting (Pujol). The anti-PT coalition kept its promise but also launched a new participatory initiative called *Governança Solidária Local* (GSL, Local Solidarity Governance). While the first initiative allows for direct citizen par-

---

2. The "two civil societies" thesis has been also formulated in other studies: Jenny Pearce uses the terms civil society "builders" and "critics;" Burgos refers to "gransciams" and "liberals" *(Da Democratização)*; and Medeiros draws the line between organizations under the umbrella of the *Associação Brasileira de Organizações não Governamentais* (ABONG, Brazilian Association of Non-Governmental Organizations) and organizations registered as Organizações da Sociedade Civil de Interesse Público (OSCIP, Civil Society Organization of Public Interest).

3. In 2001-2004, 69 of 223 large Brazilian cities, i.e. cities with more than 100 thousand inhabitants, had some variation of participatory budgeting, as did Argentina, Uruguay, Peru, Chile, Bolivia, Mexico, Canada, Italy, Spain, Germany, France, Poland, and England (Marquetti, 2007: 77).

ticipation in the public administration, the latter encourages civil society groups to participate in public-private partnerships.

This chapter argues that this seemingly archetypical case of perverse confluence is not in fact perverse. A historical examination of the political projects behind these initiatives shows that they were attempts to surmount antiquated statist models whilst avoiding the free-market option. The actions taken by the *Orçamento Participativo* and the *Governança Solidária Local* reflect their respective notions of civil society as the alternative to distrust of the political models predominant in the second half of the twentieth century. These programs used different concepts and practices to support initiatives that enhance civil society's participation in public matters. Moreover, a study of their functioning demonstrates that, contrary to political rhetoric fuelled by PT militants, the operation of the GSL is not detrimental to the OP. Indeed, interviews with activists demonstrate that Porto Alegre's civil society is diverse and experienced enough to take advantage of both participatory channels.[4] In the case of Porto Alegre, the confluence of civil society discourses and participatory practices is augmenting the democratization of the state and creating new spaces for citizens' participation. I call this a "constructive confluence." Political projects inspired in certain theoretical traditions may successfully further a particular understanding of civil society, but they are not likely to impose a homogenous behavior on social activists. The opposite is more likely to take place: political projects and political theory will have to adapt to the various practices of civil society.

The next section of this paper examines the political and theoretical developments that led to the establishment of the Participatory Budgeting, describes how the program operates, and discusses its main current challenges. The third section does the same for the Local Solidarity Governance. The fourth section discusses the experiences of citizens active in both participatory initiatives. The conclusion summarizes the main findings and returns to the perverse confluence argument.

---

4. The field research for this study was carried in the period of May to July, 2008. In these four months I attended the weekly meetings of the OP Committee; visited all the major GSL projects; interviewed various members of the team responsible for implementing the GSL, including an independent UNESCO consultant; discussed OP recent developments with members of the independent monitoring non-governmental organization CIDADE; and carried 23 in-depth open interviews with OP and GSL participants, some more than once. It was an intentional sample and the selection criterion was diversity: during OP meetings and GSL visits I selected activists with a different political discourses; most interviewees have been involved in the programs for at least five years, three were in their first year; the sample was roughly equally distributed between male and female participants.

# To Civil Society, From the Left

## Gramscian Civil Society

The history of the Latin American Left is commonly divided into four periods (Löwy, 1999). The first period began in the 1920s, when the October Revolution in Russia (1917), the Leninist Comintern, and the writings of José Carlos Mariátegui spurred the creation of communist parties with revolutionary character throughout the region. In the mid-1930s these parties adopted the Stalinist doctrine promoted by the Comintern. The "national-democratic" strategy required the expansion of capitalism and the strengthening of a national bourgeoisie. In this second period, democracy was part of Marxists' discourse; however, the adjective "bourgeois" disfigured the concept and prevented reflections on it (Garcia, 1996: 121). In the third period, the Cuban Revolution inspired a new wave of revolutionary movements. This trend was centered on the Organización Latinoamerica de Solidariedad (1967: 313), according to which "the revolutionary armed struggles constitute the fundamental line of revolution for Latin America." Overall, in these three periods democracy and civil society did not constitute a substantial part of the political program of the Latin American Left.

The fourth period was incited by a number of theoretical and political developments that lead to the abandonment of traditional Marxist strategies and the construction of a political project that valued democracy and popular participation. On the theoretical side, a new alternative emerged as the ideas of Antonio Gramsci spread through the continent. Gramsci offered a conceptualization of civil society that allowed Marxists to come to terms with the concept (Cohen and Arato, 1992: 77-82). In his *Prison Notebooks,* Gramsci argues that a dominant group must exert control of both political and civil society in order to become a hegemonic force (Hoare and Smith, 1971: 245). The political society is the sphere of legal, overt control while civil society is the arena of cultural dominance where subaltern classes "spontaneously" give consent to the hegemonic group. Civil society is also the arena where a counter-hegemonic bloc is able to challenge the established order (Howell and Pearce, 2001: 33-34).

According to Raúl Burgos (2002), Gramsci began to play a major role in Latin American academia in the end of the 1960s. The Left had failed to seize control of the state using tactics learnt from Lenin and the Cuban Revolution. At the same time, democracy had become the demand around which resistance was organized and therefore new strategies had to endorse democracy in order to gain popular support. Gramsci allowed Latin American scholars to put forward the idea that revolution is not a single explosive act but a process in which political democracy is a necessary terrain where revolutionary forces gain strength. This idea permitted a more sophisticated understanding of the conditions of the continent, the preservation of a revolutionary ideal, and the galvanizing of the latent popular support for democracy.

## PT's Political Project

Founded in 1979, the Brazilian Workers' Party (PT) did not embrace a particular Marxist doctrine or a clear socialist program. Instead, it allowed the coalescence of various unions, social movements, ecclesiastic community-based groups, student associations, and intellectuals in an internally democratic party (Cesar, 2002: 214-30). In spite of an amicable heterogeneity, two dominant factions argued over the party's political program. One faction saw the party as a popular, mass party, and emphasized democracy over socialism, while a more statist faction clung to Leninist ideals, envisioned the PT as a proletariat party, and placed less emphasis on democracy. A general trend marked the PT's discourse in the 1980s: from 1979 to the middle of the eighties, the democratic faction was paramount; in 1986-87 the country's economic and political crisis, allegedly a revolutionary opportunity, backed the raise of the statist faction; finally, the defeat of the PT in the 1989 presidential elections, the crumble of socialist role models, and a new analysis of capitalism brought the democratic faction back to the forefront in 1990-91. An analysis of official documents reveals the party's deliberations over matters of socialism, democracy, and civil society, and the consolidation of a radical democratic program.

The PT gradually modified its statement about the groups it viewed as forming its constituency. In its founding manifesto the PT declares itself to be a "mass party, ample and open, based on urban and rural workers" (Cesar, 2002: 248). Moreover, the document points out that in Brazil, "the rights of all workers are neglected, from peasants to doctors, from industrial workers to engineers to teachers." In 1980, notably breaking away from Leninist thought, the party stated, "there should be a clear *interest identity* (and not simply an 'alliance') between urban and rural workers." When the statist faction led PT more traditional statements appeared, as in, "industrial workers [are] the vanguard of all the exploited population" (Cesar, 2002: 248). In the 1990 VII National Congress, the party renounced the revolutionary vanguard attitude and civil society gained a privileged role:

> The relationship between the PT and Brazilian civil society is important not only because of the latter's growing influence, but also because the dispute for hegemony and political power by the workers and other popular social groups takes place much more intensely in the civil society sphere (Cesar, 2002: 262).

A year later, the First National Congress of the PT discussed how technological advances have changed the structure of capitalism and fragmented the contemporary working class, and the following statement was issued, "We want a Party that dialogues with other democratic and socialist forces, favoring the construction of a program and a historic bloc necessary in the promotion of an alternative development to the country" (Cesar, 2002: 265). In sum, the party goes through a discernible transition from a party that sees itself as the representation of the diverse sectors of civil society, at times the leader of these lesser groups, to a party aware of its location within it.

The party also reflected intensively on the role of democracy and the nature of socialism. In its first years the party reluctantly asserted itself as a socialist party, often making use of indirect statements, "the PT struggles so that economic and political power may be exerted directly by the workers" (Cesar, 2002: 273). In this period, the term socialism was almost unequivocally accompanied by the term democracy since, "there is no socialism without democracy, and no democracy without socialism" (Cesar, 2002: 272). In the 1987 Congress, wherein the Leninist segment was prominent, the objective of PT was clearly stated as socialism, though the term continued to be attached to the word democracy. In the 1990 Congress, the democratic faction was again strong, and the party issued statements explicitly rejecting the Soviet model; for example, "the communist parties in power drove their economies to a dead end because they failed to incorporate the concept of democracy [in their political program]" (Cesar, 2002: 286); and the PT "rejects any kind of dictatorship, and that includes the dictatorship of the proletariat" (Cesar, 2002: 288).

The concluding document of the 1990 VII National Congress of the PT posited that, "[democracy] is for us, at once a means and an end, an instrument of transformation and a goal to be achieved" (Partido dos Trabalhadores, 1990: 496-97). Later in the same document we find, "[s]ocialism, for the PT, is either radically democratic or it is not socialism" (Partido dos Trabalhadores, 1990: 500). The PT was particularly interested in the notion of participatory democracy with broad-based civic participation. The second-to-last paragraph calls for the expansion of instruments for direct democracy, "to guarantee the participation of the masses in the varied levels of organization of the political process and management of the economy" (Partido dos Trabalhadores, 1990: 503). These ideas were put into practice in one of the PT's first experiences in public administration: Porto Alegre.

## The Participatory Budgeting

In 1988, the PT's Olivio Dutra became mayor after defeating the traditional *Partido Democrático Trabalhista* (PDT, Democratic Labor Party). In Dutra's first year the city had a large deficit, the party had a minority in the municipal assembly, the new public servants had little or no experience in public administration, and the organized popular sectors were highly frustrated with unfulfilled promises of participation. Dutra's team used a 1989 federal law to rearrange the city taxation system, increasing the city budget by 40%. Next, Dutra created the Planning Office, which decided to respond to civil society's demand for participation in the formulation of the city's budget (Abers, 2000). In 1990 the Participatory Budgeting of Porto Alegre began to be implemented.

The Participatory Budgeting is comprised of three levels. (1) At the local level groups organized in various forms work all year on their issues and participate in the regional preparatory meetings in March/April. At these meetings they discuss the execution of the previous year's demands and the priorities for the next year. In April/May each of the 17 regions of the city holds a Regional Assembly. In these Assemblies the government—often represented by the mayor—accounts for the investments in the region and the overall city finances. All attendees then vote on two items: they pick four priority investment areas, out of 16 options,[5] and they choose a group of four representatives who will serve as the region's counselors at the municipal level. (2) A thematic structure functions in a way similar to the process described above. The procedure is the same except that citizens gather around six broad themes instead of geographical areas.[6] These forums tend to attract the middle-class and representatives of specific segments of the population, e.g. sports

---

5. Basic sanitation, housing, paving, education, social assistance, health, accessibility, and urban mobility, youth, transport, leisure areas, sport and leisure, public illumination, economic development and taxation, tourism, culture, and environment.

6. Transport; culture; economic development and tourism; education, sports, and leisure; city organization, urban and environment development; and health and social assistance.

and culture (Fedozzi, 1999: 142-46). (3) The Participatory Budgeting Committee (COP) is the highest-level forum and it is comprised of two counselors and two alternates from each regional forum; two counselors and two alternates from each thematic forum; one counselor and one alternate from the municipal public workers union; one counselor and one alternate from the União das Associações de Moradores de Porto Alegre (UAMPA, Union of Neighborhood Associations of Porto Alegre); and two representatives, and their alternates, from the government's executive office (appointed by the mayor, these representatives participate in the deliberations but do not have voting power). The main function of the COP is to transform the demands made at the local and thematic levels into an official municipal budget that adheres to the technical criteria negotiated with the various city departments and the city's budgetary limitations. The other two important roles of the COP are to monitor the implementation of the previous year's budget and to conduct a review of the Participatory Budgeting structure in December/January (Orçamento Participativo, 2008).

Neither the people directly involved in the OP nor researchers suggest the process is flawless. In fact the opposite is true. As a live and continuingly adapting process its deficiencies are constantly debated. In the first five years of OP, for example, technical discussions were absent. The population demanded whatever they deemed necessary. The result was upset engineers, unfinished projects, and wasted resources. In 1995 the administration asked the city agencies to define "technical criteria" and present them to participants before the conclusion of the year's budget (Abers, 2000: 203-10). Since then the Participatory Budgeting Committee discusses the technical criteria every year. Participants' ability to effectively participate in the meetings, given their educational level, has also been widely discussed (Abers, 2000: 115-33; Gret and Sintomer, 2005: 73-96). On this front the government tries to educate the population through various publications, and the non-governmental organization CIDADE offers important courses to new participants.

Another issue is whether the Orçamento Participativo should become law. So far the process has been based on a constitutional article that encourages the participation of citizens in municipal administration.[7] The final budget still requires the approval of the legislative assembly. On one hand, it is argued that the non-legalization of the OP is what allows for flexibility and inclusiveness.[8] On the other hand, in a Committee meeting of June 2008, because of the coming elections, a counselor argued that "the

---

7. Article 29 of the 1988 Constitution.

OP ought to be law, otherwise it is a concession and stays in the hands of politicians."[9] These questions do not constitute a challenge to the process: continuous evaluation and debate strengthens the program.

However, two issues defy the effectiveness of this democratizing tool. The first regards the "trivialization" of the process and the emergence of "specialist participants" responsible for mediating participation (Beras, 2008). In other words, a small group of delegates and councilors learned how to control and manipulate the process. Instead of a process of popular participation and democratic exercise, this mechanism sometimes becomes simply an instrument for the attainment of material demands, with an unwritten restrictive code that hinders the participation of inexperienced members. According to Beras (2008: 241), "the Porto Alegre OP experiment initially produces a new understanding of democracy in the Brazilian society." In a second moment, however, "this new understanding is progressively incorporated and systematized under traditional forms of political engagement," i.e. clientelism. As a consequence, he argues, "the differentiation between civil society and state is weakened, and, once again, civil society is incapable of invigorating itself, the state lapses back into an arena for the pursuit of interests, and, in short, participation gains a merely pragmatic character." In the words of a new OP counselor, "the old guys push us aside and do not teach us how things work; they want to control the process." Prior to 2004, the Participatory Budgeting Internal Statute imposed a maximum two-year term for COP councilors; recently this clause was voted out, by the councilors themselves. As a result, the turnover rate of councilors, which declined from 75% in 2000 to 34% in 2008, is likely to continue to decrease; CIDADE (2007) has alerted to the "need to reflect on leadership renovation" or risk to negate the democratic history built by the OP process.

The second relevant concern regards the proportion of the city's total budget made available to the Orçamento Participativo. Only a portion of the budget that is destined to new investments is open for discussion: between 6% and 8% of the total budget in the last eight years (CIDADE, 2008). Furthermore, once the annual investment plan has been formulated, the government still has to actually disburse the funds. It is not possible to find consistent figures for government expenditure; figures vary according to the source. The fact is that a large number of approved demands are delayed, i.e., demands entered the City's Plan of Investment, following the OP procedure,

---

8. For comparative studies of participatory budgets and legally-institutionalized popular health councils, see Cunha and Avritzer.

9. Field notes, COP Meeting (June 10, 2008).

but the administration did not execute them. As of 2008, estimates range from 801 to 1,561 delayed demands (CIDADE, 2008). The delays began in the PT's last administration but worsened in the last six years.[10] The current administration argues that the PT left a large fiscal deficit; the opposition points to R$15 million spent in government publicity in 2007 alone (the equivalent to US$8.4 million in December of that year). In either case, lack of confidence in the mechanism threatens to reduce civil society's participation in the budgeting process: the poor sacrifice valuable time and resource to participate, sometimes even a bus fare is a forbidding cost. As one interviewee noted, "the community does not attend meetings anymore because they do not see results." Moreover, with so many delayed demands, how and who decides what demands are carried out? These setbacks point to the need to improve, not abandon, the Participatory Budgeting.

## TO CIVIL SOCIETY, FROM THE RIGHT

### Neo-Tocquevillian Constructs

In the late 1970s, critiques of the welfare state advocated the adoption of neo-liberal economics, known as "the Washington Consensus." In this consensus, civil society is split into two parts: commercial society, commonly referred to as "the market," and "civil society," usually meaning non-governmental and charitable organizations. The main engine of growth and development is the market, the state has a regulatory role, and civil society has the responsibility to care for the destitute. The most important characteristic of this view is the belief in a benevolent and self-correcting market. Since the market is not harmful and the state is—as allegedly made evident by the malfunctioning of welfare programs—the best option is to replace government institutions by market mechanisms (Cohen and Arato, 1992; Howell and Pearce, 2001).

In the 1980s and 1990s, the two main proponents of the Washington Consensus, the World Bank and the International Monetary Fund, imposed Structural Adjustment Programs on developing countries that borrowed from them. The failures of these programs and the booming of East Asian economies reliant on state intervention drew attention to studies of

---

10. According to CIDADE (2008), 70% of the demands were executed in 2002-2004, and only 33% in 2004-2007.

market imperfections (Fine, 1999; Howell and Pearce, 2001). At the end of the 1990s, a number of orthodox economists began to accept the existence of market imperfections and admitted the need for state intervention.

In this context, civil society returned to the forefront of mainstream political analysis. In 1993, drawing on the work of Edward Banfield and James Coleman, Robert Putnam published a book in which he argued strong associational life and networks of civil engagement were distinctive features between more prosperous and democratic Northern Italy and less affluent and clientelistic Southern Italy (Howell and Pierce, 2001: 26). He used the term "social capital" to refer to the positive impact of associational cultural networks in the functioning of democracy. This theoretical development provided a non-market explanation for market imperfections and brought the notion of civil society to the center of neo-liberal discourse, although it would be a mistake to assume that the notions of "social capital" and "third sector" are used only by neo-liberals.

Luciana Tatagiba proposed the notion of "managerial democracy" to describe post-liberal reform governments that use civil society's participation as a mechanism to increase administrative efficiency. According to Tatagiba, governments seek partnership with the private sector and civil society in order to galvanize its limited resources. The "highly confrontational tone that used to constitute the participatory rhetoric is dissolved into the supposedly neutral, technical discourse of modern management" (Tatagiba, 2006: 142). In managerial democracy, discussions regarding what is of public interest are absent; the state retains the power to decide on this manner unilaterally. Instead, partners are asked how they can "do their part" in a specific action that aims at addressing a particular issue that "can only be solved with the contribution and solidarity of all" (Tagatiba, 2006: 146). Although associated with neo-liberal governments, this practice is not restricted to them.

## PPS's Managerial Democracy

At a first glance, the Local Solidarity Governance (GSL) seems an expression of the neo-liberal political project: the proponents of the program endorse privatization, condemn state centralism, defend fiscal responsibility, and use terms such as "social capital" and "third sector." The program is an example of the managerial democracy approach described in the previous section. In Porto Alegre, the adoption of managerial democracy combines a defeatist attitude towards the hard-nosed economic globalization with an attempt to surmount anachronistic statist models associated with Marxist ideals and nationalist-developmentalist programs.

This section offers an analysis of texts and policies put forward by the political-intellectual group behind the GSL. Central to this analysis is Cézar Busatto.[11] Although most of the texts examined were authored by Busatto, he represents a group of less-visible intellectuals and politicians that actively participated in the conceptual development and implementation of the GSL, some of whom are also referenced here.

In 1991, Busatto attacked President Collor's reckless liberalizations that set in motion the Brazilian neo-liberal program with the following words,

> the development trajectory taken will do nothing other than exacerbate the social and regional imbalances. . . this development project confronts the interests of the destitute majority of the population. . . Evidently, the forces of an oligopoly market will not incorporate millions of men and women living in absolute poverty (Busatto, 1991: 143).

Later in the same text Busatto argued the need to install a new kind of state, distinct from the outsized state of the import substitution period and the liberal minimum state. He endorsed a developmental state: small and robust with a strategic role of formulating and facilitating a development program in collaboration with the private sector and society at large.

As the Secretary of Finance, Busatto implemented a program that counted on citizens' inspection of businesses to reduce tax evasion in small commercial transactions. As a reward, the population could choose institutions, e.g. orphanages and hospitals, to receive a portion of the incremental tax revenue. The program included a series of more traditional state policies as, "it wouldn't have been enough if society did its part and the state neglected its, and vice-versa . . . Synergy is fundamental" (Busatto, 1998: 55). Still commenting on PMDB's state administration, Busatto noted, "this is the vision I have of the role of governments in whatever level: they have to be partners among themselves and with society, in order to make the world a bit better to live in" (Busatto, 1998: 88).[12] Finally, Busatto (1999b: 97-98) argued that the fiscal incentives given to multinational corporations

---

11. Busatto is a political economist trained in the Universidad Autónoma de Mexico. He is a pro-democracy militant with a brief passage in the Castroist MR-8, who served two times as state representative for the PMDB; was Secretary of Finance of PMDB's state administration (1994-1998); and was the founding secretary of the Porto Alegre's Secretariat for Political Coordination and Local Solidarity Governance.

and the privatizations in the Brazilian economy "responded to the historical necessity of spurring a dynamic regional economy."

Busatto (1999a: 21) summarized much of this thought when affirming that one of the characteristics of the turning of the century is,

> the hegemony of the economy over politics, of the internationalized markets over states, and the transformation of citizens into consumers. The consequences are dramatic; especially in the social sphere. . . There are no longer possibilities for a nation—and much less a state within this nation—to not be involved in the process. Thus, there is an increasing consensus regarding the necessity of creation of a mechanism at the global level to counter the forces of the international market. While these mechanisms are not adopted, there is a search for national policies that at least attenuate the perverse effects of globalization.

This discontented and disillusioned political group led by Busatto sought a new political project in the turbulent 1990s. The past pointed to the inefficiency of statism models, the present made evident states' lack of muscle vis-à-vis international capital. Neither past nor present offered viable alternatives. In the words of Jandira Feijó (2008: 117), a journalist in the group, "to expect that the humongous state institutions are capable of being modernized, one needs much more than hope and political will power. To believe that the market is willing to include more people is almost like believing in fairy tales." The solution found was a dynamic and competent state trying to rally civil society and "build a new mindset in our business class" (Busatto, 1998: 107). It is in this context that concepts such as social capital and social responsibility entered the group's political project.

In *Democracy, Prosperity and Social Responsibility*, Busatto draws heavily on studies of the John Hopkins Institute in order to explain the notions of third sector, social responsibility, social entrepreneur, and social capital. In *Social Responsibility: The Revolution of our Times*, he further elaborates the idea of a political program resting on citizen participation, businesses ethics, and cooperation between state, civil society, and the private sector. In a later publication, Plínio Zalewski and Busatto established the groundwork for the Local Solidarity Governance and pointed out social capital, sustainable development, local power, and social responsibility as some of the main concepts shaping the initiative. Finally, Bussato and Feijó summarized much of the group's thought in *The Fireflies' Era. The Emergence of a New Political*

---

12. The inability to work together is a fault usually attributed to PT (Plínio Zalewski, 1999: 90). A journalist member of this political group stated that, "PT is the averse of plurality, [it] is intolerant, the heir of a totalitarian socialist tradition, de-linked from the main modernizing movements taking place in the globe."

*Culture* where in fireflies are the millions of isolated citizens doing their bit in the construction of a better world. While publishing these works, Busatto's team pushed a series of social responsibility projects in the municipal and state assemblies.[13]

My own interview with Busatto confirmed the conceptual developments traced above. Busatto said that his formal education and first years of political activism fostered a conviction in statist alternatives to a more just society, "Marxism and Keynesian influenced my thought a lot; the older my texts, the more clear this influence is." In 1980, the rise of the Washington Consensus and the subsequent fall of socialist models "baffled us" and "made us start seeking a new form of state." The Soviet Union had fallen, "neo-liberalism did not convince us," and "we did not want just to keep the system rolling, we wanted to promote an alternative." Social responsibility appeared as a new paradigm, "it animated me, gave me energy to try to improve things again." This concept "allowed us to move away from a stiff and fragmented understanding of society to a more harmonious, holistic view." Terms such as governance and networks helped them to articulate this horizontal, cooperative understanding of state-society relationship. The idea of the "local" also supports the move beyond grand meta-narratives since it "permits us to focus on life where it happens." Finally, Busatto acknowledged that it was Augusto de Franco who helped to give their ideas form.

Franco is the last piece in this puzzle. In 1993, Franco left the PT after 13 years of militancy and became involved in two mid-1990s national initiatives against poverty and hunger created by President Cardoso's administration. Since then he has been an enthusiastic proponent of what has been described here as managerial democracy. A marked characteristic of his writing is the vision of a fundamentally new political culture, in which "acting here and now in networks of solidarity" is the historical synthesis between the traditional societal forms and the unrealizable modern project.[14] Thus, a "change in the political culture" is an aim of and condition for the GSL. Franco (2008: 100) disentangles for us the thorny question of whether theory informed practice or vice-versa:

> It should be mentioned that the basic idea of [Local Solidarity Governance]...
> was conceived by the team long before this idea was developed and shaped as a

---

13. The Social Responsibility Award; the Solidarity Law; the Solidarity Day, and the Special Commission in Public Social Responsibility.

14. "Acting here and now" dissolves the dialectics between traditional monastic-mythical and the modern prophetic-utopia, and "networks of solidarity" solves the hierarchical-autocracy versus autonomous-democracy tension (Franco, 2008).

program. But it should also be recognized that the more elaborate theoretical justification—which was created after the fact—for the later development of this basic idea was enthusiastically adopted by the team.

Thus, after a long decade of intense debate, this political group arrives at a participatory democracy, involving all sectors of society, as the best alternative to the 1990s' challenges. Contrary to the PT, this group did not have a distinct theoretical body in which to draw upon. Instead, they adopted terms in vogue in the international scenario and used them according to their ideals and needs.

## Local Solidarity Governance

In 2002, Busatto and a number of PMDB (Brazilian Democratic Movement Party) members broke with the party and joined the *Partido Popular Socialista* (PPS, Socialist People's Party). The PPS was created in 1992 as a renovation of the Brazilian Communist Party (PCB) and was later joined by a number of former members of the PMDB and the PT. PMDB members joined PPS alleging their party lost sight of the democratic and social justice values in which it was founded (Busatto, 2001: 166-90). According to Dacanal, the PT's radical faction became dominant within the party in the mid-to-late 1990s[15]; as a result, a number of PT members from the moderate faction abandoned the party and some, like Zalewski, joined the PPS. In the 2004 election, PPS formed a twelve-party coalition and defeated PT: José Fogaça became mayor; Bussato the head of the newly created Secretariat for Political Coordination and Local Solidarity Governance (SMCPGL); Feijó and Zalewski, received coordinating positions within the Secretariat. In 2005, Fogaça called public meetings in each of the 17 Participatory Budgeting regions, wherein he inaugurated the *Comitê Gestor Local* (CGL, Local Managing Committee) and explained the new participatory initiative. Next, governance agents were hired to spur regional networks and initiate the eight steps that constitute the Local Solidarity Governance. This section describes the CGL, explains the eight-step process, and then discuses their implementation.[16]

According to the Secretariat, Comitê Gestor Local is a public network that integrates all sectors of municipal administration" and seeks to foment

---

15. Dacanal explains that this *tendência* was weak in early 1980s, but progressively gained the support of a "new class" of a low-educated proletariat massively admitted into the party's public offices.
16. This brief description overlooks intermediary implementation steps found in Perusso et al. (2008).

endo-governance actions and facilitate society's governance programs (SMCPGL, 2005). They operate from the Centros Administrativos Regionais (CAR, Regional Administrative Centers) which are responsible for solving citizens' day-to-day problems; they serve as a link between people and the various municipal departments. At the Regional Administrative Centers, clientelism happens at its best. CAR coordinators are directly appointed by the mayor; municipal departments' personnel are permanent public workers with their own political affiliations; and the community leaders who walk in to report issues often represent a number of voters. In order to change this traditional way of doing local politics, CGLs started to bring together once a month representatives from various municipal departments, the coordinator of the Regional Administrative Centers, the Participatory Budgeting regional coordinators, and the SMCPGL person incharge of CGS. In these meetings municipal staff from various departments meet to discuss citizens' requests, draw on each other's knowledge, plan combined action, and demand cooperation. Meetings' records are posted online and the SMCPGL person follows-up on resolutions.

The backbone of the Local Solidarity Governance is an eight-step process, in which governance agents and community members: 1) receive training; 2) form a network team in their respective regions; 3) organize this team; 4) hold a "vision for the future" seminar; 5) diagnose the region's assets and needs; 6) define the participatory plans and goals; 7) set priorities; and 8) sign an agreement with all parties involved, committing themselves to the agenda. The GSL's website and materials teach the population the meaning of the concepts used above. In line with Tatagiba's definition of managerial democracy, these materials explain that actors (i.e. citizens, civil society organizations, businesses, and government agencies) ought to create local (i.e. territorially based, regional) networks that allow the flow of social and human capital; moreover, actors ought to see each other as partners whose ideological differences shall not interfere in the accomplishment of common goals; working teams are organized transversely, surpassing hierarchical structures; and decision-making is based on dialogue and consensus, moving beyond argumentative and voting methods.

In the period of August of 2006 and May of 2007, an estimate of 450 people from some 186 NGOs and social institutions attended a training course in project management, the CapacitaPOA. Augusto de Franco's consultancy group led the workshops with the support of the United Nations Education, Scientific, and Cultural Organization (UNESCO) and the

Lutheran University of Brazil (Perusso et al., 2008). The main objective of this course was to increase the administrative capacity of civil society organizations. As of November of 2008, the GSL consisted of eight large "demonstrative actions," a number of small actions, Solidarity Events, and two information portals.

The small actions function on the idea of *contrapartida* (pay back), and transversal partnerships. A circus wants an authorization to use a city's park for a month, the Regional Administrative Center coordinator gives the authorization, as *contrapartida* the circus lends their large tent for a public event, e.g. a Citizenship Day where people from poor areas can issue and renew documents, close to their homes on a weekend. An example of a "transversal partnership" is when the administration provides land (use license) and technical support (engineers) to a non-governmental organization (NGO) wanting to use private funds to build a day care. In one instance, the administration transformed an abandoned small bus terminal into a community kitchen and passed it on to a religious group who served soup to the homeless from a small house.

The Solidarity Actions are events organized with the collaboration of civil society groups, businesses, and different municipal departments. For example, a middle school wanted to bring together the rival neighborhoods in the region and decided to organize a Christmas party in the park in the area. The local YMCA bought the idea and helped to organize the event. Local businesses made donations in kind. The governance agent contacted the police, the firefighters, and the Secretariat of Culture to support the event. The party was "a success at zero cost," according to the school's principal.

Finally, the GSL has a communication structure. The *Blog da Governança* (Governance Blog) is the main engine of the regional networks. The main page shows a map of the city, the user clicks on a particular region and gains access to GSL news, Managing Committee reports, and developments of the eight-step process. The SMGL has installed a number of *TeleCentros* (Public Computer Labs) across the city to facilitate citizens' access to public information. A number of *TeleCentros* were themselves the result of partnership with businesses. The *Observatório de Porto Alegre* (ObservaPOA, Porto Alegre Observatory) "makes available a large geo-referenced data bank about Porto Alegre, contributing to the consolidation of citizen participation in the city's management."[17] According to one of its staff members, the initial idea was to create a "non-governmental public institution," in which the state

---

17. See www2.portoalegre.rs.gov.br/observatorio.

would contribute as much as the academia, the private sector, and civil society. The idea did not blossom as wished and the ObservaPOA remains a government project. In the interviewee's opinion, in Brazil a truly participatory culture is very weak; organizations' main motivation to partner with the government is to access public resources, not to contribute to society. He defends, however, that it is the state's responsibility to continuously promote a truly participatory culture. Unfortunately, ObservaPOA and the NGO CIDADE do not collaborate; both provide vital services to enhance the city's democratic cultural but political lines set them apart.

The proponents and managers of the Local Solidarity Governance offer four explanations to the slow implementation process. First, the GSL versus OP attitude prevented a more enthusiastic adoption of the program in the communities. The new administration kept its promise of maintaining the Participatory Budgeting. However, skeptical activists and the PT opposition continually incite the OP versus GSL antagonism, notably visible in OP meetings. Moreover, the GSL is referred to as a neo-liberal process attempting to release the government from its responsibilities. The administration defends the Local Solidarity Governance by arguing that the program is complementary to the Participatory Budgeting. While the latter discusses the best allocation of public funds, the former assists communities to recognize and utilize other resources (Perusso et al., 2008).

The second issue hampering the GSL is lack of capacity. Governance agents were few and unprepared. The total number of agents never passed ten, there was a high turnover, and among the current agents most do not have any experience in public administration. Both Augusto de Franco and the UNESCO consultant have expressed their frustration with this team (Franco, 2008; interview with Andréa Martins, August 10, 2008). Within the communities there is also an educational barrier that prevents people from engaging with complicated strategic plans and financial diagnosis. I asked the UNESCO consultant whether people were having a difficult time with the more intricate administrative tools; she replied that "often the problem is illiteracy." The third fact slowing this initiative is the lack of involvement of the private sector. This fact is linked to a broader phenomenon: the "lack of a truly participatory culture," the fourth and most common explanation offered to explain the slow-moving Local Solidarity Governance program. Proponents of the program often assert that the GSL involves the solidification of a new political culture, which takes time.

In my analysis, two other important factors obstruct the running of the GSL. First, responding to the political demand for new alternatives in the 2004 elections, the GSL was designed by the Socialist People's Party, as part of the electoral campaign. By contrast, in 1990-91, Participatory Budgeting proposals were drafted in consultation with the population (Abers, 2000; Fedozzi, 1999). Activists reminded me innumerable times that "It was we who created the OP!" The GSL affronted activists' understanding of participation by launching a program drafted behind closed doors. The second problem is the knotty language used by the GSL. A number of activists humbly admitted they never understood its content. In the wish to be innovative and overcome outdated models, planners overused conceptual jargons.[18] The GSL is a positive attempt to broaden participatory channels in the city. Nevertheless, in order to be effective the program needs to depart from what the city understands as legitimate forms of participation and from there build new participatory mechanisms. In order to make the Local Solidarity Governance politically accepted and functional, the administration needs to invite civil society to revise and rewrite the process. The most serious risk facing the GSL is the circular and disingenuous argument that the program does not work yet because it requires a "change in culture."

## CITIZENS' EXPERIENCES

The field research for this study included interviews with citizens active in at least one of the initiatives. The material collected does not suggest the two programs are incompatible; in fact, the opposite is true. Citizens participating in the Local Solidarity Governance tend to see it as more suitable to them than the Participatory Budgeting. A regatta coordinator who used GSL support to start a sailing school for low-income children affirmed that, "I never liked this OP stuff, I always thought this is for people to demand paving and sewage, important, but not for me." According to the president of the São Guilherme Neighborhood Association, a former OP counselor and now head of a GSL initiative, "adding the GSL to the OP was very important. . . We know there are too many demands, there is no way you can address all of them, doesn't matter whose government it is." In an interview with five

---

18. For example, one document written by the creators of the GSL defines the initiative as following: "Local Solidarity Governance is a multidisciplinary network that is territorially organized in order to promote the culture of solidarity and cooperation between government and local society. Its aim is to stimulate partnerships based on the principles of participation, autonomy, multidisciplinary, and co-responsibility in favor of social inclusion" (SMCPGL, 2008).

women leaders in the Cruzeiro neighborhood, the GSL was seen as empowering civic leaders, "With the GSL the government challenges us to go further. We don't just say what we want, but how we want it as well." One would make a tremendous error in assuming these women are co-opted, "In these 16 years of OP the government trained us politically to discuss and argue with them. Today we discuss with any government, face-to-face." Overall, GSL participants endorse the OP, but welcome the new initiative.

OP counselors are divided about the GSL; some view it with askance, others seem open to the new initiative. In an interview with two 80-year-old OP counselors with a long history of activism, one stated, "the GSL is just clientelism;" the other said she is willing to give it a chance, but admitted she cannot understand the program, though she attended many meetings and read all the material. Another OP old-timer, a chess instructor, thinks the two programs are not incongruous; he argues that "if the GSL had been implemented through the OP, it would've been a success, but the administration opted for creating a parallel, confronting structure, it was a strategic mistake, they played chess poorly." The president of one of the street vendors unions in the city declared that he attended two GSL meetings and did not like what he witnessed, "it appeared to me as if the government was trying to wash its hands on things I consider its responsibility." In September of 2008, four years after the election of Fogaça, one could still sense in OP cycles the fear for the termination of the process, and its replacement for the GSL. The government response is that the two programs are complementary: public funding is still open for public debate in the OP, while the GSL tries to facilitate partnerships and resource allocation among various non-public actors.

Finally, there is a third group of activists whose view is succinctly summarized in the words of a neighborhood leader in the north side, "We did partnerships with everyone; what is important for us is to get things." A public health care worker expressed a similar opinion in a more elaborated manner, "I think there are no intrinsic values. You can't just think, 'Is it good, is it bad?' I think it is the result that counts, the sort of door it opens." In a more confrontational tone, another OP old-timer stated that, "I will always be in opposition [to the government]; our party is the community." With the exception of some OP old-timers with a zealous attitude towards the initiative,[19] activists' allegiance rest with the "community" not with a particular program or ideal of civil society.

---

19. Fedozzi (1999) called this "the pioneer syndrome;" old-timers resent the label.

Despite their prominence and political importance, these two participatory initiatives are only part of the activists' history and repertoire of action. A number of interviewees made references to struggles against the military government; the public health care worker was active in the student movement that helped to bring down President Collor; two interviewees are committed primarily to their labor unions; some are active in party politics; two OP councilors head social movements for urban housing that occupies abandoned buildings and often have to confront the police; the list of examples goes on. A truly proactive civil society—as allegedly advocated by leftists and neo-liberals—does not limit its actions to space created by government institutions and political discourses.

## CONCLUSION

In electoral periods, PT and PMDB supporters in Porto Alegre stand in clearly demarcated sides of the Redenção Park, waving their flags and provoking each other. Likewise, Participatory Budgeting and Local Solidarity Governance supporters often stand on different sides, cheering for one program and booing the other. A hasty examination may further the antagonism created by party politics, setting one program as "radical democratic" and the other as "neo-liberal." However, a historical examination shows that the groups behind these initiatives faced essentially the same challenge: how to avoid statist models without surrendering to free-market ruling. In the PT's theoretical tradition, Gramsci's writings allowed a new understanding of the worth of civil society and democracy, and backed a proposition for the radical democratization of the state. In turn, the PPS adopted terms in vogue in the international political scenario and used them according to the group's ideal.

This study also examined the operation and current challenges of each program. The OP allows citizens, directly and through their representatives, to discuss the utilization of a small but significant portion of the public budget. This program breaks with traditional clientelism by opening public administration to popular scrutiny. Moreover, it teaches citizens about their rights and fosters reflection on collective issues. The process is now vulnerable to small groups of individuals who try to control it and limit the access of new community members. Furthermore, the large number of unattended demands threatens the program as citizens' participation is dependent on the delivery of services. In turn, the GSL attempts to facilitate partnerships among the various sectors of society, galvanizing non-public resources towards collective concerns. However, the programs still lacks a more clear language and a more transparent process that respects the city's participatory culture.

Finally, the third section of this paper drew on field interviews to show that Porto Alegre's activists are diverse and experienced enough to take advantage of both participatory initiatives. Neighborhood leaders, regatta coordinators, chess instructors, public health care workers, union leaders, housewives, students, homeless urban-dwellers, and other groups, will participate in public matters distinctively; each according to its need, ability, interest, resource, and geographic location. The OP has been a useful tool for many years and activists almost unanimously endorse it. The GSL now offers a new alternative: some groups have learned how to benefit from it; others are studying it, trying to get through its complicated language; still others remain skeptical and prefer to work with the more familiar OP. Thus, from an activist perspective the issue seems to be how to make these programs function better, not what ideal of civil society should be advanced.

The present study supports the first part of Dagnino's argument by providing a historical account of the development of two political projects with distinct understandings of civil society and participation. However, the study challenges the second part of Dagnino's argument by suggesting that in Porto Alegre, the meaning and practice of civil society and participation has been expanded by the creation of a new participatory initiative. In practice, neither program directly challenged market forces, although both increased the state apparatus as new agencies were created to manage the programs. Overall, participation in public matters increased as two programs gave citizens more choice on how to participate. Finally, the existence of two distinct programs fueled a discussion on democracy, participation, and the role of civil society—a very democratic exercise. For these reasons, in the Porto Alegre case, the confluence of civil society discourses seems constructive, not perverse.

Brazil has *one*, diverse and active civil society. The language and practices that pushed the democratizing period are now complemented by terms such public-private partnerships, social capital, and social responsibility. Initiatives based on this language ought to be welcomed as new efforts to deepen democracy, increase citizen participation, government transparency, and public awareness. To dismiss these initiatives based on *a priori* theoretical arguments is a regrettable mistake. In democratic Brazil, citizens themselves will determine the usefulness and value of participatory mechanisms. Political projects and state models can influence but not determine what civil society is or is not.

# Part II
# Social and Cultural Dimensions

# 9

# PENSION REFORM IN BRAZIL: ADDRESSING A SOCIAL PACT

*José Roberto Ferreira Savoia*

*Abstract: The following study highlights the key features that define today's social security scenario in Brazil. One of the most important issues raised is the striking lack of balance between revenue and expenditure within the social security sector against a backdrop of worrying trends such as unequal benefits rights and a large contingent of casual workers. This article proposes a number of ways toward improving the nation's pension laws and system.[1]*

Social Security reforms in Latin American countries have some peculiar characteristics that have changed the role of the State. In short, the welfare state is in decline as the importance of the private sector has increased. In Brazil, before the Constitutional Amendments of 1998, the State was viewed as the only provider of pensions. This has been slowly abandoned and individuals are being encouraged to set up their own pension savings accounts. Complementary pensions are increasing owing to new measures such as new regulation, enforcement by supervising authorities and adoption of tax incentives. Consequently, the number of participants and private

---

1. I would like to thank Albert Fishlow and Carmelo Mesa-Lago for their comments. Liliana Reyes and Shawn Pearce from ILAS-Columbia University, Bruno Buscariolli, Daniel Bergman, Ana Paula Alcântara, and Anthony de Faria Dovkants assisted me with comments and data collection.

pension plans has increased, creating a positive impact for the long-term savings culture (Savoia et al, 2007).

Nowadays, Brazil's pension system is made up of various inequalities allowing some groups to benefit while the majority of those retired end up worse off. This distortion occurs because of an old institutional arrangement, molded during the seventies, and not completely reformed. This is just one example. But overall, Brazil has the same problems observed in other countries, such as fiscal deficits, a low level of affiliation to the official system, an aggravating aging problem, differences in eligibility criteria between the sexes and an imbalance between the number of public- and private- sector workers. The government must increase affiliation levels and incorporate informal workers into the formal labor sector in order to bring balance to the social security system.

After President Luiz Inácio Lula da Silva came to power in 2003, many expected his key Social Security reform to change the imbalances created over many decades, but like any bill certain elements were watered down and compromise was reached to ensure it was passed. During the reform process, the most important parameters that were targeted for change included limiting the amount paid to pensioners, retirement criteria for public-sector workers and for the next generation of public servants an end to their full pensions involving a parity between the value of active workers' wages and their pensions. Tax measures to promote higher affiliation and institutional changes to reduce informality, however, are showing some good results on the fiscal side, and the number of self-employed people increased to 4.1 million in 2008 from 3.3 million in 2007.

This text is organized as follows: after this introduction, a background section provides a description of the Brazilian social security system. The next sections analyze the main issues to be addressed, review measures adopted by Lula's reform, indicate the bill's financial impacts and analyze the role of a social pact aimed at promoting reform.

## BACKGROUND

Historical causes explain the distortions in the Brazilian pension system. A good historical perspective is provided by Oliveira, Beltrão, and Ferreira (1997). Path dependency and the role of collective action help to clarify the current situation and the emergence of so many deep problems.

A 1998 reform cleared up some distortions such as the absence of age limits on retirement for the public servants and produced conditions to help control the Social Security deficit. However, its results were partial since an imbalance between account and benefit values continue. At that time, studies were made to calculate the cost of changing the Brazilian social security system into a capitalized system, which proved to be impracticable ranging between 188% (General Regime) and 255% of GDP (General Regime and Special Regime), depending on the transition's form. As mentioned by Nakahodo and Savoia (2008) the transition from a defined benefit to a defined contribution scheme entails high transition costs because, with creation of individual accounts, not only would the government stop collecting mandatory contributions from current workers, but it would also need to fund new individual accounts until the system became self-sustainable. Consequently, government was left with the option of stimulating complementary pensions and making a parametric reform.[2]

The pensions system in Brazil comprises:

1. The General Regime for private-sector workers and the Special Regime for employees of the public sector. The General Regime is a pay-as-you-go (PAYG) system in which contributions from both employers and employees are used to pay defined benefits to pensioners. The National Institute for Social Security, or INSS, is responsible for managing the social security of around 26.7 million active workers (in a nation of more than 190 million people). In 2008 INSS collected R$180.4 billion in contributions and paid R$242.6 billion in benefits to 26 million people, representing an average benefit of R$777.56 per month. The observed deficit of R$62.4 billion was equivalent to 2.32 percent of GDP.

2. The Special Regime, which gathers Union, State, and Municipality Civil Servants, pays high benefits and charges very low contributions, generating severe deficits. The last official Federal report from 2008 presented total expenses of R$63.2 billion whilst contributions were R$8.2 billion, which generated a deficit of R$55 billion (2.06 percent of GDP). There were around 5.3 million contributors and 1 million pensioners. The public-sector civil servants have pensions readjusted in the same way as the active workers' salaries.

   There is also a Complementary Pension Regime for the future employees of the public sector still regulated but not yet implemented. It is a mandatory Pension Fund only for the next generation of public servants.

3. A Complementary Pension Regime (RPC), working on a voluntary basis, is comprised of Closed Pensions (Pension Funds and Multi-employer Funds) and

---

2. A reform that changes parameters, or requirements for eligibility, like: years of contribution instead of years worked; the abolition of early retirement for new insured; and the adoption of minimum age criteria for civil servant retirement; total contributions and age are used for the calculation of social security payments.

Open Funds provided by financial institutions. Similar to the US, Pension Funds are voluntary and can be organized as Sponsored Funds by the businesses or in Multi-employer Form. In 2008 there were 371 pension funds, with R$442.9 billion of assets and 2.6 million participants. The value of benefits paid was R$2.2 billion. Pension Funds play a significant role in the Brazilian economy, providing a stable basis of long-term resources to finance productive investments and also are major buyers of Brazilian treasuries.

The Open Funds are managed by the financial system and offer plans to individuals and corporations. These plans are capitalized, optional, and most of them have defined contributions. In 2008, they comprised of R$147.5 billion in assets and approximately 96,000 beneficiaries who receive some type of income (ANAPP, 2008).

4. There is also a "zero" pillar that provides poverty relief to the elderly. It is financed by the Treasury and managed by the INSS. Since the passage of the 1988 Constitution, the community and casual workers have benefitted thanks to an enhancement and extension of retirement rights. These programs were implemented in the beginning of the 1990s, and have achieved important results in poverty reduction among the deprived.[3] The most important ones under the pensions regime are the Rural Pensions (Previdência Rural) and the Organic Social Security Law (Lei Orgânica de Assistência Social—LOAS). Rural Pensions started in 1991 and pay a minimum wage to approximately 7.2 million rural workers. The social assistance program (LOAS) reaches 2.9 million people. It pays one minimum wage to those who have 65 years or some kind of disability. In 2008 expenses were R$15.6 billion paid to 3.2 million beneficiaries.

## THE SOCIAL SECURITY DIAGNOSIS

The Brazilian Social Security System has some crucial issues that should be addressed as part of a process of continuous institutional change and political negotiation, addressing: the aging problem, the differences in retirement criteria between gender, the low affiliation level, the disparity between benefits of public and private employees, actions focused on reducing poverty, and the growth of the General Regime deficit.

---

3. Brazil has a great number of poor people, even though in 2008 its income per capita was around US$8,400 (63rd position in the World).

# The Aging Problem

PAYG models are sensitive to the number of beneficiaries, to the level of benefits and to the number of contributors. To establish equilibrium, it is necessary to balance the actual value of all contributions paid and the actual value of the future benefits. In this sense, averting the problems of increasing life expectancy becomes fundamental to sustain the system. Since people are living longer, the system should aim for sketching plans that deal with this new situation.

In the last few years, the problems of early retirement have been partially offset by adopting age parameters that promote an adjustment between the number of years of contributions and the value of the pension. Early retirees receive an adjusted benefit that is lowered due to the application of a formula, referred to as the Social Security Factor, an actuarial approach that adjusts the benefits value versus the period of contributions and age of retirement.

In 2008, around 10.2 percent of Brazil's total population was older than 60 years old. The average age of retired Brazilian men was close to 56 years old. This figure is considered one of the most worrisome characteristics of the social security system since it triggers serious intergenerational costs, posing a high taxation on future generations. Besides that, in the last two decades, the child mortality rate has dropped dramatically and the living conditions for the elderly have improved. In 1991 Brazilians had an average life expectancy of about 66 years of age. In 2005 this figure changed to 71.9 years of age, a growth of 6 years in 14, an impressive evolution of more than 5 months per year. Based on Brazilian historical data and numbers from some more developed economies—in which the growth rate is smaller—it is possible to affirm that the Brazilian population's average life expectancy will reach 74 by 2010, being 70 for men and 78 for women.

It is remarkable that the elderly are increasing their life expectancy, and for instance, by 2010 life expectancy at 60 years old is calculated by IBGE as 83 years for women and 80 years for men. But this will put more pressure on the expenses. One way under consideration to help resolve this issue would be to adopt a minimum retirement age—something that has been done in several countries. However, such a move would have a significant impact on the number of opportunities for young people trying to enter the workplace.

On the other hand, the Brazilian birth rate has been reduced to around 1.4 percent during the last decade amid expectations it will drop to 1.2 percent between 2040 and 2050. As a result, the net population growth rate was 2.89 in 1991, 2.39 in 2000, and 1.89 in 2008, and it is estimated that it will be by 1.50 by 2028. A smaller working force will have to support the increasing expenditures of the social security. Brazil is facing a "demographic transition," which occurs when high natality and high mortality rates are changed. In the first phase there is a sudden increase of the population, because mortality rates declines faster than natality, but it will tend to stabilize in the second step. During this period the country faces a "demographic bonus" that is characterized by a still large amount of people in working age (14-64 years) in relation to the elderly (over 65).

## The Gender Issue: Age and Contribution Time Differences

The latest pension reform runs contrary, however, to the latest demographic findings, making the retirement age for women 5 years earlier than for men. On average, in Brazil, men will live at least 3 years less than women, so there is an implicit 8-year benefit discrepancy for women. Although there are differences in the retirement age in other countries, we can identify three tendencies in the world scenario (Giambiagi and Castro, 2003). In the United States, Ireland, Iceland, Denmark, and Norway, there is no legal difference between men and women when it comes to retirement age. In Germany, Holland, Spain, United Kingdom, Finland, Sweden, Luxembourg, and Canada there is a difference that is lower than five years between men and women. Even when there is a five-year difference between men and women, in general, the women cannot retire before they are 60 years of age. This criterion is adopted in Japan, Austria, Italy, Portugal, France, Belgium, Switzerland, and Greece.

About half of the Latin America's nations do not differentiate between the retirement ages of men and women. In those countries where there is a difference, women tend to retire 2 to 5 years before men. However, some Latin America countries are reducing this minimum age differential between the sexes to the average of two years. Table 9-1 reveals the minimum retirement age and estimated period of benefits in various regions and countries.

In the European Community and North America, the minimum retirement age is being raised from 65 to 67 or 68 years of age. In the next decade, France will count on an age limit of 69 years of age and 41 years of contributions. Similar measures of age versus contribution period increases must be adopted in Brazil. Currently, the system charges future generations with the

TABLE 9-1. Minimum Age of Retirement and Estimated Period of Benefits, 2005 and 2007

| Countries | Minimum Age of Retirement (years) | | Expected Length of Retirement (years) | |
|---|---|---|---|---|
| | Men | Women | Men | Women |
| OECD (29 countries) | 64 | 63 | 16 | 21 |
| Latin America (7 countries) | 62 | 60 | 17 | 21 |
| Others (66 countries) | 62 | 60 | 16 | 21 |
| Brazil | | | | |
| Pensions by Contribution Period | 54ᵃ | 51ᵃ | 23 | 29 |
| Special Rural Pensions | 60 | 55 | 19 | 26 |

*Notes:* ᵃAverage retirement age. 2007 figures for Brazilian data and 2005 for all others.

*Source:* Rocha e Caetano (2008).

costs of current policies. In the near future, the country will not be able to adopt such generous policies if it aims to bring balance.[4]

Brazil needs to set an age limit for retirement as the population evolves. To do this, the age limit could be adjusted by using a two-stage approach. In the first stage, the minimum retirement age would be established at 65 years for men and 62 for women. In a second stage the limit is set to 65 years of age for both genders. This gradual increase of the age limit for retirement creates a natural transition and reduces conflicts.

The inclusion of a longer contribution period is crucial for dealing with the growth of a longer-lived population. The contribution time has to be slowly increased to 35 years for women and 37 years for men.

## The Disparity Between Public and Private Workers Issues

The system comprised by the General Regime and the Special Regime generates a deficit of 5.7–5.9 percent of GDP. The Special Regime accounts for 75 percent of the total deficit, and the General Regime is responsible for the other 25 percent.

In 2008, for the Public Sector (Union, States, and Municipalities) estimates are that total expenses reached R$121.25 billion and contributions R$70 bil-

---

4. According to OECD (2002), in 2001, only 8.4 percent of Brazil's total population was over 60 years of age; nevertheless, its social security expense corresponded to 11.5% of GDP. Proportionally, these expenses were greater than the ones of the richest countries, with a higher number of elderly people, for instance Sweden and the United States. These two countries had for the same period annual expenses of 9.2 percent and 6.3 percent of GDP, respectively, with 22 percent and 16.1 percent of the population being older than 60 years.

lion, generating a deficit of R$60.9 billion (2.16 percent of GDP). There are around 4.9 million contributors, 1.6 million retired, and also another 0.6 million pensioners. There are high disparities in the values of pensions as shown in Table 9-2. In the Special Regime, pensions can be up to 22 times greater in terms of value than the average pension value for the General Regime.

Inequality between General and Special Regimes benefits can be explained mostly by a public-sector worker's capacity to negotiate and keep benefits and the institutional difficulties inherent when trying to change the law.

In order to accommodate people who will soon be granted benefits, it is preferable to make progressive changes in age limits, or in the contribution period, avoiding sudden measures. Usually, the political reactions tend to be lower when the loss imposed to the beneficiary does not materialize immediately, and the perspective of its realization is in the medium to long term.

TABLE 9-2. Comparison of the Average Value of Pensions for Federal Public Servants, 2003

| Categories | | Average Value of Pensions | Ratio |
|---|---|---|---|
| General Regime | | US$259 | 1 |
| Special Regime | Executive (Civilians) | US$1,360 | 5.2 |
| Union | Military | US$2,400 | 9.3 |
| | Legislative | US$5,900 | 22.8 |
| | Judiciary | US$5,550 | 21.4 |

*Source*: Pensions and Social Security Ministries—a diagnostic of the Brazilian pensions system presented March 18 2003, and Social Pensions statistics bulletin Vol. 9 No 3.

## The Poverty Issue

In the last decade poverty in Latin America has been falling, especially among people in the base of the income pyramid. Nonetheless, the permanence of high poverty levels in the region challenges the pension model, especially because the poor are unable to contribute to the pension system. The situation in Brazil shows that social security is distributed widely although it could be much improved. Analyzing a decomposition of the "Gini Index," Ferreira (2003) noticed that the return on pensions is uneven between the elderly poor and those better off but also elderly. This happens because many elderly poor do not receive any social security benefit creating an inverted redistribution of income in which those who make less money are financing those who retire earlier and get paid more.

In this context, pensions are badly distributed when considering that social expenses are intended for poverty alleviation. Amsberg (2000) performed analysis in the Northeast and Southeast, which together have 73% of the population and 80% of the poor in Brazil. Amsberg observed only 13% of such pensions went to the poorest people. Neri (2001) noticed that the top 10% of benefits, including INSS and public-sector inactive worker benefits, consume almost half of all the benefits distributed.

## Poverty Reduction

One positive aspect is that poverty has decreased since 1998, but it is clear that there is still much to do to improve the distribution of wealth in Brazil, however, improvements in salaries and wealth distribution can be seen in economic data and the amount the government pays to those who have retired. This is demonstrated in an increase in the amount of formal contributions made and an increase in the value of the contributions, helping improve the balance between INSS revenue and expenses.

Brazil is reducing inequality and will achieve the lowest level since the inception of these measures in the sixties. Nevertheless inequality within the country is considered one of the ten largest in the world, and despite the improvement and maintaining the observed track it would take another thirty years to reach the level of developed countries, like the US.

The combination of high growth and the shortage of inequality during the period of 2003-2008, the proportion of Brazilian people living in poverty was reduced by 43%, and 19 million people went out of poverty levels. Another 32 million people became middle-class citizens in the same period.

The Gini index has constantly fallen since 1997 from 0.60 to 0.54, highlighting a drop in the inequality of the distribution of wealth. This improvement in wealth distribution is good news for the pensions sector as the number of formal workers, fiscal and pension contribution revenues, and quality of life increase.

FIGURE 9-1. Percentage of Extremely Poor People in the Total Population, 2008

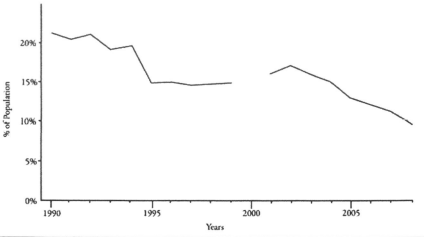

Source: IBGE and PNAD.

## The Revenue Issue

The main consequence of an imbalance in the social security system is that the Government is forced to make a decision. To use public resources to pay social security benefits is one option, which leads to a reduction of investments in other areas such as infrastructure, social assistance, and health. Essentially, it is a perverse transference of the society's income to a small portion of people who already have the retirement benefits and that in general have a per capita income much higher than the average population.

Analyses about the factors that broaden the Brazilian social security deficit were extensively explored by Cechin (2002), Giambiagi and Castro (2003). They are summarized here:

1. Since 1988 minimum wage payments are made to rural workers who had never contributed to social security.

2. Some 500,000 public-sector workers, who contributed more than the stated General Regime ceiling and moved to the private-sector, were able to retire since 1988 receiving generous benefits.

3. An increase in the number of retirement by contribution period, without a minimum age requirement, and during 2002 to 2005 its participation reached almost 40% of total expenses.

4. A real increase in the minimum wage, which serves as an index for Social Security benefits.

5.Fraud and tax evasion.

Figure 9-2 shows the evolution of the INSS benefits' expenses during the years following the approval of the 1988 Constitution. The total value went from 2.5% of GDP in 1988 to 6.6% of GDP in 2008. This growth tendency is worrisome because it is directly linked to the real minimum wages gains, which indexes social security benefits. This should be changed so that social security benefits are readjusted by a price index related to the cost of living, while the minimum wage would have the freedom to produce real income gains for workers according to economic productivity gains.

FIGURE 9-2. Expenditure on INSS Benefits, 1980-2008

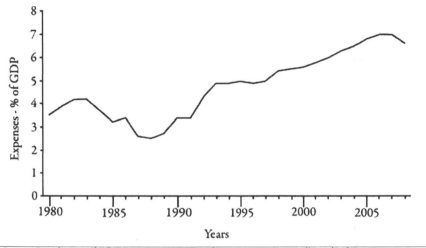

*Source*: Giambiagi and Além, 1999, p. 229; Social Security Statistics Bulletin (Boletim Estatístico Da Previdência Social)—vol.5, n°12, vol.6, n° 10 e vol.7, n°6, and Ministry of Planning's Budget Data 2005-2007.

The increase in INSS benefits payments is not just in absolute value terms but also in relative value terms between 1988 and 2007, increasing to 7% from nearly 3% of GDP (see Figure 9-2). This growth is extremely dangerous for Brazil given there is a clear absence of fail-safes aimed at controlling increasing expenses. This level will just keep rising until the government is no longer able to meet benefits payments. Another factor preventing a balancing out between revenue versus social security payments is that two thirds of all benefits are linked to the minimum wage, or rather by law no benefit payment can be inferior to the minimum monthly wage. Between 1995 to 2009 the minimum wage rose to R$465 (US$258 at US$1/ R$1.85) from R$100, which was then approximately worth US$95. This represents a more than 100% increase in the minimum wage's real buying value since 1995, and this increase was automatically passed to those who are retired. In turn pension payments rose too.

## The Low Affiliation Issue

In Latin America, statistics show that social security has not been adequately extended to the entire population and the coverage level is typically low. The reforms that happened in the region did not emphasize the low coverage level issue, although this has been pointed out by Murro (2001) as the main problem because the excluded population is almost two thirds the total (Mesa-Lago, 2000), and two countries with large public systems—Brazil and Panama—have levels of coverage much higher than the other seven that implemented some form of structural reform (Mesa-Lago, 2004).

As mentioned by Schmidt-Hebbel (1997: 10) "Coverage of affiliates—that comprise both active contributors, and non-active members—is very different from coverage of contributors." So, it is important to address the reasons for this difference and to increase compliance levels.

### *The Role of Informality*

Informality is a concept with different meanings, but in this paper it is the lack of a formal working relationship that can provide individuals with workers' rights. In this situation, there are no benefits, but there are some kinds of tax evasion, including non-payment of pension contributions. In the macro level this will lead to an increase in tax burden on formal corporations and on individuals, constraining investments and reducing productivity, in such a combination that affects economic growth.

In 2008 the average unemployment rate was 7.9%, declining from the previous levels between 9%-10% prevailing since 1999. There was an increase in the number of top educated workers within the workforce losing jobs—those with more than eleven years of schooling were 11.9 million in 1992 before reaching 30.4 million in 2005—meanwhile less skilled workers lost 6.5 million jobs during the same period (Ramos, 2007:27).

According to IBGE the casual workforce represented 48.2% of the total labor force in 2007. Casual work is more intense in intensive labor sectors and less intense in sectors with medium to high levels of technology. Formal companies totaled 5 million, and informal ones came to 10.3 million. The great majority of firms in the informal sector are micro and small companies where 60% of the entrepreneurs are women and 40% are men, and whose average age is 42 years. Eighty-five percent of the entrepreneurs have no partners, and 78% do not hire employees. Fifty-six percent of them work at home and 33% do not have a fixed place to work.

Younger workers are the most affected by casual informal work. Informal workers' salaries are 20% less than ones earned by formal workers but this difference varies according to the number of years of schooling and age.

At higher ages, 50 to 54 years, formal workers make twice the income of informal ones. Approximately 41 million workers are not covered by the social security system and only 30 million contribute. Figure 9-3 shows a drop in the total number of informal workers between 1992 and 2007 but the number still remains at a very high 48.5%. This has led to a drop in the relative number of social security contributors, impacting revenues and reducing the capacity to pay benefits to pensioners. Nowadays, the ratio is 1.2 contributors to each retired person. When analyzing the composition of the non-contributors group, families earning an average per capita income of one and a half of minimum wages make up almost 50% of that group. In other words, the group that does not contribute to the system is the very group that needs social security the most.

FIGURE 9-3. Informality: A Historical Evolution, 1992-2007

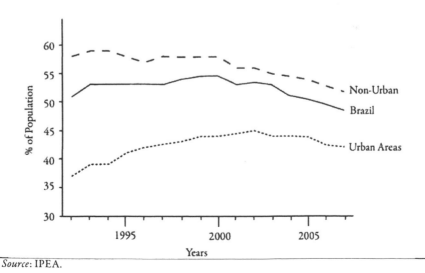

Source: IPEA.

## REFORMING SOCIAL SECURITY IN LULA'S GOVERNMENT

President Lula's Government came to power in the beginning of 2003. It was charged with widely reforming the social security system. A strong reform was expected to promote equity between private and public-sector pensions as well as parametric changes already diagnosed as necessary. What has been seen, however, is the proposition of very restricted measures essentially when it came to the Special Regimes without making any relevant changes to the workers in the General Regime. The reform oriented to the public sector, specially the future civil servants, was an option to avoid a confrontation with the current servants, facing a typical collective action problem and those reform policies contribute to lower resistance from labor unions and leftist parties (Nakahodo and Savoia, 2008).

## Analysis of the Last Reform's Measures (2003)

The most important measures,[5] approved in December 2003, were:

*Creation of a New Benefits Ceiling*: The pension ceiling was raised around 28.4% to US$1,333. This same amount was also applied to private-sector workers and to the next generation of public-sector staff. They are able to contribute to pension funds. This pension ceiling was the only general measure of the reform while all the others were related to the characteristics of the civilian workers.

Fixing the ceiling of payments to retirees at R$1,333 in the General Regime brings in income to the government and postpones benefits payments. The employees are responsible for one-third of contributions to their Social Security while the employer is responsible for the other two thirds. With the increase in the ceiling, the employee can raise his or her contribution to up to 53%. On the other hand, payments made by the employer cannot be increased. In the future, benefits will be raised without the corresponding financing by the employer. In praxis, it will be a partial subsidy of the State, there is no change or benefit with this measure for those currently retired.

*Age Limit and Contribution Length Time*: Employees who are in the public service receive a whole pension if women are 55 years of age and have 30 years of contribution; men are 60 years of age and have 35 years of contribu-

---

5. A detailed discussion is provided by Giambiagi et al. (2007, 2010).

tion; or for both it is necessary to have 20 years of public service and the last 5 in the post in which they retire. The possibility of early retirement has been maintained, beginning at the age of 48 for women and 53 for men. Nevertheless, a reduction of 5% a year is applied relating to the age reference—60 years of age for men and 55 years of age for women. For public-sector workers who previously worked in the private sector, the calculation of their benefits is being done considering the average contributions to the General Regime.

The minimum retirement age for public workers causes a 5-year delay in starting benefits and adds a valuable additional contribution period. In addition, this measure postpones the staffer's departure from his or her activities, thus postponing the necessity of hiring a substitute.

The new formula for calculating a pension's value adjusts wages and contribution period in both public and private sectors. For instance, a person who contributed for 35 years to the Social Security System is about 60 years old, has worked 30 years in Public Service and 5 years in the Private Sector, and receives a retirement pension value equivalent to his or her wage as a public servant that has been reduced by between 10% and 13%. But, in a situation in which the person decided to join the Public Sector after working 20 years for the Private Sector, the reduction applied to the wage is higher—starting at 39.3% and reaching up to 52%.

*Benefits Limit*: Active workers' remuneration and also the pensions have a maximum ceiling ranging around US$8,300 per year, as of 2008. The reduction of the pension value from its original amount is based on the argument that there are fewer people being sustained after the death of the original beneficiary.

*Pensioners' Contribution*: Retired public-sector workers and pensioners pay 11% of the pension's package that exceeds the US$1,300 ceiling. Between 1995 and 2002, the federal expense on personnel was only 2.1% per year, while the expenses on retired workers grew 2.4%. Based on these facts, it is possible to affirm that charging inactive workers was an indispensable measure. It is also important to lower the deficit of states and municipalities.

*End of Parity between Wages and Pensions*: Before the 2003 reform, a public-sector worker's pension was the same value as that of his or her last month's salary. According to the reform, the benefits are in line with the average contribution made during a person's working life—the same benefit provided in the General Regime. The end of parity between wages of active workers applies the same criteria of pension calculus to both public servants and civilian workers linked to the General Regime.

*Creation of Pension Funds to Future Public Servers*: The reform in 2003 established that every person who enters the public administration has their pension calculated by an average of contributions made with a ceiling of ten times the minimum wage. There is also a Complementary Pension Fund available to public-sector workers. The fund provides a defined contribution plan but joining the fund is optional. Although the regulation is ready and because there is much opposition to the starting of the fund, in practice the situation did not change and it must be improved only in a new legislature, after Lula da Silva.

## Analysis of the Reform's Impact

Pension expenditures are one of the two most important fiscal issues that President Lula addressed. The establishment of equal ceilings for the General Regime and the Special Regimes undoubtedly represented a first step for better social equality. Table 9-3 presents a comparison of social security contributions before and after the Government's reform. When analyzing the contributions brackets to the General Regime, it is easy to see that this has not changed, that is, it has collected more than it needs to offer the benefits level to a retired person.

In the current situation, to cover all the INSS benefits, without taking special situations into account, a contribution bracket of 17% is enough to bring the pension system into balance. Nevertheless, the current bracket is about 21%. It is possible to introduce a lower contribution bracket without changing the current benefit level. To do so, better transparency is necessary in the accounts related to assistance benefits by separating them from the General Regime budget since it is the Treasury's responsibility to finance them.

In public civil service, the percentage collected increased and the necessary contribution diminished with the reform. The necessary contribution to cover such a worker's benefit level would have been between 45 percent and 50 percent of his or her wages—very different from today's levels of between 85 percent and 16 percent of the wages. The reform produced an increase of those contributions and a reduction in benefits. Nonetheless even with such changes, the necessary contributions to provide such benefits would be from 19 to 27 percent of wages, while collecting would be between 18 and 21 percent.

TABLE 9-3. Comparison of Social Security Contributions Before and After Lula

| | Prior Situation | | Lula's Government | |
|---|---|---|---|---|
| | Contribution Needed (%) | Contribution Collected (%) | Contribution Needed (%) | Contribution Collected (%) |
| INSS | 17 | 21 | 17 | 21 |
| Public Servers | 49 | 16 | 27 | 18 |
| Judiciary | 48 | 15 | 25 | 18 |
| Legislative | 47 | 15 | 25 | 18 |
| Executive | 50 | 16 | 27 | 19 |
| Military | 47 | 9 | 19 | 12 |

*Source*: Zylbersztajn, Souza, Stancioli, Milan 2003.

The effects of leveling the benefits for future public-sector staff and workers from private companies will be observed only in the long run but it is necessary to observe an entire generation[6] for this measure to show full effects.

In 2005 the government started administrative measures to increase revenues and cut expenses. Some of them are related to a more severe control on fraud and tax evasion. Other measures included a management turnaround at the INSS and investments in technology.

## A SOCIAL PACT TO REFORM PENSIONS IN BRAZIL

In a great number of countries social security systems are not funded where active workers contribute to their respective programs to guarantee the payment of benefits to current retirees. This pay-as-you-go model is sustained by the existence of a "pact between generations" in which the current taxpayers will receive their pensions in the future thanks to payments of the next generation.

What happens when the benefit to current retirees is disproportionate to their previous contributions? Should the benefits be reduced in the future by allocating a loss to the current generation of workers? To avoid problems of this nature and ensure more solid institutions, reforms are being made

---

6. Under Brazilian law, regulation changes cannot modify acquired rights, that is, for those who already receive pensions. However, there are theses of Economic Law that guarantee State constitutional changes that alter the law's expectations, that is, the conditions for those workers who have not completed all the requirements necessary to achieve retirement status. Such changes would produce countless questions in the courts and have been avoided in practice.

with the objective of ensuring equity between contributions and promises made to each generation to create a balance between generations.

Another set of problems appears when workers, who are not affiliated to the system or who are not entitled to certain benefits, begin to pressure lawmakers to ensure they are supported in some way. At this moment, widespread benefits can be created that are not based on contributions but are instead generated by taxing the rest of the population, usually impacting the middle class the most.

However, the middle class cannot choose how its tax money is used and if there had ever existed such an opportunity to voice opinion on the use of such resources they probably would have chosen to allocate them differently into areas such as education, health, or housing for example. In this way, the problem of creating public benefits is that of finding coherent means to cover costs without imposing on less politically organized sectors to attend to organized special interest groups.

The 1998 reform cleared up some distortions such as retirement vis-à-vis service time and produced some measures aimed at controlling the Social Security deficit. However, its results were only partly successful given that the imbalance between contributions and deficit continues. Reform by President Lula's government consequently did not meet expectations because it did not alter a series of imperfections that have historically been present in the Social Security System. The government suffered various limitations throughout the reform process. Despite the political power shown in the negotiations there were no conditions, or willingness to implement all the necessary changes.

The impossibility of changing age limits and contribution time for private workers is a demonstration of political opportunism clearly brought on by a lack of interest in making the essential transformations toward better systems—a process that is happening in most countries. As mentioned before, an alternative toward diminishing the imbalance at the INSS is by progressively raising the age limit to between 60-65 years for both men and women over the next decade. To the same effect, gradual additions to the contribution time in an evolutionary course for 37 years would be a must.

In Brazil, the democratic debate prevails over the search of what Brazilian society desires and considers fair. In this sense, reforming pensions is not a consensual matter. In fact, some institutional changes have been set out, although the role of those with the power of a veto continues to stop major social changes. Brazil goes through drastic changes in its priorities and perceptions. Setting and keeping the privileges by groups is part of a culture whose roots are founded on the origin of a bureaucratic and conservative state. The array of benefits offered to public-sector workers date back to the last century when they were consolidated under a military dictatorship and are clearly rooted in Brazilian tradition.

Lula's pension reform set the limits on pension payments and allowed for private pensions for public-sector workers; however the latter is yet to be fully realized. The resistance to implement the measures voted and approved by Congress shows the lack of commitment by various groups of society.

An assessment of the main problems of the Brazilian social security system can be found in Giambiagi et al. (2007), Savoia (2007), and Brooks (2009); and can be consequently summarized in five points:

1. In the last two decades the country saw an increase in the population's life expectancy, which is explained by the strong reduction of the child mortality rate, and also by better living conditions among the elderly;

2. Early Retirement, at an average of 55 years, with no minimum age for most workers, makes spending on pensions in Brazil disproportionately high and comparable to that made by developed countries;

3. There are more than 16.4 million people receiving assistance benefits from the social security system because they were not entitled to regular pensions due to lack of contributions. In the future this figure must increase much more, reflecting informal labor markets that comprise 41% of the economically active population;

4. The low growth in gross domestic product (GDP), on average 3.0% per annum since stabilization in 1994, reduces the level of revenue, which makes it difficult to finance social security expenditures because benefits grow at higher rates than GDP growth. Benefits whose values are indexed to the minimum wage doubled over the past 15 years; and there has been an increase in pension and healthcare costs not linked to contributions;

5. There are different opinions about the changes to be adopted in Brazilian social security. However, there is a consensus that the following measures should be adopted. These measures are (i) the gradual adjustment of the minimum retirement age to 62 years for women and 65 for men, (ii) the gradual adjustment of the contribution period from 35 to 37 years, (iii) the indexing of benefits to the Index of Consumer Prices for higher pension values and the Minimum Wage Index for the lowest values, and (iv) the elimination of all exemptions for contributions.

Key issues that should be taken into consideration when making changes include respect for existing rights and care when adopting rules that lead to transition. New legislation should not undo the positive effects of existing reforms. Attention should also be paid to the combination of private and public-sector mechanisms whether they be optional or mandatory when it comes to providing pensions coverage for the population.

Another crucial point is the consolidation of the way the pension system is handled by uniting the supervising organs that take care of it and of the rules that enforce the system. Today, it is handled between two different ministries. And finally, an evaluation should be made of best practices abroad and whether there could be possible convergence with local mechanisms.

## WHY A SOCIAL PACT

According to Dion and Roberts (2008) pensions are the "third rail" of politics. Politicians cannot cut benefits without suffering electoral retribution. Reform of social security is made difficult as people above 50 vote in greater proportion than those bellow 30 and therefore insist that any changes do not affect current recipients. In this way, most countries reform their system gradually.

Pierson (1998) states that the contemporary politics of the welfare state centers on renegotiation, restructuring, and modernization rather than on dismantling the current situation. This is difficult because the simple mention of the possibility of reform creates feelings of insecurity among those who benefit from the status quo. Thus, many proposals for serious and well-intentioned social security reforms have been repeatedly destroyed (Naka-hodo and Savoia, 2008).

Social pacts were negotiated in many European countries in the 1980s and 1990s and have become a major issue in comparative research on industrial relations, corporatist policy-making, and welfare state reform (Siegel, 2005). According to Baccaro (2002, 413-414), the experiences of pension reforms in Italy (1995), Spain (1997), France (1993), Austria (1997), and Finland (1999), took the form of "centralized agreements between government and the 'social partners' (business and labor) or even, as in the case of Italy and Spain, between governments and the labor unions."

One of our main analyses will be how much validity there is in using a social pact for this process. Siegel (2005) affirms that they may provide an advantage for initiating pensions reforms in comparison to other techniques of promoting consultation and consensus building.

On the flip side, it can be said that there is little use for social pacts when it comes to reforms. Indeed, reforms have occurred without social pacts or other concerted efforts exerting a major role on such a process in countries such as Germany, Austria, Sweden, and the Netherlands. In contrast to macroeconomic coordination and reforms of wage bargaining systems, the findings reported by Jochem and Siegel (2003) imply that the impact of tripartite social pacts on welfare state reforms do vary. In many countries they were restricted, in some cases at least disputable and in others not observable at all.

A broad reform of the Brazilian Social Security System by the creation of a social pact that aligns the interests of various sectors of society within the same document would generate greater credibility and less political friction than a multilateral process of negotiation between the government and the unions.

Such a Social Pact document should be expressed as a plan, which would become a Constitutional Amendment, voted and approved by a majority of Congress without suffering opportunistic change or restrictions on scope and content. Evaluation of the program would be done in five years, with new actuarial studies, which would allow for refiguring of effects of previous measures for the correction of distortions.

# 10

# FEMINISM, THE STATE, AND GENDER EQUALITY

*Lia Zanotta Machado*

*Abstract: The paper argues that from a dynamic confrontation against dictatorship in the early seventies, the Brazilian feminist movement has changed towards logic of negotiation in the 21ˢᵗ century. My main point is that, despite these important changes, the logic of addressing the state has always been present. Lula's Government (2003-2010) set up an original and very innovative coalition to sustain political strategies with feminist movements. The building up of the National Council of Women's Rights and the proposal of National Conferences for Women's Policies led the government to approach the positions of feminist movements and vice-versa. However, when pressures became strong against key proposals of the movement, resistances, and contradictions came about within the governmental arena, stressing contradictions and setting apart political positions between government and feminist proposals concerning women's rights.*

One singular trait brought about by the Brazilian feminist movement is its strong connection with the defense of women's rights interwoven with the social rights issue, rather than the insulated notion of women's freedom or liberation. While, in the early moments, the feminist movement in the US and France claimed the right to choose and freedom in the realms of love, sex, and household issues leading to a complete freedom and autonomy in labor relations and in the political sphere, the Brazilian feminist movement stressed, since its inception in the second half of the seventies and the first half of the eighties, a demand for the rights of the women and their fight for democratization (Goldberg, 1991).

## WOMEN'S RIGHTS AND DICTATORSHIP IN THE SEVENTIES

The feminist movement for women's liberation in the US in the sixties and in France in seventies placed emphasis on sexual freedom, condemning the fact that the female body and sex were controlled by men. The battle for sexual freedom was congruent with the denouncing of sexual violation and oppressive sexual relations, at large. It consisted of politicizing the private life.

In Brazil, the feminist movement, since its beginnings in the seventies, has the presence of an international exchange of ideas and proposals with women in exile in Paris, Berkeley, and Santiago (Chile). Discussion groups were built around exiled women, writers, young university students, and left-wing party women who rapidly joined together with women such as Romi Medeiros, a lawyer from Brazilian elite who attained the approval of the Married Woman's Act in 1962. This Act was responsible for releasing the woman from a "relatively incapable condition" in relation to her husband. Before the passage of this act, a woman's right to work and to choose a place to live was dependent on her husband's decision. These discussion groups introduced proposals similar to those proposed by the American and French women's movements, but were also featured as something "good for Brazil" in the words of Goldberg (1987 and 1991). That is to say, they had been effective in bringing together the feminist struggle and the defense of citizenship rights and democracy.

To a large extent, the strength of the feminist movement's repercussion depended upon its participation in the general struggle for democracy, against dictatorship and social inequalities.

The movement's specific issues gained ground, especially in the discussion groups which got together to talk about their daily experiences, and the very same women proposed the holding of encounters and congresses, searching for visibility and political repercussion. Starting in Rio de Janeiro and São Paulo, these encounters aimed at stressing both their own struggle and the struggle for democracy, fighting the authoritarian regime, and getting heard. Male control over female bodies was strongly denounced.

The first public demonstration (1975, Rio de Janeiro) came about with the Seminar on the Role and Behavior of Woman in Brazilian Society. The main issues of the Seminar were dedicated to the daily conditions involving

Brazilian women, such as labor relations, physical and mental health conditions, racial discrimination, and female homosexuality.

As Leila Barsted (2007: 4) wrote, "still in the decade of 1970, we can record perhaps the first media manifestation in favor of abortion through *Jornal Opinião* (1973), an alternative newspaper that in 1973 published some stories on feminism, one of them about voluntary abortion, explaining new and safe abortion techniques." And further ahead: "In 1978, the Ceres group, within a funding program for research about woman from Fundação Carlos Chagas, has carried out a research about social and sexual identity from Brazilian women, also approaching life experiences and perceptions on the abortion through witnesses from many interviewees in this research" (Barsted, 2007: 5).[1]

And yet, denouncing of "the extreme case of men's power over their women's life and death" was the key point that was able to spread across the vast majority of feminists and reach public opinion and elites at that time. The specific issue of the movement with larger visibility is the murder of women, with the first watchwords relating to violence coming up in 1979. These were the denouncing of homicides committed by husbands against their wives and the fact these men were absolved or were released from prison (Sorj and Montero, 1985; Cavalcanti and Heilborn, 1985; Gregori, 1993). The critique of daily and permanent violence against women was not the key point that was able to reverberate in the political elites at that time.[2] The key was the denouncing of women's murder. In fact, women's movements concentrated on the right to survive. Public opinion had great repercussions in the press regarding the cases involving upper and middle classes homicides. Broader than the demand for sexual freedom, the voice that managed to be heard was the denouncing of misogynist and discriminating cultural values in the Penal and Civil Codes and in the jurisprudential interpretations. The repercussion of spouses' homicides from men against their partners gave rise to feminist mobilization with the creation of

---

1. See Alves, Branca Moreira, Barsted, Leila Linhares, Boschi, Sandra Azeredo, Pitanguy, Jacqueline and Ribeiro, Mariska (1981), members of the Grupo Ceres and authors from this book.

2. A well known case was the murder of Ângela Diniz by her partner, Doca Street, both from the social elite. Soon after in 1980, there were the homicides of Maria Regina Rocha and Heloisa Ballesteros. The first trial of Doca Street was in 1979. With a large audience, the trial showed the judicial practice of considering such guilty persons innocent in the category of "defense of honor." Stanciolli, murderer of Heloisa, was condemned in 1982 to two years in prison. The defense accused the victim of being more interested in her entrepreneurial activity than in her role of a mother and wife. Christel Johnston was threatened, pursued, and murdered by her husband who did not accept divorce and, despite looking for help in the police station and courts, she was not protected. See Sorj and Montero (1985) and Cavalcanti and Heilborn, (1985).

centers and of the Committee on Violence Against Women. The public sensitivity about daily violence against women was not equivalent to the debate about female homicides. Some feminist groups, depending on their voluntary work, started to build up help groups offering services targeting women who were victims of violence.

## ADDRESSING THE STATE

In the next moment, the demand from feminist movement (action) was the attempt to place their policies in the agenda of the state public policies. This demand had to do with the proposal for the creation of councils joined by feminists, legitimized by the public authorities, and serving as a consulting and proposal making at local and regional levels. The first State Council of The Feminine Condition (Conselho Estadual da Condição Feminina) was created in São Paulo in 1983. This first Council was the pioneer in suggesting the creation of the first specialized police station[3] providing service for women in 1985.

It is in this context that the idea of specialized police stations to serve women or in the defense of women became relevant. It then possible to build up a certain consensus about two assertions: the prevalence of social values and customs where the importance of violence against women tended to be minimized, and the existence of differences between the male and female approach about violence.

Without a special attention towards violence against women, it would continue invisible, unpunished, and almost legitimized by state power and ruling common sense, as if it were not a social problem. There was an understanding that the specialized police stations were the place where the female voice and denunciations could be heard as well as the place to address properly the male violent acts as crimes. In the majority, these specialized units should be run by female police inspectors. The rationale and claim for this rested upon the idea that their cultural background and identification with the issue would make women more able to give credibility to denouncements made by women.

An important result was the "stop" given by feminists to the alleging of the defense of honor as an argument leading to crime exemption or milder punishment. Under the aegis of the impact of the political voice from femi-

---

3. The specialized police stations were being created beginning in 1985 and in 2010 are still being created (Machado, L., 2001 and 2002; Silva, 2001; SPM, 2008).

nists and from repercussion in the press, it was possible to build up a comprehensive category of "violence against women" that included the "sexual violence" and the inflicting of "light and severe daily body lesions" by partners against their women.

I stress here the fact that, in common-place thought, the idea of murder reminds us of a very severe fact, but it resembles the idea of a single and extraordinary event. When this idea is brought into the field of marital violence, it can reinforce the sense that murder is unbearable, but small eventual and circumstantial violent acts are not. Murder is thought of as inadmissible, but does not point out, in its own turn, its possible inclusion into a permanent and systematic scenario of "severe and small" violence. The systematic and daily "habit" of "beating the women" or of "being beaten by men" is disguised under the curtain of silence and in the assumption of the light injuries towards the eventual and very severe happening of homicide.

And yet, the wrathful indignation towards homicides has created a context able to emerge and "spring up" the cases of systematic and permanent body lesions, more or less often. Whether or not medical symptomatology would call these lesions "severe" or "light," almost always, one and the other are the ground for enormous losses in the women's health and integrity.

The peculiar fact is that female homicide, the landmark in the creation of specialized police stations, has not been defined as pertaining to the jurisdiction of such stations. Specialized police stations being responsible for the investigation of homicide crimes against women are exceptions. It is important to stress that those police stations mostly specialized in the investigation of crimes where interpersonal relationship between victims and witnesses is intense are set apart from the carrying out of such investigation when it comes to homicides.

The slogan "our body belongs to us" gained ground in the beginning of eighties. Feminists criticized proposals for birth control, that, however, were not implemented by federal governments stimulated by international agencies such as the World Bank (Alvarez, 1990; Knudsen, 2006). Birth control turned into facts, by the sterilization provided by two nongovernmental organizations in Brazil linked to and financed by two international nongovernmental organizations. Their activities were allowed by federal and state governments (Costa, 1996). These organizations did not give women complete information either about the consequences of sterilization or about alternative forms of contraception.[4]

The feminist movement was against imposing birth control on the population, but claimed the right to family planning, the right of women to control their fertility, and the public duty to offer contraceptives alongside with information. They were understood as women's rights to autonomy and decision-making. Women's movements and Brazilian health professionals, especially sanitarians, (a term that includes all physicians and health professionals that identify themselves with the international and national movement struggling to introduce sanitary regulations and public policies in order to achieve improvement in environmental conditions and public health)[5] suggested a "Complete Assistance Health Program for Women" (Programa de Assistência Integral à Saúde da Mulher/PAISM) and managed to get an approval from the Ministry of Health in 1983 for a public health system allowing a complete service for female health. It was in opposition to the almost exclusive health service for women as mothers in child and mother's hospitals; therefore, including the right to conception and contraception.

In 1983 in Rio de Janeiro, several feminist groups organized the Encounter About Health Sexuality, Contraception and Abortion.[6] This Encounter "became a landmark for the public debate on abortion due to its national dimension. During three days, it gathered around three hundred representatives from 57 women's groups from all over the country besides parliament members (senators, congressmen, state congressmen, and town councilors) (*Jornal Mulherio*, 1983)... In this Encounter, September 28 was established as the national Day of Fight for the Right of Abortion that became the cornerstone of mobilization in the decades to follow" (Barsted, 2007: 13)

---

4. BEMFAM, Sociedade Civil do Bem-Estar Familiar (Civil Society for Familiar Welfare) was created in 1965 and was linked to the International Planned Parenthood Federation (IPPF), created in 1952. Centro de Pesquisa de Assistência Integrada à Mulher e à Criança (CPAIMC) (Center for Research and Integral Assistance to Women and Children) was linked and financed by Family Planning International Assistance. Paradoxically these two institutions, although they offered Surgical Sterilization to poor women without all the information needed, were the only institutions offering contraceptive pills. See Costa (1996).

5. In Brazil, the international Sanitarians' questions strongly influenced public health policy makers, scholars, and physicians, since the Sanitarians' inception in 1901, and especially, in the seventies and eighties, after the end of dictatorship's period. It was the need to disseminate information, in fact, that led to the establishment of the Pan American Sanitary Bureau. As the American governments became increasingly concerned about the need to collaborate on a wide range of social, economic, and political issues, the First International Conference of American States, held in Washington, D.C., in 1890, established the agency known today as the Organization of American States. That body, at its Second Conference in Mexico City in 1901, called for a "general convention of representatives of the health organizations of the different American republics" to formulate "sanitary agreements and regulations" and to "designate a permanent executive board" to be known as the International Sanitary Bureau—the precursor of the Pan American Sanitary Bureau (Pan American Health Organization, 1998: 1)

6. Grupo Ceres (Ceres Group), Casa da Mulher do Rio de Janeiro (Woman's Home in Rio de Janeiro), Coletivo de Mulheres do Rio de Janeiro, Projeto Mulher do IDAC (Instituto de Ação Cultural) (Woman Project from Cultural Action Institute), and Grupo Mulherando (Womanhood Group).

In 1985, the National Council of Women Rights (Conselho Nacional dos Direitos das Mulheres, CNDM) was created in response to the "Women's Movement for Direct Elections." Violence, since then, continues to be an issue constantly renewed in the national, state, and municipal Councils for Women's Rights. Although the equal rights to work and health are also present, the exposure of violence tends to be essential in these councils and in the feminist movements.

In 1988, the National Council of Women Rights formed an interest group, the "lipstick lobby." It presented to Congressmen of the Constituent Assembly the "Letter From Women" (CNDM, 1986), elaborated by a great number of feminists (see Pinto, 2003). Here the singularity of the Brazilian women's movement is reinforced by presenting its first agenda in the name of democracy and social issues: social justice, creation of a Unified Health System, public and free education in all levels, unions' autonomy, agrarian reform, tax reform, and negotiation of foreign debt. In the second part, the Letter referred to women's rights: labor, health, property rights, sharing in marital relations, defense of physical and psychic integrity of women as a strong point to fight violence, redefinition of penal classification of rape, and creation of specialized police stations to serve women in all towns. The Letter is more contained in relation to the proposal of legalization of abortion. A constitutional principle was suggested in the following terms: "The right to know and decide about her own body will be assured to woman."

The pressure of diversified emergent social movements for democracy in the eighties brought about new possibilities for the interlocution between the state and civil society (Paoli and Telles, 1998) that I call "informal public spaces." Different demands circulate: demands coming from distinct groups in name of different constructions of the "politics of identity" as feminist and women's movements, black people and gays, the so called "new social movements" (Alvarez, 1998; Jelin, 1998); demands for public policies as health, housing and water, and union demands for increase of salaries. (Paoli and Telles, 1998). Fraser would call these "informal public spaces" as "subaltern counter publics" or "parallel discursive arenas where members of subordinated social groups invented and circulated counter discourses, so as to formulate oppositional interpretations of their identities, interests, and needs" (Fraser, 1993: 14).

"A consciousness of the right to have rights was elaborated in this public space, an unprecedented experience in Brazilian history," as Brazilian authors Paoli and Telles (1998: 65) say referring to the eighties. This was the period of eruption of new social movements anchored in groups demanding in name of their identities access to civil rights and recognition.

In the nineties, the trend of feminist movements was to organize in nongovernmental organizations (NGOs) in the search for resources to carry out projects related to the elaboration, follow-up, and "social control" of public policies, as well as participating in the international feminist movement. In response to the need of a greater effectiveness from action proposals within public policies, from social accountability and from representation in international meetings and conferences on the women rights, there was the formation of huge networks[7] to connect local groups in a nationwide network such as the "National Feminist Network of Health and Sexual and Reproductive Rights" (Rede Nacional Feminista de Saúde e Direitos Sexuais e Reprodutivos) created in 1991 and the "Brazilian Women's National Articulation" (Articulação das Mulheres Brasileiras) created in the previous years of the preparation of the Conference of Women's Rights in Beijing in 1995. In 2000, there was the creation of the "Black Brazilian Women NGOs' Articulation" (Articulatio de ONGs de Mulheres Negras Brasileiras), and, soon after, the "Brazilian Lesbian League" (Liga Brasileira de Lésbicas).

Organized in this new way, the feminist movements focused in the nineties and in the first decade of the 2000s on the search for support in the National Congress and in the national and state-level executive institutions for the implementation of a broad range of rights: black women's rights, decriminalization of abortion, and the right to health service in the Unified Health System (Sistema Único de Saúde, SUS) for women who had an unsafe abortion, implementation in the public health system service for abortion cases allowed in the Penal Code from 1940, but not assured as rights, as in the case of interruption of pregnancy in the situation of rape and in situations in which woman's health is in danger.

From 1995 on, in the Government of Fernando Henrique Cardoso, the CNDM was linked to the Ministry of Justice. In 2002, at the end of his second term, the "Special Secretariat for Women's Rights" (Secretaria Especial para os Direitos das Mulheres) was created attached to the Ministry of Justice. The priorities set by the Secretariat were to aid women in the combat against violence against women, in their participation in the political scenario of the country, and in their entrance into the labor market (Bandeira, 2005).

---

7. See Alvarez (1998) for the "boom" of Latin American feminism.

On the other hand, the feminists were called by the Ministry of Health to look after the continuity of the Woman's Health Committee, (achieved in 1983), with a new design of a Legal Abortion Service policy to undertake public service in the case of abortions allowed in the Law so that the public health service for women would provide treatment to women who had an abortion in unsafe conditions.

## THE FEMINIST NETWORKS AND THE NEW PUBLIC SPACES

The new Constitution and the informal public spaces opened up by the social movements in eighties and nineties have turned possible the institutionalization of "formal public spaces" within the State. Formal public spaces within the State have been constructed to negotiate conflicts and social demands, such as the diverse consultative or deliberative councils established at federal, state, and municipal levels. Focusing on creation and empowerment of all kinds of Councils, the very notion of liberal citizenship has been partially transformed into "collective participation in dialogue and negotiation" as Paoli and Telles argued since 1998, much before the expansions and empowerment of these councils.

The empowerment of the councils has especially increased by the decision of Lula's Government. However, against the expectations of the nineties, its scope has been restricted, from my point of view, to fields and issues demanded by the "new social movements," not including the generalization of decisions about public budget, or social and economic policies, as proposed by Labor Party (Partido dos Trabalhadores, PT) in the eighties and nineties.

In 2003, on the first day of Lula's government, the "Special Secretariat for Women's Policies" was created (Secretaria Especial para Políticas para Mulheres, SPM), directly attached to the President's Cabinet and with the status of a Ministry. The difference in the name of the secretariat from that established by Fernando Henrique Cardoso (the State Secretariat for the Rights of Women) reflects the fact that Lula wanted to emphasize that his government was making policies for women.

The government, through the creation of this Secretariat with such status, gave it more budget autonomy than had been given to the precedent Secretariat of Women's Rights. The new government recognized the need to design specific public policies, coordinating and stimulating action on other government bodies, aiming at "transversal gender issues," meaning interconnected gender priorities in public policies that should be implemented by different Ministries, under a common initiative.

Its immediate political strategies were: (1) to establish a new form of relationship with feminist movements, women's movements, and unionized women's movements; and (2) to establish a new form of relationship with and management of state-level and municipal-level bodies.

As an upshot of the first strategy, the SPM started to include the totally restructured National Council of Women's Rights (Conselho Nacional dos Direitos das Mulheres, CNDM). Until then, the members were indicated and nominated by the governments, nevertheless they were recognized by the movement. Since 2003, the new government has introduced the possibility of participation in the Council of representatives of feminist organizations and brokering in the national women networks. One condition is that they are national networks, or exceptionally regional networks attached to diverse specific conditions, for example, such as Women living in Amazonia, as many live in forest and rural areas. The second condition is that they are demanding participation, by their own initiative, justifying and proving their existence and indicating a representative and a surrogate. Heterogeneous organizations comprised the first Council (2003-2005), and the second Council (2005-2008). They included national feminist organizations; feminist women's organizations traditionally bound to political parties, but as autonomous organizations; professional women's organizations; and union organizations that promote women's rights being represented by their women's sections. It is only in the third Council (2008-2010) that special quotas are set for two groups: a first group classified as "feminist networks and movements in the defense of women's rights" (redes feministas e de movimentos de mulheres em defesa dos direitos das mulheres) gets 14 seats and a surrogate entity as an alternate to replace one of the seats, when one of these entities are unable to attend. The second group was classified as "union organizations, associative, professional or category acting in the promotion of women rights, represented by their women's bodies' sections," (organizações sindicais, associativas e profissionais que atuam na promoção de direitos das mulheres, representadas pelas seções de mulheres) with seven seats and a surrogate. The entities present themselves as candidates and indicate their representatives. The representatives chosen by these entities are those with the right to vote and be voted.

The properly recognized feminist networks are present in all three councils: they are the Brazilian Women's Articulation (Articulação de Mulheres

Brasileiras), Black Brazilian Women NGOs' Articulation (Articulação de ONGs de Mulheres Negras Brasileiras), National Feminist Network on Health (Rede Nacional Feminista de Saúde), World Women's March (Marcha Mundial das Mulheres), Women's Forum in Mercosur (Fórum de Mulheres do Mercosul), and Articulated Amazonian Women's Movement (Movimento Articulado de Mulheres da Amazônia). Two other feminist party-leaning organizations, but which are autonomous, are the Brazil's Women's Confederation (Confederação das Mulheres Brasileiras) and Brazilian Union of Women (União Brasileira de Mulheres), that also have been present since the beginning of Lula's government. It is important to point out that in the third Council the recently created Brazilian Lesbian League, the National Forum of Black Women, and the Peasant Women's Movement, strengthened the trend to organize the feminist movements in networks accounting for the diversity of their representation. A new thematic feminist network has a place in the Council: the Economy and Feminism Network.

Differently from the First and Second Councils with a representative from the National Council of Indigenous Women (Conselho Nacional das Mulheres Indígenas) (an exclusively female organization), the native Indigenous representation in the Third Council is the Committee of Indigenous Organizations from Brazilian Amazon, (Coordenação das Organizações Indígenas da Amazônia Brasileira), a more general organization represented by its women's section.

With exclusively or mostly female members, the first group of 14 seats includes the Household Workers Federation (Federação Nacional dos Trabalhadores Domésticos) and as surrogate the Federation of Business Women Associations (Federação das Associações de Mulheres de Negócios e Profissionais do Brasil).

In the second group of the Third Council, since the beginning of Lula's Government, there is the presence of the Labor Trade Union (Central Única dos Trabalhadores), the National Confederation of Agricultural Workers (Confederação Nacional dos Trabalhadores da Agricultura), the National Teachers Union (Confederação Nacional dos Trabalhadores em Educação), and the Brazilian Association of Lawyers (Ordem dos Advogados do Brasil).[8] If in the first and second Councils, the proportion of civil society's representatives and federal government representatives is 20 to 13, without accounting for the three seats for "women with expertise on gender issues," in the third Council, this proportion is 21 civil society's representatives to 14 government representatives.

The second strategy implicated in new forms of relationship with states and municipalities. There were various political gestures to change federal relationship with states and municipalities: the proposal of the National Conferences on Women's Policies, preceded by state and municipal conferences; the support to the formation of Women's Rights Committees in the states and in towns; the signing by municipal and state bodies of the National Pacts concerning each program such as Combating Violence Against Women and Reduction of Maternal Mortality, and the incentives given to the elaboration of State and Municipal Plans.[9] I argue that the national, state, and municipalities conferences for Women's Policies proposals provided the foundation of and legitimized all the new federal relationships with states and municipalities, as well with feminist and women's movements at national, state, and municipal levels.

In its turn, the Conferences for Women's Policies were legitimized by the joint proposal of the National Council of Women's Rights and the Secretariat for Women's Policies to organize the Conference on Women's Policies. Its approval will depend, however, on the appraisal by the government and civil society representatives as well as those from municipalities and states. Although the numerical relation between civil society and government representation in the Conference will be favorable to civil society, the government has greater political weight, given its initiative being prioritizing in the political deals so far.

The initial theme proposals for the First National Conference, preceded by State and Municipal Conferences, were the initiative of the Secretariat for Women's Policies (SPM) in a discussion with National Council of Women's Rights (CNDM) through the representatives' members of the council who elected some of them, to organize the Conference. In this consulting and election process, there was a tacit allowance in the priority to nominate feminists. In relation to the elaboration of the themes, they were

---

8. Important workers confederations are not present anymore such as Labor General Confederation (Confederação Geral dos Trabalhadores) and Union Strength (Força Sindical). Both are general unions from Brazilian workers. Similarly, the National Articulation of Worker Rural Women (Articulação Nacional de Mulheres Trabalhadoras Rurais) is no longer present. For the first time at the Council, there are present the National Gathering Family Farm Workers (Federação dos Trabalhadores na Agricultura Familiar) and the Association of Graduate Courses in Public Health (Associação Brasileira de Pós-graduação em Saúde Coletiva), an association of those university centers and research centers that provide Graduate courses in Public Health. The continuities and the changes between the entities represented in the Council of Women's Rights indicates the great diversity of women's autonomous organizations as well as their diversity in specific sectors within more broad organizations and unions.

9. Federal transfers were delivered conditional on formally committing to the targets of the Federal Plan.

proposed by the Secretariat and its technical staff, with the support of feminist academics specialized in the topics in agreement with the Council. The themes for the first Conference were: "Autonomy and Equality in the Labor World;" "Inclusive and Non-racist, Non-homophobian, and Non-lesbophobian Education," "Women's Health, Sexual, and Reproduction Rights," "Combat Against all Forms of Violence Against women" and "Plan Management and Monitoring."

The same topics are reinforced in the second Conference and are expanded with two more areas suggested by the Secretariat: "Participation in the Power Spaces" and "Sustainable Development;" and four more areas suggested by civil society in the Conference: "Right to Land and Decent Living in the Rural and Urban Areas, Considering the Traditional Communities"; "Culture, Communication and Democratic and Non-discriminating Egalitarian Media"; "Combat of Racism, Sexism, and Lesbophobia"; and "Combat of Generational Inequalities Affecting Women, Especially the Youngest and the Oldest." The new topics indicate the strength of the idea of presenting claims referring to interest. They demand diversity from women according to age, race, and lifestyle. Diversity of claims coming from differences of class, race, sexuality, age, and conditions of life, between women, have been included successfully in Feminist and Women's Movements and in the "new public spaces."

## PUBLIC POLICIES FOR GENDER EQUALITY

Since the first National Conference held in 2004 and from the second National Conference held in 2007, it was possible to design policies elaborated as The National Plan for Women's Policies: I and II. These Plans covered not only proposals and activities to be carried out by the Secretariat for Women's Policies itself, but by the many ministries. For this, a Juncture and Plan Monitoring Committee with members from all Ministries was created in March, 8, 2005 by Presidential Ordinance. For the first time, a structure with such a broad scope was outlined in the Brazilian Government. However, the differentiated participation in the support of the proposals of the conferences from each Ministry is evident. The difference in participation to a large extent depends on the stronger or weaker acquaintance and tradition with topics related to women's rights, such as the cases of the Ministry of Health and the Ministry of Agrarian Development. In the same way, the many proposals do not correspond to an activity with a budget, but to a qualitative way of acting that it may not be possible to evaluate.

Still more difficult to evaluate is the impact of support and implementation from state-level and municipal-level policies.

The symbolic effectiveness, however, produces reciprocal effects between feminist movements, union movements, state and municipal committees devoted to women rights, as well as between social movements and the Special Secretariat for Women's Policies. In terms of a coordinated political maneuvering, there is a strong novelty in Lula's Government. And yet, when seen from the global scale of public policies, the budget of the Special Secretariat is pretty tiny, as well are insufficient the budgets supporting the National Plans for Women's Policies encompassing goals and resources from other Ministries.

General data concerning work, education, and health can signal achievements directly linked to new policies and new forms designed to revolutionize our understanding of gender equalities. These measurements of gender equalities can show the effects of the feminist movement and of legitimating feminist goals by the State and can also signal resistance to gender equality which is not yet possible to remove.

Among the data[10] that allow seeing issues relative to gender (in-) equality, I point out the significant rise of women's participation in the active population and labor market. While in 1996, 52.2% of women over 16 years old were active; such a figure reached 59% in 2006. However, if women's participation in the labor market reached 17.8% in 2006, male activity in that year was still responsible for 82.2% of labor market participation. The unemployment rate was smaller for men (6.4%) in comparison to 11% for women, revealing their greater difficulty in obtaining access to the labor market. While white men accounted for an unemployment rate of 5.7%, black women accounted for a rate of 12.5%. Women to a larger extent are housemaids, self-employed workers for their own consumption and without any pay, and the men are often employees, self-employed workers, and employers.

Data from the Brazilian Geographical and Statistics Institute (Instituto Brasileiro de Geografia e Estatística, IBGE) for 2006 indicate[11] that while

---

10. See *II Plano Nacional de Políticas Públicas para as Mulheres* (SPM, 2008). Also see for specific data:*Pesquisa por Amostra de Domicílios* (PNAD) from Instituto Brasileiro de Geografia e Estatística (IBGE), in IBGE. *Pesquisa Nacional por Amostra de Domicílios (PNAD) 2006.* http://www.ibge.gov.br/home/estatistica/populacao/trabalhoerendimento/pnad2006/default.shtm. Also see *Banco de Dados do Sistema Único de Saúde (DATASUS)* from Ministério da Saúde. http://tabnet.datasus.gov.br/cgi/deftohtm.exe?sim/cnv/matuf.def.

90.2% of occupied women dedicate themselves to household tasks, only 51.4% of men say they do them, although this data is probably something new. While women say they spend 25 hours looking after household tasks, men spend less than ten hours. A significant inequality is the continuity of greater income for men than for women, despite the relevance of a smaller difference with a 2% drop between 2001 and 2006. Women earned an average 65% of men's earnings. The racial issue has a strong presence. Black people earn less than the half of white people's earnings.

In education, women are stronger in comparison with men; women have higher educational levels: high school (54.06%), professional education (50.87%), and higher education teaching (62.8%) compared with men whose compared educational levels are 45.94%, 49.13%, and 37,02%.[12] Even so, they earn less in the labor market. On the other hand, there is strong inequality concerning the gender segmentation in the matter involving distribution of careers. The areas in higher education with more women are Teacher's College [pedagogy] (91.3%), Languages (80%), and Nursing (82.9%). The larger male percentages are in the careers of Computing Science (81.2%) and Engineering (79.7%).

In Brazil, the ratio of maternal mortality has been falling over the years, reaching a rate in 2005 with the adjusted figure of 74.6 maternal deaths for each 100,000 live births.[13] Even so the rate is elevated if compared with developed countries where these ratios move around 6 and 20 maternal deaths for each 100,000 live births. In the Unified Public Health System, 222,840 post-abortion curettages were made, with 37 maternal deaths. There may be an underestimation of all kinds of maternal deaths, stemming from child-bearing, from post-child-bearing and from abortion; the underestimation is still larger for maternal death result of unsafe and clandestine abortions. Maternal death is the most probable avoidable death in 95% of the cases and death by abortion is estimated as the fourth cause of maternal mortality. Estimates for abortion done according to reckoning from international organizations for Brazil, considering the figure of 222,840 post-abortion curettages, the number would be around 800,000 or 1,000,000 abortions done every year in clandestine conditions.

---

11. IBGE. *Pesquisa Nacional por Amostra de Domicílios (PNAD)* 2006. In http://www.ibge.gov.br/home/estatistica/populacao/trabalhoerendimento/pnad2006/default.shtm. See also SPM (2008).
12. Instituto Nacional de Estudos e Pesquisas Educacionais Anísio Teixeira (INEP) Ministério de Educação 2006. In http://www.inep.gov.br/superior/enade/default.asp. Also see SPM (2008).
13. Secretaria de Vigilância da Saúde. Ministério de Saúde http://tabnet.datasus.gov.br/cgi/deftohtm.exe?sim/cnv/matuf.def and SPM (2008).

According to data from the Ministry of Health for the year 2000, there were 26.7 homicides per 100,000 inhabitants. The growth of violence in the last decades in Brazil is clear if we compare the period from 1980 to 2003. It was 14 homicides per 100,000 inhabitants in 1980, reaching a peak of 28.9 for each 100,000 in 2003.[14]

Between 2004 and 2006, there was a drop in the rate of homicides to 23.9 per 100,000 inhabitants in 2006. An analytical document produced by the Ministry of Health and the Secretariat of Health Surveillance (SVS, 2006: 12) mentions as probable causes of the drop in violent deaths: "[the] disarmament act, the gathering of firearms by government authorities, and the investments in security by the Federal Government and by the states and towns which played the role of stimulating the development of structures of public security and local projects for the combat of violence."[15]

Even taking into account the impact of public policies, it is necessary to expand the international comparison to see the remarkable amount of homicides in Brazil. Data from the US in 2000 showed there were around 6 homicides per each 100,000 inhabitants, in France; the number was 4, in England, Canada, and Australia from 2 to 3. (SENASP, 2001; Souza, 2003)

Comparing homicides and female murdering and focusing on Brazilian capital cities (Souza and Carvalho, 2006), mortality data in 2003 register a difference in the victimization of men and women. Female mortality due to homicide in the Brazilian capital cities in the Northeast ranges from 1.8 per 100,000 inhabitants (João Pessoa) to 8.4 per 100,000 (Cuiabá), and male mortality ranges from 37.2 (Natal) to 134.6 (Recife).

These rates of murdering females evens out or overcomes the total rate of homicides, including men and women, from Western European countries (3 to 4), in North American countries (2 to 6), and in Australia (2 to 3). This comparison reveals the high incidence of homicides of women in Brazil, without mentioning the recognized amount of male homicides.

Such murdering of females is mainly done by former partners, ex-husbands, relatives, and acquaintances. So are the body lesions and daily threats in the

---

14. All Brazilian data about homicides are collected and informed by Ministry of Health's database (DATASUS) (http://www2.datasus.gov.br/DATASUS/index.php). The specific data from 1980 and 2000 are included in the report made by Secretaria Nacional de Segurança Pública (SENASP, 2001). The specific data from 2000 to 2003 are included in the analytical text written by Filho and Gazal-Carvalho (2007).

15. In Brazil, the "Disarmament Statute" is a federal law of December 22, 2003 that prohibits civilians from carrying, with exception for the cases where there is threat to the person's life. In those cases, there will be permission for limited duration. See Estatuto do Desarmamento Comentado. Lei n° 10.826, de 22 de Dezembro de 2003 (http://www.deolhonoestatuto.org.br/downloads/biblioteca/002.pdf).

family, marital, and domestic environments. While young men are particularly the guilty and victims of murder in the case of male homicides, women are the victims of daily violence (see Machado, L., 1998 and Bandeira, 1998). The combination of forms of violence from organized crime together with the high incidence of interpersonal violence between men and women enable us to understand that the issue of "violence against women" is the most visible form of a violent sociability lived as something unimportant.

These data give us both the confirmation of gender inequality and possibly positive results stemming from public policies and forms of feminist movement and from human rights producing its effects upon the State, but also in the forms of sociability.

However, perhaps the achievements and challenges from feminist movement can be better scrutinized when there is a focus on the two main political projects of feminist movement (action) over the last eight years and the strategic position performed by the Special Secretariat for Women's Policies towards the Federal Government in the decision to introduce the project into the political scene.

## FEMINIST DRAFT BILLS UNDER LULA'S GOVERNMENT

In Lula's Government (2003-2010) there were two ongoing projects due to the initiative from the feminist movement. There were two draft bills arising from the mobilization from feminist organizations that depended, however, on taking the leading role from the official initiative of the Special Secretariat for Women's Policies. Feminist intellectuals working in NGOs and universities, as well as their knowledge of Law, Social Sciences, Health Sciences, and other disciplines were crucial to the design of these projects.

The first draft bill is about domestic violence against women. The negotiations between a consortium of feminist nongovernmental organizations and the Special Secretariat for Women's Policies began in 2003 and a new law was presented by Lula's Government and approved by the Parliament in August 2006.[16]

The second draft provides the right to halt pregnancy during the first twelve weeks, decriminalization of the termination of pregnancy during this period, and the guarantees its coverage by the national health care sys-

---

16. Act n 11,340, August 7, 2006 (http://www.planalto.gov.br/CCIVIL/_Ato2004-2006/2006/Lei/L11340.htm).

tem and by private health insurance plans. The need to change the law that criminalizes abortion was a decision of the First National Conference on Women's Policies en 2004. A new Draft Bill was written in 2005, but has not been approved or presented and directed by Lula's Government to Parliament as of March, 2010.

The first draft presented by the Government to Parliament, the one related to violence against women, went through a broad discussion, always with the presence of feminist organizations. It was presented to Parliament as a governmental draft act akin to the initiative from the Special Secretariat for Women's Policies. It was approved by Parliament on August 7, 2006, becoming the Act 11,340, known as the Maria da Penha[17] Act. The Act is being enforced although it encounters resistance because of conservative values held by many judges, in contrast to the values expressed by public opinion and the majority of lawmakers. The idea "the women do not want to suffer violence" was legitimized. In other words, they are not embedded in symbolic violence, without any help... They do not allow it...

The juridical resistance towards the Act reveals how much the former understanding of the Penal Code hindered any measure of protection of women and of combat against violence. Today, in the places where the Act is being enforced, protection measures are being applied and force anyone convicted of violence against a woman to move from the home and not approach the woman.

Before the new Act, crimes of violence against women were under two different systems: one before 1995 and the last, between 1995 and 2006. Until 1995, under the rules of Penal Code, only about 6% of accused were condemned and very few were convicted.[18] From 1995 to 2006 there was the Act 9099/95 ("court of small causes") that included the majority of cases of violence against women (Campos, 2001). This act only demanded that the accused pay the value of a package of essential goods, representing one fifth of minimum wage, to the community when he injured his wife. As a member of the couple, the victim, in some way, had to lose some of the

---

17. The *Act: "Lei n° 11,340" (2006)* has been called the "Lei (law) Maria da Penha," in honor of Maria da Penha, a woman severely injured as the victim of her husband's violence. A document on behalf of this woman was sent by the feminist movement to the International Court, and Brazil received the recommendation to change the impunity situation of the perpetrators of violence against women. This situation has improved the favorable conditions for the government to propose this law.

18. See research on judicial sentences on Violence against Women in Rio de Janeiro in Carrara, Vianna and Enne (2000).

family's income. Besides, she wasn't even listened to by the Judge or didn't receive any protection measure...

There are at least two challenges posed by marital violence as presented in the new Act Maria da Penha to the Justice System, to specialized police stations, and to traditional and specialized courts. The first is to deal with crimes or violations inscribed in cultural hegemonic values and disseminated across all social classes and traditionally inscribed in jurisprudence:[19] the trend to tolerate daily marital violence, in the name of legitimating male control over sexual loyalty from wives and partners. The allegation of honor in Brazilian jurisprudence, accounted for the absolution of a confessed murderer, have effects even today, alleviating acts of violence against women. The allegation of the need to keep up the family currently stands out as a justification for non-punishment. The "jurisprudential tolerance" towards domestic violence against women is in favor of the strong idea of "family harmony," considered as juridical good.

Owing to his traditional role as a provider, a man can prevent, control, and demand sexual fidelity from his partner and control the role performance of "mother" and "housewife." Once more, the old legal power through which husbands could allow or not allow their wives access to paid jobs is only a cue to the strength of these assumptions in the social order (CFEMEA, 1994). Despite a great number of legal and social changes, these values are far from being eradicated and continue to guide social behavior and jurisprudential interpretations. These values are what "New History" historians call "long standing values."

The second challenge for the Justice System is the fact these crimes and infractions are in the realm of the so-called private and interpersonal, strongly loaded with emotion and affection without the traditional distancing between the accused and the victim that is very common in crimes against property.[20] The investigation, reconciling, arbitration, and judging are carried out in a context interweaving shared values and interests of a greater complexity and peculiarity that are very different from relations between accused and victim in most of crimes against property or crimes motivated by instrumental interests.

---

19. Carrara, Vianna, and Enne (2000), by researching two inquiry centers in Rio de Janeiro, point out how, in the name of the family, the petitions against domestic violence against women are systematically shelved or the guilty absolved. This is done with the agreement of prosecutors, attorneys, and judges. From the total of petitions only 6% ended up in condemnation. See also Baratta (1999) and Campos (2001).

20. For different conceptual typologies and crimes, see Machado, L. (1998 and 2004); Ratton Jr. and Luiz (1996); Suarez and Bandeira (1999); Soares, L., (1996).

The second draft act that is very worthwhile for the feminist movement is the one that legalizes the cessation of pregnancy. At the end of 2009, abortion was considered to be a crime. The present Brazilian Penal Code says, according to article 124 and 128 written in1940: To provoke abortion in herself or to consent that somebody else provokes it, has a detention of one to three years. There are two circumstances where there is no punishment: (1) if there is no other means of saving the pregnant woman's life; and (2) in the case of pregnancy resulting from rape (Codigo Penal Atualizado, 1940). In the new shape of national networks, the Brazilian feminist movement (action) for legalization of abortion has been brought back from the nineties over the last years with growing intensity. A great visibility was obtained with the proposal to legalize abortion undertaken by the decision of women during the first twelve weeks of pregnancy, elaborated and presented to a Three-party Committee (Comissão Tripartite) named by the President of the country, to the Social Security and Family Committee of the National Congress in 2005. The Ministry of Women's Policies presented the draft to the National Congress' Social Security and Family Committee. This is a draft act in the political scene that "establishes the right to voluntary termination of pregnancy, assuring the procedure is included in the Unified Health System, and determining its coverage by private health plans to provide assistance to health among other provisions" (SPM, 2005b).

The Three-party Committee joined by members of the Federal Government, from civil society and from the National Congress of Brazil and run by the Special Secretariat for Women Policies (SPM/PR) was set up with the purpose of discussing, elaborating, and furthering the proposal to review punishing legislation concerning voluntary termination of pregnancy, according to the Regulation N° 4 of April 6, 2005. The Three-party Committee was made up of 18 members, equally distributed between Government, Parliament (National Congress), and Civil Society.[21] A Committee, run by Special Secretariat for Women's Policies, finished its job on time

---

21. Representatives from Government: Maria Laura Pinheiro (SPM), Maria José Araújo (Ministério da Saúde), Pedro Abramovay (Ministério da Justiça), Denise Figueira (Casa Civil da Presidência da República), Paulo Sérgio Muçouçah (Secretaria Geral da Presidência da República), Carolina Melo (Secretaria Especial dos Direitos Humanos da Presidência da República). Representatives from Legislative Power: Câmara dos Deputados: Maria Suely Campos (PP-RR), Angela Moraes Guadagnin (PT-SP) e Elaine Carvalho Costa (PTB/RJ); Senado Federal: Serys Slhessarenko (PT/MT), João Capiberibe (PSB-AP) e Eduardo Suplicy (PT-SP). Representatives from Civil Society: Shuma Schumaher (Articulação de Mulheres Brasileiras, AMB), Maria Ednalva Lima (Central Única dos Trabalhadores, CUT), Maria Elvira Ferreira (Fórum de Mulheres do Mercosul), Lia Zanotta Machado (Rede Nacional Feminista de Saúde, Direitos Sexuais e Direitos Reprodutivos), Edmund Chada Baracat, represented by Jorge Andalaf (Federação Brasileira das Associações de Ginecologia e Obstetrícia) and Thomaz Rafael Gollop (Sociedade Brasileira para o Progresso da Ciência, SPBC).

and presented the product of this assignment in the form of a proposal of "Punishing legislation review concerning the Voluntary Termination of Pregnancy (SPM, 2005a and 2005b)."

There were two political events that played essential roles for the creation of the necessary conditions for the building of a Committee appointed by the President Cabinet to review the abortion legislation.

The first was the creation and constitution, by the initiative of the National Feminist Network from Reproduction and Health Rights from a network of feminist NGOs, of actions to bring back the proposal of legalizing abortion: the organization of "Brazilian Journeys for Legal and Safe Abortion" (Jornadas Brasileiras para o aborto legal e seguro) in February 2004 (*Jornadas*, 2005). The second was the holding of municipal, state, and national conferences by the Special Secretariat for Women's Policies and by the CNDM. Its organization started in 2003, and the holding of municipal and state conferences took place in the first semester of 2004, leading to the National Conference held in July in 2004, with more than 2,000 women and mobilizing around 120,000 women.

The message below from "Journeys" (Jornadas) reveals the importance given to debates held in the Conferences;

> Fighting against contempt and disrespect to the right of decision by women, feminism created Brazilian Journeys for Legal and Safe Abortion and called for women and men to be united and participate in the struggle to force the Federal Government to send recommendations from the First National Conference on the Policies for Women (July, 2004) supporting decriminalization and legalization of abortion (*Jornadas*, 2005: 1).

Certainly, the campaigns made by *Jornadas*[22] also were responsible for assuring the attention to and the vote on this controversial issue inside the broader women's movement, for feminism, in strict terms, is far from being the point of view of the majority of women. Among the 2,000 women or more present in the National Conference in 2004, only 200 opposed this resolution. From the State Conferences, with more than 20,000 women, only one Conference on the policies for woman from Minas Gerais did not approve the demand for the review of the legislation punishing abortion. Once the assignments from Three-party Committee were finished, the Special Secretariat for Women's Policies handed a draft of the project to Jandira

---

22. Two representatives from civil society in the Three-party Committee took part in the campaigns for the right of legal and safe abortion: representatives from "Articulação das Mulheres Brasileiras" (Brazilian Women's Articulation) and "Rede Nacional Feminista de Saúde e Direitos Sexuais e Reprodutivos" (Feminist Network for Health and Sexual and reproductive Rights).

Feghali of the Health, Security, and Family Committee (Comissão de Segu-ridade Social e Familia, CSSF). In that moment, Jandira Feghali was asked to give a statement about a precedent draft legalizing abortion presented many years before. She adopted the draft presented by the Three-party Committee as a replacement for the draft she was considering.

Her statement was in favor of the draft bill made by Three-party Comm ision. The resistance was huge in the Health, Security, and Family Commit-tee (CSSF), made more difficult by the absence in that meeting of congress-men, members of (CSSF) expected to be favorable. With the proximity of elections, and the uncertainty of the results, it was not sent out for a vote ( Machado, L., 2008; A.L. Cunha, 2007). The contrary positions in the Con-gress grew stronger with the setting up of a Congressional Front against abortion. With new Congress members elected in 2007, the Draft Bill has been tabled.

The ongoing negotiations for the agreements between the Vatican, Con-gress, and Lula's Government (Vaticano, 2008) as well as the pressure from the National Bishop's Conference of Brazil against the draft act of legaliza-tion of abortion forced the government to retreat from its earlier position regarding the voluntary termination of pregnancy. Still in the II Conference for Women's Policies, the Conference approved the official resending of the same draft bill on the Voluntary Termination of Pregnancy to the Congress, but this proposal is not included in the II National Plan for Women's Poli-cies, nor has it been accepted by the Government as a draft bill to again be presented to Congress.

In international feminist movements in the 1960s and 70s, women's rights were placed in a field of discourse in which women's emancipation was placed in polar opposition to conservative, masculine, religious, and traditional fam-ily values. The pro-life arguments were incipient as a social movement.

In Brazil today, the center of the debate is increasingly polarized between "the defense of women's rights and women's dignity" by feminist and pro-gressive movements, and the "pro-life" arguments, particularly defense, as an absolute value, without any balance, of the life of the embryo or fetus. The new approach of conservative thought is internationally organized as a movement. Against conservative movements, the "defense of women's life" has to be advocated using the techniques employed in the seventies and eighties to modify public opinion towards violence against women that only was changed with the murder of women. Female reproductive and sexual rights will only be heard by public opinion, and not always understood, if women's lives are in danger or lost.

Public opinion, despite being encouraged by the fundamentalist movement, seems to be anchored to an illusory notion of a large distance between guiding "private" behavior (in which mandatory and justifiable reasons appear in the intention of aborting in a specific situation) and guiding based upon a "collective morality." There is an idea of opposition between a notion of "us" who can decide privately with responsibility, justifying the termination of pregnancy in name of a specific and constrained situation, and a notion of "them" (all others) who are incapable of making a responsible decision, for whom, therefore, there is a need to criminalize abortion.

Despite all encompassing political difficulties and the failure to obtain government support for the legalization of abortion, the feminist movement is continuing to fight for the lives of nearly one million Brazilian women per year who abort in response to various constraints, according to national and international estimates, and are in danger of dying as a result of procedures performed in conditions that are unsafe, because they are illegal.

## CONCLUSION

Beyond the fact that building new forms for the composition of National Council of Women's Rights and the proposal of the National Conferences for Women's Policies yielded a visible by the government towards the positions of feminist movements and vice-versa, "Lula's" political strategies have helped to combine diverse approaches formulated by feminist movements and union and professional movements, and have contributed to the absorption of government mechanisms in the implementation of women's rights at the state and municipal levels.

Formal public spaces within the State have been constructed by Lula's government to negotiate conflicts and social demands. The very notion of liberal citizenship has been partially extended and transformed into "collective participation in dialogue and negotiation." The strength of the feminist movement on maintaining its goals limits the possibility of cooptation. The search for social rights for all women and the need for public policies always has been taken up as a goal by the Brazilian feminist movement. The majority of the feminist women, since the beginnings, were leftist and politically articulated against dictatorship. They assumed they could speak both in their own names and in the name of all women workers, middle and lower class women.

In 2009, the most important feminist networks included women of different classes, races, and sexual choices (or sexual identities). At same time, feminist black women and feminist lesbian women are organized in their own networks. All these feminist movements give priority to the establishment of common targets and reciprocally support their specific goals, as well as supporting the organization of indigenous women, unionized women, and rural women. Constructing NGOs and strong networks, despite the differences of power and access to financial resources between feminist groups, has made it possible to advocate gender equality to the government and to amalgamate alliances between widely differing segments of the feminist movement.

The Lula government has accepted the possibility of introducing and consolidating "public spaces" as Councils and new government bodies, as well as enacting and enforcing "public policies" against gender inequalities, and has approved the First and the Second Plan for Women's Policies. The first and the second Conferences called by the Special Secretariat for Women's Policies, for listening to and being accepted by the social movements has produced the effect of amalgamating the diverse claims of all these different segments of women's movements. The challenge will be the real implementation of all these claims, especially when resistances and contradictions come about within the government, setting apart political positions between government and feminist proposals for the rights of women.

Public opinion differs about how to accept all these new policies. In its mainstream, it has been very receptive to the idea of ending discrimination based on gender, sexual choice, and race. The most varied education policies of inclusion, as teaching ways of combating sexism, homophobia, lesbophobia, and racism as well as gender discrimination have been accepted and been legitimized as social values. They have been internalized as modern moral values. This does mean that discrimination cannot be, anymore, realized as legitimate and "natural" values. This does not mean that gender, race, and sexual discrimination have ended in the daily social relationships within the System of Public Health or the System of Public Education. It also does not mean that a new bill legalizing civil union or establishing racial quotas for entering at Universities has been accepted by the mainstream of public opinion.

Public Opinion surveys (Instituto Patricia Galvão, 2004) on violence against women show that Brazilians believe the woman should not put up with aggressions by her companion (86%). Statistics reflect the high incidence of violent social practices. Nonetheless, the generalized acceptance of the idea of ending violence against women probably is one of the results of the multiple campaigns made by the NGOs feminists and by the government.

I have argued here that the feminist movement's seeking the government as one allied and prior partner is due to the fact that portions of public opinion and parts of public institutions in Brazil are still very conservative concerning sexual and reproductive rights and women's rights for a life without violence. By the same token, the juridical institutions continue to be predominantly conservative in regard to violence against women. Moreover, conservative ideas have been reinforced by a new fundamentalism, namely by such components as "Prolife" and "Profamily Movement." These groups are strongly organized around some religious political representatives, mainly Catholics and Evangelicals. Fundamentalism is also supported by the most important organization of the Catholic Church in Brazil, the Conference of Bishops in Brazil, and by the new Juridical Catholic Association.

I also argue that addressing the government in these late years, the Brazilian feminist movement achieved some important goals: introducing and reinforcing public policies for women and public policies for gender equality, and contributing to some changes in public opinion. My point of view is that the institutionalization and partial professionalization of the feminist movement has increased the possibilities of achievements. We cannot forget the fact that, at the same time, the interconnections between feminism, black feminism, lesbian feminism, and all women's movements as unionized women and neighborhood women's association has been reinforced by the creation of "public spaces" for dialogue and negotiation.

The challenges are huge. From now on, the goals should continue to be addressed to the state, as well as interconnected with international feminism, but also addressed to civil society on the search of new alliances, while the new conservative and fundamentalist movements are also organized on national and international levels.

# 11

# NATION-STATE CONSOLIDATION AND CULTURAL PATRIMONY

*John F. Collins*

*Abstract: In Brazil cultural heritage has played a key role in nationalism even as Brazilian definitions of patrimony have shifted across the 20th century. In this discussion of the history of Brazil's federal cultural heritage institution, IPHAN, I analyze how heritage planning has tacked in different historical periods between a concern with monuments and buildings, on one hand, and people's everyday habits, on the other. I argue that at a moment when a new class of patrimony, usually called "intangible heritage," has become salient in both Brazil and the United Nations, people's everyday habits have come to be commodified as part of a patrimonialization process that is no longer based on demonstrating national sovereignty, but on producing value through the packaging of national culture.*

On November 10, 1937, shortly after President Getúlio Vargas announced the establishment of an *Estado Novo* intended to counter the "Universal suffrage...[that] has become the instrument of the astute, the mask which thinly disguises the connivings of personal ambition and greed" (Lacerda, 1938: 103), Francisco Campos, Minister of Education from 1930 to 1934 and the drafter of the new 1937 constitution, burned each of Brazil's twenty states' flags in a ceremony in Rio de Janeiro. As is well-known, and as these pyrotechnics by one of the Estado Novo's ideologues suggest, Vargas' ascension represented a restructuring of Brazilian society. This involved an "expansion within its own territory, conquering itself and the integration of the State, making its dimensions as vast as the country" (Vargas, 1938, vol. 5: 163). A crucial aspect of this "interior colonization" (Vargas, 1938, vol. 6: 88) lay in the creation of institutions that would foster "a hierarchization of activities, a coordination of means, and a continuity of action" (Martins dos Santos, 1941: 69).

The Estado Novo's expansion represented a marked increase in the production of data and the encouragement of nationalist pride around activities like mapmaking, record-keeping, and statistics. For bureaucrats, these were not simply representations of what Brazil already was, but rather important tools in nation-state consolidation since, for example, statistics is "more than a matter of representation. . . [it] is a tool of political intervention" (Asad, 2002: 82). Yet numbers and textual description were not the only tools open to experts focused on molding Brazil's population, geography, and culture.

On November 30, 1937, twenty days after the flag burning, Getúlio Vargas issued Presidential Decree Number 25 which outlined the responsibilities and organization of a new federal institution, the National Artistic and Historical Patrimony Service, (SPHAN). It defined the cultural manifestations around which SPHAN was organized as "patrimony," or the "set of mobile and immobile goods that exist in the nation whose conservation is of public interest, whether because of their ties to memorable facts of Brazilian history or because of their exceptional archaeological, ethnographic, bibliographic or artistic value."[1] In this way, at the outset of the Estado Novo and as a part of the project of national consolidation underway since Vargas gained power in 1930, the regime moved to outfit Brazil with a bureaucracy that would define, protect, and foment cultural expressions deemed representative of the nation.

SPHAN's establishment was an important step in terms of sovereignty, as it indicated that Brazil was prepared to protect and showcase its cultural treasures, an impetus gaining momentum at mid-century in Europe and North America, and which would increase markedly after World War II with the establishment of UNESCO. However, in spite of Decree 25's importance to sovereignty, there is something more important about the concern with cultural patrimony under Vargas than the establishment of a state office that might take the lead in, for example, recuperating stolen treasures. This involves the role of culture in the creation of a patriotic citizenry,

---

1. The full text, in Portuguese, of Getúlio Vargas' Decreto-Lei 25 of 1937 is available at http://www.planalto.gov.br/ccivil/Decreto-Lei/Del0025.htm (last accessed 7/13/10). All translations from Portuguese to English in this chapter, unless otherwise noted, are the author's.

and thus in the nation-building project developed during the 1937-1945 Estado Novo.

The term "cultural patrimony," or "cultural heritage" in the Anglophone world, describes sets of actions as well as the collections of objects produced by those actions that play decisive roles in the state-citizen interfaces so important to modern nation-states. This is because patrimony, in its noun form, is a collection of cultural objects, or a type of ideally shared property held by the nation for the future benefit of citizens. This heritage—I will use "patrimony" and "heritage" interchangeably in what follows—is usually produced by state governments which specify, protect, and inscribe in national or supranational ledgers the sets of relations, everyday habits, and artistic or architectural expressions deemed worth saving or celebrating as symbolic of a community's most important qualities. In other words, almost anything can be heritage, but in order to take on this special state it must be transferred symbolically from its everyday context and enshrined through research and state-directed ritual. Such collectively held goods that allow citizens to identify themselves in relation to a particular community, or what some analysts refer to as a "secular sacred" (MacCannell, 1999) in recognition of their inalienable, protected qualities, are essential to the pilgrimages to landmarks, the commemorations, and the museums so basic to nationalist fervor.

Analysts of the Estado Novo's role in the forging of a modern Brazil have emphasized, among many other themes, the state's involvement in education (Dávila, 2003), trade unions and shop floors (Erickson, 1977; French, 1992; Wolfe, 1993), social reproduction (Guzzo Decca, 1987), gendered forms of work (Besse, 1996; Weinstein, 1997), and music and radio industries that would have enduring effects on Brazilian society (McCann, 2004). Additionally, a number of works in Portuguese as well as English have examined cultural heritage during the Estado Novo (Cavalcanti, 1999; Fonseca, 1997; Williams, 2001) and the extent to which important aspects of the Estado Novo initiatives for heritage were continued across the second half of the twentieth century (Bomeny, 1995). Yet, as I will discuss below, cultural heritage management in Brazil today functions somewhat differently than it did during the mid-twentieth century, having undergone important breaks in the late 1970s and then again in the first years of the twenty-first century. In fact, heritage planning went through a shift in the first decade of the new millennium as UNESCO planners, conscious of the fact that a folkloric dance and a cathedral are quite different entities, complemented the world's existing supranational heritage ledgers of "natural" and "cultural" patrimony with a new listing called "immaterial" or "intangible" heritage.[2]

Intangible patrimony, established officially at the international level by UNESCO in 2003, is understood as,

> practices, representations, expressions, knowledge, skills—as well as the instruments, objects, artifacts, and cultural spaces associated therewith—that communities, groups and, in some cases, individuals recognize as part of their cultural heritage . . . transmitted from generation to generation, [it] is constantly recreated by communities . . . and provides them with a sense of identity and continuity (UNESCO, 2008: 7).

This newest class of patrimony has generated enormous interest in Brazil, a nation whose planners had already envisioned, but not necessarily implemented, initiatives that looked much like intangible heritage long before the end of the twentieth century. Thus the form of heritage planning being developed in the Lusophone Americas today in light of shifts in United Nations' conceptualization appears to owe much to earlier moments in Brazilian history, and not simply UNESCO edicts. This does not suggest that intangible heritage was invented in Brazil. Rather, today's immaterial heritage initiatives must be contextualized historically and understood not simply as Brazilian reactions to international programs, but as part of a long history of give-and-take between Brazil and the world.

In this essay I survey the history of Brazil's engagement with cultural heritage planning, and with associated trends in capitalist development and democratic governance, in order to situate in relation to nation-state consolidation processes some of the ways of relating to culture and the past discussed in my recent ethnography of heritage planning in Salvador, Bahia (Collins, 2008a; Collins, forthcoming). Put simply, both Lula and his predecessor Fernando Henrique Cardoso have sought in distinct as well as complementary ways to "chart a new path" (Cardoso, 2001) that might combine capitalist development with social justice in a nation long portrayed as formed on capitalism's periphery (Schwarz, 1992; Viotti da Costa, 2000). Within these recent efforts to reposition the state, Brazilian culture has come to be seen as an important source of development funds and foreign exchange earnings in manners that go beyond the export of archetypical figures like Carmen Miranda or the marketing of samba, carnival, and

---

2. UNESCO, which supervises heritage programs at the international level, is responsible for the transnational advising and registration processes that officially recognize "natural," "cultural," and "intangible" heritage. See UNESCO 2008 for an overview.

sexuality in places such as Rio de Janeiro. In the process, cultural heritage, which for most of the post-World War II period was configured as more of a symbol of national sovereignty than an economic resource, has leapt to the fore as an important component of the nation's political economy and culture industry, which is perhaps best-known today for the export of television dramas, or *telenovelas* (Kottak, 2009).

The history below suggests that culture's growing fungibility in contemporary Brazil is not simply a novel response to shifting economic conditions, but rather a complex resuscitation of earlier models of cultural management. While Brazilian approaches to national culture are constantly evolving, they do so in a manner indebted to experiences in cultural heritage management which have marked the federal institutions in charge of culture and which, in turn, provide Brazil's planners with sophisticated resources and perspectives in the creation of new cultural goods and the mobilization of vernacular culture in spurring greater democratic participation.

In exploring contemporary conceptions of political belonging produced in a historical relationship to cultural heritage planning, I look first at the origins of Brazilian cultural heritage programs in modernist circles and the Estado Novo. I then move to the post-World War II development of SPHAN into one of the world's most technically competent, but somewhat iconoclastic in terms of its relationship to other strands in Brazilian nationalism, cultural patrimony institutions. Next, I follow as the institution takes on a more politicized direction in relation to the challenges to the 1964-1985 military dictatorship. This pushes the essay toward its conclusion by forcing a consideration of the ways that a late 20$^{th}$ century fomentation of cultural heritage as a tool for political economic development has blurred the boundaries between culture and economy in ways that have transformed culture and identity into increasingly important economic resources. I then conclude with suggestions for further research on how recent reformulations of the Brazilian tradition of cultural heritage management that support efforts to turn a populace's everyday habits into a more marketable entity have impacted state-citizen interactions, and thus the nature of democratic participation today.

## A BLUEPRINT FOR A CULTURAL INSTITUTION

Histories of cultural heritage planning in Brazil typically trace the federal institution dedicated to monuments and national culture to a planning document presented in 1936 to the Minister of Health and Education, Gustavo Capanema, by Mário de Andrade, the folklorist, novelist, and leader of Brazil's modernist movement of the 1920s (Ministério da Cultura, 1980: 22). In his proposal, Andrade defined cultural patrimony, "as all pure or applied artworks, popular or erudite, national or foreign, that belong to public powers, social organisms, individual citizens, and foreign citizens resident in Brazil" (Andrade, 1993: 40). He divided conceptually such "pure or applied artworks" into eight basic categories: (1)Archaeological Art; (2) Amerindian Art; (3) Popular Art; (4) Historical Art; (5) National Erudite Art; (6) Foreign Erudite Art; (7) National Applied Arts; (8) Foreign Applied Arts (Andrade, 1993: 41).

Andrade then argued that these categories could be collapsed, and thus mobilized to begin the transformation from quotidian object into a possession of the collectivity, so as to generate four registries of the nation's patrimony. These encyclopedic, state-managed volumes, similar to those which serve around the world as the archival tools through which governments inscribe their citizens' habits as patrimony today, were:

> Archaeological and Ethnographic Registry, corresponding to the first three categories of arts: archaeology, Amerindian and popular.
>
> Historical Registry, corresponding to the fourth category, historical art
>
> Fine Arts Registry—National Gallery of Fine Arts, corresponding to the fifth and sixth categories: national and foreign erudite arts
>
> Applied Arts Registry and the Museum of Applied Arts and Industrial Technologies, corresponding to the seventh and eight categories: national and foreign applied arts (Andrade, 1993: 45).

Andrade's catalogue of cultural possessions—a method of imagining the nation that stands in importance and, given the emphasis on the gathering of information under the Estado Novo, alongside the legislation that regulated industrial trade unions or radio broadcasting or the public health initiatives directed at mothers and infants, for example—separates and defines the popular, erudite, and applied arts.[3] The divisions revolve around objects' valorization in three areas. These include an association with a Brazilian people being defined under Vargas; aesthetic or "fine" arts criteria as mobilized by Andrade and his team in tense relation to European definitions; and industry, an area of great interest during the mid-century push for mod-

---

3. Andrade also proposed that each *livro de tombo*, or patrimonial registry, be complemented by a separate museum dedicated to one of the four categories of national possessions.

ernization. This is significant in terms of an understanding, from the perspective of the cultural elite of the Estado Novo, of the future of a modernizing Brazil in which the nation is understood as composed of its "popular," "erudite," and applied or industrial sectors.

Two concerns were salient in Andrade's attempts to give substance to Brazil. The first was an interest in participant observation and concerns with the everyday life of common people that led him to a fascination with creative process, and thus with the techniques, types of knowledge, care, and creativity with which common Brazilians produced material culture. The second was an event-based theory of history in which culture stood as a mark of development. Both approaches reflect Andrade's historical moment, his prior experiences managing São Paulo's cultural office, and, as emphasized in subsequent histories of Brazil's patrimony movement, his particular genius (Gonçalves, 1996; Nogueira, 2005).

In Andrade's suggestion for listing objects to be protected, the "popular" arts came to include the Amerindian and the archaeological, thus illustrating the temporal and ethnic bases of a national popular substantially dependent on a relationship between the cultural production of Native Brazilians in the present (Amerindians) and Native Brazilians in the past (the producers of "Archaeological Arts"). Here, at a critical moment in the development of ideas about racial mixture in Brazil, and a juncture roughly contemporaneous with Gilberto Freyre's influential argument about miscegenation in the 1933 *Masters and the Slaves*, the organization of the nation's patrimony locates Amerindian and popular culture in a historical time linked to archeological investigation, and thus the past.

Andrade's contradictory attempt to unify the nation follows fairly standard moves within mid-century social scientific and museological movements. But this congruence with international norms suggests that within an ideology of supposedly egalitarian and exemplarily Brazilian culture there exist a range of distinctions and evolutionary evaluations that undermines a dominant discourse on the coeval, forward movement of a single national race. In other words, within the version of citizenship being supported in its cultural facets by the SPHAN institution that would be in charge of cataloguing, protecting, and exhibiting the nation's artistic and historical possessions, the forward-thinking folklorist Mário de Andrade created a series of social hierarchies that implicitly located rural and nonwhite peoples in the nation's past, but not necessarily its future.

To make the point that SPHAN's documents relegated certain people and their cultural manifestations to history indicates that the nation is not constructed via a homogeneous time that avoids racisms. Rather, Brazil's federal heritage institution took form in the late 1930s in relation to a national consolidation dependent, at least in part, on separations between high and low art; past, present, and future; and a particularly Brazilian configuration of the relationship between Europeans, Africans, and Native Brazilians. This means of charting the future around heritage seems to have drawn on tendencies established in the previous decade within the Brazilian modernist movement.

## Modernism and the Birth of Cultural Heritage Planning

Brazilian modernism, which gained attention in relation to the arts festival held from February 11 to February 18, 1922, or what is usually referred to as São Paulo's "modern art week," was a transformative impulse for most of Latin America. It gave form to a differentiated movement whose emphases, personnel, and politics and aesthetics shifted across the 1920s and, as many of its proponents took on posts in the Estado Novo in institutions like SPHAN, across the twentieth century. It is thus difficult to equate modernism to a discrete set of ideas. Yet there are two tendencies that are widely accepted as integral to its coherence as well as important to the development of cultural heritage institutions. First, modernists valued tradition and associated it with the activities of minority and rural populations like São Paulo's rural cowboys (Andrade, 1968). Thus tradition is central to Brazilian modernity: the nation's march into the future was grounded by a past celebrated in research and writings about citizens' everyday lives. Second, in seeking to valorize such lifeways, the modernists set out also to challenge European cultural dominance and scientific denigrations of Brazil's mixed race people.[4]

Research was essential to the modernist attempt to redeem the non-European populace and chart an independent course for Brazil. Andrade and his

---

4. This movement to counter European racisms and to valorize Brazilian nationhood on the basis of the cultural traits of its mixed race populace was not limited to the intellectuals surrounding modern art week, or even those commonly accepted as modernists. For example, the enormously influential public intellectual from Brazil's Northeast, Gilberto Freyre, is typically understood, and often presented himself, as what was known as a "regionalist" even as he is closely associated with the movement to celebrate Brazilian racial ideology and cultural independence. For discussions of these dynamics see especially Chacon (2001), as well as Gilberto Freyre's own definition of his "regionalist" focus in his 1926 Regionalist Manifesto (Freyre, 1996).

associates delved into music, art, Brazilian Portuguese, and domestic habits in an ethnographic manner which stressed the careful surveying of what people actually did, rather than the collection of objects for museums or the publication of unresearched impressions about working classes. This is apparent in Andrade's conception of SPHAN. He makes room for objects with historical or aesthetic value, but the first category of patrimony he proposed was the "Archaeological and Ethnographic Registry."

Andrade's empirical focus on vernacular culture is notable in light of the proposals for a patrimony service that preceded his 1936 outline for SPHAN. During the first three decades of the 20th century an effort to establish a national institution that would oversee monuments and historical sites had been gaining support. For example, in 1923 the State of Pernambuco's delegate, in a speech to the national congress, reported that,

> I have been able to overcome my embarrassment and natural hesitation in order to occupy myself with an issue that has not previously required our care. Nonetheless, this is an issue that is essentially Brazilian, and which holds great interest for the civic education of our people. The State should not remain indifferent to this cause. It involves the defense of our historical monuments and to this end I have just proposed a project that intends to place under State protection all buildings which present historical or aesthetic merits.[5]

Pernambuco's delegate was not alone in his interest in buildings and monuments. In 1925 the president of Minas Gerais, Mello Vianna, created a commission to study historical monuments. Minas Gerais had also been the site of early cultural heritage work in Brazil when in 1924 the Swiss poet Blaise Cendrars, after a voyage there with Mário de Andrade and other Brazilian modernists like Oswald de Andrade and the renowned painter Tarsila de Amaral, put together a draft document that suggested not only that buildings and monuments be protected, but that their surroundings also be considered patrimony (Telles, 2009: 7). Then in 1930 Bahia's representative, José Wanderley de Araújo Pinho, proposed to congress a law that synthesized important aspects of previous plans and brought together wide-ranging concerns with personal and collective property as well as historical, ethnographic, and aesthetic considerations. But Pinho's bill was interrupted as Getúlio Vargas gained power in 1930 (Fonseca, 1997). Federal heritage initiatives languished during the first years of Vargas' rule and portions of Pinho's attempt to regulate Brazil's patrimony would be retaken only in 1934 with the creation of an Inspectorship of National Monuments under the aegis of Brazil's National Historical Museum. However, this initiative

---

5. This speech is reproduced in Telles (2009: 3).

ran counter to the efforts to protect and foment national culture by the federal bureaucrats who had emerged from the modernist movement.

The National Historical Museum was run by Gustavo Barroso, well-known for his anti-Semitism, sympathies to the fascist and nativist movement known as *integralismo* which accompanied the Estado Novo's rise, and who competed with the group recruited by Gustavo Capanema for control of federal cultural policy (Fonseca, 1997). Nonetheless, Pinho's attempt is significant in that it did not focus simply on buildings.[6] He supplemented a concern with monuments with cultural goods that had ethnographic or archaeological value. In other words, a concern with the creation of a state institution that would protect and regulate Brazilian buildings and everyday practices as something conceived of as national culture, or patrimony, was an important part or result of modernist debates by the end of the 1920s.

Andrade's collaboration with a variety of modernist figures and involvement in debates about folklore and ethnography is important in two somewhat different manners. First, his approach provides a contrast to that developed within SPHAN across most of the second half of the twentieth century by another Andrade, the lawyer and administrator who would direct the institution from 1938 until 1967, Rodrigo M.F. de Andrade. Second, Mario de Andrade's insistence on a cultural heritage that moves between monuments, buildings, and more ephemeral or personal and quotidian practices raises the issue of how culture is to be defined within Brazilian nationalism, something to which I will return at the end of this essay as I consider how culture and democratic inclusion intersect in the first decade of the new millennium.

## Exceptional Brazilianness: Buildings and Monuments

Despite his influence on the modernists and role in establishing SPHAN, Mário de Andrade never served as the institution's director. Instead, Minister Capanema chose Rodrigo M.F. de Andrade to direct the new cultural heritage institution. This Andrade seemed to enjoy bureaucratic process as much as Mário de Andrade valorized the ethnographic celebration of Brazilian creativity. Under Rodrigo's guidance, SPHAN exhibited an elitist class orientation and a south and central-Brazilian geographic bias (Rubim, 1997). The institution largely ignored the discussions of miscegenation and

---

6. Getúlio Vargas took power in 1930 and remained Brazil's leader until 1945. While he was forced from power at the end of the Estado Novo, he returned to Brazil's presidency in 1951 until his suicide in 1954.

popular culture that have come to define images of Brazil, and which are a staple of analyses of mid-twentieth century Brazilian nationalism.

Instead, in the decades following World War II, SPHAN became one of the world's most technically adept heritage institutions. It concentrated not on popular culture or on Mário de Andrade's directives, but surveyed monuments and buildings in constructing a canon of Brazilianness linked tightly to ideas about Portuguese baroque contributions to the nation (Williams, 2001). This quasi-European, high cultural version did not become hegemonic in representations at home or abroad, in no small part because of cultural initiatives under Vargas, the florescence in cultural production prior to the 1964 coup that was nonetheless not linked directly to state institutions in the 1950s and 1960s, and the subsequent impact of the military's 1964-1985 authoritarian fomentation of national integration and a culture industry based on television and radio (Chaui, 2000; Cohn, 1984).

SPHAN's activities during and after the Estado Novo suggest the extent to which representations of the nation and its salient imaginaries vacillated between visions of harmonious racial mixture, on one hand, and a valorizations of enduring attachment to Portuguese traditions on the other (Cunha, 2000). This seems at least in part a reaction to an elite and southern-Brazilian based aversion to discussions of African and northeastern regional influences in the internal development of the nation as a whole. It is also emblematic of a certain class-related disjuncture between Brazil's federal cultural heritage bureaucracy and the activities, the everyday cultural manifestations, and interests of the majority of its citizenry and artists in the post-World War II period.[7] Thus, despite the interest in folklore Mário de Andrade enunciated over the course of his career and within his SPHAN blueprint, for most of the mid-to late 20th century the federal heritage bureaucracy that today champions minority rights and multicultural initiatives stood as a purveyor of Brazilian ideas about European culture (Fonseca, 1997).

Under Rodrigo M.F. de Andrade's direction, SPHAN focused on the Iberian baroque heritage of Minas Gerais and Rio de Janeiro. The states of Pernambuco and Bahia—Brazil's first capital and hence a major site of colonial architecture—dominated the attention paid to regions outside of the south-central region that concentrated political and economic power. In choosing buildings and monuments, SPHAN focused on criteria related to aesthetic and historical value that were somehow iconic of what made Brazil

---

7. In an example of the history of art, rather than social historical or archaeological, focus of SPHAN, the institution did not have an archaeologist on staff until 1979. For a discussion of IPHAN, archaeology, and national education, see Najjar and Najjar (2007).

special, or particular, among nations. The result was mainly scattered, individual interventions that restored edifices understood as exceptionally Brazilian, often because of their relationship to the Portuguese baroque which the modernists had come to valorize in their mid-1920s excursions through the state of Minas Gerais. Yet the physical areas or the social processes surrounding monuments chosen for registry attracted little SPHAN attention. Nor did the dances, ways of cooking and worshipping, music, or religious practices that interested Mário de Andrade and which were included implicitly in Bahian congressman Wanderley Araujo Pinho's 1930 proposal become an important part of SPHAN policy.

The three decades during which Rodrigo M.F. de Andrade ran SPHAN showcased the enduring existence of a section of Brazil's federal bureaucracy which was in no small degree cut off from the everyday worries or the political concerns of a majority of Brazil's citizenry. Heritage planning in this environment responded to technical criteria imposed by architects and advocated within closed planning circles by an international and Brazilian community of experts. This rarified discourse set off architectural gems as collective representations that were in reality marks of the tastes and desires of a small segment of society. The extent to which SPHAN's architectural orientation continued to predominate after the 1945 demise of the Estado Novo suggests not only a class bias within Brazilian cultural heritage, but the extent to which the corporatist reordering continued to impact the memory work and commemorations critical to the "invention of tradition" (Hobsbawm, 1983) that produced the attachments to community so important to the smooth functioning of a national community.

SPHAN's importance to the objects to which nationalist "structures of feeling" (Williams, 1977) bonded is important to understanding the reconstitution of the state undertaken in the late 1990s by Fernando Henrique Cardoso's government and retaken by the Lula government after 2002. SPHAN, unlike, for example, Brazil's health or retirement or electrical energy system, was never identified as in need of renewal due to cost overruns or a lack of efficiency. On the contrary, it was one of the world's most technically competent state heritage institutions and it balanced local and federal interests while interacting effectively with UNESCO.

The Brazilian federal heritage institution's trajectory means that the continuing influence of an orientation that arose during Vargas' corporatist restructuring is difficult to portray, in the SPHAN case and thus in relation to national culture, as an issue of an oversized bureaucracy or a heavy-handed state presence in areas supposedly more adequately served or run by private industry. The management of the nation's cultural possessions is instead a realm in which the interfaces between a citizenry and a collection of national objects that supposedly belong to all citizens have been overseen for most of the second half of the twentieth century by a well-oiled, technocratic institution. SPHAN under Rodrigo M.F. de Andrade, then, was not conceived of as a site for the production of value, but rather as a space for the development of Brazilian modernity, and thus sovereignty. SPHAN continued the modernist goal of cultural autonomy, or transnational parity among nation-states conceived of as culture-bearing entities, even as it expunged the modernist project's more democratic components. Yet this would change, due in no small part to Brazil's 1964-1985 military dictatorship.

## Patrimony, the Military, and Democratic Openings

After the Estado Novo's demise in 1945, Brazilian cultural life gained momentum even as state policies seem to have played little direct role in this effervescence. Nor did SPHAN, which continued to espouse a high cultural orientation around buildings and monuments that contributed little to the explosion in film, theatre, and the plastic arts that would be dampened only by the military's 1964 incursion into civil society. Nonetheless, during this period SPHAN did begin to work, for example, with the Cuban government to establish museums described as intended to educate the two nation's populaces. This led to meetings in Havana in 1957 and 1958, and Rio de Janeiro in 1956, overseen by UNESCO, SPHAN, and the Cuban National Committee for Museums (Trigueiros, 1958: 45).

Such cooperation was part of an expanding transnational investment in culture after World War II, a movement led within the United Nations by technicians from France, England, and the United States, and on a wider stage by U.S. post-war development efforts that sought to encourage hemispheric tourism (Schwartz, 1999). The attempts in the 1950s to establish transnational networks serve as evidence of SPHAN's continuing engagement with currents in cultural heritage management around the world, if not with Brazil's vernacular culture. This took place in an environment in which, despite the florescence of student culture and civil society more generally, "cultural policies put forth by the Brazilian state . . . are practically inexistent with the exception of SPHAN interventions [into the built environment]" (Rubim, 2007: 18).

SPHAN, reorganized as the Department of Historical and Artistic Patrimony (DPHAN) in 1946 with the fall of the Estado Novo and the Institute of Historical and Artistic Patrimony (IPHAN) in 1970, was so detached from the core of the nation's intellectual life that the 1964 coup led to little change in its orientation (Fonseca, 1997). Instead, as military planners sought to convert the relatively independent cultural initiatives of the 1950s and early 1960s into a culture industry that might produce vast fortunes and integrate the nation around its authoritarian versions of society via television and radio, SPHAN continued to focus on monuments and baroque architecture as a symbol of European influence.

The welter of programs through which military planners sought to colonize the nation's pre-1964 cultural life seem to have had little bearing on cultural heritage policy at a national level even as the sorts of popular literacy and handicrafts programs established under the military—but not supervised by SPHAN—did help residents of cultural heritage sites in the state of Bahia begin to recognize themselves as special populations who gained a certain identity from what they perceived as their close relationship to the practices identified by their state as national culture (Collins, forthcoming; Moreira, 2007). In other words, even as SPHAN cared mainly for buildings and monuments, shifts at the national level through which the military sought legitimacy came to impact residents of at least the Bahian historical center in ways that would come to alter how citizens interacted with patrimony in Brazil.

Yet SPHAN's policies were not altered significantly, even with the retirement of Rodrigo M.F. de Andrade in 1967, until the graphic designer born in the northeastern state of Pernambuco, Aloisio Magalhães, was appointed director in 1979. At this time, what had become IPHAN became joined administratively to an institution concerned with national memory, the Fundação Nacional Pró-Memória. During this late 1970s and early 1980s period of opposition to the military regime, planners working with the municipality of São Paulo like the social historian Silvia Lara and Bahian intellectuals like the anthropologist Ordep Serra, director of the Bahian Institute of Cultural and Artistic Patrimony ("IPAC"), sought to move patrimonialization policies at local, federal, and state levels toward a greater engagement with the citizenry's everyday lives. IPHAN under Magalhães supported such initiatives: In an environment of Brazilian redemocratization and United Nations' challenges to the industrialized world's stranglehold on patents in the 1970s and 1980s, IPHAN re-instated a more processual understanding of culture akin to Mário de Andrade's view of a Brazilian folklore. This was influenced by Aloisio Magalhães' more anthropological approach which emphasized not monuments, but everyday practices.

Magalhães had come to IPHAN after founding the National Center of Cultural Reference (CNRC) in Brasília. This CNRC, which he headed from 1975-1979, was a think tank and design studio concerned with popular culture. Supported by an array of state institutions like the Bank of Brazil and the University of Brasília and financed by the Ministry of Industry and Commerce, the CNRC sought to map a form of "know-how" that might somehow be translated into national business policy. In other words, the CNRC came about not simply as an attempt to define Brazil, but to mobilize its labor power in relation to something called national culture. As its name suggested, the CNRC was concerned with cultural *reference*, rather than a collection of cultural objects (Anastassakis, 2008). Yet how reference was defined is a matter of contention.

Magalhães, somewhat like Mário de Andrade, approached culture as a compendium of interactions and thus relatively ephemeral practices and representations. He linked this culture to tradition, suggesting that traditional knowledge and values were disappearing in the context of industrialization. Hence Brazil needed to document its practices before they disappeared (Magalhães, 1997). Such an emphasis on saving threatened culture permeated IPHAN at the end of the 1970s (Gonçalves, 1996) and filtered into regional heritage institutions like Bahia's IPAC by the early 1980s (Collins, forthcoming).

Brazilian popular culture came to be understood, even by a number of bureaucrats working within the state, as an arena that might open more democratic futures.[8] By politicizing culture in the service of Brazil's return to democracy by including working class people's everyday practices and Afro-Brazilian historical sites as components of the nation's heritage, planners associated with Magalhães further synthesized an understanding of vernacular culture as something special that belonged to the nation due to its origins in an authentically Brazilian people. In other words, even as popular culture was invoked in an attempt to foment a democracy rather than an authoritarian, corporate Brazil, intellectuals continued a tendency central to Mário de Andrade's approach to national culture. This involved a valorization of folklore as a redemptive and harmonious voice of the people.

---

8. For a discussion of how a variety of actors agitated for a democratic opening from within state institutions, see Cardoso (1992).

The late 1970s also saw a multiplication of municipal, state-level, federal, and quasi-governmental agencies concerned with patrimony. Intellectuals sought to reverse what they considered racist and Eurocentric criteria. This rethinking of the cultural goods imagined as evocative of Brazil's true essence led to the 1982 registry of Salvador's oldest continually functioning Candomblé temple and Palmares, the site of a sixteenth century maroon community in the state of Alagoas. These efforts to include social struggle and Afro-Brazilian and working class heritage as patrimony arose in part from the fact that from the late 1970s onward intellectuals committed to democracy looked increasingly at culture as a force that might be mobilized to open the political system. Article 216 of Brazil's new 1988 constitution made this orientation into law, defining "cultural patrimony as goods of a material and immaterial nature, taken individually or as a group, which are significant to the identity, action, or memory of the different groups that make up Brazilian society."

The constitutional article, written as indigenous rights were becoming a major issue in Amazonia and internationally, points to an incipient multiculturalism in its reference to social groups increasingly distinguished and painted as making up Brazilian society. It thus mitigates against the sort of high cultural orientation common under Rodrigo M.F. de Andrade's SPHAN by avoiding a language of monuments or simplistic exceptionality tied to a putative national essence. Instead, it defined patrimony in relation to cultural manifestations' significance to particular communities, which in turn make up the nation. The dissemination of ideas about diversity from the CNRC and IPHAN alongside Brazil's adoption of a new national constitution also created room for individual states to move to protect and foment practices that could be defined under the mantle of Brazilian culture.

Article 270 of the 1989 state constitution of Bahia specified that cultural policy should "facilitate the population's access to the production, distribution, and consumption of cultural goods" and "guarantee . . . communities' own abilities to direct popular, traditional, and contemporary cultural manifestations." But despite the beauty of the new Bahian constitution's legal language, the state's largest 20th century cultural initiative, the US$100 million transformation of its capital city's colonial center, the Pelourinho neighborhood, has taken form as a top-down packaging of culture for the benefit of elites and outsiders (Collins, 2008a). The project, begun in earnest in 1992, bears little resemblance to a grass-roots fomentation of the community's involvement with its own cultural practices and is instead directed in large part at the fabrication of representations of Afro-Bahian lifeways that might attract tourists.

The Pelourinho's reconstruction as a cash cow intended to permit local elites to dominate politics and disseminate representations of Afro-Bahiannness in manners that enrich them has lessened since the 2002-2005 demise of the political coalition run by the feared Bahian populist leader, Antônio Carlos Magalhães. In Bahia's new environment, and in spite of the continuing pressure by the federal and local states and development organizations to commodify culture, Workers Party (PT) politicians have challenged the patron-client relations developed by Antônio Carlos Magalhães around a discourse of traditional, rooted Bahiannness, or what is known as *baianidade* in Brazil. Nonetheless, the Pelourinho, now largely devoid of its pre-1992 populace forced out by state edicts, is not a place where an Afro-Bahian community of the sort usually credited by policymakers with generating popular culture has been able to remain or control what passes as its cultural production.

Instead, in a process repeated around the world during the 1990s, a constriction of possibilities that enriches a few at the expense of the majority has benefitted a small number of residents able to present themselves as community leaders or supposedly authentic avatars of Bahian tradition. These successful cultural entrepreneurs, who include members of neighborhood social movements active in redemocratization, have been enshrined as a species of symbolic ancestor to the nation represented by the restored Pelourinho. At the same time, many of their former neighbors have been exiled to peripheral neighborhoods where, in the eyes of the state, they belong. In this way selected Afro-Bahians have been permitted to gain a toehold in a neighborhood once infamous as Salvador's red light zone and celebrated as a core of Afro-Brazil but now reserved mainly for tourists, the bourgeoisie, and the money-making activities of investors from around the world (Collins, 2008a). The entwined Brazilian and transnational mechanisms for packaging culture through which this has taken place are critical technologies for understanding shifts in patrimony, and in Brazilian cultural policy, since the early 1990s.

## Marketing the Everyday as Cultural Property: "Intangible" Patrimony

As should be clear from the history recounted so far, definitions of culture and thus cultural heritage policies change over time. The renaissance in heritage planning associated with the return to democracy and Aloisio Magalhães' stewardship of IPHAN came to an end by the final years of the 1980s as President Fernando Collor de Mello sought to balance the national budget by doing away with the Ministry of Culture. Yet after Collor de Mello's impeachment and Itamar Franco's interim presidency, the election of Fernando Henrique Cardoso in 1997 led to the re-establishment of the Ministry and pragmatic attempts by the federal government to support cultural initiatives in the face of calls for fiscal restraint and shifting international development paradigms. By the late 1990s, the Ministry of Culture came to approach buildings, cultural production, and even working class, indigenous, and Afro-Brazilian lifeways as national properties that might be bundled as alienable goods to generate income and help alleviate Brazil's fiscal challenges. One of the more intriguing aspects of this way of mobilizing culture for national development, something presaged by Aloisio Magalhães' tenure at IPHAN, involved the role of cultural heritage professionals' social scientific research in the Cardoso administration's interest in cultural heritage. Rather than employing ethnography to define Brazil as a modernist project in formation, such research helped bureaucrats package something called culture that held a critical economic role in a changing Brazil. This was not an entirely novel development in world history, since visits to ruins or orientalist fascination with non-European cultural production have long been a motor for exploration and tourism in many areas of the world, especially former colonies.

But Brazil of the mid- to late 1990s represents a shift in the tenor of initiatives through which people's everyday habits were collected and exhibited by institutions that configured them as collective possessions valuable to capitalist development. In this environment culture came to stand as more than a set of traditional activities that distinguished nations or impede western-style development and market economies (Weffort, 2000). As Minister of Culture Weffort stated in a World Bank meeting in New Orleans' restored French Quarter in 2000, "We must turn history around to combine development and heritage preservation" ("IDB President," 2000).[9]

The shift away from culture as a source of independence and pride and toward culture as an economic resource—a move that mirrored developments around the world whereby the "information economy" led to an emphasis on "intangible" assets and alienation of areas of social life previously excluded from the market—came at a moment in which worldwide approaches to and definitions of patrimony underwent significant alteration (Yúdice, 2004). The engagements between institutions like UNESCO and the World Bank and national-level planners have given rise to the welter of instruments now available for the management of culture. For example, by the mid-1990s UNESCO planners found themselves responding to critiques of the anthropological conceptions of culture that focused on everyday life rather than on exceptional historical or artistic icons, and to the increasing momentum of worldwide attempts to transform social and cultural relations into social or cultural capital. UNESCO's experts thus came to recognize a need to augment "cultural patrimony" and "natural patrimony," the two existing categories available for listing national treasures under the institution's auspices. In 2003, with the "Convention for the Safeguarding of the Intangible Cultural Heritage," UNESCO officially added another, third, realm of patrimony to its supranational ledgers that, in a manner akin to Mário de Andrade's ethnographic registry proposed for SPAHN in 1936, define the epistemological and archival categories that turn into patrimony formerly unmarked or everyday practices like dancing the samba, playing the Afro-Brazilian dance/martial art *capoeira*, or cooking the fish stew known in Brazil as *moqueca*.

While statecrafting efforts of the 1930s and 1940s rested prominently on efficient statistical, public relations, and policing tools for managing everyday life, the rolling back of the Estado Novo's corporatist labor, industrial, and pension systems in the 1990s occurred in relation to a different, yet nonetheless related, alteration in the state's knowledge or research-based treatment of social relations (Mattar, 2003). Aspects of everyday life celebrated for political ends during redemocratization in the 1980s as the cultural possessions of particular social groups came to be treated in the 1990s as properties that might be bought, sold or even help the national state produce rents through the re-occupation of territories like the Pelourinho, a neighborhood left to Afro-Bahian invaders during an earlier period of "order and progress."

---

9. This document no longer appears on the IDB website even as it was available until 2004 at http://www.iadb.org/exr/am2000/release/7100.htm.

The state, in reconstructing and then overseeing spaces like Salvador's formerly abandoned Pelourinho through the regulation of residents' activities and the fomentation of folklore, came to use attention to the health and well-being of residents as a way of sanitizing their cultural practices. The goal was to exhibit folkloric manifestations in the reconstructed UNESCO center for the enjoyment of visitors. Such expansion of state activity during a period usually characterized as neoliberal and thus supposedly involving a rollback of government involvement in the economy took place in Bahia as a citizenry's everyday habits on which important democratic initiatives during redemocratization had rested, came to be configured as alienable economic goods (Collins, 2008b).

The 1988 constitution makes clear that so-called immaterial culture and its preservation had by the mid-to late 1980s become an important part of Brazilian democracy. But as something called culture has come to be conceptualized as a marketable resource by organizations like Brazil's Ministry of Culture and IPHAN of the 1990s, citizenship has come to mean something quite special to a number of Brazilians with whom I have conducted fieldwork in Salvador's Pelourinho. More than simply indicating that political subjects participate in a shared medium called culture, today's citizenship around culture in places like the Pelourinho often means that people conceptualize this culture as a thing with value that they might possess. Many Pelourinho residents argue that culture accrues to particular groups and that members of those groups may deploy it in interactions with tourists and bureaucrats so as to generate cash (Collins, 2008b). This means that culture often becomes configured as an interiorized essence, rather than as something available to all.

The extent to which residents of Salvador's Pelourinho are reinterpreting the relationship between culture and citizenship in a rather unexpected manner today is one function of an emphasis on everyday habits and identities that became a part of federal policy when, in August of 2000 and in advance of UNESCO's 2003 legal and bureaucratic definition of its new category of "intangible" patrimony, Brazil's Federal Decree number 3,551 augmented the cultural ledgers envisioned by Mario de Andrade. It specified that the nation's immaterial cultural heritage should be inscribed in four volumes:

1] The Book of Knowledges [*Livro dos Saberes*]

2] The Book of Celebrations [*Livro das Celebrações*]

3] The Book of Expressive Forms [*Registro das Formas de Expressão*]

4] The Book of Places [*Registro dos Lugares*]

The innovations promulgated by IPHAN and institutions like Bahia's IPAC are impressive in terms of their potential for supporting democratic reform. In their wake, municipal administrations like Porto Alegre's mayor's office have permitted common citizens, as opposed to experts like architects or museum staff, to draw up documents and propose the registry of aspects of a community's culture as cultural heritage (Meira, 2004). Additionally, in Brasilia planners have put together a revolutionary concept of patrimonial merit around a notion of scale whereby the relationships between plazas, buildings, and streets might be registered, and thus preserved (Ribeiro, 2005; Sinoti, 2005).

As these revolutions in heritage planning have been going on, Brazil, once described as a nation "of the future" and characterized by foreign social scientists as lacking an intense engagement with memory or history, has been undergoing a veritable memory boom (Collins, 2008a). Thus it seems that heritage legislation and practice both piggyback upon, and reveal, the existence of shifting temporal conceptualizations of the national community. Heritage also seems to have permitted citizens to gain a diverse toolkit that encourages them to perceive, and attach themselves to, the polity on the basis of cultural manifestations.

Nonetheless, the more recent innovations in heritage practice have taken place during a period characterized by a marketization of the social. Such a shifting economic picture suggests that culture and identity have come to mean something new to bureaucrats, policymakers, and citizens at the turn of the millennium (Comaroff and Comaroff, 2009; Collins, 2008b). Cultural practices' and social identities' bundling as economic goods around the world in the late 20th century have helped lead to, and make visible, a situation in which attachment to the community has come to signify something more than sovereignty or democratic participation, at least in places like the Pelourinho where visitors and residents encounter their habits as highly reified things called cultural heritage. Seemingly as a result, those residents of the Pelourinho configured by their state as valued cultural producers and able to resist IPAC attempts to dislodge them from the restored heritage center, increasingly view culture as a resource through which they may profit and demand inclusion in a Brazil, and a world, where consumption has come increasingly to stand as a mark of political belonging.

Similar shifts in emphasis in the relationship between politics and economics have been repeated to various degrees in many sites around the world over the last two decades (Yúdice, 2004). Yet given Latin America's largest democracy's position as a creator of cultural products for global export, its economic and social vitality, its return to democratic governance, the reach of its early 20th century modernist project, and its enduring class divisions, it appears that the contradictions so much a part of the marketing of social relations as a thing called culture are especially visible, or important, in Brazil.

A key facet of the growing importance of cultural heritage in Brazil's economy involves international loan programs. In the 1990s institutions like the World Bank and the Inter-American Development Bank (IDB) decided that culture was good business. In 1999 Brazil gained a US$125 million IDB program designed to support the restoration of cultural heritage centers. But this *Projeto Monumenta*, administered by IPHAN and the Ministry of Culture, is not only about monuments. Instead, the loan program, which may be transferred between different sites according to needs as put forth by Brazilian authorities, focuses on restoring buildings, the internal workings of IPHAN, and the patrimony-based education of local people. As the IDB makes explicit on its website, Monumenta supports

> the training of instructors and artisans in restoration techniques, including carpenters, stone masons, blacksmiths, stone cutters, stucco workers and painters. The training of local cultural and training agents will also be financed. The fifth component finances educational programs to inform Brazilians of their historic and artistic heritage, its care, and its use.[10]

Here the IDB made loans not for highways or dams, but for cultural heritage as culture began at the turn of the millennium to take its place alongside such industries as a major source of earnings and investment. But what interests me most in the above statement from the IDB is its hybrid nature and its focus not only on buildings, but on quotidian activities that come close to anthropological definitions of culture: The masons, carpenters, and blacksmiths will restore buildings and the IDB proposal includes these people's training as a focus of its lending. Of course, their skills involve restoring a monument—after all, workforces in any industry need to be trained and Monumenta thus continues an IDB interest in producing qualified workforces. Yet educational programs designed to "inform Brazilians of their his-

---

10. See the International Development Bank's documents for the Monumenta Project at http://www.bid.org.uy/projects/project.cfm?id=BR0261&lang=en, (site last consulted 7/15/10).

toric and artistic heritage" present an apparently trickier situation. Are these Brazilians who will be schooled in the value of heritage the ultimate consumers of national culture? Is the IDB, in an echo of mid-century development efforts to expand internal markets, fostering a public for cultural heritage products made in Brazil? Or, in a model well-known in ecotourism and sustainable conservation efforts, can governments simply do a better job of protecting their treasures if a populace is informed as to those objects' value and their roles in citizens' and their communities' identities?

The situation in Salvador, Bahia's Pelourinho during the period in which the Monumenta funding was announced suggests that the above explanations are inadequate. First, even as Salvador's Pelourinho was initially contemplated by the IDB and Ministry of Culture for financing, the Bahian historical center failed to qualify for the monies. This was due to the state's 1992-1998 removal of the overwhelming majority of residents and a lack of private investment in the area.[11] Also, IDB consultants I interviewed stated that until the Bahian government put together a more just policy towards residents, no monies would be disbursed in Bahia. To this end, the IDB sent personnel to Salvador in early 2000 to educate Bahian planners as to its cultural heritage policies and goals, but met substantial resistance (Collins, 2008a).

A concern with an overbearing, rapacious state and with the residents of historical centers underscores the IDB's suspicion of state inefficiency and the extent to which development efforts today take into greater account the well-being of populations impacted by their projects. But this does not mean the IDB is interested only in bureaucratic efficiencies, or the management of some ostensibly discrete sphere that might be called "the economy." Instead, the Monumenta Program reveals a double-sided IDB concern with IPHAN's ability to manage Brazilian culture and the people involved with that heritage, whether workers restoring antiquities or a public expected to care for these treasures and come to know themselves as a community on the basis of their appreciation of this supposedly shared cultural heritage. As emphasized in the Monumenta documentation,

> The preservation, promotion, and knowledge of national culture are essential to social development. Common understanding and appreciation of the different aspects of history and culture are important to social consensus and political cooperation. Cultural knowledge of shared symbols is essential to

---

11. Members of Antônio Carlos Magalhães' coalition sought to use the state, which they dominated throughout the 1990s and employed as a mechanism for personal gain, to further their profits extracted in the Pelourinho. For an analysis of the Magalhães' clan's enrichment in the context of a broad critique of global development and corruption, see especially Henry (2003).

communication among citizens. Many of these shared symbols are historical
references preserved materially in built heritage.[12]

The claim above helps explain why Monumenta is structured around
buildings, the training of people in architectural restoration, and the
fomentation of a public who might consume or participate in the development of national culture. All three foci revolve around specifying the proper
shape and role of the state in fostering community, a philosophical and
practical discussion at the core of Getúlio Vargas' Estado Novo whereby an
authoritarian, corporatist state was portrayed as something that might rec-
tify the vicissitudes of a supposedly corrupt liberal democracy.

In an early twenty-first century light, national symbols become an issue
not only of economic advances as the IDB makes clear that culture can be
mobilized for development, but also of the nature of governance and the
acquiescence of communities to state power. Yet as the IDB invests in culture, "social development" becomes an end in itself, rather than a necessary
correlate to an industrial development tied to the market, democratization,
and consumers and well-behaved workers. In its focus on culture, the IDB
works instead to spur such "social development" and well-being through
communication among citizens. This is supposed to lead to "social consensus and political cooperation" as an essential aspect, and goal, of its programs. Such harmony is not portrayed as emanating from just wages or full
bellies, but rather "historical references preserved materially in built heritage" which might take on the dual role of producing value and encouraging
social harmony by configuring as central to a nation's economy those so-
called "immaterial" relations between, for example, people and monuments
and craft producers and students.

## CONCLUSION

This essay has focused on a tension, and a historical oscillation, between
two sides of the Brazilian and the international cultural heritage movements. In doing so, it has put forth a history of the institution now called
IPHAN that focuses on the borders, and overlaps, between cultural policies
directed at what might be dubbed monuments, on one hand, and everyday
life, on the other. This orientation brings out the shifting nature of Brazil's
federal cultural heritage bureaucracy and links Brazilian changes to cultural

---

12. See the International Development Bank's executive summary for Monumenta at http://idb-docs.iadb.org/wsdocs/getdocument.aspx?docnum=437363, (site last consulted 7/15/10).

heritage initiatives at the supranational level and in the Brazilian city of Salvador, well known as a center of Afro-Brazilian culture. This effort reveals how, for most of the latter half of the twentieth century, people's habits as well as architectural wonders were subsumed within the same category of cultural patrimony in Brazil and the rest of the world. But by the end of the twentieth century, and thus at the moment of Brazil's redemocratization, the gap between quotidian activities and monumentalized stones and mortar came to be codified in heritage registries split by both UNESCO and the Brazilian state between cultural heritage and intangible, or immaterial, heritage. Thus the case of the rise of a Brazilian federal heritage bureaucracy, when supplemented with ethnographic data from the implementation of such policies used to restore Brazil's first capital city, the Pelourinho UNESCO World Heritage Site in Salvador, Bahia, reveals some of the ways culture and social development have come to play changing roles in modern governance, nationalism, and the global production of value.

My argument has charted not only a back and forth between buildings and everyday practices, but also a more linear movement toward a commodification of the cultural heritage that has become so important to fomenting nationalism and recognizing cultural and ethnic groups' contributions to nations around the world. In the hands of Aloisio Magalhães' patrons in the Ministry of Industry and Commerce, culture appeared a way to get at the mythic, traditional core of the nation which also promised to unlock that nation's potential in terms of its people's creativity. But this was understood mainly in relation to production, or goods that offered an alternative to modern manufacturing. However, by the late 1990s when Minister of Culture Weffort and the intellectuals associated with Fernando Henrique Cardoso put together their cultural policy, concerns with so-called immaterial labor and social capital had come to the fore. In this context, everyday cultural practices were treated as valuable in terms of their performance. This version of culture promised also to attract lending, rather than simply fostering the production of goods of the sort envisioned in Aloisio Magalhães' time. Thus culture came to be seen in the late twentieth century as not simply a correlate to economic development and an aspect of democracy, but rather a core component of the both.

The perambulations of the concept of cultural heritage suggest the importance of attending to the ways that today's emphasis on reconstructing Brazil's heritage may be altering the nature of democratic participation and national belonging.[13] This is not to say that something resolutely new has taken place—after all, SPHAN/IPHAN history demonstrates the extent to which institutions have drawn on and reinterpreted enduring concerns and problems in Brazilian national life. But it is to suggest that at a moment when people's quotidian practices come to be valued and defined in new ways, so too might their politics. The issue is best addressed empirically, and via research that tacks between everyday life and government initiatives and includes collaboration among different social sciences. Such cooperation underscores in turn the prescience of the Estado Novo bureaucrats who sought to define a nation through the development of ever sharper, and powerful, social scientific instruments. After all, how else might one turn a dance or a recipe into a collective possession of the nation that attracts outside funding? And, finally, how else might one convince an international organization to dedicate US$125 million to training masons and restoring crumbling baroque ruins in a move that suggests culture may be a motor for, and not just the effect of, development policies directed at one of the world's most dynamic economies?

---

13. These early descriptions of intangible heritage and "living human treasures" may be found at http://www.unesco.org/culture/heritage/intangible/html_eng/index_en.shtml, (site last consulted on 1/20/07).

# Part III
# Financial Crisis and Response

# 12

# THE FINANCIAL SERVICES INDUSTRY

*Fernando Sotelino*

*Abstract: One characteristic of the Brazilian banking industry as it stands today is the balance of power between private and public sector banks; another is the balance of power within the private sector between domestic and foreign banks; a third is that it ranks among the world's best capitalized and supervised; and a fourth is that most of the financing of investment is shouldered by public sector banks. This paper examines how this unique industry profile came to be and explores the prospects for the consolidation of a strong domestic long term credit market in Brazil.*

It is now the aftermath of the global financial crisis triggered by the US sub-prime meltdown in 2008. Most analysts are back to projecting GDP growth for Brazil for 2010 and beyond in the 5 percent plus range. They also rejoice with a gradual return to normality of domestic credit markets and a renewed flow of global equity offerings by Brazilian companies. Plus, the leading Brazilian banks have come out not only unscathed from the crisis but in an even stronger relative position in terms of market value vis-à-vis peers around the world.

One characteristic of the Brazilian banking industry—as it stood prior to the subprime meltdown and stands today—is the balance of power (in terms of shares of deposits and loans) between private and public sector banks; another is the balance of power within the private sector between domestic and foreign banks. This is a unique profile when compared not only to OECD countries—where domestic private sector banks are dominant and the role of public sector banks is modest—but also to other large emerging economies such as Mexico, where foreign banks are dominant and the presence of public sector banks is relatively modest, or India, where the public sector banks are dominant and the market share of foreign banks is modest.

The Brazilian banking industry is also perceived to be among the world's best capitalized and supervised. On the other hand, long term lending by Brazilian private sector banks is very small by any standards when matched against private or public sector banks of both the OECD and other leading emerging economies; public sector banks provide most of the financing of investment by businesses (industries and infrastructure) and families (housing).

How did this unique profile come to be? Is it likely to change? How was it indeed affected by this last global financial crisis? Is the Brazilian financial sector finally becoming capable of transforming short-term savings into long term availability of credit at costs competitive with important economies in the world?

Section 2 provides a historical perspective of Brazilian banking from its origin in 1808 to the eve of the *Plano Real* (Real Plan) in 1993. Particular attention is given to exploring how private sector banks came to be and managed to develop a firm foundation so that the they never ceased to exist, and to examining the evolving roles of public and private sector banks in the financing of consumption and investment in Brazil from the late 1830s to the early 1990s.

Section 3 begins with an assessment of the effects of *Plano Real* (the stabilization plan put in motion in December 1993 to finally, with a strong fiscal adjustment and no element of surprise, extinguish hyperinflation in Brazil) and the late 1994 Mexican crisis on bank behavior and systemic risk, and proceeds to examine in some detail what the author characterizes as three quite distinct stages of industry consolidation that followed: government assisted (1995–1998), market driven (1999–2007), and subprime meltdown induced (2008–2009).

Section 4, concluding remarks, revisits the strengths and weaknesses of the Brazilian financial system as it stands today and highlights the obstacles to be overcome for the consolidation of a strong domestic fixed income securities market.

## BANKING IN BRAZIL, FROM 1808 TO *PLANO REAL*

## Early Banking, 1808–1889

Commercial banking in Brazil began with the foundation of Banco do Brasil in 1808, when the King of Portugal, Dom João VI and his court, in flight from the imminent invasion of Lisbon by the Napoleonic troops, arrived in Rio de Janeiro (Smith, 2002: 39).

The Banco do Brasil was conceived as both a commercial bank for takings deposits and discounting commercial paper, and a central bank for issuing paper money. It could also engage in trading commodities and foreign exchange. Its intended minimum capital upon foundation was 1,200 contos.[1] But after four years of operation, paid-in capital was only 126 contos. Additional incentives were put in place, allowing the original minimum capital to be reached in 1818.[2] But, by 1821, as a result of year-after-year printing of money to finance the Crown, over 70 percent of Banco do Brasil's assets were government bonds and only less than 15 percent of its notes in circulation were backed by metallic reserves.

Upon Independence in 1822, withdrawals by the Portuguese royal suite returning to Lisbon exposed the bank's delicate liquidity situation. Additional remedial rounds of capitalization approved by the new Brazilian Emperor, Dom Pedro I, were not sufficient to avoid continued deterioration. By mid-1829 gold coins commanded a 200 percent premium over Banco do Brasil's paper money. On September 23, the bank's liquidation was declared. The Banco do Brasil's notes in circulation were gradually replaced by new Treasury notes explicitly backed by the Nation. Brazil's first commercial banking venture, characterized by a hybrid (public-private) ownership, dangerously conflicting objectives (bank of issue of paper money and commercial bank), and poor governance (favored treatment of related parties and high dividend distributions on accounting profits) had ended.[3]

---

1. 1 conto equals 1,000 "mil réis." Réis is the plural of Real, the standard unit of account for the Brazilian currency. So 1 conto equals 1 million "réis." In August 1808 one thousand réis (or the "mil réis") was equivalent to 67.5 British pence. The "mil réis" appreciated to 96 pence in May 1814 and, then, devalued continuously to 54 pence in January 1821, and 21 pence in January 1831 (see Cavalcanti, 1999: 523-25).
2. Incentives included knightly honors to capital subscribers to a Government commitment to subscribe 100 shares per annum from tax collections with the dividends on these shares for the first 5 years being paid to the private shareholders.
3. For more details on the sequence of events between the foundation of Banco do Brasil and the end of the Empire see Ribeiro and Guimarães (1967: 37-117).

When Brazil's Emperor, Dom Pedro I, returned to Lisbon in 1831 to become King of Portugal, he abdicated in favor of his five year old son. Brazil's government was temporarily entrusted to the Regency.[4] The Regency government (1831-1840) had to face several regional revolts (including the Farrapos War in Rio Grande do Sul, 1835), but managed to keep the country whole and to restore financial order. Coffee exports grew significantly and the occupation of the country's interior by industrial and agricultural enterprises accelerated. As a result, the demand by society for banking services—payments and collections, deposit taking and credit—increased substantially.

The creation of a new government sponsored Banco do Brasil was again attempted in 1833. Proposed bank's by-laws established that bank notes issued would be exchangeable on demand for gold or silver and prohibited the bank from lending to the government without approval by Congress. But not enough public trust had yet been built to allow for the initiative to materialize. So, private sector banking began to flourish in Brazil.

Private sector banks were born in Ceará (1836), Rio de Janeiro (1838), Bahia (1845), Maranhão (1846), Pará (1847), and Pernambuco (1851). Brazil's first multi-state banking enterprise was private. It was named "Banco do Brasil." It was established in 1851 by the Barão de Mauá, and had headquarters in Rio de Janeiro and branches in São Paulo and Rio Grande do Sul.[5]

Notes issued by private sector banks began to be accepted as means of payment in their own geographic vicinity. But lack of a paper medium with countrywide acceptance remained an obstacle to economic development. In July 1853 a major new arrangement was announced: a new Banco do Brasil would be formed through the merger between the country's two largest private sector banks (Mauá's Banco do Brasil and Banco Comercial do Rio de Janeiro) plus new capital subscriptions by the provinces interested in having Banco do Brasil's commercial branches and by investors at large. The resulting ownership structure was 11/15 private (1/3 Maua's Banco do Brasil, 1/5 Banco Comercial, 3/15 other investors) and 4/15 public. Representation on the board of directors was proportional to shareholdings; but the bank's President and Treasurer had to be appointed by the Emperor.

The new Banco do Brasil was, again, authorized to operate as a commercial bank (deposit taking, payments and collections, credit, and foreign exchange and commodities trading) and had the mandate of a central bank

---

4. Initially a triumvirate, after 1834, one single Regent was chosen every four years by the General Assembly (Smith, 2002: 48).
5. For more details on Maua's Banco do Brasil see Caldeira (1995), chapter 18.

(the country's monopoly issuer of paper money). This time the bank's by-laws established clear liquidity and leverage guidelines[6]: paper emissions should not exceed two times metallic reserves and total loans should not exceed two times net worth.

Unfortunately, however, this was another short-lived attempt. In 1857, Banco do Brasil, weakened by higher leverage and lower levels of metallic reserves than specified by its by-laws, refused to borrow abroad to lend to the government. The government then broke the Banco do Brasil's monopoly of issuing currency (Ribeiro and Guimarães, 1967: 80). In 1866, with notes outstanding in excess of 5 times its metallic reserves, it lost (together with the other banks also granted the right to issue currency in 1857) the right to issue paper money.[7] Another two decades would go by before the Brazilian government would again entrust any financial institution with the right to issue paper money.[8] But private sector banks had begun to learn when to expand or contract their balance sheets in response to external conditions and perceived risks, and would never cease to exist in Brazil.

## From "Encilhamento" to the Great Depression, 1889–1930

The winds of liberalization towards the last days of the Empire had not been limited to the end of slavery. In May 1888, the government had already granted three private sector banks the right to issue paper money. Proclamation of the Republic (on November 15, 1889) reinforced the trend. With the goal of stimulating credit and economic growth, the new government decided to allow a plurality of paper money emissions. Commercial banks could be formed with the right to issue notes that were legal tender backed by bonds deposited with Treasury. No restriction on bank leverage was imposed and shareholders' liability was limited to the invested capital. The free market should be capable of self-restraint.

---

6. Bank liquidity is defined as the bank's ability to meet its financial obligations as they come due without incurring losses of a magnitude that could threaten its solvency. Bank solvency is defined as the bank's capacity to meet all financial obligations to third parties in full and on time. Bank leverage is the ratio between the bank's total financial obligations to third parties and its shareholder's capital.

7. The debate on who should be entrusted with the right to issue money (paper notes with legal tender) was also in debate in the US in the late 1800's. For a detailed discussion see Knox (1969).

8. Law 401 of September 1846 debased the gold standard from 2.5 *mil réis*/ounce to 4 *mil réis*/ounce. The following amount of metallic money was minted in Brazil (assuming the 4 *mil réis*/ounce standard) until 1888: 45.7 contos de réis in gold coins, 21.0 contos in silver, 3.9 contos in bronze, and 2.7 contos in nickel. Old Portuguese coins also circulated as metallic money. In addition, in 1849 the government gave legal tender status to English money. For more details on money in Brazil during the Second Empire (1831-1889) see Ribeiro and Guimarães (1967: 100-02).

The response was phenomenal (Ribeiro and Guimarães, 1967: 117). Registered capital by the (private) banking industry increased forty-fold, from 18.5 thousand contos in May 1888 to 828 thousand contos in October 1890. Private sector joint stock corporations were created throughout the country, with banks taking the lead. In Rio de Janeiro alone, 57 banks of issue were in operation. It was what historians would call the "Encilhamento," the saddling-up and frenetic betting which precedes a horse race.

Not all banks issued paper money and/or pursued unsecured optimistic lending. Several chose to simply ride the wave of other people's money and engage in basic commercial banking activities. But, as a result of the extraordinary monetary expansion, inflation permeated the economy, causing Brazil's currency to devalue by more than 100 percent between 1889 and 1892. Uncertainty regarding the soundness of banks began to mount. The Treasury eventually had to intervene to rescue the financial system. It cancelled all banks' licenses to issue paper money, liquidated many weaker banks, and pressured the shareholders of the private sector Banco República dos Estados Unidos do Brasil and the public-private Banco do Brasil to merge the two banks to form Banco República do Brasil. Banco República do Brasil's registered capital was 190 thousand contos. But initial paid-in capital was only 25.5 thousand contos and loan losses between 1893 and 1900 were more than 60,000 contos. By the end of 1900, the Treasury had begun the liquidation of the bank.

A period of fiscal and monetary orthodoxy ensued.[9] Finally, by legislation of December 30, 1905, a new (the fourth to operate) Banco do Brasil was formed to absorb the now smaller and cleaner balance sheet and the banking operations of Banco República do Brasil. Paid-in capital was 70,000 contos, 1/3 each approximately provided by the Banco da República's shareholders, the federal government, and the public. Born to be the country's leading commercial bank, the new Banco do Brasil would not be granted the right to issue paper money this time around. The bank's management was formed by five directors, two (the president and the director for foreign exchange) appointed by the government and three elected proportionately by the stockholders. As a result, the government obtained the effective control of the enterprise. By 1921, Banco do Brasil had 40 branches (from Manaus, in the Amazon Region, to Porto Alegre, in Rio Grande do Sul)

---

9. M1, currency plus demand deposits, stayed constant at 670,000 contos from 1900 to 1905 (Onody, 1960: 28).

and operated a clearing house for checks and a rediscount window for liquidity support to other banks.

The post–World War I economic euphoria lasted until 1920.[10] In the second semester of 1920 Brazil was dragged into a global, brief but severe, recession. This triggered increasing complaints throughout the economy against the scarcity of credit (Neuhaus, 1975: 60). Inspired by prevailing economic models in more developed economies,[11] Minister of Finance Homero Baptista proposed the establishment of an independent central bank to control the supply of money and credit, therefore freeing the economy from the negative influences of Treasury (fundamentally concerned with the financing of government deficits) in this area. Concerns regarding potential abuse of the power to issue paper money by a new central bank led to the approval of Law 4182 (1920) creating the Carteira de Emissão e Redesconto within Banco do Brasil but to be run by a director appointed by the President and having an initial authorized ceiling of 200,000 contos for future emissions. Decree-Law 4635 of January 8, 1923 (under President Artur Bernardes) gave Banco do Brasil absolute central banking powers, as it abolished the ceiling on emissions which had been set in 1920. But Decree-Law 5108 of December 18, 1926 (under President Washington Luiz) determined a return to the gold standard[12] suspending, for all practical purposes, the paper money issuing powers of Banco do Brasil (Neuhaus, 1975: 86) leading to a contraction of the monetary base[13] and suspending the central banking powers of Banco do Brasil.

Brazil's economic stability and growth potential had stimulated in the 1910's the entry of foreign banks (e.g. Banco Francês e Italiano para a América do Sul, later Sudameris, 1910; First National City Bank, later Citibank, 1915; Banco Holandês Unido, later ABN, 1917). Restored tranquility to the banking system as a result of the establishment of the Carteira de Emissão e Redesconto had given rise to new private sector Brazilian banks (e.g. Banco Moreira Salles, later Unibanco, 1924 and Banco da Lavoura de Minas Gerais, later Banco Real, 1925). But, perhaps as a result of the monetary tightening of the late 1920's, provinces around the country

---

10. GDP growth was 5.9 percent in 1919 and 10.1 percent in 1920 (Neuhaus, 1975: 58).

11. The U.S. Federal Reserve System (FED) had been established in 1913.

12. This would be a short lived attempt. Decree-Law 19423 (November 22, 1930) would determine the end of the gold standard and Decree-Law 19525 (December 24, 1930) would re-establish the Carteira de Redesconto do Banco do Brasil (Neuhaus, 1975: 105).

13. The monetary base (defined as the stock of paper money issued) expanded from 1,748 thousand contos in 1920 to 2,649 thousand contos in 1923; and remained stable at around 2,600 thousand contos through mid-1927 (Neuhaus, 1975: 158).

felt that insufficient support was available from the Banco do Brasil and the private sector for financing agricultural and manufacturing initiatives in their regions. So, government controlled state banks (e.g.: Piauí, 1926; São Paulo, 1927; Paraná and Rio Grande do Sul, 1928) (Baer and Nazmi, 2000: 5) were formed. This may have been well intended, but the clean-up of state banks was quite costly to society at large seven decades later.

## From Great Depression to "Fifty Years in Five," 1930–1961

The 1930's were particularly tumultuous, both politically and economically in Brazil. On the political front, President Washington Luís decided to break an alliance between São Paulo and Minas Gerais for rotation in power. He backed Julio Prestes, governor of São Paulo for President. Antônio Carlos Ribeiro de Andrada, the governor of Minas Gerais, reacted by throwing his support behind Getúlio Vargas, the governor of Rio Grande do Sul, for the presidency, and João Pessoa, the governor of Paraíba, for the vice-presidency. Júlio Prestes defeated Getúlio Vargas in the March elections. But, in July, still prior to his taking office, João Pessoa was assassinated in his home state of Paraíba. This added fuel to flames of country-wide dissatisfaction with what was perceived as excessive dominance by São Paulo on all relevant national affairs. In early October, Julio Prestes was arrested by the country's military command and told to resign, and the presidency was handed to Getúlio Vargas.

President Vargas dissolved Congress and replaced state governors with individuals of his personal choice. This generated further political dissent. A bloody revolt erupted in July 1932 in São Paulo, the richest state and by far the largest contributor to the federal coffers. The paulistas' revolution lasted three months and ended with their defeat, but with Vargas' commitment to call for congressional elections in 1933 and enact a new constitution in 1934 (Calógeras, 1939: 340). The political situation would, however, deteriorate further. Following a communist leaning mobilization in 1935, Vargas shut down Congress and suspended individual rights protected under the 1934 Constitution, making it clear that his regime, which lasted until 1945, was a dictatorship.

On the economic front, as previously indicated, Brazil had entered the 1930's highly dependent on coffee exports. With the advent of the Great Depression, coffee prices dropped from 22 cents per pound in 1929 to 9 cents in 1931. Every aspect of the Brazilian economic life was affected. Private sector banks, "known for a tradition of prudent lending" (Neuhaus, 1975: 115), adjusted their deposit taking and lending activities to the extremely volatile environment surrounding them. As a result, Banco do Brasil reinforced its central role in the provision of credit in domestic currency.

The economic odds for Brazil began to turn as the world gradually stepped out of depression and would substantially improve with the advent of World War II. Devaluation of the Brazilian mil réis (from 44.4 mil réis per British pound in 1930 to 65.7 in 1931) (Ribeiro and Guimarães, 1967: 149) and import taxes (imposed by the government to diminish the outflow of foreign exchange) had already triggered an initial process of imports substitution[14] and industrialization. Brazil's cotton production, for example, had increased six fold from 1932 to 1939 with a growing share being absorbed by a rapidly expanding domestic textile industry. World War II would make textiles Brazil's main export earner (Smith, 2002: 171-173). Coffee prices also rebounded back to 20 cents per pound, further reinforcing export surpluses. Brazil had regained the ability to invest and put it to use: installed production capacity of energy, cement, and steel more than doubled between 1938 and 1945.

This new wave of economic growth stimulated the demand for banking services. Private sector banks formed during this period include Banco Mercantil de Minas Gerais (1941), Banco Bradesco (1943), Banco Nacional (1944), and Banco Itaú (1945). The movement initiated in the late 1920's by a handful of provincial governments of establishing their own banks also gained force. By year-end 1945, the country's banking network had expanded from 860 to 2,035 branches, the number of processed checks had increased from 1.9 million to 4.8 million, the monetary base had grown from 4.8 million to 20.5 million cruzeiros;[15] and every state of the federation owned a commercial bank.

This expansion posed enormous challenges of systemic coordination and risk. In the words of José Whitaker (Ribeiro and Guimarães, 1967: 166) (former Vargas' Minister of Finance) in 1944: "We live, in reality, in the illogical situation of having banks but not a banking system; we live in a regime of sudden and frequent alarms, without tranquility, without confidence, with insufficient credit not so much because of lack of money but

---

14. Imports substitution: development policy characterized by the imposition of trade barriers to increase the competitiveness of local firms for faster domestic industrialization. For a detailed discussion see Södersten (1970: 375-80).

15. The Cruzeiro "(1 CR$= 1,000 réis) became the Brazilian monetary standard in October 1942.

because of its slow and defective circulation." An old debate[16] about the creation of an independent central bank was revived.

Contemporary to this domestic debate was Brazil's participation in the United Nations International Monetary Conference in Bretton Woods in 1944—which resulted in the adoption of a new international fixed exchange rates regime and the establishment of the IMF. It served as lender of last resort to sovereign nations to help ease temporary balance of payments disturbances, and of the World Bank, to assist governments with the financing of investments in reconstruction and development.

In this historical context, Brazil's Superintendência de Moeda e Crédito (SUMOC) was created (Decree-Law 7293 of February 2, 1945)[17] with the objectives of coordination of monetary policy and preparation of the basis for the establishment of an independent central bank. SUMOC's managing board was chaired by the Minister of Finance and had as directors the President of Banco do Brasil and its directors for Foreign Exchange and International Trade, and SUMOC's Executive Director.

In 1946, under democratically elected President Eurico Dutra (1946-1950), a proposal for a major banking reform was put forward by Minister of Finance Corrêa e Castro. It called for the creation of a 100 percent government owned Central Bank (under the direct supervision of an independent Monetary Council) to act as the sole issuer of paper money and the controller of foreign exchange flows in and out of the country. The new Central Bank would have to maintain gold (or hard currency) reserves of at least 25 percent of the total value of notes in circulation. The Banco do Brasil would become purely a commercial bank and five new specialized banks of joint public-private ownership—Rural, Mortgage, Export-Import, Industry, and Investment—would be formed to provide and stimulate the availability of credit to key areas of economic activity. Corrêa e Castro's proposal was not implemented but many traces would later be found in the major banking reform finally carried out twenty years later.

An initial post-war movement in the direction of free trade and economic liberalism was reversed in 1947, as massive imports of consumer goods caused

---

16. In the context of the successful negotiation of Brazil's foreign debt in the early 1930's he conducted, Minister of Finance José Whitaker himself had presented to Sir Otto Niemeyer, Director of the Bank of England, a program calling for a balanced fiscal budget and the creation of an autonomous central bank (Ribeiro and Guimarães, 1967: 151).

17. SUMOC's main functions were to decide upon the need of paper money emissions and request Treasury authorization to execute them, be the depositary bank for the reserve requirements of commercial banks, monitor interest rates, act as the primary dealer in government securities, monitor the exposure to other banks of Banco do Brasil's Carteira de Redesconto, and bank supervision (Neuhaus, 1975: 141).

rapid depletion of foreign exchange reserves accumulated during the war. By the end of Dutra's term in office, Brazil enjoyed a significant trade surplus (US$425 million, up from US$130 million in 1947) and had averaged real GDP growth close to 8 percent per annum for the previous 4 years.[18]

When Getúlio Vargas took office as president in 1951—this time through direct elections—the benign external economic environment of the previous years had begun to sour. Lower export revenues from coffee (due to new entrants to this market) added to stockpiling of basic materials (to protect the Brazilian industry from potential shortages as a result of the Korean War), causing a major reversal in the balance of trade (from a US$425 million surplus in 1950 to a US$277 million deficit in 1952).

On the political front, a climate of unrest brewing since the elections deteriorated rapidly in 1954 as a consequence of an attempt against the life of a journalist by Vargas' chief of security. Under the demand of senior military commanders to resign, "Vargas shot himself in the heart on August 24 (1954)"(Smith, 2002: 160). With Vargas' death his vice-president, Café Filho, took office and conducted the country without major policy changes until the orderly elections of 1955, won by Juscelino Kubitschek, then governor of Minas Gerais.

Still, Brazil's industrialization had marched on. In the three years from 1951 to 1954, electric power generation capacity had increased by 47 percent (from 1.9 to 2.8 million kilowatts); steel production, by 43 percent (from 840 thousand to 1.2 million tons); and cement production, by 66 percent (from 1.5 to 2.5 million tons) (Ribeiro and Guimarães, 1967: 157). GDP growth had still averaged over 6 percent per annum; but the monetary base had more than doubled (from 31.2 billion cruzeiros in 1950 to 65 billion cruzeiros in 1954)(Ribeiro and Guimarães, 1967: 158), bringing the annual inflation rate to approximately 30 percent in 1954.

The most important banking event of this period was the foundation in 1952 of the 100 percent government-owned Banco Nacional do Desenvolvimento Econômico (BNDE).[19] Embodying, in essence, the missions outlined for two of Corrêa e Castro's proposed banks in 1944 (the Industry Bank and the Investment Bank), BNDE was formed to provide, and to stimulate the availability—in cooperation with the private sector—of long term credit for investment in industrialization and infrastructure. For pri-

18. Instituto de Pesquisa Econômica e Aplicada (IPEA), www.ipeadata.gov.br.
19. BNDE, the Brazilian government owned development bank, was renamed BNDES (Banco Nacional do Desenvolvimento Econômico e Social) in 1982.

vate sector banks, this was a time for consolidation and gains in efficiency: the total number of banks dropped from 444 in 1946 to 357 in 1957 and the total number of branches increased from 1,783 in 1946 to 4,628 in 1957 (Bouzan, 1975 and Toledo, 1994: 137).

President Kubitschek (1956-1960) sought to deliver on his campaign promise of "fifty years in five." Import substitution policies were further reinforced and greater emphasis placed on central economic planning to stimulate domestic and foreign investment. There was rapid development of the automobile industry (130,000 vehicles produced in 1960, up from 30,000 in 1957) and other core industries such as shipyards, chemical, capital goods, and agricultural equipment. There was also massive public sector investment in transportation (primarily highways), hydroelectric plants and, last but not least, the construction and inauguration of the country's new capital, Brasília. As Kubitschek left office, Brazil was a fast growing (7 percent on average during his term) and significantly more industrialized country; but it was also one facing increasing balance of payments challenges and escalating inflation.[20]

Extreme political instability was to follow Kubitschek's relatively calm period in office. His immediate successor, Jânio Quadros, introduced austerity measures and managed to temporarily mitigate balance of payments pressures. He negotiated an important loan with his successor President João Goulart (1962-1964) and took an expansionist path under deteriorating financial conditions. Paper money emissions escalated (M1 up from 206 billion cruzeiros in 1956 to 890 billion in 1963 (Ribeiro and Guimarães, 1967: 162), and annual inflation reached almost 100 percent (annualized) during the first quarter of 1964. A growing sense of economic disorder created the political conditions for the March 31, 1964 military coup, and marked the beginning of two decades of authoritarian rule in Brazil.

For the banking sector, the 1956-1964 period was, again, a time for further consolidation (328 banks in 1964, down from 351 in 1957) and expansion of branch networks (6,424 branches in 1964, up from 4,628 in 1957). The economic optimism of the Kubitschek years had been tempered by the financial reality of monetary uncertainty. Higher inflation made it also harder for banks to perform their function of transforming short-term savings into medium-term loans at acceptable risks.[21]

---

20. Trade balance reversal, from US$194 million surplus in 1956 to US$430 million deficit in 1960; inflation approaching 40 percent for 1960, as a result of expansion of the monetary base from 80 billion cruzeiros in 1956 to 206 billion cruzeiros in 1960 (Ribeiro and Guimarães, 1967: 161).

## From Economic Miracle to Monetary Chaos, 1964–1993

The military junta (formed by the heads of the Army, Navy, and Air Force) was quick to instruct Congress to choose a new president and vice-president. On April 11, 1964, General Castelo Branco was elected by a large majority and took over the government under the motto "economic development and national security." While political liberties were severely restricted, a highly qualified team (under the leadership of Octávio Bulhões, Minister of Finance, and Roberto Campos, Minister of Planning) undertook the mission of reshaping public policies to attack Brazil's chronic inflation and balance of payments problems. It was in this context that perhaps the most important set of economic reforms in Brazilian history, with major consequences for the workings and organization to-date of the financial system, was put in place.

First, the concept of monetary correction was born. Law 4357 (July, 1964) imposed adjustment for inflation on overdue taxes and introduced the first inflation indexed financial asset, the ORTN (monthly adjusted treasury bill); and Law 4380 (which also created the Banco Nacional da Habitação, BNH) authorized financial institutions to monetarily correct both installments on mortgage financing and interest paid on savings deposits.[22]

Second, an autonomous central bank—operating under the supervision of a Monetary Council chaired by the Minister of Finance and formed by the Minister of Planning, the Minister of Industry and Commerce, the President of the Central Bank,[23] the President of Banco do Brasil, the President of BNDE, three Central Bank directors and two representatives of the private sector appointed by the President of the Republic—was finally created. Law 4595 (Lei da Reforma Bancária, December 1964), created the Banco Central do Brasil (through conversion of SUMOC), for managing the money supply, for controlling foreign exchange flows into and out of the country, and for supervising banks.[24]

---

21. The spread (the margin added to the cost of funds a bank charges a borrower) incorporates a charge for credit risk (the risk of default by the borrower) and a charge for market risk (the risk of loss resulting from an interest rate and/or a currency mismatch); the higher and more volatile the inflation rate, the higher (to the limit of becoming prohibitive) the charge for market (or mismatch) risk.

22. These measures restored banks' ability to manage interest rate risk, therefore increasing their willingness to lend.

23. The President and the directors of the Central Bank are appointed by the President of the Republic and have to be confirmed by Congress; but differently from the US, their terms do not cross presidential electoral terms.

Third, a major push towards the rapid development of the domestic securities market was undertaken. Law 4728 (July, 1965) imposed new rules for securities underwriting and trading; it introduced a wide range of new tradable instruments, and established that dedicated companies, also subject to Central Bank supervision, should be formed to pursue specific financial services activities (e.g. investment banking, asset management, consumer finance, mortgage lending).[25]

Fourth, a 100 percent government owned federal housing bank (Banco Nacional da Habitação—BNH, Law 4380, 1964) was created and new guidelines for mortgage lending (including a minimum required allocation by banks of savings deposits to mortgage loans) were imposed.

And last but not least, the compulsory savings mechanisms of FGTS (Fundo de Garantia de Tempo de Serviço, Law 5107, 1966) and PIS (Programa de Integração Social, Lei Complementar 07/70) were created.[26] FGTS and PIS are funds constituted by contributions made by employers on behalf of workers managed by the government. The below market remuneration (monetary correction plus a small spread) would make them the key sources of long term funding in domestic currency for investment in Brazil, a situation which persists to our days.

These measures fell under the umbrella of PAEG (the program for government action, 1964-1968) which also included more effective tax collection, reduction of government expenses, restrictions to the automatic transmission passing of inflation to labor costs (there was an estimated purchasing power loss of 30 percent for the minimum wage between 1964 and 1967), export incentives, and the introduction of the mini-devaluations system to continue the competitiveness of Brazilian exports, by making the exchange rate more realistic.

---

24. Decree-Law 4635 of January 8, 1923 (under President Artur Bernardes) gave Banco do Brasil the monopoly right to issue paper money, as it abolished the ceiling on emissions which had been set for the Carteira de Emissão e Redesconto in 1920 (200,000 contos). Decree-Law 5108 of December 18, 1926 (under President Washington Luís) determined a return to the gold standard suspending, for all practical purposes, the central bank authority of Banco do Brasil.

25. Differently from the US market (then under the restrictions of the 1933 Glass-Steagall Act), these specialized companies could be part of a financial group that also controlled a commercial bank.

26. The FGTS fund is constituted by monthly deposits made by all employers in the amount of 8 percent of every worker's salary in an account kept for this employee at Caixa Econômica Federal. PIS is similarly constituted but as a percentage of gross revenues, with deposits being made at Caixa Econômica Federal for private sector workers, at Banco do Brasil for public sector workers. Caixa Econômica Federal and Banco do Brasil act as fiduciary agents for the funds. Withdrawals by workers of their FGTS savings are restricted to certain specific events (purchase of a home in value not to exceed R$300,000, dismissal without just cause, and upon retirement). PIS benefits can only be paid in situations of temporary unemployment, major disease, and old age. For further details on origin and uses of FGTS and PIS-PASEP/FAT refer to the IPEA website, www.IPEA.gov.br.

The seeds had been planted for the Brazilian economic miracle. Inflation went down from 100 percent in 1964 to 25 percent in 1967 and to 12 percent in 1970. GDP growth averaged 11 percent per annum between 1968 and 1973.

For the financial sector, greater monetary stability and economic growth stimulated expansion and structural changes. Bank loans grew over 20 percent per annum in real terms between 1965 and 1974, and private sector banks more than doubled their share of total loans, from 17 percent 1963 to 46 percent in 1974.[27] Government incentives to industry consolidation combined with market driven pursuit of scale economies to increase private sector mergers and acquisitions.[28] Also, the Brazilian domestic securities market received a major boost. Larger financial groups established their investment banking arms (in some cases in partnership with foreign interests).[29] Independent broker-dealers were formed.[30] And the legal framework for capital markets activities was refined further through enactment of Lei das Sociedades Anônimas (1972) and establishment of the Comissão de Valores Mobiliários (CVM, the Brazilian equivalent to the SEC).

Unfortunately, however, Brazil's economic miracle had become too dependent on oil imports and foreign borrowings. In November 1973, OPEC imposed its first oil embargo. Oil prices more than tripled (from US$3 to US$10/barrel), Brazil's import bill doubled (from US$6.2 billion in 1973 to US$12.6 billion in 1974), and the current account deficit quadrupled (from US$1.7 billion to US$7.1 billion[31]). Relatively cheap external funding available from the Eurodollar market[32] would still permit the newly empowered Ernesto Geisel government (1974-1978) to postpone a major fiscal adjustment. PND II (Plano Nacional de Desenvolvimento II, an ambitious government sponsored investment program in infrastructure—primarily transportation and basic industries—to last the entire presidential term) launched in December 1974, was maintained through the end of President Geisel's term, as well as the trend of gains in real wages were maintained. By year-end 1978, GDP growth had dropped by more than half but still stood at 4.8 percent for the year. Inflation, however, was back

---

27. Source: Banco Central do Brasil.
28. The number of banks dropped from 152 in 1970 to 80 in 1978 while the total number of branches increased from 5,576 in 1970 to 6,583 in 1978 (Baer and Nazmi, 2000: 7).
29. e.g. Banco de Investimentos do Brasil (BIB), 1966.
30. e.g. Corretora Garantia, 1971.
31. Baer, 2008, chapter 6.
32. Petrodollars accumulated by oil exporters with leading international money center banks.

to 40 percent (up from 16 percent in 1974) and foreign indebtedness had more than tripled to reach US$43 billion.

General Figueiredo (empowered in March 1979 to be the last military president and prepare the country's transition back to democracy) was almost immediately confronted with the dramatic consequences for Brazil of the Iran-Iraq war. Oil prices went from US$12/barrel in 1979 to US$36/barrel in 1981 and the US FED raised its federal funds target rate[33] from 7 percent to 13 percent in 1979—and, subsequently, in additional increments to almost 20 percent in 1982 (with immediate pass through to the LIBOR[34] market).

Brazil's path to growth and development had suffered a most severe double hit: a (second) tripling of the price of its major and critical import plus the doubling of the interest cost on its fast growing foreign indebtedness. By early 1981 it was clear that strong medicine was required. Monetary tightening, reduction in government expenditures, and acceleration of the mini-devaluations mechanism followed. The economy contracted 6 percent between 1980 and 1983, to grow back 5.5 percent in 1984 and 8 percent in 1985. But, by then, inflation was over 200 percent per annum and high frequency indexation had spread throughout the economy. Five economic stabilization plans (Cruzado, Bresser, Verão, Collor I, and Collor II) would be put forward between 1986 and 1991 and fail. Brazil would be eventually forced to impose a moratorium on its non-trade related foreign debt service (1987), to only reestablish normal relations with the international banking community in the early 1990s upon implementation of Plano Brady.[35]

It should be no surprise that this fifteen year period (1978-1993) of high uncertainty would cause private sector banks to make fewer high risk loans. Still, private sector banks managed to remain profitable and continue to develop their asset-liability management, credit, and client servicing skills by limiting themselves to very short-term (and often collateralized) lending in domestic currency; foreign currency match-funded international trade

---

33. The federal funds rate is the rate of interest at which depository institutions lend money to one another overnight. By trading government securities, the FED can affect the federal funds rate. The Federal Open Market Committee establishes the target for trading in the federal funds market.

34. The London Interbank Offered Rate (LIBOR) is a daily reference rate based on the interest rates at which banks lend to one another in the London wholesale for certain tenors. The most common base interest rate for international sovereign borrowings is the LIBOR for 6 months.

35. Brady Plan stands for the framework for restructuring of the sovereign debt of most Latin American countries in the aftermath of the late 1980s. Named after the US Treasury Secretary Nicholas Brady, it offered banks a menu of choices to swap their exposures with some debt reduction (either through a discount on face value for LIBOR based bonds or through fixed below market rate bonds without a discount on face value). Specific Brady plans were reached by Mexico and Costa Rica (1989), Venezuela (1990), Uruguay (1991), and Argentina and Brazil (1992). For further details see Vásquez (1996).

finance activities; match-funded floating rate medium term lending to industry; and growing exploitation of inflation revenues (spread between the daily yield on Treasury bills and the cost of third party funds parked in the bank) through expansion of their branch networks.

From an organizational standpoint, private sector banks were quick to capitalize on the benefits of pooling of capital and managerial synergies arising from Central Bank Resolution 1254, enacted in 1988. Resolution 1254 authorized financial groups to consolidate into a single balance sheet (the multiple bank)[36] their different specialized financial companies (commercial banks, broker-dealers, investment banks, asset managers, consumer finance companies, Savings and Loans). Between 1988 and 1993 (Studart, 2000: 30), 206 multiple banks were formed and the number of single-purpose financial institutions reduced dramatically (commercial banks, 106 to 36; investment banks, 56 to 17; finance companies, 107 to 40). Universal banking—later to become the dominant form of organization for most of the large publicly traded financial institutions globally—had arrived in Brazil.

## BANKING IN BRAZIL POST *PLANO REAL*

## Fast Start and Sudden Stop

Brazilian society's exhaustion with life under hyperinflation (approaching 1,000 percent in 1993) brought about the political conditions for the *Plano Real* (Baer, 2008, chapter 7), proposed to Congress by Finance Minister Fernando Henrique Cardoso in December 1993. Differently from previous stabilization attempts, the *Plano Real* did not carry any element of surprise or impose any sort of price controls. A full indexation system was put in place to remain until a certain moment in the future, to be known by all in advance, when society's confidence on the fiscal adjustment being made would allow the introduction of the new currency, the Real. This general sense of credibility was built through a major initial fiscal adjustment[37] and a commitment by the executive branch to work with Congress to pursue

---

36. There is, actually, a great similarity between the scope of Brazil's Lei do Banco Múltiplo (Resolution 1254) and the US Bank Holding Act (1999) which revoked the forced separation between commercial banking and any type of securities underwriting activities that had been imposed by the 1933 Glass-Steagall Act.

37. A 5 percent tax increase across the board plus the establishment of the Social Emergency Fund comprising 15 percent of all tax revenues for discretionary use by the Federal Government.

constitutional amendments to reduce the amount of fiscal transfers from the Federal to state governments.

The new indexing system created a shadow currency (the Unit of Real Value, URV) tied to the US dollar on a one-to-one basis, therefore adjusting daily to a higher equivalent in the circulating currency, the Cruzeiro Real (Cr$). From paychecks to products on the shelves of retailers, every transaction was denominated in both, the official currency (Cruzeiro Real) and the shadow currency (the URV). Full indexation lasted for five months. On July 1, 1994, the Real (BRL) was finally introduced (equal to 1 URV and CR$2,750). A quite restrictive monetary policy (high real interest rates and 100 percent compulsory reserve requirement on new demand deposits) was put in place to curb excessive expansion of aggregate demand and minimize the chances of an early return of inflationary pressures.

The initial achievements of *Plano Real* were highly impressive. The monthly inflation rate fell from 46.6 percent in June to 2.5 percent in October, and 0.6 percent in December (Baer, 2008: 132); aggregate consumption increased over 20 percent in real terms between July and December; and GDP growth reached 5.9 percent for the full year. Fueling the rapid growth in consumption was the substantial increase in the purchasing power of the population as a result of the sharp drop in inflation as well as the willingness of banks to expand credit. Eager to compensate for the loss of float revenues,[38] banks—some more aggressively than others—increased lending. Bank loans grew by over 25 percent between June and December, leading to a total bank debt to GDP ratio of 36.6 percent in December 1994, up from 28.9 percent in December 1993.

Unfortunately, trouble brewed elsewhere in Latin America. A delicate political transition in Mexico was further complicated by the assassination of a presidential candidate, triggering massive capital flight. Between October and December, Mexico's foreign exchange reserves fell 75 percent (from US$17.6 billion to US$4.4 billion) and the Mexican peso devalued by 50 percent (from 3.4 to 5 Mexican pesos/US dollar). The crisis would be eventually resolved with financial assistance from the US Treasury and the IMF, but it would also cause the Mexican banking industry, highly exposed to the Mexican peso to US dollar currency mismatch, to come close to collapse. This time around no banking industry wide nationalization would take place in Mexico, as it had happened in the early 1980s. But the Mexican

---

38. Estimated at 35 percent to 40 percent of total revenues for most banks (Baer and Nazmi, 2000: 8).

banking sector would eventually re-emerge largely dominated by foreign banks (Tschoegl, 2006).

Serious threats were posed to balance of payments equilibrium and exchange rate stability throughout Latin America where countries had just begun to reengage with the international financial community after the implementation of their Brady plans. Seeking to avoid a major devaluation of the BRL[39]—which could result in significant inflationary pressures—the Brazilian Central Bank reacted swiftly. The Central Bank's target base rate, the SELIC,[40] was raised sharply (from 50 percent in January to 70 percent in March) and new reserve requirements and lending restrictions (e.g. strict limitations on credit card borrowings) imposed. This abrupt pulling on the monetary breaks after such a fast start of lending had to cause damage to banks' balance sheets. Past due loans for the system increased from under 6 percent of total loans in mid-1994 to over 17 percent by mid-1995.[41] The survival of a number of private sector banks and of most public sector banks was under question. By November 1995 it was clear that a major government intervention was necessary to rescue the financial system.

## Government Assisted Consolidation, 1995–1998

By year end 1995 three government programs had been put in place to support the reorganization and recapitalization of the financial sector: the Programa de Estímulo à Reestruturação e ao Fortalecimento do Sistema Financeiro Nacional (PROER), to facilitate the transfer of the banking operations of endangered financial institutions to healthier private sector banks; the Programa de Incentivo à Redução do Estado na Atividade Bancária (PROES), for the restructuring and subsequent privatization of state banks; and the Programa de Fortalecimento dos Bancos Federais, to recapitalize federal banks. In addition, foreign banks were permitted to acquire Brazilian banks.

---

39. BRL is the International Organization for Standardization code for Brazil's currency, the Real.
40. The SELIC (Sistema Especial de Liquidação e Custódia) rate is Banco Central do Brasil's equivalent to the FED's federal funds rates.
41. Central Bank statistics on past due loans excluded FCVS (Fundo de Cobertura de Variação Salarial) exposure, a substantial portfolio of federal government obligations held by banks resulting from the difference accumulated since the mid 1980s between the monetary correction on mortgage contracts under SFH (the National Housing System) and the nominal increase in minimum wages. By mid-1995 some banks had 100 percent provisions against their FCVS exposure; but others carried it at face value. As it turned out, FCVS obligations ended up being swapped for Treasury bonds at a present value for banks' FCVS obligations at an estimated at 1/3 of their face value. For a complete discussion see Barbosa (2008).

The largest transactions under PROER were the absorptions of the banking operations of Banco Nacional by Unibanco,[42] Banco Bamerindus by HSBC (UK), and Banco Econômico by Banco Excel (shortly thereafter acquired by BBVA, Spain).[43] The largest privatizations under PROES were of BANERJ (Rio de Janeiro), BEMGE (Minas Gerais) and BANESTADO (Paraná), acquired by Banco Itaú; and of BANESPA (São Paulo), acquired by Banco Santander (Spain). The most important transaction under PROEF was the R\$8 billion recapitalization of Banco do Brasil in 1996. It is estimated that the combined fiscal cost of the three financial rescue programs reached approximately 9 percent of GDP (0.9 percent for PROER, 2.1 percent for PROES, 5.7 percent for PROEF) (Goldfajn, 2003: 16).

Specific measures to help prevent future systemic banking crises included the creation of the FGC (Fundo Garantidor de Crédito)[44] in 1995 and the enactment between 1997 and 1999 of a series of Central Bank resolutions imposing strict and closely monitored credit rating and provisioning rules for loans as well as capital charges for currency and interest rate mismatches. In addition, the minimum capital adequacy ratio for banks operating in Brazil was set by the Central Bank at 11 percent, significantly above Basel's minimum of 8 percent.[45]

The extraordinary expansion in bank credit after the introduction of the Real on July 1, 1994 had caused total bank debt-to-GDP to increase from

---

42. The first good bank/bad bank transaction under PROER was the absorption, in November 1995, of Banco Nacional, the fourth largest private sector Brazilian bank, by Unibanco, the fifth largest. Bad loans absorbed by the government exceeded R\$5 billion; in exchange for the good bank being transferred to Unibanco, the government was able to retain a 1/3 equity stake in the new Unibanco (now the third largest private sector bank). This equity stake was sold in May 1997, in the first major global public offering by a Brazilian bank, for US\$1.2 billion.

43. Bamerindus, Nacional, and Econômico were the sixth, seventh, and thirteenth largest commercial banks in Brazil on June 30, 1994. Their total assets in BRL equivalent (1BRL = Cr\$2,750) were R\$12.0 billion, R\$9.8 billion, and R\$5.0 billion respectively. Source: Banco Central do Brasil, Informações Contábeis, Ranking dos Bancos, www.bcb.gov.br.

44. FGC, formed on August 31, 1995, is funded by contributions from all banks; it currently guarantees individual deposits up to R\$60,000.

45. Per the Basel I accord of 1988, the Bank of International Settlements (BIS) declared that banks had to maintain a minimum capital ratio of 8 percent of maximum expected losses (weighted risk assets, WRA), where WRA was defined as the sum of each of a bank's loans multiplied by a weight which differentiated between sovereign risks (OECD versus non-OECD country) (Apostolik et.al., 2009). Per the 1996 Market Amendment to the Capital Accord to Incorporate Market Risks, the minimum capital ratio became 8 percent of maximum expected losses not only for credit risk (as per Basel I) but also market risk (Apostolik et.al., 2009); per Basel II in 2004, the minimum capital ratio became 8 percent of maximum expected losses from credit risk (now with WRA methodology making use of either external or internal ratings for credit exposure), market risk, and operating risk (BIS, 2004). As of 1997, Banco Central do Brasil not only imposed a higher minimum capital ratio than per Basel accord (11 vs. 8 percent) but also more specific and stringent requirements, and capital charges for credit risk and market risk. For further details on the Basel accords see BIS (2004).

29 percent in year-end 1993 to 36.6 percent in 1994; the sudden stop, as a result of the Mexican crisis, brought this ratio back to 28 percent in December 1998. But PROER, PROES, PROEF had not only reinvigorated the Brazilian financial system but also contributed to fundamental changes in the structure of the industry.

In July 1998 ABN-Amro (Holland) announced the conclusion of negotiations for the acquisition of Banco Real. This was a purely market driven (non-PROER) transaction in which ABN-Amro managed to outbid the competition to acquire the country's fourth largest private sector banking franchise, an early sign of a new stage of consolidation to come.

The number of public sector banks among the top 21 had dropped from 9 in 1995 to 6 in 1998; the number of foreign banks had increased from 3 to 7 (2 among the top 10);[46] private sector banks had expanded much faster than public sector banks; but, by year-end 1998, the two largest public sector banks (Banco do Brasil and CEF) still had over twice the total assets of the largest private sector bank (Bradesco).

## Market Driven Consolidation, 1999–2007

Brazil's *Plano Real* was once again threatened, this time by the eruption of the Russian economic crisis in the second half of 1998 following the 1997 financial market upheaval in Asia. Capital flight caused Brazil's foreign exchange reserves to drop abruptly, from US$75 billion in August to US$35 billion in January. An emergency line of credit was put in place in November with IMF and US Treasury support (US$41.5 billion in total). But open political dissent regarding the scope of the fiscal adjustment necessary to maintain the recently acquired relative monetary stability continued to feed uncertainty. In January 1999 the BRL was finally allowed to float, devaluing over 70 percent in a few weeks. The inflation rate shot up from close to zero during the last quarter of 1998 to 4.5 percent per month in February.

From then on Brazil's macroeconomic policy took a major shift: from dependence for monetary stability on an exchange rate anchor (defended via very high real interest rates) and only secondary attention to fiscal discipline, to adherence to pre-established targets for the inflation rate and the primary fiscal surplus, and a floating exchange rate regime.

---

46. ABN-Amro (#14) was soon to join the also foreign Santander (#6) and HSBC (#10) among the top 10 as a result of its acquisition of Real (#8).

Tight monetary policy (SELIC in excess of 1.5 percent per month in real terms) combined with fiscal austerity measures kept inflation in check (11.3 percent for the year 1999) and the exchange rate relatively stable (R$1.7 per U.S. dollar in March to R$1.85 per U.S. dollar in December[47]). Tax increases (Goldfajn, 2003: 16) plus cuts in government expenditures produced a 3.9 percent primary fiscal surplus[48] in 1999 (well above the 3.1 percent target promised to the IMF in 1998). In addition, to enhance fiscal sustainability going forward, three important sets of initiatives were put in place: restructuring of the debt of each individual state with the federal government; enactment of the Fiscal Responsibility Law, comprising a legally binding framework for budgeting, execution, and reporting for all levels of government (federal, state, and local); and setting of the stage for discussion of the so-called structural reforms (labor, fiscal, and social security).

The first two sets of initiatives were implemented during President Cardoso's second term in office (1998-2002). Regarding the third set, some modest progress has been made on social security by President Lula's administration; fiscal and labor reforms remain a work-in-progress.

Brazil's GDP would remain flat for 1998 and 1999, and grow 4.5 percent in 2000. But a severe drought, with resulting major disruption to energy generation and distribution, caused the economy to slow to 1.3 percent growth in 2001. First quarter 2002 annualized projections were for GDP growth to again reach the 4 percent to 5 percent range. But, this time, an entirely domestic event—coming of the elections for President and the consequent uncertainty regarding future economic policy and the treatment of holders of Brazilian domestic and foreign debt by an increasingly likely to win opposition—caused a new and major reversal of capital flows. This time even short-term trade finance lines (on which Brazil had never defaulted) from international banks to their Brazilian correspondents (including the leading Brazilian banks) were cut, causing the BRL to devalue 70 percent (from R$2.3/US dollar in March to R$3.9/US dollar in September). Consistent with its inflation targeting policy, the Central Bank was forced to sharply raise the SELIC rate. The yield on the one-year fixed rate Treasury note jumped from 19 percent in March to 29 percent in July and 34 percent in November, to finally come back to below 20 percent only eighteen months later (September, 2003), after the dissipation of market fears. As a result, GDP growth slowed

---

47. IPEA, Taxa de Câmbio Comercial, www.ipea.data.gov.br.
48. Primary fiscal surplus equals total federal government revenues minus total federal government expenses excluding the interest cost of the federal government's debt.

(2.6 percent in 2002, 1.1 percent in 2003)[49] and credit expansion remained subdued (9.2 percent in 2002, 5.6 percent in 2003).[50]

The extraordinary exchange rate and interest rate movements brought about by such a succession of financial crises (Asia, Russia, and Brazil[51]) could have caused a serious weakening of the Brazilian financial sector. But, actually, the opposite occurred. Private sector banks did retract from expanding credit (private sector bank debt- to-GDP dropped from 15.4 percent 1998 to 14.8 percent in 2003[52]) but, well capitalized; confident on a just tested (under PROER and PROES) capacity to implement acquisitions; and motivated to pursue further gains of scale and/or scope (Davis, 2000, chapter 3), they went shopping, acquiring smaller commercial banking franchises[53] and the larger independent consumer finance companies in the market.[54]

By early 2004 private sector Brazilian banks had already begun to see the benefits of their strategic repositioning over the previous ten years reflected in their market values. The yield on the one-year Treasury note would still go up from 15.5 percent in January 2004 to 19.5 percent in April 2005 (due to another round of monetary tightening by the Central Bank in response to inflation fears), causing a slowdown of GDP growth from 5.7 percent in 2004 to 3.1 percent in 2005. But it would then drop continuously for the following 32 months, from 19.5 percent in April 2005 to under 12 percent in December 2007. Monetary stability had been re-conquered, bringing with it robust economic growth (average GDP growth of 4.7 percent per annum for 2004-2007) and substantial credit expansion (25 percent per annum growth in total loans for 2004-2007, compared to 7.5 percent per annum for 2001-2003).

Two pieces of legislation further contributed to the willingness and ability of banks to lend: specific payroll lending legislation, enacted in 2004, allowing a bank to deduct interest and principal on personal loans from the paychecks of individuals; and a new bankruptcy law, approved by Congress in February 2005, significantly strengthening creditor rights (Queiroz and Anselmo, 2005). Higher margins in consumer lending, combined with a

---

49. IPEA, PIB (preços 2009), www.ipea.data.gov.br.
50. Banco Central do Brasil, Sistema Financeiro Nacional, 50 Maiores Bancos e Consolidado do Sistema, Relatório de Ativos, www.bcb.gov.br.
51. Argentina's foreign debt default in late 2001 had not caused significant foreign exchange volatility for Brazil; but its disastrous consequences for investors and banks (domestic and foreign) certainly contributed to the market panic regarding the potential implications of the political transition in Brazil.
52. Banco Central do Brasil, Sistema Financeiro Nacional, Relatório de Ativos, www.bcb.gov.br.
53. e.g. Bandeirantes, by Unibanco; Noroeste by Santander; BBVA by Bradesco; Bank Boston, by Itaú.
54. e.g. Fininvest, by Unibanco; Finasa and Zogbi, by Bradesco; Losango, by HSBC.

gradual return of larger corporate borrowers to the capital markets, also led to a change in the structure of banks' balance sheets: loans to businesses dropped from over 65 percent of total in 2002 to under 50 percent in 2007. In addition, as shown in Table 12–1 below, private sector banks gained share on public sector banks.

TABLE 12-1. Loans by Private and Public Banks, 2003–2007

| Year | Private Sector (% of GDP) | Public Sector (% of GDP) | Total (% of GDP) |
|---|---|---|---|
| 2003 | 14.8 | 9.8 | 24.6 |
| 2004 | 15.8 | 9.9 | 25.7 |
| 2005 | 17.8 | 10.4 | 28.3 |
| 2006 | 19.6 | 11.3 | 30.9 |
| 2007 | 23.2 | 12.0 | 35.2 |

Source: Banco Central do Brasil, "Sistema Financeiro Nacional, Operações de Crédito do Sistema Financeiro."

In the capital markets arena, greater confidence in the direction of the country's economic policy had also helped revive expectations for fast growth of brokerage, underwriting, and asset management businesses. Some of the leading universal banks since 1998 had begun to revisit segmentation strategies and organizational structures to better compete with the investment banks in capital market activities. By 2002, most large private sector banks had formed strong wholesale banking divisions by combining renovated in-house corporate and investment banking platforms and by acquiring independent wholesale banks (e.g. Bozano Simonsen by Santander, Credibanco by Unibanco, BBA by Itaú). International banks also expanded their Brazil dedicated teams (at headquarters and in the field) and increased capital commitments to participate in the Brazilian primary and secondary securities markets; and some of them pursued acquisitions, the most visible having been the purchases of Garantia by Credit Suisse (1998) and of Pactual by UBS (2006).

The last and major event of this market driven period of consolidation was the acquisition in September 2007 in Europe of ABN-Amro by a consortium formed by Banco Santander, Royal Bank of Scotland, and Fortis Bank. Banco Santander's targets were ABN's Italian franchise (Banco Antonveneta, sold shortly thereafter to Banca Monte dei Paschi de Siena) and ABN-Real in Brazil (valued at US$17 billion) (Babington and Barrett, 2007). Consolidation between the banking operations of Santander-Banespa and ABN-Real in Brazil only took place the following year. But, for all practical purposes,

Santander ended 2007 ranked among the top three private sector banks in Brazil, with a scale comparable to those of Bradesco and Itaú.

Table 12-2 portrays the structural changes the Brazilian banking industry went through over this 1995-2007 period of fundamentally market driven consolidation. The Brazilian banking industry experienced large structural

TABLE 12-2. Industry Ranking, Top 10 plus BNDES, 1995, 1998, and 2007

| December 30, 1995 | | December 30, 1998 | | December 30, 2007 | |
|---|---|---|---|---|---|
| Bank | Total Assets in R$bn | Bank | Total Assets in R$bn | Bank | Total Assets in R$bn |
| 1. CEF | 80.0 | 1. Banco do Brazil | 121.4 | 1. Banco do Brasil | 316.4 |
| 2. Banco do Brasil | 79.1 | 2. CEF | 114.3 | 2. Itaú | 267.0 |
| 3. BNDES | 43.6 | 3. BNDES | 76.7 | 3. Bradesco | 254.9 |
| 4. BANESPA | 37.0 | 4. Bradesco | 57.5 | 4. Santander -ABN | 253.5 |
| 5. Bradesco | 25.1 | 5. Itaú | 44.8 | 5. CEF | 239.0 |
| 6. Unibanco | 20.7 | 6. Santander | 35.8 | 6. BNDES | 198.7 |
| 7. Itaú | 18.7 | 7. Unibanco | 26.7 | 7. Unibanco | 132.8 |
| 8. Bamerindus | 14.3 | 8. ABN-Real | 24.1 | 8. HSBC | 69.4 |
| 9. Real | 10.9 | 9. Banrisul | 15.0 | 9. Safra | 65.8 |
| 10. Nossa Caixa | 8.7 | 10. HSBC | 13.9 | 10. Votorantim | 60.6 |
| 11. BANRISUL | 7.6 | 11. Nossa Caixa | 13.6 | 11. Citibank | 54.7 |
| Sub-total (Top 11) | 345.7 | | 543.8 | | 1,912.8 |
| Top 11 - BNDES | 302.1 | | 467.1 | | 1,714.1 |
| System Total | 532.0 | | 753.4 | | 2,382.5 |
| Total - BNDES | 488.4 | | 676.7 | | 2,183.8 |
| Public in Top 11 | 256.0 | | 341.0 | | 754.1 |
| Priv. Br. in Top 11 | 89.7 | | 129.0 | | 781.1 |
| Foreign in Top 11 | 0 | | 76.8 | | 377.6 |
| Top 11/System Total | 65% | | 72.2% | | 80.3% |
| Top 10/System Total (w/o BNDES) | 61.8% | | 69% | | 78.4% |
| Public in Top 11 | 48.1% | | 45.3% | | 31.6% |
| Private in Top 11 | 16.9% | | 17.1% | | 32.7% |
| Foreign in Top 11 | 0% | | 9.8% | | 16.8% |
| Bank debt - GDP | 32.1% | | 28% | | 34% |

*Source*: Banco Central do Brasil, Sistema Financeiro Nacional, Informações Contábeis, 50 Maiores Bancos, www.bcb.gov.br.

change over this 1995–2007 period of fundamentally market driven consolidation. Private sector banks among the top 11 had expanded by 5 to 6 times (compared to 2 to 3 times for the public sector banks). Brazilian private sector banks had almost doubled their share of total assets (from 17.1 percent to 32.7 percent); foreign banks among the top 11 had also gained (from 9.8 percent to 16.8 percent); and public sector banks had lost, (45.3 to 31.6 percent). Industry concentration had firmly marched on: the top 10 banks' (BNDES excluded) percent share of total assets having reached 78.4 in 2007, up from 69 in 1998 and 62 in 1995.

## Subprime Meltdown–Induced Consolidation, 2008–2009

The world entered 2008 projecting another year of strong economic growth. For Brazil, the global boom had translated into consistently higher volumes of exports (primarily commodities) at continuously higher prices, and robust trade surpluses (4 percent of GDP in 2007). Most analysts' projections for the year pointed to a relatively stable exchange rate (around R$1.8 per US dollar) and a declining SELIC rate (then, 11 percent). Brazil had accumulated enough foreign exchange reserves to become a net creditor in US dollars and finally enjoyed investment grade status for its sovereign risk. But net public sector debt remained too high (over 40 percent of GDP) for its cost (a real interest rate of 7 percent per annum). And big trouble had been brewing up North.

Lax US monetary policy (particularly between December 2001 and November 2004) had not only stimulated high levels of consumption (in great part of products made in China at stable prices in US dollars) but also a real estate bubble (real estate prices rose on average around 10 percent per annum between 2002 and 2006 versus 3 percent between 1990 and 2000). Subprime lending (100 percent of home value mortgage financing at subsidized rates in the early years to be reset later) had become hugely popular. Capital markets' creativity, lax regulatory supervision, less than adequate credit ratings and generalized greed had conspired to bring about additional levels of poorly priced financial instruments. As real estate prices peaked in late 2006 (to start falling in 2007) the bubble began to crack. At its roots, the subprime meltdown crisis was not very different from other previous financial crises: first, generalized expectations of continued economic stability and growth leading to excessive optimism by lenders and borrowers; then, the surprise of an economic slowdown causing asset prices to stabilize and begin to fall; and, finally, severe balance sheet problems for banks. The trouble this time around was that the so-called subprime meltdown crisis had been nurtured over a long period of time in the world's largest and most globally interconnected economy, and the one home to both, the most creative financial market and the most widely accepted currency.

By mid 2008, early hopes that the US Federal Reserve Bank could continue to fight the battle alone, without major involvement by the US Treasury, began to dissipate.[55] In June, the US Congress authorized the Treasury to purchase shares of the government sponsored Fannie Mae and Freddie Mac.[56] In early September, Fannie Mae and Freddie Mac, as well as the country's largest insurance company, AIG, had to be put into conservatorship.[57] Congress approved TARP (the Troubled Assets Relief Program), committing up to US$700 billion for recapitalization of banks in October 2008, and President Obama's US$780 billion fiscal stimulus plan in March 2009. All combined, US$2.2 trillion (15 percent of GDP) had been committed by the Treasury alone to prevent the collapse of the financial system and to attenuate the social impact of a major recession.

The difficulties in the US financial markets had begun, since early 2008, to spill over internationally, with greater impact on the economies with banking systems more interconnected with the US financial markets. Central banks and treasuries around the world were gradually forced to act in accordance with their perceptions of—and ability to deal with—the problems faced by their own financial systems and the threat of the recession to come.

While claims of decoupling between the developed world and the emerging economies had continued to dominate the media and the sell side reports from Wall Street during the first semester of 2008, the global credit crunch ended up having a major impact on Brazil. In spite of the country's position as a net creditor in US dollars, investment grade status, and minimal interconnectedness with the US domestic financial markets, the BRL suffered in less than 4 months a 50 percent devaluation (from R$1.56 to R$2.32/US dollar between August and October). Opposite to what was being done in most countries around the world, the Brazilian Central Bank, consistent with its inflation targeting policy, was forced to raise the SELIC rate by 25 percent (from 0.9 percent/month in June to 1.2 percent/month

55. A lot had already been done by the US Federal Reserve including continued lowering of the FED funds rate to below 2 percent, acting as lender of last resort for liquidity support to banks with greater flexibility regarding collateral required, and liquidity assistance to induce absorption of large problem companies (such as the mortgage bank Countrywide by Bank of America and the investment bank Bear Stearns by JPMorgan Chase).

56. The Federal National Mortgage Association (Fannie Mae) was established as a federal agency in 1938 to make mortgages more available to low income families. In 1968 it was chartered by Congress as a private shareholder-owned company. Rather than making home loans directly to consumers, Fannie Mae acted in the secondary markets, acquiring mortgage portfolios, and financing itself in the domestic and international capital markets. The Federal Home Mortgage Corporation (Freddie Mac) was chartered by Congress in 1970 to compete with Fannie Mae. Because of their congressional charters, Fannie Mae and Freddie Mac are considered government-sponsored enterprises (GSEs), therefore being perceived by the market as (almost) US sovereign credit risk. For further details refer to www.fanniemae.com and www.freddiemac.com.

57. For all practical purposes (at least temporarily) nationalized through capital injections from Treasury in exchange for over 80 percent equity stakes.

in October), leading the yield on the one-year Treasury note to increase to 15.25 percent on October 30, up from 11.9 percent on January 1, 2008.

The consequences for the financial sector were severe. Small and medium sized banks, largely dependent on the institutional market for funding, were faced with tremendous liquidity challenges. The liquidity squeeze was also felt by the larger banks, in proportion to the market perception of their leverage and sustainability of their funding sources.

As it turned out, prompt action by the Central Bank—in the form of liquidity support against collateral to small banks and the use of foreign exchange reserves to provide US dollar lines of credit to banks for them to be able to meet immediate foreign currency needs of important corporate clients—was sufficient to shore-up the financial sector without the need for Treasury involvement. But the sequence of events since May, more significantly felt by those more dependent on market counterparts for their total funding, forced all banks to revisit their strategic plans.

On November 3, the merger of Itaú and Unibanco, the largest ever in Latin America, was announced. The transaction consisted in a share exchange by which Unibanco shareholders received one Itaú non-voting share for either 3.4782 Unibanco non-voting shares (reflecting the average relative price between the two stocks for the 45 days prior) or 1.1797 Unibanco voting share (implying in a 195 percent premium for voting over non-voting stock).[58] From Itaú's shareholders standpoint it meant paying 1.6 times book value for Unibanco non-voting stock, 4.8 times for voting stock, 2.3 times overall (approximately R$30 billion) for 100 percent of Unibanco. The new Itaú-Unibanco would close 2008 as Brazil's largest bank by equity and total loans, although still second to Banco do Brasil in number of branches.

On November 20, Banco do Brasil completed the acquisition of 71.25 percent of the São Paulo state bank Nossa Caixa for R$5.45 billion (100 percent ownership to be achieved later, in October 2009, via a share swap); and on January 9, 2010, Banco do Brasil announced the purchase of 50 percent of privately held Banco Votorantim, regaining the position of Brazil's (and Latin America's) largest bank by total assets. This was a cash transaction in the total amount of R$4.2 billion (Banco do Brasil S.A., 2009), R$3 billion paid to Votorantim's shareholders for 49.9 percent of the voting stock and R$1.2 billion as fresh capital in the form of non-voting shares. In July, Banco Santander (Spain), the controlling shareholder of Santander-

---

58. Itaú-Unibanco Banco Múltiplo S.A., 2009.

Brasil, announced that it would conduct a global public offering to raise capital to boost growth across the whole spectrum of its activities in Brazil. This public equity offering, the largest in the world in 2009 (and to mid-May, 2010 in Brazil), attracted R$13.2 billion in fresh capital (Banco Santander, 2009) (for approximately 1/6 of the bank) bringing Santander-Brasil's capital adequacy ratio to 33 percent, three times the minimum required by the Central Bank. These movements significantly impacted the structure of the industry.

First, banking industry concentration increased sharply: the shares of total assets of the country's top 6 banks (BNDES excluded) increased from 67 percent in 2007 to 76.5 percent in 2009, a variation of the same order of magnitude as the one observed for the nine year market driven stage of consolidation (from 59 percent in 1998 to 67 percent in 2007). Second, public sector banks increased their share of total assets (from 31.6 percent in 2007 to 39.4 percent in 2009), in a clear reversal of the trend observed during the market driven consolidation stage (1999-2007). Third, the balance of power remained relatively unchanged between private sector Brazilian and foreign banks, approximately 32 percent of total assets for the former, 16 percent for the latter. And fourth, BNDES had by far the largest organic growth, in great part due to the government's decision to have the Treasury provide an extra R$100 billion to enable the BNDES to lend for infrastructure and industry. As of December 30, 2009 BNDES had R$280 billion in loans, 20 percent of the countries total bank debt of R$1.4 trillion (45 percent of GDP).

## CONCLUSION

The recent development of the Brazilian financial system has been impressive, particularly after 1999, as a result of the government assisted industry re-structuring stage described in section 3 and of the beginning of a decade long adherence to a macroeconomic policy characterized by firm compliance with inflation and primary fiscal targets, and a floating exchange rate.

As of year-end 2009, two Brazilian private sector banks (Itaú and Bradesco) ranked among the top 20 most valuable banks in the world. Santander-Brasil had conducted a most successful global offering and accounted for approximately one-third of Banco Santander's (Spain) total market capitalization. Total bank debt had expanded from 25 percent of GDP in 1999 to 45 percent of GDP in 2009. Medium term (typically 3 to 5 year) fixed rate automobile financing, inexistent a decade ago, had reached R$94.1 billion (approximately 3 percent of GDP). And banks ended 2009 showing very high capital adequacy levels by any world standards, therefore enjoying a quite comfortable position to engage in significant additional credit expansion without immediate pressure on capital base.

The equities market has also been another bright spot of financial activity in Brazil. Benefiting from the country's market size, continuous development of important companies across the different sectors of the economy, consistent progress in the legal and regulatory framework (from the creation of the Comissão de Valores Mobiliários[59] in the early 1970s through the New Market legislation in 2002), continuous investment in the quality of trading platforms and, last but not least, top notch standards of transparency and corporate governance by publicly traded companies, BOVESPA (Bolsa de Valores de São Paulo) ranks today among the most respected equity exchanges globally.[60] An increasing number of Brazilian companies have also been listed on other international stock exchanges (mainly the New York Stock Exchange) and Brazilian global equity offerings have made, particularly since 2004, the headlines of the business media around the world.

But equity capital should always be the smaller part of the capital required for investment, that part which is permanent and the basis for borrowings (from lenders or in the fixed income securities market) at a financial cost below the expected rate of return on investment. The Brazilian process of economic development is constrained by the limitations of its domestic long term credit markets, more specifically, by the availability of affordable long term credit in reais, the currency in which most businesses earn their revenues and individuals earn their salaries.

Mortgage loans outstanding have increased by almost 80 percent over the past ten years, in great part as a result of the Central Bank imposed minimum lending requirements of 65 percent on savings deposits. But, at year-end 2009, the total amount of mortgage loans outstanding was only 3 percent of GDP (R$91.9 billion),[61] versus 15 percent for Mexico (Investment Properties Mexico, 2010) and 20 percent for Chile (Global Property Guide,

---

59. CVM, the Brazilian securities and exchange commission.

60. Total market capitalization of the companies traded in the São Paulo Stock Exchange reached US$1.34 trillion in December 2009, approximately equal to those of the Deutsche Borse and the Bombay Stock Exchange, half those of the London and Shanghai stock exchanges (World Federation of Exchanges).

61. Banco Central do Brasil, "Operações de Crédito do Sistema Financeiro, Saldos com Recursos Livres e Direcionados," www.bcb.gov.br.

2010). Also, 85 percent of total mortgage lending in Brazil was still provided by the public sector (mainly, CEF).[62]

Long-term financing in reais for investments by businesses and in infrastructure continues to come, in almost its entirety, from BNDES. Benefiting from stable compulsory social contributions (remunerated at below market rates) for over 2/3 of its funding, BNDES has had a long history of praiseworthy support of important companies and projects, as well as an effective partnership with the private sector banks to whom it also lends at preferential rates in order for them to be able to finance—in domestic currency, on a matched basis, and at their own credit risk—their corporate clients. But how can BNDES continue to expand its balance sheet to support higher levels of investment in Brazil without resorting to the market? And if so, how can it do this without passing on to borrowers the higher free market financial cost? For the moment, Treasury has been the solution. In 2009, BNDES received an extra R$100 billion in transfers from Treasury (in what was, perhaps, the most important fiscal measure by the government) to help mitigate the impact on the economy of the credit crunch. As a result, BNDES' loan book reached R$283 billion,[63] corresponding to 20 percent of total bank credit in Brazil. What can we expect for 2010 and thereafter?

The evolution of the Brazilian fixed income securities market towards establishment and enforcement of high standards of transparency, corporate governance, and protection of lenders' rights has also been impressive when compared to any other emerging economy. But the capacity of the Brazilian debt securities market to provide long term credit for the financing of investment is still extraordinarily modest. As of September 2009, the total amount of medium-term corporate bond issues in reais outstanding stood at R$271 billion[64] (under 10 percent of GDP, 1/5 of total bank debt) and consisted entirely of floating (as opposed to fixed) rate instruments, for the most part issued by leasing subsidiaries of financial conglomerates, not by businesses tapping the market directly to finance their investments.

The Brazilian Treasury remains, fifteen years after the introduction of the Real, incapable of issuing long term notes in reais at a fixed interest rate competitive with other major emerging market economies in their domestic currencies.[65] This has prevented the development of a strong domestic long

---

62. Ibid.
63. Ibid.
64. CETIP - Initiating Coverage, Credit Suisse Equity Research, December 10, 2009.
65. Yields on 10 year treasury notes in domestic currency: 3.3 percent for U.S., 5.4 percent for Australia, 7.5 percent for India, 12.7 percent for Brazil (www.bloomberg.com, government bonds)

term credit market. And Brazil has become increasingly dependent on public sector banks' long term investment.[66]

Let us hope that the coming 2010 elections in Brazil can bring together
the necessary degrees of conviction and political commitment to move forward with the structural reforms necessary for the conquest of a long term
fiscal credibility that has been pursued for two centuries. Were that to happen, one of the world's most robust long term fixed income securities market would rapidly materialize, consolidating the pre-conditions for a much
more vigorous and sustainable process of economic growth.

---

66. On May 20, 2010 the Brazilian newspaper *O Estado de São Paulo* reported an additional R$80
billion loan made in April by the Brazilian Treasury to BNDES at below market rates (Fernandes,
A. e Veríssimo, R., "Tesouro aumenta subsídio a BNDES," *O Estado de São Paulo*, Economia, 20 de
maio de 2010).

# 13

# REGULATION & COMPLIANCE: ANTI–MONEY LAUNDERING

*Monica Arruda de Almeida*

*Abstract: As an active member of the Financial Action Task Force (FATF), an international agency that combats money laundering and financial terrorism, Brazil supports the global anti-money launder-ing (AML) regime as a means to improve the reputation of its financial institutions, and ultimately their capacity to attract foreign capital. This study finds that although Brazil's AML compliance is considered credible by international players, the recent improvement of its international reputation is attributable to other government initiatives such as the improved management of its debt portfolio and more effective monetary and fiscal policies.*

The global effort to combat money laundering, promoted by the G-7 coun-tries in the last twenty years, has stirred a great deal of criticism among skep-tics who are suspicious of the motives of the leading economies that "name and shame" countries that do not adopt anti-money laundering (AML) practices.[1] As an active member of the Financial Action Task Force (FATF), an international agency whose sole mandate is to combat money laundering

---

1. Most non-adopting countries are offshore financial centers (OFCs). One reason for such wariness is the concern that the pressure on offshore tax havens to adopt anti-money laundering controls is being used by the G-7 members to diminish the competitiveness of the financial centers' tax schemes. According to the OECD's *Harmful Tax Competition* of 1998, tax havens jurisdictions are characterized by: (1) little or no tax on relevant income; (2) ineffective system of information sharing; (3) lack of transparency, and (4) the existence of activities claimed by a haven location that are unsubstantiated (Kudrle, 2008).

and financial terrorism, Brazil has regulated and monitored money laundering cases and other financial crimes since 1998.

The Brazilian government has endorsed the global AML effort on many occasions as a means of improving the international reputation of its financial institutions, and ultimately their capacity to attract foreign capital. As Antonio Gustavo Rodrigues, a Brazilian former president of the FATF stated, "an international financial center perceived to be open to dirty money will eventually lose trust—and investments."[2] This rationale for adhering to the G-7 countries' anti-money laundering agenda is, in many ways, novel. The question of whether to adopt the AML standards is generally seen by scholars as a prisoner's dilemma. Because states can gain from stricter financial regulations elsewhere, there are substantial benefits for free-rider countries (see for example, Hülsse and Kerwer, 2007). Hence, it is commonly assumed that countries will limit restrictions on foreign capital inflows to gain a competitive edge.

One of this study's goals is to examine Brazil's declared reasons for the support of international AML efforts. The literature on the political economy of financial flows is mostly silent about the economic benefits that countries derive from restricting the cross-border flow of illicit money or its flow within domestic boundaries.[3] With the passage of the Law No. 9,613 in 1998, Brazil's federal government attained the mandate to regulate, monitor, and prosecute illegal financial activities, particularly cases of money laundering. Two questions that arise from its AML initiative are whether its regulatory reforms are credible and whether they have tangibly improved the country's financial standing. This study finds that, contrary to the position maintained by Brazilian authorities, there is no evidence that adherence to the AML standards has yielded an economic benefit. I argue that although Brazil's AML compliance is considered credible among international players, the recent improvement of its international financial status is attributable to other governmental initiatives, such as the improved management of its debt portfolio and more effective monetary and fiscal policies. A significant side effect of Brazil's AML program is the strengthening of the law enforcement capabilities of the Executive branch in areas traditionally within the ambit of the judicial system. Hence, in the context of post-neoliberal reforms of the 1990s, Brazil's recent experience of federal

---

2. Keynote address delivered on November 24, 2008. Antonio Rodrigues was president of the FATF until early 2009. He is currently the president of Brazil's Council for Control of Financial Activities (COAF), the main Ministry of Finance agency responsible for combating financial crime.

3. Veiga and Andrade (2006) and Kudrle (2008) are exceptions, as reviewed later.

reregulation has allowed the executive government to exert greater control over the country's financial affairs.

The following is a brief description of the initial years of the global anti-money laundering effort and a review of the literature concerning the political economy of financial flows. My goal is to search for both scholarly and empirical justifications for the global anti-money laundering regime. Later, I review certain aspects of the AML policymaking process in Brazil and examine the reception that the effort has received internationally. I conclude this study by arguing that even though Brazil's current justification for combating money-laundering is unsubstantiated, the program might nevertheless be worthwhile because of its utility in combating corruption.

## RATIONALE FOR AN AML REGIME

Money laundering is defined in legal terms as the concealment of funds and the illegality of their origin (Machado, M.R., 2008). Money laundering was first criminalized by the US in the mid-1980s as part of its war on drugs. The US later led other G-7 to promote a global effort against the activity and in 1989 they founded the Financial Action Task Force (FATF), whose exclusive mandate is to combat global money laundering. The FATF standards consist of forty financial practice recommendations that, although not binding on members, are enforced by sanctions that vary from warnings to outright expulsion from the organization (Hülsse and Kerwer, 2007).[4] After the 9/11 terrorist attack, nine special recommendations were added to the FATF regime to combat terrorism financing. In practice, countering the finance of terrorism (CFT) functions as a subset of the AML standards. A feature of the AML global effort is that it involves numerous international and regional organizations, including the United Nations, the OECD, the World Bank, and the IMF.[5]

---

4. The FATF began blacklisting non-participating countries in 2000 but that was abandoned six years later because it was perceived as being too confrontational in addition to raising concerns of double standards between member and non-member states (Sharman, 2006).

5. Sharman explains that the IMF and World Bank were "recruited" by the G-7 nations to offer financial expertise to members and surveillance of illegal financial activity. For that purpose, there has been a division of labor between these two institutions whereby the IMF works with developed countries and offshore centers, and the World Bank with developing countries. Sharman argues that the high number of institutions participating in the AML regime pays testimony to the priority placed by the G-7 countries on the issue, despite the challenges involving the coordination and overlapping of many initiatives (Sharman, 2006).

Currently there are thirty-five full member states and jurisdictions that observe the AML standards. The FATF's financial regime is not only expensive to implement but also technically challenging, particularly to countries lacking sophisticated financial sectors.[6] But if on one hand the widespread adoption of the FATF's recommendations is seen as a successful case of transnational policy convergence, on the other hand this outcome is puzzling, because of the lack of evidence regarding the regulations' efficacy. Due to the "naming and shaming" strategy pursued by the OECD and the FATF, for example, many authors have argued that states adopted the AML/CFT regime primarily because of reputational concerns (Helleiner, 2000; Simmons, 2000; Sharman, 2006; Hülsse and Kerwer, 2007).

One of the questions that this article raises is whether the reputational concerns are justified. Studies that have attempted to measure the effects of adhering or failing to adhere to the anti-money laundering standards on a country's investment level fail to convincingly establish a direct link. Veiga and Andrade (2006) analyze, among other questions, whether the existence of anti-money laundering institutions and regulations affects a country's economic performance. They find that Latin American and African countries' efforts to criminalize money-laundering for offenses that are not drug-related have a positive association with investment and economic growth. However, they observe an opposite result in the OECD countries, whose AML efforts do not translate into additional economic rewards. Unfortunately, one has to be skeptical of Veiga's and Andrade's results because they use data from 1991 to 2000, a period when the implementation of the AML standards had barely begun anywhere.

Kudrle (2008), on the other hand, examines whether the blacklisting program pursued by the OECD (2000–2007) and the FATF (2000–2006) negatively affected financial activities in tax haven jurisdictions.[7] Using data on financial flows to and from 38 jurisdictions, Kudrle finds no systematic evidence of a negative impact on the volume of their financial transactions due to blacklisting. However, this author recognizes that the reputational liability of a blacklisting might have prompted the tax havens to adhere to the AML/CFT standards given their current high level of compliance.

---

6. A survey by Celent Communications, a consultancy firm, finds that in order to adhere to the AML/CFT standards, the US and European financial firms spent over US$5 billion only in 2003 (*The Economist*, 16 October 2004). A different survey organized by KPMG, another consulting firm, shows that among Latin American banks alone spending with anti-money laundry controls rose by 73 percent from 2001 to 2004 (*Valor Econômico*, 21 June 2005).

7. The OECD and the FATF had separate blacklists. However, their lists overlapped considerably. Of the 45 jurisdictions ever to be blacklisted, 20 were the target of both organizations.

But if the literature on the economic impact of a country's adopting, or declining to adopt, an anti-money laundering program is still scarce and inconclusive, there is consensus among scholars about certain economic and political variables associated with changes in perceptions of a country's risk. Moreira et al. (2008) remark that scholarly understanding of emerging markets' vulnerability to external shocks has evolved rapidly, especially after the Asian (1997) and Russian (1998) currency crises. Since then, important economic and institutional determinants of financial risk have been identified. For example, investors tend to be watchful of (1) the scope of a country's financial liberalization, (2) the quality of its foreign debt management program (to assess a government's ability to repay its debt), (3) its fiscal and monetary policies (to assess the probability of nominal exchange rate devaluations), (4) its growth sustainability, and (5) its institutional guarantees of property rights, as measured by the quality of its laws and regulations as well as the effectiveness of their enforcement (Ibid.).

There is also a very interesting branch of scholarly work that studies the determinants of bond spreads in emerging countries, namely, the difference between interest rates paid on bonds issued by emerging countries and those offered on the US 10-year Treasury note. Most work in this area tends to focus on investors' response to changes in countries' macroeconomic fundamentals. A good example is Akitoby and Stratmann (2008), who examine the effect of policy changes on interest rates in the bond markets of 32 emerging countries. The authors contend that investors' reactions to a country's fiscal adjustment vary according to the makeup of the particular economic policy. For instance, they find that revenue-based adjustments (i.e., increases in tax collection) lower spreads more than spending-based adjustments (i.e., government spending cuts). In addition, the authors show that cuts in current spending are more effective in reducing spreads than cuts in investment, and that tax-financed current spending lowers spreads, as opposed to debt-financed current spending, which increases sovereign risk. Financial investors appear to be more nuanced in their assessment of a country's risk than previously believed.

A recent phenomenon related to bond markets in emerging economies is that since mid 2002 spreads have narrowed to record lows. Puzzled by this event, scholars noticed that the overall improvement in the countries' macroeconomic indicators was insufficient to explain the spread reduction. They found instead that lower spreads were also caused by a surge in international liquidity, which in turn is attributable to the overall reduction in interest rates in industrialized countries (IMF, 2004; Hartelius et al, 2008; Moreira et al., 2008).

Arguably, Brazil has taken advantage of the favorable international financial environment in recent years by considerably reducing its sovereign risk and, starting in 2008, by achieving an investment-grade debt rating.[8] One of the main benefits for a country whose debt is rated at investment grade, and is therefore considered more likely to meet its payment obligations, is that interest rates charged on foreign debt tend to be lower, which in turn makes capital cheaper for domestic borrowers.

In addition to the Lula administration's efforts to improve Brazil's macroeconomic indicators and debt portfolio (as detailed below), Moreira et al. (2008) cite various reforms that have raised Brazil from the 25th percentile to the 75th percentile in least vulnerability among emerging markets between 1998 and 2007. These reforms include, for example, the reduction of currency exchange transaction costs, greater incentives for foreign investors to participate in public ventures, and the standardization of accounting practices among companies traded in the open market. None of these reforms is related to the control of money laundering.

Nonetheless, there is evidence that political institutions, events, and scandals can affect the performance of a country's sovereign debt. Although comparatively new, the literature on this subject is rich, especially in relation to developing countries, which tend to have weaker institutions and present greater uncertainty in the sustainability of their economic policies when compared to developed societies. Financial investors' confidence in a country's economic performance (as measured, for example, by the volatility of the exchange rate, bond spreads, and stock earnings) is tested in particular during election seasons, when governments in both developed and developing countries are tempted to adopt expansionary (and inflationary) fiscal policies. Such policies often cause exchange rate depreciation, which many times can lead to increases in its foreign debt denominated in international currencies.[9]

Recent Brazilian history offers good evidence of the negative effect that political scandals and perceived uncertainties have on a country's financial market. A case in point is Brazil's 2002 presidential election when the "Lula

---

8. The Lula administration has indeed been very fortunate to experience an almost crisis-free international economic environment, with notable exception of the current major crisis that started in late 2008. That wasn't the case in the decade that preceded the Lula administration. Before then, Brazilian financial authorities had to cope with the Mexican crisis (1994-1995), the Asian crisis (1997-1998), the Russian crisis (1998), the September 11th 2001 attacks, the Argentine crisis (2001-2002), and finally the financial turmoil caused by the 2002 Brazilian presidential election.

9. For a review on related studies, see Parra and Santiso (2008).

effect" caused a substantial increase in the country's bond spreads. The crisis was also fed by prominent investment banks that one after another downgraded Brazil's credit ratings in a domino effect. There also have been other politically motivated financial crises that, although not as dramatic as the 2002 episode, have forced the Brazilian government to respond to international pressure by enacting legislation that addresses institutional vulnerability as it surfaces.[10] The events leading to Brazil's adoption of anti-money laundering legislation in 1998 seem to fit this pattern.

## BOND MARKETS AND CREDIT RATINGS

International authorities encourage participation in the global effort to combat money laundering with promises of future financial market rewards. They preach that legitimate investors will lose confidence in, and decline to invest in, countries that provide safe havens for tainted funds. This paper challenges this doctrine by focusing on the Brazilian AML program. It contends, instead, that Brazil's money-laundering policy has had no effect on the country's financial reputation. Although Brazil's financial rating has risen significantly in the last decade or so, the improvement in its economic reputation is attributable to the better management of its macroeconomic indicators and debt portfolio. Two sets of data presented in this paper (qualitative and quantitative) substantiate this conclusion.

One measure of the markets recognition of Brazil's efforts to combat money-laundering is the favorability of the reports published by companies specializing in investment analysis and forecasting. One need not be a day trader to appreciate the massive amount of research put into financial forecasting and investment-risk assessment for companies and countries. I choose to track the Country Report and the Financial Report, both published by The Economist Intelligence Unit (EIU), a leading research and advisory firm that is part of The Economist Group, along with the weekly magazine *The Economist* and the American news outlet *Congressional Quarterly (CQ)*.[11] I examined 131 editions of the Country Report and 37 editions of the Financial Report published from 1996 to 2009.[12] I searched for "money laundering" using the search utility of Adobe's "PDF" (portable document format)

---

10. Martinez and Santiso (2003) present an excellent study of the Brazilian financial crises in the 2002 and other presidential elections.

11. The Economist Group is, in turn, half owned by the daily newspaper *Financial Times*.

12. Country Report is published more frequently than Country Finance.

TABLE 13-1. Brazil Country Report, August 1996 to September 2009

| Date/Mentions | Content | Context |
|---|---|---|
| Sept. 2003<br>1 mention, 38 pages | 1) Notes involvement of some members of the PFL (Partido da Frente Liberal) in a money laundering scandal associated with the Banestado Bank. | Political analysis. Assesses the clout of the PFL as opposition party. |
| Sept. 2004<br>1 mention, 33 pages | 1) Highlights Brazil's efforts to police its borders with Colombia Paraguay, and Argentina, and the cooperation among those countries in the war against money laundering. | International relations. Analyzes whether the Lula administration is more likely to partner with the US or to align with other leftist governments with an anti-US stance. |
| Dec. 2004<br>1 mention, 37 pages | 1) Calls attention to the resignation of president of the Banco do Brasil on November 16, 2004, who was accused of money laundering. | Description of the reshuffles taken place in government posts. |
| June 2005<br>1 mention, 33 pages | 1) Appointment of Romero Jucá as minister of Social Security. Mentions the involvement with money laundering of one of his main finance contributors, a money changer from the state of Roraima. Jucá was governor of Roraima (1988-1990) and currently represents the state as senator.<br>2) Supreme Court decides to proceed with an investigation against the president of the Central Bank, Henrique Meirelles, who was accused of engaging in tax evasion and money laundering in the late 1990s. | Describes some of the corruption probes the government has faced. |
| Dec. 2005<br>2 mentions, 35 page | 1) Describes the downfall of Severino Cavalcanti, who stepped down of the presidency of the Chamber of Deputies under accusations for receiving kickbacks on restaurant concessions in Congress. | A currency dealer convicted of conspiring to evade tax and money laundering helped law enforcement officials in the investigation against Cavalcanti. |
| Sept. 2007<br>1 mention, 36 pages | 1) Mentions the expulsion from Congress of Roberto Jefferson, a deputy of the PTB (Partido Trabalhista Brasileiro), who was accused of money laundering. | Describes some of the indictments of the "mensalão," a major political scandal of vote-buying that took place in mid-2005. |
| August 2008<br>1 mention, 24 pages | 1) Describes the arrests, and subsequently releases by habeas corpus, of banker Daniel Dantas, who was accused of tax evasion and money laundering. | Story exposes the constitutional crisis that was occurring between the minister of Justice, the federal tribunal, and lower courts, which publicly criticized each other's decisions. |

*Source:* The Economist Intelligence Unit. Country Finance on Brazil.

reader in all 168 editions for coverage on the topic. Tables 13-1 and 13-2 show only the editions in which the term "money laundering" was found. The Country Reports tend to mention money laundering only as part of their political analysis, in the context of assessing the stability of the federal government. They look for political crises that can adversely affect the executive branch's capacity to push for reform or the ability of Congress to pass legislation. The September 2007 edition contains an edifying example of a country political risk analysis. It mentions the mensalão, a major scandal in 2005 involving President Lula's party, the PT (Workers' Party), which allegedly paid a number of Congress members around US$12,000 a month in exchange for votes on legislation favored by the PT. Despite the resignation of many executive officials and Congress members, President Lula was able to distance himself from the episode and was reelected in 2006. Although the reports abound with political scandals, there are relatively few mentions of money laundering and, when they do happen, they have little relevance to the country's AML program. The publishers of the Country Report do not appear to consider Brazil's anti-money laundering program a noteworthy effort for improving the government's international image.

My analysis of the Country Finance editions yields similar results. I found one mention of the creation of the COAF in 2003, which is repeated using the same language in subsequent years. The reports also cite the passage of Law No. 10,406, which, among other things, recognizes factoring firms as financial entities and therefore subject to government regulations. The same language is also repeated in subsequent editions.

Since Brazil's anti-money laundering efforts are barely mentioned by the EIU reports, two of the most prominent international publications in country-risk analysis, it appears that the Brazilian authorities have overestimated the impact of the policy on the country's reputation.

As already mentioned, certain economic policies adopted in recent years reduced Brazil's vulnerability to external economic shocks. One outcome of the country's improved performance was an upgrade in its investment status by Standard & Poor's, Fitch, and Moody's, three major credit rating agencies. This change has helped Brazil to reduce the interest paid on its internal and external debt to historically low levels.[13] For example, by the end of 2009, the difference in interest paid on Brazil's and the US's Treasury bonds was less than 5 percent (500 basis points), a far cry from the 2002 presidential election year, when interest on the Brazilian bonds reached almost 25% (2,500 basis points).

But if Brazil's AML program did not contribute to its recent economic recovery, what else can explain such a change? This study posits that a series of initiatives by the Cardoso and Lula administrations placed the country on a more stable financial footing. Brazil's pursuits of greater debt portfolio management efficiency, of higher accumulation of foreign reserves, and of

---

13. Note that in Brazil, as in most of the other Latin American countries, the capital market is still dominated by government bonds. For example, by 2007, the stock of Brazil's government bond was about 60 percent of the country's GDP, whereas bonds issued by corporate and financial companies make up only about 10 percent of the Brazilian GDP (Banco Central do Brasil, Financial Stability Report, 2008).

TABLE 13-2. Country Finance, Brazil, 1996–2009

| Publication Date | Content | Context |
|---|---|---|
| February 2003<br>2 mentions, 22 pages | 1) Mentions a new Civil Code (Law no. 10,406) that recognizes factoring firms as financial agents. Until then, factoring firms were not considered financial institutions and thus were not regulated.<br>2) In a paragraph cites that Brazil has met all international standards related to the control of money laundering. Also mentions the law that created the COAF. (Exact same words used in earlier editions) | 1) Brazil's national association of factoring (Anfac) approved the change because it will help to improve the reputation of the sector, which was being damaged by some firms that have been involved with money-laundering schemes in the past. |
| February 2004<br>1 mention, 53 pages | 1) In a paragraph cites that Brazil has met all international standards related to the control of money laundering. Also mentions the law that created the COAF. (Exact same words used in earlier editions) | |
| December 2004<br>2 mentions, 53 pages | 1) Mentions a new Civil Code (Law no. 10,406) that recognizes factoring firms as financial agents. Until then, factoring firms were not considered financial institutions and thus were not regulated.<br>2) In a paragraph cites that Brazil has met all international standards related to the control of money laundering. Also mentions the law that created the COAF. (Exact same words used in earlier editions) | |
| February 2005<br>1 mention, 80 pages | 1) Mentions a new Civil Code (Law no. 10,406) that recognizes factoring firms as financial agents. Until then, factoring firms were not considered financial institutions and thus were not regulated. (Exact same words used in earlier editions) | |
| February 2006<br>1 mention, 85 pages | 1) Mentions a new Civil Code (Law no. 10,406) that recognizes factoring firms as financial agents. Until then, factoring firms were not considered financial institutions and thus were not regulated. (Exact same words used in earlier editions) | |
| April 2007<br>1 mention, 90 pages | 1) Mentions a new Civil Code (Law no. 10,406) that recognizes factoring firms as financial agents. Until then, factoring firms were not considered financial institutions and thus were not regulated. (Exact same words used in earlier editions) | |
| April 2008<br>1 mention, 90 pages | 1) Mentions a new Civil Code (Law no. 10,406) that recognizes factoring firms as financial agents. Until then, factoring firms were not considered financial institutions and thus were not regulated. (Exact same words used in earlier editions) | |
| April 2009<br>1 mention, 75 pages | 1) Mentions a new Civil Code (Law no. 10,406) that recognizes factoring firms as financial agents. Until then, factoring firms were not considered financial institutions and thus were not regulated. (Exact same words used in earlier editions) | |

*Source*: The Economist Intelligence Unit. Country Finance on Brazil.

more stable exchange rates were among the most important. For example, to reduce the country's debt exposure, the government started gradually buying back some of the highest yielding bonds and replacing them with new bonds with lower interest rates (therefore, making foreign capital cheaper at home) and longer maturities. As Table 13-3 shows, by February of 2008, 63% of the debt issued by the federal government consisted of fixed-rate and inflation-indexed securities, a portfolio mix that tends to do a better job

TABLE 13-3. Domestic Federal Debt Held by the Public

| Financial return per bond type | 2004 Dec | 2005 Dec | 2006 Jun | Dec | 2007 Feb | Apr | Jun | Aug | Oct | Dec | 2008 Feb |
|---|---|---|---|---|---|---|---|---|---|---|---|
| Fixed rate | | | | | | | | | | | |
| Value in R$bn | 163 | 273 | 320 | 395 | 396 | 417 | 464 | 433 | 422 | 457 | 443 |
| % | 20 | 28 | 31 | 36 | 35 | 36 | 39 | 36 | 35 | 37 | 36 |
| Selic rate | | | | | | | | | | | |
| Value in R$bn | 425 | 522 | 470 | 440 | 456 | 454 | 451 | 463 | 464 | 449 | 466 |
| % | 52 | 53 | 46 | 40 | 41 | 39 | 38 | 39 | 39 | 37 | 37 |
| Price index | | | | | | | | | | | |
| Value in R$bn | 121 | 152 | 221 | 246 | 253 | 269 | 286 | 295 | 313 | 322 | 334 |
| % | 15 | 16 | 22 | 23 | 23 | 23 | 24 | 25 | 26 | 26 | 27 |
| Exchange rate | | | | | | | | | | | |
| Value in R$bn | 80 | 11 | -15 | -12 | -12 | -14 | -30 | -30 | -27 | -28 | -27 |
| % | 10 | 1 | -1 | -1 | -1 | -1 | -2 | -3 | -2 | -2 | -2 |
| Others | | | | | | | | | | | |
| Value in R$bn | 22 | 21 | 20 | 24 | 26 | 27 | 27 | 28 | 27 | 26 | 26 |
| % | 3 | 2 | 2 | 2 | 2 | 2 | 2 | 2 | 2 | 2 | 2 |
| Total in R$bn | 810 | 910 | 1016 | 1093 | 1120 | 1151 | 1199 | 1189 | 1199 | 1225 | 1242 |

*Source*: Ministry of Finance, Banco Central do Brasil. Financial Stability Report (May 2008).

of insulating the country from exchange-rate volatility and even possibly an international currency crisis. That was an important improvement over 2004, when these financial instruments made up just 35% of the country's portfolio. The government's goal is to phase out the offering of floating-rate and foreign exchange-indexed securities. In addition, Brazil became in 2006, for the first time ever, an international creditor and no longer owes debt in a foreign currency.[14] Still the government has not been very successful in extending the maturity of its bonds when compared to other 10-year government bonds issued by OECD countries, very popular among international investors. As Figure 13-1 shows, Brazil's average of bond maturity has stubbornly remained below eight years. Another highlight of Brazil's performance is the significant reduction in the size of its total external debt, which is currently just above 10 percent of the GDP, its lowest level since the 1970s.

Equally important in the effort to secure greater financial stability is the accumulation of foreign exchange reserves. Here, Brazil has also made significant progress over the years, especially considering that it does not adopt the economic strategy of trade-surplus-oriented nations, but relies instead on the bond and stock markets to attract foreign capital. Some important indicators of financial liquidity point to a favorable forecast for Brazil. The

---

14. Brazil repaid all its debt to the IMF in December 2005 (*Bloomberg News*, February 21, 2008).

FIGURE 13-1. Debt Characteristics, 1971–2008

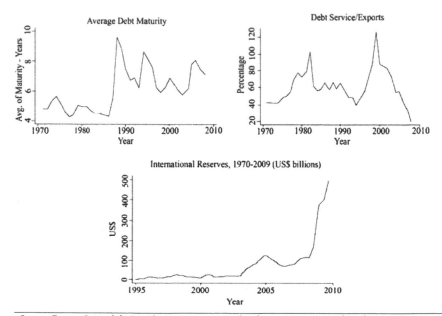

*Source*: Banco Central do Brazil: Sistema Gerenciador de Séries Temporais (SGS).

proportion of the country's debt service to exports, for example, is at the lowest level since the 1970s, just below 20 percent (Figure 13-1). Other indicators of financial liquidity also performed excellently in recent years, improving Brazil's ability to pay for its short-term external debt and to defend itself against speculative attacks on its currency (see Figure 13-2).

FIGURE 13-2. International Reserves

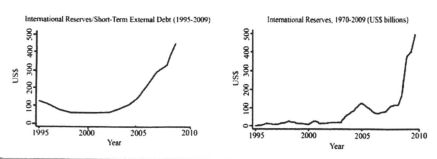

*Source*: Banco do Brasil, Sistema Gerenciador de Séries Temporais.

A third set of economic indicators that deserves attention relates to Brazil's exchange rate performance, which has been considerably stable in relation to other major international currencies. The anti-inflationary policies that started in 1994, year in which Brazil's Real was created, has allowed for greater stability of its exchange rate. One of the reasons for the Brazilian government's success in controlling inflation is that it has kept public debt in check. However, this objective is being accomplished by greater taxation of the productive sector rather than by cuts in government spending.

All in all, the economic indicators highlighted above were very positive for Brazil. The country's recent rise to an investment-grade level corroborates the findings of studies that were reviewed earlier in this chapter. With the exception of few areas that still display some economic vulnerability (e.g., Brazil's inability to cut public spending), the country's experience is almost a textbook for financial stability.

Next, I examine the Brazilian authorities' rationale for adopting the FATF's AML standards.

## THE BRAZILIAN AML INITIATIVE

Despite the absence of empirical support for Brazil's economic rationale for adopting the AML standards, there seems to be a link between the country's increased vulnerability to external economic shocks and the push for an anti-money laundering program. Teixeira's (2005) account of the policy-making process that led to the signing of the 1998 money-laundering legislation suggests that the government used legislation as political cover for the lack of effective policies. She writes that whenever Brazil needed to improve its international reputation because of a domestic political scandal or to ward off the contagious effect of an economic crisis elsewhere, advances in the country's AML program were made. Teixeira contends that the government's goal was to reassure investors by signaling its commitment to curb financial misconduct and corruption. In the absence of such pressures, the governmental agencies in charge of drafting money-laundering legislation were unable to achieve consensus.[15]

After the first internal evaluation of Brazil's existing money-laundering controls, spearheaded by the central bank and the revenue service in 1993, it took 19 different drafts of the bill and the advocacy of Minister of Justice

---

15. Brazil's constitution allows the executive government to introduce legislative proposals to Congress.

Nelson Jobim before the government sent the bill to Congress for an "urgent" vote in late 1997.[16] The bill was part of a legislative package sent to Congress to improve the image of Brazil's financial institutions in the aftermath of the Asian currency crisis (Teixeira, 2005).

There are two important aspects of the decision-making process that led to the submission of the bill to Congress. One is the dominance of the executive branch in the drafting of Brazil's AML legislation. Among the offices that contributed to the AML bill were the President's cabinet, the ministries of Planning, Justice, and Foreign Relations, the central bank, the federal tax service, and the Department of Federal Police. The private sector also participated in government meetings, including representatives of the Brazilian Federation of Banks (FEBRABAN) and the stock exchange. The legislative and the judiciary branches had little or no involvement in the drafting (Teixeira, 2005; Machado, M.R., 2008). As a result, the creation of the Council for Control of Financial Activities (COAF), Brazil's financial intelligence unit (FIU), strengthened the executive branch's law enforcement capacity in areas traditionally under the jurisdiction of the judicial branch. According to Machado, countries such as China, Indonesia, and South Korea, for example, have in the past dealt with cases of financial regulatory reform by shifting power from executive agencies to legislatures and to the courts. Brazil is an outlier in this regard. Moreover, the pattern of Brazil's regulatory reform is inconsistent with the Cardoso administration's approach to governing, which emphasized deregulation as part of the administration's liberalization program.

Another fact worth noting is the relative absence of legislative debate on the executive bill. The document that was ultimately signed into law contained no material alterations. Teixeira argues that this reflects a lack of expertise in Congress about such a complex financial regulatory matter rather than an ideological endorsement of the President's proposal. Another significant feature of Brazil's AML law is that it incorporates, with little deviation, the financial practice standards promoted by the FATF. One may thus conclude that the Cardoso administration opted to closely comply with the AML guidelines promoted by international actors.

Brazil's compliance with international money-laundering protocols arguably enhanced its international credibility. Since becoming a full member of

---

16. As minister of Justice (1995-1997), Jobim gained praises for being an effective political articulator of the Fernando Henrique Cardoso administration (1995-2002) in Congress. Even after being nominated justice to Brazil's Supreme Court in April 2007, he continued to work on behalf of the executive until the passing of the AML legislation in March 1998.

the FATF in 2000, Brazil has been evaluated twice, in 2001 and 2005. On both occasions it was considered compliant with the organization's standards. Nonetheless, the international reviewers sometimes have found vulnerabilities in Brazil's AML program, including vulnerabilities related to financial secrecy: the reviewers believed that Brazil needed to improve its mechanisms for disclosure of data. Another common problem involves the "know your customer" practices, where greater government pressure on financial entities is required so that they properly identify users or issuers of all sorts of monetary instruments, such as pre-paid credit cards that are easily available at street vendors. On many occasions, the Cardoso and, later, the Lula administrations acted rapidly to address the shortcomings of the Brazilian program and, whenever called for, promptly requested Congress to pass additional legislation.[17] The FATF evaluations are performed with on-site visits and conducted in a system of mutual review by its members. Overall, Brazil's commitment to combat money laundering has been considered very credible by international actors. In fact, COAF's president Antônio Rodrigues was President of the FATF in the 2008–2009 term.

## FOLLOWING THE MONEY TRAIL

In COAF's online statement in celebration of its twelfth anniversary, the council claimed to have frozen $2 billion Brazilian reais (US$1.1bn) in banking accounts involving over 63,000 people investigated for money laundering and other crimes. Subordinated to the Ministry of Planning, COAF has the authority to analyze financial data sent by the national banking system and other economic entities that are mandated by law to report monetary transactions that fit the category of "suspicious," such as accounts of R$100,000 (US$55,600) or more. Companies that fail to report the transactions to the COAF are subject to fines.[18]

It is important to note, however, that the COAF can only analyze the data it receives from the financial system, which by law need to be handled with confidentiality. Among the reports that are actually investigated by the council's intelligence officials, the ones that are confirmed as suspicious

---

17. Machado recounts some of the initiatives taken by the executive office to have Congress pass legislation either in response to, or in anticipation of, FATF's evaluations (Machado, M.R., 2008).

18. The COAF has received more than $4.1 million (US$2.3 million) in proceeds from such penalties. The guideline issued by Brazil's central bank also cites other lesser amounts that are subject to inspection by the COAF. For further information, see "Circular no. 3,461 (July 24, 2009)" at https://www.coaf.fazenda.gov.br/.

become subject of an intelligence financial report (RIF). The RIFs are then forwarded to other federal agencies that will perform the actual investigation, such as the federal police and prosecutors. However, law enforcement authorities will still need judicial authorization to freeze somebody's bank account or confiscate its property, for example.[19]

Among the almost 8,500 RIFs produced, there is a significant number of high profile cases of money laundering, embezzlement, and tax evasion that received wide coverage in the news media. In retrospect, if the decision-making process that led to the passage of the AML legislation lacked public debate, one cannot say the same about the financial intelligence work performed at the COAF. Arguably, the agency has become a household name among those who follow corruption scandals in Brazil. "Operação Furacão," for example, was a police operation that unveiled a scheme of illegal gambling that was being run thanks to the bribes paid to numerous police officers and highly placed public officials, including a judge from the Federal Appellate Court. According to COAF's 2008 report, 25 people went to prison for this crime. Another important case was "Operação Aquarela," when 19 people ended up in prison after law enforcement officials stopped a scheme involving private companies and non-governmental organizations that received payments from government agencies for services that they did not provide. The president of Bank of Brasília, a state bank, and public agencies from São Paulo, Goiás, Distrito Federal e Paraná were was also implicated in this crime, which had the involvement of around 300 individuals and cost R$20 million (US$11 million) of stolen money from the public sector.

Other police operations cited in the 2008 report include "Operação Kasper," where 22 people were sentenced to prison and 52 others received arrest warrants, and "Operação Exodus," resulting in seven prison sentences and 15 arrest warrants. Although the combat of corruption has been a central element of COAF's policy agenda, the agency has also the mandate to pursue cases against those who avoid paying tax in Brazil by sending their money abroad illegally. The report claims that the council's exchanges of financial intelligence with similar agencies in over 70 countries, including Portugal, Belgium, Switzerland, Uruguay, and the US, has helped on that front. Factor-

---

19. The sharing of confidential financial data among governmental agencies predicted in Brazil's AML legislation has caused some controversy. Justice Marco Aurélio Mello of the Supreme Federal Court, for example, has been quite vocal against the measure citing it as being unconstitutional (see for example, *Folha de São Paulo*, January 11, 2008).

ing firms, real estate, bingos (illegal in Brazil), and lotteries are the sectors with the highest number of reported irregularities in the country.

## CONCLUSION

This study's primary goal is to examine Brazil's reasons for the adoption of money-laundering controls. According to Antônio Rodrigues, who was head of the FATF and is currently president of Brazil's COAF, a financial center whose image is blemished by the presence of tainted money will "eventually lose trust and investment." This study finds Rodrigues' claims to be empirically unsubstantiated. Instead, it contends that Brazil's AML program has had no effect on the country's economic standing. Although Brazil's financial rating has improved significantly in recent years, the advancement in its reputation is better explained by the more efficient management of the country's macroeconomic indicators and debt portfolio.

However, despite the legitimacy problems caused by the relative absence of legislative debate on Brazil's anti-money laundering policy, the program has shown a surprising utility in the fight against public corruption with the arrest of public officials involved in high profile criminal cases (e.g., "Operação Furacão"). This is an important accomplishment especially because the bulk of the money laundered in the country is stolen from the public sector. I believe this development should offer enough rationality in support of an anti-money laundering program that is better tailored to serve the needs of Brazil in its fight against financial crimes.

# 14

# FINANCIALIZATION, CRISIS, AND A NEW MANIA IN BRAZIL

*Elaine da Silveira Leite*

*Abstract:* The Brazilian financial market has developed several institutions to create a stable environment and encourage savings and investment from the majority of the population who were previously unfamiliar with the financial system. This "financialization process" was unique in Brazil, because it involved the Brazilian state, corporate governance practices, democracy, and equality issues that appeared associated to self-help ideals, paving the way for the emergence of financial intermediaries that legitimize personal economic activities. This chapter presents the roots of personal finance, the principal institutions and intermediaries, and their roles in the development of financial issues. I argue that this cadre has grown and is becoming an important agent in the production and diffusion of social values as "moral entrepreneurs" of finance.

The Brazilian economic scenario at the beginning of the twenty first century presented a reasonable growth of the stock market. The Brazilian capital market reached impressive valuations; consequently, the market witnessed a large increase of its investor base, attracting individuals that earlier were unimaginable into the market.

In recent years, the São Paulo Stock Exchange (Bovespa)[1] has grown over 500 percent; this growth is related to the number of individual investors. In

---

1. São Paulo Stock Exchange (Bovespa) is the principal stock exchange of Brazil. The State of São Paulo has more individual investors in Bovespa than do other states; it contains 233,490 individual investors.

2002, there were 85,249 individual accounts in brokerages and banks. In 2005, the number rose to 155,183 accounts; an increase of 82 percent in three years ("Investidores individuais," 2008). In July 2008, this number went up to 516,000 and also recorded 555,768 individual investor accounts in October 2009, even after a period of uncertainty related to the economic crisis that shook the world ("Número de investidores," 2009).

In addition, many people participate in the market indirectly. They invest in long-term funds, private pension plans, mutual funds, and investment clubs that purchase stocks from companies listed on Bovespa.[2]

Recent economic growth confirms this positive outlook. The Brazilian media justifies this sudden interest in the financial market as a result of the country's recent economic growth. The decline in interest rates, along with other measures, stabilized the economy and increased GDP.[3]

An additional contributing factor in Brazil's economic growth is the well-publicized reconfiguration of its principal stock exchange. Bovespa adopted corporate governance ideals and implemented a transparent approach to reach ordinary people. In effect, Bovespa's major campaign focused on popularizing the stock market, which contributed to the capital market's increased competitiveness.

Other important policy initiatives were essential for the growth of the Brazilian financial market, including new laws for corporations offering strong protection for minority shareholders;[4] strengthening of the Securities and Exchange Commission of Brazil, whose activities were restructured to support financial market development;[5] establishing benefits for companies that adopt the corporate governance practices of the Brazilian Development Bank;[6] and Bovespa's guiding the creation of a capital market plan[7] that was to guarantee the sustainability of the stock market. These recent

---

2. Milton Gamez. "Os investidores estão voltando." *Revista Bovespa*, Janeiro/Março, 2006. Online.
3. From 2002 to 2007, real GDP in US dollars almost doubled, going from US$714 billion to US$1.313 trillion, with constant growth from 2004 onwards. Brazil is today the tenth-largest economy in the world, ahead of Russia and India, and the largest in Latin America. The country was classified by the United Nations Development Program (UNDP) as having a high Human Development Index (HDI), ahead of the other BRIC countries (Russia, India, and China). Data taken from "A favorable economic, political, and legal environment" Brasscom. Web 10 Oct. 2009.
4. Adriana Dias, "Impactos positivos da nova lei das Sociedades Anônimas." Empreendedor. 15 Fev. 2008. Online.
5. "FIDC: novas instruções da CVM devem trazer mais proteção ao investidor" in *Administradores* 12 December, 2006. Online.
6. Catherine Vieira. "Os pioneiros da governança corporativa." *Valor Econômico* 29 Jun. 2004.
7. "Plano Diretor do Mercado de Capitais, o que muda para o investidor?" in *Portal Acionista* 10 August, 2009. Online.

events increased security and ensured the creditability of the Brazilian financial market.[8]

Therefore, in April 2008, Brazil was classified as investment grade. It suggests that the country is regarded as having low risk of default and the nation is safe to receive investment. The news affected the stock market and the Bovespa index registered a new record score. It is important to mention that Brazil also received substantial foreign investment as a consequence of the world attention on the BRIC countries (Brazil, Russia, India, and China).[9]

Symbolically, at least, Brazil achieved a greater position in the international scenario and it is now seen as having a solid economic, political, and legal environment. In this context, the Brazilian financial market developed institutions to create a stable environment and encourage savings and investment from a sector of the population which was previously unfamiliar with or marginalized by the financial system.

In this scenario, new agents emerged; they are considered financial intermediaries that entice ordinary people to enter the finance field through different activities such as production of books, lectures, and coaching. I argue that it is attractive to map the financial market intermediates and their activities to understand how some actors are able to bring such a different pool of individuals into the same market for the first time.

This paper begins with a review of the bibliography to explain how the Brazilian state assimilated some market practices, providing autonomy to financial institutions to allow the growth of the capital market. These circumstances were unique in Brazil because they involved issues of corporate governance, democracy, and equality that appeared related to self-help ideals. In all, it paved the way for the emergence of financial intermediaries that legitimate personal economic activities.

As a second step, the paper presents the roots of personal finance, the principal institutions and intermediaries—commonly known as "gurus"—and their role in the development of finance issues. As a result, a huge cul-

---

8. It is important to mention Apolinário et al. (2002) who states that the Brazilian government has adopted new strategies to make the national stock market stronger. The "desestatização," which has been observed for the last years by selling government's stocks from the two biggest Brazilian companies, Petrobras and the Companhia Vale do Rio Doce, represents the last stage of privatization process, which was initiated in 1997. This process is called "Stock Market Democratization." The success in moving funds from FGTS (Time Service Warranty Funds) to Petrobras Privatization Mutual Funds (FMP) greatly increased Brazilians' interest in investing their money into the FMPCVRD, causing the biggest stock sale operation that has ever happened in Brazil.

9. Anne Warth and Francisco Carlos de Assis, "Brasil é o 10° em ranking mundial de investimento estrangeiro." *Agência Estado* 17 Sep. 2009. Web. 10 Nov. 2009.

ture of investment—emerging as a new mania—is blending concepts of success and happiness to the wealth in Brazilian society.

## STATE, DEMOCRACY AND SELF-HELP

The debate about the role of the state and the economic model in Brazil led to a series of studies, mainly from the 1980s to the present, about the state's role and the debate between regulation and economic liberalization.

After the failure of welfare state principles, the economic position taken at first by England and then by the United States spread throughout the world. It was organized around the notion of a minimalist state that should not interfere in economic issues. Supporters of this perspective see the state as promoting delays, inefficiency, and economic irrationality. Thus, it is argued that this creates the need to reduce the duties performed by the state in promoting economic development (Evans, 1995).

Overall, the 1980s was characterized by a neo-conservative wave and its proposal of a minimal state. In the 1990s, the movement shifted toward reform. More specifically, state reconstruction began to be a dominant program, as Bresser-Pereira (2000b) sums up in the following extract:

> The great political task of the 1990s is to reform or to rebuild the state. Between the 1930s and 1960s, the state became a significant factor in fostering economic and social development. During that period, and particularly after World War II, we witnessed a time of economic prosperity and an increase in standards of living as never before in the history of mankind. Yet, since the 1970s, because of its distorted growth coupled with the globalization process, the state entered into a crisis and became the main cause for the drop in economic growth rates and the increase in unemployment and inflation rates that have taken place throughout the world. A neo-conservative wave and market oriented economic reforms were respectively the ideological and political responses to the crisis—reforms which neo-liberals or neo-conservative politicians and intellectuals hoped that would bring about the size of the state reduced to a minimum. But, in the 1990s, when the neoconservative proposal of a minimum state proved not to be feasible, the true nature of the reforms was disclosed: the rebuilding of the state was essential for it to undertake not just its classical tasks of assuring property rights and contracts, but also those required to ensure social rights and promote competitiveness in the country (Bresser-Pereira, 2000b: 176).

According to Bresser-Pereira and Grau (1999), the globalization process of the 1990s required new methods of more efficient public administration. Consequently, new actors for executing social services guaranteed by the state became increasingly important. At the same time, the state was seen as inefficient and corrupt. This dichotomy provided the rise of new agents and organizations such as non-governmental organization (NGOs) and self-help groups that were concerned with bringing social and economic development to the country (Bresser-Pereira and Grau, 1999).

This framework helps us understand not only the evolution of state reform but also the development of the Brazilian financial market and the emergence of corporate governance issues in Brazil (Grün, 2003). Corporate governance—shaped by the financial sphere—appeared as a requirement for transparency via society, emerging as a criticism of the Brazilian bureaucratic model.

The corporate governance movement is evidenced clearly during the Fernando Henrique Cardoso government (1995-2002). Transparency was key to warm up the capital market and attract investors in the context of privatization and reform during this period. Therefore, the government was required to adopt corporate governance strategies to increase transparency (Grün, 2003).

Carvalho (2002) argues that changes of institutional investors' attitudes are evident during the Cardoso government. As a result, very important facts emerge, such as the internationalization of the Brazilian capital market; the increasing number of companies accessing international markets through American Depositary Receipt (ADR);[10] the opening of the financial system for multinational institutions; and the increasing importance of foreign investors in the domestic stock market.

In 2002, then presidential candidate Luiz Inácio Lula da Silva of the Workers Party visited Bovespa. At that time, he wanted to demonstrate adherence to economic and corporate governance practices established in the financial market. At least from a symbolic approach, corporate governance has gained much attention in the nation (Grün, 2003).

After 2002, the pension funds grew and adopted the corporate governance practices as an instrument for their protection. The pension funds are essential to understand the advancement of corporate governance, since the corporate governance conflict is between institutional investors (the pension fund is considered a minority shareholder) and owners (the majority shareholders) in Brazil.

It is important to emphasize that the principal leaders of unionism control the major pension funds in Brazil (Jardim, 2009). From this perspec-

---

10. "International Investing: get the facts." *Securities and Exchange Commission.* Division of Corporation Finance. Online.

tive, Jardim (2009) states that the unions stopped answering simply "no" to the market, and began to consider the possibility of negotiation, discussing questions such as worker's savings.

The dialogue established between the left and the financial market, created a base for the "domestication" and/or "moralization" of capitalism in Brazil (Jardim, 2009). Jardim (2009) shows that certain social projects implemented by Lula's government go through the market—such as microcredit projects—negating the idea of the quest for profit and redefining the concept of financial market. Through these projects the popular classes start to interact with the financial market.

Jardim (2009) also illustrates how the Lula government promotes active participation of some unions in the financial market through corporate governance. For example, at the micro level, the unions begin to discuss democracy and transparency as workers gain access to their employer's shares becoming "owners" and gaining the new title of shareholders. Consequently, this also introduces social, ethical, and worker perception in the financial market field resulting in a social and financial integration never before seen in Brazilian society.

It is important to highlight, according to Sá (2003), that the corporate governance discourse is associated with economic progress. The financial actors claim that it is through the economic growth that Brazilian nation will achieve social development. Symbolically, this discourse forms a "mix" in the common sense about what is social and economic development. In general, social and economic development came to be seen as part of the same political approach.

For these reasons, corporate governance is becoming the great solution for Brazilian society. It is recognized not only as a neoliberal prescription to solve the problem of companies' capitalization, but also as a means to enlarge not only the financial markets and economy but also the social field (Grün, 2004).[11]

---

11. At the same time, it is important to examine some research that focus on the entrepreneurial changes and their effects on the Brazilian enterprise structure. Diniz and Boschi (2003) state that crisis of the national development model and the transition to a market model provided the keynote of the 1990s. In addition, reforms and their impacts have influenced the composition of plans and business elites' collective action. Filho and Silva (2001) state that some enterprises decided to move to a new control (from the traditional and family control to a professional management); as a result, there was a redefinition of the family enterprises' priorities. On one hand, family businesses (which represent the majority of Brazilian enterprises) have found themselves under strong pressure, such as difficulties in establishing their own capital structure and inability to open their capital to foreign and other investors. On the other hand, institutional investors begin to gain significance in the control of large national companies. As a result, corporate governance practices that institutional investors are supposed to follow began to shape the national economy.

Also important to the development of corporate governance is the "New Market" (2002), created by Bovespa. This segment of the stock market is dedicated to shares issued by companies that voluntarily adopt governance rules and implement strong corporate governance practices. The capital of listed companies in the "New Market" is composed only of shares with voting rights; an important factor in Brazil where most of the market's liquidity is concentrated in non-voting shares.

The "New Market" has inaugurated a new phase of the capital market in Brazil. It is supported by corporate governance practices of transparency, accountability and social responsibility that are designed to reduce uncertainties in the financial market. According to Bovespa, the value and liquidity of listed shares are positively influenced by levels of security rights to shareholders and by quality of information disclosed by companies. Bovespa also has companies qualified as Level 1; these are required to provide improvement in the provision of information, including requirements for consolidated financial reports. They must also maintain 25 percent of their shares on the market. On the other hand, companies qualified as Level 2—in addition to the practices of Level 1—have to adopt strong practices related to minority shareholders rights such as extending 70 percent tag-along rights to non-voting shares.[12]

In 2001, Bovespa also initiated a campaign focused on educating the general population about the stock market. The principal program, which is called "Bovespa Goes to You," aims to bring the capital market closer to civil society. The key point is to make the stock market more popular. In order to spread this campaign, Bovespa focuses on the idea that the market is transparent and democratic. As part of this project, other initiatives have been developed such as "Bovespa at the Beach," "Bovespa at the Factory/Company," "Bovespa at the University."

This new dynamic created by the market gave rise to new economic actors that appeared as a solution to change the "uncertainty" of the economic and political scenarios. At the same time, there is also a boom of the self-help literature. McGee (2005) explains that in a period of declining security there is no surprise if one finds a marked increase in the number of self-help titles. In this way, McGee emphasizes how the promise of self-help can lead indi-

---

12. "Tag along" is a mechanism to protect a minority shareholder. For example, if a majority investor buys the control of the company, then the minority shareholder has the right to join the transaction or sell his or her minority part in the company.

viduals into a new sort of enslavement and into a cycle where the self is not improved but endlessly belabored.

As the financial market is being reshaped, there is an increase of personal finance literature that it is linked to self-help schemes in Brazil. Bookstores' shelves are filled with books and releases that deal with money and financial education. These books focus on the idea of getting rich, that is, they establish the "steps" to reach the "first million."

Thus, the pathway of corporate governance in Brazil—ranging from economic and political issues to the capital market—opens a new way to understand how actors try to change the traditional perception of the market through their symbolic strategies (Grün, 2007). Moreover, regarding the popularization of financial market issues, the Brazilian state is watching its expansion, but to some extent, without control over the situation.

## THEORETICAL BACKGROUND

In this part of the chapter, I review the literature that reports on current economic processes through studies about financialization in order to provide theoretical elements offering some connections between the current bibliography and the empirical data that will be presented.

Financialization is a relatively new term that refers to the increasing importance of financial markets, financial tools, and financial actors in the economy's operation. According to Martin (2002), financialization, like other recently coined concepts of postmodernism and globalization, gets stretched and drives us in numerous directions. "Part of the complexity of these terms is that they stand simultaneously as subject and object of analysis—something to be explained and a way of making sense out of what is going on around us" (Martin, 2002: 08).

Brazil, like other emerging nations, is experiencing rapid financialization. This process is shaped by financial changes in the global financial market and involves restructuring of the country's financial organization through privatization, fiscal and monetary reform, and the creation of new programs and institutions that encourage economic growth and popular investment (Grün, 2009). Financialization includes not only financial intermediaries but also self-help ideals. The country's financialization processes are formed by an interesting dynamic in which corporate governance practices gain significance in the context of the critique of the inefficient state.

Nowadays, the economic changes and increases in market tools are discussed as part of a new context. According to Thrift (2008), they are considered a "new economy" perspective. Thrift argues that the "new economy" is spread by investors who seek protection and information; and as a result creates a "cultural circuit of capital." Mainly business schools, advisors, and gurus—intermediaries who increasingly gain space in this new financial expansion—create and participate in this cultural circuit.

However, the "new economy" is different from other periods of economic change because the principal agents are intermediaries who try to motivate the masses (ordinary people) to create and establish a new market culture. "The growth in the number of shareholders and in shareholder choice was buttressed by the increasing mediation of finance, which meant that narratives like the new economy could travel further" (Thrift, 2008: 264).

In this context, discussions about financialization have increased and have had increasing importance among academics, media, and the business world (Erturk et al. 2008). For Erturk et al. (2007), there are several differences among researchers about their emphases in analyzing the financialization processes. The cultural economy analysis, which is the main mode of financialization studies nowadays, includes terms such as "corporate culture," "market culture," and the "knowledge economy." Crotty (2003) emphasizes the non-financial corporation. On the other hand, some researchers such as Martin (2002) focus on the individual analysis and identity that is changed with the implementation of financial tools.

In general, Erturk et al. (2008) highlight that the actual financialization process is different from other forms that previously existed. This new format is particular in some points, such as: structure, where there is a creation of mass markets in the domestic economy (for example, in the United States); the growth of financial intermediaries; and in the popular reaction to certain facts released by companies. Thus, it is possible to argue that Brazil is currently going through the financialization process. Moreover the Brazilian case has been regarded as an extreme example of "financialization" because interest rates and bank spreads between borrowing and lending rates are considered the highest in the world, and, more recently, because of the apparent submission of Lula's government to the financial markets (Jardim, 2009). It is also important to stress that the markets are international and it is through them that most of globalizing pressures are internalized in the Brazilian society (Grün, 2009). Within this context, international economic events impact Brazil's economy and add to uncertainty about Brazil's economic future.

In a dramatic period of social change, the general promise of self-help is increasingly important, because the self-help offers "comfort and consoles us, suggesting that vast material, social, and personal success are available to anyone who is willing to work long and hard enough to improve the self" (McGee, 2005: 13).

This evidence shows a great "combination" that is the onset of financialization, at least beginning with Fernando Henrique Cardoso's government. It was further developed by Lula's government (2003-2010) and now by Bovespa and private sector financial advisors and nonfinancial intermediaries. The latter were incorporated by self-help ideals that employ concepts of democracy shaped by corporate governance.

So economic development has become embedded into the ideals of democracy (corporate governance) and self-help schemes; simultaneously, it allocates to individuals the need to rely on private financing rather than on the government. It formed the basis for the development of a new way of thinking in Brazil in which individual ideals of self-help stimulate economic growth. "The fantasy has maintained considerable appeal, despite its troubling corollary: if success is solely the result of one's own efforts, then the responsibility for any failure must necessarily be individual shortcomings or weaknesses" (McGee, 2005:13).

Based on McGee's arguments about the self-help industry in the United States, where this phenomenon has a long tradition, one can argue that at the moment when self-help in Brazil emerges, the country is focused on issues of democracy, equality and the financial market's embeddedness in society.

Beginning in 1990, according to Bresser-Pereira and Grau (1999), there was an incredible growth of private and non-private organizations (such as NGOs) that developed together with self-help practices. At this time, the national discourse was about equal positions both in the economic and in the political sphere.

However, the varieties of the financialization processes present some similarities among different nations. These include the broadening of their activities to include a mass audience and the spread of financial literature for ordinary people. Erturk et al. (2008), based on a survey, found that among Anglo-Saxons, the finance literature was responsible for bringing financial education to Americans, which enabled and taught the public about investments and the varieties of financial products.

Therefore, based on these studies, I argue that the personal finance literature supported by self-help is an important point of convergence in the theoretical financialization debate, both in the international and national spheres. The market euphoria boosted the personal finance industry related to self-help schemes in Brazil. This literature seeks to reach the general population; it is not restricted to a portion of society able to save and invest in the markets.

Again, I reinforce the importance of mapping financial market mediators and their activities because it provides sound evidence about the emergence of new actors. It also offers some analytical elements for discussing the role of the state related to the growth of the financial market in Brazil.

The next part of this article presents some empirical data about the roots of personal finance; its principal institutions and agents (commonly known as "gurus"); and their role in the expansion of personal finance. These created a stable environment to encourage savings and investment by the majority of the population who were unfamiliar with or had been marginalized by the financial system.

## ROOTS OF PERSONAL FINANCE

The onset of financial speculation has been attributed to medieval Europe, where the carnivals caused by Lent and other cultural events were amongst the few social spaces in which economic activity for profit was sanctioned. More importantly, investments in stocks of companies could be sold in such events, along with municipal bonds and lottery tickets. At this time, according to Harrington (2008), financial bubbles were caused by two factors: innovation, like fashion in the Netherlands by the Turkish tulip; and necessity, such as the plan to nationalize the debt of the British government through the issuance of South Sea Company's shares. The boom of populist investment in the 1990s could be described as a combination of innovation and necessity, driven in part by technological innovation (World Wide Web and e-commerce, in particular) and by the requirement for many Americans to meet the needs of private funding instead of relying on the government or the employer's safety net (Harrington, 2008).

In the same way—through the great results brought by corporate governance that was motivated by the democratic ideal (Grün, 2003)—the view that popular investment in the stock market would lead to economic development was popularized in the press beginning in the year 2000 in Brazil.

As indicated above, there were about 85,000 individual investors in 2002 in Brazil while in 2009, the number of investors exceeded 550,000, even with the effects of the global economic crisis.

Meanwhile, the number of female investors increased by more than seven times (647.74 percent), from 15,030 in 2002 to 112,386 at the end of 2007, and the growth of the male audience in this period was 390.14 percent. In 2009, Bovespa had 136,062 women investors.[13]

In an interview with a shareholder at Bovespa, I was asked if I had read the book *Rich Dad, Poor Dad*. *Rich Dad, Poor Dad: What the Rich Teach Their Kids About Money—That the Poor and Middle Class Do Not!* was first published in 2000, by Robert T. Kiyosaki and Sharon L. Lechter. This narrative, largely based on Kiyosaki's own upbringing and education in Hawaii, focuses on the idea that the poor and middle classes work for money and the rich men have money work for them. The Poor Dad is based on Kiyosaki's real father—a PhD holder and graduate of Stanford University, University of Chicago, and Northwestern University—who was the head of the Department of Education of the Hawaii. In the book, he is greatly respected until he decides, late in his career, to go against the governor of Hawaii. As a consequence, Poor Dad loses his job, and is unable to find comparable work. Since he never learned how to handle money, and instead depended on the government (his employer) for support, he dies in severe debt.

In contrast to this character is Rich Dad, his best friend Michael's father, and Kiyosaki father's partner. Rich Dad dropped out of school in eighth grade, but became a self-made multi-millionaire regardless. He taught Kiyosaki's son and Michael a variety of financial lessons, and emphasized that the boys need to learn how to make money work for them to avoid spending their whole life working for money.

In Brazil, Paula and Wood Jr. (2002) highlighted that the first signs of demand for personal finance issues were noted after the release of the books *Seu Futuro Financeiro* by Louis Frankenberg[14] and *Rich Dad, Poor Dad*.

Yet another empirical landmark of personal finance in Brazil was the publication of the Personal Investments Guide in 2006 by an important Brazil-

---

13. "Número de mulheres na Bolsa cresce nove vezes em sete anos." *Infomoney* 11 Jan. 2010. Online.
14. Louis Frankenberg is considered to be the first financial planner in Brazil.

ian economic journal. It offered a list of books to help readers make their money increase without much effort.[15] The guide presents some best-selling books in Brazil, such as *Casais Inteligentes Enriquecem Juntos* (Gustavo Cerbasi); *Rich Dad, Poor Dad for Teens*; *Rich Dad in Comics* (these two books were written by the same authors of *Rich Dad, Poor Dad*); and *Nice Girls Don't Get Rich* (Lois P. Frankel). The only Brazilian book is *Young Couple Be Rich Together*, by Gustavo Cerbasi. Today, he is the main author of personal finance books in Brazil. The segment of personal finance became one of the most significant of the Brazilian publishing market and each month, there are several new titles related to finance.

The recent expansion of publications related to personal finance—and classified as self-help—is evidence of the popularization of finance in Brazil representing a new mania. Since its release, *Rich Dad, Poor Dad* has been classified as a best-seller.[16]

## ACTORS, ACTIONS AND MOTIVATIONS[17]

The personal finance phenomenon has spread to television programs, courses, magazines, web sites, communities, and events such as Expo Money. Expo Money is considered the most important event on financial education in Brazil.[18] Each month, it takes place in a different Brazilian state, but the principal one happens in São Paulo. In 2008, the three-day gathering received more than 20,000 visitors.[19]

Expo Money produces a collection of books with the main purpose to educate children, explaining how to escape from consumerism, help with the budget, and be financially independent. For example, there are titles such as *The Tree of Money*; *The Traps of Consumption*; *Investing in Options*; *How to Increase Your Money*; *Financial Education*; *500 Questions (and*

15. "Investimentos pessoais." *Guia Exame*. Editora Abril, 2006. Print.

16. Ibid.

17. I have analyzed the literature about self-help and finance in Brazil to map the "moral entrepreneurs" of personal finance. The number of books related to personal finance phenomenon is "amazing," so I selected the books that are considered best-sellers in the vehicles of information about finance, business, and careers in Brazil. I also participated in courses, attended lectures, and interviewed some gurus of finance.

18. Expo Money is produced by the World Money Show, the traditional event about investments in the United States. It also happens in Japan, China, Russia, United Kingdom, Australia, Germany, Canada, South Africa, and Vietnam.

19. Expo Money 2009. http://www.expomoney.com.br.

*Answers) about Finance*; and *The Pocket Diet*. The collection is written by financial advisors.[20]

The Expo Money collection is organized by Gustavo Cerbasi, the principal financial advisor and author of personal finance in Brazil. Cerbasi was considered by Revista Época to be one of the 100 most influential Brazilian personalities in 2009.[21] After 500,000 copies sold since the release of his book *Young Couples Be Rich Together* in 2004, a special edition was issued in which the author's preface emphasized the importance that the book had reached in Brazilian society.

In this field, there is also a segment that works to introduce financial education for children; the goal is encouraging the culture of savings and introducing concepts of credit in schools and universities (Savóia, 2006). In this sense, many institutions have worked to introduce financial education in their curriculum including The Financial Education Institute that offers courses to guide people on investment and money.[22] This segment also applies "steps" to teach how to achieve wealth following the same script used by Expo Money and its advisors. Bovespa also maintains an educational program focused on assisting students of public and private schools with information about capital markets. Its focus is to explain basic economic and finance concepts that are used in daily life.

In general, the personal finance segment that is directed to women shows how the financial sector reached important segments of society. There are a lot of books for women, such as, *Rich Woman* by Kim Kiyosaki. The formula she uses is her husband's idea—he is the author of *Rich Dad, Poor Dad*. Kim Kiyosaki employs her own history to teach how to be financially independent.

*Meninas Normais Vão ao Shopping—Meninas Iradas Vão à Bolsa* by Andréia Assef and Mara Luquet stresses the concept that "you do not know, but you were made to invest" focusing on how women are educated to hate money.

In general, advice for women emphasize the idea that they do not enrich themselves because they focus on needs of others rather than their own, preventing women from becoming truly independent. The literature highlights that women always hear messages such as "don't be greedy" or "learn

---

20. "Coleção Expo Money." *Expo Money.* 2009. Online at http://www.expomoney.com.br/2009/colec.asp.
21. "Os 100 brasileiros mais influentes de 2009." *Revista Época* 05 Dec. 2009.
22. *Instituto de Educaçao Financeira.* Online at http://www.edufinanceira.org.br.

to be happy with what you have." Furthermore they explain how these messages are forms of interference that keep women from having a prosperous future. The following extracts are from the book *Normal Girls Go Shopping; Expert Girls go to the Stock Market:*

> You do not get married waiting to divorce. You do not start to work on a new job waiting to be dismissed. But these things happen and, now, increasingly often. I have already said, but it is important to repeat: If you're dependent on someone—husband, boss or anyone else—about your financial future—you must think twice. Sometimes, we don't perceive how we are dependent, until the moment that we have to take control of our lives.

> "Don't be greedy" or "Learn to be happy with what you have." These messages are forms of interference that avoid your seeing a great future. To accumulate wealth, no matter how much, requires a clear vision that could show you surrounded with money on all your sides.

*Normal Girls Go Shopping; Expert Girls Go to the Stock Market* reached a great importance, so much so that the "*Geração Futuro*" brokerage created the first investment club for women. The club is called "Girl Experts" and it is based on precepts of sustainability. In this context, Bovespa also created the "Women in Action," which is a project about financial education for women. The program focuses on approaching women and teaching them stock market concepts.[23]

In general, the contents of books, lectures, and fieldwork already examined are advice that aims to guide individuals. The advice is more or less practical, for example, "Do Something!" or "Where and Why to Invest." But, it also gives advice, such as "you need to be self-confident, think positively." In general, these kinds of advice are combined, and the general public does not distinguish them and they understand them as a coherent actions and values.

Behind these exhortations, there are "gurus" who are mediators that explain, instruct, educate, and illustrate the advice with case studies. Gurus' performances help to instill in the public a new perception about the financial world. According to Becker (1977), social norms are created by groups or individuals that are called "moral entrepreneurs." So these gurus are significant to spread new social values. They are "moral entrepreneurs" of finance.

Gurus and their advice lead individuals to believe that acting "economically" is a good action. The books and contents analyzed try to educate, and to introduce items to be mimicked. This allows for the transformation of the

---

23. "Mulheres em Ação" in *Bovespa*. Online.

social meanings given to people and social activities. The mechanism used by gurus transforms individuals in their collective experience and thus contributes to the (re) production of habitus (Bourdieu, 1997). The personal finance field gave legitimacy to personal activities that were not previously valued.

There is a moral influence being created that transforms attitudes and modes of action. Personal finance promoters have created a new social space, supported by performances, miraculous calculations, magic, and science, therefore, connecting happiness and satisfaction to the possession of money (Zelizer, 1994; Simmel, 1990).

> The tremendous importance of money for understanding the basic motives of life lies in the concept that money embodies and sublimates the practical relation of man to the objects of his will, his power, and his impotence; one might say, paradoxically, that man is an indirect being. I am here concerned with the relation of money to the totality of human life only in so far as it illuminates our immediate problem, which is to comprehend the nature of money trough the internal and external relationships that find their expression, their means or their effects in money (Simmel, 1990: 211).

In this sense, the segment of personal finance targeted to women highlights the setting described above. The personal finance field emphasizes that women do not enrich themselves because they focus on the needs of others, so they avoid taking the necessary "steps" to become financially independent.

"When personal finance becomes the way in which ordinary people are invited to participate in that large abstraction called the economy, a new set of signals are introduced as to how life is to be lived and what it is for" (Martin, 2002). The argument supported by Martin reinforces what happened in Brazil. The personal finance advice creates an obsession for money that dominates lifestyle, personal ambitions, and decisions. Consequently, the risk becomes part of everyday life. The moral entrepreneurs of personal finance (gurus) also use the argument that, currently, people have no more security in daily life. In a period where instability and unemployment worry the population, personal finance books show cases of business or professional success based on self-help schemes.

However, the period of crisis is an inspiring situation for personal finance gurus, because they create a new advice market about "how and where to invest in time of crisis" with a certain emotional appeal. While the rest of the world went into panic, the gurus showed how this can be the best time for financial investments. As a result, it was exactly at the period of great turbulence in financial markets that individual investors became more attracted to the stock exchange.[24]

These gurus are important to disseminate social values. They act as "moral entrepreneurs" of finance and provide advice about how to operate in times of crisis, creating new speculative manias. Their advice has increased the legitimacy of personal economic activities that were not previously valued in Brazilian society.

## CONCLUSION

The literature reviewed in this chapter provides evidence that the scenario of the reconstruction of the state in Brazil made possible the legitimization of corporate governance practices; consequently, allowing the expansion of financialization in the country. Bovespa's campaign and the boom of personal finance have also shaped the Brazilian lifestyle to include increased participation in the stock market.

This context allowed the emergence of new actors—the gurus. They are moral entrepreneurs of finance, educating on ways to invest honestly to achieve economic security, if not profits, even during times of crisis. By capitalizing on instability and uncertainty, they educate how these can be the best time for the development of financial skills and economic character. Yet these institutions and agents also renew themselves and expand their market by creating speculative manias.

The expansion of this culture of investment is strongly linked to and popularized by models of self-help. This phenomenon has "magically" been consolidated into a new model of society that supports the growth of the popular investor in Brazil and legitimizes personal economic activities that were not valued in this society.

In other words, this paper calls attention to future research that may provide additional empirical evidence that self-help has been moving from a parlor game to serious initiatives that force the state to institute rules of corporate governance and thus broaden the financial market.

---

24. Milton Gamez, "Os investidores estão voltando." in *Revista Bovespa*, Janeiro/Março, 2006. Online.

# Part IV
# Shifting Global Relations

# 15

# BRAZIL AND THE TRANSATLANTIC COMMUNITY

*Thomas J. Trebat*

*Abstract: In this study, the changing role of the Brazilian state in matters of global economic and political governance is examined in an effort to define areas of cooperation and areas of conflict between Brazil and what is referred to in the paper as the transatlantic community, i.e., basically the United States and Europe. It is appropriate to talk of cooperation and also of conflict because, on the one hand, Brazil's model of economic and political development in recent decades has drawn it ever closer to the transatlantic community in numerous ways. On the other hand, conflict and misunderstanding arise because the relative success of the Brazilian model has also fed Brazil's long-held aspirations to be an independent regional and global power-broker outside the tutelage of the wealthier countries of the North.*

As the global financial crisis of 2008–2009 recedes, it seems an opportune time to reconsider relations between Brazil, an emerging market that weathered the crisis relatively well, and the broader transatlantic community, especially the United States and the European Union. Could relations between Brazil and the West improve to a point that the stability of the global economy might increase? Brazil is hardly an unfriendly nation; in fact, its close integration with the global economy suggests quite the contrary. At the same time, Brazil has changed significantly over the last two decades of economic reform and political stability. Its long-held aspirations to be an important and independent regional and global power-broker are now more in line with its resources and self-confidence. This evolution is not fully appreciated in the North though awareness is spreading.

This paper sets forth the hypothesis that a new and more productive period in Brazil's relations with the US and Europe is possible and that this improved state of relations would contribute to a more stable global economy in the future. This positive outcome derives from numerous factors, most especially Brazil's peaceful rise to a more prominent global economic role and to political changes in the United States and, prospectively, in Brazil as well which faces presidential elections in October 2010. Specifically, the arrival of the Obama administration in 2008 and its promise of a new and less muscular, less unilateral emphasis in US foreign policy has been greeted with enthusiasm in Brazil even though several irritants have cropped up in the bilateral relationships recently. Meanwhile, in Brazil itself, the 2010 presidential elections will choose a successor to President Luis Inácio (Lula) da Silva who will be provided with a natural opportunity to re-examine the state of relations between Brazil and the countries of the North that it both admires and distrusts.

Brazil's foreign policy has incorporated traditionally a strong element of nationalism, especially with respect to creating and maintaining space for an industrial sector to develop in a global economy dominated by the United States and other center economies (Lafer, 2009). This tone of foreign policy was muted during the presidential terms of Fernando Henrique Cardoso (1994–2002), but regained emphasis and vigor during the two terms of President Lula (2002–2010) (Almeida, 2009). During this Lula period, Brazil's foreign policy elite in the foreign ministry (known as Itamaraty) has experienced turmoil as diplomats considered more amenable to forging closer alliances with the West have been pushed aside in favor of those considered more attuned to the objective of creating a distinct voice for Brazil in all global matters and a leader of the global South. This more recent, more autonomous tone in Brazilian foreign policy would seem to set Brazil farther apart from the United States and Europe in matters that go beyond Western hemispheric affairs, including the standoff with Iran regarding uranium enrichment in 2010 and the ongoing peace process in the Middle East where Brazil seeks an independent role as a mediator between Israel and Palestine.

While contentious issues will arise in the relationship between Brazil and the West, three observations about Brazil suggest that a closer, more productive engagement with the West is possible given Brazil's stature in global politics and economics. First, Brazil has developed, over several decades, a role as an effective bridge to the global South and an influential voice for more inclusive global economic management. Second, the global post-2008 financial crisis and its aftermath did reveal some weaknesses in the Brazilian economy which could limit its aspirations. These include deficient levels of savings, investment, technology, and human capital. In order to address these weaknesses, which are long-standing, Brazil is keenly aware of the need for a more productive interaction with the North. Third, ambivalence permeates Brazil's approach to global reform and governance. Brazil clearly benefits from the global status quo, i.e., integration with the world market and established institutions. At the same time, Brazil is anti-status quo, seeking opportunities to distance itself from Western ideals and institutions (Schirm, 2009).

Incorporating Brazil on its terms into established institutions of global governance will be challenging, but also worth the effort. The US and the global North have recognized this already to some extent by expanding the Group of Eight (G-8) group of leading world economies to a successor Group of Twenty (G-20) that prominently includes Brazil (and several other Latin American countries).[1] For the long run, the goal for the West should be to integrate Brazil as a partner into reformed multilateral institutions (in finance, trade, and regulation) as a means of assuring stable global growth on the basis of more inclusive global management.

To understand the reasoning behind this recommendation, three issues are considered:

- the areas of common interests in foreign economic policy between Brazil and the transatlantic community;

- the roots of Brazil's traditional divergences with the North; and

- the domestic dynamics in Brazil that are leading to a change in its world view. These issues are considered in turn in this paper, followed by recommendations on how to incorporate Brazil more effectively into a transatlantic partnership.

## AREAS OF CLOSE COOPERATION

Brazil, Europe, and the US share fundamental foreign policy goals. Dealing with the post-2008 global crisis has reinforced a need for global policy

---

1. The G-20 group annually gathers finance ministers and central bank presidents to consider cooperation and policy coordination in view of the state of the global economy. It has been particularly active during the global economic crisis following the collapse of Lehman Brothers in 2008. The most recent meeting was held in Busan, South Korea, in June 2010. For more on this organization, see: http://www.g20.org/.

coordination. This has been particularly clear in the area of stimulating global demand where Brazil, a large trade surplus economy prior to the onset of the global crisis, has clearly made an effort to boost consumption and investment at home, thus contributing to the global economic recovery that is underway in mid-2010 (OECD, 2009).

Brazil was able in 2009–2010 to engage in counter-cyclical fiscal and monetary policies at home that stabilized most components of domestic demand. The Central Bank of Brazil, for example, has delivered substantial monetary stimulus through an accelerated program of interest rate reductions which brought overnight rates from pre-September 2008 levels close to 12 percent down to 8.65 percent at their low point in August 2009, one of the lowest levels for interest rates in recent memory in Brazil. Meanwhile, the government announced a number of emergency fiscal measures which amounted to about 3 percent of GDP, among these significant reductions in taxes on the purchase of new vehicles, increases in the minimum wage which boosted pension payments throughout the country, an acceleration in government infrastructure spending, and a rapid expansion of credit via the lending programs of the BNDES, Brazil's national development bank (OECD, 2009).

Brazil was able to deliver this stimulus to domestic demand while still recording a primary fiscal surplus (i.e., surplus on government operations before the payment of interest on the government debt) in each month following the crisis. Thus, Brazil benefited during the crisis from a relatively strong starting position in terms of the government fiscal accounts (see Figure 15-1).

The results of the government's aggressive stimulus policies, while not without some risks of overheating the domestic economy leading to inflation, were impressive. Economic growth in Brazil was set to expand by about 7 percent in 2010 after plunging and virtually coming to a halt in late 2008 and early 2009. While Brazil experienced a great fright, this economic recovery was one of the fastest anywhere in the world in the wake of the financial crisis (see Figure 15-2 below on GDP growth). Moreover, as the financial crisis receded and GDP rebounded, the jobless rate in Brazil approached an historic low in 2010. The level of industrial production, which had plunged in the post-Lehman days of global financial turmoil, fully recovered lost ground and moved higher by mid-2010.

The most revealing indication of Brazil's contribution to global stimulus was the shift in the current account deficit of the balance of payments from

FIGURE 15-1. Government Primary Budget Surplus, 2007–2010

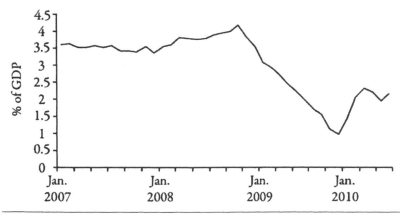

*Source*: Central Bank of Brazil.

a small surplus in the heady, pre-Lehman days of 2007, to a deficit estimated at about $40 billion, close to 3 percent of GDP in 2010 (see Figure 15-3). The Brazilian exchange rate which, like most non-dollar global currencies, depreciated sharply after September 2008, soon recovered to pre-crisis levels as global investors expressed confidence in the recovery prospects of the Brazilian economy (see Figure 15-4) Lula had boasted at the outset of the crisis that Brazil would be among the first economies to recover; in this respect, he appears to have been correct. In the process, Brazil not only contributed (albeit modestly because its size in the global economy is not large) to global recovery, it also strengthened its hand for future. discussions with the United States and Europe on reform of the global economy.

One of these areas for reform will be the shared governance of the main institutions of the global economy, including the International Monetary Fund (IMF). Brazil has also been an important part of global conversations to bolster the IMF as a source of emergency financial liquidity to the most vulnerable emerging economies. In 2009, Brazil agreed to subscribe to $10 billion in IMF notes in order to bolster the Fund's Special Liquidity Facility designed to help emerging economies hard hit by the global financial crisis. According to IMF Managing Director Dominique Strauss-Kahn, through this action to help other countries weather the effects of the global crisis, Brazil was not only "fulfilling the commitment of G-20 leaders," but reaffirming "its strong role as a leading emerging market economy."[2]

---

2. See the IMF press release: http://www.imf.org/external/np/sec/pr/2009/pr09207.htm.

FIGURE 15-2. Real GDP Growth Before and After Sept. 2008 (Quarterly Growth at Annual Rate)

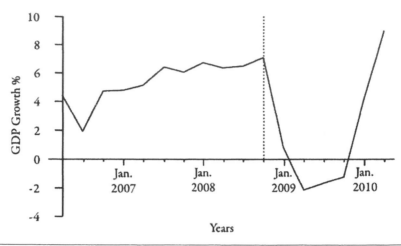

*Source*: IBGE

While Brazil and the wealthier countries have found common ground in global finance, the level of congruence is far less in terms of global management of the world trade system. Brazil has often found itself at odds with the United States and the West, in fact, allying itself with China and India, to resist reducing tariff barriers to permit greater access to their domestic markets. At the same time, Brazil has been aggressive, within the rules of the World Trade Organization, in efforts to protect its exporters from unfair trade practices by the West. In mid-2010 Brazil and the US were locked in a dispute about subsidized US cotton production which has caused harm to Brazilian producers (the dispute was settled by the WTO in Brazil's favor in 2010 although Brazil has refrained from adopting the retaliatory measures to which it is entitled by virtue of the WTO's finding).

The recurrent conflict between Brazil and the United States on trade matters is real, but it also masks large areas of congruence in global trade. While China has moved quickly up the chart in terms of Brazil's largest export markets and may well continue to climb, trade with the developed markets of the United States and Europe is still more important for Brazil. The US and Europe as recently as 2008 still account for some 35 percent of Brazil's total trade[3] (see Table 15-1 below). Brazil obviously has an interest

---

3. Cooperation in trade matters should certainly not be overstated as conflicts occur frequently, often assuming a high profile in Brazil.

FIGURE 15-3. Balance of Payments Current Account 2007–2010 (Accumulated last 12 months)

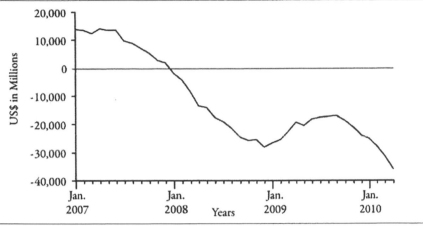

*Source*: Central Bank of Brazil (http://www.bcb.gov.br/?SERIEBALPAG).

in maintaining market access to these rich country markets and recognizes that the quid pro quo will be (eventually) improved access to its own market. Moreover, it is interesting that Brazil and the United States are the largest agricultural exporters in the world. While they clash on issues of industrial protection and the liberalization of trade in services, Brazil and the US have basically closed ranks in terms of the need for liberalization of global agricultural trade. It is this shared interest by US and Brazil in opening up global trade in agriculture (in particular, by breaking down protectionist barriers in Europe) that could provide the emphasis for the conclusion of the current round of global trade talks, known as the Development Round or Doha Round (these talks are basically deadlocked eight years after the launch of the Round in 2002).[4]

## Foreign Investment Ties

Brazil's stable laws on foreign direct investment stand in sharp contrast to the wave of populist nationalizations of foreign and domestic companies that is occurring in Venezuela, Ecuador, Bolivia, and Argentina. Europe, the US, and Brazil are tied together as well by the accumulated stock of foreign direct investment in Brazil and the accompanying connections that this

---

4. In the 2008 negotiations of the Doha Round, Brazil actually broke ranks with more protectionist emerging markets, such as Argentina, China, and India, in order to support a last-minute compromise with the wealthy countries that might have given new energy to the talks.

FIGURE 15-4. Exchange Rates (Reais per Dollar), 2008-2010

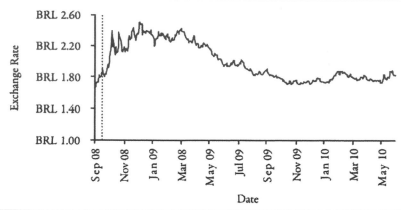

*Source*: Central Bank of Brazil (http://www4.bcb.gov.br/pec/taxas/port/ptaxmpesq.asp?id=txco-tacao&id=txcotacao).

inflow brings in terms of access to technology, management, and global marketing networks. The overall net foreign investment in Brazil in a recent (1999-2009) period was about $265 billion; the share of the US, Europe, and Japan in the total foreign investment in Brazil is close to two-thirds, with the US accounting for the largest single-country share, followed by Spain (ECLAC, 2010: 62). Most major US and European multinationals

TABLE 15-1. Structure of Brazilian Trade in 2008

| Share in world total exports (%) | 1.23 | Share in world total imports (%) | 1.11 |
|---|---|---|---|
| By main commodity group (% of total) | | By main commodity group (% of total) | |
| Agricultural products | 31.0 | Agricultural products | 5.6 |
| Fuels and mining products | 22.2 | Fuels and mining products | 23.9 |
| Manufactures | 43.7 | Manufactures | 70.5 |
| By main destination (% of total) | | By main origin (% of total) | |
| 1. European Union (27) | 23.5 | 1. European Union (27) | 20.9 |
| 2. United States | 14.0 | 2. United States | 14.9 |
| 3. Argentina | 8.9 | 3. China | 11.6 |
| 4. China | 8.3 | 4. Argentina | 7.7 |
| 5. Japan | 3.1 | 5. Japan | 3.9 |

*Source*: WTO Trade Profiles 2009 (http://stat.wto.org/CountryProfile/WSDBCountryP-FView.aspx?Country=BR).

have operations of some importance in Brazil; US firms have been particularly active in the expansion of Brazil's agribusiness. The huge investment push by Spanish companies in the late 1990s and early 2000s has led to the achievement by these companies of truly dominant positions in key sectors, including banking and telecommunications, led by such names as Banco Santander and Telefónica. By creating competitive pressures in areas of the Brazilian economy long dominated by US firms, the rise in the importance of Spanish firms balances the large US investment presence in Brazil and leads to new linkages for Brazil to the global economy (ECLAC, 2010).

The presence of foreign firms, mainly from the West, is expected to increase substantially in the oil sector as Brazil moves to develop its large, "pre-salt" oil reserves which are located in very deep waters off the south-eastern coast. While the state-owned oil company, Petrobras, will take the lead in developing these oil reserves, Brazil will also rely substantially on foreign investment and technology in what is likely to be a gargantuan investment effort. Petrobras' own expected capital expenditure program, mostly to develop these reserves, is anticipated to be on the order of US$225 billion and that is just over the next five years. In September 2010, Petrobras raised almost US$70 billion of this amount in a single global share offering, the largest operation of its type in history. While this indicates very significant investor interest indeed in Petrobras' future, the Brazilian government will also be required to put substantial investment resources of its own into Petrobras to finance the pre-salt investment program.

Foreign oil companies will be invited to participate on a production-sharing basis in the development of these reserves, and foreign companies, mainly from the West, will be crucial to Brazil as well in the supply of drilling equipment and transportation logistics. While the emphasis in developing the pre-salt reserves will be on Petrobras and state-led investment, Brazil will be far more open to foreign participation in the pre-salt region than would be imaginable under the more restrictive foreign investment regimes in place in the oil sectors of other Latin American nations, notably Mexico and Venezuela.

While Brazil has been traditionally a recipient of foreign direct inflows, it has also emerged in the last decade as a source of direct foreign investment in other nations of growing importance. In something of a twist, Brazil has also spawned a large number of so-called "multilatinas," domestically based corporate giants such as Vale and Gerdau who have expanded aggressively into the US, Europe and elsewhere (ECLAC, 2010; Brainard et al., 2009). Petrobras is, by a wide margin, the most aggressive of the Brazilian firms in pursuing opportunities abroad, but the list of companies with important foreign operations is growing as Brazil's global connections broaden and deepen (see Table 15-2).

TABLE 15-2. Brazilian Firms with Large Foreign Operations in 2009

| Firm | Sales 2009 (US$mm) | Foreign Sales (%) | Investment Abroad (%) | Workers Abroad (%) | Sector |
|---|---|---|---|---|---|
| Petrobras | 101,948 | 29 | 34 | 10 | Oil and Gas |
| Itaú-Unibanco | 44,242 | 11 | 3 | 10 | Banking |
| Vale | 27,852 | 35 | 47 | 20 | Mining |
| Grupo JBS | 20,458 | 85 | 85 | 77 | Agribusiness |
| Gerdau | 15,242 | 53 | 58 | 46 | Iron and Steel |
| Camargo-Correa | 6,950 | 22 | 47 | 28 | Construction |
| Embraer | 6,812 | 86 | 45 | 13 | Aerospace |
| Cia Siderurgica Nacional | 6,305 | 23 | 13 | 6 | Iron and Steel |
| Tam | 5,780 | 31 | 5 | 6 | Airlines |
| Sadia | 5,577 | 39 | 40 | 35 | Agribusiness |
| Marfrig | 5,317 | 39 | 40 | 35 | Agribusiness |
| Odebrecht | 4,800 | 69 | 56 | 49 | Construction |
| Andrade Gutierrez | 4,500 | 15 | 10 | 5 | Construction |
| Votorantim | 3,110 | 36 | 48 | 35 | Cement |

Source: United Nations, ECLAC, *Foreign Direct Investment in Latin America and the Caribbean*, 2009, p. 62.

## Climate Change Talks

The development of alternative energy sources and approaches to climate risk mitigation seem to be drawing Brazil closer to the transatlantic community after a long history of tense relations. Brazil is justly renowned for its pioneering research and production of biofuels; a 2007 agreement with the US pledged joint efforts to develop a global market for ethanol and other biofuels. More generally, Brazil's supply of energy has always featured a relatively high percentage of supply from renewable sources, including hydroelectricity and ethanol.

Brazil's position on climate change and deforestation has also evolved in ways that favor a global accord on the reduction of carbon emissions to move beyond the 1998 Kyoto protocol of the United Nations Framework Convention on Climate Change. Neither Brazil nor the United States ever became signatories of the Kyoto protocol, so the evolution of their respective positions in future climate talks is a matter of great international concern. At the inter-governmental climate meetings in Copenhagen in December 2009, Brazil surprised world opinion by announcing planned cuts in carbon emissions that went well beyond earlier expectations of what Brazil would be willing to offer. In announcing its intent to achieve a 35% cut in annual carbon emissions by 2020, Brazil has sought to seize the initiative by laying down a clear challenge to the rich nations (most especially, the United States) which have been reluctant to embrace such an ambitious target for emission reductions.

About one-half of Brazil's planned reduction in emissions is slated to come through a reduction in deforestation.[5] While Brazil's management of the Amazon forest is likely to remain controversial, recent advances in satellite technology to detect hot spots and improvements in land titling process in the Amazon to more clearly define ownership and discourage illegal economic activities have allowed the Brazilian government to claim a substantial reduction in rates of deforestation due to illegal logging and ranching. Brazil's evolving role toward greater cooperation with the global community in matters of climate change is more than a tactical move to deflect international criticism of its forest management policies and of its regional development policies which have featured road construction in the Amazon and dam construction which have led to flooding in vast areas. A greater ecological awareness has permeated Brazilian policy for at least the last fifteen years. As one symbol of the evolution of public opinion in Brazil on environmental matters, Lula's former minister of the environment, Marina Silva, is mounting a serious campaign for the presidency of Brazil in 2010 as a candidate of the Green Party.

## DIVERGENCES WITH THE NORTH: BRAZIL'S SOUTH-SOUTH ORIENTATION

In both political and economic matters, Brazil and the global North are not always in agreement about how the world should work or be governed. Strong evidence exists, in fact, that Brazil seeks to play an important role as an independent power broker on a global scale and a bridge to the global South. In order to do so, it is not reluctant to stake out policy positions that are at odds with the United States and other global powers on important matters.

This independent role in global matters that Brazil seeks to play was clearly on view in early 2010 when Brazil, acting in close partnership with Turkey, brokered a proposed agreement on nuclear enrichment with Iran which was intended to head off tough new UN sanctions against Iran which the US had been proposing. In Brazil's view, it was acting as part of a good faith effort to promote dialogue and to avert a rush toward sanctions,

---

5. http://www.guardian.co.uk/environment/2009/nov/10/brazil-emissions.

increased conflict between Iran and West, and, inevitably, the possibility of another war. Obviously, its actions (along with those of its partner, Turkey) were seen as a rebuke of United States diplomacy and a criticism of faulty US intelligence which had helped pave the way to a war in Iraq which Brazil opposed. Brazil's mediation efforts in this case apparently came to naught. The US pronounced them "dangerously naïve" and the UN Security Council (with Brazil, a temporary member, opposed) promptly went ahead with broad sanctions against Iran. The upshot is that while the Brazilian-Turkish effort fell short of its goals and Brazil was exposed in its aftermath to criticism both domestic and foreign, the action did send a strong signal to the global community that Brazil's leadership ambitions are not geographically circumscribed to its own neighborhood in South America. In particular, Brazil will continue to look for ways to play a constructive role more broadly in the Middle East, including by playing a mediating role in negotiations between Israel and Palestine.

Looking more broadly at Brazilian foreign policy, areas of disagreement between the United States and Brazil in hemispheric affairs appear to abound. In the case of the Honduran political crisis of 2009, for example, Brazil refused to go along with the US decision to recognize the government elected in Honduras in November 2009 and as of mid-2010 was one of a relatively small number of Latin American nations not to have re-established relations with Honduras. Brazil's embrace of Cuba and the Castro brothers has been another bone of contention with the United States; Brazil has been a supporter of Cuba's readmission to the Organization of American States, a position clearly at odds with the long-standing policy of the United States, and maintains active trade and diplomatic relations with the island in the face of the long-standing US embargo.[6]

In other hemispheric political matters as well, Brazil does seem to be pursuing an agenda that is not consistent with US policy and which is designed to maintain a certain distance between the two countries. For example, Brazil is the chief architect between a new regional organization created in 2008 and known as the South American Union of Nations (or UNASUR using the Spanish acronym) which specifically excludes the United States (and Mexico, too, a potential rival for regional leadership which Brazil perceives as too close to the United States).[7] UNASUR could be seen as a regional structure to mediate conflicts in South America and, as such, an

---

6. In 2009, Brazil was a strong supporter of an OAS decision to lift Cuba's suspension from the OAS, though this did not automatically open the door to renewed membership (see: http://www.cnn.com/2009/WORLD/americas/06/04/cuba.oas/index.html).

alternative to the Organization of American States, long dominated by the United States and US foreign policy concerns.

Still other examples of Brazil's regional assertion of leadership would be its decision, backed by Argentina, to invite Venezuela to join Mercosul, the customs union arrangement comprised heretofore of Argentina, Brazil, Paraguay, and Uruguay. The action was probably intended as a counterpoint to US policies to isolate and ignore President Hugo Chavez of Venezuela. Along similar lines, Brazil has expressed its concern to the United States regarding the proposed creation of US military bases in Colombia. In all these matters of political governance in the hemisphere, Brazil seems to be signaling that while it values good relations with the United States, it also feels free to challenge the US position as it sees fit.

Similarly in many issues of global economic diplomacy, Brazil can often seen to be at odds with the United States, and the West more generally, even while valuing the benefits of closer integration with the global economy.

The predominant economic ideology underlying Brazil's approach in economic matters could be referred to as a national development mindset, rooted in a world view that global economic relations reinforced an unequal power distribution between the developed and richer countries of the center North and the capital-dependent and technology-challenged countries of the periphery South. The traditional foreign policy framework of a large divide between the North and South (also characterized as a division between industrial powers and commodity producers such as Brazil and most of the other economies of Latin America) has led Brazil practically since the 1930s to be very protectionist in terms of trade policies to promote development of its industrial sector, in particular, by shielding industry in São Paulo (and elsewhere in Brazil, of course) from competition deemed to be unfair coming from companies based in the North (Baer, 2008).

Buffered from foreign competition by a complex set of tariffs, non-tariff barriers, and export promotion schemes, the favored sectors in Brazilian industry have always included automobiles, electric and electronic devices, textiles, clothing, and footwear (Motta Veiga, 2009). While tariffs were reduced unilaterally through a broad program of trade liberalization introduced by the Collor administration in the early 1990s, protection from international trade competition remains relatively high in Brazil.

---

7. For more on UNASUR, see: http://www.upi.com/Top_News/Special/2010/06/16/Ambitious-UNASUR-seeks-to-make-impact-without-conflict/UPI-62331276717712/.

To be fair, the value-added weighted-average tariff in Brazil has been reduced substantially since the late 1980s, from 57% to about 13% in the early 2000s (Moreira, 2009: 139). While the subsequent years under Lula saw some reversal in trade policy liberalization, including an increase in tariffs to 35% for some apparel and footwear, the Lula administration has not significantly increased protection. However, it should be emphasized that protection remains relatively high in international comparative perspective and that Brazil has ruled out any further reduction or rationalization of its tariff structure unless and until a broad multilateral agreement is reached in the context of the Doha Round. Moreover, the stated level of average protection does understate, in some cases significantly understate, the actual protection provided to Brazilian industry. If the concept of effective protection is used, which takes into account not only tariffs on final products, but tariffs as well on the inputs used to produce these products, protection for certain important branches of Brazilian industry is extraordinarily high, e.g., almost 140% in the case of passenger cars and light trucks (Moreira, 2009: 142-43). While economists would argue that tariffs of these levels is damaging to economic growth, the need to maintain protection is close to an article of faith among both São Paulo elites and general public opinion in Brazil.

The deeply ingrained belief in Brazil that increased global engagement with the North will inevitably (and unfairly) reduce the "space" for autonomous industrial development has been reinforced by a general onset of "reform fatigue" that followed the Cardoso era in which an aggressive pace of economic reform failed to raise the level of Brazilian economic growth. This belief has stiffened Brazil's inherent tendency to be dubious about the benefits of bilateral or regional free trade agreements with the North. In the post-2002 period of the Lula administration, this traditional tendency is most in evidence in the downgrading of bilateral US-Brazil trade talks and discussions between Mercosul and the European Union on a free trade agreement. Of course, and in addition, Brazil's opposition to the mid-1990s US initiative to negotiate a Free Trade Area of the Americas (or FTAA) eventually and inevitably led to a sidelining of the initiative and its eventual abandonment.

Tensions on trade issues are also evident at the multilateral or global level. Brazil has resisted efforts to negotiate new disciplines in the World Trade Organization in such sensitive areas as investment, trade in services, and government procurement, all of which are intended to remove non-tariff barriers to global trade in goods and services. As Schirm reminds us, Brazil has been instrumental in successfully organizing a larger group of emerging market economies (including India and China) in the context of the Doha Round talks to oppose particular European Union and United States initiatives seen as tilting the deck in favor of developed country interests at the expense of the South (Schirm, 2009).

Brazil has complemented what might be perceived as something less than wholehearted engagement in global trade talks by pursuing other, more limited and region-specific accords that further its goal of being seen as a leader of the global South interested above all in South-South economic cooperation. Brazil has embraced its association with the so-called BRIC group of nations (including Russia, India, and China) and promoted greater collaboration in trade and economic matters among this potentially powerful set of economies in a series of trade initiative international summits which have taken place since 2008. Brazil's India-Brazil-South Africa Initiative is an innovative structure launched in 2006 which seeks to knit together south economies which traditionally have had very limited trade and commercial interaction.[8] Brazil has reached out to sign agreements with minor countries as well, including Cuba and Morocco, with which even the potential for trade is limited. More broadly, Brazil has engaged in an ambitious program to build its diplomatic presence through Africa as a means to improve trade relations and to seek the support of these nations for Brazilian initiatives in international forums, such as the United Nations.

To round out the picture, various Brazilian initiatives in South America also embody the South-South thrust in foreign policy. Obviously, Brazil has worked hard to keep the Mercosul arrangement together despite a slow pace of growth in trade between Brazil and Argentina over the last decade and despite the unhappiness with the regional tariff structure expressed by the more junior partners, especially Uruguay, but also Paraguay. As mentioned, the initiative to invite Venezuela to participate reflects Brazil's long-term foreign policy goals although the economic rationale to include Venezuela in the arrangement is not crystal clear as trade ties are quite limited. The UNASUR arrangement, mentioned above, also has an economic component in that it is designed to help promote infrastructure projects, in energy and transportation especially, that would lead to a greater integration of the South American economies traditionally separated by vast physical distances.

To conclude this section on Brazil's South-South orientation and how this sets the country apart from the agenda of the richer nations, one might

---

8. For more on IBSA, see http://www.ibsa-trilateral.org/.

consider Brazil's evolving role in the G-20 group of powerful economies, the successor to the G-7, an informal club of the largest economies in the world. Along with China, Brazil seems destined to be the influential voice on behalf of the global issues of greatest concern to the emerging nations. These issues would include liberalization in agricultural trade, which would benefit most of the poorer nations of the world, while including also Brazil. The issues would include reform of the leading institutions of international economic governance, especially the International Monetary Fund and the World Bank, in which the voting power has always tilted heavily toward the US, Europe, and Japan. Brazil has long called for a larger voting share in both the Fund and the Bank with the stated intent of altering the mission of these institutions toward development and economic assistance issues which are of primary concern to the developing countries.

## BRAZIL'S CHANGING WORLD VIEW

In the first two sections, two somewhat opposing forces shaping Brazil's role in global economy and politics have been examined. In Part I, the numerous and powerful forces leading to a greater integration of Brazil within the global community seem to indicate clearly that the country has much to gain indeed from greater globalization. In Part II, the strong pull of Brazil's history, including decades-long traditions of foreign policy, seems to set up countervailing pressures upon Brazil to set itself apart from the North and to assert its leadership of the global South. The interplay of these two factors could, at first glance, create a somewhat muddled image for Brazil in global affairs. In particular, is this new Brazil a reliable partner for the United States and the transatlantic community? Or is it an emerging new power with its own distinct policy goals and also with the resources and confidence to pursue an agenda that might conflict with the West in important areas?

The answer to this apparent puzzle is likely to be found in dynamics within Brazil itself, in particular, in profound alterations in Brazil's view of the world and its role within it. On balance, understanding this changing perception requires a closer look at what is happening within Brazil itself. The argument will be made that these changes, which are unfolding in Brazil and shaping both elite and popular opinion, are likely to move Brazil more firmly into the transatlantic community with benefits for both.

The changing nature of the Brazilian economy itself is one factor favoring greater, rather than lesser, integration with the West. One of these factors has already been alluded to—Brazil recognized the need for shared management of global risks in the post-2008 financial crisis and has been able to make positive contributions to domestic and international stability despite the serious nature of the shock Brazil endured. One of the reasons for Brazil's relatively safe passage through the global crisis is the economic stability produced over at least the two decades (or, roughly, since the Collor administration in the early 1990s) by the application of a rules-based approach to economic management. These rules, or economic practices, have consolidated in Brazil a model of economic management that approximates the Western ideal of a market-oriented economy with an important role for government as a regulator of economic activity and provider of social services.

Some of the hallmarks of Brazilian economic management have included a concern for macroeconomic stability as one of the foundations of sustained economic growth. This stability had eluded Brazil in the decades that followed the decline of the import-substitution model of economic growth after the 1970s. The essential policy components have included fiscal, monetary, and exchange rate policies that have produced in Brazil relatively low government budget deficits, a reduced risk of sovereign debt problems, low and stable rates of inflation, and a large supply of foreign exchange reserves. The overall impact of these policies was to permit a period of strong economic growth in Brazil in the period from 2003–2008. While growth plunged in 2009 in line with the downturn in the global economy, Brazil's resilience because of its improved economic policies and the large accumulated stock of international reserves effectively buffered Brazil during the global turmoil of 2008–2009. In 2008, one of the major rating agencies recognized the policy improvements in the Brazilian economy by assigning an investment-grade rating for Brazil's sovereign debt which has meant that Brazil can now access international capital markets (on which it is dependent for development finance) on more favorable terms.

Important changes are occurring in the external structure of the Brazilian economy that are leading to a fuller engagement with the world economy. Following the strong surge in exports in 2003-08, much of it the result of Chinese demand for the commodity exports in which Brazil specializes, the importance of the external sector to Brazil's growth and stability is now more evident. Combined with a very vigorous growth in imports during the same period of the early 2000s, the surge in exports has contributed to boosting the openness of the Brazilian economy; the ratio of external trade to GDP, the main measure of how open an economy is, has increased to 25 percent of GDP in the late 2000s, close to the level of other large economies, and almost twice the level of a decade ago in Brazil when Brazil was far more closed to the outside world in economic terms.[9]

Much of Brazil's export growth is commodity-based, including both industrial raw materials, such as iron ore and agricultural products, including soybeans and meat products. Motta Veiga reports that agribusiness exports grew at annual rates in excess of 16 percent in the mid-2000s, with significant diversification occurring in terms of markets reached and products exported (2009: 125-26).[10] The author further observes that Brazil is the world leader in such exports as sugar, ethanol, beef, and chicken and among the top exporters of soybeans and orange juice.

In the past, Brazil may have been reluctant to embrace this role of a food and raw material exporter to the rest of the world as it seemed that the economy would be limited by a specialization in sectors involving low levels of technology and innovation and, consequently, generating few spillover benefits to the rest of the economy. This attitude seems to be fading as export growth, based on both agribusiness and industrial exports, is seen not only as a means of relieving Brazil's chronic foreign exchange problems, effectively insulating the economy from the periodic external shocks which in the past, such as in the 1980s and again in the late 1990s, have cut off capital inflows to Brazil and interrupted economic growth. In other words, Brazil's growing success as an exporter has allowed the country to diminish one of the principal obstacles to sustained growth which in the past has been the perception by international investors that the country was permanently on the cusp of sovereign debt problems. It has probably also helped that the agribusiness boom has acted to spread prosperity regionally across many areas of the interior of Brazil and that much of the boom has been based on the successful application of technology to permit the cultivation of semi-arid land. Much of the research on which this technology has been based is authentically Brazilian having been produced in the laboratories of EMBRAPA, a state-supported research entity dedicated to agriculture (Mueller, 2009).

---

9. Ipeadata. The overall level of openness of the Brazilian economy is still relatively low compared to other fast growing emerging economies, however.

10. In the period from 2001-2005, for example, growth to developing markets (including, importantly, China) grew at even higher rates of 26 percent annually.

With the success of Brazil's trade policies and the growth and global integration of the economy, new forces may be emerging within the Brazilian business community which could be in favor of freer trade, possibly countering to some extent the still strong influence of the São Paulo elites and the foreign policy establishment. Motta Veiga cites the example of the Confederação Nacional de Indústria (CNI, or National Confederation of Industry) which in 2006 produced an important document arguing for a new strategy of trade negotiations with countries such as Mexico which would be based solely on the economic benefits accruing to Brazil, including greater access to larger markets for its exports. He adds: "It is the first time that the Brazilian manufacturing sector has formally adopted an offensive stance in trade negotiations and pushed for a comprehensive and ambitious agreement" (Motta Veiga, 2009: 127).

Moreover, the emergence of a global agribusiness based in Brazil has raised the profile of sectors which would benefit very importantly from greater liberalization of global trade, thus infusing what is called an offensive or market-opening element in Brazil's global trade posture as opposed to the more traditional, defensive agenda focused on protecting Brazilian industry from external competition.

Along the same lines, the important growth of the large Brazilian companies with a global reach, companies such as Gerdau, Odebrecht, and Vale, is also challenging the way in which Brazilians think about the role of multinational enterprise and the ease with which it should be allowed to cross and operate beyond borders. While Brazil does not have an official policy to support the expansion of private-sector firms abroad, the growing success of these firms and their increasing presence abroad is a matter of national pride. As a matter of conjecture, the growth of these "national champions" in international markets is likely to make Brazil more, rather than less, likely to back global efforts to facilitate international investment flows.

The case of the state-owned oil company, Petrobras, is a special case of a multinational which shows the extent to which Brazil's role in international investment flows is changing from passive recipient to active participant exposed to the risks and rewards of such activity. Petrobras was, by a large margin, the most important investor in oil and gas properties in neighboring Bolivia when the newly elected government of President Evo Morales in May 2006 nationalized all fields and ordered the army to occupy all foreign-owned facilities. At the time, Petrobras' investment in gas properties in Bolivia was valued at about $1.5 billion. Resisting calls to take harsh measures against Bolivia to retaliate for the nationalization, Brazil eventually negotiated an agreement later in 2006 that essentially acquiesced in Bolivia's sovereign actions in exchange for a share of profits and a continued management role in the subsidiary. The company continues to operate in Bolivia and remains responsible for the flow of most gas exports to Brazil.

## AN AGENDA FOR COOPERATION

In sum, the argument is that while Brazil will continue to seek a "world without the West" and to strengthen its South-South ties, the factors promoting Brazil's greater global integration are very powerful. The predominant tendency for Brazil in the future is in this light likely to be one of increasing cooperation, rather than confrontation with the United States and the richer countries of the West. Because Brazil's long-term strategic interests overlap to an important degree with those of the North, it makes sense for the transatlantic community to incorporate and accommodate Brazil within the institutions that govern the global economy rather than exclude or isolate Brazil. A number of policy areas come to mind where greater inclusion of Brazil would be helpful. Some of these are reviewed below by way of conclusion.

### Reform of global governance

Brazil has been a leading voice for increased representation of the developing countries in global economic decision-making and norm-setting. Reform of the IMF is the starting point. The reform agenda includes increasing the resources of the Fund, revising conditionality requirements, and improving its governance to increase the voting shares of countries other than the United States, Europe, and Japan. The idea that the IMF should be governed more democratically so that its actions more appropriately reflect the interests of the global economic community, not just the wealthier countries, gained new urgency in the context of the post-2008 global financial crisis. Provided that its own voting share increased in the Fund were to increase, Brazil would be very supportive of reforms to place the IMF at the center of global policy coordination with an enhanced ability to lend more freely to poorer economies grappling with sharp declines in government revenues and export earnings following future global financial crises.

## Reform of global financial regulation

Global financial sector reform is needed to create a well functioning network of national and regional authorities to prevent a reoccurrence of the 2008 financial crisis attributed to poor financial regulation and excessive risk-taking by international banks. In this area of international financial flows in which North-South cooperation is essential, Brazil has been in the forefront of this debate to provide truly international supervision of financial institutions with a global reach as these institutions have proven to be channels by which financial shocks originating in the North are transmitted quickly to the South. Brazil's credibility in this area was enhanced by the relatively smooth passage of its own financial sector through the post-2008 financial crisis which was attributable to the broad ranging nature of financial regulation in Brazil. Some of the elements of the Brazilian regulatory framework, such as the comprehensive oversight of all financial institutions by a single regulator (the Central Bank) are aspects of financial reform that were absent in the regulatory systems of the United States and other richer nations prior to the financial crisis (Meirelles, 2010).

## A new consensus on global trade liberalization

An obvious area for cooperation would be for the transatlantic community to enlist Brazil's support in stemming the tide toward increased protectionism that has been spawned by the decline of global trade in 2009. Brazil is well placed in global trade talks to bridge longstanding differences between North and South particularly in the areas of market access and agricultural trade. Elements of a global grand bargain are liberalized trade in agricultural products, including ethanol, in exchange for significant movement by emerging economies on industrial sector liberalization and trade-related disciplines, such as government procurement. The evolution of trade strategy in Brazil itself points in this direction (Motta Veiga, 2009: 128-36) If so, and if Brazil signals a clearer intent to make concessions in exchange for benefits, it could have a powerful impact on the G-20 grouping of nations within the broader WTO talks.

## A global framework on energy and climate change

Brazil plays an important role in global energy and climate change discussions, policy areas where more North-South collaboration is needed. Brazil is a leader in the use and production of biofuels, including ethanol, and is committed to further research and to the development of global markets for trade in greener forms of energy. In March 2007, the US and Brazil reached a landmark agreement for shared research and technology in the production and international trade of biofuels.[11] These types of agreements between the world's leading producers of ethanol could well be revisited and to expanded to include other countries. On climate change, Brazil plays a role as steward of the resources of the Amazon region. Perhaps because of this global responsibility and the perception that this responsibility places limits on its own domestic development objectives, Brazil has not been an enthusiastic participant in climate change discussions. As discussed earlier, however, Brazilian public opinion and public policies appear to be changing. Brazil made a bold policy proposal at the 2009 Copenhagen meetings to success a successor global agreement to the Kyoto Protocol. This change in Brazilian policies has coincided with the advent of the Obama administration in the United States and its greater amenability to accepting limits on emissions as part of a global compact.

*Development beyond trade: new sources of financing for emerging economies*

The post-2008 global crisis has pointed to the need for more secure sources of long-term financing for low-income emerging economies, especially in periods during which private financing via bank lending or bond markets dries up. Brazil itself in 2008 benefited during the crisis from availability of dollar financing in a currency swap arrangement with the Federal Reserve Bank of the United States. In part, the global task involves creating a more important and permanent role for multilateral and regional development banks, a position that Brazil has favored through increasing the capital of these global institutions. Obviously, strengthened capital for the World Bank and the Inter-American Development Bank, among other institutions, would improve their ability to extend loans for development purposes. These entities could also prove useful, as they have in the case of Brazil, in helping Latin American economies to strengthen their financial markets and develop their own bond markets.

The point is that a more balanced flow of investment financing, one which assures a more reliable source of credit to the emerging economies

---

11. For background, see http://www.nytimes.com/2007/03/03/business/worldbusiness/ 03ethanol.html.

than private markets are capable of providing, could produce a more stable world economy by directing more surplus savings to economies (such as Brazil's) where the rates or return on investment are the highest. Besides being an advocate for less developed emerging economies, Brazil itself could obviously benefit from a more powerful and better capitalized network of multilateral and regional official lenders as it seeks to overcome chronically low levels of public investment, including poor economic and social infrastructure.

While for Brazil and for many developing countries, the issue of greater reliance for development finance on official lenders raises longstanding issues of conditionality, i.e., that increased lending will come with demands for changed public policies that developing countries will view as impinging on their sovereignty. In part, these concerns could be addressed by increasing the voting rights of the developing countries. In part, as well, conditionality may be for developing countries the lesser of two evils for developing economies, especially when private sector financing is suddenly not available due to a global financial crisis and the poorer economies have limited resources of their own to fall back upon.

## Conclusions

Brazil's peaceful rise in global affairs makes it an attractive partner in global initiatives for the US and the EU. While often wishing to project an image of anti–status quo, the argument here is that Brazil actually would welcome a more meaningful role in managing and reforming the institutions and practices of global governance. Indeed, the main objective of its foreign policy has long been to obtain a permanent seat on the Security Council of the United Nations. While this may or may not be a realistic goal in the foreseeable future, it does demonstrate Brazil's commitment to multilateralism and the objective should not be seen as an impediment to improved cooperation between Brazil and the United States. The shock of the global crisis underlines needed reforms in global governance and the positive role that Brazil can play as a nation closely tied to the West and yet able and willing to act as a bridge to the global South.

# 16

# REGIONAL INTEGRATION: POLITICAL USES OF ENERGY POLICY

*Christine A. Gustafson and Leslie Elliott Armijo*

*Abstract: This chapter analyzes the role of the Brazilian state in regional energy policy from 1990 to 2009. It compares Brazil's vision of energy cooperation in the Americas with those of two other important states, the United States and Venezuela. It finds that in each case, energy policy forms an integral piece of the countries' larger plans for organizing the region. It argues further that the Brazilian government's vision of "South American" energy integration may be more likely to be realized than either the "hemispheric" integration plans of the United States or the "Latin/Caribbean" energy framework of Venezuela.*

State goals for the energy sector are important to any consideration of the contemporary economic role of the Brazilian state. This chapter examines one often-overlooked aspect of national energy planning. We ask how the ongoing competition among Western Hemisphere governments over the contours of 21st century international cooperation has influenced energy sector development. That is, we analyze energy policy from the perspective of foreign policy. We find, first, that contemporary "national" energy strategies form integral pieces of states' larger plans for organizing the region. Thus the United States, Venezuela, and Brazil each promote distinct regional cooperation projects that imply non-trivial differences in hemispheric energy integration. Our second, and subsidiary, thesis is necessarily speculative, foreshadowing rather than reporting on actual events. Our reading of evidence suggests that key aspects of the Brazilian government's vision of "South American" energy integration may be more likely to be realized than either the "hemispheric" integration plans of the US or the "Latin/Caribbean" energy framework envisioned by Venezuela.

The chapter has six parts. Following section one's brief review of the history of regionalism in the Americas, section two provides essential empirical information about energy production, consumption, investment, and trading patterns in the Western Hemisphere. The third through fifth sections analyze three competing visions of regional energy integration. We end with tentative conclusions about a still unfolding process.[1]

## REGIONALISM IN THE AMERICAS

Efforts at regional cooperation and economic integration have a long history in the Americas. Mace and Thérien (2007) identify three periods of hemispheric cooperation, the first beginning with the first Pan-American conference in 1889-90, the second with the formation of the Organization of American States (OAS) in 1948, and the most recent era commencing in 1994 with the first Summit of the Americas meeting. Mace and Thérien note a cyclical pattern in which each period began strongly, with enthusiasm and real cooperative gains, and then lost steam as balance of power disparities and true differences in national interests came ineluctably to the fore.

Regarding the more specific issue of regional *economic* integration,[2] scholars identify two periods (Devlin and Estevadeordal, 2001; Gómez-Mera, 2008; Grugel, 2006). The first, today called the "old regionalism," began just after the Second World War and lasted until the 1980s. The old regionalism was greatly influenced by the developmentalist ideology of the United Nations Economic Commission for Latin America (ECLA—now the Economic Commission for Latin America and the Caribbean or ECLAC),

---

1. The authors thank Sean Burges, Maxwell Cameron, Laura Gómez-Mera, Eric Hershberg, Anil Hira, Andrew Hurrell, Alberto Pfeifer, Shawn Smallman, Maria Regina Soares de Lima, Laura Randall, and William Smith for their comments on previous versions of this work.

2. Regional economic integration is the process by which two or more countries become increasingly interlinked via trade, production, or finance. Formal integration arrangements range from "free trade areas" to "common markets." A "free trade area" consists of a group of countries that have free trade with one another but maintain separate trade policies with outside countries. A "customs union" unites countries that have free trade with one another and a common external tariff for trade outside the group. A "common market" exists when a group of countries forms a customs union, and in addition allows free movement of labor and capital among group members (Black, Hashimzade and Myles, 2009).

founded in 1948.[3] ECLA economists saw regional integration as a strategy for promoting import substitution industrialization (ISI). They believed that eliminating tariff barriers among the member nations of the regionally integrated area, while maintaining them against other nations, would increase the size of markets and thus allow industries to take advantage of economies of scale, lower "unit costs," and enjoy "protection against imports from third countries" (Bulmer-Thomas, 1994: 299). Although three regional trade organizations (RTOs) formed in the 1960s under this rationale—the Latin American Free Trade Association (LAFTA), the Andean Pact (AP), and the Central American Common Market (CACM)—none were very successful. Although the CACM increased industrialization, its members were the least developed in the region, and therefore even modest gains seemed huge. All of the RTOs also struggled with distributing benefits equitably, with finding reliable mechanisms for compensating their poorest members, and with agreeing on tariff reductions for key products (Felix, 1969). By 1975, intraregional trade's share in total exports was only about 18 percent (Bulmer-Thomas, 1994: 305). By the early 1980s, the old regionalism was moribund. The RTOs continued to exist, some with new names (LAFTA became the Latin American Integration Association or ALADI in 1980), but integration as a development strategy seemed to get scrapped along with ISI when the pro-market or "neoliberal" economic ideology took hold in Latin America following the 1980s debt crisis (Kearney, 2001).

The second period, called the "new regionalism," began in the late 1980s and continues to the present. It emerged as part of neoliberalism's emphasis on macroeconomic stabilization and structural reform of the national economic regulatory framework. The International Monetary Fund (IMF) and World Bank promoted regional integration, not as a means of stimulating industrialization, but rather with the goals of advancing free trade and locking in other liberalization efforts. What became known as "open regionalism," both in Latin America and East Asia, was an ideology that championed the private sector and favored the withdrawal of the state from economic activity. The new regionalism coincided with the conclusion of the Uruguay Round in 1994 and the acceleration of market liberalization and integration worldwide after the end of the Cold War. In this new ideological and global economic climate, some of the old RTOs reinvented

---

3. Developmentalism in the Latin American context is an ideology asserting that the shortest path to economic growth and prosperity for poor countries is through industrialization, usually led by the state and with the protection of high tariffs (Bulmer-Thomas, 1994: 278-279).

themselves as free trade associations, while others disbanded and formed new groupings. The Central American Common Market endured, but with new goals; the countries of the Southern Cone formed the Common Market of the South (MERCOSUR) in 1991; the Andean countries created the Andean Community (CAN) in 1993; and the United States, Canada, and Mexico inaugurated the North American Free Trade Agreement (NAFTA) in 1994. Devlin and Estevadeordal (2001: 25-35) argue that these newer RTOs contrast markedly with those of the old regionalism: they are market driven rather than state driven; they aim to attract foreign investment rather than restrict it; they are outward-looking, creating demand for greater rather than less participation in extra-regional trade forums; they are very little concerned with special and differential treatment of members; and their institutional architecture is much scaled down in comparison to the RTOs of the 1960s and 1970s (see also de la Reza, 2006).

The cross-regional comparative literature, much of which has focused on Western European integration, also stresses the more pro-market, globally-integrated forms of economic regulation today as compared to integration efforts of the 1950s and 1960s. It suggests that the *politics* of the integration process are notably less state-centric and more reliant on leadership from private business and transnational groups, as well as more influenced by existing international institutions, than in the past (Katzenstein, 2005; Buzan and Waever, 2003; Acharya, 2007). Observers of Latin America, in contrast, highlight the continuing dominance of the state in integration decisions (Gómez-Mera, 2008; Hurrell, 2005).[4] Moreover, the straightforward division of "old regionalism" as representing the structuralist vision of ECLA, and "new regionalism" as embodying neoliberalism and the embrace of globalization, describes NAFTA better than the universe of contemporary integration options in South America.

At present, there are multiple formal institutions in the Americas that embody aspects of political cooperation and economic integration. Nonetheless, they may be summarized into three distinct regional integration projects or visions for the hemisphere (cf. Burges, 2007).[5] Each has both political and economic dimensions, and each is championed by one of the hemisphere's important states. The United States prefers a vision of regional

---

4. Structuralism is related to developmentalism. It has several meanings, but we refer here to the idea that the world economy is structurally biased against poor countries. Specifically, the terms of trade between primary product exporters (normally poor countries) and exporters of manufactures (normally rich countries) tend to decline over time—the Singer-Prebisch thesis. Thus, in order to grow and prosper, primary product exporters must industrialize, usually via state-sponsored import-substituting policies (Prebisch, 1949; Furtado, 1959).

integration, embodied in NAFTA, that incorporates all countries in the Western Hemisphere, excepting Cuba, and in which the US is the dominant player. Venezuela promotes a Latin American vision that explicitly excludes the US and Canada, but includes Cuba and other Caribbean nations whose friendship can help Venezuela in its aspirations for regional leadership. Its institutional manifestation is the Bolivarian Alliance for the Americas (ALBA). Brazil's preferred regional design is manifest in the Union of South American Nations (UNASUR). It includes all of South America, but locates both North and Central America, including the island states of the Caribbean, outside.

What is interesting for a volume on the future role of the Brazilian state is that the three integration alternatives currently in play in the Americas offer three distinct visions of the state's appropriate economic role. Together they evoke a rough right-to-left political continuum, running from NAFTA through UNASUR to ALBA, though there is also considerable overlap among them (Burges, 2007; Kellogg, 2007). Each of these integration alternatives began as a vision of *trade integration*, involving mechanisms to promote the exchange of goods and services among members, and of the group with the outside world. But each of these contemporary regional integration initiatives also involves a number of other dimensions, including explicit and implicit promotion of foreign direct investment (FDI), collaborative infrastructure, harmonization of domestic regulatory frameworks, joint political positions in international affairs, and transnational citizen links. Rather than examining tariff arrangements or trade-related negotiations per se, we prefer to explore an issue arena that clearly possesses profound regional and international dimensions, but that is less often addressed by the regional integration literature. This chapter's task, then, is to treat energy integration (a work in progress, by definition) as a critical case study for understanding the region's broader integration dynamics.

---

5. Laura Randall, in an e-mail communication in late 2009, noted the striking similarities between the three contemporary regional integration visions profiled here and the colonial governance structure, centered in present-day Mexico but including much of what is now US territory (Viceroyalty of New Spain, established 1535), the Andes (the Viceroyalty of Peru, established in 1544, from which the Viceroyalty of New Granada, headquartered in Caracas, separated off in 1717), and Brazil (the Viceroyalty of Brazil, governed from Portugal after 1640).

## ENERGY IN THE WESTERN HEMISPHERE

This section provides a brief factual overview of Latin America's contemporary energy profile in terms of production, consumption, and resource endowments. It compares the region's situation in the early 1990s with data from the latest available sources. In accordance with statistical norms, we consider "Latin America," and sometimes "Latin America and the Caribbean," as the relevant region.

In 1991, Latin America's total energy production was 13.9 million boe/d (barrels of oil equivalent per day), distributed among the major countries as shown in Table 16-1. Total production was 59% petroleum, 16% natural gas, 6% hydroelectric, 4% coal, and half a percent nuclear, with the remaining 14% dispersed among firewood, sugarcane products, geothermal, and a host of other nontraditional sources. Energy resources were unequally distributed: Venezuela and Mexico together accounted for 92% of Latin America's proven oil reserves[6] and 70% of oil production, while countries like Paraguay and Uruguay had no oil at all. In terms of total energy consumption, in the early 1990s fossil fuels dominated, as shown in Table 16-1.

TABLE 16-1. Energy Production and Use in Latin America, 1992 and 2006

|  | Energy imports, net (% of energy use) | | Energy Production (kilotons of oil equivalent) | | Energy use (kg of oil equivalent per capita) | | Fossil fuel energy consumption (% of total) | |
|---|---|---|---|---|---|---|---|---|
|  | 1992 | 2006 | 1992 | 2006 | 1992 | 2006 | 1992 | 2006 |
| Argentina | -8.7 | -21.4 | 54,322 | 83,865 | 1,491.5 | 1,765.7 | 88.8 | 88.4 |
| Bolivia | -68.5 | -144.3 | 5,058 | 14,290 | 429.8 | 625.3 | 70.8 | 83.1 |
| Brazil | 27.6 | 7.8 | 104,280 | 206,717 | 933.0 | 1,183.8 | 52.7 | 53.7 |
| Chile | 47.2 | 66.5 | 8,412 | 9,970 | 1,166.4 | 1,811.9 | 69.3 | 73.5 |
| Colombia | -84.9 | -180.0 | 48,443 | 84,588 | 759.3 | 695.5 | 69.9 | 73.4 |
| Ecuador | -186.9 | -165.3 | 18,355 | 29,819 | 595.8 | 851.4 | 80.4 | 88.2 |
| Mexico | -53.1 | -44.3 | 200,321 | 255,967 | 1,514.7 | 1,702.4 | 88.0 | 89.1 |
| Paraguay | -42.7 | -68.9 | 4,520 | 6,708 | 709.9 | 660.1 | 24.0 | 30.5 |
| Peru | -0.9 | 15.4 | 9,597 | 11,470 | 420.4 | 491.3 | 65.1 | 68.5 |
| Uruguay | 53.3 | 75.4 | 1,261 | 784 | 856.9 | 962.4 | 64.0 | 67.8 |
| Venezuela | -226.4 | -214.3 | 165,780 | 195,547 | 2,458.5 | 2,301.9 | 90.9 | 88.2 |

*Source*: World Bank, 2009.

Nonetheless, almost 72% of Latin America's electricity came from hydropower plants. Table 16-2 shows that every South American country used

---

6. Proven oil reserves are "those quantities of petroleum which, by analysis of geological and engineering data, can be estimated with a high degree of confidence to be commercially recoverable from a given date forward, from known reservoirs and under current economic conditions" (CIA World Factbook 2009, https://www.cia.gov/library/publications/the-world-factbook).

hydropower as a principal source for electricity, a fact that has created supply problems in times of drought (Wu, 1995: 1-5).

Latin America in the early 1990s had a net energy surplus with the rest of the world. In 1991, the region's net energy exports were about 4 million boe/d, representing 26% of all energy produced in the region. With about 12% of the world's proven oil reserves (124 billion barrels in 1992), and 12% of world crude oil production, Latin America was a net exporter of oil, refined petroleum products, and coal. 73% of Latin American oil exports went to the United States, with Western Europe taking 19%, and the Asia-Pacific region another 5%. Venezuela, Mexico, Colombia, and Ecuador

TABLE 16-2. Energy Production by Source in Latin America, 1992 and 2006

| | Hydroelectric (% of total) | | Oil (% of total) | | Natural Gas (% of total) | | Coal (% of total) | | Nuclear (% of total) | |
|---|---|---|---|---|---|---|---|---|---|---|
| | 1992 | 2006 | 1992 | 2006 | 1992 | 2006 | 1992 | 2006 | 1992 | 2006 |
| Argentina | 34.7 | 33.0 | 13.7 | 7.0 | 37.3 | 50.2 | 1.5 | 1.8 | 12.7 | 6.7 |
| Bolivia | 52.4 | 40.8 | 6.3 | 16.7 | 38.1 | 39.3 | 0.0 | 0.0 | 0.0 | 0.0 |
| Brazil | 92.4 | 83.2 | 2.6 | 3.0 | 0.0 | 4.4 | 2.1 | 2.4 | 0.7 | 3.3 |
| Chile | 82.2 | 59.5 | 3.8 | 1.6 | 1.2 | 19.9 | 10.6 | 17.1 | 0.0 | 0.0 |
| Colombia | 67.6 | 78.7 | 2.2 | 0.2 | 15.0 | 12.4 | 14.0 | 7.5 | 0.0 | 0.0 |
| Ecuador | 69.1 | 46.3 | 30.9 | 44.1 | 0.0 | 9.6 | 0.0 | 0.0 | 0.0 | 0.0 |
| Mexico | 19.8 | 12.2 | 54.0 | 21.6 | 12.5 | 45.5 | 6.3 | 12.7 | 3.0 | 4.4 |
| Paraguay | 99.9 | 100.0 | 0.0 | 0.0 | 0.0 | 0.0 | 0.0 | 0.0 | 0.0 | 0.0 |
| Peru | 73.8 | 78.5 | 23.8 | 8.4 | 1.4 | 9.5 | 0.0 | 3.0 | 0.0 | 0.0 |
| Uruguay | 89.0 | 64.0 | 10.3 | 35.1 | 0.0 | 0.1 | 0.0 | 0.0 | 0.0 | 0.0 |
| Venezuela | 70.1 | 72.0 | 6.8 | 14.6 | 23.1 | 13.4 | 0.0 | 0.0 | 0.0 | 0.0 |

*Source*: World Bank, 2009.

were the main oil exporters, and Chile and Brazil the main importers. All of the natural gas produced in the region was consumed in the region, with Bolivia being the only net exporter, and Argentina the only net importer. Coal represented only 2% of total net energy exports (Wu, 1995: 1-5).

The energy scenario at the end of the first decade of the 21st century reveals subtle but important differences from the early 1990s. Given economic growth, both production and consumption have increased. Total Latin American consumption reached 3.6 million kbep (thousands of barrels of oil equivalent) in 2006 (World Energy Council, 2008; OLADE, 2007), with Mexico accounting for about 21% of Latin American consumption and Brazil 36% (OLADE, 2007). Fossil fuels still dominate both total regional energy production and total consumption, with oil products now accounting for about 50% of energy consumption on average in all countries. Firewood is still a major factor in Paraguay (40% of the energy mix). Venezuela uses virtually no natural gas, while in Argentina it is 50 percent of energy use. Coal is not significant in the region. In contrast, biofuels have become much more important, especially in Brazil over recent decades. Brazil produced 46% of world ethanol in 2006, and flex fuel cars in the same year accounted for 65% of Brazilian car manufactures (World Energy Council, 2008: 10-11). As before, hydroelectric dams generate the majority of electricity in Latin America, especially throughout South America.

TABLE 16-3. Estimated Oil and Gas Reserves in Latin American, Jan. 2010

| | Oil | | Gas | |
|---|---|---|---|---|
| | Volume (billion barrels) | % Total | Volume (trillion cubit feet) | % Total |
| Argentina | 2.5 | 1.9 | 14.1 | 2.4 |
| Bolivia | 0.5 | 0.3 | 26.5 | 4.5 |
| Brazil | 12.8 | 9.5 | 12.9 | 2.2 |
| Chile | 0.2 | 0.1 | 3.5 | 0.6 |
| Colombia | 1.4 | 1.0 | 4.0 | 0.7 |
| Ecuador | 6.5 | 4.8 | 0.3 | 0.0 |
| Mexico | 10.4 | 7.7 | 12.7 | 2.2 |
| Peru | 0.4 | 0.3 | 11.8 | 2.0 |
| Suriname | 0.1 | 0.1 | | |
| Trinidad and Tobago | 0.7 | 0.5 | 15.4 | 2.6 |
| Venezuela | 99.4 | 73.7 | 176.0 | 30.0 |
| Total | 134.8 | | 586.1 | |

Source: Radler, 2009.

Some individual countries within the region have become more energy-independent, but others less so. Venezuela still has the largest proven oil reserves by far and is the region's largest producer of oil and oil products. Until recently, Mexico came second in terms of proven reserves, but recent discoveries off the Brazilian coast already have pushed Brazil to second place, as shown in Table 16-3. Venezuela and Mexico remain the region's top producers and net exporters of oil and oil products. In 2008, they ranked tenth and seventh in the world respectively for oil production, and eighth and thirteenth in the world respectively for net oil exports (US Energy Information Administration, 2010). Argentina and Bolivia are the region's top natural gas exporters (Sullivan, Rush, and Seelke, 2008). Looking at relative changes, Table 16-1 shows that net imports as a share of domestic energy consumption are up since 1992 in Chile, Peru, and Uruguay, while Mexico, Ecuador, and even Venezuela are exporting somewhat smaller shares of their production. In contrast, Argentina, Bolivia, Brazil, Colombia, and Uruguay all have bettered their national net energy positions since 1992. In absolute terms, Venezuela, Ecuador, Bolivia, and perhaps Colombia can fairly be described as natural resource economies, with

93, 59, 49, and 38%, respectively, of their merchandise exports in 2006 consisting of fuel exports (World Bank, 2009). Mexico, Argentina, and surprisingly also Paraguay (due to its share in the hydropower from the Itaipú Dam) are all comfortable net energy exporters, although energy provides less than 20% of their merchandise exports. Brazil too is rapidly approaching energy balance, and may soon become a net energy exporter. Net energy importers currently include Brazil, Peru, Chile, and especially Uruguay (World Bank, 2009).

In 2009, Latin America as a whole still had a net energy surplus and was a net exporter of energy to the rest of the world. Latin American proven oil reserves were down slightly from the early 1990s as a percentage of the world's total, constituting approximately 11% in 2009 (US Energy Information Administration, 2009a). The United States remained the region's most important customer. Some 60% of Venezuela's oil exports, for example, went to the United States in 2006 (Sullivan, Rush, and Seelke, 2008; Caspary, 2007). But China is rapidly becoming an important consumer of Latin American energy. For example, in May 2009 the China Development Bank and Sinopec, a Chinese oil company, lent Petrobras, Brazil's state oil company, US$10 billion. In exchange, China will receive up to 200,000 barrels per day of crude oil for ten years from Brazil's new deep-sea oil fields. China and Venezuela have also set up a joint investment fund. Formed in 2007, the fund was increased to US$12 billion in February 2009, with the China Development Bank lending two thirds of the total. The goal is for Chinese companies to use this fund to invest in the Venezuelan energy sector and, ultimately, to increase Venezuelan oil exports to China ("The Dragon in the Backyard," 2009: 19-21).

Industry observers have characterized Latin America as having vast untapped energy potential, but as suffering from a lack of investment. *The Banker* estimated in 2008 that from now until 2030, the region will be the site of about 7% of global project investments in energy, and that, of these investments, Brazil will probably garner about one third (Rumsey, 2008). The President of the Inter-American Development Bank (IDB) has said that in order to meet demand, investment in Latin America's energy sector will need to be $1,380 billion by 2030 (Moreno, 2008), while the International Energy Agency has cited a figure of US$1,337 billion for the same period (IEA, 2003). Over the past two decades, however, energy projects have made up only about 20% of foreign direct investments. For this reason, supply, distribution and service have been unreliable. Some blame this situation on the regulatory systems of South American governments, which arguably tilted more toward resource nationalism in the first decade of the 21st century (Rumsey, 2008).

Some analysts also view investment in the renewable energy sector as insufficient, but note that many efforts are currently being made to stimulate it.[7] 21 countries signed the Brasilia Platform on Renewable Energies in 2003.[8] They agreed that 10% of energy should be derived from renewable energy sources. The wording of the agreement, however, is loose, saying that the countries should try to meet the target "on the basis of voluntary efforts and taking into account the diversity of national situations" (Rumsey, 2008). Local private investment in the sector faces obstacles, such as failure of governments to provide subsidies and lack of access to loans. Problems of scale and newness of technology are also important. Multilateral institutions and state development banks, however, are filling the gap. The IDB, for example, wants to spend $300 million on renewable energy in Latin America over the next five years. It is actively promoting programs on sustainable biofuels, energy efficiency, solar and wind power, small-scale hydropower, and energy from waste. In Brazil, the National Development Bank (BNDES) is taking a leading role, especially in cases where local currency is needed and commercial banks have trouble hedging their foreign exchange risk on long-term contracts (Rumsey, 2008).[9]

In this discussion of investment, however, we do not wish to imply that foreign investment is essential in order to meet the region's future energy needs and goals. First, if investment is to be subsidized by local or multilateral development banks, it is not clear why foreign direct investors, rather than local ones, should be the main private sector partners, or why other sectors of the economy should not take precedence over the energy sector. Second, such investment might not be needed if domestic tax systems and the pricing of energy products could be designed and managed better by Latin American governments.[10]

---

7. Renewable energy is any energy source that is "naturally regenerated" and "virtually inexhaustible," but whose flow may be limited. Sources include "biomass, hydro, geothermal, solar, wind, ocean thermal, wave action, and tidal energy" (US Energy Information Administration, 2010, http://www.eia.doe.gov).

8. For more information on the Brasília Platform, see ECLAC's web page on the agreement: http://www.eclac.cl/cgi-bin/getProd.asp?xml=/dmaah/noticias/discursos/5/13555/P13555.xml&xsl=/dmaah/tpl-i/p4f.xsl&base=/tpl/top-bottom.xslt.

9. Energy investments, especially in developing countries tend to be risky. They involve large amounts of capital, take a long time to yield a profit, often involve many investors, and are subject to changes in host-country government policies and economic climate (such as exchange rates). For more information, see Razavi (1996).

10. The authors thank Laura Randall for these insights.

Energy integration—the process of interlinking states' energy infrastructure, institutions, and investments—has been on the agenda in Latin America for decades now. Several regional organizations have been created. In the 1960s and 1970s, the Regional Association of Oil and Natural Gas Companies in Latin America and the Caribbean (ARPEL), the Regional Electrical Integration Commission (CIER), and the Latin American Energy Organization (OLADE) formed. All have regional integration as priorities in their mission statements (Caro, 2008). Energy integration has also been a priority of multilateral lending institutions, such as the IDB and the World Bank. More recently, initiatives emerged from the Summits of the Americas process, the most important being the "Hemispheric Energy Initiative" now overseen by the OAS. Finally, the first South American Presidential Energy Summit took place in April 2007. Its purpose was to begin developing a joint energy strategy for the region and to institute regular meetings (Caro, 2008). The following sections review how the United States, Venezuela, and Brazil view these efforts.

## THE UNITED STATES' VISION: NAFTA-PLUS

We use the term "NAFTA-plus" to describe the United States' approach to hemispheric policy, as the US's goal has been to embrace the entire hemisphere within trade and investment rules that closely parallel those embodied in the North American Free Trade Agreement among the US, Canada, and Mexico. The NAFTA-plus vision's principal incarnation has been the Free Trade Area of the Americas (FTAA), an initiative first launched by US President George H. W. Bush at the 1992 Summit of the Americas in Miami.[11] Since the stalling of the FTAA in November 2005, the United States instead has pursued bilateral trade and investment agreements.[12] While some hoped the 2008 election of Barack Obama would jumpstart the Summit process, as of late 2009 they had been disappointed (LeVine, 2009).

---

11. There have been five Summits to date: Miami (1994); Santiago, Chile (1998); Quebec City, Canada (2001); Mar del Plata, Argentina (2005); and Port-of-Spain, Trinidad and Tobego (2009). The sixth is scheduled for 2013 in Colombia.

12. The main reason for the halt has been disagreements between the United States and Brazil, but Venezuelan inflexibility and rhetorical attacks on other member states have also been factors. Brazil and the United States are the co-chairs of the FTAA. At a trade meeting in Miami in 2003, they changed the basis of the FTAA from a "comprehensive, single undertaking principle" to "a two-tier framework comprising a set of 'common rights and obligations' for all countries, combined with voluntary plurilateral arrangements with country benefits related to commitments" (Hornbeck, 2005: 1).

The US approach to regional integration is broad and deep. US negotiators seek market access through both bilateral and multilateral free trade agreements covering all aspects of trade, and extending the major provisions of the North American Free Trade Area to the Caribbean, Central America, and South America. NAFTA-plus is notably friendly to transnational business interests, often requiring that trade agreements include the obligation to submit any disputes with transnational investors to international arbitration, rather than trying them in home-country courts. At the same time, the proposed FTAA places special emphasis on "harmonizing" foreign direct investment, intellectual property, and government procurement rules. The US strategy is sometimes termed "competitive liberalization," as its focus is less on traditional merchandise trade and more on encouraging countries to compete with one another to liberalize their domestic regulatory regimes sufficiently to attract the most foreign investment. More recently, additional issues have been added to this deep trade and market access agenda. The US Congress has been debating the labor and environmental standards that future free trade agreements must protect. It has agreed basically that US trade partners must comply with International Labor Organization (ILO) rules, as well as with any multilateral environmental agreements to which the US is a signatory (ECLAC, 2008: 125-127).

The United States' approach to energy policy in particular is much influenced by its status as the world's largest consumer of oil. As of 2006, the United States consumed about 21 million barrels of oil per day (mbd). Net oil imports were about 12 mbd or 60% of this total. Latin America supplied about 32% of total US crude oil imports in 2007, with Venezuela alone accounting for 12% and Mexico 14%. South America provided about 17% (Sullivan, Rush, and Seelke, 2008). The energy needs of the United States are enormous, and its dependence on foreign oil is a crucial component of its foreign policy. South America is an important part of the mix.

Not surprisingly, energy security is a crucial element of President Barack Obama's foreign policy. Reducing dependence on foreign oil, especially from the Middle East, is critical. There is disagreement among the US elite as to how this goal should be accomplished, but most proposals include cultivating sources closer to home, which includes Latin America, as well as developing renewables. The US prefers energy initiatives that are hemisphere-wide, market based, and led by the private sector. The Obama administration also has added a greater concern with climate change. When Senator Hillary Clinton was being vetted for the post of Secretary of State, she echoed all of these positions. She assured the Senate Foreign Relations Committee that she would work to reduce US dependence on foreign oil and to form partnerships with other countries to overcome threats to the environment. Clinton said that in this regard Obama wants an energy partnership with Latin America, "looking to find ways through technology and other activities [that] we can work together to become more energy independent in this hemisphere" (Snow, 2009: 28). She added that this partnership would require overcoming resource nationalism disputes with key oil and natural gas exporting states like Venezuela and Bolivia, as well as helping other countries to meet their energy supply needs. The Secretary of State also voiced an interest in working through the International Energy Agency (IEA), noting that demand for energy is shifting from the developed to the developing world, and arguing that it will be important to have developing countries, particularly China and India, involved in "agreeing on energy standards and principles such as transparent energy markets, to ensure the coordinated release of strategic petroleum reserves during a major market disruption, and to maintain IEA's position as the voice of the world's major energy consuming nations" (Snow, 2009: 28).

Clinton also echoed the usual US concern for promoting the private sector, and called attention to problems with resource nationalism in Latin America and other developing countries. She said, "Most of the required investment [for energy] . . . must come from the private sector. In order to mobilize that investment, major policy and regulatory reforms are needed in many countries. Neither public nor private utilities and their investors can generate the capital required to expand access to clean, sustainable energy supplies, for example, when regulatory regimes prevent them from recovering their direct and indirect operating costs" (Snow, 2009: 28). She offered two kinds of assistance to developing countries willing to reform their energy sectors: technical assistance to "establish the overall regulatory and policy environment to stimulate new public and private investments," and "project-based financial guarantees [that] can help to reduce the perceived risks and costs of mobilizing the much larger flows of private sector financing [which will be] required" (Snow, 2009: 28).

However, resource nationalism in Venezuela, Bolivia, and Ecuador has dogged US attempts to see its energy vision realized in the hemisphere. Although the United States had great hopes for the Summits of the Americas process in general, and specifically for its "Hemispheric Energy Initiative," the Summits forum has stagnated in recent years. Venezuela's

President Hugo Chávez has been perceived in the US as a particular cause for concern. Since taking office in 1999, he has increased state control of Petróleos de Venezuela (PDVSA). He has directed its earnings and projects toward social purposes and asserted control over foreign investment. By early 2006, President Chávez had forced the conversion of operating agreements with foreign oil companies into joint ventures in which the Venezuelan state retained the upper hand. The new joint ventures also carry an income tax increase from 34 to 50%. Some companies voluntarily turned operating agreements over to PDVSA, but Chávez confiscated two operations when companies rejected his terms, and in 2007 also altered associations with foreign companies in the Orinoco River Basin. Three of the six companies involved were based in the United States (ExxonMobil, ConocoPhillips, and Chevron). ExxonMobil entered into a long dispute over its compensation, filing a request for arbitration with the International Center for Settlement of Investment Disputes in 2007. Other Andean governments also recently have challenged the property rights of multinational energy firms. Bolivia's President Evo Morales nationalized his country's gas sector, which is substantial and had strong involvement from US companies. Ecuador increased its share of windfall profits from foreign oil companies and also terminated the contract of Occidental Petroleum after a lengthy disagreement over the sale of drilling rights (Sullivan, Rush, and Seelke, 2008: 7-8).

As a result, US companies are looking for investments in other parts of the region and the world. Moreover, the US government and think tanks have expressed concern about what Chávez and his followers mean for energy security in the region. Senator Richard Lugar (R-Ind), the ranking member of the Senate Foreign Relations Committee, has sponsored two bills. The Energy Diplomacy and Security Act of 2007 contained a proposal for establishing a "Western Hemisphere Energy crisis mechanism" and a ministerial forum called the "Hemisphere Energy Cooperation Forum" (Sullivan, Rush, and Seelke, 2008: 19). Lugar also sponsored the United States-Brazil Energy Cooperation Pact of 2007. This bill calls on the Secretary of State to "accelerate the development of biofuels production, research, and infrastructure" (Sullivan, Rush, and Seelke, 2008: 19). A US business association, the Council of the Americas, has issued a report specifically recommending hemispheric energy cooperation as an engine for regional development and growth. The group favors expanding on the

NAFTA framework. Finally, the US Southern Command has taken up energy security as a key concern (Sullivan, Rush, and Seelke, 2008: 17).

In sum, the United States' NAFTA-plus vision of energy integration would (ideally) use the proposed FTAA or similar bilateral agreements to tie Latin American energy producers to the US market by a combination of long-term contracts and foreign direct investment. It envisions a minimal role for the state in managing the energy sector. The state would regulate, but only with the goals of protecting property rights, enforcing contracts, and, perhaps, ensuring basic labor and environmental standards. The bulk of the investment, exploration, extraction, and distribution of energy would be left to private actors.

## THE VENEZUELAN VISION: THE BOLIVARIAN ALLIANCE (ALBA)

The second integration option prominent today is the Bolivarian Alliance for the Americas (ALBA), the brainchild of Venezuelan President Hugo Chávez Frías (Burges, 2007; Kellogg, 2007). Chávez first mooted ALBA in December 2001 at a Summit of the Association of Caribbean States, and formally launched it in December 2004 in a joint declaration with Cuba's Fidel Castro. Bolivia's New Left President Evo Morales formalized Bolivia's entrance into ALBA in April 2006. Nicaragua joined the group in January 2007, just as ALBA was holding its fourth leaders' summit. A fifth summit took place in April 2007, and the governments of Haiti, Ecuador, Uruguay, Dominica, Saint Kitts and Nevis, and Saint Vincent and the Grenadines sent representatives, after which Dominica became a full member. Ecuador and St. Vincent and the Grenadines joined in 2009.

ALBA is Chávez's alternative to the United States' plan for a Free Trade Area of the Americas. David Harris and Diego Azzi note enthusiastically, "[ALBA] includes the promotion of trade relations between countries, and even the elimination of tariff barriers on certain products, but its core purpose goes far beyond this. The explicit aim of ALBA is to promote the 'social' side of development, eliminating poverty and combating social exclusion in a cooperative effort by Latin American states" (Harris and Azzi, 2006: 6). More skeptically, Sean W. Burges characterizes ALBA as a realist strategy designed to protect Chávez from internal and external enemies. By sharing Venezuelan petro-profits with neighbors, forging alliances with like-minded regional allies, and employing the rhetoric of the historic liberator Simón de Bolívar,

Chávez hopes to secure his domestic rule and counteract US hegemony (Burges, 2007). Indeed, the ideological symbolism of ALBA is strong, and reactions to it tend to fall clearly along ideological lines.

Of the three visions for regional energy policy, Venezuela's is the most explicitly political and social. Energy policy is a tool for development, but more importantly it is a weapon for fighting imperialism and inequality. President Hugo Chávez's proposals for energy integration thus follow closely the lines set out in his Bolivarian vision (ALBA). ALBA's stated goals are wide ranging. They include: fostering trade and investment "based on cooperation, and with the aim of improving people's lives, not making profits;" providing universal free healthcare and education; integrating members' energy sectors "to meet people's needs;" creating alternative media outlets "to counterbalance the US and regional neo-liberal media and promote an indigenous Latin American identity;" promoting land redistribution and food security; founding state-owned enterprises; developing basic industries "so that ALBA member states can become economically independent;" supporting "workers' movements, student movements, and social movements;" and ensuring that ALBA projects are environmentally sustainable (Hattingh, 2008).

Venezuela has the largest proven oil reserves and oil exports in Latin America (see Tables 16-1 and 16-3), and President Chávez has endeavored to use this wealth to build an anti-imperialist coalition in the region. There are several examples of this policy. First, as already mentioned, Chávez thoroughly restructured PDVSA, nationalizing it and reorienting its mission toward achieving social development goals. At the same time, Chávez fired the majority of PDVSA senior executives and many workers, horrifying many Venezuelan and foreign elites, (Dittrick, 2009). Second, there is PetroCaribe, an initiative launched in 2005. Through it, Venezuela supplies poor countries in the region with oil on preferential terms.[13] PetroCaribe aims to establish "a regional supply, refining, and transportation and storage network," and it includes a development fund for participating countries (Sullivan, Rush, and Seelke, 2008: 14). As of late 2009, PetroCaribe included most Caribbean countries plus Nicaragua and Honduras. Third, Venezuela has formed an accord with Bolivia, called PetroAndina, which will supply about 8,300 bpd to Bolivia via a joint venture. Fourth, PDVSA

---

13. PetroCaribe is just the latest in a long line of such programs, however, and some of them predate Chávez. Also, Chávez, through PDVSA's US-based refining subsidiary, Citgo, Venezuela even has provided low-cost heating oil to needy families in the US (Sullivan, Rush, and Seelke, 2008; James, 2006).

has spearheaded the Petroamerica initiative, the aim of which is to use the region's vast energy reserves in hydroelectric power and fossil fuels as the "backbone" for a modern regional economy and continental integration (Wertheim, 2004). Finally, Venezuela has invested in the energy sectors of several of its Latin American neighbors. It has plans to invest $1.5 billion in the Bolivian gas industry, has an agreement with Ecuador for joint ventures in oil, gas and refining, and has a refinery project in Northeastern Brazil that began construction in 2007. In 2006, Venezuela and Colombia agreed to construct a gas pipeline project. There is a joint hydrocarbon exploration and development project with Argentina (signed in 2006), and numerous cooperative projects in Cuba (Sullivan, Rush, and Seelke, 2008).

Another of President Chávez's strategies for securing regional leadership has been to cultivate outside allegiances, particularly with US rivals. Venezuela was a founding member of the Organization of Petroleum Exporting Countries (OPEC) in 1960, well before Chávez's time, but since taking office he has tried to use the organization to promote his socialist goals and to criticize the United States (Williams and Chmaytelli, 2007). He has also sought closer ties with Russia, based on the commonality of being major energy producing states. He has said he would offer Russia a military base in Venezuela if President Medvedev wants one. The two countries have formed a "strategic partnership," which seems mainly to consist of Russia selling arms to Venezuela. Chávez has also tried to cultivate Iran. All three countries dislike the United States and all three have an interest in trying to keep energy prices from falling too much. The point, however, is the strong symbolism and the recurring anti-American theme in Venezuela's regional vision (Watkins, 2008).

Despite ALBA's rhetorical commitment to building "21st Century Socialism," Venezuela's petroleum wealth clearly provides much of the organization's glue, a fact that makes Chávez's regional plans dependent on the world oil market. Oil is 90% of Venezuelan exports and provides over half of government income. "For each $10 drop in the oil price, the government gets $5 billion (1.4% of GDP) less in revenue" ("An Axis in Need of Oiling," 2008: 71-72). World petroleum prices have been highly volatile in the past decade, rising from about US$17 dollars per barrel in 1998 to over $95 dollars per barrel in 2007, then plummeting by mid 2009 to below US$50 dollars per barrel.[14] During the crash that began in early 2008, many proj-

---

14. All figures are in constant 2008 dollars. See "Oil price history and analysis" and the table "Crude Oil Prices, 1947-August 2009" at www.wtrg.com, accessed 26 February 2010.

ects advocated by President Chávez stalled, including a continental gas pipeline from Venezuela to Argentina, and as many as eight refineries throughout the region. Venezuelan aid to its neighbors also became more difficult. In May 2009, *The New York Times* reported that Venezuela was expected to spend only US$6 billion overseas in 2009, compared with US$79 billion in 2008, and noting further that Venezuelan allies like Argentina and Ecuador were looking elsewhere for support ("Venezuela's Hope," 2009: A8). In 2009 Argentina closed a trade deal with China, Ecuador renewed relations with the IMF and the United States, and even Cuba began exploring improved ties with Washington and the new Obama administration. The larger countries in Latin America have also seemed to be cultivating energy relationships away from Venezuela, turning to Russia, Trinidad and Tobago, and even Brazil, with its new deep sea oil and natural gas discoveries ("Venezuela's Hope," 2009: A8). Whether these efforts were politically motivated or the result of economic prudence (or both), however, is not clear.

The 2008-2009 drop in world oil prices, combined with President Chávez's management of his domestic oil sector, has also created problems for him at home. In 2010, Venezuela suffered from high inflation, labor union tension, and slowing economic growth. The oil industry is still reeling from Chávez's nationalizations of PDVSA and foreign oil contracts, and there is insufficient technology and expertise to develop the Orinoco fields or to embark on further off shore exploration. There is also illegal smuggling of fuel to Colombia, export delays, and increasing debts. In early 2008, Chávez seized the assets of several domestic and foreign oil contractors rather than pay more than $10 billion in debts owed to them ("Venezuela's Hope," 2009: A8). All of these factors reflect the vulnerability of Venezuela's regional vision to the vagaries of the world oil market.

Nevertheless, Venezuela still has a great deal of influence, and a strengthening of world oil prices, as now seems to be occurring, can significantly improve both Venezuela's domestic economic prospects and its ability to fund ALBA's energy vision. As of early 2010, energy prices seem to be rising again, with oil futures on the New York Mercantile Exchange (NYMEX) increasing steadily from $34 dollars per barrel in March 2009 to $78 dollars per barrel in February 2010.[15] Venezuela has closed deals with both Russia and China to exploit the Orinoco fields (Tockman, 2009), and in February 2010 once again awarded contracts to western foreign oil companies,

---

15. From graph of "NYMEX Crude Oil Futures" at www.wtrg.com, accessed 26 February 2010.

including Chevron (Romero, 2010). Many Central American and Caribbean countries are dependent on Venezuelan oil subsidies and special payment arrangements. In 2008, they had debts to Venezuela of $5.5 billion. Venezuela's idea for a Bank of the South also seems to be making progress, though there is no set starting date for operations. And ALBA still has wide ideological appeal, especially to the region's poorest countries ("Venezuela's Hope," 2009: A8). Finally, the smaller and poorer countries of the hemisphere question the ability of Obama to offer an alternative attractive to them (Weisbrot, 2009).

With regard to the role of the state in the energy sector, the ALBA vision is the most state-directed of the three visions we discuss. ALBA explicitly calls for the state to use energy wealth to improve social welfare and reduce inequality. Market considerations, and the interests of private actors are clearly subordinate to the "social good." If Chávez's domestic energy policies are indicative of his broader regional vision, then the role for private capital in regional energy extraction and distribution would be tightly circumscribed by states. The energy assets themselves also would not be left in the hands of private companies, but rather, administered by states in the name of their people.

## THE BRAZILIAN VISION: FROM MERCOSUR TO UNASUR

We use "UNASUR approach" to describe the efforts at regional cooperation pursued by the countries of MERCOSUR and the Andean Community. These efforts culminated in the creation of UNASUR in 2008, although the idea for such a union existed as early as 2004. UNASUR was formalized in the Constitutive Treaty of the South American Union of Nations, signed by the MERCOSUR and Andean countries, as well as Chile, Guyana, and Suriname. Its goals are very ambitious, moving well beyond economic cooperation and integration. Its preamble states that UNASUR will work "to eliminate socio-economic inequality, achieve social inclusion and civil-society participation, strengthen democracy, and reduce asymmetries" (ECLAC, 2008: 103). It also has a range of more specific goals, including energy integration. UNASUR's institutions include four bodies: the Council of Heads of State and Government, the Council of Ministers of Foreign Affairs, the Council of Delegates, and the General Secretariat. The General Secretariat is to be headquartered in Quito. However, as of early 2010, UNASUR's constitutive treaty had yet to be signed and ratified by member countries.[16]

Brazil has been a prime mover in the formation of UNASUR, just as it was in the formation of MERCOSUR in 1991 (Armijo and Kearney, 2008). At the same time, UNASUR's proposed institutions and even its name reflect accommodations with the sensitivities of other states, particularly Venezuela. Even so, UNASUR's incipient approach to regionalism reflects to a large extent Brazil's approach to regional and economic development, which puts the state, as well as political interests, front and center. Scholars have noted MERCOSUR's deviation from the "new regionalism" model of bottom-up, market, and civil-society generated integration (Gómez-Mera, 2008). MERCOSUR began and has continued to be as much about political alliances and state building as it has been about freer trade per se. With its weak institutionalization, low participation of economic interest groups, and reliance on government leaders to keep it alive, MERCOSUR retains elements of the "old regionalism" (Grugel, 2006; Gómez-Mera, 2008). In a similar vein, Brazil's vision of regionalism, as manifest in the UNASUR initiative, retains a strong role for state leadership in economic development (Burges, 2006). Where the NAFTA-plus vision focuses on regulatory integration of all of the hemisphere's economies by rewriting domestic economic legislation to give transnational businesses a stable environment for investment, Brazil's UNASUR vision represents a contemporary, more pro-market incarnation of South America's tradition of structuralism, which recognizes that the state has an ongoing and crucial role to play in guiding and promoting economic development (Prebisch, 1949; Furtado, 1959).

Brazil's preferences for the energy sector lie between those of the United States and Venezuela. Brazil has regional and global leadership aspirations, but it takes a pragmatic approach. Its attitude toward the United States is conciliatory but firm, as reflected in a recent statement by foreign minister Celso Amorim: "We want to have a good relationship with the United States. But we don't depend on external tutelage" ("The Samba Beat," 2008: 57). Brazil takes a middle position in the debate over whether the state or the private sector should take the lead in the energy sector, emphasizing

---

16. In using UNASUR as a short hand for Brazil's vision of regionalism, we do not wish to suggest that all of the countries that signed the treaty agree with Brazil's vision of economic and energy integration. Both CAN and MERCOSUR have been plagued by internal divisions, Chile has initiated and terminated associations with both groups, and UNASUR itself is already experiencing disagreements. For more extensive treatment of these dynamics see Gómez-Mera (2008), Malamud (2005), and ECLAC (2008).

that there is a role for both. Petrobras, Brazil's leading oil company, is evidence of this stance, being mostly state-owned but having a substantial number of private shareholders too.[17] In terms of scope, Brazil privileges South American initiatives over hemispheric ones, and on the social welfare aspects of energy policy, it shows more explicit concern than does the United States, but is far less militant and populist than Venezuela. In an interview with Newsweek, for example, President Lula mildly noted that recent Brazilian oil discoveries are important because they can be used to help overcome social problems like poverty and lack of education ("Lula Wants to Fight," 2009: 43).[18]

Like Venezuela, Brazil has significant energy wealth. As of January 1, 2010, its estimated proven oil reserves were 12.8 billion barrels and its natural gas reserves were 12.8 trillion cubic feet, ranking fourth and seventh largest respectively in the western hemisphere (Radler, 2009). Brazilian oil reserves were only about 1% of the world's estimated total in 2007, but recent discoveries in pre-salt fields[19] off the southern coast may amount to as much as 40 billion barrels, which would place Brazil eighth in the world ("More Bounty," 2008: 82; IEA, 2009). Brazil is also significant in terms of production and consumption. In 2006, Brazil was the third largest producer of oil after Venezuela and Mexico, and the fifth largest producer of natural gas after Mexico, Argentina, Venezuela, and Trinidad and Tobago. It had the largest installed capacity for the generation of electricity (about 36 % of the regional total), and it accounted for well over a third of Latin America's total final energy consumption (OLADE, 2007). Currently, Brazil is one of the top ten oil consumers in the world (IEA, 2009).

Brazil is also an important energy actor because of its industry leadership. Petrobras, the state oil company, is Brazil's largest company. Founded in 1953, it was instrumental in the development of Brazil's capital goods industry, and it currently has projects and investments in more than 25 countries, including almost all of the countries in South America. Projects involve exploration and production, refining, marketing and transportation, petrochemicals, distribution, biofuels, and natural gas. Its proven reserves in 2007 were the equivalent of 15 billion barrels of oil (boe). It also

---

17. The structure of Petrobras is complex, and includes multiple subsidiaries. See the Petrobras website: http://www2.petrobras.com.br/ingles/index.asp.

18. Some in the Brazilian Congress, however, think that President Lula's plan for tying Brazil's health and education funding to Petrobras' revenues will place these programs' future funding at risk ("Brazil's Lula meets foes," 2009).

19. The fields are called "pre-salt" because the oil is located deep beneath the ocean floor under a thick layer of salt, which makes extracting it difficult.

had 15 refineries, thousands of kilometers of ducts and close to 6000 service stations. Petrobras' net income in 2007 was $13 billion, which enabled it to fund investments of $21 billion. It plans to invest $174.4 billion between 2009 and 2013, with an annual average of $34.9 billion in Brazil and $3.2 billion abroad. The company actively seeks partnerships with companies in other countries ("New Horizons," 2009) Petrobras' investments abroad may be one of the reasons that for the first time, in January 2008, Brazil became a net foreign exchange creditor (Parra-Bernal and Pimentel, 2008). The Brazilian National Development Bank (BNDES) also provides a significant amount of financing for energy projects in the region, lending not only to Brazilian entities, but also to foreign governments, as in a recent controversial case with the government of Ecuador involving a hydropower project (discussed further below). The BNDES also partners with multilateral lending agencies, such as the Inter-American Development Bank, which is a major sponsor of the IIRSA initiative (also discussed below).

Brazilian companies are also large players in energy construction. At the South American Presidential Summit in August of 2000, the Brazilian government began to promote a plan called Integração da Infraestrutura Regional na América do Sul (IIRSA, South American Regional Infrastructure Integration), whose purpose is to create "axes of development" that will connect different regions of South America via "corridors" of energy, transportation, and communications infrastructure. The idea is to foster "regional production chains" that will help South America exploit its global competitive advantages (Burges, 2006). Energy is a big part of IIRSA, and companies like Odebrecht are involved in building power plants and dams throughout the region. Odebrecht is the largest construction company in Latin America and the third largest company in Brazil. It was founded in 1944, operates in 20 countries—including all of the South American countries—and had recorded earnings in 2007 of $17 billion (Zibechi, 2009: 3). As Raúl Zibechi (2009) notes, this figure is more than the GDPs of Bolivia and Paraguay combined. Overall, Brazilian foreign direct investment (FDI) was $71 billion by 2005, much of it in Latin America. By comparison, Mexico was a distant second with FDI of only $28 billion (Zibechi, 2009: 1).

The regional energy projects and partnerships that involve Brazil are far too numerous to list here. But several have been in the news recently due to disputes with other countries. As the Brazilian economy continues to grow and strengthen, and Brazilian companies engage in foreign investment, other Latin American countries are making accusations of imperialism, which Brazil's neighbors periodically have leveled against it since the nineteenth century. The Andean countries have been the most vocal, perhaps inspired by Hugo Chávez and his Bolivarian socialist ideology. In 2006, Bolivia nationalized two Brazilian oil refineries built by Petrobras, as part of a more general effort on the part of President Morales to gain national control over energy production ("The Samba Beat," 2008: 57). In September 2008, Ecuador had a significant dispute with Odebrecht regarding a hydroelectric plant it failed to build to specification, which resulted in power losses due to dam shutdowns, as well as damage to aquifers and springs. President Rafael Correa had the Army surround four Odebrecht projects, froze the company's assets, and threatened to stop payment on a $243 million loan from the Brazilian national development bank. Correa then kicked Odebrecht out of the country and said he would oust other Brazilian companies too, including Petrobras. He accused the Brazilians of "disrespecting national sovereignty" (Margolis, 2008: 52-53). Shortly thereafter, in November 2008, Venezuela's President Chávez charged Odebrecht with $282 million in "extra" taxes, leading to a serious dispute with the Brazilian government. The company claimed it had already paid its full tax bill, and there was speculation that the additional taxes were levied as punishment for the company's behavior in Ecuador ("Update 2," 2008). Regarding Venezuelan accession to MERCOSUR, Chávez also called the Brazilian Congress "Washington's parrot" (Margolis, 2008: 52-53).

Brazil has also had conflicts with Paraguay. Paraguay's president, Fernando Lugo, ran on an "energy independence" platform, and upon election embarked on negotiations with Brazil over the Itaipú dam, which the two countries share. Paraguay has long held that Brazil does not pay enough for power imports from the plant. When construction began on the dam in 1973, the two countries signed a treaty specifying that each country had a right to 50% of the energy generated by the dam's power plant, but that they had to sell any unused energy to one another. The power plant began generating electricity in 1984, and for its entire history, Paraguay has used far less of its electricity than has Brazil. It is estimated that 90% of the plant's electricity goes to Brazilian industry. In 1985, Paraguay agreed to sell its unused electricity to Brazil at below-market prices in order to help Brazil with its balance of payments problems. This situation continued, however, until very recently, and was the focus of President Lugo's complaints to Brazil. He wanted Brazil to pay Paraguay more for Itaipú electricity, and he wanted the right to sell electricity to third parties (Barrionuevo, 2009; Margolis, 2008).

On the surface, Brazil seems not to do much about actions from neighboring countries that seemingly threaten its interests. Unlike its reactions to industrialized countries, where it has not hesitated to bring World Trade Organization (WTO) cases, with Latin American countries Brazil appears tolerant. In the Paraguayan case just discussed, although Brazil at first refused to renegotiate the Itaipú agreement, it ultimately relented in July 2009. The two countries signed a new deal, which will triple what Brazil pays yearly for Paraguay's unused electricity (from $124 million to $360 million) and allow Paraguay to sell electricity directly to the Brazilian market, bypassing Brazilian state electricity companies. Referring to the deal, Lula said in a speech in Asunción, "Brazil is not interested in growing and developing if its partners don't grow and don't develop" (Barrionuevo, 2009: A10). When Bolivia nationalized Petrobras' refineries, Brazilian officials said that Morales was "exercising his country's sovereign rights" (Margolis, 2008: 52-53). Lula asked rhetorically, "What do you want us to do, invade Bolivia?" (Margolis, 2008: 52-53). He said further that powerful countries like Brazil "must show solidarity with the poorer countries" (Margolis, 2008: 52-53).

On the one hand, Brazil seems to understand that these outbursts are the price of success. Brazil's diplomats note that their country's rising economic power means that at every meeting on trade, they are confronted with a demand to do more for their neighbors ("The Samba Beat," 2008: 57). At the same time, these neighbors are supplying Brazil with essential resources, and Brazil cannot afford to alienate them. Perhaps for this reason Brazil refrains from open criticism. Lula refuses to be bated into criticizing Venezuelan democracy, for example. There are Brazilians that want their country to do more in the face of these actions by neighbors. Brazilian political analyst Amaury de Souza has said, "We're getting our butts kicked by mice" ("The Samba Beat," 2008: 57). Also, in October 2008, the Brazilian Defense Ministry formulated a new National Mobilization Strategy, which Lula has signed. It has stronger rules for responding to "rogue nations" and "actions that damage national sovereignty" (Margolis, 2008: 52-53). For the most part, however, Brazil is subtle. "Brazil never criticises Mr. Chávez in public but it increasingly seeks to outflank him" ("The Samba Beat," 2008: 57).

Two final energy issues concerning Brazil's role in the region are worth mentioning. First, as discussed above, Brazil has taken the lead on efforts to promote biofuels and renewable energy. Given the currently large and growing demand internationally in this sector, the Brazilian government views expansion as both imperative and highly lucrative. Brazil has actively pursued greater market access for its sugar and ethanol exports in international trade fora, winning a 2004 case in the WTO against European Union (EU) sugar subsidies. It has also made sugar and ethanol part of a broader agricultural export drive, one that has been highly successful. Finally, at home and abroad Brazilian policy makers have been pushing ethanol as a substitute for gasoline, on both economic and environmental grounds. Brazil has even agreed to help other poor countries, such as Jamaica and India, develop their own self-sustaining ethanol industries (Beattie, 2006). Brazil sponsored the Brasília Platform on Renewable Energies in 2003, and in 2007 partnered with the United States to promote biofuels in the western hemisphere.

Second, Brazil is thinking of joining OPEC. Lula has recently said that Brazil will participate very soon. The initial invitation from Saudi Arabia came in September of 2008. The renewed invitation came in March 2009. Brazil initially declined, saying that it planned to export refined petroleum products like gasoline and not crude oil. Lula reiterated this intention earlier this year. If Brazil joins OPEC, it could mark a major shift in policy. At any rate, Brazil cannot join immediately because it would not be able to implement OPEC production cuts. Brazil uses all the oil it produces and still imports oil (Watkins, 2009).

## CONCLUSIONS

As we noted in this chapter's beginning, energy integration in the Americas is incipient but likely to be on going and ultimately profound. We have described three visions for regional integration, each promoted by an important state, and each with a distinct vision of energy policy. The United States' NAFTA-plus approach is in general pro-private enterprise and pro-market. For energy integration, it would use multilateral and bilateral free trade agreements to tie Latin American energy producers to the US market by a combination of long-term contracts and foreign direct investment. It sees the proper role for the state in the economy as a minimal, regulatory one. Venezuela's ALBA vision takes much the opposite view. The role for the state is extensive, both in its general integration vision and its energy policy initiatives. It would use Chávez-brokered deals to exchange subsidized energy or finance for other goods and services, such as Cuban medical personnel, and political support for Venezuela-centric energy infrastructure. The stated goal in all cases would be to improve social welfare. Finally,

Brazil's UNASUR vision lies between the two extremes. Regional integration would have roles for both states and private actors. For energy policy specifically, it would involve a perhaps uneasy coexistence of "green energy" promotion and a push for continental energy infrastructure, such as binational or multinational hydroelectric projects built via the IDB-funded IIRSA initiative.

For several reasons, we find that Brazil's vision of energy integration is the most likely to endure in South America. First, there is the seriousness of Brazil's commitment to South America. One sign of this is Brazil's allocation of diplomatic resources over the past seven years. Since 2002, the number of diplomats from Itamaraty (Brazil's foreign ministry) posted in South America has nearly doubled, while the number in Europe has declined substantially. Brazil hopes regional involvement will promote better relations with Argentina, strengthen democracy and political stability in the region, and "consolidate regional support for the expansion of [Brazil's] presence in world affairs" (Soares de Lima and Hirst, 2006: 31). In achieving all of these goals, Brazilian participation and financing of infrastructure and energy projects are important bargaining tools. Not only do improvements in these areas help insure Brazil's continued economic health and expansion, but they also offer opportunities to Brazil's poorer neighbors, and they potentially foster good will in regional inter-governmental relations (Burges, 2006). Countries in the region have had specific disputes with Brazilian corporations and with the Brazilian government, but these do not seem to have detracted from the broader appeal of Brazil's vision and leadership. Brazil's low-key management of its power has helped it to weather disputes and maintain good relations with neighbors, while Lula in particular has been a popular and revered role model (Margolis, 2008).

Second, contemporary economic debates may favor Brazil's model, especially as the larger emerging markets seek to deepen their investments in infrastructure and energy. Commitment from multilateral institutions like the IDB to the energy and infrastructure projects of the IIRSA is already strong. With world class institutions like Petrobras and the BNDES offering partnerships or deals to private firms, foreign governments, and international governmental institutions alike, Brazil's integration plans may well have the best chance of surviving tough economic times—especially given new discoveries and growing demand in the region.

Third, but perhaps least recognized in the often highly-technical debates over economic integration, is the fact that the UNASUR vision, and Brazil's prominent but not overwhelming role within the UNASUR institutional framework, receives enormous political benefits in the other capitals of South America by the existence of realistic, but potentially more threatening, integration alternatives both to the right and to the left. The UNASUR approach to energy integration is notable for the moderate stance it strikes between the perhaps overly private-enterprise-friendly positions of the United States on the one hand, and the anti-market hostility of Venezuela on the other. Brazil has a long history of state economic management, production, investment, and regulation, and pragmatism is widely agreed to characterize Brazil's overall foreign policy stance. Evidence from the energy sector suggests that South America is rather likely to integrate with a continental, rather than a Latin/Caribbean or a hemispheric scope.

# APPENDIX
# ECONOMIC AND SOCIAL
# INDICATORS

*Laura Randall*

Table A-1: Brazil Economic Indicators, 1980–2009

| | Brazil GDP per capita, PPP[a] | World GDP per capita, PPP[a] | GDP growth (annual%) PPP[a] | Gross capital formation (% GDP) | Gross fixed capital formation (% GDP) | Gross savings[c] (% GDP) | FDI[b], Net inflow (% GDP) | FDI[b], Net outflow (% GDP) |
|---|---|---|---|---|---|---|---|---|
| 1980 | 7,572 | 5,949 | 9.11 | 23.35 | 22.90 | 17.87 | 0.81 | 0.16 |
| 1981 | 7,072 | 5,961 | -4.39 | 23.08 | 22.94 | 18.64 | 0.96 | 0.08 |
| 1982 | 6,950 | 5,890 | 0.58 | 21.09 | 21.44 | 15.29 | 1.03 | 0.13 |
| 1983 | 6,562 | 5,939 | -3.41 | 16.68 | 18.13 | 13.32 | 0.79 | 0.09 |
| 1984 | 6,756 | 6,107 | 5.27 | 15.74 | 16.89 | 15.76 | 0.76 | 0.02 |
| 1985 | 7,139 | 6,224 | 7.95 | 19.20 | 16.95 | 19.09 | 0.65 | 0.04 |
| 1986 | 7,554 | 6,327 | 7.99 | 19.09 | 19.09 | 17.12 | 0.13 | 0.05 |
| 1987 | 7,674 | 6,448 | 3.60 | 22.30 | 19.09 | 21.81 | 0.40 | 0.05 |
| 1988 | 7,524 | 6,627 | -0.10 | 22.72 | 22.30 | 23.94 | 0.85 | 0.05 |
| 1989 | 7,632 | 6,755 | 3.28 | 26.90 | 22.72 | 35.81 | 0.27 | 0.12 |
| 1990 | 7,179 | 6,813 | -4.30 | 20.17 | 26.90 | 18.92 | 0.21 | 0.14 |
| 1991 | 7,168 | 6,796 | 1.51 | 19.77 | 20.66 | 18.66 | 0.27 | 0.25 |
| 1992 | 7,022 | 6,807 | -0.47 | 18.93 | 18.42 | 20.09 | 0.53 | 0.04 |
| 1993 | 7,238 | 6,822 | 4.66 | 20.85 | 19.28 | 20.18 | 0.29 | 0.11 |
| 1994 | 7,510 | 6,934 | 5.33 | 22.15 | 20.75 | 21.27 | 0.56 | 0.19 |
| 1995 | 7,724 | 7,054 | 4.42 | 18.03 | 20.75 | 15.54 | 0.63 | 0.18 |
| 1996 | 7,771 | 7,213 | 2.15 | 17.04 | 18.32 | 14.08 | 1.33 | -0.06 |
| 1997 | 7,913 | 7,397 | 3.37 | 17.43 | 16.87 | 13.58 | 2.26 | 0.12 |
| 1998 | 7,799 | 7,475 | 0.04 | 17.03 | 17.37 | 13.03 | 3.78 | 0.32 |
| 1999 | 7,704 | 7,637 | 0.25 | 16.38 | 16.97 | 12.06 | 4.87 | 0.29 |
| 2000 | 7,921 | 7,883 | 4.31 | 18.25 | 15.66 | 13.94 | 5.08 | 0.35 |
| 2001 | 7,911 | 7,951 | 1.31 | 18.03 | 16.80 | 13.81 | 4.06 | -0.41 |
| 2002 | 8,010 | 8,058 | 2.66 | 16.20 | 17.03 | 15.16 | 3.29 | 0.49 |
| 2003 | 7,994 | 8,239 | 1.15 | 15.77 | 16.39 | 17.99 | 1.84 | 0.05 |
| 2004 | 8,344 | 8,547 | 5.71 | 17.12 | 15.28 | 20.36 | 2.74 | 1.43 |
| 2005 | 8,505 | 8,825 | 3.16 | 16.21 | 16.10 | 18.79 | 1.71 | 0.29 |
| 2006 | 8,744 | 9,166 | 3.96 | 16.77 | 15.94 | 18.68 | 1.72 | 2.59 |
| 2007 | 9,181 | 9,530 | 6.09 | 17.31 | 16.43 | 17.66 | 2.53 | 0.29 |
| 2008 | 9,559 | 9,688 | 5.14 | 18.21 | 17.10 | 16.86 | 2.75 | 0.52 |
| 2009 | 9,455 | 9,514 | -0.18 | 16.60 | 18.26 | 14.78 | 1.65 | 1.25 |

*Notes:* [a] Purchasing Power Parity in constant 2005 international dollars. [b] Foreign Direct Investment

*Source:* http://data.worldbank.org/country/brazil.

Table A-1: Brazil Economic Indicators, 1980–2009

| Year | Exports (% of GDP) | Imports (% of GDP) | Current account balance (% of GDP) | Money and quasi money (% of GDP) | Total debt service (% of exports)[a] | Interest payments on external debt (% of exports)[a] | Total reserves (% total external debt) | Tariff rate (%)[b] | Official exchange rate[c] | Inflation, GDP deflator (annual %) |
|---|---|---|---|---|---|---|---|---|---|---|
| 1980 | 9.05 | 11.31 | -5.46 | 18.49 | 63.25 | 33.90 | 9.61 | — | 0.05 | 87.31 |
| 1981 | 9.42 | 9.80 | -4.46 | 18.53 | 66.22 | 38.71 | 9.18 | — | 0.09 | 107.21 |
| 1982 | 7.61 | 8.27 | -5.79 | 18.97 | 81.76 | 49.50 | 4.26 | — | 0.18 | 104.83 |
| 1983 | 11.42 | 9.01 | -3.36 | 20.75 | 54.62 | 39.54 | 4.63 | — | 0.58 | 140.20 |
| 1984 | 13.55 | 7.92 | 0.02 | 20.89 | 45.34 | 30.94 | 11.52 | — | 1.85 | 212.79 |
| 1985 | 12.25 | 7.10 | -0.13 | 21.26 | 39.10 | 31.06 | 11.21 | — | 6.20 | 231.72 |
| 1986 | 8.82 | 6.35 | -1.98 | 16.03 | 46.19 | 30.96 | 6.19 | — | 13.66 | 145.27 |
| 1987 | 9.46 | 6.19 | -0.49 | 11.87 | 41.59 | 25.52 | 6.24 | — | 39.23 | 204.10 |
| 1988 | 10.89 | 5.69 | 1.26 | 38.71 | 45.72 | 34.29 | 6.89 | — | 262.38 | 651.11 |
| 1989 | 8.93 | 5.46 | 0.24 | 58.44 | 36.29 | 13.42 | 7.63 | 42.92 | 0.00 | 1,209.12 |
| 1990 | 8.20 | 6.96 | -0.83 | 17.25 | 22.13 | 6.13 | 7.68 | 33.50 | 0.00 | 2,735.49 |
| 1991 | 8.68 | 7.91 | -0.36 | 20.43 | 22.55 | 9.57 | 7.24 | 27.53 | 0.00 | 414.24 |
| 1992 | 10.87 | 8.39 | 1.56 | 32.11 | 20.23 | 8.91 | 18.03 | 23.45 | 0.00 | 968.18 |
| 1993 | 10.50 | 9.10 | 0.00 | 48.21 | 23.64 | 8.80 | 22.04 | 15.73 | 0.03 | 2,001.35 |
| 1994 | 9.51 | 9.16 | -0.21 | 24.62 | 30.04 | 11.68 | 25.26 | 14.46 | 0.64 | 2,251.70 |
| 1995 | 7.26 | 8.78 | -2.36 | 27.48 | 36.57 | 17.84 | 32.08 | 13.23 | 0.92 | 93.52 |
| 1996 | 6.57 | 8.37 | -2.77 | 31.36 | 42.22 | 17.50 | 32.92 | 15.05 | 1.01 | 17.09 |
| 1997 | 6.82 | 9.02 | -3.50 | 34.72 | 62.64 | 18.46 | 26.05 | 14.42 | 1.08 | 7.64 |
| 1998 | 6.93 | 8.93 | -4.01 | 38.10 | 79.45 | 23.90 | 18.18 | 17.15 | 1.16 | 4.23 |
| 1999 | 9.41 | 10.82 | -4.33 | 40.37 | 117.81 | 29.40 | 14.89 | 15.89 | 1.81 | 8.48 |
| 2000 | 9.98 | 11.74 | -3.76 | 43.37 | 93.55 | 24.68 | 13.67 | 16.55 | 1.83 | 6.18 |
| 2001 | 12.18 | 13.50 | -4.19 | 45.27 | 75.72 | 23.86 | 15.66 | 14.80 | 2.35 | 8.97 |
| 2002 | 14.10 | 12.58 | -1.51 | 44.02 | 69.40 | 19.94 | 16.38 | 14.56 | 2.92 | 10.55 |
| 2003 | 14.99 | 12.08 | 0.76 | 44.40 | 65.56 | 18.37 | 20.99 | 14.37 | 3.08 | 13.72 |
| 2004 | 16.43 | 12.55 | 1.77 | 46.38 | 46.63 | 12.82 | 24.12 | 13.28 | 2.93 | 8.04 |
| 2005 | 15.13 | 11.52 | 1.59 | 49.62 | 44.73 | 9.48 | 28.70 | 12.39 | 2.43 | 7.21 |
| 2006 | 14.37 | 11.47 | 1.25 | 53.58 | 37.30 | 8.87 | 44.36 | 12.20 | 2.18 | 6.15 |
| 2007 | 13.35 | 11.85 | 0.11 | 56.63 | 27.81 | 7.53 | 75.94 | 12.22 | 1.95 | 5.87 |
| 2008 | 13.79 | 13.63 | -1.72 | 59.12 | 22.73 | 6.49 | 75.81 | 12.22 | 1.83 | 7.39 |
| 2009 | 12.83 | 13.29 | -1.55 | — | — | — | — | 13.08 | 2.00 | 4.79 |

*Notes:* [a] Percent of exports of goods, services and income. [b] Applied, simple mean, all products. [c] LCU per US$, period average.

*Source:* http://data.worldbank.org/country/brazil.

I

## Table A-1: Brazil Economic Indicators, 1980–2009

| Year | Alternative and nuclear energy (% of total energy use) | GDP per unit of energy use (constant 2005 PPP $ per kg of oil equivalent) | Agricultural land (% of land area) | Fuel Imports (% merchandise imports) | Fuel Exports (% merchandise exports) | Labor participation rate, female (% of female pop. ages 15+) | Labor participation rate, total (% of total pop. ages 15+) |
|---|---|---|---|---|---|---|---|
| 1980 | 9.74 | 8.09 | 26.51 | 23.35 | 9.11 | 38.20 | 61.50 |
| 1981 | 10.32 | 8.08 | 26.69 | 23.08 | -4.39 | 39.40 | 62.10 |
| 1982 | 10.98 | 8.01 | 26.97 | 21.09 | 0.58 | 40.00 | 62.40 |
| 1983 | 11.45 | 7.52 | 27.05 | 16.68 | -3.41 | 41.00 | 63.00 |
| 1984 | 12.20 | 7.45 | 27.18 | 15.74 | 5.27 | 41.30 | 63.10 |
| 1985 | 12.56 | 7.53 | 27.31 | 19.20 | 7.95 | 41.60 | 63.10 |
| 1986 | 11.64 | 7.77 | 27.67 | 19.09 | 7.99 | 43.50 | 63.30 |
| 1987 | 11.56 | 7.75 | 27.87 | 22.30 | 3.60 | 43.50 | 64.50 |
| 1988 | 12.15 | 7.64 | 28.10 | 22.72 | -0.10 | 43.80 | 64.50 |
| 1989 | 12.49 | 7.75 | 28.30 | 26.90 | 3.28 | 43.90 | 64.50 |
| 1990 | 13.16 | 7.70 | 28.56 | 20.17 | -4.3 | 44.70 | 64.70 |
| 1991 | 13.44 | 7.67 | 28.95 | 19.77 | 1.51 | 48.50 | 66.50 |
| 1992 | 13.69 | 7.55 | 29.16 | 18.93 | -0.47 | 52.20 | 68.40 |
| 1993 | 13.81 | 7.71 | 29.49 | 20.85 | 4.66 | 52.30 | 68.30 |
| 1994 | 13.48 | 7.72 | 29.72 | 22.15 | 5.33 | 52.90 | 68.50 |
| 1995 | 14.04 | 7.80 | 30.55 | 18.03 | 4.42 | 53.60 | 68.60 |
| 1996 | 13.92 | 7.56 | 30.62 | 17.04 | 2.15 | 53.50 | 66.90 |
| 1997 | 13.95 | 7.41 | 30.68 | 17.43 | 3.37 | 51.80 | 67.60 |
| 1998 | 14.22 | 7.24 | 30.75 | 17.03 | 0.04 | 52.80 | 67.60 |
| 1999 | 14.04 | 7.07 | 30.82 | 16.38 | 0.25 | 53.20 | 67.60 |
| 2000 | 14.70 | 7.29 | 30.90 | 18.25 | 4.31 | 54.80 | 68.30 |
| 2001 | 14.09 | 7.34 | 31.14 | 18.03 | 1.31 | 54.70 | 68.00 |
| 2002 | 14.44 | 7.33 | 31.16 | 16.20 | 2.66 | 56.20 | 68.60 |
| 2003 | 15.02 | 7.30 | 31.16 | 15.77 | 1.15 | 56.60 | 68.70 |
| 2004 | 14.62 | 7.31 | 31.18 | 17.12 | 5.71 | 57.60 | 69.40 |
| 2005 | 14.70 | 7.34 | 31.21 | 16.21 | 3.16 | 58.50 | 70.10 |
| 2006 | 15.12 | 7.38 | 31.21 | 16.77 | 3.96 | 59.50 | 70.80 |
| 2007 | 15.10 | 7.41 | 31.15 | 17.31 | 6.09 | 59.10 | 70.30 |
| 2008 | — | — | — | 18.21 | 5.14 | 59.90 | 70.70 |
| 2009 | — | — | — | 16.60 | -0.18 | — | — |

*Source*: http://data.worldbank.org/country/brazil

Table A-2: Brazil Population and Social Indicators, 1980–2009

| | Population growth rate | Rural Population (% of total population) | Telephone lines (per 100 people) | Fertility rate (births per woman) | Birth rate, crude (per 1,000 people) | Death rate, crude (per 1,000 people) | Life expectancy at birth (years) | Life expectancy at birth, female ages (years) | Population ages 0-14 (% of total) | Population ages 65 and above |
|---|---|---|---|---|---|---|---|---|---|---|
| 1980 | 2.34 | 32.60 | 4.07 | 4.07 | 31.95 | 8.67 | 62.49 | 65.30 | 38.08 | 4.11 |
| 1981 | 2.34 | 31.82 | 4.28 | 3.97 | 31.53 | 8.50 | 62.89 | 65.87 | 37.81 | 4.12 |
| 1982 | 2.32 | 31.04 | 4.57 | 3.85 | 30.99 | 8.33 | 63.28 | 66.43 | 37.59 | 4.12 |
| 1983 | 2.28 | 30.26 | 4.83 | 3.72 | 30.34 | 8.15 | 63.66 | 66.96 | 37.40 | 4.12 |
| 1984 | 2.22 | 29.48 | 5.03 | 3.59 | 29.57 | 7.98 | 64.04 | 67.47 | 37.20 | 4.13 |
| 1985 | 2.13 | 28.70 | 5.29 | 3.45 | 28.71 | 7.80 | 64.42 | 67.95 | 36.98 | 4.15 |
| 1986 | 2.04 | 28.00 | 5.36 | 3.31 | 27.78 | 7.63 | 64.80 | 68.40 | 36.72 | 4.18 |
| 1987 | 1.96 | 27.30 | 5.51 | 3.17 | 26.82 | 7.47 | 65.17 | 68.84 | 36.43 | 4.22 |
| 1988 | 1.88 | 26.60 | 5.73 | 3.04 | 25.88 | 7.31 | 65.54 | 69.27 | 36.10 | 4.28 |
| 1989 | 1.80 | 25.90 | 5.98 | 2.92 | 25.00 | 7.17 | 65.92 | 69.70 | 35.72 | 4.35 |
| 1990 | 1.73 | 25.20 | 6.29 | 2.81 | 24.20 | 7.05 | 66.30 | 70.13 | 35.29 | 4.43 |
| 1991 | 1.65 | 24.60 | 6.63 | 2.72 | 23.52 | 6.94 | 66.69 | 70.57 | 34.80 | 4.53 |
| 1992 | 1.58 | 24.00 | 7.02 | 2.64 | 22.97 | 6.83 | 67.09 | 71.01 | 34.26 | 4.64 |
| 1993 | 1.53 | 23.40 | 7.21 | 2.58 | 22.53 | 6.74 | 67.49 | 71.44 | 33.69 | 4.75 |
| 1994 | 1.51 | 22.80 | 7.70 | 2.54 | 22.20 | 6.66 | 67.91 | 71.88 | 33.10 | 4.87 |
| 1995 | 1.51 | 22.20 | 8.20 | 2.50 | 21.95 | 6.59 | 68.32 | 72.30 | 32.49 | 4.97 |
| 1996 | 1.51 | 21.52 | 9.20 | 2.47 | 21.76 | 6.53 | 68.72 | 72.71 | 31.89 | 5.08 |
| 1997 | 1.50 | 20.84 | 10.22 | 2.45 | 21.59 | 6.48 | 69.11 | 73.10 | 31.28 | 5.17 |
| 1998 | 1.50 | 20.16 | 11.82 | 2.43 | 21.41 | 6.44 | 69.49 | 73.47 | 30.68 | 5.27 |
| 1999 | 1.47 | 19.48 | 14.55 | 2.40 | 21.18 | 6.41 | 69.85 | 73.82 | 30.12 | 5.37 |
| 2000 | 1.44 | 18.80 | 17.76 | 2.36 | 20.88 | 6.39 | 70.19 | 74.15 | 29.60 | 5.49 |
| 2001 | 1.42 | 18.20 | 21.19 | 2.32 | 20.48 | 6.37 | 70.50 | 74.45 | 29.13 | 5.61 |
| 2002 | 1.38 | 17.60 | 21.67 | 2.27 | 20.00 | 6.36 | 70.81 | 74.72 | 28.71 | 5.75 |
| 2003 | 1.34 | 17.00 | 21.60 | 2.21 | 19.44 | 6.35 | 71.10 | 74.99 | 28.31 | 5.89 |
| 2004 | 1.27 | 16.40 | 21.53 | 2.14 | 18.82 | 6.34 | 71.38 | 75.23 | 27.93 | 6.03 |
| 2005 | 1.19 | 15.80 | 21.42 | 2.08 | 18.15 | 6.34 | 71.65 | 75.47 | 27.55 | 6.17 |
| 2006 | 1.11 | 15.34 | 20.62 | 2.01 | 17.48 | 6.35 | 71.91 | 75.70 | 27.16 | 6.30 |
| 2007 | 1.04 | 14.88 | 20.72 | 1.94 | 16.81 | 6.36 | 72.16 | 75.93 | 26.77 | 6.44 |
| 2008 | 0.97 | 14.42 | 21.43 | 1.88 | 16.19 | 6.38 | 72.40 | 76.16 | 26.36 | 6.58 |
| 2009 | 0.91 | 13.96 | — | — | — | — | — | — | 25.93 | 6.73 |

*Source:*http://data.worldbank.org/country/brazil.

Table A-2: Brazil Population and Social Indicators, 1980–2009

| Year | Unemployment, total (% of total labor force) | Unemployment, male (% of male labor force) | Unemployment, female (% of female labor force) | Female labor force (% of total labor) | Poverty gap at $1.25 a day (PPP) (%) | Poverty gap at $2 a day (PPP) (%) | Poverty headcount ratio at $1.25 a day, PPP (% of population) | Poverty headcount ratio at $2 a day, PPP (% of population) |
|---|---|---|---|---|---|---|---|---|
| 1980 | - | - | - | 31.27 | - | - | - | - |
| 1981 | 4.30 | 4.20 | 4.40 | 31.96 | 5.18 | 12.38 | 17.10 | 31.12 |
| 1982 | - | - | - | 32.32 | 5.46 | 12.68 | 17.52 | 31.32 |
| 1983 | 4.90 | 4.90 | 4.80 | 32.85 | 6.64 | 14.96 | 20.86 | 36.01 |
| 1984 | 4.30 | 4.10 | 4.60 | 33.08 | 6.36 | 14.74 | 20.56 | 36.08 |
| 1985 | 3.40 | 3.90 | 3.90 | 33.12 | 5.33 | 12.63 | 17.51 | 31.48 |
| 1986 | 2.40 | 2.20 | 2.70 | 33.29 | 3.13 | 8.99 | 12.29 | 24.80 |
| 1987 | 3.60 | 3.30 | 4.00 | 34.20 | 5.47 | 12.15 | 16.68 | 29.42 |
| 1988 | 3.80 | 3.50 | 4.30 | 34.47 | 5.93 | 12.83 | 17.66 | 30.48 |
| 1989 | 3.00 | 3.00 | 3.00 | 34.58 | 4.29 | 10.53 | 14.59 | 26.75 |
| 1990 | 3.70 | 3.80 | 3.50 | 35.14 | 4.81 | 11.22 | 15.49 | 27.83 |
| 1991 | - | - | - | 37.13 | - | - | - | - |
| 1992 | 6.40 | 5.40 | 7.90 | 38.89 | 4.30 | 9.81 | 13.29 | 24.42 |
| 1993 | 6.00 | 5.20 | 7.30 | 39.05 | 3.78 | 9.49 | 12.97 | 24.69 |
| 1994 | - | - | - | 39.41 | - | - | - | - |
| 1995 | 6.00 | 5.10 | 7.20 | 39.90 | 2.56 | 7.74 | 10.51 | 21.92 |
| 1996 | 6.80 | 5.50 | 8.60 | 39.56 | 3.05 | 8.36 | 11.43 | 22.64 |
| 1997 | 7.70 | 6.20 | 9.80 | 39.93 | 3.31 | 8.75 | 11.98 | 23.32 |
| 1998 | 8.90 | 7.10 | 11.50 | 40.24 | 2.78 | 8.10 | 11.03 | 22.55 |
| 1999 | 9.60 | 7.80 | 12.10 | 41.04 | 2.76 | 8.20 | 11.15 | 23.00 |
| 2000 | - | - | - | 41.17 | - | - | - | - |
| 2001 | 9.30 | 7.50 | 11.90 | 41.30 | 2.83 | 8.06 | 10.96 | 22.28 |
| 2002 | 9.10 | 7.30 | 11.50 | 41.96 | 2.24 | 7.30 | 9.81 | 21.32 |
| 2003 | 9.70 | 7.80 | 12.30 | 42.22 | 2.60 | 7.71 | 10.43 | 21.74 |
| 2004 | 8.90 | 6.80 | 11.70 | 42.55 | 3.84 | 7.58 | 11.68 | 20.93 |
| 2005 | 9.30 | 7.10 | 12.20 | 42.80 | 1.59 | 5.93 | 7.76 | 18.34 |
| 2006 | 8.40 | 6.40 | 11.00 | 43.11 | 1.84 | 5.62 | 7.36 | 16.38 |
| 2007 | 9.30 | 7.40 | 11.60 | 43.14 | 1.26 | 4.15 | 5.21 | 12.69 |
| 2008 | 7.90 | 6.10 | 10.00 | 43.50 | - | - | - | - |
| 2009 | - | - | - | - | - | - | - | - |

*Source:* http://data.worldbank.org/country/brazil.

# ABBREVIATIONS AND ACRONYMS

| | |
|---|---|
| ABDI | Agência Brasileira de Desenvolvimento Industrial (Brazilian Agency of Industrial Development) |
| ABI | Associação Brasileira de Imprensa (Brazilian Press Association) |
| ABONG | Associação Brasileira de Organizações Não Governamentais (Brazilian Association of Non-Govermental Organizations) |
| AIG | American International Group |
| ALADI | Associação Latino-Americana de Integração (Latin American Integration Association) |
| ALBA | Alianza Bolivariana para los Pueblos de Nuestra América (Bolivarian Alliance for the Americas) |
| ANP | Agência Nacional do Petróleo (National Petroleum Agency) |
| ARPEL | Asociación Regional de Empresas de Petróleo y Gas Natural en Latinoamérica y el Caribe (Regional Association of Latin American and Caribbean Oil and Natural Gas Companies) |
| BIB | Banco de Investimentos do Brasil (Investment Bank of Brazil) |
| BNDE | Banco Nacional de Desenvolvimento Econômico (National Bank of Economic Development) |
| BNH | Banco Nacional da Habitação (National Bank of Housing) |
| Bovespa | São Paulo Stock Exchange |

375

| | |
|---|---|
| CACM | Central American Common Market |
| CAR | Centros Administrativos Regionais (Regional Administrative Centers) |
| CDES | Conselho de Desenvolvimento Econômico e Social (Council of Economic and Social Development) |
| CEF | Caixa Econômica Federal (Federal Savings and Loans Bank) |
| CETIP | S.A. Balcão Organizado de Ativos e Derivativos (Over-the-Counter Fixed Income and Derivatives Trading and Custody Organization) |
| CFEMEA | Centro Feminista de Estudos e Assessoria (Feminist Center for Studies and Consulting) |
| CGL | Comitê Gestor Local (Local Managing Committee) |
| CIER | Comisión de Integración Energética Regional (Regional Electrical Integration Commission) |
| CLT | Consolidação das Leis do Trabalho (Labor Code) |
| CNDI | Conselho Naciuonal de Desenvolvimento Industrial (National Council of Industrial Development) |
| CNDM | Conselho Nacional dos Direitos das Mulheres (National Council of Women's Rights) |
| CNI | Confederação Nacional da Indústria (National Confederation of Industry) |
| COAF | Conselho de Controle de Atividades Financeiras (Council for Control of Financial Activities) |
| COAL | Coordenadoria de Assuntos Legislativo (Coordination Office for legislative Affairs) |
| COP | Comitê do Orçamento Participativo (The Participatory Budgeting Committee) |
| CPAIMC | Centro de Pesquisa de Assistência Integrada à Mulher e à Criança (Center for Research and Integral Assistance to Women and Children) |
| CSN | Companhia Siderúrgica Nacional (National Steel Company) |
| CSSF | Comissão de Seguridade Social e Familia (Health, Security and Family Committee) |
| CUT | Central Única dos Trabalhadores (Unified Worker's Central) |
| DASP | Departamento Administrativo do Serviço Público (The Public Service Management Department) |
| DPHAN | Department of Historical and Artistic Patrimony |
| ECLAC | United Nations Economic Commission for Latin America and the Caribbean |
| EMBRAPA | Empresa Brasileira de Pesquisa Agropecuária (Brazilian State Company for Research in Agriculture) |
| EMBRATEL | Empresa Brasileira de Telecomunicações (Brazilian Telecom Company) |

ERP            European Recovery Program (Marshall Plan)

FAT            Fundo de Amparo ao Trabalhador (Workers Assistance Fund)

FEBRABAN Federação Brasileira de Bancos (Brazilian Federation of Banks)

FGC            Fundo Garantidor de Crédito (Federal Deposit Insurance Fund)

FGTS           Fundo de Garantia de Tempo de Serviço (Social Security Fund)

FIESP          Federação das Indústrias do Estado de São Paulo (Federation of Industries of the State of Sao Paulo)

FINATEC   Fundação de Empreendimentos Científicos e Tecnológicos (Foundation for Scientific and Technological Projects)

FIU            Financial Intelligence Unit

FTAA           Free Trade Area of the Americas

GATT           General Agreement on Tariffs and Trade

GDP            Gross Domestic Product

GNP            Gross National Product

IBGE           Instituto Brasileiro de Geografia e Estatística (Brazilian Institute of Geography and Statistics)

IDB            Inter-American Development Bank

IEA            International Energy Agency

IEDI           Instituto de Estudos para o Desenvolvimento Industrial (Institute for the Study of Industrial Development)

ILO            International Labor Organization

IMF            International Monetary Fund

INTAL          Institute for the Integration of Latin America and the Caribbean

IPEA           Instituto de Pesquisas Econômicas Aplicadas (Applied Economic Research Institute)

IPAC           Institute of Cultural and Artistic Patrimony

IPHAN          Institute of National Artistic and Historical Patrimony

IPI            Imposto sobre Produtos Industrializado (Tax on Industrialized Products)

ISI            Import-Substituting Industrialization

ITO            International Trade Organization

LAFTA          Latin American Free Trade Association

LIBOR          London Interbank Offering Rate

MARE           Ministério da Administração Federal e Reforma do Estado (Ministry of Federal Administration and State Reform)

MERCOSUR Mercado Común del Sur (Common Market of the South)

NAFTA          North American Free Trade Agreement

NATO           North Atlantic Treaty Organization

NPM            New Public Management

| | |
|---|---|
| NYMEX | New York Mercantile Exchange |
| OAB | Ordem dos Advogados do Brasil (Brazilian Bar Association) |
| OAS | Organization of the American States |
| OECD | Organization for Economic Co-operation and Development |
| OLADE | Organización Latinoamericana de Energía (Latin American Energy Organization) |
| ONIP | Organização Nacional da Indústria do Petróleo (National Organization of Industry and Petroleum) |
| OP | Orçamento Participativo (Participatory Budgeting) |
| OPEC | Organization of the Petroleum Exporting Countries |
| ORTN | Obrigação Reajustável do Tesouro Nacional - Inflation Adjusted Treasury Note |
| OSCIP | Organizações da Sociedade Civil de Interesse Público (Civil Society Organization of Public Interest) |
| PAC | Programa de Acelaração do Desenvolvimento (Accelerated Growth Program) |
| PAEG | Plano de Ação Econômica do Governo (Plan for Government Economic Action) |
| PAISM | Programa de Assistência Integral à Saúde da Mulher (Complete Assistance Health Program for Women) |
| PDVSA | Petróleos de Venezuela (Venezuelan Petroleum Company) |
| Petrobras | Petróleo Brasileiro S/A (State Oil Company) |
| PIS | Plano de Integração Social (Plan for Social Integration) |
| PITCE | Programa de Inovação Tecnológica e Comércio Exterior (Industrial, Technological, and Trade Policy) |
| PMDB | Partido do Movimento Democrático Brasileiro (Party of the Brazilian Democratic Movement) |
| PMN | Partido da Mobilização Nacional (National Mobilization Party) |
| PNAD | Pesquisa Nacional por Amostra de Domicílio (Household National Sample Survey) |
| PND II | Plano Nacional do Desenvolvimento II (National Plan for Development II) |
| PRONA | Partido da Reedificação da Ordem Nacional (Party of the Reedification of National Order) |
| PR | Partido da República (Party of the Republic) |
| PROEF | Programa de Fortalecimento dos Bancos Federais (Program for the Strengthening of Federal Banks) |
| PROER | Programa de Estímulo à Reestruturação e ao Fortalecimento do Sistema Financeiro Nacional (Stimulus Program for the Restructuring and Strengthening of the Brazilian Financial System) |

| | |
|---|---|
| PROES | Programa de Incentivo à Redução do Estado na Atividade Bancária (Stimulus Program for the Reduction of State Involvement in Banking Activities) |
| PSB | Partido Socialista Brasileiro (Brazilian Socialist Party) |
| PSDB | Partido da Social Democracia Brasileira (Brazilian Social Democratic Party) |
| PSoL | Partido de Socialism e Liberdade (Party of Socialism and Liberty) |
| PSTU | Partido Socialista dos Trabalhadores Unificado (Unified Socialist Labor Party) |
| PT | Partido dos Trabalhadores (Workers' Party) |
| PTB | Partido Trabalhista Brasileiro Brazilian Labor Party |
| SAL/MJ | Secretaria de Assuntos Legislativos/Ministerio de Justiça (Legislative Affairs section at the Justice Ministry) |
| SELIC | Sistema Especial de Liquidação e Custódia (Special System for Trading and Custody) |
| SENASP | Secretaria Nacional de Segurança Pública (National Secretariat for Public Safety) |
| SMCPGL | Secretaria Municipal de Coordenação Política e Governança Local (Secretariat for Political Coordination and Local Solidarity Governance) |
| SPHAN | National Artistic and Historical Patrimony Service |
| SPM | Secretaria Especial para Políticas para Mulheres (Special Secretariat for Women's Policies) |
| STF | Supremo Tribunal Federal (The national level Supreme Court) |
| STJ | Superior Tribunal de Justiça (Highest level federal appeals court) |
| TSE | Tribunal Superior Eleitoral (Brazil's national level election) |
| SUMOC | Superintendência da Moeda e do Crédito (Superintendency for Money and Credit) |
| SUS | Sistema Unico de Saude (Unified Health System) |
| SVS | Secretaria de Vigilância em Saúde (Secretariat for Health Surveillance) |
| TELEBRAS | Telecomunicações Brasileiras (State Telephone Company) |
| UAMPA | União das Associações de Moradores de Porto Alegre (Union of Neighborhood Associations of Porto Alegre) |
| UNASUR | Unión de Naciones Suramericanas (Union of South American Nations) |
| UNCTAD | United Nations Conference on Trade and Development |
| UNESCO | United Nations Educational, Scientific and Cultural Organization |
| URV | Unidade Real de Valor (Unit of Real Value) |

# BIBLIOGRAPHY

Abers, Rebecca Neaera. 2000. *Inventing Local Democracy: Grassroots Politics in Brazil.* Boulder, Colo.: Lynne Rienner Publishers.

Aberbach, Joel, R. Putnam, and B. Rockman. 1981. *Bureaucrats and Politicians in Western Democracy.* Cambridge, Massachussets: Harvard University Press.

Abranches, Sérgio. 1988. "O presidencialismo de coalizão: o dilema institucional brasileiro," *Dados*, 31(1): 5-33.

———. 1996. "Governabilidade e reformas: dilemas de transição." In J.P. Reis Velloso, ed., *O Real, O Crescimento e as Reformas.* Rio de Janeiro, Brazil: José Olympio.

Acharya, Amitav. 2007. "The Emerging Regional Architecture of World Politics." *World Politics* 59 (4): 629-52.

Aggarwal, Reena 2003. "Capital Market Development and Nurturing," In Litan, Pomerleano and Sundararajan, eds., *The Future of Domestic Capital Markets in Developing Countries.* Washington, D.C.: Brookings Institution Press.

Akitoby, Bernardin and Thomas Stratmann. 2008. "Fiscal Policy and Financial Markets." *Economic Journal* 118: 1971-85.

Aldcroft, Derek H. 1977. *From Versailles to Wall Street. 1919-1929.* London, U.K.: Allen Lane Penguin Books.

Almeida, Paulo Roberto de. 2009. "Lula's Foreign Policy: Regional and Global Strategies." In Joseph L. Love and Werner Baer, eds., *Brazil Under Lula: Economy, Politics, and Society under the Worker-President.* New York, N.Y.:

Palgrave-MacMillan, 167-186.

Almeida, Rodrigo. Forthcoming. "Entrando no clube: o BNDES e a inserção Brasileira no capitalismo internacional." In Renato Boschi ed., *Variedades de capitalismo: política e desenvolvimento na América Latina.* Belo Horizonte, Brazil: Ed.UFMG/IUPERJ.

Alvarez, Sonia E. 1990. *Engendering Democracy in Brazil: Women's Movements in Transition Politics.* Princeton, N.J.: Princeton University Press.

———. 1998. "Latin American Feminisms 'Go Global': Trends of the 1990s and Challenges for the New Millennium." In Sonia E. Alvarez, Evelina Dagnino, and Arturo Escobar, eds., *Cultures of Politics/Politics of Cultures: Re-visioning Latin American Social Movements.* Boulder, Colo.: Westview Press.

Alves, Branca Moreira, Leila Linhares Barsted, Sandra Azeredo Boschi, Jacqueline Pitanguy, and Mariska Ribeiro. 1981. *Espelho de Vênus: identidade social e sexual da mulher.* São Paulo, Brazil: Grupo Ceres, Editora Brasiliense.

Amable, Bruno. 2003. *The Diversity of Modern Capitalism.* Oxford, London: Oxford University Press.

Amsberg, Joachim von, Peter Lanjouw, Kimberly Nead. 2000. "A focalização do gasto social sobre a pobreza no Brasil." In R. Henriques, ed. *Desigualdade e pobreza no Brasil.* Rio de Janeiro, Brazil: IPEA, pp. 685-718.

"An Axis in Need of Oiling: the Anti-West." 2008. *The Economist*, 25 October: 71-72.

ANAPP. 2008. *Estatísticas de Mercado.* December. www.anapp.org.br.

Anastasia, Fátima, Carlos Ranulfo Melo, and Fabiano Santos. 2004. *Governabilidade e representação política na América do Sul.* São Paulo, Brazil: Editora da UNESP/Fundação Konrad Adenauer.

Anastassakis, Zoy. 2008. "Um projeto de design nacional: Aloisio Magalhães e o Centro Nacional de Referencia Cultural." Anais do 8o Congresso Brasileiro de Pesquisa e Desenvolvimento em Design. São Paulo, Brazil: AEND.

Andrade, Mário de. 1968. "O movimento modernista" In Gilberto Freyre, ed., *Temas Brasileiros.* Rio de Janeiro, Brazil: Casa do Estudante do Brasil.

———. 1993. "Anteprojeto do patrimônio." In Lauro Cavalcanti, ed., *Modernistas na repartição.* Rio de Janeiro, Brazil: Editora UFRJ, 39-56.

Assef, Andrea and Mara Luquet. 2006. *Meninas normais vão ao shopping—meninas iradas vão à bolsa.* São Paulo, Brazil: Editora Saraiva.

Andrews, Edmund and Larry Rohter. 2007. "U.S. and Brazil Seek to Promote Ethanol in West." *The New York Times*, 3 March.

Apolinário, Alessandro A., Alessandro Rocha da Silva, Carlos Eduardo Marinho Diniz, Erica Pelicano Ribeiro, and Emerson de Oliveira Capistrano. 2002. "O impacto do FGTS na alavancagem do mercado de capitais brasileiro." Paper presente at the "XXII Encontro Nacional de Engenharia de Produção," Curitiba, Brazil, October 23-25.

Apostolik, Richard, Christopher Donohue, and Peter Went. 2009. *Foundations of Banking Risk.* Hoboken, N.J.: Wiley, John & Sons, Inc., 68-70.

Araújo, Clara. 2001. "As cotas por sexo para a competição legislativa: o caso brasileiro e comparação com experiências internacionais." *Dados*, 44 (1): 155-94.

Arbix, Glauco. 2000. "Beyond Market Fundamentalism and the Developmental State." Paper presented at the conference, "Regional Powers, New Developmental States, and Global Governance: BRICS in the New World

Order," Watston Institute for International Studies, Brown University, March 13-14.

Arbix, Glauco and Zil Miranda. 2009. "Tecnologia e internacionalizacão." *Folha de São Paulo*, 19 October.

Arbix, Glauco and João A. Negri. 2006. "Uma nova competitividade da indústria e o novo empresariado: uma hipótese de trabalho." *São Paulo em Perspectiva* 19 (2).

Armijo, Leslie Elliott and Christine A. Kearney. 2008. "Does Democratization Alter the Policy Process? Trade Policymaking in Brazil." *Democratization* 15 (5): 991-1017.

Arretche, Marta. 2004. "Toward a Unified and More Equitable System: Health Reform in Brazil." In Robert R. Kaufman and Joan Nelson, eds., *Crucial Needs, Weak Incentives: Social Sector Reform, Democratication, and Globalization in Latin America*. Baltimore, Md. and London, U.K.: Johns Hopkins University Press, 155-88.

Asad, Talal. 2002. "Ethnographic Representation, Statistics, and Modern Power." In Brian Axel, ed., *From the Margins: Historical Anthropology and its Futures*. Durham, N.C.: Duke University Press, 66-94.

Avelar, Lúcia, and Antônio Cintra, ed. 2007. *Sistema político Brasileiro: uma introdução*. 2nd Ed. São Paulo, Brazil: UNESP/Konrad Adenauer Stiftung.

Avritzer, Leonardo. 2009. *Participatory Institutions in Democratic Brazil*. Baltimore, MD: The Johns Hopkins University Press.

Avritzer, Leonardo, and Fátima Anastásia, ed. 2006. *Reforma política no Brasil*. Belo Horizonte, Brazil: Editora da UFMG.

Baaklini, Abdo and Antonio Carlos Pojo do Rego. 1988. "The Congress and the National Policy on Computer Science." *Revista de Administração Pública* 22 (2).

Babington, Deepa and Jane Barrett. 2007. "Santander sells Antonveneta to M. Paschi." Reuters, 8 November.

Baccaro, Lucio. 2002. "Negotiating the Italian Pension Reform with the Unions: Lessons for Corporatist Theory." *Industrial and Labor Relations Review* 55 (3): 413-431.

Baer, Werner. 1995. *The Brazilian Economy: Growth and Development.*. 4th Ed. Westport, Conn.: Praeger Publishers.

———. 2008. *The Brazilian Economy: Growth and Development*. 6th Ed. Boulder, Colo.: Lynne Rienner Publishers.

Baer, Werner and Nader Nazmi. 2000. "Privatization and Restructuring of Banks in Brazil." *The Quarterly Review of Economics and Finance* 40 (1).

Baier, Scott L., Jeffrey H. Bergstrand, and Erika Vidal. 2007. "Free Trade Agreement in the Americas: Are the Trade Effects Larger than Anticipated?" *World Economy* 30 (9): 1347-77.

Baiocchi, Gianpaolo. 2005. *Militants and Citizens: The Politics of Participatory Democracy in Porto Alegre*. Stanford, Calif.: Stanford University Press.

Banco Central do Brasil. 2008. *Financial Stability Report 7.1*. Brasília, Brazil: BCB.

———. *Informações Contábeis, 50 Maiores Bancos*. www.bcb.gov.br.

———. *Operações de crédito do sistema financeiro, saldos com recursos livres e direcionados*. www.bcb.gov.br.

———. *Series temporais*. http://www.bcb.gov.br/?SERIETEMP.

———. *Sistema financeiro nacional. relatório de ativos*. www.bcb.gov.br.

Banco do Brasil S.A. 2009. "Conclusion of Banco Votorantim Strategic Partnership." Press Release, 28 September.

BIS. 2004. *International Convergence of Capital Measurements and Standards: A Revised Framework.* Basel, Switzerland: Bank of International Settlements.

BID. 2009. *INTAL - Carta Mensal no. 152*, March.

Banco Santander, 2009. "Material Fact, Complementary Information on IPO of Banco Santander (Brasil) S.A," 10 November. www.santander.com.

Bandeira, Lourdes. 1998. "O que faz da vítima, vítima?" In Ricardo Limam, Djaci Oliveira, and Elen Geraldes, eds., *A Primavera já Partiu.* Petrópolis, Brazil: Ed. Vozes e M.N.D.H.

———. 2005. *Brasil: fortalecimento da Secretaria Especial de Políticas para as Mulheres avançar na transversalidade da perspectiva de Gênero nas Políticas.* Brasília, Brazil: CEPAL and SPM.

Baratta, Alessandro. 1999. *Criminologia crítica e crítica do Direito Penal.* Rio de Janeiro, Brazil: Instituto Carioca de Criminologia.

Barbosa, Fernando. 2008. "Jogo de Ponzi, PROER e FCVS," *Revista de Economia Política* 28 (1).

Barreto, Leonardo, and David Fleischer. 2008. "Reformas políticas y democracia en Brasil." In Daniel G. Zovatto, and José Henríquez, eds., *Reforma política y electoral en América Latina.* México: UNAM and IDEA, 315-52.

Barrionuevo, Alexei. 2009. "Energy Deal with Brazil Gives Boost to Paraguay." *New York Times*, 27 July: A10.

Barros, Ricardo and Miguel Foguel. 2000. "Focalização dos gastos públicos sociais e erradicação da pobreza no Brasil." In *Desigualdade e pobreza do Brasil.* Rio de Janeiro, Brazil: IPEA.

Barsted, Leila Linhares. 2007. "O movimento de mulheres e o debate sobre o aborto." Presented at the "Seminário Estudos sobre a Questão do Aborto." Campinas, Brazil: Unicamp.

Beattie, Alan. 2006. "Ethanol Puts Power in Brazil's Tank." *The Financial Times* (London), 16 May.

Becker, Howard S. 1997. *Uma teoria da ação coletiva.* Rio de Janeiro, Brazil: Zahar.

Becker, Uwe. 2007. "Open Systemness and Contested Reference Frames and Change: A Reformulation of the Varieties of Capitalism Theory." *Socio-Economic Review* 5.

Beltrão, Hélio. 1984. *Descentralização e liberdade.* Rio de Janeiro, Brazil: Record.

Benevides, Maria Victória. 1976. *Governo Kubitschek: desenvolvimento econômico e estabilidade política.* São Paulo, Brazil: Brasiliense.

Benevides, Maria Victória, Paulo Vannuchi, and Fábio Kerche, eds. 2003. *Reforma política e cidadania.* São Paulo, Brazil: Fundação Perseu Abramo.

Beras, Cesar. 2008. "Orçamento participativo de Porto Alegre e a democratização do Estado: a configuração especifica do caso de Porto Alegre: 1989-2004." Ph.D. Diss. Universidade Federal do Rio Grande do Sul.

Besley, Timothy and Burgess, Robin. 2003. "Halving Global Poverty." *Journal of Economic Perspectives* 17 (3): 3-22.

Besse, Susan. 1996. *Restructuring Patriarchy: The Modernization of Gender Inequality in Brazil, 1914-1940.* Chapel Hill, N.C.: University of North Carolina Press.

Black, John, Nigar Hashimzade, and Gareth Myles. 2009. *A Dictionary of Economics.* Oxford, London: Oxford University Press.

Bomeny, Helena Bousquet. 1995. "O patrimônio de Mário de Andrade." In Márcia Chuva et al., eds. *A invenção do patrimônio: continuidade e ruptura na constituição de uma política oficial de preservação no Brasil.* Rio de Janeiro, Brazil: Minc/IPHAN.

Boschi, Renato. 2004. "Instituciones políticas, reformas estructurales y ciudadanía: dilemas de la democracia en Brasil." *Política* 42.

———. 2006. "Setor privado, reestruturação econômica e democratização na América Latina." In José M. Domingues and María Maneiro eds., *América Latina hoje.* Rio de Janeiro, Brazil: Civilização Brasileira.

———. 2008. "Capacidades estatales y políticas de desarrollo en Brasil: Tendencias Recientes." In Manuel Alcántara Sáez and Carlos Ranulfo Melo eds., *La democracia Brasileña, balance y perspectivas para el siglo XXI.* Salamanca, Spain: Ediciones Univesidad de Salamanca.

———. 2009. "Elites parlamentares e a agenda pós-neoliberal: Brasil e Chile." In Fátima Anastasia et al. eds., *Elites parlamentares na América Latina.* Belo Horizonte, Brazil: Ed. Argvmentvm.

Boschi, Renato and Flávio Gaitan. 2008a. "Intervencionismo estatal e políticas de desenvolvimento na América Latina." *Caderno CRH* 21 (53): 301-17.

———. 2008b. "Gobiernos progresistas, agendas neodesarrollistas y capacidades estatales: la experiencia reciente en Argentina, Brasil y Chile." In Maria Regina S. de Lima, ed., *Desempenho de governos progressistas no Cone Sul.* Rio de Janeiro, Brazil: Edições IUPERJ.

———. 2009. "Outra volta no parafuso desenvolvimentista: um manifesto." *INSIGHT Inteligencia* 45: 131-45.

Boschi, Renato and Maria Regina S. de Lima. 2002. "O Executivo e a construção do Estado no Brasil: Do Desmonte da Era Vargas ao Novo Intervencionismo Regulatório." In Luiz Werneck Vianna ed., *A democracia e os três poderes no Brasil.* Belo Horizonte, Brazil: Ed. UFMG/IUPERJ.

Bourdieu, Pierre. 1997. "Le Champs Économique." *Actes de la Recherché en Sciences Sociales* 119: 15-57.

Bouzan, Ary. 1975. *Os bancos comerciais do Brasil (1964-1972).* São Paulo, Brazil: FEBRABAN.

Boyer, Robert. 2005. "How and Why Capitalisms Differ." *Economy and Society* 34 (4): 509-57.

Braga, Isabel. 2003. "Bancada evangélica pressiona o governo contra a reforma política." *O Globo,* 13 July: 4.

Bragon, Ranier, and Maria Clara Cabral. 2009. "Troca-troca engorda PSC e PR; oposição encolhe 17%." *Folha de São Paulo,* 3 October.

Brainard, Lael and Leonardo Martinez-Diaz, eds. 2009. *Brazil as an Economic Superpower? Understanding Brazil's Changing Role in the Global Economy.* Washington, D.C.: Brookings Institution Press.

Brasil Jr., Olavo. 1998. "As reformas administrativas no Brasil: modelos, sucessos e fracassos." 49 (2).

"Brazil's Lula meets foes to new oil plan." 2009. *Reuters,* 31 August. www.reuters.com.

Bresser-Pereira, Luiz Carlos. 1972. *Tecnoburocracia e contestação.* Petrópolis, Brazil: Editora Vozes.

———. 1977. *Estado e desenvolvimento industrializado.* São Paulo, Brazil: Brasiliense.

——. 2000a. *The New Left and the Moving Center.* Brasília, Brazil: Instituto Teotônio Vilela.

——. 2000b. "State Reform in the 1990s: Logic and Control Mechanisms." In Leonardo Burlamaqui, Ana Célia Castro, Ha-Joon Chang, eds., *Institutions and the Role of the State.* Cheltenham, U.K.: Edward Elgar, 175-219.

——. 2004. "O novo desenvolvimentismo." *Folha de S. Paulo*, 19 September.

——. 2005. "Proposta de desenvolvimento para o Brasil." In João Sicsú, Luís Fernando de Paula and R. Michel, eds., *Novo-desenvolvimentismo: um projeto nacional de crescimento com eqüidade.* São Paulo, Brazil: Editora Manole.

——. 2006. "O novo desenvolvimentismo e a ortodoxia convencional." *São Paulo em Perspectiva* 20(1).

——. 2009. *Mondialisation et Competition: Pourquoi Certains Pays Émergents Réussissent et d'Autres Non.* Paris, France: Editions la Découverte.

Bresser-Pereira, Luiz Carlos, and Nuria C. Grau. 1999. "Entre o Estado e o mercado: o público não estatal." In L.C. Bresser-Pereira and Nuria C. Grau, eds., *O público não-estatal na reforma do Estado.* Rio de Janeiro, Brazil: Editora FGV, 15-48.

Brooks, Sarah M. 2009. *Social Protection and the Market in Latin America: the Transformation of Social Security Institutions.* New York, N.Y.: Cambridge University Press.

Bulmer-Thomas, Victor. 1994. *The Economic History of Latin America Since Independence.* Cambridge, Mass.: Cambridge University Press.

Burges, Sean. 2006. "Without Sticks or Carrots: Brazilian Leadership in South America During the Cardoso Era, 1992-2003." *Bulletin of Latin American Research* 25 (1): 23-42.

——. 2007. "Building a Global Southern Coalition: the Competing Approaches of Brazil's Lula and Venezuela's Chavez." *Third World Quarterly* 28 (7): 1343-58.

Burgos, Raúl. 2002. "The Gramscian Intervention in the Theoretical and Political Production of the Latin American Left." *Latin American Perspectives* 29 (1): 9-37.

——. 2007. "Da democratização política à radicalização da democracia: novasdimensões estratégicas dos movimentos sociais." In Evelina Dagnino and Luciana Tatagiba, eds., *Democracia, sociedade civil e participação.* Chapecó, Brazil: Argos, 125-66.

Busatto, Cézar. 1991. "Notas sobre desenvolvimento, Estado, planejamento e orçamento." In Cézar Busatto, ed., *Democracia, prosperidade e responsabilidade social.* Porto Alegre, Brazil: Editora Sulina, 38-57.

——. 1998. *Anjos anônimos: exemplo de luta e solidariedade humana.* Porto Alegre, Brazil: L&PM Editores.

——. 1999a. "O significado histórico do Governo Britto." *Democracia: Cadernos de Reflexão Política* 3: 94-106.

——. 1999b. "Política e desenvolvimento paraviver melhor." In Cézar Busatto, ed., *Democracia, prosperidade e responsabilidade social.* Porto Alegre, Brazil: Editora Sulina. 15-36.

——. 1999c. *Democracia, prosperidade e responsabilidade social.* Porto Alegre, Brazil: Editora Sulina.

——. 2001. *Responsabilidade social: revolução do nosso tempo.* Porto Alegre, Brazil:

CORAG.

———. 2008. Personal Interview. August 31.

Busatto, Cézar, and Jandira Feijó. 2006. *A era dos vagalumes: o florescer de uma nova cultura política.* Porto Alegre, Brazil: Universidade Luterana do Brasil.

Busatto, Cézar, and Plíno Zalewski. 2004. *Governça Solidária Local: fundamentos políticos da mundança em Porto Alegre.* Porto Alegre, Brazil: Prefeitura Municipas de Porto Alegre.

Buzan, Barry and Ole Waever. 2003. *Regions and Powers: The Structure of International Security.* Cambridge, Mass.: Cambridge University Press.

"Caderno Economia." *O Globo,* 2006. 3 August.

Caiado, Ronaldo. 2007. "Com o atual sistema, não há salvação." *Plenarium* [Câmara dos Deputados] 4 (2): 4-29.

Caldeira, Jorge. 1995. *Mauá empresário do Império.* São Paulo, Brazil: Editora Schwartz.

Calógeras, João P. 1939. *A History of Brazil.* Chapel Hill, N.C.: University of North Carolina Press.

Câmara dos Deputados. 2007. "Reforma política." *Plenarium* 4.

Campbell, John L. and Ove Pedersen. 2007. "The Varieties of Capitalism and Hybrid Success: Denmark in the Global Economy." *Comparative Political Studies* 40 (3): 307-32.

Campello de Souza, Maria do Carmo. 1976. *Estado e partidos políticos no Brazil.* São Paulo, Brazil: Editora Alfa-Omega.

Campos, Carmen. 2001. "Violência doméstica no espaço da Lei." In Cristina Bruschini, and Céli Pinto, eds., *Tempos e Lugares de Gênero.* São Paulo, Brazil: Fundação Carlos Chagas and Editora 34.

Cardoso, Fernando Henrique. 1975. *Autoritarismo e democratização.* Rio de Janeiro, Brazil: Paz e Terra.

———. 2001. *Charting a New Course: The Politics of Globalization and Social Transformation.* Maurício Font, ed., New York, N.Y.: Rowman and Littlefield.

Cardoso, Ruth. 1992. "Popular Movements in the Context of Democracy in Brazil." In Escobar and S. Alvarez, eds., *The Making of Social Movements in Latin America: Identity, Strategy and Democracy.* Boulder, Colo.: Westview Press.

Caro, Ariela Ruiz. 2008. "Energy Integration and Security in Latin America and the Caribbean." Americas Policy Program 27 March. www.americas.irc-online.org.

Carrara, Sérgio, Adriana Vianna, and Ana Lúcia Enne. 2000. "Crimes de Bagatela: a violência contra a mulher na justiça do Rio de Janeiro." In Mariza Corrêa, ed., *Gênero e cidadania.* São Paulo, Brazil: Unicamp.

Carvalho, Antonio G. 2002. "Governança corporativa no Brasil em perspectiva." *Revista de Administração de Empresas* 37: 19-32.

Carvalho, José Murilo. 1997. "Mandonismo, coronelismo, clientelismo: uma discussão conceitual." *Revista Dados* 40(2), Rio de Janeiro, Brazil.

Caspary, Georg. 2007. "The Energy Sector in Latin America: Key Prospects, Risks and Opportunities." Latin America Current Issues, Deutsche Bank Research, 7 September.

Castañeda, Jorge. 2006. "Latin America's Left Turn." *Foreign Affairs,* May-June.

Castro, Mônica. 2006. "Cláusula de barreira." In Leonardo Avritzer, and Fátima

Anastásia, eds., *Reforma política no Brasil.* Belo Horizonte: Editora da UFMG, 188-91.

Cavalcanti, Amaro. 1983. *Meio circulante nacional (1808-1835).* Brasília, Brazil: Editora Universidade de Brasília.

Cavalcanti, Lauro. 1999. "Modernistas, arquitetura e patrimônio." In Dulce Pandolfi, ed., *Repensando o Estado Novo.* Rio de Janeiro, Brazil: Editora FGV, 178-196.

Cavalcanti, Maria Laura and Maria Luiza Heilborn. 1985. "SOS—Mulher do Rio de Janeiro: uma entrevista." In Bruna Franchetto, Maria Laura Cavalcanti e Maria Luiza Heilborn, eds., *Perspectivas antropológicas da mulher: sobre mulher e violência.* Rio de Janeiro, Brazil: Zahar Editores.

Cechin, J. 2002. "A previdência social reavaliada-II." *Conjuntura Social* 13 (1): 7-54.

"Central Planning: Rediscovering the Charms of BNDES." 2009. *The Economist,* 16 April.

Cerbasi, Gustavo. 2004. *Casais Inteligentes Enriquecem Juntos.* São Paulo, Brazil: Editora Gente.

Cesar, Benedito Tadeu. 2002. "O projeto político-societário petista." In *PT: a contemporaneidade possível. base social e projeto político (1980-1991).* Porto Alegre: Editora Universidade Federal do Rio Grande do Sul.

CFEMEA. 1994. *Jornal Fêmea.* n°11, January.

Chacon, Vamireh. 2001. *A construção da brasilidade: Gilberto Freyre e sua geração.* São Paulo, Brazil: Marco Zero.

Chang, Ha-Joon. 2002. *Kicking Away the Ladder: Development Strategy in Historical Perspective.* London, U.K.: Anthem Press.

———. 2003. *Globalization, Economic Development and the Role of the State.* London, U.K.: Zed Books.

———. 2007. *Bad Samaritans: Rich Nations, Poor Policies, and the Threat to the Developing World.* London, U.K.: Random House.

Chaui, Marilena. 2000. *Brasil: mito fundador e sociedade autoritaria.* São Paulo, Brazil: Fundação Perseu Abramo.

CIA World Factbook. 2009. Washington, D.C.: Central Intelligence Agency.

CIDADE. 2007. "Renovação de lideranças e democracia: uma reflexão necessária." *Boletim Cidade* VI (39).

———. 2008. "Um fantasma assombra o governo municipal." *Boletim Cidade* VII (43).

Cintra, Antônio. 2008. "Majoritário ou proporcional? Em busca do equilíbrio na construção de um sistema eleitoral." In João Paulo Viana, and Gilmar Nascimento, eds., *O sistema político brasileiro: continuidade ou reforma.* Porto Velho, Brazil: Edufro, 17-46.

CNDM. 1986. Carta das Mulheres. Brasília, Brazil.

Coates, David. 2005. *Varieties of Capitalism, Varieties of Approaches.* New York, N.Y.: Palgrave McMillan.

Código Penal Atualizado. 1940. Decreto-Lei no 2.848, de 7 de Dezembro.

Cohen, Jean L. and Andrew Arato. 1992. *Civil Society and Political Theory.* Cambridge, Mass.: MIT Press.

Cohn, Gabriel. 1968. *Petróleo e nacionalismo.* São Paulo, Brazil: DIFEL.

———. 1984. "A concepção oficial da política cultural nos anos 70." In Sérgio Miceli, ed., *Estado e cultura no Brasil.* São Paulo, Brazil: Difel, 85-96.

Collins, John. 2008a. "'But What if I Should Need to Defecate in Your Neighborhood, Madame?' Empire, Redemption and the 'Tradition of the Oppressed' in a Brazilian Historical Center." *Cultural Anthropology* 23: 279-328.

———. 2008b. "Patrimony, Public Health, and National Culture: The Commodification and Redemption of Origins in Neoliberal Brazil." *Critique of Anthropology* 28: 237-55.

———. Forthcoming. *The Revolt of the Saints: Memory and Redemption in the Twilight of Brazil's 'Racial Democracy.'* Durham, N.C.: Duke University Press.

Comaroff, Jean and John Comaroff. 2009. *Ethnicity, Inc.* Chicago, Ill.: University of Chicago Press.

Constanzi, Rogério N. 2009. "Crise global e impactos no Brasil: o problema da estabilidade da instabilidade financeira," *Informações FIPE*, August.

*Correio Braziliense.* 2000. 28 August: 6.

Costa, Ana Maria. 1996. "Planejamentofamiliar no Brasil." *Revista Bio* 2 (4).

Costa, Vanda Maria Ribeiro. 2006. "Os conselhos do CDES: experimento sem conclusão." *Insight Inteligência* 32: 146-61.

Crotty, James R. 2003. "The Neoliberal Paradox: the Impact of Destructive Product Market Competition and Impatient Finance on Nonfinancial Corporations in the Neoliberal Era." *PERI Research Brief.* Amherst, Mass.: University of Massachusetts Press.

Crouch, Colin. 2005. *Capitalist Diversity and Change: Recombinant Governance and Institutional Entrepreneurs.* Oxford, London: Oxford University Press.

Crouch, Colin and Henry Farrell. 2004. "Breaking the Path of Institutional Development? Alternative to the New Determinism." *Rationality and Society* 16 (5): 5-43.

Cruvinel, Tereza. 2003. "Regras próprias." *O Globo*, 15 July: 2.

"Cuba rejects OAS membership, official says." 2009. *CNN*, 4 June. http:// www.cnn.com/2009/WORLD/americas/06/04/cuba.oas/index.html.

Cunha, Anna Lucia. 2007. "Pessoa e direito, corpo e ciência: negociando preceitos cosmológicos em torno da legalização do aborto." M.A. Diss. Universidade de Brasília.

Cunha, Eleonora Schettini Martins. 2007. "O potencial de conselhos de políticas e orçamentos participativos para o aprofundamento democrático." In Evelina Dagnino and Luciana Tatagiba, eds., *Democracia, sociedade civil e participação.* Chapecó, Brazil: Argos, 25-44.

Cunha, Olívia Maria Gomes da. 2000. "Sua alma em sua palma: identificando a 'raça' e inventando a nação." In Dulce Pandolfi, ed., *Repensando o Estado Novo.* Rio de Janeiro, Brazil: Editora FGV.

D'Araujo, Maria Celina. 1982. *O segundo governo Vargas (1951-54).* Rio de Janeiro, Brazil: Zahar Editores.

———. 2007. "Governo Lula: contornos sociais e políticos da elite do poder." *CPDOC/FGV.*

Dacanal, José Hildebrando. 1999. *A nova classe no poder.* Porto Alegre, Brazil: Editora Novo Século.

Dagnino, Evelina. 2004. "Sociedade civil, participação e cidadania: de que estamos falando?" In Daniel Mato, ed., *Políticas de ciudadanía y sociedad civil en tiempos de globalización*. Caracas, Venezuela: FACES, Universidad Central de Venezuela, 95-110.

———. 2007. "Citizenship: A Perverse Confluence." *Development in Practice* 17 (4 and 5): 549-56.

Dagnino, Evelina, Alberto J. Olvera, and Aldo Panfichi. 2006. "Para uma outra leitura da disputa pela construção democrática na América Latina." In Evelina Dagnino, Alberto J. Olvera and Aldo Panfichi, eds., *A disputa pela construção democrática na América Latina*. São Paulo, Brazil: Editora Paz e Terra, 13-91.

Dalland, Robert. 1968. *Brazilian Planing*. Chapel Hill: University of North Carolina Press.

DATASUS. Ministério de Saúde. http://www2.datasus.gov.br/DATASUS/index.php.

Dávila, Jerry. 2003. *Diploma of Whiteness: Race and Social Policy in Brazil, 1917-1945*. Durham, N.C.: Duke University Press.

Davis, Steven. 2000. *Bank Mergers: Lessons for the Future*. London, U.K.: MacMillan Press.

De la Reza, Germán A. 2006. *Integración económica en América Latina: hacia una nueva comunidad regional en el siglo XXI*. Mexico City, Mexico: Universidad Autónoma Metropolitana Azcapotzalco; Plaza y Valdés.

De Vries, Margaret G. 1972. *The International Monetary Fund. 1945-1970*. Washington, D.C.: International Monetary Fund.

Deeg, Richard. 2005. "Path Dependency, Institutional Complementarity, and Change in National Business Systems." In Glenn Morgan, Richard Whitley and Eli Moen, eds., *Changing Capitalisms? Internationalization, Institutional Change, and Systems of Economic Organization*. Oxford, London: Oxford University Press.

Deeg, Richard and Gregory Jackson. 2007. "The State of the Art: Towards a More Dynamic Theory of Capitalist Variety." *Socio Economic Review* 5:149-79.

Devlin, Robert and Antoni Estevadeordal. 2001. "What's New in the New Regionalism in the Americas?" In Victor Bulmer-Thomas, ed., *Regional Integration in Latin America and the Caribbean: the Political Economy of Open Regionalism*. London, U.K.: Institute of Latin American Studies, 17-44.

Dezalay, Yves and Bryant G. Garth. 2002. *The Internationalization of Palace Wars: Lawyers, Economists, and the Contest to Transform Latin American States*. Chicago, IL: University of Chicago Press.

Diebold, William Jr. 1952. "The End of ITO." *Princeton Essays in International Finance* 16.

Diniz, Eli. 1997. *Crise, reforma do Estado e governabilidade*. Rio de Janeiro, Brazil: Fundação Getulio Vargas

———. 2000. Globalizacão, reformas econômicas e es empresariais. Rio de Janeiro, Brazil: FGV Editora.

Diniz, Eli and Renato Boschi. 2003. "Empresariado e estratégia de desenvolvimento." *Revista Brasileira de Ciências Sociais* 18 (52).

———. 2004. *Empresários, interesses e mercado: dilemas do desenvolvimento no Brasil*. Belo Horizonte, Brazil: Ed. UFMG.

———. 2007. *A difícil rota do desenvolvimento: empresários e a agenda pós-neoliberal*. Belo Horizonte, Brazil: Ed. UFMG.

Dion, Michelle and Andrew Roberts. 2008. "Sources of Support for Pension Reform: A Cross-National Perspective." Center for Retirement Research at Boston College Working Paper Series 23.

Dittrick, Paula. 2009. "Latin American oil, gas policies remain in flux." *Oil and Gas Journal*, 13 April: 20.

Domingues, José Maurício. 2008. *Latin America and Contemporary Modernity: A Sociological Interpretation*. New York, N.Y./London, U.K.: Routledge.

Doner, Richard F. and Ben Schneider. 2000. "Business Associations and Economic Development: Why Some Associations Contribute More Than Others." *Business and Politics* 2 (3).

"The Dragon in the Backyard." 2009. *The Economist*, 15 August: 19-21.

Draibe, Sônia M. 1985. *Rumos e metamorfoses: um estudo sobre a constituição do Estado e as alternativas industriais no Brasil (1930-1960)*. Rio de Janeiro, Brazil: Paz e Terra.

———. 2004. "Federal Leverage in a Decentralized System: Education Reform in Brazil." In Robert R. Kaufman and Joan M. Nelson, eds., *Crucial Needs, Weak Incentives: Social Sector Reform, Democratization, and Globalization in Latin America*. Baltimore, M.D.: Johns Hopkins University Press.

Drucker, Peter F. 1986. *The Frontiers of Management. Where Tomorrow's Decisions are Being Shaped Today*. New York, N.Y.: Penguin Putnam Inc.

Easton, David. 1965. *A System Analysis of Political Life*. New York, N.Y.: Wiley.

ECLAC. 2008. *Latin America and the Caribbean in the World Economy 2007, 2008 Trends*. Santiago, Chile: United Nations.

———. 2010. *Foreign Direct Investment in Latin America and the Caribbean, 2009*. New York, N.Y.: United Nations.

Erickson, Kenneth. 1977. *The Brazilian Corporative State and Working-Class Politics*. Berkeley, Calif.: University of California Press.

Erturk, Ismail, Julie Froud, Sukhdev Johal, Adam Leaver, and Karel Williams. 2007. "The Democratisation of Finance? Promises, Outcomes, Conditions." *Review of International Political Economy* 14 (4): 553-75.

———. 2008. *Financialization at Work: Key Texts and Analysis*. New York, N.Y.: Routledge.

Esping-Andersen, Gosta. 1985. *Politics Against Markets: The Social Democratic Road to Power*. Princeton, N.J.: Princeton University Press.

Estatuto do Desarmamento Comentado. Lei n° 10.826, de 22 de Dezembro de 2003. http://www.deolhonoestatuto.org.br/downloads/biblioteca/002.pdf

Evans, Peter. 1992. "The State as Problem and Solution: Predation, Embedded Autonomy, and Structural Change." In Haggard and Kaufman, eds., *The Politics of Economic Adjustment: International Constraints, Distributive Conflicts and the State*. Princeton, N.J.: Princeton University Press, 139-81.

———. 1995. *Embedded Autonomy, States & Industrial Transformation*. Princeton, N.J.: Princeton University Press.

———. 1997. "The Eclipse of the State? Reflections on Stateness in an Era of Globalization." *World Politics* 50 (1) :62-87.

———. 2005a. "Harnessing the State: Rebalancing Strategies for Monitoring and Motivation." In Matthew Lange and Dietrich Rueschemeyer eds., *States and Development: Historical Antecedents of Stagnation and Advance*. New York, N.Y.: Palgrave MacMillan.

———. 2005b. "Neoliberalism as a Political Opportunity: Constrain and

Innovation in Contemporary Development Strategy." In K. Gallagher ed., *Putting Development First: The Importance of Policy Space in the WTO and International Financial Institutions.* London, U.K.: Zed, 195-215.

———. 2008. "Constructing the 21st century Developmental State: Potentialities and Pitfalls." Presentation delivered at the DBSA/HSRC conference on "The Potentials for and Challenges of Constructing a Democratic Developmental State in South Africa," Magaliesburg, South Africa, 4 June.

Faletto, Enzo. 1996. "La CEPAL y la sociologia del desarrollo." *Revista de La CEPAL* 58.

Fausto, Boris. 2001. *História concisa do Brasil.* São Paulo, Brazil: Edusp e Impresa Oficial.

Fedozzi, Luciano. 1999. *Orçamento Participativo: reflexões sobre a experiência de Porto Alegre.* 2nd ed. Porto Alegre, Brazil: Tomo Editorial.

Feijó, Jandira. 2008. "My View Is Perplexed." In Jandira Feijó and Augusto de Franco, eds., *Views on the Local Solidary Governance in Porto Alegre. Porto Alegre, Brazil.* Porto Alegre, Brazil: EDIPUCRS.

Feinberg, Richard E. with Paul Haslam. 2007. "Problem of Coordination: the OAS and the IADB." In G. Mace, J.P. Thérien, and P. Haslam, eds., *Governing the Americas: Assessing Multilateral Institutions.* Boulder, Colo.: Lynne Rienner, 68-94.

Felix, David. 1969. "The Political Economy of Integration in Latin America." *Studies in Comparative International Development* 5 (5): 87-102.

Ferraz Junior, Vitor Emanuel. 2008. "Poder judiciário e competição política no Brasil: uma análise das decisões do TSE e do STF sobre as regras eleitorais." Ph.D. Diss. PUC, São Paulo. www.sapientia.pucsp.br//tde_busca/arquivo.php?codArquivo=7260.

Ferreira, Carlos Roberto. 2003. "Participação das aposentadorias e pensões na desigualdade da distribuição de renda no período de 1981 a 2001." Ph.D. Diss. Escola Superior de Agricultura Luís de Queirós da Universidade de São Paulo.

Figueiredo, Argelina, and Fernando Limongi. 1999. *Executivo e legislativo na nova ordem constitucional.* Rio de Janeiro/São Paulo: Editora FGV/FAPESP.

Filgueira, Carlos H. and Fernando Filgueira. 2002. "Models of Welfare and Models of Capitalism: The Limits of Transferability." In Evelyne Huber, ed., *Models of Capitalism: Lessons for Latin America.* University Park, Pa.: Penn State University Press, 127-158.

Filho, Adauto, Maria de Fátima Souza, and Cynthia Gazal-Carvalho. 2007. "Análise da mortalidade por homicídios no Brasil." *Epidemiol. Serv. Saúde* 16 (1): 7-18.

Filho, Nelson S. and Carla S. Silva. 2001. "As grandes empresas nos anos 90: respostas estratégicas a um cenário de mudanças." Banco Nacional de Desenvolvimento Econômico, Working Paper: 375-410. http://www.bndes.gov.br/SiteBNDES/export/sites/default/bndes_pt/Galerias/Arquivos/conhecimento/livro/eco90_11.pdf.

Fine, Ben. 1999. "The Developmental State is Dead—Long Live Social Capital?" *Development and Change* 30: 1-19.

Fleischer, David. 1998. "Reelección a Brasileña: las elecciones generales de 1998." *Contribuciones* 15 (4): 175-95.

———. 2002. "As eleições municipais no Brasil: uma análise comparativa (1982-

2000)." *Opinião Pública* 8 (1): 80-105.

——. 2004a. "Political Reforms: Cardoso's 'Missing Link.'" In Mauricio Font, and Anthony Spanakos, eds., *Reforming Brazil*. Lanham, Md.: Rowman & Littlefield, 112-39.

——. 2004b. "O impacto da reforma política sobre a Câmara dos Deputados." Plenarium [Brasília] 1: 123-41.

——. 2004c. "Reforma política en Brasil: una historia sin Fin." *América Latina Hoy* 37: 81-99.

——. 2006. "A política de coligações no Brasil—antes e depois da verticalização: impactos sobre os partidos." Paper presented at the "VII Congress of the Brazilian Studies Association," Nashville, Tennessee, 13-16 October.

——. 2007a. "Os partidos políticos." In Lúcia Avelar, and Antônio Cintra, ed., *Sistema político Brasileiro: uma introdução*. 2nd Ed. São Paulo: UNESP/Konrad Adenauer Stiftung, 303-48.

——. 2007b. "Reforma política no Brasil: os partidos políticos em questão." In Lúcio Rennó, ed., *Reforma política em questão*. Brasília: Editora da UnB, 163-90.

Fligstein, Neil. 2001. *The Architecture of Markets: an Economic Sociology of Twenty-First Century Capitalist Societies*. Princeton, N.J.: Princeton University Press.

Fonseca, Marcia Cecilia Londres. 1997. *O patrimônio em processo: trajetória da política federal de preservação no Brasil*. Rio de Janeiro, Brazil: UFRJ/Minc.

Font, Mauricio A. 2002. *Transforming Brazil: A Reform Era in Perspective*. Boulder and New York: Rowman & Littlefield.

Font, Mauricio A. and Anthony Spanakos, eds. 2004. *Reforming Brazil*. Boulder and New York: Lexington Books.

Fourcade-Gourinchas, Marion and Sarah L. Babb. 2002. "The Rebirth of the Liberal Creed: Neoliberal Transitions in England, France, Mexico and Chile." *American Journal of Sociology* 108 (3): 533-79.

Franco, Augusto de. 2008. "My View on Local Solidary Governance." In Jandira Feijó and Augusto de Franco, eds., *Views on the Local Solidary Governance in Porto Alegre*. Porto Alegre, Brazil: EDIPUCRS, 91-114.

Frankenberg, Louis. 2001. *Seu futuro financeiro*. Rio de Janeiro, Brazil: Campus Elsevier.

Fraser, Nancy. 1993. "Rethinking the Public Sphere: A Contribution to the Critique of Actually Existing Democracy." In B. Robbins, ed., *The Phantom Public Sphere*. Minneapolis: University of Minnesota Press.

French, John. 1992. *The Brazilian Workers' ABC: Class Conflict and Alliances in Modern São Paulo*. Chapel Hill, N.C.: University of North Carolina Press.

Freyre, Gilberto. 1996. *Manifesto regionalista*. Recife, Brazil: Fundação Joaquim Nabuco.

Frischtak, Claudio R. 1986. "Brazil." In Francis W. Rushing and Carole B. Brown, eds., *National Policies for Developing High Technology Industries: International Comparisons*. Boulder, Colo.: Westview Press, 31-70.

Furtado, Celso. 1959. *Formação econômica do Brasil*. São Paulo, Brazil: Companhia Editora Nacional.

——. 1976. *Economic Development of Latin America-Historical Background and contemporary problems*. 2nd Ed. Cambridge, Mass.: Cambridge University Press.

Gallagher, Kevin, ed. 2005. *Putting Development First: The Importance of Policy Space in the WTO and International Financial Institutions*. London, U.K.: Zed.

Galle, Juliano Morais and Sandro Bertolli. 2004. "As finanças públicas brasileiras do início da década de 1980 até a implantação do Plano Real," *Intertemas* 8 (8).

Garcia, Marco Aurélio. 1996. "Esquerdas: rupturas e continuidades." In Evelina Dagnino, ed., *Os anos 90: política e sociedade no Brasil*. São Paulo, Brazil: Editora Brasiliense, 119-36.

Gardner, Richard N. 1956. *Sterling-Dollar Diplomacy*. Oxford, London: Clarendon Press.

Geddes, Barbara. 1990. "Building State Autonomy in Brazil, 1930-1964," *Comparative Politics* 22(2): 217-235.

———. 1996. *Politician's Dilemma: Building State Capacity in Latin America*. Berkeley, Calif.: University of California Press.

Gerschenkron, Alexander. 1962. *Economic Backwardness in Historical Perspective*. Cambridge, Mass.: Belknap Press.

Giambiagi, Fabio, Ana Claudia Além. 1999. *Finanças públicas teoría e práctica no Brasil*. Rio de Janeiro, Brazil: Campus.

Giambiagi, Fábio and Paulo Tefner. 2010. *Demografia a ameaça invisível*. São Paulo, Brazil: Campus Elsevier.

Giambiagi, Fábio and Lavínia Barros de Castro. 2003. "Previdência social: diagnósticos e propostas." *Revista do BNDES* 10 (19): 265-292.

Giambiagi, Fabio, Hélio Zylbersztajn, Luís Eduardo Afonso, André Portela Souza, and Eduardo Zylbersztajn. 2007. "Impacto de reformas paramétricas na previdência social brasileira: simulações alternativas." *Pesquisa e Planejamento Econômico* 37 (2).

Glatzer, Miguel and Dietrich Rueschemeyer, eds. 2005. *Globalization and the Future of the Welfare State*. Pittsburgh, PA: University of Pittsburgh Press.

Global Property Guide. 2010. 7 February. www.globalpropertyguide.com/ Chile.

Goertzel, Ted G. 2002. *Fernando Henrique Cardoso e a reconstrução da democracia no Brasil*. São Paulo, Brazil: Saraiva.

Goldberg, Anette. 1987. "Feminismo e autoritarismo: a metamorfose de uma utopía de liberação em ideología liberalizante." M.A. Diss. Universidade Federal do Rio de Janeiro.

———. 1991. "Le Dire et Le Faire Feministes: une approche socioculturelle du Brésil Contemporain." Ph.D. Diss.Université de Paris VII.

Goldfajn, Ilan. 2003. "The Brazilian Crisis, the Role of the IMF and Democratic Governability." Pontifícia Universidade Católica do Rio de Janeiro, 19 October. www.econ.puc-rio.br

Goldsmith, Raymond W. 1986. *Desenvolvimento financeiro sob um século de inflação: Brasil 1850-1984*. São Paulo, Brazil: Bamerindus.

Gómez-Mera, Laura. 2008. "How 'new' is the 'New Regionalism' in the Americas? The Case of Mercosur." *Journal of International Relations and Development* 11 (3): 279-308.

Gonçalves, José Reginaldo Santos. 1996. *A retórica da perda: os discursos do patrimonio cultural no Brasil*. Rio de Janeiro, Brazil: Editora UFRJ/Ministério da Cultura-IPHAN.

Gourevitch, Peter Alexis. 1986. *Politics in Hard Times*. Ithaca, N.Y.: Cornell University Press.

Gourevitch, Peter Alexis and James Shinn. 2005. *Political Power and Corporate Control: The New Global Politics of Corporate Governance*. Princeton, N.J.: Princeton University Press.

Gouveia, Gilda. 1994. *Burocracia e elites burocráticas no Brasil*. São Paulo, Brazil: Editora Sumaré.

Gregori, María F. 1993. *Cenas e queixas: um estudo sobre mulheres, relações violentas e a prática feminista*. São Paulo, Brazil: Paz e Terra.

Gret, Marion, and Yves Sintomer. 2005. *The Porto Alegre Experiment: Learning Lessons for Better Democracy*. London, U.K.: Zed Books.

Grugel, Jean. 2006. "Regional Governance and Transnational Collective Action in Latin America." *Economy and Society* 35 (2): 209-31.

Grün, Roberto. 2003. "Atores e ações na construção da governança corporativa Brasileira." *Revista Brasileira de Ciências Sociais* 18: 139-61.

———. 2004. "A evolução recente do espaço financeiro no Brasil e alguns reflexos na cena política." *Revista Brasileira de Ciências Sociais*. 47: 5-47.

———. 2007. "Decifra-me ou te devoro! As finanças e a sociedade Brasileira." *MANA* 13: 381-410.

———. 2009. "A crise, a guerra cultural e as surpreendentes transformações do espaço econômico brasileiro em 2009." Paper presented at the "Colóquio Internacional—A internacionalização das ciências sociais francesas e a cooperação científica com o Brasil." http://www.fe.unicamp.br/focus/textos/GRUN-Coloquio2009.pdf

Guerreiro, Gabriela. 2009. "Ministros entregam ao Congresso proposta de reforma política sem brecha para 3° mandato." *Folha de São Paulo*, 10 February.

Guzzo Decca, Maria Auxiliadora. 1987. *A vida fora das fabricas: cotidiano operario em São Paulo, 1920-1934*. São Paulo, Brazil: Paz e Terra.

Haggard, Stephan and Robert R. Kaufman, eds. 1992. *The Politics of Economic Adjustment*. Princeton, N.J.: Princeton University Press.

Haggard, Stephan and Robert R. Kaufman. 2008. *Development, Democracy, and Welfare States: Latin America, East Asia, and Eastern Europe*. Princeton, N.J.: Princeton University Press.

Hagopian, Francis and Scott Mainwaring, eds. 2005. *The Third Wave of Democratization in Latin America: Advances and Setbacks*. New York, N.Y.: Cambridge University Press.

Hall, Peter. 2007. "The Evolution of Varieties of Capitalism in Europe." In Bob Hancké, Martin Rhodes and Mark Thatcher eds., *Beyond Varieties of Capitalism: Conflict, Contradictions, and Complementarities in the European Economy*. Oxford, London: Oxford University Press.

Hall, Peter, and David Soskice, eds. 2001. *Varieties of Capitalism: The Institutional Foundations of Comparative Advantage*. Oxford, London and New York, N.Y.: Oxford University Press.

Harrington, Brooke. 2008. *Pop Finance: Investment Clubs and the New Investor Populism*. Princeton, N. J.: Princeton University Press.

Harris, David, and Deigo Azzi. 2006. "ALBA: Venezuela's Answer to 'Free Trade': The Bolivarian Alternative for the Americas." Focus on the Global South, Occasional Paper 3.

Harris, Richard L. 2008. "Latin America's Response to Neoliberalism and

Globalization." *Nueva Sociedad* 214.

Hartelius, Kristian et al. 2008. "Emerging Market Spread Compression: Is it Real or is it Liquidity?" Working Paper 08/10. Washington, D.C.: IMF.

Hattingh, Shawn. 2008. "ALBA: Creating a Regional Alternative to Neoliberalism?" Venezuelanalysis, 13 February. www.venezuelanalysis.com.

Helleiner, Eric. 2000. "The Politics of Global Financial Reregulation: Lessons from the Fight against Money Laundering." CEPA Working Paper Series III. Working Paper 15.

Henisz, Witold. J., Bennet Zelner and Mauro F. Guillén. 2005. "The Worldwide Diffusion of Market-Oriented Infrastructure Reform, 1977-1999." *American Sociological Review* 70 (6): 871-97.

Henry, James. 2003. *The Blood Bankers: Tales from the Global Underground Economy.* New York, N.Y.: Four Walls Eight Windows.

Hill, Lawrence. 1947. *Brazil.* Berkeley, Calif.: University of California Press and London, U.K.: Cambridge University Press.

Hirschman, Albert O. 1958. *The Strategy of Economic Development.* New Haven, Conn.: Yale University Press.

Hoare, Quintin, and Geoffrey Nowell-Smith. 1971. *Selections from the Prison Notebooks of Antonio Gramsci.* New York, N.Y.: International Publishers.

Hobsbawm, Eric. 1983. "Introduction." In Eric Hobsbawm and Terence Ranger, *The Invention of Tradition.* Cambridge, Mass.: Cambridge University Press.

Hollingworth, Joseph Rogers, Philippe Schmitter and Wolfgang Streeck, eds. 1994. *Governing Capitalist Economies: Performance and Control of Economic Sectors.* Oxford, U.K.: Oxford University Press.

Hornbeck, John F. 2005. "A Free Trade Area of the Americas: Major Policy Issues and Status of Negotiations." CRS Report for Congress RS 20864. Washington, D.C.: Congressional Research Service.

Howell, Jude, and Jenny Pearce. 2001. *Civil Society and Development: A Critical Exploration.* Boulder, Colo.: Lynne Rienner Publishers.

Huber, Evelyne, ed. 2002. *Models of Capitalism: Lessons from Latin America.* University Park: Pennsylvania University Press.

Huber, Evelyne et al. 2006. "Politics and Inequality in Latin America and the Caribbean." *American Sociological Review* 71 (6):943-63.

Hülsse, Rainer and Dieter Kerwer. 2007. "Global Standards in Action: Insights from Anti-Money Laundering Regulation." Organization 14: 625-42.

Hurrell, Andrew. 2005. "Hegemony and Regional Governance in the Americas." In Louise Fawcett and Mónica Serrano, eds., *Regionalism and Governance in the Americas: Continental Drift.* London, U.K.: Palgrave Macmillan, 185-208.

Ianni, Octavio. 1971. *Estado e planejamento no Brasil (1930-64).* Rio de Janeiro, Brazil: Civilização Brasileira.

IBGE. *Contas nacionais trimestrais.* www.ipeadata.gov.br.

——. 2006. *Pesquisa Nacional por Amostra de Domicílios (PNAD).*

——. 2007. *Pesquisa Nacional por Amostra de Domicílios (PNAD)*

——. 2008. *Indicadores sociais, 2008.* www.ibge.gov.br.

——. 2010. *Resultados do 1° Trimestre de 2010—Indicadores de volume e valores correntes.*

http://www.ibge.gov.br/home/estatistica/indicadores/pib/defaulttabelas.shtm

"IDB Aims to Stay Relevant." 2008. *The Banker* 1 July.

"IDB President Calls for Heritage Preservation to Spur Economic and Social Development." 2000. Press Release, World Bank Headquarters 29 March.

IDB. 2006. *The Politics of Policies.* Washington, D.C.: IDB.

———. 2009. "Our History." Washington, D.C.: Inter-American Development Bank.

IEA. 2003. *World Energy Investment Outlook: 2003 Insights.* Paris, France: Organization for Economic Cooperation and Development/International Energy Agency.

———. 2009. *Oil Market Report,* 14 May.

ILO. 2009. "Brazil Extends Bolsa Familia During the Economic Crisis," ILO News, 20 March.

IMF. 2004. *Global Finance Stability Report.* Washington, D.C.: IMF.

———. 2009. "IMF Managing Director Dominique Strauss-Kahn Welcomes Brazil's Intention to Invest Up To US$10 Billion in Notes Issued by the IMF." 10 June.

INEP. 2006. http://www.inep.gov.br/superior/enade/default.asp.

Instituto Patricia Galvão. 2004. *Pesquisa Ibope: O que a sociedade pensa sobre a violência contra as mulheres.* Rio de Janeiro, Brazil.

International Development Bank. *Monumenta—Executive Summary.* http://idbdocs.iadb.org/wsdocs/getdocument.aspx?docnum=437363.

———. *Projects at the International Development Bank.* http://www.bid.org.uy/projects/project.cfm?id= BR0261&lang=en.

Investment Properties Mexico. www.goarticles.com/cgi.

IPEA. *PIB (preços 2009).* www.ipea.data.gov.br.

———. 2006. *Relatório de avaliação da Bolsa Família,* Brasília, Brazil.

———. 2008a. *Mercado de trabalho, trabalho infantil e previdência: primeiras análises.* Brasília, Brasil.

———. 2008b. *PNAD 2007: primeiras análises.* October.

———. *Taxa de câmbio comercial.* www.ipea.data.gov.br.

Itaú-Unibanco Banco Múltiplo S.A. 2009. "Approval of the Merger between Itaú and Unibanco." Press Release, 20 February.

Jackson, Gregory and Richard Deeg. 2006. "How Many Varieties of Capitalism? Comparing the Comparative Institutional Analyses of Capitalist Diversity." MPIfG Discussion Papers, 06/2.

James, Ian. 2006. "Chavez Boost Heating Oil Program for U.S. Poor; Goes After Bush Again." *The Washington Post,* 21 September.

Jardim, María C. 2009. "Domesticação e/ou moralização do capitalismo no governo Lula: inclusão social via mercado e via fundos de pensão." *Revista de Ciências Sociais* 52: 123-59.

Jelin, Elizabeth. 1998. "Toward a Culture of Participation and Citizenship: Challenges for a More Equitable World." In Sonia E. Alvarez; Evelina Dagnino and Arturo Escobar, eds., *Cultures of Politics, Politics of Cultures: Revisioning Latin American Movements.* Boulder, Colo.: Westview Press.

Jochem, Sven and Nico A. Siegel, eds. 2003. *Konzertierung, Verhandlungsdemokratie und Reformpolitik im Wohlfahrtsstaad.* Oplanden: Leske/Budrich.

*Jornadas pelo Aborto Legal e Seguro.* 2005.

*Jornal Mulherio.* May/July 1983.

*Jornal Opinião.* 1973. no 19.

Katzenstein, Peter J. 2005. *A World of Regions: Asia and Europe in the American Imperium.* Ithaca, N.Y.: Cornell University Press.

Kearney, Christine A. 2001. "The Comparative Influence of Neoliberal Ideas: Economic Culture and Stabilization in Brazil." Ph.D. Diss. Brown University.

Keck, Margaret E. 1992. *Workers' Party and Democratization in Brazil.* New Haven, Conn.: Yale University Press.

Kellogg, Paul. 2007. "Regional Integration in Latin America: Dawn of an Alternative to Neoliberalism?" *New Political Science* 29 (2): 187-209.

Kennedy, Paul M. 1988. *The Rise and Fall of the Great Powers.* London, U.K.: Fontana Press.

Kindleberger, Charles P. 1987. *The World in Depression, 1929-1939.* Middlesex, U.K.: Penguin Books.

Kitschelt, Herbert, et al. 1999. *Continuity and Change in Contemporary Capitalism.* Cambridge, Mass.: Cambridge University Press.

Kiyosaki, Kim. 2006. *Rich Woman: A Book on Investing for Women.* Rich Publishing, LLC.

Kiyosaki, Robert T. and Sharon L. Lechter. 2000. *Rich Dad, Poor Dad: What the Rich Teach their Kids Abou Money—That the Poor and Middle Class do Not!* Warner Business Books.

Klein, Cristian. 2007. *O desafio da reforma política: conseqüências dos sistemas eleitorais de listas aberta e fechadas.* Rio de Janeiro, Brazil: Mauad.

Knight, Jack. 2001. "Explaining the Rise of Neoliberalism: Mechanisms of Institutional Change." In John L. Campbell and Ove K. Pedersen, eds., *The Rise of Neoliberalism and Institutional Analysis.* Princeton, N.J.: Princeton University Press.

Knox, John. 1969. "Contest Between Legal-Tender Note and National Bank Note, 1862-1878," In *A History of Banking in the United States, Reprints of Economic Classics.* New York, N.Y.: August M. Kelley Publishers.

Knudsen, Laura M. 2006. *Reproductive Rights in a Global Context.* Nashville, Tenn.: Vanderbilt University Press.

Kohli, Atul. 2004. *State Directed Development: Political Power and Industrialization in the Global Periphery.* Cambridge, Mass.: Cambridge University Press.

Kottak, Conrad. 2009. *Prime-Time Society: An Anthropological Analysis of Television and Culture.* Walnut Creek, Calif.: Left Coast Press.

Kuczinsky, Pedro-Pablo and John Williamson. 2004. *Depois do Consenso de Washington: retomando o crescimento e a reforma na América Latina.* São Paulo: Editora Saraiva.

Kudrle, Robert T. 2008. "Did Blacklisting Hurt the Tax Havens?" Paolo Baffi Centre Research Paper Series 23. http://papers.ssrn.com/sol3/papers.cfm?abstract_id=1243695.

Kurtz, Marcus. 2001. "State Developmentalism without a Developmentalist State: The Public Foundations of the 'Free-Market Miracle' in Chile." *Latin American Politics and Society* 43 (2): 1-25.

Lacerda, João. 1938. *O Estado Novo: democracia e corporatismo, a posição do Brasil.* Rio de Janeiro, Brazil: Editora Nacional.

Lafer, Celso. 1970. *O sistema político brasileiro.* São Paulo, Brazil: Perspectiva.

——. 2009. "Brazil and the World." In Ignacy Sachs et al., eds., *Brazil: A Century of Change.* Chapel Hill, N.C.: University of North Carolina Press, 101-19.

Lamounier, Bolivar and Raquel Meneguello. 1986. *Partidos políticos e consolidação democrática.* São Paulo, Brazil: Brasiliense.

Lange, Matthew and Dietrich Rueschemeyer, eds. 2005. *States and Development: Historical Antecedents of Stagnation and Advance.* New York, N.Y.: Palgrave MacMillan.

Lavalle, Adrián G., Peter P. Houtzager, and Graziela Castello. 2006. "Democracia, pluralização da representação e sociedade civil." *Lua Nova,* 67: 49-103.

Leff, Nathaniel. 1977. *Política econômica e desenvolvimento no Brasil (1947-64).* São Paulo, Brazil: Perspectiva.

Lei Maria da Penha, Lei n° 11.340, de 7 de Agosto de 2006. http://www.planalto.gov.br/ccivil_03/_Ato2004-2006/2006/Lei/L11340.htm.

LeVine, Steve. 2009. "Free Trade in the Slow Lane." *Business Week,* 21 September: 59.

Levy, María B. 1967. *História dos bancos comerciais no Brasil.* Rio de Janeiro, Brazil: IBMEC.

Lindblom, Charles E. and Edward J. Woodhouse. 1993. *The Policy Making Process.* New Jersey: Prentice Hall.

Lins, Alvaro. 1962. *Rio-Branco.* São Paulo, Brazil: Cia. Editora Nacional.

Loureiro, Maria Rita. 1997. *Os economistas no governo: gestão econômica e democracia.* Rio de Janeiro, Brazil: Editora FGV.

Loureiro, Maria Rita, and Fernando Abrucio. 1999. "Política e burocracia no presidencialismo brasileiro: o papel do Ministério da Fazenda no primeiro governo Fernando Henrique Cardoso." *Revista Braileira de Ciências Sociais* 14(41): 69-89.

Löwy, Michael. 1999. "Pontos de referência para uma história do Marxismo na América Latina." In Michael Löwy, ed., *O Marxismo na América Latina: uma antologia de 1909 aos dias atuais.* São Paulo, Brazil: Editora Fundação Perseu Abramo, 9-64.

"Lula Wants to Fight; Invigorated by the Crisis, Brazil's President says He's Praying for Obama." 2009. *Newsweek,* 30 March: 43.

Lustig, Nora. 2009. "Poverty, Inequality, and the New Left in Latin America," Presentation given at Woodrow Wilson International Center for Scholars, Wasghinton, D.C., July 21.

MacCannell, Dean. 1999. *The Tourist: A New Theory of the Leisure Class.* Berkeley: University of California Press.

MacDonald, Austin. 1954. *Latin American Politics and Government.* New York, N.Y.: Thomas Y. Crowell Company.

Mace, Gordon and Jean-Philippe Thérien. 2007. "Inter-American Governance: a Sysyphean Endeavor?" In G. Mace, J.P. Thérien, and P. Haslam, eds., *Governing the Americas: Assessing Multilateral Institutions.* Boulder, Colo.: Lynne Rienner, 45-67.

Machado, Lia Zanotta. 1998. "Matar e morrer no masculino e no feminino." In

Ricardo Lima, Djaci Oliveira, and Elen Geraldes, eds., *A primavera já partiu*. Petrópolis, Brazil: Editora Vozes e M.N.D.H.

———. 2001. *Eficácia e desafios das delegacias especializadas no atendimento às mulheres: o futuro dos direitos à não violência*. Brasília, Brazil: Conselho Nacional dos Direitos da Mulher.

———. 2002. "Atender vítimas, criminalizar violências: dilemas das delegacias da mulher." *Série Antropologia* 319. Brasília: UnB Press.

———. 2004. "Masculinidades e violências: o mal-estar da contemporaneidade." In Mônica Schpun, ed., *Masculinidades*. São Paulo, Brazil: Boitempo.

———. 2008. "Os novos contextos e os novos têrmos do debate contemporâneo sobre o aborto: a questão de gênero e o impacto social das novas narrativas biológicas, jurídicas e religiosas." *Série Antropologia* 419. Brasília, Brazil: UnB Press.

Machado, Maíra Rocha. 2008. "Financial Regulation and International Criminal Policy: The Anti-Money Laundering System in Brazil and Argentina." Paper presented at the 2006 Law and Society Meeting, Baltimore, Maryland.

Machado, Sérgio. 1998. *Reforma político partidária: relatório final*. Brasília, Brazil: Senado Federal.

Machinea, José Luis and Narcís Serra, eds. 2007. *Visiones del desarrollo en América Latina*. Santiago, Chile: CEPAL.

Magalhães, Aloisio. 1997. *E triunfo? a questão dos bens culturais no Brasil*. Rio de Janeiro, Brazil: Nova Fronteira.

Mahoney, James. 2000. "Path Dependence in Historical Sociology." *Theory and Society* 29 (4).

Mainwaring, Scott. 1993. "Presidentialism, multipartism and democracy: the difficult combination." *Comparative Political Studies* 26(2):198-228.

Mainwaring, Scott and Timothy R. Scully, eds. 1995. *Building Democratic Institutions—Party Systems in Latin America*. Palo Alto, Calif.: Stanford University Press.

Malamud, Andrés. 2005. "Mercosur Turns 15: Between Rising Rhetoric and Declining Achievement." *Cambridge Review of International Affairs* 18 (3): 421-36.

Mancuso, Wagner P. 2004. "O lobby da indústria no congresso nacional: empresariado e política no Brasil contemporâneo." *Dados* 47 (3): 505-47.

———. 2007. "O empresariado como ator político no Brasil: balanço da literatura e agenda de pesquisa." *Revista de Sociologia e Política* 28: 131-46.

Margolis, Mac. 2008. "Cutting Things Down to Size; As Brazil Becomes a More Powerful Player, its Neighbors are Becoming Increasingly Aggressive." *Newsweek*, 24 November: 52-53.

Marques, Myriam Silva. 1999. *Não é o certo, mas foi o certo prá mim: um estudo sobre aborto provocado entre adolescentes*. M.A. Diss. Bahia/Minas Gerais, Brazil: Grupo Ânima.

Marques Pereira, Jaime and Bruno Théret. 2009. "Mediations Institutionnelles de la Regulation Sociale et Dynamiques Macro-economiques." *Ponto de Vista* 9.

Marquetti, Adalmir. 2007. "Experiências de orçamento participativo no Brasil: uma proposta de classificação." In Evelina Dagnino and Luciana Tatagiba, eds., *Democracia, sociedade civil e participação*. Chapecó, Brazil: Argos, 77-95.

Martin, Randy. 2002. *Financialization of Daily Life*. Philadelphia, Penn.: Temple

University Press.

Martínez, Juan and Javier Santiso. 2003. "Financial Markets and Politics. The Confidence Game in Latin American Emerging Economies." *International Political Science Review* 24 (3): 363-95.

Martins, Andréa. Personal Interview. August 10, 2008.

Martins, Carlos E. 1974. *Tecnocracia e capitalismo.* São Paulo, Brazil: Brasiliense/ CEBRAP.

Martins, Luciano. 1985. *Estado capitalista e burocracia no Brasil pós-64.* Rio de Janeiro, Brazil: Paz e Terra.

Martins dos Santos, Francisco. 1941. *O fato moral e o fato social da década getuliana.* Rio de Janeiro, Brazil: Z. Valverde.

Mattar, Eliana. 2003. "Dos arquivos em defesa do Estado ao Estado em defesa dos arquivos." In Eliana Mattar, ed., *Acesso à informação e política de arquivos.* Rio de Janeiro, Brazil: Arquivo Nacional.

Mattos, Paul and Diogo Coutinho. 2008. "Law and the New Developmental State: Pilot Project on Brazil," unpublished project document.

Maxwell, Kenneth. 1999. "The Two Brazils." *The Wilson Quarterly* 23.

McCann, Bryan. 2004. *Hello, Hello Brazil: Popular Music in the Making of Modern Brazil.* Durham, N.C.: Duke University Press.

McGee, Micki 2005. *Self-Help, Inc.: Makeover Culture in American Life.* London, U.K.: Oxford University Press.

McGillivray, Warren. 2001. "Contribution Evasion: Implications for Social Security Pension Schemes." *International Social Security Association Review* 54 (2): 3-22.

McKinsey & Company, Inc. 2004. *Eliminando as barreiras ao crescimento econômico e a economia formal no Brasil.* São Paulo, Brazil: McKinsey & Company.

Médici, André Cezar and Marco Maciel. 1996. "A dinâmica do gasto social nas três esferas de governo: 1980-92," *Decentralização e políticas sociais.* São Paulo, Brazil: FUNDAP.

Medeiros, Rogério de Souza. 2007. "Crítica e resignação nas atuais relações entre as ONGs e o Estado no Brasil." In Evelina Dagnino and Luciana Tatagiba, eds., *Democracia, sociedade civil e participação.* Chapecó: Argos, 167-202.

Meira, Ana Lúcia. 2004. *O passado no futuro da cidade: políticas públicas e participação dos cidadãos na preservação do patrimônio cultural de Porto Alegre.* Porto Alegre, Brazil: Editora da Universidade Federal do Rio Grande do Sul.

Meirelles, Henrique de Campos. 2010. "Estabilidade macroeconomica e crescimento." Presentation on Central Bank of Brazil website. http://www.bcb.gov.br/?RED1-APRESPRONUNC.

Melo, Carlos Ranuflo. 2004. *Retirando as cadeiras do lugar: migração partidária na Câmara dos Deputados (1985-2002).* Belo Horizonte, Brazil: Editora da UFMG.

———. 2006. "Sistema partidário, presidencialismo e reforma política no Brasil." In Gláucio Soares, and Lúcio Rennó, *Reforma política: lições da história contemporânea.* Rio de Janeiro, Brazil: Editora da FGV, 157-75.

Melo, Marcus André. "Institutional Choice and the Diffusion of Policy Paradigms: Brazil and the Second Wave of Pension Reform." *International Political Science Review* 25 (3): 320-41.

Meneguello, Rachel. 1998. *Partidos e governos no Brasil contemporâneo (1985-1997).* São Paulo, Brazil: Paz e Terra.

Menz, Georg. 2003. "Re-regulating the Single Market: National Varieties of Capitalism and their Responses to Europeanization." *Journal of European Public Policy* 10 (4): 532-55.

Mesa-Lago, Carmelo. 2000. "Comentarios a la reforma de la seguridad social en Venezuela." Caracas: ILDIS-GTZ.

———. 2002. "The Politics Pension Reform in Latin America." *Journal of Latin America Studies* 34 (3): 687-715.

———. 2004. "Las reformas de pensiones en América Latina y su impacto en los principios de la seguridad social", *Financiamiento del desarrollo* 144, Santiago de Chile, Comisión Económica para América Latina (CEPAL).

Meynaud, Jean. 1964. *La Technocracie: Mythe ou Realite*. Paris, France: Payot

Miliband, Ralph. 1983. *Class Power and State Power*. London, U.K.: Verso.

Ministerio da Cultura. 1980. *Proteção e revitilização do patrimônio cultural no Brasil: uma trajetória*. Brasília, Brazil: SPHAN/Pro-Memória.

Ministério da Fazenda. 2008. *Relatório de atividades da COAF*. Brasília, Brazil: Ministério da Fazenda.

Ministério da Previdência e Assistência Social. 1999. *Informe da previdência* 11 (11).

———. 2004. *Informe da previdência* 16 (1).

———. 2004. *Resultado do regime geral de previdência social*. Nota Técnica n° 003/04.

Ministério da Previdência Social. 2008. *Overview of Brazilian Social Welfare*, Brasília, Brazil.

Ministério do Planejamento, Orçamento e Gestão. 2003a. *Boletim estatístico de pessoal* 92. Brasília, Brasil: MP.

———. 2003b. *Projeções do orçamento para 2004*. Brasília, Brazil: MP.

———. 2008. *Boletim estatístico de pessoal* 152. Brasília, Brazil: MP.

"More Bounty." 2008. *The Economist*, 19 April: 82.

Moreira, Ajax et al. 2008. "O papel dos fundamentos domésticos na vulnerabilidade econômica dos emergentes." Texto para Discussão 1358. Rio de Janeiro, Brazil: IPEA.

Moreira, Mauricio Mesquita. 2009. "Trade Policy: Old and New Issues." In Lael Brainard and Leonardo Martinez-Diaz, eds., *Brazil as an Economic Superpower? Understanding Brazil's Changing Role in the Global Economy*. Washington, D.C.: Brookings Institution Press.

Moreira, Vicente Deocleciano. 2007. "Vivaldo e o Maciel." In Jeferson Bacelar and Claudio Pereira, eds., *Vivaldo da Costa Lima: intérprete do Afro-Brasil*. Salvador, Brazil: EDUFBA.

Moreno, Luis Alberto. 2008. "Enhancing Competitiveness in Latin America: the Role of Infrastructure." Speech given at Canning House Conference, London, 21 January.

Morley, Samuel and David Coady. 2003. *From Social Assistance to Social Development: A Review of Targeted Education Subsidies in Developing Countries*. International Food Policy Research Institute, Washington, D.C., February.

Motta Veiga, Pedro da. 2009. "Brazil's Trade Policy: Moving Away from Old Paradigms." In Lael Brainard and Leonardo Martinez-Diaz, eds., *Brazil as an Economic Superpower? Understanding Brazil's Changing Role in the Global Economy*. Washington, D.C.: Brookings Institution Press, 113-136.

Mueller, Charles C. 2009. "Agricultural, Agrarian, and Environmental Policy

Formation under Lula: The Role of Policy Networks." In Joseph L. Love and Werner Baer, eds., *Brazil Under Lula: Economy, Politics, and Society under the Worker-President.* New York, N.Y.: Palgrave-MacMillan, 136-50.

Müller. Lucia. 2006. *Mercado exemplar: estudo antropológico sobre a bolsa de valores.* Porto Alegre, Brazil: Zouk.

Murro, Ernesto. 2001. "As tendências na América Latina e a reforma Uruguaiana da previdência social." Paper presented at the Conference, "Previdência Social e Pública—desafios para sua preservação," Brasília, Brazil, October.

Najjar, Jorge and Rosana Najjar. 2007. "Reflections on the Relationship between Education and Archaeology: An Analysis of IPHAN's Role as Collective Educator" *Archaeologies* 3: 169-78.

Nakahodo, Sidney Nakao, and José Roberto Ferreira Savoia. 2008. "Reforma da previdência no Brasil: Estudo Comparativo dos Governos Fernando Henrique Cardoso e Lula." *Revista Brasileira de Ciências Sociais* 23: 45-58.

Nau, Henry R. 1990. *The Myth of America's Decline: Leading the World Economy into the 1990's.* New York, N.Y.: Oxford University Press.

Neri, Marcelo. 2001. "Recursos existem, falta qualidade." *Conjuntura Economica* 55(11) Nov.: 78-79.

———. 2002. "Decent Work and the Informal Sector." *Ensaios Economicos EPGE* 461.

Neuhaus, Paulo 1975. *História Monetária do Brasil 1900 -1945.* Rio de Janeiro, Brazil: IBMEC.

"New Horizons: Petrobrás." 2009. *The Banker,* 10 March.

Nicolau, Jairo. 2004. "Receita para reduzir escândalos." *O Globo,* 4 March: 7.

———. 2006a. "Lista aberta-lista fechada." In Leonardo Arvitzer, and Fátima Anastásia, eds., *Reforma política no Brasil.* Belo Horizonte, Brazil: Editora da UFMG, 133-36.

———. 2006b. "Voto personalizado e reforma eleitoral no Brasil." In Gláucio Soares, and Lúcio Rennó, eds., *Reforma política: lições da história contemporânea.* Rio de Janeiro, Brazil: Editora da FGV, 23-33.

———. 2007. "Cinco opções, uma escolha: o debate sobre a reforma do sistema eleitoral no Brasil" Plenarium [Câmara dos Deputados] 4: 70-79.

Nóbrega, Maílson da. 2005. *O futuro chegou: instituições e desenvolvimento no Brasil.* São Paulo: Editora Globo.

Nogueira, Antonio Gilberto Ramos. 2005. *Por um inventario dos sentidos: Mario de Andrade e a concepção de patrimonio e inventario.* São Paulo, Brazil: Editora Hucitec.

Novaro, Marcos. 2000. *Representación y liderazgo en las democracias contemporaneás.* Rosario, Argentina: HomoSapiens Ediciones.

Nonneman, Gerd, ed. 1996. *Political and Economic Liberalization: Dynamics and Linkages in Comparative Perspective.* Boulder, Colo.: Lynne Rienner Publishers.

North, Douglas. 1990. *Institutions, Institutional Change and Economic Performance.* Cambridge, Mass.: Cambridge University Press.

———. 1998. "Economic Performance Through Time." In M. C. Brinton and V. Nee. *The New Institutionalism in Sociology.* Stanford, CA: Stanford University Press.

———. 2005. *Understanding the Process of Economic Change.* Princeton, N.J.: Princeton

University Press.

Northcote, Stafford H. and Charles E. Trevelyan. 1854. *Report on the Organization of the Permanent Civil Service, 1853.* London, House of Commons: Her Majesty's Stationery Office.

"Número de investidores de varejo na BM&F Bovespa bate recorde em outubro." 2009. *Infomoney*, 6 November.

Nunes, Edson. 1997. *A gramática política do Brasil: clientelismo e insulamento burocrático.* Rio de Janeiro, Brazil: Zahar.

Nylen, William. 2003. *Participatory Democracy Versus Elitist Democracy: Lessons from Brazil.* London, U.K.: Palgrave Macmillan.

O'Donnell, Guillermo. 1975. "Sobre o corporativismo e a questão do Estado." *Cadernos DCP*, Belo Horizonte, Brazil.

OECD. 2002. Social Expenditure Database 1980-1998. November. www.oecd.org.

———. 2009. Brazil: OECD Economic Survey. Paris: OECD Development Center, July.

"Oil price history and analysis." WTRG Economics. www.wtrg.com.

OLADE. 2007. *Energy Economic Information System: Energy Statistics.* Quito, Ecuador: Latin American Energy Association.

Oliveira, Francisco, Kaizô Beltrão, and Mônica Ferreira. 1997. "Reforma da previdência." Texto para discussão n° 508. Rio de Janeiro, Brazil: IPEA.

Olivieri, Cecília. 2007. "Política, burocracia e redes sociais: as nomeaçõ es para lo alto escalão do Banco Central do Brazil." *Revista de Sociologia Política* 29.

———. 2010a. *A lógica política do controle interno: o monitoramento das políticas públicas no presidencialismo brasileiro.* São Paulo, Brazil: Annablume.

———. 2010b. *Política e burocracia no Brasil: o controle sobre a execução das políticas públicas.* Tese de Doutorado, EAESP/FGV, São Paulo.

Olson, Mancur. 2000. *Power and Prosperity. Outgrowing Communist and Capitalist Dictatorships.* New York, N.Y.: Basic Books.

Onody, Oliver. 1960. *A inflação brasileira, 1820-1958.* Rio de Janeiro, Brazil: [s.n.]

Orçamento Participativo. 2008. *Regimento interno—critérios gerais, técnicos e regionais—2008/2009.* Porto Alegre, Brazil: Prefeitura Municipal de Porto Alegre.

Organización Latinoamerica de Solidariedad. 1967. "Declaración General de La Primera Conferencia Latinoamericana de Solidaridad." In Michael Löwy, ed., *O Marxismo na América Latina: uma antologia de 1909 aos dias atuais.* São Paulo, Brazil: Editoria Perseu Abramo, 303-14.

Packeman, Robert. 1994. *The Politics of Economic Liberalization: Argentina and Brazil in Comparative Perspective.* Ft. Wayne, Ind.: University of Notre Dame/Kellogg Institute, April.

Palermo, Vicente. 2000. "Como se governa o Brasil? O debate sobre instituições políticas e gestão do governo". *Dados* 43(3): 521-558.

Palier, Bruno and Yves Surel. 2005. "Les 'Trois I' et l'Analyse de l'Etat en Action." *Revue Française de Science Politique* 55 (1): 7-32.

Panizza, Francisco. 2006. "'Brazil needs to change': Change as iteration and the iteration of change in Brazil's 2002 presidential election." *Cuadernos del CLAFH* 1, Special ed.

Paoli, Maria Célia and Vera da Silva Telles. 1998. "Social Rights: Conflicts and Negotiations in Contemporary Brazil." In Sonia E. Alvarez; Evelina Dagnino and Arturo Escobar, eds., *Cultures of Politics. Politics of Cultures: Revisioning Latin American Movements.* Boulder, Colo.: Westview Press.

Parra, Sebastián Neto and Javier Santiso. 2008. "Wall Street and Elections in Latin American Emerging Democracies." *Latin American Economic Outlook.* Working Paper 272.

Parra-Bernal, Guillermo and Lester Pimentel. 2008. "Brazil Became Net Creditor for First Time in January (Update 4)." *Bloomberg LP* 21 February. www.bloomberg.com.

Partido dos Trabalhores. 1990. "Resolução do 7 encontro nacional do PT." In Michael Löwy, ed., *O Marxismo na América Latina: uma antologia de 1909 aos dias atuais.* São Paulo: Editora Fundacão Perseu Abramo, 496-503.

Paula, Ana Paula Paes de and Thomaz Wood Jr. 2002. "Pop-management: contos de paixão, lucro e poder." *Encontro de Estudos Organizacionais* 9 (24): 39-51.

Pearce, Jenny. 2004. "Collective Action or Public Administration?: Civil Society and the Public Sphere in Post-Transition Latin America." In Marlies Glasius, David Lewis and Hakan Seckinelgin, eds., *Exploring Civil Society: Political and Cultural Contexts.* New York, N.Y.: Routledge, 61-70.

Pedersen, Jorgen D. 2008. *Globalization, Development and the State the Performance of India and Brazil since 1990.* London, U.K.: Palgrave Macmillan.

Peixoto, João Paulo M. (Org). 2008. *Governando o governo: modernização da administração pública no Brasil.* São Paulo, Brazil: Atlas.

Perusso, Mari, et al. 2008. "The Practice. The Initial Experience of Implementation in the 17 Regions of Porto Alegre." In Jandira Feijó and Augusto de Franco, eds., *Views on the the Local Solidary Governance in Porto Alegre.* Porto Alegre, Brazil: EDIPUCRS, 63-92.

Phillips, Tom. 2009. "Brazil pledges deep emission cuts in 'political gesture' to rich nations." *The Guardian,* 10 November.

Pierson, Paul. 1998. "Irresistible forces, immovable objects: post-industrial welfare states confront permanent austerity." *Journal of European Public Policy* 5 (4): 539-60.

——. 2004. *Politics in Time, History, Institutions and Social Analysis.* Princeton, N.J.: Princeton University Press.

Pinto, Céli Regina Jardim. 2003. *Uma história do feminismo no Brasil.* São Paulo, Brazil: Editora Fundação Perseu Abramo.

Polanyi, Karl. 1944. *The Great Transformation.* Boston, Mass.: Beacon Press.

Power, Timothy J. 1997. *A Social Democracia no Brasil e no Mundo.* Porto Alegre, Brazil: Instituto Teotônio Vilela/Fundação Pedroso Horta.

Prebisch, Raúl. 1949. *The Economic Development of Latin America and Some of its Problems.* Santiago, Chile: Economic Commission for Latin America.

Preda, Alex. 2001. "The Rise of Popular Investor: Financial Knowledge and Investing in England and France, 1840-1880." *The Sociological Quartely* 42: 205-32.

Przeworksi, Adam. 1985. *Capitalism and Social Democracy.* Cambridge, Mass. and New York, N.Y.: Cambridge University Press.

Przeworski, Adam and Carolina Curvale. 2007. "Instituciones políticas y desarrollo económico en las Américas: el largo plazo." In José Luis Machinea and Narcís Serra, eds., *Visiones del desarrollo en América Latina*. Santiago, Chile: CEPAL.

Przeworski, Adam, Susan Stokes, and Bernard Manin, eds. 1999. *Democracy, Accountability and Representation*. Cambridge: Cambridge University Press.

*Públicas*. 2005. Brasília, Brazil: CEPAL and SPM.

Pujol, Júlio. 2008. Personal Interview. 13 May.

Putnam, Robert. 1993. *Making Democracy Work: Civil Traditions in Modern Italy*. Princeton, N.J.: Princeton University Press.

Queiroz, Jose Eduardo and Marina de Carvalho Anselmo. 2005. "The New Brazilian Bankruptcy Law." *International Finance Law Review* 01 Mar.

Radler, Marilyn. 2009. "Oil, gas reserves rise as oil output declines." *Oil and Gas Journal*, 21 Dec.: 18.

Ramos, Lauro. 2007. "O desempenho recente do mercado de trabalho brasileiro: tendências, fatos estilizados e padrões espaciais." Texto para discussão n° 1255. Rio de Janeiro, Brazil: IPEA.

Ratton Jr., Amorin and José Luiz. 1996. *Violência e crime no Brasil contemporâneo*. Brasília, Brazil: Cidade Gráfica Editora.

Razavi, Hossein. 1996. *Financing energy projects in emerging economies*. Tulsa, Okla.: PennWell Publishing.

Rego, Antonio Carlos Pojo and João Paulo M. Peixoto. 1998. *A Política das reformas econômicas no Brasil*. Rio de Janeiro, Brazil: Expressão e Cultura.

Reinert, Erik. 2007. *How Rich Countries Got Rich...and Why Poor Countries Stay Poor*. London, U.K.: Constable.

Reis, Bruno. 2007. "O presidencialismo de coalizão sob pressão: da formação de maiorias democráticas à formação democrática de maiorias." Plenarium [Câmara dos Deputados] 4: 80-103.

Relativo ao Estatuto Jurídico da Igreja Católica no Brasil, 2008. Website. http://www.camara.gov.br/sileg/integras/637903.pdf

Renault, Sérgio, and Pierpaulo Bottini. 2005. *Reforma do judiciário*. São Paulo, Brazil: Saraiva.

Rennó, Lúcio, ed. 2007. *Reforma política em questão*. Brasília, Brazil: Editora da UnB.

Ribeiro, Benedito and Mário M. Guimarães. 1967. *História dos bancos e do desenvolvimento financeiro do Brasil*. São Paulo, Brazil: Editora Pro-Service.

Ribeiro, Renato Janine. 2003. "Sobre o voto obrigatório." In Maria Victória Benevides, Paulo Vannuchi, and Fábio Kerche, eds., *Reforma política e cidadania*. São Paulo, Brazil: Fundação Perseu Abramo. 182-91.

Ribeiro, Sandra Bernardes. 2005. *Brasília: memória, cidadania e gestão do patrimônio cultural*. São Paulo, Brazil: Editora Annablume.

Roberts, Kenneth. 1998. *Deepening Democracy? The Modern Left and Social Movements in Peru and Chile*. Stanford, Calif.: Stanford University Press.

Rocha, Roberto and Marcelo Caetano. 2008. "O sistema previdenciário brasileiro: uma perspectiva comparada." Texto para discussão no. 1331. Rio de Janeiro, Brazil: IPEA.

Rodrik, Dani. 2004. "Rethinking Growth Policies in the Developing World" Luca d'Agliano Lecture in Development Economics, Torino, Italy. October.

———. 2007. *One Economics, Many Recipes: Globalization, Institutions, and Economic*

*Growth.* Princeton, N. J.: Princeton University Press.

Romero, Simon. 2010. "Sealing Shift, Chávez Gives Contracts to Western Oil Companies." *New York Times,* 12 February.

Rosado Nunes, Maria José and Regina Kurjewicz. 1999. "Aborto: un tema en discusión en la Iglesia Católica.: El Surgimiento de las Católicas por el derecho de decidir." In Lucila Scavone, ed., *Género y salud reproductiva en América Latina.* Cartago, Costa Rica: LUR.

Rostow, Walt W. 1960. *The Stages of Economic Growth: A Non-Communist Manifesto.* Cambridge, Mass.: Cambridge University Press.

Rubim, Antônio Albino Canelas. 2007. "Políticas culturais no Brasil: tristes tradições, enormes desafios." In Antônio Albino Canelas Rubim and Alexandre Barbalho, eds., *Políticas culturais no Brasil.* Salvador, Brazil: EDUFBA, 1-37.

Rueschemeyer, Dietrich, Evelyne Huber Stephens and John Stephens. 1992. *Capitalist Development and Democracy.* Cambridge, Mass.: Polity Press.

Rumsey, John. 2008. "Latin America: Energy Rich, Cash Poor." *The Banker,* 2 June.

Sá, Graciano. 2003. "A revolução cultural no mercado acionário." *Revista de Administração da USP* 38: 112-125.

Sadek, Maria Tereza. 2002. *Reforma do judiciário.* Rio de Janeiro: Konrad Adenauer Stiftung.

——. 2004. "Poder judiciário: perspectivas de reforma." *Opinião Pública* [Campinas] 10 (1): 01-62.

Sallum Brasílio. 1996. *Laberintos: dos generais à Nova República.* São Paulo: Editora Hucitec.

"The Samba Beat, with Missteps." 2008. *The Economist,* 20 December: 57.

Sandbrook, Richard, Marc Edelman, Patrick Heller, and Judith Teichman. 2007. *Social Democracy in the Global Periphery: Origins, Challenges, Prospects.* Cambridge, Mass. and New York, N.Y.: Cambridge University Press.

Santana, Carlos Henrique V. Forthcoming. "Conjuntura crítica, legados institucionais e comunidades epistêmicas: limites e possibilidades de uma agenda de desenvolvimento no Brasil." In Renato Boschi, ed., *Variedades de capitalismo, política e desenvolvimento na América Latina.* Belo Horizonte, Brazil: Ed.UFMG/IUPERJ.

Santos, André Marenco. 2006a. "Regras eleitorais importam? Modelos de listas eleitorais e seus efeitos sobre a competição partidária e o desempenho institucional." *Dados* 49 (4): 721-49.

——. 2006b. "Regras eleitorais, deputados e fidelidade partidária." In Gláucio Soares, and Lúcio Rennó, eds., *Reforma política: lições da história contemporânea.* Rio de Janeiro, Brazil: Editora da FGV, 176-92.

Santos, Eurico Cursino. 2004a. "Comentários ao PL 2.679/2003, da Comissão da Reforma Política da Câmara dos Deputados." *Revista de Informação Legislativa* 161: 15-22.

——. 2004b. "Da obrigatoriedade do voto." *Revista de Informação Legislativa* 161: 101-06.

Santos, Fabiano. 2006. "Governos de coalizão no sistema presidencial: o caso do Brasil sob a égide da Constituição de 1988." In Leonardo Avritzer, and Fátima Anastásia, eds., *Reforma política no Brasil.* Belo Horizonte, Brazil:

Editora da UFMG, 223-36.

Santos, Wanderley Guilherme dos. 2004. "A reforma política convoca impolutos." *Valor*, 4 March: A-9.

Santos Filho, Raimundo, and Vinícius Miguel. 2008. "Coligações proporcionais no sistema eleitoral brasileiro." In João Paulo Viana, and Gilmar Nascimento, eds., *O sistema político brasileiro: continuidade ou reforma?* Porto Velho, Brazil: Edufro, 199-211.

*São Paulo em Perspectiva.* 2006. 20 (3) Jul-Sept.

Sardenberg, Carlos Alberto. 1987. *Aventura e agonia: nos bastidores do Plano Cruzado.* São Paulo, Brazil: Companhia das Letras.

Savóia, José Roberto Ferreira. 2006. "A urgência na inserção da educação financeira no Brasil." *Valor Econômico*, 12 September.

———. 2007. "Reforma previsional en Brasil: el desafio de la inclusión laboral." *Estudios de la Seguridad Social* 100: 65-90.

Savóia, José Roberto Ferreira, André Taue Saito, and Flávia de Angelis Santana. 2007. "Paradigmas da educação financeira no Brasil." *Revista de Administração Pública* 41 (6).

Schamis, Hector E. 2002. *Re-Forming the State: The Politics of Privatization in Latin America and Europe.* Ann Arbor: The University of Michigan Press.

Schirm, Stefan A. 2009. "Brazil's Rise as an Emerging Power: Implications for the U.S. and Europe," paper presented at the conference "Brazil's Rise: A U.S.-European Assessment," Center for Transatlantic Relations, SAIS, Johns Hopkins University, Washington, D.C., June 1-2.

Schmidt-Hebbel, Klaus. 1997. "Pension Systems: From Crisis to Reform." EDI Conference volume.

Schmitter, Philippe. 1971. *Interest conflict and political change in Brazil.* Stanford, Conn.: Stanford University Press.

Schneider, Ben. 1994. *Burocracia pública e política industrial no Brasil.* São Paulo, Brazil: Editora Sumaré.

———. 1995. "El abrazo esquivo: sinergia entre el sector privado y el Estado en los países de industrialización reciente." *Política y Gobierno* 2 (1).

———. 2004. *Business Politics and the State in Twentieth Century Latin America.* Cambridge, Mass.: Cambridge University Press.

———. 2008. "Comparing Capitalisms: Liberal, Coordinated, Network, and Hierarchical Varieties." Mimeo.

Schneider, Ben R. and Sylvia Maxfield, eds. 1997. *Business and the State in Developing Countries.* Ithaca, N.Y./London, U.K.: Cornell University Press.

Schumpeter, Joseph A. 1982. *The Theory of Economic Development: An Inquiry into Profits, Capital, Credit, Interest, and the Business Cycle.* Edison, N.J.: Transaction Publishers.

Schwartz, Rosalie. 1999. *Pleasure Island: Tourism and Temptation in Cuba.* Lincoln, NE: University of Nebraska Press.

Schwarz, Roberto. 1992. *Misplaced Ideas: Essays on Brazilian Culture.* Trans. John Gledson. New York, N.Y.: Verso.

Schwartzman, Simon 2001. *Um espaço para a Ciência: a formação da comunidade científica no Brasil.* Brasília, Brazil: Ministério da Ciência e Tecnologia/CNpq and Centro de Estudos Estratégicos.

SENASP. 2001. *Diagnóstico da criminalidade no Brasil.* Brasília, Brazil: Ministério da

Justiça. http://www.mj.gov.br/services.

Seixas, Sigmaringa, and Edgar Proença. 2005. "Reformas necessárias ao Estado brasileiro." Plenarium [Câmara dos Deputados] 2: 216-42.

Senghaas, Dieter. 1985. *The European Experience: A Historical Critique of Development Theory.* Leamington Spa: Berg Publishers.

Sharman, Jason C. 2006. "The Global Anti-Money Laundering Regime and Developing Countries: Damned if they Do, Damned if they Don't?" Paper presented at the Annual ISA Convention, March 22-25, San Diego, California.

Sheahan, John. 1987. *Patterns of Development in Latin America: Poverty, Depression and Economic Strategy.* Princeton, N.J.: Princeton University Press.

Shonfield, Andrew. 1965. *Modern Capitalism.* Oxford, U.K.: Oxford University Press.

Sicsú, João, Luiz Fernando de Paula and Michel Renaut, eds. 2005. *Novo-desenvolvimentismo: um projeto nacional de crescimento com equidade social.* São Paulo, Brazil: Manole, Konrad Adenauer Stiftung.

Siegel, Nico A. 2005. "Social Pacts Revisited: 'Competite Concertation' and Complex Causality in Negotiated Welfare State Reforms." *European Journal of Industrial Relations* 11: 107.

Silva, Kelly. 2001. *As DEAMs, as corporações policiais e a violência contra as mulheres: representações, dilemas e desafios.* Brasília, Brazil: Conselho Nacional dos Direitos da Mulher.

Silva, Mônica Corrêa da. 2002. *Voto eletrônico: é mais seguro votar assim?* Florianópolis, Brazil: Editora Insular.

Simmel, George. 1990. *The Philosophy of Money.* New York, N.Y.: Routledge.

Simmons, Beth. 2000. "International Efforts against Money Laundering." In Dinah Shelton, ed., *Commitment and Compliance: The Role of Non-binding Norms in the International Legal System.* New York, NY: Oxford University Press.

Singer, Paul. 1974. *Desenvolvimento e crise.* São Paulo, Brazil: DIFEL.

Sinoti, Marta Litwinczik. 2005. *Quem me quer, nao me quer: Brasília, metropole-patrimônio.* São Paulo, Brazil: Editora Annablume.

Skidmore, Thomas E. 1967. *Politics in Brazil, 1930-1964: An Experiment in Democracy.* Oxford, U.K. and New York, N.Y.: Oxford University Press.

——. 1971. *Brasil: de Castelo a Tancredo.* São Paulo, Brazil: Paz e Terra.

——. 2006. Amanhã 217, January/February.

SMCPGL. 2005. *Governança Solidária Local.* Documento-de-referência. Porto Alegre, Brazil: Prefeitura Municipal de Porto Alegre.

——. 2008. "Definition: Local Solidarity Governance." In Jandira Feijó and Augusto de Franco, eds., *Views on the Local Solidarity Governance in Porto Alegre.* Porto Alegre, Brazil: EDIPUCRS.

Smith, Joseph. 2002. *History of Brazil 1500-2000.* London, U.K.: Pearson Education Limited.

Smith, William, Carlos H. Acuña and Eduardo A. Gamarra, eds. 1994. *Latin American Political Economy in the Age of Neoliberal Reform, Theoretical and Comparative Perspectives for the 1990s.* New Brunswick/London: Transaction Publishers.

Snow, Nick. 2009. "Clinton: Energy Security a Major US Foreign Policy Element." *Oil and Gas Journal,* 2 February: 28.

Soares de Lima, Maria Regina and Mônica Hirst. 2006. "Brazil as an Intermediate State and Regional Power: Action, Choice and Responsibilities." _International Affairs_ 82 (1): 21-40.

Soares, Gláucio, and Lúcio Rennó, eds. 2006. _Reforma política: lições da história contemporânea._ Rio de Janeiro, Brazil: Editora da FGV.

Soares, Luiz, ed. 1996. _Violência e política no Rio de Janeiro._ Rio de Janeiro, Brazil: ISER/Relume Dumará.

Soares, Paulo Henrique. 2004a. "Vantagens e desvantagens do voto facultativo." _Revista de Informação Legislativa_ 161: 107-16.

———. 2004b. "Reeleição e estado democrático de direito." _Revista de Informação Legislativa_ 161: 117-20.

Soares, Sérgio et al. 2007. "Conditional Cash Transfers in Brazil, Chile, and Mexico: Impacts Upon Inequality." Working Paper 35, International Poverty Centre.

Södersten, Bo. 1970. _International Economics._ London, U.K.: Harper & Row Publishers.

Sola, Lourdes. 1998. _Idéias econômicas e decisões políticas._ São Paulo, Brazil: Edusp/ FAPESP.

Sorj, Bila and Paula Montero. 1985. "SOS-Mulher e a luta contra a violência." In Bruna Franchetto, Maria Laura Cavalcanti and Maria Luiza Heilborn, eds., _Perspectivas antropológicas da mulher: sobre mulher e violência._ Rio de Janeiro, Brazil: Zahar Editores.

Soskice, David. 1999. "Divergent Production Regimes: Coordinated and Uncoordinated Market Economies in the 1980's and 1990's." In H. Kitschelt et al, eds., _Continuity and Change in Contemporary Capitalism._ Cambridge, Mass.: Cambridge University Press.

Sotelino, Fernando. 1997. "O mundo mudou, e osbancos?" _Gazeta Mercantil,_ 25 September.

———. 2008. "Brazil, Failing to Turn the Corner," Working Paper Series. New York: Columbia University Press.

Souza, Ednilsa Ramos de and Maria Luiza Carvalho de Lima. 2006. "Panorama da violência urbana e suas capitais." _Ciências da Saúde Coletiva_ 11: 1211-22.

Souza, Robson Sávio Reis. 2003. _Homicídios Brasil: comparativo de fonte de dados._ SENASP and CRISP.

SPM. 2005a. Portaria n° 4, de 6 de Abril. Brasília, Brazil.

———. 2005b. _Relatório final dos trabalhos da Comissão de Revisão da Legislação Punitiva,_ 1 August, Brasília.

———. 2008. _II Plano nacional de políticas para as mulheres._ Brasília, Brazil: Secretaria Especial de Políticas para as Mulheres.

Stallings, Barbara and Rogerio Studart. 2006. _Finance for Development: Latin America in Comparative Perspective._ Washington D.C.: Brookings Institution Press.

Stiglitz, Joseph E. 2003. _The Roaring Nineties: a New History of the World's Most Prosperous Decade._ New York, NY.: W. W. Norton & Co.

Stokes, Susan. 2001. _Mandates and Democracy: Neoliberalism by Surprise in Latin America._ Cambridge, Mass.: Cambridge University Press.

Studart, Rogerio. 2000. "Financial Opening and Deregulation in Brazil in the 1990's." _The Quarterly Review of Economics and Finance_ 40 (1).

Suárez, Mirey and Lourdes Bandeira. 1999. "Introdução." In Mireya Suárez and

Lourdes Bandeira, eds., *Violência, gênero e crime no Distrito Federal.* Brasília, Brazil: Editora Universidade de Brasília.

Sullivan, Mark P., Rebecca G. Rush and Clare Ribando Seelke. 2008. "Latin America: Energy Supply, Political Developments, and U.S. Policy Approaches." CRS Report for Congress (RL 33693). Washington, DC: Congressional Research Service.

SVS. Tabela de Estimativas Vitais. Website. http://tabnet.datasus.gov.br/cgi/deftohtm.exe?sim/cnv/matuf.def.

———. 2006. *Redução de homicídios no Brasil.* Brasília, Brazil: Ministério de Saúde.

Tatagiba, Luciana. 2006. "Os desafios da articulação entre sociedade civil e sociedade política sob o marco da democracia gerencial: o caso do projeto Rede Criança em Vitória/Es." In Evelina Dagnino, Alberto J. Olvera and Aldo Panfichi, eds., *A disputa pela construção democrática na América Latina.* São Paulo, Brazil: Editora Paz e Terra, 137-78.

Tavares Filho, Newton. 2005. "Emenda Constitucional No. 45 e a reforma do Poder Judiciário: algumas observações." Plenarium [Câmara dos Deputados] 2: 202-15.

Taylor, Matthew. 2006. "Veto and voice in the courts: Policy implications of institutional design in the Brazilian Judiciary." *Comparative Politics* 38 (3): 337-55.

———. 2007. "O Judiciário e as políticas públicas no Brasil." *Dados* 50 (2): 229-57.

———. 2008. *Judging Policy: Courts and Policy Reform in Brazil.* Stanford, Calif.: Stanford University Press.

Taylor, Matthew and Luciano da Ros. 2008. "Partidos de dentro e de fora do poder: a judicialização como resultado contingente da estratégia política." *Dados* 51 (3): 438-69.

Teixeira, Letícia Miranda. 2005. "A política contra a lavagem de dinheiro no Brasil: o processo de absorção de um regime internacional." MA Diss. Universidade de Brasília.

Teixeira, Rodolfo. 2009. "Reforma política: dilemas brasileiros e experiências estrangeiras." Ph.D. Diss. Universidade de Brasília.

Telles, Mário de Pragmacio Ferreira. 2009a. "Attractive upside on high growth profile." *Credit Suisse Equity Research,* 10 December.

Telles, Mário de Pragmacio Ferreira. 2009b. "Entre a lei e as salchichas: analise dos antecedents do Decreto-Lei 25/37." Paper presented at the 5th meeting of Estudos Multidisciplinares em Cultura, Federal University of Bahia, Salvador, Brazil.

Thelen, Kathleen. 2004. *How Institutions Evolve: The Political Economy of Skills in Germany, Britain, the United States and Japan.* Cambridge, Mass.: Cambridge University Press.

Thomson, David, ed. 1982. *Political Ideas.* London, U.K.: Penguin Books.

Thrift, Nigel J. 2008. "The New Economy and a New Market Culture." In Ismail Erturk, Julie Froud, Sukhdev Johal, Adam Leaver, and Karel Williams, eds., *Financialization at Work: Key Texts and Commentary.* New York, N.Y.: Routledge.

Tockman, Jason. 2009. "Multipolar Machinations: Chávez Endeavors to "Sow the Oil" with Russia and China." *NACLA,* 15 October.

Toledo, Roberto Pompeu de. 1994. *História do Unibanco, 1924-1994.* São Paulo, Brazil: Instituto Moreira Salles.

Topik, Steven. 1989. "The Old Republic." In Michael L.Conniff and Frank McCann eds., *Modern Brazil: Elites and Masses in Historical Perspective.* Lincoln, NE: University of Nebraska Press.

Torre, Augusto, Juan Carlos Gozzi and Sergio L. Schmukler. 2007. "El desarrollo económico en América Latina." In José Luis Machinea and Narcís Serra, eds., *Visiones del desarrollo en América Latina.* Santiago, Chile: CEPAL.

Triffin, Robert. 1960. *Gold and the Dollar Crisis: The Future of Convertibility.* New Haven, Conn.: Yale University Press

Trigueiros, Florisvaldo dos Santos. 1958. *Museu e educação.* Rio de Janeiro, Brazil: Irmãos Pongetti.

Trubek, David M. 2008. "Developmental States and the Legal Order: Toward a New Political Economy of Development and Law," Paper presented at the Conference "Social Science in the Age of Globalization. National Institute for Advanced Study on Social Science," Shanghai, China, December.

Tschoegl, Adrian E. 2006. "Foreign Ownership in Mexican Banking: A Self Correcting Phenomenon," Philadelphia, Pa.: The Wharton School of the University of Pennsylvania.

Ulyssea, Gabriel. 2005. "Informalidade no mercado de trabalho brasileiro: uma resenha da literatura." Texto para discussão n° 1070. Rio de Janeiro, Brazil: IPEA.

UNCTAD. 2009. *Trade and Development Report, 2009.* New York and Geneva: United Nations Publication.

UNESCO. *Intangible Heritage.* Web.

———. 2008. *World Heritage Information Kit.* Paris, France: UNESCO.

United Press International. 2010. "Ambitious UNASUR seeks to make impact without conflict." Jun. 16. http://www.upi.com/Top_News/Special/2010/06/16/Ambitious-UNASUR-seeks-to-make-impact-without-conflict/UPI-62331276717712/.

"Update 2 - Venezuela Gives Brazil's Odebrecht $282 mln Tax Bill." 2008. *Reuters,* 4 November.

Urbinati, Nadia. 2006. *Representative Democracy, Principles and Genealogy.* Chicago, Ill.: The University of Chicago Press.

U.S. Energy Information Administration. 2009a. "World Proved Crude Oil Reserves, 1 January 1980 - 1 January 2009, Estimates."

———. 2009b. "Country Analysis Briefs: Brazil."

———. 2010. "Renewable Energy Consumption and Electricity Preliminary 2006 Statistics."

Vargas, Getulio. 1938. *A nova política do Brasil.* Rio de Janeiro, Brazil: José Olympio.

Vásquez, Ian. 1996. "The Brady Plan and Market-Based Solutions to Debt Crises." *Cato Journal* 16 (2).

Vaticano. 2008. Acordo entre a República Federativa do Brasil e a Santa Sé Relativo ao Estatuto Jurídico da Igreja Católica no Brasil. http://www.camara.gov.br/sileg/integras/637903.pdf

Veiga, Luiz H. Cavalcante and Joaquim P. Andrade. 2006. "Money Laundering, Corruption, and Growth. An Empirical Rational for a Global Convergence on Anti-Money Laundering Regulation." Berkeley Program in Law and Economics, Paper 32. Berkeley: University of California Press.

"Venezuela's Hope of Greater Sway Dims as Riches Dip." 2009. *New York Times*, 20 May: A8.

Venzin, Markus. 2009. *Building an International Financial Services Firm*. Oxford, U.K.: Oxford University Press.

Viana, João Paulo, and Flávia Coelho. 2008. "Democracia ou partidocracia? Pontos e contrapontos da lista fechada no Brasil." In João Paulo Viana, and Gilmar Nascimento, eds., *O sistema político: continuidade ou reforma?* Porto Velho: Edufro.

Viana, João Paulo, and Gilmar Nascimento, eds. 2008. *O sistema político brasileiro: continuidade ou reforma?* Porto Velho, Brazil: Edufro.

Vianna, Luiz Werneck. 1999. *Judicialização da política e das relações sociais*. Rio de Janeiro, Brazil: Editora Revan.

———. 2002. *Democracia e os três poderes no Brasil*. Belo Horizonte, Brazil: Editora da UFMG.

Vianna, Luiz Werneck, Marcelo Baumann, and Paula Martins Salles. 2007. "Dezessete anos de judicialização da política." *Tempo Social* 19 (2): 39-85.

Viotti Da Costa, Emilia. 2000. *The Brazilian Empire: Myths and Histories*. Chapel Hill: The University of North Carolina Press.

Wallerstein, Immanuel et al. 2003. *Uma nova fase do capitalismo?* São Paulo, Brazil: Xamã.

Watkins, Eric. 2008. "Mixing Oil and Politics." *Oil and Gas Journal*, 28 July: 27.

———. 2009. "Brazil Considering OPEC's Renewed Membership Invitation." *Oil and Gas Journal*, 6 April: 30.

Weber, Max. 1984. *A Bolsa*. Lisbon, Portugal: Relógio d'água.

Weffort, Francisco. 2000. *A cultura e as revoluções da modernização*. Rio de Janeiro, Brazil: Edições Fundo Nacional de Cultura.

Weinstein, Barbara. 1997. *For Social Peace in Brazil: Industrialists and the Remaking of the Working Class in Sao Paulo, 1920-1964*. Chapel Hill: University of North Carolina Press.

Weisbrot, Mark. 2009. "More of the Same in Latin America." *International Herald Tribune*, 12 August: 6.

Weiss, Linda, ed. 2004. *States in the Global Economy: Bringing Domestic Institutions Back In*. Cambridge, Mass. and New York, N.Y.: Cambridge University Press.

Weiss, Linda. 2010. "The State in the Economy: Neoliberal or Neoactivist?" In Glenn Morgan et al, eds., *Oxford Handbook of Comparative Institutional Analysis*. Oxford, U.K.: Oxford University Press.

Werneck Vianna, Maria Lúcia Teixeira. 1987. *A administração do "milagre" o Conselho Mentário Nacional, 1964-1974*. Petrópolis: Vozes.

Wertheim, Peter Howard. 2004. "Rodriguez Reaffirms PDVSA's Energy Integration Plans." *Oil and Gas Journal*, 18 October.: 32.

Weyland, Kurt. 1996. *Democracy without Equity: Failures of Reform in Brazil*. Pittsburgh, Pa.: University of Pittsburgh Press.

Wheatley, Jonathan. 2009. "Brazil Urged to Lead at Climate Summit." *The Financial Times* (London), 5 October.

"Whose Side is Brazil On?" 2009. *The Economist*, 15 August: 10.

Williams, Daniel and Maher Chmaytelli. 2007. "Chavez Tells OPEC to Use Politics, Curb 'Imperialism.'" *Bloomberg LP*, 19 November.

Williams, Daryle. 2001. *Culture Wars in Brazil: The First Vargas Regime, 1930-1945.* Durham, N.C.: Duke University Press.

Williams, Raymond. 1977. *Marxism and Literature.* New York, N.Y.: Oxford University Press.

Williamson, John, ed. 1990. *The Progress of Policy Reform in Latin America in Latin American Adjustment: How Much Has Happened?* Washington, D.C.: Institute of International Economics.

Wirth, John Davis. 1970. *The Politics of Brazilian Development (1930-45).* Stanford, Conn.: Stanford University Press.

Wolfe, Joel. 1993. *Working Women, Working Men: São Paulo and the Rise of Brazil's Industrial Working Class, 1900-1955.* Durham, N.C.: Duke University Press.

Wood, B. Dan, and Richard W. Waterman. 1994. *Bureaucratic Dynamics—The Role of Bureaucracy in a Democracy.* Boulder, Colo.: Westview Press.

Wilson, Woodrow. 1887. "The Study of Administration," *Political Science Quarterly,* June.

World Bank. 2009. "World Development Indicators Online." Washington, D.C.: World Bank. http://data.worldbank.org/indicator/PA.NUS.FCRF.

World Energy Council. 2008. *Regional Energy Integration in Latin America and the Caribbean.* London, U.K.: World Energy Council.

WTO. 2007. *World Trade Report 2007.* Geneva, Switzerland.

———. 2008. *WTO Statistics 2008.* Geneva, Switzerland.

———. 2009. *WTO Statistics 2009.* Geneva, Switzerland.

Wu, Kang. 1995. *Energy in Latin America: Production, Consumption, and Future Growth.* Westport, Conn.: Praeger.

Yúdice, George. 2004. *The Expediency of Culture: Uses of Culture in the Global Era.* Durham, N.C.: Duke University Press.

Zakaria, Fareed. 2008. *The Post American World.* New York, N.Y.: W.W. Norton & Co.

Zalewski, Plínio. 1999. "O governo do PT." *Democracia: Cadernos de Reflexão Política* 3: 89-91.

Zelizer, Viviana. 1994. *The Social Meaning of Money.* New York, N.Y.: Princeton University Press.

Zibechi, Raúl. 2009. "Is Brazil Creating Its Own Backyard?" Americas Policy Program, 3 February. www.americas.irc-online.org.

Zovatto, Daniel G. and José Henriquez, eds. 2008. *Reforma política y electoral en América Latina.* México: UNAM e IDEA.

Zylbersztajn, Hélio, André Souza, Anderson Stancioli, and Marcelo Milan. 2003. "Aposentadoria e Eqüidade." *Folha de São Paulo,* 6 August: A3.

# INDEX

# ABOUT THE CONTRIBUTORS

**Monica Arruda de Almeida** is Adjunct Professor in Latin American Studies at the Edmund A. Walsh School of Foreign Service at Georgetown University.

**Glauco Arbix** is Professor of Sociology at the University of São Paulo (USP).

**Leslie Elliott Armijo** is Visiting Scholar at the Mark O. Hatfield School of Government at Portland State University.

**Renato Boschi** is Full Professor at the Instituto de Estudos Sociais, Políticos e Econômicos (IESP) at the Rio de Janeiro State University.

**John F. Collins** is Associate Professor of Anthropology at Queens College and The Graduate Center of City University of New York.

**David Fleischer** is Professor Emeritus of Political Science at the University of Brasília.

**Mauricio A. Font** is Professor of Sociology at The Graduate Center of the City University of New York, and director of the Bildner Center for Western Hemisphere Studies.

**Christine A. Gustafson** is Associate Professor in the Politics Department at Saint Anselm College.

**Elaine da Silveira Leite** is a Ph.D. candidate in Sociology at the Federal University of São Carlos (UFSCar).

**Maria Rita Loureiro** is Full Professor at the Fundação Getulio Vargas and at the University of São Paulo (USP).

**Lia Zanotta Machado** is Visiting Professor at Columbia University (2009-2010) and Full Professor of Anthropology at the University of Brasília.

**Ana Cristina Braga Martes** is Professor of Sociology at the Fundação Getulio Vargas (FGV-EAESP).

**Scott B. Martin** is Part-Time Faculty at the Graduate School of International Affairs at The New School and Adjunct Assistant Professor at the School of International and Public Affairs at Columbia University.

**Cecília Olivieri** is Professor of Graduate Studies at the School of Arts, Sciences and Humanities at University of São Paulo (USP).

**João Paulo M. Peixoto** is Professor of Government at the University of Brasília.

**Laura Randall** is Professor Emerita of Economics at Hunter College of the City University of New York.

**Janaina Saad** is Research Associate at the Bildner Center for Western Hemisphere Studies.

**Eiiti Sato** is Professor of International Relations at the University of Brasília.

**José Roberto Ferreira Savoia** is Professor of Finance at the University of São Paulo (FEA-USP).

**Fernando B. Sotelino** is Adjunct Professor at the School of International and Public Affairs (SIPA) at Columbia University.

**J. Ricardo Tranjan** is a Ph.D. candidate in Global Governance at the Balsillie School of International Affairs at the University of Waterloo.

**Thomas J. Trebat** is the Executive Director of the Institute of Latin American Studies and the Center for Brazilian Studies at Columbia University.